KNIVES
IN THE
SOUTH

P.F. Chisholm is an author and journalist. She is a graduate of Oxford University with a degree in History. Her first novel, *A Shadow of Gulls*, published when she was eighteen, won the David Higham Award for Best First Novel.

KNIVES
IN THE
SOUTH
P.F. CHISHOLM

Comprising

A PLAGUE OF ANGELS

A MURDER OF CROWS

AN AIR OF TREASON

HEAD
ℓ ZEUS

This omnibus edition first published in the UK in 2017
by Head of Zeus, Ltd

A *Plague of Angels* first edition 1998
A *Plague of Angels* Copyright © P.F. Chisholm, 1998

A *Murder of Crows* first edition 2010
A *Murder of Crows* Copyright © P.F. Chisholm, 2010

An Air of Treason first edition 2014
An Air of Treason Copyright © P.F. Chisholm, 2014

Knives in the South Copyright © P.F. Chisholm, 2017

9 7 5 3 1 2 4 6 8

A CIP catalogue record for this book is available
from the British Library.

ISBN 9781786694720

Printed and bound in Germany by CPI Books GmbH

Head of Zeus Ltd
5–8 Hardwick Street
London EC1R 4RG
WWW.HEADOFZEUS.COM

CONTENTS

A PLAGUE OF ANGELS

An introduction from Diana Gabaldon

A MURDER OF CROWS

AN AIR OF TREASON

Historical Note

Glossary

A PLAGUE OF ANGELS

To Kay, with thanks

INTRODUCTION

I am something of a connoisseur of opening lines, and the first line of P.F Chisholm's *A Plague of Angels* is right up there with the best:

> You could always tell when you were near a town from the bodies hanging on the gibbets by the main road, thought Sergeant Dodd.

Past the first line, Chisholm's Sir Robert Carey novels are the sort of books that cause one to rush out of the house and leave the supper burning for fear of finishing one after the bookstore has closed and the others are out of reach. And the main reason for this addictive readability is the way in which complete matter-of-factness meets historical picturesqueness, thus resulting in a thoroughly convincing illusion of reality.

Wildly entertaining reality, to be sure, but reality nonetheless.

Historical events are all very well—and P.F. Chisholm obviously has her setting by the short hairs—but the reality of a *story* rests on the personalities of the characters.

One historical author of my acquaintance describes something she calls "historical serendipity." This is the condition of knowing one's period so well and so intimately that when one reaches a point in the story where it's necessary to…(gasp) make something *up*, one's fictional choices are not only historically plausible—but very often turn out to be the *ex post facto* honest-to-goodness truth, as well.

I'd say that Chisholm operates with great aplomb in this rarefied state of serendipity; while she makes no bones that these are novels, her conscientious—and thoroughly unconscionable—handling of historical persons, such as William Shakespeare, keep the reader alternately giggling and drop-jawed, but never incredulous. No one *knows* that William Shakespeare did such things; but no one can prove he didn't, either, and Chisholm's version is so perfectly in tune with time and attitude that we're more than willing to believe it.

She pays the debt of accuracy that any historical novelist owes to the honor of the dead—and yet where history leaves lacunae, her imagination leaps gleefully in to fill the gap.

In Chisholm's fiction, the historical characters—including Sir Robert Carey himself—are as believable as the fictional ones; this is a feat in a genre where "real" characters are sometimes so constrained by documentation and "what's known" as to come off as paradoxically wooden, by contrast with the purely fictional—and thus fancy-free—characters, who can cavort and speak as they please.

And that's the chief trick, of course, in creating lively, vivid characters; no trick at all, but only allowing the characters to speak for themselves. Chisholm does this brilliantly, and I can do no less:

Sir Robert Carey, gallant courtier, valiant soldier, and noble deadbeat:

'Don't kill anybody, Sergeant,' Carey said. 'Even if there's a fight.'

'Why not?'

'You've no idea what a bloody nuisance it is to fix juries in London,' Carey snapped. 'So don't get yourself hanged.'

Sergeant Henry Dodd, suspicious and canny Land Sergeant of Gilsland, a force to be reckoned with on his native Border, and not entirely helpless even in the strange stews of London:

'Ay tell you what,' he said conversationally, and trying hard to talk as much like Barnabus as he could so they would understand him. 'Since ye're all a bunch o' catamites wi' nae bollocks at all, I'll take three o'ye at once so I dinnae outnumber ye.'

Henry Carey, Lord Hunsdon, illegitimate half-brother to the Queen, and patriarch to a brood of reckless sons:

'ROBIN!' bellowed Hunsdon, nose to nose with Carey. 'Do I have to hit you to calm you down?'

And Barnabas Cooke, so much more effective as a pickpocket than as a valet, who leads our heroes through the myriad dangers of the urban jungle:

Dodd gobbled. He heard himself do it, but couldn't stop. *Twenty-five shillings*, for a *hat*? 'Barnabus…' he growled and Barnabus took his elbow and whisked him round the side of the stall.

'Look, Sergeant, it sounds a lot, but it'll be worf it, believe me. There's nuffing ladies like better than 'ats and she'd never ever get one this good nor this fashionable anywhere norf of York.'

To say nothing of the articulate and picturesque characters who people Chisholm's London:

'I know a lot of poets. Good company.'
'Yarrargh warra gerk…' said the poet, and puked over Dodd's boots.

Not only dialogue but narrative is carried on the giddy whirls of language like spun sugar; so elegant and delightful that you want to read each line over several times for the sheer pleasure of seeing it again.

This gift of language, combined with that masterly appreciation for the small pleasures and inconveniences of life—

'Och,' said Dodd, enjoying himself. 'Is the light too bright for ye, sir. Will I shut the shutters for ye?' Perhaps he did bang them a bit hard but it was such fun to watch Carey wince. That'll learn ye to be happy in the morning, Dodd thought savagely.

—gives the book a feeling of complete reality, no matter whether the setting is a plague-stricken neighborhood, a Cheapside jeweler's, or the beggar's ward of the Fleet prison.

From opening line to bottom line, the felicity of the language leads us through a neatly dove-tailed plot that ranges from high comedy to genuine pathos, but never loses its sense of engagement—because it's dealing with characters who are Real People.

And the *real* bottom line is that while I adore Sir Robert Carey *and* his father, I am just hopelessly in love with Sergeant Dodd.

Diana Gabaldon
Scottsdale
July 3, 2000

A PLAGUE OF ANGELS

WEDNESDAY, 30TH AUGUST 1592,

LATE AFTERNOON

You could always tell when you were near a town from the
bodies hanging on the gibbets by the main road, thought Sergeant
Dodd. London was no different from anywhere else they had
passed on the interminable way south. As their horses toiled
up the long hill from Golders Farm, Dodd could just glimpse a
robber's corpse dangling from a big elm tree, up on the brow.
Of course Sir Robert Carey had told him how close they were to
London when they turned off the Great North Road and passed
through the village of Hendon, but they had been delayed by
Carey's horse throwing a shoe. The afternoon crowds of people
were gone now so that the dusty rutted road was quite empty. It
could have been anywhere.

A bit of knowledge gleaned from Carey's manservant floated
to the front of his mind.

'Ay,' he said with interest, and turned in the saddle to speak to
Barnabus himself who trailed lumpenly along behind them on a
sulky looking horse. 'Would that be Tyburn Tree up ahead there?'

Barnabus was frowning with concentration as he tried to get
his mount to move faster up the hill.

'Nah, mate,' he puffed, kicking viciously at the horse's flanks.
'Tyburn's off to the west, where the Edgeware Road meets the
Oxford Road, and it's a lot fancier than that. That's only the
Hampstead Hanging Elm.'

The road was curving round into a deep cutting with scrubby
heathland trees growing on the banks. Ahead, the Courtier's ugly
and obstinate replacement horse was balking at something again,
probably the smell of rot from the corpse. Carey had glanced
without interest at the Elm with its judicial fruit. The horse neighed,
tossed his head and skittered sideways.

9

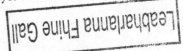

'God damn it,' Carey snarled to the horse. 'You flyblown lump of dogsmeat, get over!' He brought his whip down on the animal's flank and the horse crow-hopped and tried to turn to run back down the hill to its home in Golders Green.

Dodd wasn't liking the look of the place either. You couldn't see past the curve of the road and those high banks on both sides were perfect siting for an ambush.

He tried to urge his own horse up to a canter to bring him level with Carey, but the mare had her head up too, and her nostrils flared. Forelegs straight and the hairs of her mane up, she refused to pick up the pace. Dodd frowned.

'Whit's ahead of us, sir?' he called to Carey whose nag was slowly turning round in circles and shaking his head.

'The Cut, then Hampstead horse pond,' said the Courtier and whacked the animal again. 'Will you get on, blast you...!' he roared at it.

Drawing his sword, Dodd slid from the saddle, took the mare's bridle and led her forward at a run, then dodged behind and hit her on the rump with the flat of the sword. The mare reared and bolted past the Courtier and young Simon Barnet on his pony.

As she galloped up the road through the Cut, whinnying and shaking her head, Dodd heard the unmistakeable *whip-chunk!* of a crossbow being fired.

'Och,' he said to himself as he instantly changed direction and sprinted softly up the narrow path he had spotted on the right hand side of the Cut. 'Ah might have guessed.'

The bank reared higher on the right of the road, soft sandy earth held together by tree roots and bushes. Just below him, overlooking the narrowest part, he saw a man hunched in hiding, a bolt ready in his crossbow as he squinted down the sight ready for them to pass by.

Dodd had been storing up an awful lot of rage on the journey south from Carlisle. He gave an inarticulate roar at the sight, hopped like a goat down the high crumbling earthbank and cut down on the man with his sword.

The footpad had heard something coming, turned just in time to see his death, dropped the crossbow and reflexively put up his hands to defend himself. He took Dodd's swordblade straight down through his armbone and the middle of his face. Dodd slashed sideways to finish the job, then turned at another man who was lungeing out of a bramble bush waving the biggest sword Dodd had ever seen in his life, a great long monster of a thing that the robber was wielding two-handed, his face purple with effort.

Somewhere behind him, Dodd heard one of Carey's dags fire and an incoherent screaming follow it. As he dodged the whirling blade in front of him, a particle of thought noted that for the first time in his memory, Carey had finally managed to shoot somebody with his fancy weapon.

Balancing in a crouch, Dodd watched how the robber handled his stupid great sword, ducked again and waited for the instant when the momentum of it was whirling it round the back of the robber's head. That was when Dodd jumped inside the man's guard, slashed once with his sword and kicked as hard as he could at the man's balls.

The soft earth crumbled under him, he missed his target as he toppled and slipped on his bum down the bank. The robber danced after him, hefted up the long blade to bring it down on Dodd's head; the blade arced through the sky and Dodd rolled and slithered frantically, caught a rowan trunk to stop himself pitching eight feet down, and then saw the man grunt, stand still for a moment with his mouth wide open. The double-handed sword thudded to the ground and its wielder pitched headfirst down the bank and into the road.

Barnabus stood behind him, puffing for breath and dusting off his hands. Dodd nodded his thanks, clambered back up to the tiny narrow path and ran on to find the rest of the bastards, his blood properly up, just itching to find someone else to kill.

He saw the flash of legs and then glimpsed three more men off across the bare hill, running as fast as they could past the Hanging Elm. He sprinted after them, roaring 'A Tynedale, A Tynedale, Out! Out!' and the cowardly southron pigs only ran faster, splitting up as they dodged down the other side of the hill through the brambles and bushes.

Years spent on the Border not getting himself killed won through

11

Dodd's rage and he stopped. They might have kin within hailing range, there might be men and horses lying in wait behind one of the hedges, hiding in a double ambush to catch them when they thought they'd won the fight. No. He was a Dodd from Upper Tynedale and he'd pulled that trick too often himself in the past to be fooled by it.

He caught his breath and wiped his swordblade with some of the tussocky grass next to the Elm, where the sandy soil was more fertile, glanced up at the corpse in its soiled suit of brown wool with black velvet trimmings. A bit prosperous-looking for a thief; must have been a murderer. The smell wasn't bad at all, though the face was a terrible mess.

Horsehooves beat the earth behind him, and Dodd whisked round into a crouch again, sword at the ready. It was only the Courtier though, laughing fit to burst his ribs, dag in his left hand and his sword in his right.

'By God, Sergeant,' he said. 'That was a bloody good piece of work.'

Dodd tried hard not to look pleased. 'Ay,' he said. 'They've run though.'

'Of course they have. No soft southern footpad is a match for a Tynedaler and never will be.'

As this was undoubtedly true, Dodd nodded his head. 'How long afore they fetch their kin?' he asked, squinting around himself. Apart from the Elm, there were no proper trees, though a multiplicity of hedges split the fields below. Not much cover up here, he thought, plenty down there; I don't like it.

Carey was laughing again, putting his still-wound second dag back into its case on the horse's withers, and twirling his sword around his gloved fingers in an absurd swordmaster's flourish.

'They won't,' he said with the unwarranted certainty that always enraged Dodd. 'This is Hampstead Heath, not the Bewcastle Waste. Every man jack of them will have to change his breeches now they've lost three of their friends, including the big ugly bastard that almost fell on Simon, who I think was their leader.'

'Ye killed one, then, sir?' Dodd said as he followed Carey down the slightly better path that led back to the road on the southern side of the Cut.

'Shot one, slashed another.'

'Nae trouble wi' yer hands now?'

Carey grinned with satisfaction and flexed the fingers of his left hand in the embroidered kid gloves he was wearing. 'No, my grip's as good as it ever was,' he said. 'The kick didn't even hurt.'

Dodd nodded once, unwilling to be as delighted with Carey as Carey was with himself.

'I swapped a couple of blows with somebody who had a polearm, might have got him with a slash, and then you killed the big one and the lot of them ran like rabbits.'

'Nay sir, that werenae me, it were Barnabus,' Dodd said dolefully, annoyed with himself for not doing better. 'Got him in the back with a throwing knife. I killed anither man with a crossbow.'

Carey laughed again and sheathed his sword. 'I've never regretted the day I hired Barnabus,' he said untruthfully. 'Even though I was drunk at the time. Come on, let's make sure he doesn't strip all the corpses.'

Dodd glowered at the thought of being bilked out of his rightful spoils and ran back through the Cut to find Barnabus bending over the man Carey had evidently shot, since his chest was a mashed mess of bone and blood. He was still flopping feebly and Barnabus appeared to be trying to act as a surgeon on him.

'Barnabus, really,' admonished Carey from his horse, which was spinning and sidling again. 'Wait until the poor bugger's dead.'

Barnabus looked furtive. 'Well, sir, I was...ah...going to put him out of his misery, so to speak.'

'Ay,' said Dodd, coming close and looking down. 'Were ye now? What are they, then?' He pointed at the round bright gold coins scattered about the dying man, some of them embedded in the ruined flesh of his chest. 'Buttercups?'

Barnabus had the grace to look embarrassed. 'Just wondering,' he muttered.

Even the sniff of gold had the Courtier off his horse, tying it to a bush and coming over to look.

'Hm,' he said. 'That's peculiar.'

Dodd was gathering up the coins on the ground, though he

couldn't quite bring himself to start plucking coins out of the man's body. Barnabus wasn't so fussy.

'What's a scrawny Hampstead footpad doing with a purseful of gold?' Carey asked. 'And why did they try it on with us if they already had money?'

Dodd shrugged and went to look at the big bruiser that Barnabus had killed. Somebody else had got there first though, and he scowled at Barnabus who coughed and brought out the purse he had taken.

Simon came trotting down from the bank looking disappointed. 'Nothing up there, Uncle Barney,' he said. 'Sorry.'

Pointedly, Carey held out his hand for the spoils which Barnabus handed over. Dodd was very reluctant to give up a purse full of money, even if it had blood and chips of bone mixed in, but wasn't quite annoyed enough with the Courtier to hold onto it.

Carey hefted the purses and frowned. 'What wealthy little footpads,' he said, and bent over the man he had shot, who was finally still. Staring eyes told him he'd get no information.

'Hm,' said Carey again, putting the purses into one of his saddle bags. 'Come on, let's get the horses watered and try and make it into London before nightfall.'

* * *

As expected, Dodd's nag was at the horsepond slurping up greenish water and swishing at flies with her tail. She made a great drama about shying when she saw him and trotting further round the pool. Dodd pretended he wasn't interested in her, wandered up to the trampled banks of the pond, looked everywhere but at the horse and then when she put her wary head down again, nipped her bridle.

'Got ye,' he whispered to her and she snorted resignedly.

Carey's mount was still pulling on the reins and sidling stupidly until he caught the smell of water and then he lunged for it. Carey tied him to one of the posts and disappeared into a bramble bush a little way off. Simon came up from the Cut with Barnabus, leading the other two horses. They had no packponies and were riding strange southern horses because Carey had been in a hurry and they had been riding post. They were due to change mounts again at the Holly Tree in Hampstead, and Dodd, for one, couldn't wait to be rid of the latest batch of useless knacker's rejects. Also, he was thirsty, but he would have to be a great deal worse off to consider the stuff in the horsepond. What he wanted was a quart of ale, Bessie's for preference, bread, cheese, a meat pie, pickled onions...Dodd sighed. Maybe the Holly Tree would have some food. Maybe Carey would let them stop for half an hour to drink.

Maybe he wouldn't. Dodd wasn't very hopeful. Out of sheer habit, he stared out across the horsepond at the countryside around them and at the thatched roofs of the village which began a little way down the other side of the hill. His horse had finished and was looking at him expectantly, but he didn't have a feedbag hidden anywhere on him, so he tied her to the hitching post near the pond. Then he wandered to the other side of the hilltop, to see if he could spy London town yet, even though the milestone had said they were five miles away still.

His mouth fell open. It was a fine lookout spot, that hill, good siting for a pele tower, not that the soft southrons had thought of building one. They had a pathetic beacon on a raised bracket that must have been put up in the Armada year from the rust on it, but there was no wood around to light it with. You could see for miles when it was clear, which it was; a pale golden evening with not a hint of autumn.

And if you looked southwards, there it lay, a baleful brackish sea of houses, the foremost city in England. The craggy flotsam of church steeples poked up among the cluttered roofs, with smoke dirtying the sky above even on a warm day. Dodd had never seen such a thing. The day before he had been impressed with York, but this...A city that had burst its walls in all directions with so many people that came and stayed, as if the city ate them and got fatter each time. Dodd narrowed his eyes and pursed his lips. London might impress him, but eat him it would not.

'Makes yer heart sing, don't it?' said a guttural voice beside him. Barnabus Cooke was standing there, squinting in the south-westering light of the sun. Either the light was stronger than Dodd thought, or the ferret-faced little man had tears in his eyes. 'Seems a hundred years gone since I left,' he sighed.

'Hmphm,' said Dodd noncommitally.

Barnabus heard his lack of enthusiasm and waved an expressive arm. 'That, Sergeant Dodd, is the greatest city in Christendom. Everything any sane man could ever want you can get right there, no trouble, money to be made, never any reason to be bored.'

'Ay, and the streets are all paved wi' gold,' said Dodd straight-faced, 'so I've heard tell.'

'No, they ain't,' piped up Simon. 'Don't you listen to 'em, Sergeant. Me and my friend Tom, we dug down for two days solid looking for gold paving stones and we never found nuffing except more paving stones.'

Dodd nodded at Simon. At some time on the long weary journey, a mystery had happened to the lad's speech again. From sounding quite Christian really, at least as comprehensible as the Carlisle stable lads, Simon had turned back into the guttural creature with hiccups for 't's that he had been when he first came north. God save me, Dodd thought, feeling for the little lump of his wife's amulet under his shirt; alien men with alien notions and words like cobblestones.

'Nay lad,' he said gravely to Simon. 'I never thought it were, or why are the Grahams no' laying siege to it?'

'Figures of speech, Sergeant,' said Barnabus patronisingly. 'Only true in a manner of speaking. Like what you get at the playhouse? You ever seen a play?'

'I've seen the players that come to Carlisle some years,' said Dodd, who hadn't thought much of them. 'Garish folk, and ay arguing.'

Barnabus tutted. 'Nah. Plays. At a playhouse. With guns for thunder and the boys tricked out in velvets and satin and trumpets and a jig at the end. Best bit, the jig, I've always thought. Worf waiting for.'

'Why?'

Barnabus grinned knowingly and tapped his bulbous nose. 'You'll see.'

Dodd grunted and looked around for the cause of this whole stupid expedition into foreign parts. Carey came striding impatiently out of his sorry-looking stand of thorns, his good humour after a fight obviously destroyed by what had sent him hurrying into it. Dodd was quite recovered from the vicious Scottish flux they had both picked up in Dumfries, but Carey's bowels were clearly made of weaker stuff. He saw them gazing into the distance and turned to look as well, scowling at the view of London before turning back to scowl at all of them. To his clear dissatisfaction, the horses were all drinking nicely, none of them was lame for a change, and there was nothing to complain about. God, but he was in a nasty temper and had been all the way south, starting with an eyeblinking explosion of profanity when he first got the letter from his father. Dodd had heard it in the new barracks building while Carey was in the Carlisle castle yard.

It had been very wearying, riding with a man as chancy as a bad gun, all the way to Newcastle and every step of the Roman road south. They had changed horses luxuriously twice a day and pressed on at a pace that Dodd thought indecent, even with the Courtier having to stop and find cover every couple of hours. It wasn't the length of time it took—Dodd was no stranger to long rides and three days was not the longest he'd been on by several days—it was the sheer dullness of the business. Hour after hour of cavalry pace, walk a mile, trot a mile, canter for two, then lead the horses again, and never a familiar face to greet nor a known tower to sight by. Dodd felt marooned. Even with the straight dusty Roman road, he doubted he could find his way back home again from so far away, though Carey knew the way well enough. After all, he was used to flinging himself across the entire country on the Queen's account.

The countryside had changed around them as they went, so you might think they were still and the country moving, changing itself magically from rocky to flat and back to hills, fat and golden with straw after the harvest, the gleaners still combing painstakingly through the fields. They passed orchards—Dodd had not been certain what the little woods full of fruit trees might be, but had found out from Simon; they passed fields full of sheep and kine and only children guarding them, so it made you sad to think how many you could reive if only the distances weren't so great. Even the size of the fields changed, from small and stone-walled to vast striped prairies and then back to small squares quilted with hedges. The road was generally full of strangers as well, crowded with packponies, carriers' wagons, even newfangled coaches jolting along with silkclad green-faced women suffering inside them. Once a courier carrying the Queen's dispatches had galloped down the grassy verge, shouting for them to make room, and leaving the rest of the travellers bathed in dust. Carey had coughed and brightened up a little, and they had talked for an hour about the technicalities of riding post. They had agreed that the key to speed was in making the change of horses every ten miles as fast as possible and paradoxically in taking the first half mile slowly so the animal had a chance to warm up.

Once a trotting train carrying fish from Norwich went past them, little light carts pulled by perkily trotting ponies, trailing a smell of the ocean behind the smart clatter. Once they had passed a band of beggars and Dodd had loosened his sword, but the upright man at the head of them had not liked the look of three men and a boy, well-armed and with the gentleman at the head of them ostentatiously opening his dag case before him. Dodd had thought it was a pity, really: he'd heard tell of southern beggars and a fight would at least have broken the monotony. Dodd was also short of sleep, thanks to Carey's efforts at economising. At each inn they stayed at, Carey had put them all in the one room so Dodd could get the full benefit of Carey and Barnabus's outrageous snoring. In desperation he had offered to sleep with the horses in the stables, but Carey had turned the idea down.

The south was a dreamworld where all the familiar normal animals had suddenly turned fat and handsome and he could only understand one word in three that was spoken to him. Dodd felt naked without his jack and morion, and thought wistfully that it would have been nice if his brother could have come too so he could have had someone to talk to. But Carey had refused to pay for any more followers than he had to on the grounds that it was Dodd himself that the Lord Chamberlain, his father, wanted to speak to, not Red Sandy.

'What do you make of it, Sergeant?' Carey asked him, nodding at the ambush of houses ahead of them.

'Ah dinna ken, sir,' said Dodd at his most stolid. 'I've no' been there yet.' Was Carey actually planning to keep all the spoils for himself? Damn him for a selfish grasping miser; he'd only killed one of the footpads and if it hadn't been for Dodd, they would have been helpless in the Cut when the robbers attacked...

As if reading Dodd's mind, Carey had squatted down and was emptying out the gold and silver coins onto a flat stone, sorting them briskly into shillings and crowns and angels, and then into three piles which he then doled out. The few pennies left over he gave to Simon.

'Will we get to see the Queen, sir?' asked Simon as he stowed his money away.

Carey shrugged. 'We might, if she's in London. She's more likely to be on progress.'

'Will yer father no' be with her then, sir?' Dodd said, having picked up the vague notion that Lord Chamberlains were supposed to look after courtiers and the court and such. 'How will we tell him our tale if he isnae there?'

'How the hell should I know?' snapped Carey. 'Father's brains have addled, I expect. Bloody London. What the devil's the point of making me come back to London now?'

'Ay, the Grahams will be riding, and the Armstrongs forbye,' said Dodd dolefully. 'Once the Assize judge has gone home after Lammas torches, and the horses are strong and the kine are fat, that's when we run our rodes.'

Carey snorted. Dodd, who was tired of treating Carey with tact, decided to live dangerously. 'Ah, that'll be it, sir,' he said comfortably. 'Your father will have got wind the Grahams have a price on yer head and he'll want ye safe in the south again.'

Lord, Carey could glare fit to split a stone when he wanted. 'I very much doubt it,' he said frostily, 'seeing he knows perfectly well I'd rather be in Carlisle and take my chances with the Grahams.'

'Hm,' said Barnabus. 'Not an easy choice, is it, sir? With all the people wanting to see you in London.'

Carey didn't answer, but went to his horse and started turning up hooves looking for stones. The animal nickered and licked at his neck, searching for salt and knocking his hat off in the process.

Uncharacteristically, Carey elbowed the enquiring muzzle away with a growled 'Get over, you stupid animal.'

'Mr Skeres will want to talk to you, won't he, sir?' Barnabus went on, sucking his teeth and scratching his bum. 'And Mr Barnet and Mr Palavicino's agent and Mr Bullard and then there's Mr Pickering's men...'

Involuntarily, Carey winced.

'Got some feuds waiting for ye, have ye, sir?' asked Dodd with interest. It didn't surprise him at all, knowing Carey by now, but he wouldn't have thought southerners would have the spirit.

'No,' Carey admitted as he checked the girth and mounted. 'Not feuds. Much worse.'

'Och ay?'

'Much much worse,' Barnabus explained gloomily, using the mounting stone to clamber into the saddle.

'What then?'

'Creditors,' Carey said hollowly. 'London's bloody crawling with my creditors.'

***

The nags supplied by the Holly Tree were, if anything, worse than the ones they had been riding before and true to Dodd's gloomy expectation, Carey refused even to pause long enough for a quart of beer. Nor would he roust out the village Watch to go and find the footpads, though that was sensible enough since they were more than likely the same people or at least their relatives.

As they clopped briskly down Haverstock Hill, Carey's face got longer and longer. He looked just like a man whose blackrent to the Grahams was late, waiting for the torch in his thatch.

'Could ye not pay 'em off with the spoils fra the footpads?' Dodd asked solicitously.

Carey blinked at him, as if checking to see whether he was making fun, and then laughed hollowly.

'Christ, Dodd, you've no idea,' he said. 'I wish I could. The only thing I've got going for me is the fact they don't know I'm coming.'

'Wouldn't be too sure of that, sir,' said Barnabus from behind them.

Carey had been in a tearing hurry all the way south, but now he slowed to a walk.

'I don't know,' he said. 'What do you think, Barnabus? I was hoping to come down Gray's Inn Road and into Holborn just about the time when the law students come out of dinner and use them as cover, but we're too late for that.'

'Mm,' said Barnabus thoughtfully. 'I shouldn't think there'll be too many duns out on Holborn—why bother? If I was trying to catch you, I'd hang around Somerset House, wiv a boat on the river. After all, they don't know which way you're coming.'

'If they know I'm coming at all.'

'You're planning to rely on that, are you, sir?'

Carey shook his head. 'It's the Strand that's the problem then.' He nibbled the stitching on the thumb of his glove. 'I simply can't afford to wind up in the Fleet.'

'What's that, sir?'

'A debtor's prison,' said Carey in a voice of doom.

'Och,' said Dodd and considered. 'Have ye kin in London? Yer father's there, is he no'?'

'I hope so, since he's forced me to ride a couple of hundred miles just to talk to him face to face and do business that could be perfectly well done by letter.'

'Ay. It's no' difficult, then. They willnae ken ma face as one o' yourn, so ye tell me the lie of the land and where your father's castle is, I ride hell fer leather intae it, he calls out yer kin and comes out to meet ye and none o' yer enemies can do a thing about it.'

A short silence greeted this excellent plan which Dodd realised was not the silence of admiration. Carey cleared his throat in a way which Dodd knew meant he was trying hard not to laugh and Simon sniggered behind his hand.

'Well?' demanded Dodd truculently. 'What's wrong with that idea?' He could feel his neck reddening.

'Among other things, the fact that Somerset House is only one of the palaces on the Strand and I doubt you could find it,' said Carey. 'Not to mention the fact that the Queen is highly averse to pitched battles being fought on the streets of London.'

'You could let 'em take you, we talk to your dad and he bails you tomorrow,' suggested Barnabus. 'You'd only need to spend one night inside...'

'Absolutely not,' snapped Carey, and his face was pale.

Dodd thought he was being overdramatic and called his bluff. 'Ye can allus change clothes wi' me, sir, if ye're so feart o' being seen; none will know you in my clothes,' he offered. Perhaps it was cruel to tease the Courtier; Dodd knew perfectly well that Carey would probably rather die than enter even London's suburbs wearing Dodd's sturdy best suit of homespun russet. Certainly he would hang before going into his father's house like that.

Carey's blue glare narrowed again but it seemed he was learning to know when Dodd was pulling his leg. He coughed.

'Thank you for your offer, Dodd,' he said, 'but I doubt your duds would fit me.'

'Ay, they would,' said Dodd, who was only a couple of inches shorter than Carey and not far off the same build. Though he thought no one would actually confuse them in a thousand years since Carey had dark chestnut hair, hooded blue eyes, a striking family resemblance to the Queen along his cheekbones and slightly hooked nose, and a breezy swagger that breathed of the court. Dodd knew he was no beauty though he felt it was unfair the way his wife sometimes compared his usual expression to a wet winter's day. The best you could say about his brown hair was that it was quite clean and he still had all of it.

'We dinna have to go straight in,' Dodd pointed out. 'There's surely no shortage of fine inns. Ye could stay at one o' them, Barnabus could scout out yer dad's castle for ye, see was the approaches laid wi' ambush, and then we could bring out a covered litter for ye and take ye in that way.'

'That might work,' said Barnabus. 'At least we could bring out some of your father's liverymen for cover.' Dodd forebore to point out that this was exactly the plan he had first suggested and they had laughed at.

For once Carey looked as if he was being tempted to act sensibly but as Dodd expected, it didn't last.

'No,' Carey said. 'News travels fast in London. If anyone spots you, Barnabus, they'll know I'm back and come looking for me when you return. Dodd wouldn't know the way and Simon's too young. Also nobody knows them at Somerset House so they might have trouble getting in. Besides, I'm not skulking into my father's house in a blasted litter like some bloody trollop from the stews. No, if we move fast enough and quietly enough, by the time they realise it's me, we'll be in.'

'And yer father's henchmen can see 'em off.'

'No,' said Carey. 'My father's lawyers.'

'Whit use are lawyers?' laughed Dodd, who had never heard good of one. 'It's fighting men we lack, as usual.'

'You'd be surprised, Sergeant. Right, so it's down Gray's Inn Road to Holborn, turn right on Holborn and past Chancery Lane, cut across Lincoln's Inn Fields, then down Little Drury Lane at a trot, turn right into the Strand where we'll walk so as not to be too dramatic and besides the ground's awful there, then in at my father's gatehouse. Stick close, Dodd, I don't want you getting lost.'

What did a London bailiff look like? wondered Dodd as they cut across the fields to the gate at the top of Gray's Inn Lane, cattle almost blocking it as they stood waiting to be taken in for milking. They were lovely beasts, fat as butter, huge udders groaning. As they manoevred round the herd, Dodd rode up behind Carey and let out a soft cough.

'Look at them,' he said longingly. 'Could we no'...er...borrow a few, sir? I could drive at least five o' them maself, and more if ye gave me a hand. We could use 'em to pay off yer creditors.'

Carey stared for a moment and then shouted with humourless laughter. 'For God's sake, Dodd, keep your sticky hands off those beasts, they're the Earl of Essex's. See the bear and ragged staff brand? Don't touch 'em.'

'Och,' said Dodd sadly, not very surprised. 'He's a big lord, is he, sir?'

'Er...yes,' said Carey. 'Also, I'm still his man and you'd get me in a lot of trouble.'

Gray's Inn Road must have been a horror in winter, what with the depth of dust. It was lined with houses, like streets in Edinburgh, and then they came out on a wide road. Carey was looking about him and had his hat pulled down. They crossed some fields crisscrossed with paths that looked badly overgrazed and came through a gate beside a high garden wall. Across another dusty road was a lane that led due south between tall narrow houses. Simon shut the gate and they unconsciously bunched together as they went into the lane. The sun was a low copper bowl now and the people milling around not paying them any attention. Dodd thought that Londoners were very rude folk not to wave, even. Carey was biting the corner of his lip and looking nervous, while Barnabus had the narrow-eyed thoughtful expression he wore when he was waiting for trouble. Dodd loosened his sword and wished for a bow.

'Don't kill anybody, Sergeant,' Carey said. 'Even if there's a fight.'

'Why not?'

'You've no idea what a bloody nuisance it is to fix juries in London,' Carey snapped. 'So don't get yourself hanged.'

Their horses' hooves slipped and scuffed on the dusty clay as they negotiated a whole fine litter of red piglets plugged into their dam across the middle of the lane. There was a stone water conduit at the end of the lane, where city women stood waiting to draw water—fine ladies too, by the looks of their velvet trimmed kirtles and outrageously feathered hats. The Strand was wide and choking with dust, the biggest houses Dodd had ever seen in his life rearing up like cliffs on either side of it.

'Hell's teeth,' said Carey, catching sight of the decorative gathering at the conduit. 'The wives are out to watch.'

Dodd gestured at an impressive house opposite the conduit. 'Is that yer father's house...?' he asked. Carey shook his head and pointed at the gatehouse of a towering elaboration of a palace that Dodd had taken for the Queen's court itself.

'And here they come,' said Barnabus, as a crowd of large men in buff coats, waving pieces of paper and clubs and coshes, moved suddenly in their direction.

Just for a second, Dodd saw Carey on the verge of running like a rabbit. If he hadn't known why Carey was so afraid of arrest he would have thought it funny, but since he did, he decided that he wasn't going to allow it and the hell with London juries, they had to catch him first.

Dodd drew his sword and drove his horse into the thick of

the shouting crowd of men. As he'd thought, they wanted their bounties for arresting Carey, but not at the expense of their heads, and they fell back in front of him. At least Carey, Barnabus and Simon had the sense to stick close behind him. The boom of Carey's second dag rang out by Dodd's ear as he discharged it into the air. A couple of bailiffs clutched desperately for Carey's reins and stirrup leathers. One fell back with a broken nose from a vicious kick from Carey's boot, and Barnabus's horse co-operatively trod on another one's foot, making him howl.

And then they were through, the whole bunch scattering at the edges, the other people in the street staring, a couple of children laughing and pointing and the women round the conduit clapping.

They clattered inside the shelter of the gatehouse, Dodd turning at the opening with his sword ready and his teeth bared. The bailiffs had followed them, though at a safe distance. A hubbub rose from them in which the words 'writs', 'warrants' and 'Westminster Hall' could be heard and more papers were waved.

'Och,' said Dodd, spitting deliberately at the feet of the biggest one. 'If ye think ye can take a Dodd fra Tynedale, come on and try it.'

Carey was shouting at the gatekeeper in his lodge. Surely to God they weren't at the wrong place? Was Carey's father not there? What was going on? Dodd had his horse placed sideways on to block any rushes, but he didn't think the bailiffs had the stomach for a real fight.

'Ay tell you what,' he said conversationally, and trying hard to talk as much like Barnabus as he could so they would understand him. 'Since ye're all a bunch o' catamites wi' nae bollocks at all, I'll take three o' ye at once so I dinnae outnumber ye.'

The biggest bailiff stopped and frowned in puzzlement. How much longer would it take Carey to get into his father's house? If this had been anywhere in Cumberland, they would all have been dead by now. A coach bowled past like the Devil himself.

Surely somebody would have a go soon? Even Londoners couldn't be that soft. Dodd gripped his sword more tightly and wished again for his nice comfortable jack and helmet, and a lance as well while he was at it. He looked about in case the bailiffs had sent for reinforcements. How far did a messenger have to go to find men? How long would Carey be chatting in the gatehouse…?

The postern gate opened finally and Carey beckoned. Instinctively Dodd sent the boy in first leading the horses, then Barnabus, before backing his own horse through the gate. That was the bailiffs' last chance to hit him but by that time his already low opinion of southerners was at rock bottom.

'Off ye go, lads,' he sneered at the bewildered bunch. 'Ye've lost us. Best get back to yer mams and yer fancy-boys.' He gave a hard final stare at the biggest bailiff as the postern gate shut and Carey barred it.

He turned to see a small yard beetled over by high stone and brick walls. A groom came to take the horses. Someone else in yellow and black livery, wearing a badge that looked like a duck in the throes of delirium, came hurrying out, bowing to Carey who greeted the plump little man with a familiar clap on the shoulder. The servant led them through a stunning marble entrance hall and into a small parlour lined with painted cloths and dotted with benches and stools padded in primrose yellow. In a corner was a virginals, painted with enamel people, mostly naked and winged, with the cover on. Another man in glaring livery brought wine which Dodd tasted with habitual suspicion before finding it quite smooth and hardly sour at all. Carey knocked his back in one and held out the silver goblet for a refill. Then he threw himself onto a bench, stretched his long legs in front of him, crossed them at the ankles and grinned.

'Can't think what I was so worried about,' he said to Dodd.

Dodd himself was still worried. Magnificent and palatial though Carey's family house was, it didn't look very defensible, with no proper pele tower, no battlements, no moat, no mound, no visible ordnance. There didn't seem many men around either.

'Ay,' he said. 'But how long before we have your...creditors around our ears like flies?'

Carey laughed. 'Well, they won't have pikes and muskets like the Grahams' debt-collectors.'

'Oh? What then?' asked Dodd, interested to know what weapons Londoners preferred.

'Writs,' said Carey. 'Blizzards of paper.'

Dodd began wondering irritably what all the fuss had been

about. Barnabus took Simon off with him to see to the small amount of luggage they had brought with them in their saddlebags and Carey wandered familiarly round the room with another goblet of wine in his hand.

'Place seems deserted,' he commented. 'Where the devil's Father gone?'

On that instant there was the sound of a female voice raised in argument outside the door which opened to let the owner of the voice come in. It was a young woman trailed by a maidservant and a young man in Hunsdon's livery who was still arguing with her back.

'Mistress, this is unwise, this is very very foolish, my lord Hunsdon will...' droned the servingman in a voice that sounded as if it had been flattened with a hot iron. The maidservant elbowed him and he finally fell silent, looking crestfallen.

Dodd gawked. For all the cunning cut of her green velvet English gown, it was quite obvious the lady was pregnant. She was also tall, lushly built with a haughty expression on her face, light hazel eyes, skin creamy and hardly painted at all, and magnificent rich glossy black hair tumbling down her back in a proudly maidenlike display, only slightly controlled by a rope of pearls and emeralds wound about it.

Dodd felt quite pleased to see something so restful to the eye, especially as her neckline was cut temptingly low. He heard Carey's breath check infinitesimally beside him. A second later Carey was on his feet, sweeping a tremendous bow. Dodd's eyes were trapped by the velvet valley above the short bodice as she curtseyed in response. Then the lovely view was cut off because the lady had opened her arms, put her head on one side and Carey had folded her to his chest with a most disrespectfully thorough kiss on her mouth.

'Mistress Bassano,' he said caressingly when he had come up for air. 'What a splendid joy to see you again.'

Mistress Bassano laughed, put up a hand to stroke Carey's cheek. 'Whatever are you doing in London, Robin?' she asked. 'I thought you'd run away from me forever.'

Good God, thought Dodd in despair, not another loose bitch, and then bitterly, and not for the first time, how the devil does he draw the women to him like that?

'I could say that my despair at being parted from you so poisoned my meat and drink that in order to survive I was forced to return,' Carey suggested.

Mistress Bassano tossed her head haughtily. 'And I would say you were lying to me.'

'Well, I am,' Carey admitted, his blue eyes sparkling. 'My blasted father ordered me south.' A worrying thought obviously struck him. 'It isn't...er...He hasn't...er...?'

Mistress Bassano shook her head. 'No, no. I'm sure he doesn't know.'

Dodd caught the knowing glance from the maidservant to the servingman and felt his heart sink even further. What the hell was going on here?

'His lordship was in Chelsea this afternoon,' put in the manservant. 'We expect him at any minute. He...er...didn't leave any orders about you, sir.'

'Mm,' Carey smiled kindly on the man. 'How is it with you, Will, any luck?'

Will shook his head, looking doleful. 'No, sir. If it weren't for your father giving me his livery, I'd be in the Fleet.'

'Bit of a comedown, isn't it, after this spring?'

Will shrugged. 'Can't be helped, sir.'

Mistress Bassano had swept a glance at Dodd which instantly dismissed him, moved to the virginals in the corner and lifted the cover. She sat down and pressed some of the notes, tilted her head consideringly and then leaned down to find the tuning key. Dodd tried to stop himself from staring at those milky plump breasts that seemed fashionably on the point of bursting out of the bodice. Would they? Could they?

She caught him at it and gave him a coldly knowing glare as she twiddled one of the pegs that was not to her satisfaction. Then she put the key back on its hook and placed her fingers to play.

Carey stood over her, no doubt getting a leisurely eyeful of the view and she smiled over her shoulder at the manservant.

'Will,' she said. 'Would you fetch me the Italian songsheets?'

Will's pointed face went pink. 'Yes, mistress,' he said and hurried over to delve in a chest by the wall, bringing out sheaves of paper dotted over with music. When he brought them to her, Dodd saw his hands shake as he arranged them on the music stand. He too seemed to be fighting the urge to stare and then Dodd was shocked to see one of Mistress Bassano's slim hands lift from the keyboard and briefly brush his leg. Carey was craning over, ostensibly to read the music, and Mistress Bassano's other hand went quietly out of sight somewhere in the vicinity of Carey's trunkhose.

Dodd's mouth had to be shut consciously. It turned down in stern disapproval of the whole proceedings.

'Sir,' said Mistress Bassano, turning from between her two admirers and finally favouring him with a dazzling smile that seemed to promise worlds of pleasure. 'Robin has been very rude to you, not introducing you.'

Dodd coughed, pulled off his hat, did the best bow he could muster which he knew, to his despair, was a lumpen misshapen thing in comparison to Carey's grace.

'Sergeant Henry Dodd,' he growled. 'Land Sergeant of Gilsland.'

The pointed chin on its proudly held neck tilted a little in acknowledgement. 'Can you sing, Sergeant Dodd?'

'Ay I can, a bit,' he allowed.

'And what is your voice?'

Her own voice was deeper than most women's but as velvet as the rest of her. Dodd's mouth had gone dry as the old Adam in him went skipping off into sinful daydreams. He licked his lips.

'Ah. I dinna ken. It's just a voice.'

Carey was smiling knowingly at him, over the top of Mistress Bassano's gleaming head. 'I've never heard you sing, Dodd?'

You bastard, thought Dodd. 'Ay, well, I wouldnae claim to be a gleeman, see,' he said. 'But I can hold ma own wi' a lay.'

Delicate frown lines appeared on Mistress Bassano's smooth forehead. 'What is he saying, Robin?' she asked. 'Is he a northerner?'

Carey bent and whispered in her ear and her magnetic smile dimmed a little to become patronising. 'Well, but I am disappointed. Robin and Will are both tenors, and it would be good if we had a basso. Do you have a deep voice, Sergeant?'

Dodd coughed again, suppressing the wistful wish that she

would call him Henry. 'Ay, I reckon. But I cannae read music, mistress. Words, ay, but not notes.'

The full pink lips pouted in disappointment as Carey whispered his translation. 'Oh what a pity. Never mind. You can be our audience and make useful criticisms.'

I could criticise you, mistress, Dodd thought, as he watched a blush going all the way up into what was left of the manservant's hair under his cap, *I could criticise you with a will, ay, criticise you till ye squealed for more, but it doesnae suit me to take thirds.* Mistress Bassano's hands reappeared to be placed on the keyboards and she launched into the beginning of one of Carey's favourite Court songs, a ditty that had all the pointless complexity of a lace ruff.

Carey's voice rang out, taking the main part and Mistress Bassano's voice rose with his. Somewhere in the background Will was adding his own voice, in a key that was awkward for him so he growled in the deeps.

It was very good. Even Dodd had to admit that Carey's voice was far better than ordinary and Mistress Bassano's was a marvel of poured cream, while the ruthlessly pre-empted Will still seemed to know what he was about. Personally, Dodd had no taste for foreign songs, preferring familiar tunes like the Ballad of Chevy Chase, but you could tell it was a clever thing they were doing even if you couldn't understand a word of it and the shape of the music was strange.

They wound sinuously to a halt, Mistress Bassano gazing full into Carey's eyes while he smiled down at her, both mouths open, carolling like birds in spring. Will had been completely outbid, and he knew it, for once his part finished he moved away from the virginals to stand by the door with a face as miserable as a leaking roof.

A trumpet sounded from the water just as Carey bent to kiss Mistress Bassano's mouth again. Jesus, did the man have no shame? But then Dodd was honest enough to admit to himself that if he had the chances Carey seemed to attract, he wouldn't waste one of them either. What would it be like to kiss that curving mouth, Dodd wondered; could you get your hand between the bodice and the tit or would you have to mess about with her lacings first? Carey seemed to know the answers to these important questions. Over by the door, Will looked deliberately away from the scandalous sight, his mouth and nose pinched with distress.

The shouting and trumpets from the other side of the house grew louder. Dodd moved swiftly to the windows facing the noise and found himself looking out on a vast garden, as big as the Maxwells' or bigger, where more men in yellow livery were hurrying up the paths from a gate in a wall. Doors crashed open, someone shouted something about my Lord Chamberlain Hunsdon and Mr Vice Chamberlain Thomas Heneage. At the last possible minute, Carey straightened up, moved smoothly away from Mistress Bassano and sat down at his ease on a bench again.

The doors to the parlour burst open.

Standing framed there was a broad elderly man in black velvet and gold brocade, his hair rusty grey, his face red, his eyes a shrewd dark grey. He was wearing a terrifying expression of disgust and rage. The sheer physical presence of the man almost blotted out the second richly-dressed courtier standing next to him, not as tall, not quite as broad in the shoulder, but a great deal more fleshy. That one had a round face and a prim mouth, though his face was presently decorated with a smile.

Carey leapt to his feet.

'Robert!' boomed Lord Hunsdon. 'What the Devil are you doing here? God damn your eyes!'

Carey swept a bow to his father so poetical in its elaboration of courtesy that it came out the other side into insolence. Hunsdon glowered, and swept forward to bring his white Chamberlain's staff slamming down on a nearby table. 'By Christ, Robert,' he roared. 'I've told Heneage here, if you've got yourself into trouble with Her Majesty again, I'll disinherit you.'

Dodd, who had lost his own father to an Elliot polearm at the age of twelve, watched in fascination. Something shifted subtly inside Carey. He bowed again, including the other rich courtier this time.

'My good lord and respected Father, and Mr Vice Chamberlain, may I present my most able second-in-command at Carlisle, Mr Henry Dodd, Land Sergeant of Gilsland.'

Not knowing what else to do with himself, Dodd managed a clutch at his cap and an ungainly bow. The small parlour was suddenly crowded with people. A liveryman bustling about behind him, lighting unnecessary candles, made him twitch. Another man brought up a carved armchair for his lord, yet another poured more wine. Plates of wafers and nuts appeared seemingly invisibly.

Hunsdon threw his bulk into the armchair which creaked under him. Mr Vice Chamberlain Heneage sat more circumspectly a little behind and to the right on a yellow padded stool. Hunsdon rapped his white staff on the floor.

'Right,' he growled. 'Scotland.'

'Most reverend sir,' said Carey. 'I would prefer to have cleaned off the dust of our rather hurried journey before I rendered my report to...'

'Ay, no doubt. But we want to hear it now, since you're here, you bloody idiot.'

The tips of Carey's ears had gone red. He put his hat back on his head and sat himself back down on the bench very pointedly, without being asked. Dodd decided to stay standing.

'Where should I start, my lord?' Nobody smiled that sweetly without intending it as an insult. Hunsdon's bushy eyebrows almost met over his nose.

'How is His Majesty of Scotland?' put in Heneage, mellifluously.

'Very well indeed and received me most kindly on account of the love he bears Her Majesty the Queen.'

Hunsdon grunted. 'And the business over the guns? Lowther sent some nonsensical tale that you had substituted them for scrap iron. Is that true?'

Carey waved gloved fingers airily. 'A complete mare's nest, sir. There was indeed an arrangement between His Majesty of Scotland and the Wardenry of Carlisle, as it turned out, only no one saw fit to inform me.'

'I'd heard that some of the guns we sent were faulty,' said Heneage with oily concern. 'I do hope no one was hurt?'

'One man lost his hand and died of it, but no other harm done,' Carey told him callously. 'Really, the guns were a side-issue. We rode to congratulate my Lord Maxwell on being made Warden and of course to learn what support the King might want when he harried Liddesdale...'

Dodd's eyes were nearly popping out with shock. The tale Carey told his father...Improved was too mild. A tissue of lies spun convincingly from Carey's smiling mouth. There had been no problems whatever at the Scottish Court. Lord Maxwell had been kindness itself and of course Sir John Carmichael sent his regards. The King had been at his most affable, only a little sad at the smallness of his bribe...er, pension. Spanish spies? What Spanish spies? Oh, those Spanish spies. Well, Carey had not suspected the Italian wine merchant and his charming wife, but he had heard that Lord Spynie was deep in dangerous business with the Papists, for what that was worth. These rumours will fly around, won't they, Mr Vice Chamberlain, shocking really, what people will say in the hope of payment. Sir Henry Widdrington? Well, yes, admitted Carey, he had met the man. A little too warm to the Scots perhaps, and another one with Papist leanings, he was sure. My Lord Hunsdon might want to warn his Deputy Warden, brother John, up in Berwick, about the Widdringtons, seeing how powerful they were...

After a while Dodd stopped trying to follow exactly where Carey was sticking to the truth and where he was lying to his father, and sat back to admire the barefaced way he did it. Heneage and Hunsdon both asked pointed questions that sounded as if Lowther had been busy with his pen. Carey actually laughed when Heneage wanted to know if King James had given him a pension. No, said Carey, he had been lucky with some bets, that was all. And of course he had sold Thunder to the King.

'Hmf,' said Hunsdon. 'Pity. Best piece of horseflesh you ever owned.'

'I know sir,' said Carey with genuine regret. 'But what could I do? The King wanted him. I was quite pleased he paid for the nag, really.'

'Hah!' said his father, standing and striding out into the entrance hall while he shouted for the steward. Carey elaborately gave way to Heneage as they followed and then muttered quietly over his shoulder, 'Back me up, Dodd.'

Before Dodd could answer, Carey had hurried after his father. Dodd was pressed to keep up, reflecting that the Carey family were very tiring people, the way they were always rushing about.

Hunsdon had decided to take a turn in the garden while they waited for supper to be readied, which displeased Dodd who would have been perfectly happy with a hunk of bread and some cheese, so long as he could put something in his growling belly immediately. But no, it seemed courtiers did things differently.

Dodd had never seen the point of gardens really, except for herbs and salads and the like. Janet had a garden at their tower in Gilsland and Lord knows, she had given him grief when his favourite horse got out and ate all the pea plants. This was nothing like anything he had seen. In the pale blue dusk, the garden stretched itself down to the wall, everything in it shouting of wealth, from the rose bushes and the maze to the grass which was scythed short and green as velvet, to the trees which were politely trimmed. Dodd wandered across the grass and peeked out of the gate which gave onto the water. He saw a little landing with yellow boats drawn up and a man standing watching them. The man touched his cap to Dodd and Dodd nodded back in lordly fashion, thoroughly enjoying himself. There was an hysterical duck carved in the stone lintel of the watergate and another one on the boatman's sleeve. Dodd wondered why Lord Hunsdon had chosen such a daft badge for himself. He was impressed with the Thames, though. It was wide and fast flowing and looked an unchancy water to cross even at low tide. Good thing there was the Bridge. Even Dodd had heard tell of the glories of London Bridge, though mostly from Barnabus who couldn't really be trusted.

Someone coughed softly at his elbow and Dodd looked sideways to find he was being quietly accosted by the Vice Chamberlain.

'Mr Dodd.'

'Ay, sir,' said Dodd, wondering had the man not heard he was Land Sergeant of Gilsland or did he not know how to address him?

'Perhaps you can help me.'

'If Ah can, sir.'

'What was your impression of the King's court in Scotland?'

Dodd thought for a moment. Heneage's face was full of friendliness and affability, which was all wrong. Dodd knew he was very small fry compared to the Vice Chamberlain of the Queen's court, and no great lord was that affable to his inferiors without he wanted something.

'Ah dinna ken, sir,' he said. 'I've no' seen any ither court, sir, for comparison.'

'Did the King seem well-affected?'

What the Devil did the man mean by that? Well-affected?

'Ah dinna ken, sir.'

'Well, did His Majesty grant Sir Robert an audience?'

'Oh ay, sir, he did that.'

'And what happened?'

'Ah dinna ken, sir, I wasnae there.'

'Sir Robert was alone, unattended?'

'I didnae say that, sir, only I wasnae there.'

'Well, was my Lord Spynie present at the audience?'

'Ah dinna ken, sir.'

Heneage coughed. 'Come, Mr Dodd, you're a man of parts, I can see, Sir Robert wouldn't employ you if you weren't.' Dodd felt pricklish. He wasn't Carey's servant, even if he was under the Courtier's command. He was a free man, with his own tower and kin to back him. What the Devil did Heneage think he was, some kind of hanger-on?

Heneage was smiling. Was Dodd supposed to be pleased he thought well of Dodd? Bugger that, thought Dodd.

'Do you think Sir Robert will be returning to the Scottish court soon?' From the casual way in which it was asked, that sounded an important question.

Dodd took refuge in stolidity. 'Ah dinna ken, sir. And it isnae my place to say, forbye, sir.'

Heneage coughed again, but would he leave off? No, he would not. Where the hell was Carey when he was needed?

'Well, perhaps you can tell me how Signor and Signora Bonnetti fare?'

'Eh, sir?'

Heneage's round little smile was becoming somewhat fixed. 'The Italian wine merchant and his wife. Perhaps you recall them?'

Dodd thought about it for a while. 'Ay, I mind 'em.'

Another silence. Heneage took a deep breath, held it and coughed again. 'Did...ah...did Signora Bonnetti seem well-affected to Sir Robert?'

Dodd looked even more blank. 'Sir?'

'Surely you met the lady?'

Heneage had come closer, had taken Dodd's elbow in a proprietorial fashion. 'Come, Dodd, we can deal together,' he said softly. 'Do you know who I am?'

'Ay, sir,' said Dodd, wishing to flick Heneage's importunate fingers off his arm but controlling himself. 'Ye're the Queen's Vice Chamberlain.'

'One of my offices is to thoroughly investigate all potential... ah...foreign problems. You can be sure I ask my questions with good reason.'

'Ay, sir.' Was there some kind of threat in Heneage's silky confiding manner? Did he expect Dodd to be frightened or flattered? The plump fingers were nipping quite hard now, they were stronger than they looked. Dodd's eyes narrowed and he could feel anger starting to wash up the back of his neck. Was the fat courtier trying to bully him? *Him?*

'I have other sources regarding Signora Bonnetti,' breathed Heneage. 'You needn't fear that you will tell me anything I don't already know about your master. I am only looking for confirmation.'

Carey was standing over by a tree next to his father. Their eyes met briefly and Dodd could have sworn the Courtier winked knowingly at him. Dodd had never been so angry in his life without he punched somebody, but Carey steadied him. He took a deep shaky breath.

'I'm sorry, sir, but I cannae help ye, for I never met the lady.'

'Surely you saw her, for she danced with Sir Robert.' Jesus, would Heneage never let up?

'Ay, she did, sir, but I niver spoke to her.'

'Sir Robert was friendly with her? Hm?'

'She's a fair lady,' said Dodd, not bothering to keep his voice as low as Heneage's. 'I never saw Sir Robert but he was friendly to a good-looking woman.'

Heneage chuckled softly. 'Did they deal together?'

Much more of this, thought Dodd, and I surely will punch the bugger. Once again Carey caught his eye, still speaking to his father. Looking very amused, the Courtier shook his head infinitesimally.

Dodd felt as if he was drowning. What did Carey want him to do? Lie? But he didn't know what to say.

'Ah'm sorry, sir,' he said to Heneage at last when he was sure his voice wouldn't shake. 'But I cannae help ye as ye think I can. I'm no' Sir Robert's servant, I'm nobbut a Sergeant o' the Carlisle garrison.'

At last Heneage let go of him, leaving tingling prints on Dodd's elbow. He didn't seem dissuaded, only calculating. 'Perhaps we can talk at some other time. Perhaps I should invite you to my residence at Chelsea.'

Even Dodd could hear that there was a threat in the man's voice, though the words seemed harmless enough.

'That's kind of ye, sir,' he said, struggling to be urbane.

Heneage frowned as if Dodd had insulted him. 'Don't under-estimate me, Dodd.'

What the hell had he said that was wrong? 'I dinna follow ye, sir.'

'No? Perhaps you should ask your Captain to elucidate.'

'Ay, sir,' said Dodd, taking refuge in stolidity again.

Heneage sighed and shook his head. 'Was there nothing at all that struck you about the Scottish court?'

Dodd took a deep breath. 'They was an awfy lot of buggers there, sir. Ah didnae take to it mesen.'

Heneage's brow wrinkled as he tried to make out what Dodd was saying.

'I'm afraid Sergeant Dodd thoroughly disapproved of the Scots court and the whole proceedings generally, didn't you, Sergeant?' translated Sir Robert who had finally drifted over to them. His father was still under the apple tree, poking with his staff at the green apples weighing the branches.

'Ay, sir. I'm no' a courtier, sir.'

Both men heard the compressed distaste in his voice. Heneage smiled; Carey's eyebrows went up quizzically.

'Well, each to his own,' he said comfortably. 'Eh, Mr Vice Chamberlain? Good thing not everyone is desperate for the court, or the place would be even more infernally crowded than it is now. How are the accommodations at Oxford? Colleges being co-operative?'

Heneage sniffed. 'Helpful enough, though not perhaps as willing as one would like, Sir Robert.'

'You'll be doubling up the Gentlemen, no doubt. I remember one Progress when I had to share a bed with Sir Walter Raleigh. Though he was still a plain mister then—it was a few years ago now. And the only reason we didn't have a third man in bed with us was because we bribed him to sleep on the floor.'

Dodd found to his astonishment that his hands were shaking. Never had he felt such pure rage and been forced to do nothing about it. His arm felt unclean where Heneage had dared to pinch it. And what the hell was he hinting about his residence in Chelsea? Dodd would personally eat his helmet if the Queen's Vice Chamberlain was planning to invite him to a dinner party, no matter how eager he was to pick Dodd's brains on the subject of Carey's doings in Scotland.

They were moving back towards the house, Carey prattling about Raleigh's sleeping habits. Raleigh, it seemed, had been unreasonably insulting to Carey, claiming he snored like a wild sow in farrow, which was manifestly unfair. Was it true that Raleigh was in the Tower now, over one of the Queen's maids of honour? Heneage allowed that it was and Carey displayed an almost infantile pleasure at the juicy nugget of gossip—Bess Throgmorton, well, he was damned, would never have thought she'd have it in her, though he knew Raleigh did, and now it seemed she had more in her than she rightfully should...Carey put his head back and laughed. Serve Raleigh right, the man's arrogance was insufferable.

Mistress Bassano came out, gliding over the grass, very lithe and graceful for a woman in her condition, with two of her women, one on either side of her and her bald manservant trotting at her heels like a bloodhound. A small hairy dog followed close behind him completing the symmetry.

Hunsdon joined them from the apple tree, and Mistress Bassano smiled like a cat as he caught her hand and put a large arm proprietorially around her shoulders. She kissed Hunsdon as lingeringly on the lips as she had earlier kissed Carey. Dodd could almost feel his eyes bulging from their sockets. Was Carey really ploughing his father's field? Was that why he had come to be Deputy Warden in Carlisle? By God, it made sense of why a popinjay Courtier would want to move north in a hurry.

Carey was showing not a single sign of guilt. He was laughing and chatting to Heneage in the most natural and carefree way, taking the trouble to flatter the Vice Chamberlain as he had buttered up Lord Maxwell in Scotland.

A liveryman came out and announced that supper was served, and as he followed Hunsdon and his mistress, Carey, Heneage and flocks of attendants, Dodd's head was reeling.

***

Supper involved eight different kinds of meat in sixteen different sauces, salads decorated with orange nasturtium flowers, a piece of a pie which must originally have been the size and weight of a millstone, and yet more of the wine. Dodd had always thought he didn't like wine but now realised that what he didn't like was cheap wine. If this was the way the better stuff tasted, he felt he could well get used to it.

The pity of it was having to sit down with Carey, his dad, his dad's mistress, and Heneage in another room hung with tapestries. Servants filed in with the food under silver covers on silver dishes as ceremoniously as if this were some fine feast, which only meant further delay before Dodd could fill his belly. Lord Hunsdon said grace. After all that, Dodd had almost lost his appetite again. Heneage tucked in enthusiastically, though.

Dodd concentrated on eating as neatly as he could, despite the way the Vice Chamberlain had soured his stomach. He watched out of the corner of his eye to see how Carey handled his eating knife and silver spoon and tried hard to copy him. The funny foreign sauces on the meats didn't help and he dropped a big piece of pheasant into the rushes. Mistress Bassano's lapdog was onto the tidbit at once, slurping and growling at it. Trying to pretend he had meant to drop the food, Dodd patted the hairy head and had his fingers nipped at for his pains, which made Mistress Bassano smile at him again.

'Little Willie is a very naughty dog,' she told him with a teasing note in her voice. 'You really must not indulge him, Sergeant, or he'll get fat.'

Dodd smiled at her apologetically while he mentally took all her clothes off and bulled her up against a wall. As if reading his mind and enjoying it, she bent over and scooped the dog into her arms, while Dodd tried desperately to stop himself wondering if her arse was as smooth and round as her tits. He concentrated on the meat again. Much more of this, he thought, and he wouldn't be able to rise from the table.

The talk went right over his head too, though it seemed to be swirling repeatedly around the twin whirlpools of Carey's relations with the Scottish King and the question of the Italian woman. Mistress Bassano must have been foreign herself with that name but spoke like any other southerner. She was sitting next to Lord Hunsdon and leant against him scandalously. Carey's father seemed not exactly smitten—more pleased and smug like a bull next to his favourite heifer. Carey sat opposite her and next to Heneage. Thank God, the Courtier was studiously avoiding the lady's eye.

Mistress Bassano talked, laughed, preened and, unless Dodd was much mistaken, the whole pleasing display was aimed straight at Carey and not his dad. That was distinctly tactless and Carey seemed a little worried by it. He struck up another gossipy conversation with Heneage in a bid to avoid the noonday glare of Mistress Bassano's dangerous flirtation. It didn't work, for she kept interrupting.

At last the food was finished—or at least they had eaten their fill for there was too much to be got down in one sitting. Dodd wondered what happened to the leftovers—the Hunsdon pigs must live like kings and be fat as butter.

The leavetaking was prolonged and jovial, Carey talking rather at random as Heneage and his followers went down to the river again and took a few of the boats. Dodd was more than ready for his bed. Mistress Bassano went ostentatiously to her chamber, kissing Lord Hunsdon fondly on the lips and giving Carey's fingers a squeeze when he bent to kiss her hand.

Dodd had half-expected to be put in the servants' quarters or on a truckle bed in Carey's room, but it seemed the Hunsdon steward knew more about what a Land Sergeant was than did Heneage. He was stunned at the magnificence of his bedchamber—a fashionably golden oak-panelled cavern and no less than a four-poster bed complete with a tester and pale summer curtains. The servingman who led him there through a bewildering number of corridors and rooms advised him to shut his bed curtains against bad ague airs from the Thames and asked with a careful lack of expression and no hint of a glance at his homespun if the Land Sergeant would require a man to help him undress. Dodd told him no and decided on his usual ale and bread for breakfast at a restful 7 o'clock in the morning, well after sun-up. Now that was something to look forward to—a nice lie-in when he was neither wounded nor sick.

For a while, Dodd wandered around the room admiring the vast quantity of things in it; the painted cloths, the clothes chests, the carved folding chair, the fireplace laid with logs in case he should feel cold and a tinderbox beside it. There were candles everywhere, at least five of them and not a speck of tallow but the finest beeswax. Dodd firmly crushed the urge to slide them into his pocket. The rushes on the floor were new all the way down to the floor and the windows were glass with wooden shutters, so that not only was there no draught but you could even look out of them quite well. In awe Dodd touched the carved babies rioting with grape vines across the mantelpiece: he liked to whittle on wood himself and appreciated fine workmanship.

At last he shucked his clothes down to his shirt, left them folded on the chest, drew the curtains around the bed and climbed gingerly in, sliding between ice-smooth linen sheets that had not only never been slept in by another body but must have been ironed as well. By God, what it was to have hordes of servants, he thought, as he shut his eyes and snuggled into the softness of the pillows.

Half an hour later he turned over for the forty-fourth time and opened his eyes. It was no good. He couldn't sleep. He was used to sleeping alone—the jealously guarded privilege of his own cubbyhole next to the bunkroom of the barracks at Carlisle was normally his sole domain. But the fact remained that this bed was bigger than that entire tiny room. The vast spaces of the chamber outside the curtains, unpeopled by friendly farting snoring humanity, made him as nervous as a horse in an empty stable.

He got up, wandered around the room again, peered out of the window, swatted an enterprising mosquito and then found the jug of spiced wine. That was a blessing. Sipping lukewarm spiced syrup from the silver goblet provided, he looked again out of the window and saw someone moving on the Strand. Those bailiffs weren't giving up; two men in buff coats were watching the gatehouse like cats at a mousehole.

Thursday, 31st August 1592, Morning

Next morning Dodd had a slight headache from the spiced wine but felt happier than he could remember after sleeping so late and waking in solitary state with no one hammering on the door telling him the Grahams were over the Border or Gilsland was under siege. God knew what was going on at home with the whole Border Country as stirred up as it was, but what could he do about it? A manservant brought in his breakfast on a tray and seemed surprised to find him already up and dressed.

Sitting by the window again, he ate fine white manchet bread with fresh-made butter and cheese and drank ale as nutty and sweet as Bessie's. It was fine to look down on all the folk milling around, working hard, and the shops opening up with a rattle of shutters. And it was staggering the wealth here; even the prentices had velvet sleeves and the kitchen maids wore silk ribbons and fine hats. How would you pillage London, Dodd wondered, where would you begin? Fetching the spoils away might be a problem—there didn't seem to be many horses around. Most people were on foot.

There was a knock on the door and Carey entered, resplendent in black velvet and brocade, a suit Dodd didn't think he had seen before. He had obviously been up since well before sunrise and was full of plans. He instantly destroyed the restful peace of the morning.

'Morning, Sergeant,' he said cheerfully, strode to the window and peered out. His brows knitted. 'Christ, we're under siege.'

Dodd looked out again at once, but couldn't see any armed concourse of men, so assumed the Courtier was exaggerating about debt-collectors again. 'Oh ay?'

Carey paced up and down tiringly. 'I was going to slip out by river this morning, have a look round, but there was a whole boatload of 'em waiting by the steps. And there are four that I recognise on the Strand now.'

Dodd nodded mournfully, though in fact he had rarely been more tickled by a situation in his life. God, whatever else you could say about the Courtier, he was very entertaining.

'Ay, they were keepin' watch here last night.'

'Were they?' Carey was only confirmed in his disgust. Off he went pacing again.

'Er...sir,' said Dodd tactfully. 'Yer father's a man o' substance and wealth.'

'Yes?'

'Could he not...er...pay 'em off, sir?'

The Courtier smiled sadly, wandered over to check the wine jug, lifted his eyebrows at Dodd and then poured himself a gobletful and knocked it back.

'Well, he could and he won't,' said Carey. 'He's rich, certainly, but most of it's in land and buildings. Very hard to get liquid cash off property like that; if you sell them you lose badly on the deal and mortgaging's even worse. Plus my esteemed eldest brother George would have a fit if Father sold any of his patrimony to pay more of my debts.'

'More?'

'He's already settled about four thousand pounds for me and lent me another thousand.'

Dodd's jaw dropped. He could not get used to the way Carey casually bandied about sums that he had never even thought about before, much less owned or spent.

'And then there's brother Edmund who's not cheap to maintain either, and John's expenses in Berwick are crippling. Father says if he kept paying off his sons' debts he'd be begging at Temple Gate in a year and stark raving mad into the bargain.'

'But sir! What on earth d'ye spend all this money on? Not just clothes, surely?'

'Oh clothes, armour, horses, masquing, occasional little bets, women, plays, cockfighting…God, I don't know. It just flows away from me somehow.'

'Ay. So how much d'ye owe?'

Carey shook his head. 'I'm not sure. Somewhere about another two or three thousand, I should think. Thereabouts.'

Very carefully Dodd shut his mouth and swallowed hard.

'Two or three thousand pounds?' he asked, just to get it straight. Carey looked mildly irritated.

'Well, it's not pennies, unfortunately.'

'And the creditors are feeling a mite impatient?'

'They're terrified because I got away from them last time and they think I'll do it again—go north and stay there until the lot of them are dead or in debtors' gaol themselves.' Dodd blinked at this admission. Even Carey had the grace to look a little shamefaced. 'Well, what else could I do?'

'Ay, sir. What?' echoed Dodd, thinking of a whole variety of sensible and economical things.

'Anyway, you have to spend money to get money. Which reminds me—did Heneage give you a bribe?'

'Nay, sir, he didnae,' said Dodd, feeling aggrieved. 'Nae such thing. He said he might invite me tae his residence in Chelsea, but nae more than that…'

Carey frowned. 'That was bloody cheeky of him.'

Dodd felt confused. 'It was?'

'Who does he think he is, threatening you in front of me and my father?'

'Ah…Was that what he wis doing, sir?'

Carey's frown lightened. 'Well, you'll have confused him at least. What did you say?'

'I said he wis kind, sir. Nae more.'

Carey shouted with laughter. 'I wish I'd been closer to see his reaction. You must be the first person he's said that to who didn't instantly quiver with fright.'

'Ay, he seemed puzzled. He said I should ask you, sir.'

'How would you react if Richie Graham invited you to Brackenhill to discuss your blackrent payments?'

'Och.' Dodd sucked his teeth. 'I see. What is Mr Heneage, exactly, sir?'

'One of the most powerful men in the kingdom and getting stronger every day. I'd say he's even keeping the Cecils up at nights.'

'Why? He disnae seem much of a fighting man.'

'Did you ever hear of Sir Francis Walsingham?'

'Ay, sir, ye've told me about him. The Queen's Secretary.'

'And chief intelligencer, until his death. Well, Heneage has taken over Walsingham's activities in collecting information here and abroad, and in hunting down Papist priests. Unlike Walsingham, he isn't an honest man. Interrogations of suspected traitors used to take place in the Tower of London, under warrant from the Queen. Now they happen at Chelsea.'

'But he couldnae arrest me, could he, Sir Robert? I'm no' a traitor.'

Carey said nothing to that, just looked at him until Dodd felt embarrassed by his naivety.

'It is certainly true,' said Carey eventually, in a distant tone of voice, 'that all suspected traitors who are taken to Heneage's house in Chelsea eventually confess to treason.'

'Ay,' said Dodd, his mouth gone dry. 'I see now what he was trying. What should I do, sir? He seems to think I know what went on in Scotland. And I dinna, sir, I was wi' the Johnstones when ye...er...when ye were talking to the King.'

'A piece of advice for you, Dodd,' Carey said, fiddling with the embroidered cuffs of his fancy gloves. 'If Heneage offers you a bribe, take it. Answer his questions, tell him whatever you can; by all means play stupid, but convince him that you are frightened enough of him to want to co-operate. He likes that.'

'Ay.'

Carey squinted through the window glass again and then sat down and ran his hand through his hair.

'My blasted father's disappeared off with Heneage to have a look at some property Mr Vice wants to buy. God knows why they're both here when the Queen's on progress in Oxford and they're thick as thieves as well. I thought Father loathed the man.'

'Perhaps Heneage wants blackrent fra yer father?' offered Dodd. Carey gave him one of those very blue considering looks of his.

'You catch on fast, don't you Dodd?' he said. 'Yes, I'm beginning to think something like that is going on, but I'm damned if I can work out what. Father ought to be untouchable by the likes of Heneage.'

Dodd knew this was because Lord Hunsdon was in fact the Queen's bastard half-brother. Carey was staring out of the window and the expression on his face was one that Dodd had never seen there before; a cold, wary, calculating look.

'Anyway, he says he wants me to write a report for him about Scotland. Presumably, one he can show to Heneage.'

'Ay, sir. Which tale will ye tell?'

Carey looked amused at Dodd's tone. 'The one for public consumption, of course. It seems nobody the Cecils or Heneage is paying for news from Scotland actually recognised me at the crucial time, which is a blessed relief. Thanks for backing me with Heneage, by the way, you did it perfectly. I nearly bust a gut trying not to laugh at his expression when you were stonewalling him.'

Dodd tilted his head in acknowledgement. 'Ay, sir. I'll own I was surprised to hear ye…er…tell such a strange tale to your dad.'

'What? You mean, lie to him?' Carey, who would have instantly called Dodd out if he'd said the word himself, grinned. 'I didn't. He's already got the real report from me. He warned me to be tactful with Heneage, so I was.'

'Er…how?'

'Called me Robert. Never does that, not ever. Usually it's Robin, boy or bloody idiot, depending. I wanted to talk to him about it last night but his man said he was…ah…busy and passed the message about the report. Now it seems I'm stuck here indoors scribbling away like some damned clerk—God, how I hate paperwork. But I want you and Barnabus to go and do some scouting for me. See what's going on. Barnabus will want to put a notice up in St Paul's to find a new master and if you see any likely looking northerners who might make a decent *valet de chambre* for me, get their names. I may have to borrow somebody from Father, seeing the Court's not in town and the law term not started yet. And something's wrong here but I'm not sure what.'

'With your father?'

'And with London too. It's too quiet. Strand's half-empty. Where is everybody? Bartolmy's fair just packed up and Southwark due to start, but all the traders seem to have made off as fast as they can with their woolsacks and bolts of cloth. I want to know why. Stick close to Barnabus, and if you get lost, head south for the river and then go westwards until you find Somerset House. Or take a boat.'

'Ay, sir.'

'And leave any of your money behind that you don't want stolen. London pick-pockets are famous the world over.'

As Dodd had brought what had once seemed to him like the large sum of three shillings from his pay and also had an angel and some shillings from the footpads, he nodded at this good advice.

***

St Paul's was surrounded by a market full of little stalls filled up with booksellers and papersellers, more books than Dodd had ever seen in his entire life before. Even the Reverend Gilpin had never had such a lot of books. How could a man tell which he wanted to read? It was indecent. And the place was full of people standing around reading books or talking and arguing with each other. Two poorly-dressed, hungry-looking men were arguing loudly with a fat man in an ink-stained apron who they seemed to think owed them money for their writing of a book, which he was strenuously denying.

Barnabus threaded through purposefully, swatting boys away from his pockets and disentangling Dodd from a pretty young piece in a mockado gown who seemed to think Dodd was her long-lost cousin.

They climbed the steps and went into the cathedral of London town, which was a great echoing monster of a building. The nave was full of little stalls and scriveners tables, the aisle was full of young men who paraded in clothes that made Dodd gasp for the colours of them, the outrageous size of their cartwheel ruffs, the

47

velvets, damasks and satins, the vast padded breeches and the long peascod bellies, the slashings and panes and embroideries. The human butterflies were in constant motion, bowing to each other, talking, laughing.

'Mm,' said Barnabus, staring about critically. 'Now where is everybody?'

'Eh?' said Dodd.

'Nobody here,' Barnabus said over his shoulder as he threaded across the circling stream of haberdashery to one of the huge round pillars near the high altar screen with its blaze of gold and silver and red silk banners. There were a number of men in jerkins or buff leather standing around the pillar, looking hopeful, pieces of paper pinned to a noticeboard behind them. Barnabus went straight to it, stole two pins from one of the older notices, and stuck up his own paper.

'There,' he said. 'I'll be sorry to leave 'im, but what can you do?'

'You're resigning from the Courtier's service?'

'I've had enough,' sniffed Barnabus. 'Carlisle don't suit me, what with nuffing to do and nearly getting hanged in the summer. I'll leave 'im when I've found a new master.'

'Hmf,' said Dodd. He'd never thought much of Barnabus, who rode like a sack of meal and half the time made no sense at all. Mind you, he had good skills at knife-throwing and the Courtier seemed to rate him, but that was all you could say in his favour really.

Barnabus squared his shoulders and looked round at the competition, some of which seemed large and ugly enough.

'Don't know what I'll find though,' said the little man gloomily. 'What with nobody being here.'

'But...look at 'em all.'

'Nah,' said Barnabus, folding his arms and leaning against another pillar to glare disapprovingly down the aisle. 'The Mediterranean's half-empty for the time of year. Must all be up at Oxford, arse-licking the Queen.'

How did they all fit in when they were here, Dodd wondered? He craned his neck to look up at the roof which seemed very new, the upper walls part burned. St Paul's had no proper spire, only a

48

temporary roof where it should have been. Barnabus was beckoning one of the urchins playing dice by the altar steps.

'Here, you, boy. Show my friend here round Paul's for me and if nobody's nipped his purse by the time he gets back, I'll pay you a penny extra.'

Dodd shrugged and followed the mucky-faced child who pointed self-importantly at a large monument full of moping angels and rampant lions and the like on the south side, with a little chapel next to it. Apparently it was Duke Humphrey's tomb for certain sure and definite though some scurvy buggers said it was some John Beauchamp fellow or other, which it wasn't but Duke Humphrey's, did he understand?

Dodd shrugged again and said it could be Good King Henry's tomb for all he cared, to be told sharply that that one was in Westminster, didn't he know nuffing?

Tomb after tomb was knowledgeably pointed out, one with a lot of reverence as Sir Philip Sidney's, and they made the circuit of the nave where pie-sellers, stationers and the apple-women cried their wares. It all seemed crowded and noisy enough for Dodd.

At least the Londoners seemed to be friendly folk. Overfriendly, perhaps. Twice Dodd was hailed as an old friend by men he had never met before, one of them a southerner from Yorkshire by his speech.

The third time a complete stranger clasped his arm and demanded to know what he was doing in London, bless him, Dodd decided to play along with the game.

'Och, good day,' he said with as big a smile as he could muster. 'If it's no' Wee Colin Elliot himself,' he added, naming his family's bitterest enemy. 'What are ye doing here?'

The man, who was as tall as Dodd and by his speech had never been north of Durham in his life, laughed and bowed.

'I could ask the same of you, friend.'

'It's too long a tale to tell,' said Dodd who couldn't be bothered to make one up. 'How's yer wife and the bairns?'

'Well enough,' said the man. 'Well enough indeed. I thought it was you; I was just saying to my friend here, that's him to the life and it was.'

'Ay,' said Dodd, still smiling unnaturally until his face ached

49

with the exercise. The friend was shorter and darker and both were well-dressed in wool suits trimmed with velvet.

'It does ma heart good to find a fellow Berwick man here in this nest of Southerners,' said the shorter of the two in a passable imitation of the Berwick way of talking. 'Mr Dodd, you must have a cup of wine with us. Will ye do that? Us northerners should stick together, after all.'

'Oh ay, we should. O' course,' said Dodd, glancing across at Barnabus who was deep in obsequious conversation with an elaborately taffeta'd young man. Dodd shrugged. If he wasn't feared of the Bewcastle Waste or the Tarras Moss, why should he be feared of London, strange place though it was?

He went along with his two new friends, smiling and laughing like the Courtier, and making out that he was there to deal wool. Oh and that was lucky, because they happened to dabble in the wool trade themselves, and the one that was calling himself Wee Colin Elliot had a number of sacks in a warehouse near Queen's Hythe just begging for a buyer since they'd missed the fair...

Dodd's heart began to beat hard as they went out of a side door he hadn't noticed, through the churchyard. It seemed they were heading for a narrow alleyway. A little bit late it occurred to him that actually, when he was on his own with neither his kin nor the men of the Carlisle guard to back him, he was feared of both the Waste and the Moss because they were normally full of robbers.

'They serve the finest wine in the world just around this corner...' said the smaller man, hurrying him into the alley.

Suddenly Dodd decided he'd had enough of the game. He balked just inside the alley, felt a hand clutching at his elbow, ducked instinctively, swung about and caught the arm of the bigger man who was bringing a small cudgel down on where Dodd's head would have been. Dodd snarled. This was something he understood. He headbutted the man so his nose flowered red, bashed the hand holding the cudgel up against the wall until the weapon dropped. There was a metallic flash in the corner of his eye, so he kneed the man to put him down, whirled around sweeping his broadsword from its sheath and caught a rapier on the forte of his sword. The rapier flickered past his ear a couple of times and terrified him by nearly taking out his eye. Dodd knew that a rapier which could thrust had all the advantage over a broadsword, especially when he wasn't wearing a jack, so he pulled out his dagger and went properly into the attack, crowding the smaller man up against the opposite wall and raining blows down on him so he had no chance to pull any fancy moves.

Something grabbed his leg and bit his calf and Dodd glared down to see that the larger man had crawled over, still sobbing, and had caught him. He stamped down with his other boot to get the teeth off and went after the one with the rapier again. Unfortunately the bastard southerner was running away, so Dodd shook his foot free again and gave chase.

Barnabus appeared in the mouth of the alley and thoughtfully tripped the man up. Dodd was onto him, kicked the dropped rapier away, hauled him up by a fistful of doublet and slammed him against the wall.

'Careful, mate,' said Barnabus confidentially over his shoulder from where he was robbing the man on the ground. 'Don't kill 'im; Sir Robert's right about juries round here.'

Dodd was snarling at his prize. 'If ye ken who I am, ye'd ken that Wee Colin Elliot's dad killed mine, ye soft wet southern fart. Wis it robbery ye were after, eh? Eh?!'

The man's eyes were swivelling in his head and he was gobbling. Dodd slammed him again. 'By Christ, did ye think I wear ma sword for a fucking decoration, ye long slimy toad's pizzle, who the hell d'ye think...'

'Well, 'e wasn't to know, was he?' said Barnabus reasonably. 'He just thought you was some farmer up for the law-term, what with yer homespun suit and funny talk. Poor bugger, look at 'im, he's gone to pieces.'

Dodd realised to his disgust that the man was actually crying now, and dropped him in a convenient pile of dung. Barnabus rolled him expertly, tutted and led the way out of the alley back to Ave Maria Lane, with a quick glance either side at the turning for further ambushes. Dodd, whose blood was up, rather hoped there would be someone, but put his sword away again when Barnabus hissed at him.

Feeling witty, Dodd paused, went back, found the rapier and broke it in two with his boot. Barnabus shook his head at the waste.

'Nasty foreign weapon,' Dodd explained. 'When d'ye think they'll come after us wi' their kin?'

Barnabus laughed. 'Never,' he said. 'Not the way you think. Though I'd keep a weather eye out for coney-catchers—they'll want your purse one way or the other, believe me.'

'What's a coney-catcher, for God's sake?'

Barnabus rolled his eyes at this display of ignorance. 'Someone what wants to help you rob yourself, someone what fools you and draws you in with your own greed and fear. It's philosophical, really. They say nobody can coney-catch an honest man. Mind you, I shouldn't think there's ever been one come to London before.'

Dodd grunted, suspicious of compliments, however back-handed. Not that it mattered. With luck, once the Lord Chamberlain and Vice had satisfied themselves that Carey wasn't working for Spanish spies nor likely to become King James's new catamite, the lot of them could go north again.

A scurrying down by the entrance to the crypt caught his eye. There were black rats on the steps, crawling over and under each other brazenly in daylight. Two rat corpses lay close by, swollen out of shape by death.

'Good God, look at that,' he said in horror. 'Look at the size o' them.'

Barnabus glanced over and shrugged. 'Oh yes,' he said off-handedly. 'They say the biggest rats in the world prance up and down Paul's aisle.'

'Ah hadnae thought they meant real rats.'

'Well both: it's one of them witty comments, innit? You coming in again?'

Suddenly he felt choked by all the buildings rising up around him, hemmed in and trapped. Your eyes were always coming up short against a wall, and he was trammelled and crowded with people; the stink would fell an ox. And he had always hated rats.

He stopped at the side door of the church, unable to bear the thought of entering the high solemnity of the place with its faded paintings too high up to be whitewashed and the human trash prancing to and fro nibbling meatpies beneath the hard-faced old-fashioned angels. And God knew what horrors were underneath, in the crypt where no-one went.

'I'll take a turn round about the churchyard,' he said, hoping Barnabus wouldn't notice how pale he felt. 'Take the air.'

Barnabus nodded. 'You'll be safe enough, I should think. It'll take them a day to work out what to do about you. You could buy yourself a book.'

'Good God, what would I want to do that for?' said Dodd. Barnabus grinned and winked at him, before disappearing into the gloom.

Dodd glowered around but found no more would-be friends. He ambled past the stalls of the churchyard, looking with growing astonishment at all the different books, just casually lying there, higgledy-piggledy in piles with the first pages pinned up on the support posts of the awnings and the brightly coloured signs over the stalls—there was a cock, a pig, a blackamoor, a mermaid, all different like inns.

He stopped under one awning, picked up a small volume and opened it, squinted to spell out the words under his breath. It was poetry—some tale about foreigners, he thought, from the funny names. Dodd couldn't be doing with such nonsense.

Suddenly he caught sight of a familiar face: Mistress Bassano's servant, the balding young man called Will. He was not in livery but wearing a dark green woollen suit trimmed with brocade and a funny-looking collar that wasn't a ruff, but looked like a falling band starched so it stood up by itself. He was standing with his hat off in front of another of the men with inky aprons, though skinny this time, under the sign of a black swan. Will was proffering a sheaf of closely-written paper. The printer shook his head, arms folded, legs astride.

'Nobody's interested in rehashes of Ovid,' grumbled the printer. 'I've told you before, there's no demand for that kind of thing.'

Will's response was too soft for Dodd to hear it, though he caught a whining note. The printer rolled his eyes patiently.

'I know the market, see,' he said. 'It's my business. Your stuff wouldn't sell, believe me. I'm always looking for new talent, of course I am, but I've never known trade so slow and I have to be careful what I take on. Now if you could do me a nice chivalrous romance, or a coney-catching pamphlet or two, like Mr Greene's work—there's something that sells like hot cakes.'

Will's answer to that was sharp.

'Oh, did I?' sniffed the printer. 'Well, listen, mate, not everybody can write like Greene or Nashe or Marlowe. Maybe you should just stick to playing, hmm?'

Will turned away, looking dejected, with his papers under his arm. Not wanting to be caught eavesdropping, Dodd slung the book he was holding back amid all the piles of them, and went reluctantly back into St Paul's to find Barnabus. There was no sign of him. Dodd made two circuits of the Cathedral, trying to spot him amongst the throng, then decided he was no wean to be feared of getting lost; he'd go back to Somerset House on his own.

Dodd had never got lost since he was a lad. He always knew instinctively where he was and where his goal was in relation to him. He knew where Somerset House was now, could have pointed to it, but the trouble was, you couldn't just head straight across country to it; you had to walk along the streets, and the streets were uncooperative. They kept starting in roughly the right direction and then twisted round bewilderingly to spit you out heading away from your goal again. The people and the noise from the shopkeepers roaring out their wares and the children and the dogs and the pigs and goats made him feel breathless and confused. In his own country he was a man to respect, people made way for him even in Carlisle. Here they jostled past him and not one face was familiar, face after face, all strange, more people than he had ever met in his life before and he didn't know one of them. Rudely, not one of them so much as acknowledged he was there. They were so finely dressed, even the streetsellers wore ancient wool trimmed with motheaten fur, not homespun russet. Once or twice Dodd thought he heard people snickering at him for his countryfied clothes. His neck stiffened and his face got longer and sourer by the minute as street after street seemed to conspire to bewilder him and drive him further from Somerset House.

At last he stopped and decided to take the Courtier's advice and head for the river. Once there he could follow the bank westwards, he thought, or even take a boat. That would be the sensible thing to do.

Half an hour later he was wondering in despair where in God's name the Londoners could hide a river. He had just passed the same overdecorated water conduit for the fourth time. Dodd used the little cup chained to it to take a drink, and leaned on the side to think for a bit.

'Excuse me, sir,' said a nasal drone beside him. 'You serve my Lord Hunsdon's son, don't you?'

'Who wants tae know?' growled Dodd, glaring suspiciously at the man. By God, it was the bald-headed manservant that had been trying to sell papers to the printer in Paul's Churchyard.

'Och,' he snarled. 'Were ye following me? Whit the hell d'ye want?'

'N...nothing. Nothing, sir. Only...er...I've seen you pass by here three times now and it occurred...er...it seemed to me you might...er...'

'Spit it out, man.'

'...be lost?'

Dodd decided to let the little man live, since what he said was true. 'What of it?'

'I...I could lead you back to Somerset House.'

Dodd wasn't going to fall for any more scurvy southern tricks. 'Ay, to be sure. If ye dinna take me down some foul wynd and slip a blade in me.'

The man looked shocked and offended. 'Why would I do that? I'm no footpad.'

'Ay, I mind ye. Ye're Mistress Bassano's singing servant, Will.'

He coughed and made a reasonably graceful bow. 'Will Shakespeare, sir, at your service.'

Dodd thought it was a remarkably stupid name for a man with arms no thicker than twigs and sorrowful brown eyes like a spaniel, so he grunted.

'Ay. I'm Sergeant Dodd. What's the way back tae Somerset House, then?'

They walked in silence through dizzying alleys and passageways under houses that actually met over the pavements, until at last they came in sight of the great galleon of St Paul's moored amongst its attendant houses.

'What was it ye were trying to sell tae the bookseller?' Dodd asked. Will flushed and looked even more miserable than usual.

'Only some verses.'

'Poetry, eh? Ballads?'

'Er...no. A classical theme, the sorrowful tale of Pyramus and Thisbe.'

'Och,' said Dodd, who had never heard of the story but wasn't inclined to admit it. 'And did the man no' like it?'

'Seemingly not.'

'But ye found someone else to buy it, did ye no'?'

'No.'

'Well, where are the papers then?'

'I threw them in the Thames.'

'What? That's a powerful waste o' paper.'

Will shrugged. 'I was angry.'

'What did he mean about ye should stick to playing?'

'I am—or I was until I lost my job when the theatre was closed—a player.'

'I thocht ye were Mistress Bassano's servingman.'

Brown spaniel eyes stared into the distance and seemed to well with tears. 'At the moment, sir, I am, yes. My Lord Hunsdon was kind enough to take me in when I...when everything went wrong.'

'How did ye come to know the Lord Chamberlain?'

Something subtly out of place crossed the would-be poet's expression. 'He had seen me acting with my Lord Strange's troop and he's a good friend to poetry; he said he thought my version of *Henry VI* showed great promise and he would be happy to tide me over until...until, well, my problems were solved.'

The ugly flattened vowels had turned down at the end of the sentence, closing the door to more questions. Dodd thought it all sounded odd, a respectable lord like Hunsdon giving house space to a mere player, but then none of the Careys seemed to worry about things like scandal.

They had come down Ludgate Hill and over Fleet Bridge and Dodd was starting to recognise familiar buildings. He could even see the Thames, glinting tantalisingly between the houses.

'I think I can find ma own way now,' he said.

Will nodded, still lost in thought. As Dodd turned to take his leave, Will seemed to come to a decision. 'Sir,' he said. 'Sergeant Dodd.'

'Ay.'

'Would you...would you do me a favour?'

Dodd's eyes narrowed. 'Depends.'

Will smiled faintly. 'I was only wondering if you would pass a letter to Mistress Bassano?'

'Why can ye no' do it yerself?'

Pink embarrassment was edging the player's jaw. 'It's my day off, and, well...I think it would be better this way.'

'What is it? The letter. And who's it from?'

'It's...from me, but...er...well, really it's only a few lines I've written in her honour.'

'It's nothing scandalous, is it? It willnae make the lady greet and get me intae trouble?'

Will shook his head. 'I'm sure the poems will please her—she likes poetry. And I think these are...er...quite good. You'd only have to give them to her and...er...say they're from an admirer too humble to offer them personally.'

Dodd frowned. 'It all sounds verra strange.'

'Oh, believe me, sir, ladies like that kind of thing. They like mystery.'

For a moment it was on the tip of Dodd's tongue to ask if Will had any claim to the babe Mistress Bassano was carrying, but then he stopped himself. Really it was none of his business, fascinating though the doings in the Hunsdon household were.

Will was holding out his precious letter which he had taken out of the front of his doublet; good creamy paper, carefully folded and sealed. Dodd shrugged, took it and put it in the front of his leather jerkin.

At the gate of Somerset House Dodd was carefully inspected and then admitted without argument. Behind him on the Strand, the heavyset men in their buff coats leaned in doorways or stood in alleyways, waiting patiently for their quarry to reappear.

He asked in the yard where Sir Robert was and then headed where the manservant pointed, towards the stables that looked over the garden. Mistress Bassano was sitting under a cherry tree heavy with fruit, her two maidservants sitting prettily disposed around her, all three of them stitching busily at some large embroidery. Best get it over with, thought Dodd, and marched over to her, made the best bow of his life and stood before her with his cap off, trying to get his thoughts in order. The way she was sitting on cushions with her pale green silk skirts spread out around her, you only had to tilt your head to get a full view of those magnificently rich breasts, riding high over the fertile swell of her belly. Dodd had never bedded a pregnant woman, since Janet was yet to fall for a babe, alas. How did you do it? Could you do it? What would it be...

'Why, Sergeant Dodd,' said Mistress Bassano. 'Can I help you?'

Dodd cleared his throat. 'Ay. Ah...I was given a letter for ye by...eh...by an admirer.'

Full pink lips curled up in a slow smile, the ends tucking themselves into a pair of dimples, and the heavily-lashed lids came down a little. Dodd knew he was staring at the woman's chest but couldn't stop himself; he felt like a tranced chicken.

'How romantic. And who is he?'

'Ah...he asked me not to say on account of it...er...being better left a mystery.'

'Oh.' The maid on Mistress Bassano's left giggled and Mistress Bassano pouted her maddening lips at the girl. 'Now, be sensible. These are important matters.'

'Ay,' croaked Dodd, wanting a quart of beer and wishing the sun wasn't so hot. 'Ah...here it is.'

He clutched the letter from the inside pocket of his leather jerkin, and held it out to Mistress Bassano who reached up a hand to take it. Her fingers brushed the back of Dodd's hand and made it tingle and prickle.

'How charming to receive a *billet doux* from such an unexpected messenger,' she said. And oh, the curve of her neck as she looked up at him, he could kiss his way all down the side of it, and...

Dodd found his breath was coming short. What did the woman do to radiate desire like that? Was she a witch? Had she laid some kind of spell on him? Ay, maybe that was it. God's truth, he was beginning to hate the Courtier and his father both.

'Thank you, Sergeant Dodd,' said Mistress Bassano as she lifted the edge of her kirtle and tucked Shakespeare's letter away in the pocket of her petticoat. Surely it was no accident that she let Dodd have a flash of her ankle and bare foot…Scandalous, no stockings, no shoes, a clear line all the way up her bare leg to her…

Dodd clutched his cap, jerked a bow and stepped back, nearly tripping on a miniature box hedge surrounding a bed of herbs.

'D'ye ken…have ye seen Sir Robert?' he asked, having to whisper because his mouth was so dry.

A tiny frown crossed the creamy brow under its wings of black hair dressed with pale green stones. 'Oh, I think I heard him shouting in the stables,' she said.

'Ay. Thank ye kindly, Mistress.'

Dodd very nearly turned tail and ran across the smooth green lawn to the complex of buildings around the stable yard. Before he got there he heard the unmistakeable sound of Careys having an argument, as Mistress Bassano had said.

'I came here because you ordered me to,' Carey was saying, obviously trying not to shout though his voice was probably audible in Westminster. 'Your letter, sir, ordered me away from my responsibilities in Carlisle where I am still very far from secure, and where the reivers will no doubt be playing merry hell in my absence. *You*, sir, ordered me to London where I have absolutely no wish to be. *Sir*. If you didn't want me to come to Somerset House, you shouldn't have written your bloody letter. SIR!'

Carey was nose to nose with his father, whose face above its ruff was going purple. Behind them in the kennels, hunting dogs barked and whined in alarm.

'Damn your impudence, boy,' roared Hunsdon. 'Why the hell didn't you go to the Liberties like I told you to? What the devil did you think you were at, prancing into this house when I specifically told you the bailiffs were out in force, you stupid boy?'

'Don't call me *boy*,' Carey ground out through his teeth, his fists bunched. 'And your letter said not a damned thing about bailiffs, as you well know, unless you've bloody forgotten it, you senile old goat.'

Hunsdon roared inarticulately and threw a punch at his son, who ducked, backed and put his hand to his sword. Entertaining though the scene certainly was, Dodd decided he had to intervene. Hunsdon had his own sword half-drawn.

'Sir, my lord.' He had stepped between the Careys, his hands up to fend them off.

'Out of my way, Sergeant,' bellowed Hunsdon.

'Dodd, this is none of your business,' growled Carey.

'Ay, it is. If ye kill each other who's gonnae guide me back home? And forebye, I dinnae understand what yer quarrel is.'

'It's simple enough, Sergeant. When I order my son to make sure he doesn't come into Somerset House but should go to one of my properties in the Liberties of Whitefriars, where he can at least move without being hunted by bailiffs, I expect to be obeyed.'

'How the hell can I obey an order I never received?' bellowed Carey. 'You said nothing about Whitefriars in your letter.'

'Of course I didn't, you overdressed halfwit; I sent a verbal message by Michael.'

'What bloody message? I never got it.'

'Nay, sir, he didnae. Who's Michael?'

'Used to be my *valet de chambre*,' Carey said. 'Father, I never saw Michael.'

'What do you mean, you never saw him?' Hunsdon's voice was now modulating down to a shout. 'I sent him out to meet you at Hampstead horsepond.'

Carey's bewilderment was so clear on his face, even his father began calming down. 'He wasn't there. We were jumped by footpads, but...'

The thought struck both Carey and Dodd at the same time. Carey paled and sat down on the edge of the horsetrough. 'What was he wearing when you sent him? Livery?'

'No, of course not. I didn't want to advertise who he worked for. He was wearing a brown wool suit. Why?'

'Ay,' said Dodd mournfully. 'That was him, all right. Brown doublet and hose, wi' some fancy work in black velvet ribbons.'

'That's right,' Hunsdon growled.

'Oh,' said Carey, putting his hand over his mouth. 'Poor bastard.'

Hunsdon's bushy eyebrows were meeting over his nose. 'I thought you said you didn't see him.'

Carey seemed too upset to answer so Dodd cleared his throat and did the job.

'Ay, we saw him, but he couldnae tell us yer message, my lord, on account of he wis hanging from the Hampstead Hanging Elm at the time, and nae face on him neither.'

'What? He was dead?'

'Ay. And not long dead, now I come to think of it. The body wasnae rotted.'

'I should have spotted it,' Carey said to himself. 'What was a fresh body doing on the Elm when the Assizes couldn't have sat for a month?'

Lord Hunsdon sat down on the horsetrough edge next to his son.

'Well,' he said as if the breath had been taken out of him too. 'Who could have thought it? Poor Michael. You're sure?'

Carey nodded once then shook his head. 'It's the only explanation. You sent him with a message about the bailiffs and somebody...stopped him delivering it.'

'Ay,' added Dodd dolefully, though in fact he didn't know Michael from Adam and didn't much care that he was dead. 'And they hid his body where naebody would notice it.'

'Very imaginative of them,' said Hunsdon.

There was a short silence. 'Will you tell his wife, or should I do it?' Carey asked.

Hunsdon sighed. 'I'll send some men up to Hampstead first to fetch the body, make absolutely sure. Then I'll tell her myself. Good God. What a bloody mess.'

Carey turned his head and looked consideringly at his father. 'Father, what's going on here?'

'Damned if I know, Robin. It's all a mystery to me. Why the devil did they have to kill him? All they had to do was knock him on the head.'

'That can kill a man by itself,' said Carey. 'Maybe they did it accidentally. Or maybe somebody wanted to make a point, as it were.'

'His father served me, you know, cared for my guns and armour in '72, when we did for Dacre.'

'Yes, I remember.'

'Good man. Died of flux, I seem to recall, a couple of years after. I remember Michael as a page, eager little lad, always willing. Poor Frances.'

'Is she here?'

'No, I've set them up in a house in Holywell Street, near the Cockpit. Two whippersnappers and another on the way. He was acting under-steward here. Only sent him because you'd be sure to know him. Thought he'd gone home to his wife when you arrived last night.'

'And you could hardly ask with Heneage hanging about.'

'No.' Hunsdon's face hardened. 'God rot his bowels.'

'You think it's...er...'

Hunsdon looked up, though he didn't seem to see the gargoyle waterspout on the stable guttering that he was glaring at.

'Don't know who else it could be. Damn him.'

'Perhaps it might be worth going to Oxford?' Carey asked.

Hunsdon shook his head, then clapped his hand on Carey's shoulder and stood up. 'I'd best organise a party to go up to Hampstead, fetch the body and give him a decent burial. I'll draft a letter to Mr Recorder Fleetwood, as there'll have to be an inquest, and I want it conducted properly.'

'If the corpse is still there,' Carey said.

'Hmf. Well, what can you do? You have to try.'

'Perhaps it would be better if we didn't make it too public that we know what's happened.' Carey was speaking very quietly and thoughtfully. 'After all, Heneage will have at least one paid man here.'

'Of course he does. What do you...ah. I see. Well, I don't like it. Goes against the grain to leave a man of mine hanging on a gibbet. What if Frances went past and saw him?'

'Excuse me, sir,' said Dodd. 'I verra much doubt he'll still be on the Elm. But could ye no' make a song and dance about they footpads we saw off at the Hampstead Cut and, while ye were at it, maybe find out about your man?' Dodd found himself caught in a crossfire of stares and wished he'd kept his mouth shut. 'Only, there'd be nae secret about that, my lord, since we left three kills of our own there.'

'You omitted the detail of the footpads, Robin,' Hunsdon said drily to his son.

Carey waved airy fingers. 'Fairly cack-handed attempt at an ambush in the Cut as we came through, which was foiled by Sergeant Dodd who spotted what was going on well before I did. Nothing much to say, really, since there was no harm done. To us, anyway.'

'Hm. That was why your gun was loaded.'

'Of course.'

'When you discharged it in the Strand I felt certain you were only defying me and had come prepared to bully your way in,' Hunsdon explained, standing up and brushing down his elaborately paned trunk-hose. 'Excellent suggestion of yours, Sergeant; I'll write to Mr Recorder this afternoon about the attempted robbery. With luck we'll be able to find and hang the men who murdered my servant.'

'If not the man who paid them to do it,' murmured Carey, also standing up.

Hunsdon tilted his head cynically. 'It's the way of the world, Robin, you know that. Now would the pair of you care to view the finest pack of hounds this side of Westminster?'

***

The hounds were very elegant beasts, and included a yellow lymer with a heavy head and a serious expression. One of the dog-pages explained at length about the thorn in his paw, which the dog held up to show the neat bandage. Both Careys examined it carefully, Lord Hunsdon squatting down with his arm across the dog's back. Dodd examined it himself.

'What do you think, Dodd?' Carey asked. 'It looks clean enough to me.'

Dodd felt around the dog's leg, in case there were any lumps in the animal's groin. You could sometimes get early warning of trouble with a wound if you found lumps, but there were none and the dog panted at him in puzzlement.

'Ay,' said Dodd thoughtfully. 'But I wouldnae hunt with him till it's all healed up, of course.'

'No, of course not,' said Lord Hunsdon. 'You're on sick leave, aren't you, Bellman, old fellow?' The dog panted and licked Hunsdon's face and the old lord pummelled his ears.

'Is he any relation of my lord Scrope's lymer bitch that pupped on yer bed?' Dodd asked, thinking he saw a family resemblance.

'Yes,' smiled Carey, who was rubbing the dog's high chest as the animal groaned with pleasure and plopped himself over on his side. 'He's her brother. Father gave Scrope the bitch as a present a couple of years ago.'

'Pupped on your bed?' Hunsdon laughed. 'What did Philadelphia say about it?'

'She wasn't very pleased. I had a great long lecture about the impossibility of cleaning counterpanes properly, as if I'd told the silly animal to do it. But it was a good thing she did, because she had trouble with the last pup of the litter.'

Hunsdon listened to the tale and agreed that a ruined counterpane was a small price to pay for saving a fine gentle bitch like Buttercup. Robin should take care with the pup though, because this particular line of lymers seemed to be even more greedy than the general run of hunting dogs and they got fat very easily. In fact Bellman himself was a bit tubby, and Jimmy the dog-page must remember not to feed him too much while he couldn't run.

As if to confirm this wisdom, Bellman farted extravagantly and all three of them retired coughing to look at the horses. Dodd was greatly impressed with Hunsdon's stable which held bigger and glossier beasts than any he had seen outside the contraband animals that the Grahams had harvested from the Scottish king's stables. The pathetic nags that they had ridden in from the Holly Tree the day before looked as if they knew how useless they were in comparison.

A bell rang, calling the household to dinner, and Dodd found himself borne along to the parlour where the Careys generally ate their meals, seven covers of meat this time and still nothing

Dodd rightfully recognised as food. Afterwards Sir Robert, who had drunk far more than he ate and was evidently going mad with boredom at being cooped up in his father's house, announced he would go and talk to the falconer and see if the birds had finished their moult. Hunsdon grunted and told Dodd he wanted his opinion on some arrangements for the Berwick garrison—would he come along to the old lord's study in an hour? He wished to see Robin privately first; he could come to Hunsdon's study in half an hour.

An hour later one of the grooms led Dodd along the corridors. It was astonishing how many rooms there were in the place—you couldn't count them all—and how peculiar to have one for each thing you might do in a day, such as a parlour for eating and a study for reading and writing, and every single one of them painted and decorated with hanging cloths and furnished with carved oak. Surely to God, Hunsdon could afford to pay Sir Robert's debts, even enormous ones?

Hunsdon's study was a room lined with books and cluttered with papers and official dispatch bags hanging on hooks. Dodd knocked on the door, entered at the single bark of 'Come', and stood straight with his cap off in front of the desk. Hunsdon had been leafing dispiritedly through a pile of letters and looked up at him.

'Sergeant Dodd. Good of you to come so promptly. What do you think of the mews?'

'I'm no' a falconer, my lord, and I canna say I've ever hunted with a bird, though I've watched when I was beating. Yer man at the mews says they might fly next week, being cautious, but we'll be back on the road tae Carlisle by then.' Hunsdon wasn't really listening.

'Hm. Dodd,' he said thoughtfully. 'There was a Dodd under my command when we took Dacre's hide—any relation?'

'Ay, sir. Me father, sir.'

Hunsdon beamed. 'That's right, of course he is. You've exactly the look of him. Damned fine soldier, if a bit serious. Scouted for me, as I recall, with his Upper Tynedalers.'

'Ay, sir.'

'Spotted Dacre's cavalry, I think.'

'Did he, sir?' Dodd could feel his ears going pink. He preferred not to think of his father. It brought back the horrible hollow feeling in the pit of his stomach that he'd had all through his teens.

'How is he?'

'Ma father, sir? He's died.'

Hunsdon sighed. 'I'm sorry to hear it, Sergeant.'

Strangely enough he did genuinely seem sorry though he could hardly have given a thought to Dodd's father between the Revolt of the Northern Earls and this day.

'Ay, sir. Er...thank ye, sir.'

'And what's this I hear about my son's behaviour at the Scottish court?'

The ambush was the more deadly for coming from behind a cover of sympathy.

'My lord?' Dodd kept his face carefully blank. Hunsdon made a 'hrmhrm' noise that was obviously where the Courtier had got his throat clearing and leaned back in his carved chair, causing it to creak at the joints.

'Sergeant,' he said gently, 'I like discretion in a man under my command and I've no doubt my son does too, but I must have the full tale.'

'The one Mr Heneage heard?'

Hunsdon chuckled without the least trace of humour. 'Certainly not. The one in which my son becomes somehow sufficiently deranged to deal in armaments with a couple of Italians who had Papist Spy all but branded on their foreheads, as he saw fit to boast in his letter? The one which explains the rumours about him being arrested for high treason, which he did not mention? The one which accounts for the damage to his hands which makes him embarrassed to take his blasted gloves off in my presence? That tale?'

'Och,' said Dodd firmly, resisting any impulse to smile at the exasperation in Hunsdon's voice. 'That one?'

'Yes,' said Hunsdon patiently. 'That one.'

Dodd told him, or at least all of it that he knew. At the end of his story, Hunsdon passed his palm across his eyes.

'Good God,' he said. 'And his hands?'

'What he said to me was they got caught in a door.'

'Oh really?'

'But considering two fingers was broken—which are fine now, my lord, his grip's good enough to fire a dag—and he's lost four fingernails which arenae grown back yet, my guess is someone had at him wi' the pinniwinks.' Hunsdon raised his eyebrows. 'Ah, thumbscrews, sir.'

Carey's dad had the same capacity as his son for instantly radiating compressed fury. His grey eyes had gone cold as ice.

'King James?'

'I doubt it, seeing how much he likes the Cour...Sir Robert, and seeing he give us the guns back.'

'Then Lord Spynie.'

'Ay, my lord. And Sir Henry Widdrington.'

There was a short heavy silence. It was noticeable that Carey's father did not ask why Widdrington should want to mistreat his son. Hunsdon was staring into space. Dodd kept his mouth shut because he recognised that look, and if Lord Chamberlain Hunsdon was meditating on ways and means for a startling piece of vengeance, it wasn't Dodd's place to interrupt him. Eventually Hunsdon looked shrewdly at Dodd.

'My youngest son's capacity for getting himself into trouble and then out again has never ceased to astound me,' he said. 'Is that it, the full tale?'

'All I know, my lord.'

'Barnabus claims to be even more ignorant. Is it true Robin left him in Carlisle when he went into Scotland?'

'Ay, my lord. He was...ah...he was indisposed.'

Hunsdon grinned. 'So I gathered, poor fellow. Clap's the very devil, isn't it?'

Dodd wasn't at all sure how to answer this as he had no personal experience of clap at all, but was saved by the slam of a window being opened and an indistinct shrieking of a woman's voice on the side of the house overlooking the Strand. Hunsdon opened the window of his office himself, and leaned out to look. Dodd peered over his shoulder.

Mistress Bassano was leaning out of an upstairs window, her magnificent hair flying in the breeze, her magnificent breasts bulging over the top of her pale green bodice and two high spots of colour pointing up the hectic flash of her eyes.

'You pathetic bookworm, you *pillock* of a man, how dare you send this trash to me, how *dare* you!'

She was waving a couple of pieces of writing which had the painful regularity of something much laboured over.

'You look at me with your stupid dog's eyes and you whine of love, but do you see *me*? No. Look at this piece of drivel, you pox-blinded bald nincompoop!'

Mistress Bassano was screaming at Will Shakespeare, who stood in the street unaware of the way the passing throngs were pausing to turn and stare, his face full of misery.

With passionate ceremony Mistress Bassano tore up the papers, dug obscenely under her petticoats with them and then dropped them in a jordan held by her giggling maid. Hunsdon was leaning against the window-frame enjoying himself. Shakespeare stood with his mouth open and his hands out in desperation at this sacrilege. Mistress Bassano nodded to her maid who threw the contents of the jordan with deadly aim at his head. The other walkers in the street had scattered away from him as soon as they saw the jordan, but Shakespeare just stood there, with soiled sheets of paper fluttering around him and something horrible stuck to his doublet.

Lord Hunsdon cheered and applauded, his good-humour slightly edged with malice. Mistress Bassano dusted off her fingers fastidiously, turned a satin shoulder and disappeared from the window. The maid impudently added a finger at Will before the shutters banged closed again.

Suddenly Dodd felt very sorry for the little man. Hunsdon was coming away from the window still chuckling.

In case Carey's father thought to ask how Mistress Bassano had come by Shakespeare's letter, Dodd asked hurriedly, 'My lord, when are we heading back to Carlisle?'

Hunsdon was sitting down, picking up a pen, shaking his head and laughing. 'Splendid girl, Mistress Bassano, full of fun,' he was saying contentedly. 'You still there, Sergeant? No, you're not going back yet. Robin's got a job to do for me first.'

'Och,' said Dodd hollowly, suddenly realising how much he hated London town. 'What's that?'

The door opened and Mistress Bassano appeared alone in a rustle of pale green silk. Hunsdon smiled.

'Stupid bastard,' she was muttering. 'My lord, you should have him arrested.' She curtseyed and then glared at Dodd before emphatically ignoring him. Her back view was almost as delectable as the front, the way the gown was cut tight at the waist to flow over her bumroll, and of course that was how you could do it with a pregnant woman, like a horse, which was a wonderful thought and brought a whole new perspective to Dodd's distracted mind.

'On what grounds? Writing you untruthful sonnets?' Hunsdon was still chuckling.

'Plotting against the Queen.'

Hunsdon tutted. 'No need to hang, draw and quarter the silly poet, my dear; it'll only make him think he's important. Sergeant, Sir Robert will tell you what he's up to in his own good time, I'm sure. It boils down to finding another of my bloody sons who has succeeded in losing himself somewhere in London.'

'Who's that, my lord?' Dodd was fighting the urge to groan with disappointment and frustration.

The eyes had gone cold. 'Edmund. He's Robin's elder brother by two years but...well, I expect you'll find out.' Mistress Bassano had taken Hunsdon's velvet hat off and was blowing on a bald spot in the rusty grey.

'I cannot have Will serve me any more, my lord,' she said. 'He is impertinent.'

'Oh clearly. Can't have an ex-player making up to you, sweetheart. I'll tell the steward to assign him somewhere else.'

'Kick him out.'

'Now, my darling, there's no need to be vengeful. The poor chap only scribbled some verses for you—which poets do perpetually, my sweet, they can't help it, it's a kind of sickness. You should be kind to the afflicted, no matter how annoying they are.'

Mistress Bassano tossed her head. 'You are such a generous lord,' she said. 'Are you not afraid sneaking little lechers like him will take advantage of your good nature?'

'No, no,' said Hunsdon, putting the pen back in the ink bottle and shaking sand inaccurately. Mistress Bassano had her arms around his waist and her chin on his shoulder and something she was doing was clearly distracting him. 'Not while you are like a tigress in your loyalty, darling, that's the important part. Mmmmm.'

Mistress Bassano glared at Dodd and jerked her head at the door. Dodd gave her stare for stare and stayed put. Lord Hunsdon hadn't dismissed him yet. And besides, he thought, I know more about you than you think, missy. Loyal as a tigress, eh? As a she-cat, more like.

'Oh ah, Dodd,' said Hunsdon with his eyes half-shut. 'Would you...ah...ask Mr Blaine my steward to attend on me here in about...ah...half an hour?'

'Ay, my lord,' said Dodd neutrally. He went to the door and made the best bow he could.

'Make that an hour,' Hunsdon called after him.

'Ay, my lord.' Dodd shut the door behind him and left them to it. Outside in the passageway he sighed wistfully, feeling that it was very unfair that he had to watch the Careys, father and son, being happily seduced by beautiful women at every turn. Was it wealth or looks, he wondered, and decided that it must be both. That Bassano woman was a peach, by God, and the scandalous way she had her smock pulled down meant that every time you looked at her there was the mesmerising possibility that one of her breasts would pop out of its prison and you would be able to see her nipple...Dodd liked breasts, he liked nipples, particularly pink and pointed ones, he liked the creamy softness of Mistress Bassano's skin, he liked...Of course, he also liked counting his wife's freckles. She would hardly ever let him do it because she hated them. Unaccountably she bleached the ones on her face with lemon juice. There were squeaks and deep-voiced chuckles coming through the door now, and an instantly recognisable rhythmic sound.

Dodd scowled. And none of the blasted courtiers had any shame either.

As he hurried off to find Sir Robert, he wondered what the

famous London bawdyhouses might be like and how much they might cost. Janet would never hear of it if he paid one a visit, he was sure: there were hundreds of miles between him and her. And dear God, it would be worth it.

***

In the casual way of a man with a large staff, Lord Chamberlain Hunsdon decided to give a little supper party that night for his son's benefit. Servants were sent running with invitations, the steward hurried fretfully through the house carrying a sheaf of papers and the kitchens seemed to explode into activity.

Dodd took cover in the room he had been given, where Carey ran him to earth a little later, followed by a manservant carrying a bag containing a fine doublet and hose, a cramoisie marvel of fine wool trimmed with black velvet, padded doublet, padded sleeves and a pair of paned trunk hose. These he laid out on the bed.

'Och,' Dodd said, putting down the book he had been lent by the falconer and coming to his feet. 'What's that, sir? Are ye wearing it the night?'

'No,' said Carey, his eyes dancing with mischief. 'You are.'

'What? Ah'm no' a courtier, sir. I cannae wear fancy gear like that; forbye I'm wearin' ma best suit the day an' there's nae reason tae...'

'Dodd, shut up and listen to me. Nobody is impugning your wife's honour or her skills at weaving and tailoring. Janet is a gem of a woman and your best suit is the *dernier cri* in Carlisle, I'm sure, but I cannot and will not have you sitting at my father's supper table wearing homespun.'

'That's nae bother, sir. I'm not invited.'

'Yes, you are.'

'Och, sir, but I dinnae want...'

'Who asked you what you wanted, Dodd? Not me. Now this is Anthony who is my father's *valet de chambre*, and who has very kindly agreed to help you dress properly.'

'Nay sir, I willna. It's no' fit.'

'You will, Dodd,' snapped Carey. 'With or without a fight.'

71

Dodd started to lose his temper. 'I dinna think ye mean that, sir,' he said, trying to give the Courtier a chance to back out.

Carey drew a wound and loaded dag from under his arm and pointed it at Dodd.

'I do. Now go quietly, will you, there's a good fellow?'

Surely to God, Carey wouldn't shoot him over clothes? Surely? Was it worth the risk? Dodd shut his mouth firmly and glared at Anthony who was looking down at the rushes.

After an awkward silence in which Carey sat down on the window seat, put his legs up onto a stool and cradled the gun on his arm so it could point at Dodd with the minimum of effort, the door opened and two more servants appeared carrying a large wooden bath tub. Dodd's mouth dropped open again.

'Get your clothes off, Sergeant. I'm afraid we haven't time to go down to the stews and do the job properly, so this will have to suffice.'

The servants opened out a sheet and lined the bath with it. Then they went out again and reappeared staggering under enormous jugs of water.

Dodd was almost gobbling with rage. 'Are ye saying I'm dirty?'

Carey rolled his eyes. 'When was the last time you had a bath, Sergeant? I mean all over, not just a rinsing at a pump?'

'I...I...'

'Quite. Come on.' Carey gestured lazily with the dag. 'Clothes off.'

Anthony was arranging the fancy suit on the bed. Water poured and was mixed into the tub. The other two servants left the jugs behind and tiptoed out and Anthony took a dish of soap, a towel and a scrubbing brush and stood beside the tub with a completely blank face, like a statue.

Slowly, heart thumping with fury, Dodd undid his laces, hung his jerkin on a hook on the back of the door, and stripped off to his shirt.

'All the way,' Carey said.

'But it's no' Christmas,' Dodd pleaded. 'Why would I need a bath in August? And I swam in the Esk in June.'

'Humour me, Sergeant. Put it down to a chronic madness instilled by a Queen who bathes every single month, winter or summer.'

'Every month? Ye dinnae do that, d'ye sir? It's no' healthy.'
'No, of course I don't, unless I'm actually at court. Nonetheless. Even when it's not Christmas, if you are going to sit at my father's supper table, you are going to do it in a civilised manner.'

Mad. The Courtier and all his family were clearly as lunatic as they come. Carey in particular should be in Bedlam hospital, not casually pointing a dag at his Sergeant. Setting his jaw, Dodd pulled off his shirt and dipped a toe into the water, which had rosemary leaves in it, by Christ. What did they think he was, some kind of cat-amite? The water was hot but he decided not to complain about it as he got in and sat down cautiously, putting his hand out for the soap.

Half an hour later, skin tingling from the soap and the scrubbing brush, Dodd got out again and resentfully allowed himself to be towelled dry by Anthony, who had also trimmed and nit-combed his hair while he was helpless in the bath.

'Now what?' he growled at Carey who was still sitting at ease by the window, dag beside him on a little table, reading the book about hunting. For answer Carey lifted his eyebrows at Anthony.

The shirt was of the finest linen Dodd had ever seen, and astonishingly clean, though at least it had no fancy embroidery on it. He pulled it on while Anthony carefully toed his own shirt and netherstocks into a pile by the door. The valet then began the ridiculously complicated business of dressing Dodd in a fashionable suit. He even used needle and thread to alter it on Dodd's body, shortening and letting out the waist. The shoulders were tight but when Dodd mentioned it, Carey smiled.

'They're meant to be tight, it's the padding. Now what are you going to wear on your neck? I've brought a ruff and a falling band.'
'Not a ruff, please, sir,' begged Dodd. 'I cannae wear a ruff.'
'Fair enough. The falling band it is, Anthony.'

How the Courtier could bear to wear such tight clothes all the time, Dodd had no idea. His chest felt imprisoned and his shoulders were firmly pulled back by the cut of the doublet. The servants who had brought the bathwater returned, wheeling a large mirror, and Dodd squinted at the stranger standing awkwardly in it, wearing his face.

'There,' said Carey with satisfaction. 'That's much better.'

'Is it, sir?' said Dodd hollowly. 'Ah cannae see it maself.'

Carey stood up. He was already trimly turned out in brocade and tawny satin, Dodd noticed, the width of his ruff just this side of looking daft. But it suited him. Dodd felt he was a laughing stock, all dollied up in clothes he had no business wearing.

Anthony handed him his sword belt which he shrugged over his shoulder.

'I've brought some jewels, if you care to wear them,' offered Carey.

'No, sir,' said Dodd firmly.

'Suit yourself. Now listen to me, Dodd. This is London. Nobody knows who you are or what a Land Sergeant of Gilsland might be, or who your family connections are or anything about you. That means that if you want to be treated right, you have to look the part. What you're wearing is no fancier than what any middling London merchant would wear and that puts you at about the right level.'

'I'm not a gentleman, thank God, sir.'

'Nor is a middling London merchant. You're not wearing anything approaching fashion; what you're wearing is respectable, no more. It's actually one of my own old suits, so please try not to drop anything on it. All right?'

Dodd growled inarticulately. Carey grinned.

'It also ups your price if anyone wants to bribe you. Now if I discharge my dag out the window, will you promise not to hit me?'

Dodd scowled at him. 'I'm no' stupid, sir.'

'No, of course not. You can hit me tomorrow, if you must, but just for tonight bear with me.'

Carey opened the window, peered out at the reddening sky, pointed the dag upwards and fired. 'Come on. The guests are arriving.'

Dodd followed him awkwardly, suddenly understanding where some of Carey's swagger came from—it was the only way you could walk if you were wearing great stupid padded hose round your thighs.

***

Afterwards, when Dodd tried with all his might to remember the details of that long summer evening, he found it had disintegrated in his mind to a whirl of brilliantly dressed ladies and gentlemen who greeted him politely enough, addressed a few words to him and then slipped away to laugh and talk with Carey.

The Courtier was clearly in his element, flirting extravagantly with all the women, gossiping delightedly with the men about the doings of Sir Walter Raleigh, regretting that the South Bank theatre was shut as punishment for a riot over a glover, and, with total disregard for truth, reprising events at the King of Scotland's court. They sat down to more unrecognisable food, including a swan dressed in a full suit of white feathers and stuffed with a pheasant, and finished playing primero at separate tables under blazing banks of wax candles until the sweat ran down Dodd's back in rivulets.

Will was there, serving at table with the other liverymen, standing with his back to the wall next to the sideboard loaded with a glittering display of Hunsdon's plate, dividing his time between glowering at his shoes and staring like a motherless calf at Mistress Bassano.

She was radiant in black velvet and grass green silk, her neck milky with pearls, her hands dancing on the virginals' keys while the wealthy Londoners played at cards.

Dodd spent most of the evening watching, since he simply could not bring himself to play for entire shillings at a time. Eventually he tired of the heat, noise and sense of being completely out of place and chokingly wrapped in finery that suited neither his body nor his mind. He put down his cards, bowed to Lord Hunsdon who was roaring 'eighty-four' at the other end of the room, and went blindly out into the garden, where the summer air was a strange tapestry of flat salt and dirt from the Thames, overlaid with roses and herbs, and a familiar whiff of horses and dogs from the stables.

He stood on the grass, blinking up at the stars. Though it was a balmy summer night not all of them were visible, but he could make out the North Star right enough and he looked at it with longing. That was the way home. That was where there would be doings tonight; on such a clear night, the reivers' trails would be busy with soft-footed horses and their bridles padded with cloth to stop any jingling. He sighed.

'Mr Dodd,' came a voice in the darkness, and Dodd tensed, dropped his hand to his sword.

'Ay,' he said, noncommittally, taking a quick glance over his shoulder in case anybody was coming up behind him.

'I have a message for you from Mr Heneage.'

Dodd squinted, saw somebody wrapped in a cloak who didn't look very large, and was talking in a hoarse muffled whisper.

'Ay?'

'Please, Mr Dodd, put your hand out.'

Dodd drew his sword. 'Why?'

'I want to put something in it.'

'A dagger-blade?'

'No, no. A purse.'

Carey had said he should accept any bribes from Heneage. 'Hmf,' he said, and did as he was asked.

The purse was soft leather, bulging and heavy.

'I've been bidden to tell you to think about it,' said the whisper. 'That's all.'

Dodd whirled around, sword at the ready, looking for anyone intending to enforce the warning, and when he looked back at where the cloaked man had been, there was nobody there except a bush. Dodd hurried after him, following the traces in the dew-soaked grass and the movement of leaves. The figure whisked in at the kitchen door where the storehouses were and by the time he reached it, all he could see were scullery boys clearing up, scrubbing tables and washing floors, and liverymen whisking past the hatch picking up more plates of Seville orange suckets and rose-water jellies.

'Did ye see a mon wi' a cloak come through?' Dodd asked.

The scullery boys were staring in fright at his sword. Dodd put it away hastily. 'Did ye?'

'What, sir?'

'A man wi' a cloak...'

'Sorry, sir?'

'A man wi'...Och, never mind.'

Dodd went out into the garden again, stood near one of the windows where the light from all those candles was spilling onto the gravel and emptied the purse. There was gold and silver in it, three pounds three shillings to be exact, and a tightly folded piece of paper.

"'With good wishes and in hopes of future friendship, Thomas Heneage, Vice Chamberlain.'"

It was, as Carey would say, quite unexceptionable. A gift, a sweetener, you might say, not exactly a bribe. What was he supposed to do in return? No doubt Heneage would let him know.

Dodd scowled and stared into the velvet darkness. He couldn't give it back and what would be the point of that anyway? But something about this universal assumption that he could be bought grated on him. Still, as Janet would say, what was he complaining about? With the money from the footpads, he had already netted more than a month's pay from this trip. Dodd took out the footpad's spoils, counted the whole lot together. Five pounds and some change. Nearly two months' wages, cash in hand, no stoppages.

He picked out a couple of shillings and put them in the convenient pocket sewn into his puffed-up braid-decorated left sleeve and hid the rest of his money in the hollow of his crotch, where his codpiece would keep it in place. The next day he would buy a proper money-belt.

***

Dodd was happier than he had been for years. He was surrounded by warm silky naked flesh, by quivering crinkle-tipped breasts, by smooth round buttocks. Mistress Bassano had his head in her arms so he could suckle her. Thunder rumbled through the sky and Janet, clad only in her beautiful suit of golden freckles, was doing something sinfully obscene for him that made him feel he might explode and...

A mighty earthquake struck London and hammered through Dodd's head. He opened one eye to see that God-cursed bastard of a Courtier shaking the bed and grinning at him, with a candle next to him turning his face into a nightmare.

77

'What...what...' Dodd spluttered, reached guiltily to cover up Mistress Bassano and then realised that she had turned into a pillow. His groin throbbed and he turned over, buried his head in the other pillow.

'Very sorry, Sergeant,' said Carey in a voice which suggested he might have some notion of exactly how good a dream it was he had spoiled. 'Er...You have to get up.'

'Why, for Christ's sake?' moaned Dodd.

Carey coughed. 'We're doing a moonlight flit.'

'What?'

'We're moving out. I can't function here, I'm practically a prisoner.'

'But...'

'My father's going to pay off my tailor, Mr Bullard, who's the most dangerous of my creditors. If I can keep clear of any others, I should be all right. Anyway, I'm moving into the Liberties which still has the right of sanctuary.'

Tantalising woman-shapes were still fading in Dodd's abused head and he felt very unwell. Had he been visited by succubi, the female demons who sucked out your soul by your privy member at night? Perhaps. London must be full of them.

Groaning he sat up and tried to rub the sleep out of his eyes. 'So ye're movin?' he whined. 'Why do I have to move too? I like it here.'

Carey looked sympathetic. 'I'm sorry. I need your help.'

'Och' whimpered Dodd, giving his face another rub and wishing very much that the Courtier needed more sleep. Above all things, he hated being wakened in the middle of the night. Or the early morning. Or at all. What he hated was being woken. God, how he hated it.

'Are you awake now?' Carey said solicitously. 'I left you till last. We're all ready. Can you get up now, get dressed?'

Dodd groaned again. 'Ay,' he said at last. 'Ay. I'll be with ye in a minute.'

When he came through into the entrance hall, comfortable in his homespun and leather jerkin, the place was lit by wax candles and seemed full of people. As he sorted out who was there, the people turned into Barnabus and Simon, both yawning and looking shattered, carrying bundles. Carey strode through and smiled at them, fresh as a daisy, newly shaved and smartly turned out in black velvet slashed with flame-coloured taffeta and a clean ruff. Dodd burned with hatred for him.

There was a distinct 'hrmhrm' from one of the doorways. Lord Hunsdon was standing there, wrapped in a sable-fur dressing gown with his embroidered nightcap making him look older.

'Father,' said Carey and bowed. Hunsdon beckoned him over. Dodd was just close enough to hear the tail-end of their muttered conversation. 'Find him if you can, Robin, but for God's sake, be careful.'

Carey smiled at his father. 'You don't mean that, my lord?'

Hunsdon scowled back. 'I do, you bloody idiot. Don't get yourself killed.'

Carey kissed his father's hand with affectionate ceremony, but Hunsdon pulled him close and embraced him like a bear.

When Carey had gone ahead, with Barnabus and Simon trailing unhappily in his wake, Hunsdon growled at Dodd.

'Sergeant.'

'Ay, my lord.'

'You know that my son can sometimes be a little rash.'

Dodd remained stony-faced despite this outrageous understatement. 'Ay, my lord.'

'You seem like a man of good sense and intelligence. Try and restrain him.'

Dodd made an unhappy grimace. 'Ay, my lord. I'll try.'

'Every day I thank God that I have such a fine son. Keep him alive for me, and I'll not be ungrateful.'

Dodd's heart sank at the impossibility of the task. 'Ay, my lord,' he said hollowly.

Hunsdon grinned piratically at his dismay. 'Do your best, man. That's all I ask.'

'Ay, my lord.'

To Dodd's private amusement, instead of going through the postern gate like Christian men, Carey led the three of them into the moonlit garden and over a wall into the garden of the next house, which was a grassy mound with some trees down by the river. Then they went over another wall and into a narrow dirty alley that smelled of the salt and dirt in the Thames at the open end of it. They went the other way and came out into the dark early morning Strand just past the conduit. Nobody was there, not even the nightsoil men, because it was so horribly early in the morning that it was still the middle of the night. Dodd yawned again at the thought. They had no torches but didn't need them thanks to the moonlight, and Dodd thought of the uses of moonlight and the dangers. Cats flashed their eyes and ran for cover and more black ugly things scurried away with their naked tails slithering. Except once, Dodd had never seen so many rats in his life as he'd seen in London.

Carey led them briskly through back streets to Temple Bar where a couple of beggars were huddled up against the inner wall of the arch, with carved headless saints watching over them. They passed a church with a square tower, surrounded by a churchyard, and a vast towering midden that looked ready to topple at any minute; they passed the Cock tavern and at last Carey turned right down another tiny alley, ducked through archways that took the street under part of a house and then turned left into a jumble of small ancient houses and up four flights of stairs under a headless figure of a woman standing precariously on a coiled rope. At the top he used a key to unlock the door and they went into a little attic room with a crazily pitched ceiling that smelled musty and damp with emptiness. The floorboards were bare of rushes except for a few scraps in a corner and there was a bed with a truckle under it and a straw palliasse under that. The fireplace was empty; there was a table under the window with a candlestick on it, three stools and that was all.

Barnabus bustled straight in with bags over his shoulder, looked around and nodded. 'Not bad,' he said approvingly. 'This one of your father's investments?'

'Yes, I think so. At least we don't have to pay rent.' Carey was busy with a tinderbox and a candle he had taken out of the pocket in his sleeve. It was a wax candle, Dodd noticed, outrageously extravagant. He looked longingly at the bed where Barnabus had put the bags, though he had no expectation at all that Carey would let him rest.

He was right, though at least Simon unpacked one of his bundles and produced clean pewter plates and a large loaf of bread, fresh butter wrapped in waxed paper and some cheese. Barnabus put a large leather jack full of encouraging sloshing sounds on the table and they sat down to breakfast. Dodd was still feeling too queasy with the morning to eat much, though Carey had an excellent appetite. That worried Dodd who had learned that the Courtier tended to go off his fodder when he was bored and to eat heartily when he was anticipating excitement.

'Now then,' said Carey washing down a third hunk of bread and cheese with beer. 'Edmund.'

'Ay, sir,' said Dodd mournfully. 'Who's he?'

'Edmund is my elder brother by two years, and between you and me he's a complete pillock. He was serving in the Netherlands for a while and he did quite well after Roland Yorke sold Deventer to the Spanish; he led the loyal soldiers out of the place and got them home across enemy territory, but he took it hard since Yorke was a friend of his and he's been pretty much drunk ever since.'

Dodd munched slowly on his cheese and forbore to comment. Carey poured himself some more beer.

'Obviously he's the real reason why Father was so anxious for us to come to London—after all, he could have heard our tale at Oxford where he'd be near the Queen and that would have been useful because I could have asked Her Majesty what's happened to the five hundred pounds she's supposed to pay me.'

'And she wouldn't 'ave told you, would she, sir?'

'No, Barnabus, she wouldn't, but she would at least have been reminded of it. Now, I didn't see Edmund when I left for Carlisle in June, but as far as I knew he was planning to go back to the Netherlands again, try and loot some more cash and pay off the moneylenders. His wife had a bit of land when she married him, but of course that's all mortgaged now and the dowry's long spent. Then, according to my father, some time in early August he disappeared. Father didn't worry at first, he thought perhaps Edmund might be doing a job for Mr Vice Chamberlain Heneage, though Mr Vice denied it of course. But Edmund still hasn't turned up, Heneage is adamant that he doesn't know where he is, and furthermore my father has heard that Heneage is looking for him as well, which means he may have done something to annoy Mr Vice and that is very unwise.'

'Sir,' said Dodd with an effort. 'What sort of thing would your brother do for the Vice Chamberlain?'

'Ah. Yes. Well, as I told you, Mr Vice is currently Her Majesty's spymaster. So it was probably something shady and difficult, not to say treasonous if viewed in the wrong light.'

'Och. But I thocht your family didnae take to Heneage?'

'Edmund is a bloody idiot. He'll do almost anything for money. Walsingham would never have let him near intelligence work, so Heneage must have been desperate. He has some Catholic contacts through his friend Yorke, of course, but still...God knows what he was up to. My guess is he made a complete balls up of it, whatever it was, and has gone into hiding, but my father's worried and so we've got to find him. Which is a blasted nuisance.'

Dodd thought about London and the huge number of people in it. How could you find one man amongst all that lot, especially if he didn't want to be found? It was impossible. Dolefully he asked, 'But where will we start, sir?'

'Well, my father was paying a poet to make some enquiries, but he hasn't heard from that man either.'

'Will, d'ye mean?'

'Who?'

'The little bald-headed man that was...er...Mistress Bassano's servant. He...er...he helped me find ma way back to Somerset House yesterday and had me carry some rhymes to Mistress Bassano, the ones that annoyed her so badly, damn him.'

Carey wrinkled his brows in puzzlement for a moment and then laughed. 'Oh, him. Skinny, nervous, Wiltshire accent?'

'Ay, sir.'

'No.' Carey laughed at the thought. 'Not that little mouse of a man. Anyway, he's a player not a poet. Didn't do badly with his first try at play-making though—I saw his *Henry VI* at the Theatre in Shoreditch; can't remember which number—there were three of them...'

'What, three Henries?'

'*Henry VI*, part 1, part 2 and part 3. Same sort of style as *Tamburlain*.'

'Eh, sir?'

'You got to 'ave heard of *Tamburlain*,' put in Barnabus, his face glowing. 'Now that's proper play. "*Holla, you pampered jades of...*" of somewhere, can't remember where. Foreign.'

'Pampered jades of Israel? India?' Carey was trying to remember too, 'It's a wonderful play, plenty of battles...'

'And the Persian king pulling a chariot,' said Barnabus reminiscently. 'You remember, they had him done up like the King of Spain. I did laugh.'

'Anyway, if Shakespeare can pull off anything half as good as Marlowe, he'll be doing well,' said Carey judiciously. 'I don't think he will, though; he hasn't got the boldness.'

'So he's not the man your father had looking for your brother,' Dodd prompted, tired of all this discussion of plays he had neither seen nor wanted to.

'No, no,' Carey laughed again at the idea. 'He's been hanging around my father's household for months—before I left he even had me talk Berwick for some character he was thinking about. He wants a patron like any other would-be poet and thinks my father might be mad enough, but also he's desperately in love with Mistress Bassano.'

'She doesn't like him, though?'

'Of course not. She's not stupid and anyway, he's got no money and isn't likely to get any as a common player. Mistress Bassano has a very clear head.'

'Not that clear, sir,' said Barnabus slyly. 'I thought she had a fancy to you, didn't she?'

Carey's eyes chilled suddenly to ice. 'No, she doesn't.'

Thinking of the scene in the parlour on the day they arrived at Somerset House, Dodd regarded Carey with a grave lack of expression.

Carey did his family's explosive throat-clearing and went back to the real topic of conversation.

'My father hired Robert Greene to find Edmund, seeing as Greene's a well-known poet and he also knows his way around

London's stews and slums and he has family contacts with the King of London. Greene claimed to be hot on the trail, got five pounds off my father and since then Father's heard nothing, so the first thing we'll do is find Robert Greene and ask him what he's up to.'

Dodd sighed. 'Find another man first, sir.'

'This one's easier than my brother. I know where he lives and more importantly, I know where he drinks. The second line of enquiry is to find out who murdered Michael to stop him talking to me and why.'

FRIDAY, 1ST SEPTEMBER 1592,

EARLY MORNING

All four of them plunged into the roaring smelly chaos of London's back streets, Carey very cautiously avoiding the Strand and the Thames where the bailiffs still waited, Dodd with his hand twitching to his swordhilt every five minutes and thinking sadly of the civilised joys of Carlisle.

They first of all went to Edmund Carey's house, another one of his father's property speculations in the old Blackfriars monastery. Carey explained this system for making gold breed gold. First you found a place that was cheaper and less classy than it should be considering its location. Then using lawyers and intermediaries you quietly bought up the freeholds of all the houses in it, paying as little as you could. Doing only the most basic maintenance work you waited until you owned the whole place, then you used your court contacts to sort out any legal problems, evicted any disreputable tenants, replaced roofs, redug jakes and generally revamped the area, and then you sold off the freeholds again for quintuple what you paid for them.

Dodd shook his head at such amazing longterm planning.

Edmund Carey's house was a tall narrow building looking out over the old monastery courtyard, a wilderness of pigpens, chicken coops, overgrown herb beds, a jakes, a choked pond and a dead walnut tree, with a long wall of rubble along one side, out of which poked occasional pillars still decorated with fragments of tracery, like stone trees. Carey gestured at it while they waited for someone to answer the door.

'You see that? Used to be full of beggars living in the cloister carrells before the roof collapsed a couple of years ago. Now it would take about a month to fill the pond, cut down the walnut tree, tidy up the courtyard and repave it, after which the houses round about would be worth twice what they are now. If you cleared the rubble from the cloisters and built some houses on the site, you'd make even more.'

Dodd nodded, not all that interested. The door was opened by a pretty blonde woman with a velvet cap and little frown lines marking the smooth brow between her eyes. Her face lit up when she saw Carey.

'Robin!' she shouted and flung her arms around her brother-in-law. 'Oh Robin, you're back. Kate, Eddie, come out and see your uncle back from the wild north. Oh Robin, Robin. I don't know where he is. I haven't heard from him for weeks. Have you seen him? He didn't follow you to Berwick, did he?'

Carey shook his head and disentangled her arms. 'Susannah, my dear, that's why I'm back in London. Father wants me to find the silly bastard.'

'Don't swear.'

'Sorry. Hello, Kate, hello, Eddie.'

Two children threw themselves into Carey's arms squealing, demanding presents and asking was it true that Scotsmen had tails. He told them gravely that he rather thought it was, seeing how big their padded breeches were, and introduced Dodd.

The house had two rooms on the ground floor, one a parlour and the other a kitchen where a grim-looking woman was trying to relight the fire. Kate was sent out to get some proper beer, since Susannah was quite sure their Uncle Robin didn't like mild ale, bread and meat from the cookshop on the corner if it was open yet and if not come straight back, don't talk to any naughty street children, and when would Kate learn to comb her hair before she put her cap on, for goodness' sake, and why wasn't Eddie properly dressed and ready for school, did he think his clothes would magically climb on his back by themselves? No, and where was his hornbook, this was the third he'd lost in two weeks and she could not afford to keep buying them, he'd just have to share someone else's and if the schoolmaster beat him, then perhaps he'd take better care of his belongings in future…?

Carey and Dodd retired from the shouting to sit in the parlour where the benches were carved but padded with old cushions and the hangings clearly came from Lord Hunsdon's house because they were too big for the walls. Eventually Kate came trotting in, red-faced, carrying a jug of beer and two pewter mugs, while Eddie sprinted out of the door with his mother yelling at him that if he lost another cap, he could go bareheaded and catch lungfever and serve him right.

Finally she came into the parlour carrying her own mug, sat down and smiled wanly at them while Carey poured her some beer.

'The children think their father's in the Netherlands again,' she said. 'I know he's silly, but I wish he'd come back. I do worry so much…'

Carey fished in the pocket of one of his padded sleeves and produced a purse full of money which he handed to her.

'From Father.'

The frownlines, that had no business on such a pretty face, tightened further. 'Oh no, I shouldn't, really; Edmund gets so cross when I take more money from my lord Hunsdon. He's really too generous.'

'Rubbish,' said Carey easily. 'Doesn't want his grandchildren to lack for anything, no matter how cretinous their father. What was he up to the last time you saw him?'

Susannah Carey leaned forward, put her elbows on the worn velvet of her kirtle and caged her fingers round her nose and mouth.

'He was…He was full of plans, full of optimism, quite sure he would sort out our finances once and for all.'

'Oh, God.'

'Yes. I know. He wouldn't tell me what the secret was.'

'Reselling brocades?'

'No, he's learnt his lesson on that one, though he still notionally owes Ingram Frizer a lot of money.'

'Let the little turd sue.'

Susannah shook her head, clearly fighting tears. 'Obviously, I was worried when he was so pleased with himself. But he wouldn't tell me and...and...I lost my temper. We had a big fight and he stormed out saying he'd be back when he had hundreds of pounds and then he'd...he'd take the children away and...and...'

Silently Carey handed over his handkerchief, and stared at the ceiling for a bit. After a while he patted his sister-in-law's shoulder and said, 'There, there.'

Eventually the sniffling stopped and Susannah blew her nose.

'What was the secret, Susannah?'

She rolled her eyes and sighed. 'I think it might have been alchemy,' she said tragically.

Carey barked with laughter. 'Oh, bloody hell. I suppose it's one thing he hasn't tried.'

'You see he was talking about how he needed seed-gold.'

'Oh, yes?'

'He sold the last of his rings and my pearls that I had from the Queen when we married, and off he went. He was buying a gold plate off a sailor, he said, before we started fighting, then that gold would be the seed and he'd harvest ten times as much gold from it.'

'Let me guess. The alchemist took the seed-gold, started the reaction, some disaster happened and it didn't work and Edmund needed more money to pay for more seed-gold. Yes?'

Susannah shook her head. 'Well, no. He did come back, drunk, one night in early August and he showed me a big purse full of gold angels. He said he'd bred ten gold angels for each angel of gold he started with. He was very happy, said we'd soon be out of hock, we made up our quarrel and off he went again. That was the last time I saw him.'

Carey rubbed his chin slowly. 'It *worked*?'

'I was surprised myself. I never heard of alchemy working before.'

'Nor me. Did he let slip any names?' Susannah shook her head. 'Well, can I go upstairs and have a look round, see if he left any bits of paper or anything else?'

Susannah gestured at the stairs and finished her beer. Carey went up the stairs and jerked his head for Dodd to follow him.

The main bedchamber was on the next floor, overlooking the courtyard, smelling musty and much used. The enormous fourposter bed hadn't been made yet and the two clothes chests were open and higgledy piggledy. Carey looked around.

'Poor Susannah. She never was any good as a housekeeper, any more than Edmund has ever been worth a farthing as a provider.'

'Why do they not live wi' yer father?'

Carey shrugged. 'Edmund doesn't get on with Father at all, mainly because Father keeps trying to stop him drinking and gambling and Edmund resents it. They had a really bad fight in May after the Frizer business when Father had to pay the man off, and after the surgeon had reset Edmund's nose, he said he'd rather die in gaol than speak to Father again. All very stupid. Now then, let's have a look here.'

Carey pawed through Susannah's clothes and then did the same with the other chest which was rather more full of fashionable men's clothes, rich black velvet sprinkled with pearls, pale creamy satin. When the chest was empty he thumped the bottom of it in case there were any secret compartments. Dodd narrowed his eyes.

'What's that, sir?'

'What? Oh, yes. How odd.'

Little tiny beads of silver were clinging to the padded leather lining of the chest. Dodd prodded one with his finger and it bounced back, rolled down a seam and joined another bead like two raindrops on a windowpane. Carey tore off a little piece of paper from the small notebook he kept in a pouch in his belt, chased and caught a couple of the little beads, then twisted the paper closed and put it in the pouch.

There was nothing else in the room except for a couple of books of sermons, an empty jewel box and some dirty pewter plates which Dodd brought down with them.

Susannah had a bit more colour in her cheeks from the beer.

'Did you find anything?'

Carey shook his head. 'I'll ask Father to send a woman and a boy to you until Edmund turns up again. When he does you can send the boy to tell us. By the way, did you...er...did you check the gaols?'

Susannah nodded vigorously. 'Of course I did, it was the first thing I thought of. I went to all of them, the Clink, the Fleet, all of them, but nobody had heard of him. Oh, it's so worrying. What if he's dead?'

She was dry-washing her hands helplessly, her mouth wrung sideways with anxiety. 'What shall I do if he's dead?'

Carey put his arm across her shoulders and kissed her forehead. 'Darling, you know my father won't let you and the children starve. At least if my idiot brother is dead, you'll be able to find someone better to marry, won't you?'

'But I don't want anybody better, I want Edmund.'

'I can't imagine why, he's never treated you properly.'

'Well, you know, he is a bit silly with drinking and card-playing and money-making schemes, but he's a very good man, he's a good father, he's never beaten me once, not even when I've called him names, he...he...He's not so bad, really.'

'He doesn't deserve you,' said Carey firmly, kissing her again. 'Never has. Now dry your eyes. If the fool isn't at the bottom of the Thames, I'm going to find him. All right?'

Susannah nodded anxiously, blinking up at Carey.

Dodd felt dispirited as Carey bade goodbye to Kate and tipped her sixpence. If folk as rich as the Careys could have money troubles, what hope was there for him?

***

'Where now?' asked Dodd as they stood in Blackfriars' courtyard.

'We're finding Robert Greene,' said Carey as he struck off eastwards along St Peter and Thames Street. Carey tried Greene's lodgings first, over a cobbler's shop, but found a locked door at the top of the narrow ill-smelling stairs and nothing else. Barnabus and Simon were waiting dutifully outside as they'd been ordered to earlier that morning.

Carey went out into the smoke-dimmed sunlight and rubbed his gloved hands. Over the next two hours they quartered London for Robert Greene and it turned out that knowing the places where the poet liked to drink didn't narrow the field very much since there were so many of them.

After a while Barnabus got restless and asked if he could go off to St Paul's with Simon to see if he could find a new master. Carey told him sharply he could wait until they'd found Greene, and Barnabus lapsed into a sulk.

'If he could just wait a month or two, I could guarantee him a place with George Clifford, who'd employ him like a shot,' Carey said to Dodd.

'Don't want to risk no more northern wastelands,' muttered Barnabus.

'Clifford?' asked Dodd, not surprised that Barnabus had no appreciation for decent places. 'Is that any relation of the Earl of Cumberland, sir?'

'No, it *is* the Earl of Cumberland.'

Every so often Carey would do or say something that completely took the wind out of Dodd's chest. 'The Earl, sir?'

'Yes. Old friend of mine, we ran off from Court in 1588 to serve against the Armada, which we did on the old *Elizabeth Bonaventure*. He saved my life when I managed to catch gaol-fever that nearly did for me.'

'Sir?'

'Very embarrassing, you know. I'd risked the Queen's displeasure in the hopes of killing me a few Spaniards and getting enough loot to pay off the moneylenders. We certainly fought the Spaniards but it was all done with cannonfire and scurrying the ships around the big galleons and of course the fireships at Calais, so I never saw a penny of any treasure. Somewhere around Flamborough Head I lost ten shillings playing dice with the Ship's Master and the Surgeon, got a blinding headache and then went completely off my head with the fever. Apparently I spotted some likely looking cattle and a chest of gold in the crow's nest—you know, the look-out place on the top of the mast—climbed up the rigging in a storm and had a damned good battle with some sails. George was the one who led the sailors up to get me and knocked me out cold so they could bring me down. The Spanish ships had turned tail by then and were well on their way to Scotland, so as soon as the ship docked at Tilbury, he strapped me to a litter and sent me back to Philadelphia and Lady Widdrington in Westminster. Nice chap. Very good friend.'

'Ay, sir.' Dodd was unwillingly fascinated.

'He was the one said I should take up Scrope's offer, said I'd enjoy myself in Carlisle and he was absolutely right.'

Unwillingly, Dodd warmed to the Earl. He wasn't quite sure how much back rent he owed the Cumberland estate for some of the land he ran cattle on, but he was certain he couldn't pay it. He supposed it wasn't the Earl of Cumberland's fault. Maybe if Carey was his friend, he could put a good word in some time.

He looked around. The aggravating man had disappeared again. Dodd blinked at a tiny hovel with brightly painted red lattices and followed Carey inside.

There was no doubt that London was a drinking man's heaven. From the big coaching inns, with their great yards where the carriers' wagons were hitched ready for their long journeys to strange places like Bristol or Exeter, to tiny sheds where widows sold the ale and mead they brewed themselves, it was clear a man need never be thirsty in London. Provided he had money. Even river water cost a penny a quart if you bought it off a water-seller and was as brown as the beer and much less pleasant tasting.

Dodd stuck with beer. Carey's guts at last seemed to have settled down and his were fine, but he didn't want to spend another week sitting on the jakes with his bowels exploding and everyone knew it was diluting your humours with too much water that gave it to you.

At last, as the morning drew on, Carey went into yet another tiny boozing ken, peered around in the choking fumes of tobacco smoke, and cried, 'Ahah!' He shoved his way over to the corner where a man built like a beer barrel was propped up on a bench, mouth open and snoring, his hat drawn down over his eyes and a beard exactly the colour of carrots rising and falling with his snores.

Carey sat down next to him and grinned happily, just like a sleuthdog next to his quarry. Dodd put his hands on his hips.

'That's him,' he said.

'It certainly is,' said Carey. 'Nobody else in London has a beard exactly that shade.'

'I should 'ope not,' said Barnabus, bustling back from the woman next to the barrels with a large jug of ale and some greasy horn cups. 'Let's celebrate. Oh, she says his slate's up to ten shillings and if we want 'im, we've got to pay it.'

Carey shook his head in admiration. 'How the devil did you manage to drink five pounds in two weeks and have a slate?' he asked the snoring poet, who didn't answer and probably couldn't have explained anyway. Dodd thought he looked exactly the way anyone would after drinking five pounds in two weeks, which was to say, unhealthy, red-nosed, stertorous but happy.

'Could we not wake him up, sir?' Dodd asked as he sipped cautiously at the brown liquid in his cup. Carey had finished his.

'We could,' he said. 'Possibly.'

Dodd thought that would probably be a good idea, seeing as the man looked as if he weighed at least sixteen stone.

In the end they lurched out of the ken with one of the poet's arms over Carey's shoulder and one over Dodd's and his legs making occasional stabs at finding the floor.

'Why in God's name did yer dad use a drunk to find your brother?'

'You set a drunk to find a drunk,' said Carey with some edge in his voice. 'I expect that's what he was thinking. Also he doesn't know Greene as well as I do.'

'How d'ye know a poet, sir?'

'I know a lot of poets. Good company.'

'Yarrargh warra gerk...' said the poet, and puked over Dodd's boots.

They dropped him while he got it over with and Dodd found some grass growing out of a yard wall and used it to wipe the worst off. Barnabus cleaned up Greene's jerkin as best he could, they slung his arms over their shoulders again and set off once more.

'Where are we going with him sir?' Dodd puffed, trying to breathe sideways so as not to catch anything from Greene's breath.

'Down to the river.'

'Mrrrghh...'

'Och, Christ.'

It took two further sessions of unspeakable noises and effort from Greene before they emerged onto one of the little boatlandings that studded the Thames bank. Carey set Greene down on the planks with his back against the riverwall, took his hat off and mopped his face. He looked critically at his black velvet suit but had miraculously managed to avoid any spattering. Not for the first time, Dodd wondered how he did it and borrowed Barnabus's handkerchief to have a scrub at his best clothes.

'Robert Greene,' roared Carey in the man's ear. 'If you don't wake up, I'm going to dunk you in the river.'

'Horrrargh...grr,' said Greene, sliding down comfortably and starting to snore. Carey shook his shoulder and one large paw swiped his hand away. 'Fuck off,' said Greene quite distinctly, before settling back into snores.

Carey's lips tightened at this defiance. 'Right,' he said. 'You can't say I didn't warn you.'

One fist in the scruff of Greene's doublet, he hauled the drunk over to the edge of the boatlanding, where the Thames water at high tide flowed as dark as beer. Dodd helped him and then Carey judiciously ducked the poet's head into the water.

'I suppose if it don't kill him, it might wake him,' Barnabus commented thoughtfully.

Dodd watched Greene flailing in Carey's grip. 'Ye could let him breathe, sir,' he said after a moment.

Carey lifted Greene's head, listened to his whooping and gasping, then dunked him again.

There was nothing wrong with Carey's hands now, Dodd thought, as he watched the poet start to fight. Carey let him up again.

'...I'll kill you, I'll rip your head off and shit...blrggggle ggrrrg...'

Carey lifted the head out of the water again. 'You awake yet, Greene?' he asked conversationally.

'Herrrck, herccck...' said Greene, eyes popping and water streaming down his beard which still managed to glow like a beacon. He sat on the edge of the planks and whooped and spat for several minutes and then grabbed for his sword hilt.

Carey dunked him once more. 'Get his sword, Dodd,' he said.

Dodd got his sword, which was another of those nasty foreign rapiers the Londoners seemed to like so well, though the blade was dull and didn't look like it had been sharpened or oiled for a long time. He tutted at such carelessness, collected the man's poignard dagger as well and waited for Carey to let Greene breathe again.

'Huyuhhhh...herrrr...huyhhhh...'

'Are you awake?' bellowed Carey right in Greene's horribly stinking face. 'Do you know me?'

'Huuuuyuuh...I'll...herrrgh....I'll kill you. Where's my sword... hugggh...'

'I'll fight you any time, Greene, but first I want to talk to you. Do you understand me?'

Greene pushed him away and lurched to his feet, wiping his eyes and coughing fit to crack his chest. 'You shit...' he gasped. 'You fucking bastard...'

Carey was standing too, with Dodd at his back. 'My father gave you five pounds for information about my brother Edmund. Now I want to know what you've discovered...'

Greene flailed a fist at Carey, which he ducked, shouldered Dodd into the riverwall and stumbled up the alleyway. They went after him and caught up quickly because he was rolling from side to side so much.

'Tell me what you've learned,' demanded Carey.

'Go to hell, you bastard.'

'No,' said Carey with a dangerous glint in his eye. 'My father's the bastard, I'm the bastard's get.'

Greene blinked at him cross-eyed for a second. 'Oh yes,' he slurred. 'So you are. Well, you can go to hell, you cocksucking bastard's get and your whore of a mother with...'

Carey punched Greene in the face. He stood swaying like a maypole for fully thirty seconds, then said something that sounded like 'Whuffle' and collapsed.

'Och, sir,' said Dodd wearily. 'Now we'll have tae carry him.'

'Sir, sir,' Barnabus was calling from the boatlanding behind them. Dodd looked over his shoulder and saw that Barnabus had

had the sense to call a boat. The boatman was backing his oars against the tide's ebb and Barnabus had the painter in his hand, was wrapping it round one of the posts.

'Our friend's been taken sick,' said Barnabus and the boatman nodded understandingly.

Carey shook his hand from the wrist and flexed his fingers, rubbing at his knuckles in their elegant kid gloves. He had the grace to look embarrassed, though not very.

Between them they hauled Greene back down the alley and got him into the boat, where the boatman solicitously arranged his head so it flopped over the gunwale. He was at least still breathing. At a nod from Barnabus, Simon jumped out and collected Greene's ironmongery.

'Mermaid Steps,' said Carey.

'That'll be a shilling then, sirs, to include the baggage.'

Dodd opened his mouth to protest at this wicked overcharging but Carey just nodded. Well, it was his money but you could see how he got through so much of it.

Mermaid Steps were slippery and dangerous. It took all four of them including Simon to haul Greene up, and when they stood at the top, Carey growled, 'Bugger this for a game of soldiers, we'll take him in there.'

It looked like a reasonably respectable place, despite having a scandalous bare-breasted mermaid in pink and green on its sign, so Dodd bent his back to the burden again and they managed to get Greene through the door and lay him down on one of the benches just inside.

The innkeeper came bustling over. 'I'm sorry, sir, he can't come in. He's banned.'

'What?' said Carey, who was looking frazzled by now and had a small smear of blood and snot from Greene on his shoulder.

'On account of the damage what he hasn't paid for.'

'He's a poet. You let poets drink in here, don't you?'

'I do, sir,' allowed the innkeeper. 'When they behave in a respectable fashion. Which he don't. So he's banned.'

'Well, he's not going to do any damage now, he's been cold-cocked.'

'That's as may be, sir. But he's banned.'

'How much was the damage?'

'Two pounds, one shilling and eightpence. Sir.'

Carey handed it over, while Dodd shook his head and Barnabus sighed.

'I'll get us all a drink and a bite to eat, shall I, sir?' he said after a suitable pause.

Carey nodded and sat down next to Greene who had rolled on his side and started to snore.

'I suppose we'll just have to wait for him to recover again,' he said. 'Damn it, Greene, you're a bloody nuisance.'

Dodd rested his weary frame on the opposite bench, peered around the gloom. It seemed like a nice place, this time, fresh sawdust on the floor and some tallow candles in sconces on the walls to light up the dim places. Even the tables were clean. Barnabus came over with two trays laden with a light second breakfast of bacon, sausage, fried onions, cheese and pease pudding, beer and some bread.

They ate in tactful silence while Carey cracked his joints and rubbed his knuckles every so often. Dodd hoped his hand was really hurting him. At last Barnabus belched softly, wiped his mouth on a napkin and coughed.

'Well, sir, since you've found him, I was wondering if you could excuse me for the rest of the day, like you said, sir?'

Carey shrugged. 'Well, I shouldn't think Greene's going to wake for a while yet, so why not? I can't give you the whole day, I'll probably need you later, but you can have the rest of the morning off until dinnertime. Will that do?'

'Thank you, sir.'

Barnabus and Simon finished their beer and bustled out of the Mermaid. Five minutes after they had gone, Will Shakespeare came hurrying in, looked around him and waved when he saw Dodd and Carey, who had started a game of primero.

'Sir Robert,' he gasped nasally. 'I've got a message for you from your father, sir. He says he's going down to Hampstead with Mr Recorder Fleetwood to investigate the footpads who tried to ambush you there. He said he'd be grateful if you and Sergeant

Dodd could join him, identify them perhaps, and I've brought two horses for you.'

Carey sighed and put away his cards, which Dodd felt only showed that the man had the luck of the devil since Dodd had a flush.

'That's an infernal nuisance,' he said, looking down at the body of Greene, prone on the bench beside him and snoring a fanfare. 'What am I going to do with this? I daren't leave it behind in case it bloody wanders off again.'

Shakespeare blinked at the man on the bench, caught sight of the carroty beard and twitched. Then he said thoughtfully, 'Well, I could look after him for you, sir.'

Carey smiled. 'Would you do that? I'd be most grateful.'

'Certainly I could do it.'

'If he wakes up and starts causing trouble, don't mess about. Just call the innkeeper to help, all right?'

Shakespeare went pink at this patronage but he only nodded humbly. 'Yes, sir.'

'Splendid. Where did you say the horses were?'

'Hitched outside.'

'Come on then, Sergeant. You'll have to beggar me some other time.'

'Ay, sir.'

FRIDAY, 1ST SEPTEMBER 1592, MORNING

Carey led the way through the clutter and crowding of the London streets, through the City wall at Ludgate and up the Old Bailey, across the wide expanse of Smithfield which was full of men practising horsemanship and swordplay, some of whom shouted drunken challenges at Dodd and Carey, up Turnmill Street to the little village of Clerkenwell which seemed to be amazingly full of dazzlingly fine women, and then westwards along country lanes until they joined the Gray's Inn Road again. There at last Carey put his heels in and went to a canter and Dodd followed, instantly feeling happy to be away from the constant press of humanity. With fresh horses out of Lord Hunsdon's stables they were there well within the hour, and found Carey's father, the Recorder of London and a large number of buff-coated men. Hunsdon was leaning on his saddlehorn as Carey and Dodd came up, their horses blowing and panting after the long hill. Carey flourished off his hat in a splendid bow from the saddle taking in his father and the Recorder while Dodd touched his cap.

'Ah, there you are,' said Hunsdon. 'About time. Where have you been? I sent Shakespeare out to find you this morning.'

'Talking to Susannah.'

'Hmf. How are the children?'

'Kate forgot to comb her hair this morning and Eddie lost his third hornbook in a month, otherwise they're well.'

Hunsdon smiled. 'Mr Recorder Fleetwood and I have been considering, and we've decided not to interview the locals yet. We're going to start by searching for fresh graves.'

'Good idea, my lord,' said Carey. 'Who have you brought?'

'Who do you think? Here he is. His paw shouldn't take any harm from a little light sniffing around, eh boy?'

Jimmy the dog-page was holding Hunsdon's yellow lymer on a long leash and the dog went sniffing delightedly up to Carey's horse, who put down his head and snorted in welcome.

'Hasn't been fed this morning so he should be fairly sharp.'

'Oh, poor fellow,' said Carey sympathetically to the dog, who panted and looked hopeful for a while. 'Well, let's see what you can find.'

Watched warily by the Hampstead villagers, they left most of the buff-coated men by the horsepond and went into the Cut so that Bellman could sniff the traces left by the deaths of the footpads. Dodd and Carey both went to look for any other traces and found hoofprints and dragmarks in the dust. Then Dodd took Bellman's leash and went up the little path that led up to the Hanging Elm and had the dog sniff around its base for a while. As expected, the body was no longer there.

'Why do you think they bothered to put poor old Michael up on the Elm in the first place?' asked Hunsdon.

Dodd shrugged. 'They knew our nags might smell the corpse and hid him in plain view. And to give a reason for them spooking if they smelled the ambush too.'

'That's what I thought. Barbarous. All right, Bellman. Find. There's a good boy. Find.'

Wagging his tail happily the lymer pottered around the Elm, snorting rhythmically through his large blunt yellow nose. He found a trail, followed it enthusiastically and eventually stood barking in triumph by a large sandy bank full of rabbitholes.

'No, Bellman,' said Hunsdon patiently, and produced a blue velvet cap from a bag by his saddle, handed it down to Dodd to show the dog. 'Find.'

It took several tries but eventually the lymer found another trail and went off down into the village, snorting and sniffing as he went. Out the other side, the southern flank of Hampstead Hill was covered with market gardens being worked by more of the villagers, who stopped and leaned on their hoes as Dodd trotted by, pulled by the lymer, followed by the dog-page and then Carey, his father, the Recorder and two of the Recorder's men. Halfway down, a thick wood began and the lymer bounded into its eaves and stopped in a clearing.

There was an unmistakeable bank of newly disturbed earth where Bellman started digging and barking, so Dodd pulled the dog off in case he ate something he shouldn't. Lord Hunsdon patted the lymer and praised him extravagantly, then produced a large marrowbone from another bag hanging behind his saddle and gave it to the dog who wagged his tail ecstatically, took the bone and lay down with his paws over it, growling if one of the horses or men came too near his treasure. The Recorder sent up the hill for more men and his attendants began working with their spades. After a while they struck something that thudded.

'Four bodies,' announced the Recorder eventually. 'Sirs, would you care to identify them...?'

It wasn't difficult and not even very smelly—the bodies had been in the earth for only a day and their bellies were just beginning to swell. Looked at closely, you could tell that Michael's face had been destroyed by a gun put close to it and fired, though whether that was what had killed him was anybody's guess. He was stripped down to his shirt, as were the dead footpads.

Recorder Fleetwood was talking to his men. Dodd thought it was all very orderly and efficient. Michael was put on a horselitter, decently covered, while the footpads' bodies were loaded on packponies to go back up to the Hanging Elm for display.

'Could we search the village houses for that suit of Michael's?' Carey asked.

Hunsdon and Fleetwood exchanged cynical looks. 'I'm afraid I would need search warrants for each house,' said the Recorder.

'Why?' asked Carey. 'Her Majesty's pursuivants regularly tear London apart looking for priests.'

'Ah yes, but that is a matter of high policy and treason. This is only a murder.'

'Besides, they'll have sold the suit, I should think,' said Hunsdon. 'Surely even Hampstead peasants would have more sense than to wear a suit from a murdered man. Never mind, Robin. I'm going to try something else. Mr Fleetwood, would you and your men kindly assemble the villagers by the horsepond?'

Hunsdon addressed the assembled people from horseback.

'Now, as you know, goodmen and goodwives of Hampstead, three wicked footpads were killed by my son and his followers the day before yesterday when they tried an ambush at the Cut. I would not dream of suggesting that any of you would be concealing such criminals, which is of course a crime in itself.'

Some of the villagers shifted their feet. Dodd wondered if he recognised a couple of them.

'However, earlier that day, those same wicked footpads had probably killed my servant, Michael Lang, a good decent married man, that leaves a wife and three children. He had served me since he was a boy.' Hunsdon paused impressively. 'I will pay three pounds sterling for any genuine information about that murder. Three pounds in gold. No questions asked. Understand? You may find me at Somerset House in the Strand and I will receive any such informer personally.'

**

Carey seemed subdued as they rode back down Haverstock Hill and followed a roundabout route to return to the Mermaid Inn while avoiding the dangers of the Strand. They found Shakespeare sitting quietly next to Greene, reading a book. He had covered Greene with a solicitous if rancid blanket and put his head on a greasy bench cushion and Greene looked comfortable and happy. Carey tipped Shakespeare and sent him back to Somerset House with the horses.

After they had eaten, Dodd had no further luck with the cards and was led into a couple of very rash bets by sheer irritation with the Courtier's breeziness—as Carey sternly lectured him after each game.

Carey resorted to tossing a coin over and over.

'All right,' he said. 'Now we've had two heads in a row. What are the chances the next time it will be tails?'

'A bit higher, I'd say, sir,' Dodd opined.

'No, no, no!' said Carey, who had not been intended by Nature for a schoolmaster. 'The chances are exactly the same.'

'Why?' Dodd was frowning at the offending coin, lying innocently on the blackened table. Barnabus and Simon had come in while Carey was at his tutoring and now Barnabus gave a delicate cough.

'Only there's nothing doing in the Mediterranean, sir, and I was wondering if you'd mind if I took Simon off to see his mum, see if she's got any news, you know.'

'Of course, it doesn't work if the coins are heavier one side than the other. What's that, Barnabus? Is that the woman with the fighting cock?'

'Tamburlain the Great, sir. Yes. I wouldn't mind seeing how he's shaping now he's finished his moult.'

Dodd, who was desperate to get away from Carey and his notions about cards and the like, stared hard at Barnabus.

'Sergeant Dodd could come too. I could teach him 'ow to navigate 'is way around a city.'

'Ay, sir,' said Dodd quickly, heartily sick of card-playing. 'I wouldnae mind a breath of fresh air.'

It was certainly true that Greene had been farting with the

creativity of the very drunk, but mainly Dodd's head was hurting from adding up his points and then comparing the score with Carey's numbers.

Carey looked disappointed. 'Oh, very well.'

'Ye willnae have any trouble wi' bailiffs, sitting here alone, sir?'

'No, no. The Mermaid's in the Blackfriars Liberty, I should be safe enough. I might meet some old friends here as well if I stay long enough for them to wake up and venture out of their pits.'

Barnabus led the way up Water Lane, under the Blackfriars Gateway and into the broadest street Dodd had seen in the city, where the cobbles were worn with deep ruts. They walked eastwards along it with St Paul's looming over the houses north of them and Barnabus dinning Dodd's ears with a continuous stream of reminiscence, anecdote and the occasional history lesson attached to some landmark or other that they passed. It seemed that navigating in the city was less a matter of knowing where you were going than remembering landmarks and turning left or right at them. Barnabus took them up a long narrow street and out at a big old-fashioned market cross that he claimed was called Eleanor Cross after some Queen or other. Dodd blinked around himself. They were in a dazzlingly wealthy shopping street lined with barred windows where gold and silver plate and magnificent jewels studded with pearls, rubies, sapphires, emeralds glinted tantalisingly. Large buff-coated men with swords stood at every door, giving Dodd considering looks when he went up to gawp at the displays. He knew he was gawping and it annoyed him, but he couldn't help it. Never in all his life had he seen so much money laid out before him, so many vast golden cups and bowls, so much wrought jewellery. It made your mouth water, truly it did.

'This is Cheapside,' said Simon Barnet at Dodd's elbow. 'Good, innit?'

Dodd nodded, speechless.

'Up that way,' Barnabus added, waving an arm to the north, 'that's where the big guildhalls are and Gresham's Exchange is that way on Cornhill.'

'Does yer sister live here?'

'Nah. It's too pricey round here, I just thought I'd show you

Cheapside, seeing it's your first visit. I mean, you couldn't come
to London and miss the Cheapside jewellers, could you?'

Dodd shook his head. They wandered along for a while and came
to a row of stalls selling ruffs of astonishing width, embroidered
shirts, women's wigs sparkling with gold chains and pearls, and
some extraordinary hats. Dodd's mouth fell open again before he
shut it with an irritated click of his teeth. Never in his life had he
felt such a yokel, but this made Edinburgh look like Longtown
by comparison. Where in God's name did folk get the money to
spend on such things?

'Here,' nudged Barnabus. 'Why don't you buy something for
your wife. Eh?'

'What, for Janet?'

'Yeh. She's your wife, in't she?'

'Well, but...These are fer fine court ladies, not Janet.'

'She may not be a fine lady, though she's always seemed pretty
fine to me, but you're a man of importance in Carlisle and she
should show it, shouldn't she? Here, look, why don't you buy her
a hat?'

'What, one of them?'

'Yeh. Why not? You got Heneage's bribe money on you and
nobody's nipped it out of yer crotch yet.'

'How did ye ken...' Barnabus rolled knowing eyeballs at Dodd
and darted forwards to speak confidentially to the woman behind
the stall. She looked hard at Dodd.

'A hat for your wife, sir?' she said. 'A French hood, perhaps?'

'Nay,' said Dodd looking at the thing she was pointing at. 'She's
got one of them, there's plenty of wear in it yet. What about that
one?' He pointed at a high-crowned confection of green velvet with
a pheasant's feather in it. 'That would look well wi' her bright hair.'

'And what colour is your wife's hair, sir?'

'Red.'

'How charming,' said the woman with a smile. 'Just like the
Queen. Well, I think you've made a very good choice, sir. That
will be twenty five shillings exactly, sir, and cheap at the price.'

Dodd gobbled. He heard himself do it, but couldn't stop. *Twenty-
five shillings*, for a *hat*? 'Barnabus...' he growled and Barnabus took

his elbow and whisked him round the side of the stall.

'Look, Sergeant, it sounds a lot, but it'll be worf it, believe me. There's nuffing ladies like better than 'ats and she'd never ever get one this good nor this fashionable anywhere norf of York.'

'But...but I could buy a field for that.'

'No doubt you could, round Carlisle, where land's so cheap, but would Mrs Dodd like that so much?'

'Ay, she would, she's a sensible woman.'

'Look, mate. You've treated me right and I'm giving you some good advice 'ere. You give her the hat, and every time she looks at it, she'll forgive you for whatever it is you've done.'

Dodd shook his head to clear it. 'Ah've niver heard of such a thing.'

'Look, let's see what I can do for you, eh? I know Mrs Bridger...'

'Och, so that's it...'

'Come on. You've got to get her somefing while you're in London or she'll never speak to you again.'

This was incontrovertibly true. Dodd hesitated.

'So you might as well give your money to somebody I know, right? Anyway, let me see what I can do.'

Barnabus trotted round the back of the stall and had a long chat with Mrs Bridger, while Dodd got his breath back and resignedly pulled out his purse.

Barnabus beckoned him close again. 'Mrs Bridger has very kindly on account of our friendship agreed to cut her price by a fifth, which pretty much wipes out her profit, so this is quite a favour...'

Dodd counted out two of the golden angels Heneage had given him and handed them over. Mrs Bridger looked at them sharply, and bit both of them. Then she handed one back with an ugly look on her face and glared at Barnabus.

'Are you up to your tricks again, Cooke?'

'What's wrong?'

'That one's false. If your gentleman's got no gold in 'is purse, he shouldn't come buying things at my stall.'

'False?' echoed Dodd, looking at the coin.

'It's pewter with gold on the outside. Look at it.'

Dodd squinted closely at it and had to admit he could see grey metal in the pits made by her teeth. Simon stood on tiptoe to peer at it too, shook his head and tut-tutted.

'You could be hanged for uttering false coin, you know that, Cooke.'

'On my soul, Mrs Bridger, I'd no idea. Look at the other ones, Sergeant, see if they're all right.'

Dodd fished out another angel and bit it himself and it seemed right enough. Mrs Bridger took it suspiciously, bit it, then weighed it on a pair of little scales she had under the counter. At last she nodded. 'That one's all right too.'

With a meaningful sniff and another scowl at Barnabus she took the magnificent hat, wrapped it in a linen cloth, stuffed the inside with hay and put it in a round bandbox with a handle which she gave to Simon to hold.

A horrible idea occurred to Dodd. He poured all the angels onto his palm, bit the three remaining and found one other was the same as the false one. On Barnabus's advice he put the two false angels in his jerkin and the rest of his money back in his crotch and they walked on. Dodd felt he had been robbed, even though he was still carrying more money than he ever did except on rent day.

'We'll 'ave to talk to Sir Robert about that,' said Barnabus. 'I wonder if it was Heneage's bribe or the footpad's money?'

'Have ye got any bad ones?'

'Dunno. I left mine at Somerset House.' His small eyes narrowed with suspicion. 'Hem. Let's go see my sister first, then we'll take a boat.'

They finally came to New Fish Street and ducked down a little alley. 'Of course, there's always a bit of coining going on, but they don't generally bother with gold coins, it's too hard to spend what you make...Now, you mind that box, Simon; if anybody swipes it or sits on it, I'll sell you to the Falcon's Chick to pay for it. You should be worth that much, what d'yer reckon?'

Barnabus was still talking as he bustled up to a narrow fronted house with the shutters on the two lower windows still closed, and lifted his arm to bang on the door.

He stopped stock still, frozen in mid-move, made a little short grunt in his throat as if he'd been stabbed. Dodd saw the thing a moment after and felt the blood drain down from his face in horror and fear.

There was a cross branded into the wood of the door, red paint daubed into the burnt furrows which had dripped down the door as it dried. The latch had been nailed shut, and so had the shutters. Below the cross was pinned a piece of printed paper.

Barnabus ripped it down and his lips moved as he read it.

'"May the Lord have mercy on us."'

Dodd had backed away from the door, looked up and down the street which he now realised was suspiciously empty for London. There were other red crosses on other doors.

'Nah, nah,' Barnabus croaked. 'It's a mistake. Easily done. Just a mistake, Simon, don't you worry.'

Simon had his face screwed up and tears in his eyes as he looked up at the cross. 'Mum?' he shouted, 'Mum?'

'Margery!' bellowed Barnabus, hammering on the door. 'MARGERY! It's me, it's Barnabus. Where are you?'

One of the windows opened on the upper storey and a girl poked her head out. She was very pale and she had bandages round her neck.

'That you, Uncle Barney?' she called.

'Letty! Letty, what's happened? What's all this?'

Letty was crying and looked as if she'd done a lot of it, lately. 'Oh, Uncle Barney. It was Sam got it first, and then Mary, and then George and me, and then dad got it and mum's got it, and dad's dead and they took him off yesterday and now mum's all black and she won't wake up and...and...' She made her hands into fists and howled into them.

Barnabus was panting as he looked up while Simon had placed the bandbox carefully on the step, sat down beside it and was weeping into his sleeve.

'I...I don't believe it. She's too good for this. She never done nuffing. She's the best of the lot of us. Letty, are you sure...?'

For answer the girl pulled down the bandage under her chin and they could see the scabbed pit under her ear where a buboe had burst. Dodd had looked coolly at the pointed end of all manner of weapons, but this nearly made him lose his water. 'I'm getting better now and so's George, but...but Mary's looking poorly and the baby's...Well, the baby's dead, of course, but me mam...It's me mam I'm feared for, she's all black, all black spots all over and she smells horrible. I think she's still breathing but...Oh, Uncle Barney.'

For fully five minutes Barnabus stared up at his niece, breathing hard through his mouth and his hands opening and closing into fists. Dodd was rooted to the spot and the hair on the back of his neck standing up like a hedgehog. He had seen plague. Years ago, back when he was a little wean still in skirts, there had been plague in Upper Tynedale and his cousin Mary had died of it and his uncle had staggered through the village roaring, his face turned into a monster's by the huge lumps on his neck and the black blotches and he'd collapsed over by the stream and none of the grown-ups had dared go near, except poor mad Peter...Big strong grown-ups, men that had forayed hundreds of times into Scotland and come back triumphantly with Elliot cattle and sheep, they had smelled of fear and some of them had disappeared forever. Dodd's memory was confused but he knew that one of his sisters, the one he hated because she was littler than him, she had turned black and become a stiff doll-like thing and they had buried her...

He found he hadn't been breathing and he took in a deep harsh breath. Simon was still howling on his doorstep. My legs'll move soon, Dodd told himself, and then I'm off, I'm going, I'm out of London and I'm going north whether the Courtier likes it or not...

'All right, Letty. You got any food in the house?' How was it Barnabus's voice was so calm. He wasn't even shouting.

Letty shook her head. 'We ate the last hen two days ago,' she sniffled. 'And the bread yesterday.'

'We'll get you some. What happened to Margery's fighting cock? Did you eat him?'

Letty shook her head again and winced. 'No, Uncle Barney, mum wouldn't let us. She said he could make our fortunes if we got through this. But she's gone all black and she won't wake up...'

'Now you calm down, Letty, you hear me? You've got to be a good girl and look after the others. Me and Sergeant Dodd 'ere, we'll go get you some food. Have you got a basket and some rope?'

She nodded.

'Good. Now, Simon, you stay here and look after Sergeant Dodd's hatbox and don't you move, you hear me? You stay there. You can get plague just by going in the house, so don't you move!'

'B...but me mam...'

Barnabus's face crumpled and there were tears in his eyes too. He stroked Simon's hair. 'Son, your mum's dead. If she in't now, she will be soon. If all you've got is buboes, there's some chance for you, but if you get the black spots all over you, that's it, you're done for. And don't forget, you can take the plague just from the bad smell of it, so don't you set foot in that house.'

Dodd nodded at this sense. Barnabus jerked his head at him, and they went back up the silent little street. Dodd knew he was shaking all over, but he wasn't sure enough of his legs to start running yet.

Barnabus's shifty little ferret-face was grim and cold. 'Now we know what's going on 'ere,' he said. 'That's why there's hardly anybody about and the Queen's still in Oxford when the lawterm should be starting soon. Good Christ Almighty.'

'Are we going back to Sir Robert?' Dodd asked, knowing his voice sounded funny because of his mouth being dry.

Barnabus looked straight up at him. 'You can, mate, I'm not asking you to stick around. This is family business.'

'Ay.' Dodd wanted to explain that he was afraid of getting lost again and maybe stumbling into some other plague spot, but couldn't because it sounded so weak. Him, Sergeant Dodd, afraid? But he was, afraid of the plague and afraid of this huge city full of people, any one of whom might be sick to death and not even show it yet.

'Why didn't anybody say what was happening?'

Barnabus sucked his teeth judiciously. 'Well, there's always a bit of plague about in London, but it's usually only brats and babies that get it. They don't start shutting the playhouses and having days of penance and preaching and so on until the parishes are showing more than thirty deaths a week from plague.'

'Thirty deaths a week!' Dodd echoed, horrified again at the numbers.

'Plus of course there's plenty of rich people that want to keep it quiet because of the damage to business.'

'Ay.'

They were in New Fish Street again, according to a dirty sign up on one of the houses. Barnabus looked thoughtfully at the various fishmongers' shops, several of them shut up tight, and carried on down the street until he came to a little grocer's just under a magnificent clock hanging over the street like an inn sign.

They ranged about the nearby streets, buying bread and salt fish and cheese and finished with two big leather bottles of beer that Dodd carried. And that was amazing by itself, not having to wait for market day, being able to just go to shops and buy all that food whenever you wanted. When Barnabus ran out of money, Dodd handed over one of his false angels which made Barnabus grin cynically at him.

The afternoon was sliding away by the time they came back and found no Simon on the doorstep, but Dodd's hatbox sitting there still. That sight made Dodd feel queasy all over again. A twenty-shilling hat, left unattended in the middle of London, and nobody had stolen it.

'Where's that boy?' growled Barnabus. 'If he's gone in, 'e can stop there.'

They shouted up at the window again, until Letty put her head out and let down a basket on a rope. First the bread, then the cheese, then the salt fish, then the beer. They did it in silence, nobody having anything to say.

'We'll go to the river and fetch you some water, Letty,' said Barnabus, still quite calmly. 'You got any water barrels?'

'Simon's bringing it round from the yard,' said Letty.

'You didn't let him in the house, did you?'

She shook her head. Simon appeared in one of the tiny passageways between the houses rolling the barrel in front of him in a little handcart.

'Did you go in?'

'No, Uncle,' said Simon glibly, tears still shining on his cheeks. ''Course I didn't.'

'Not to say goodbye to your mum or nuffing?'

'No, Uncle, I wouldn't.'

'Where'd you get the barrel?'

'Well, I went in the yard, I 'ad to, see if Tamburlain the Great was all right.'

'And is he?'

'Well, he's still alive, but he don't look very well, he's huddled up in his cage looking all sad and bedraggled 'cos his hens is dead.'

Barnabus grunted. 'Come on.'

They threaded through little alleys down to some worn riversteps where Barnabus heaved the barrel on its rope into the oily water, waited until it sank and then with Dodd's help, hauled it back up again and heaved it onto the cart. Dodd pushed the barrel up New Fish Street into the alley. Letty still had her head out the window.

'Can you get it in our yard, Uncle Barney?' she called, looking a little bit more cheerful and munching on some of the bread.

'No problem, Letty.'

They manoeuvred the cart up the passageway and found the passage-gate nailed shut as well. Simon showed them where he'd climbed over the yardwall.

'I'll get in and you heft the barrel to me, Sergeant.'

'Ay.'

It was a gut-busting business hauling the heavy sloshing barrel up over the wall and into the yard. Barnabus disappeared for a minute and Dodd's neck hairs stood up again with the suspicion that he'd been mad enough to go into the house himself, but then he was lifting a wooden cage full of squawking red and bronze feathers up to the brow of the wall. Dodd took it from him, nearly getting his fingers pecked by the wild-eyed fighting cock inside, and then Barnabus climbed back into the passage, dusting himself down and shaking his head.

'The cat's dead of it too. I don't believe it.'

Dodd stared at him suspiciously. 'Ye didnae go in yerself?'

Barnabus sighed. 'No, mate, I'm not stupid. The yard should be safe enough, no bad airs there. Come on, Simon, I need a drink.'

They trailed round to the front of the house again and Dodd gingerly picked his hatbox up off the doorstep.

'You all right for the moment, Letty?'

She nodded and licked her fingers. 'Thanks, Uncle Barney. I'll tell mum when she wakes up.'

'All right, sweetheart. I'll come back tomorrow if I can, or the next day.'

'Bye, Uncle Barney. See yer.'

Barnabus nodded and swallowed hard. Dodd heard him mutter, 'Bye, Margery, God keep you, girl.'

They went back into New Fish Street again and looked at each other, exhausted. Barnabus was as grey as a man who had been badly wounded.

'Ay,' said Dodd. 'Ye do need a drink. Where's the nearest boozing ken?'

Barnabus scrubbed his sleeve along his face and coughed. 'That'll be Mother Smith's, up that way.'

Mother Smith's had a red cross on the door and the shutters nailed together. They stared at it dully and carried on up to Eastcheap and along to another little house with red lattices. Dodd bought three large horn cups of aqua vitae and some beer with the change from his false angel, and they sat by the window drinking in silence.

'What'll we tell the Courtier?'

Barnabus thought carefully about this. 'Nuffing,' he said decisively at last. 'Don't want to worry him and I'll have trouble finding a new master if they think I've got plague.'

But you could have it, yammered the scared wean inside Dodd's head, you could and not know it, the death marks could be growing on you out of sight right now, they could...He shook his head and swallowed the rest of his aqua vitae.

None of them felt like hefting a clumsy heavy cage full of outraged fowl all the way back to the western suburbs, so they took a boat. Simon sat in the back on the cushions and trailed his fingers in the water and wouldn't look at either of them. Barnabus stared at him the whole way, until Dodd was unnerved just watching.

'Take us past Mermaid Steps, boatman,' Barnabus said. 'I want Whitefriars.'

The boatman nodded, and when they landed Dodd paid him, including a tip after Barnabus elbowed him. He thought he had never ever spent so much money in one day in his life before. He couldn't even bring himself to count it up, it came to so much, and some of it was false and the plague on top of it all.

'We'll take Tamburlain the Great back to the room so he can rest and keep his strength up. Now you've looked after him before, haven't you, Simon?'

Simon nodded and perked up a little with enthusiasm. 'Me dad was teaching me to handle 'im, how to feed him up before a match and make sure he wasn't got at and how to put the spurs on. Dad says...' His voice trailed off. Then he shrugged and went back to staring at the water.

'Well, you look tired,' Barnabus said. 'How do you feel? Peaky? Got a headache?'

Simon shook his head.

'Well, you can go to bed so you can keep an eye on Tamburlain. If I know Sir Robert he's playing primero by now and we're in for a late night.' Gloomily Dodd thought he was probably right. London was a den of iniquity and no mistake, full of evil greedy folks just plotting to take your money by any way they could, and no wonder it was being visited by the Sword of God's Wrath.

But would God's vengeance hit Dodd as well, even though he hadn't done anything bad? Well, nothing iniquitous, anyway, just the routine normal sins that everybody committed. But the Reverend Gilpin had said that there wasn't any such thing as a normal sin, a venial sin like the Papists said, they were all sins and that was bad enough to draw down God's wrath. God had good reason to be angry with every man or woman. Dodd shook his head and tried to stop thinking about it. If he let his mind go down that road he'd be a gibbering wreck by the next morning (or dead of plague, if God was angry enough with him). What could you do? If you got the plague, you got it, there wasn't anything you could do to stop it except stay out of plague houses and away from sick people and repent of your sins. And even that wouldn't necessarily help you. Barnabus had said his sister was a good woman, she'd done nothing to deserve such a visitation. Deep in the recesses of his soul, Dodd found it terrifying that God was so much less reasonable than Richie Graham of Brackenhill. At least if you paid your blackrent on time and didn't kill any Grahams,

Richie Graham wouldn't burn you out.

On the way to the river they had bought grain to feed the fighting cock. It seemed tame enough when they cautiously let it out of its cage in the attic room, fed it grain on the bare floorboards which magnified every footstep and peck, every creak. It glared at Dodd and Barnabus suspiciously, but it seemed to know Simon and even let him smooth down some long feathers that had been disarranged by being in the cage. At last they left the cock roosting on the head of the bed and Simon curled up in his blankets on the pallet by the wall. Barnabus called him to get up and bolt the door from the inside, which he did.

They clattered down the stairs and hurried to Fleet Street to get back into the City before the gates shut. By the time they arrived at the Mermaid, the sun was drowning in a brilliant red blaze that set light to the water and gilded the little boats scurrying across it. All Dodd wanted was to go to bed and sleep.

Barnabus caught his arm just as they went in. 'Keep quiet for me, Sergeant.'

Dodd sighed. 'He willnae like it when he finds out.'

'He won't find out.'

'All right, if ye want.'

'You're a prince, Sergeant. I owe you one. Not many would have stuck around like that for people that weren't even related.'

Dodd ducked his head in embarrassment, not able to explain that he had stuck around because he was afraid of getting lost in London again.

Carey was happily calling his point score as they came in, putting down more money on a terrifyingly large pile. Beside him was bundled the still unconscious mound of Robert Greene. When he saw Dodd and Barnabus, Carey closed up his cards and smiled.

'Oh, there you are. Greene's no better, as you can see, though I think it's now the booze not the blow that's made him so sleepy. Pull up a stool, Sergeant, I'll introduce you.'

Dodd nodded politely as Carey went round the circle of cardplayers, firing off names like a bowman in a battle. Unfortunately not one of them hit the mark and all were instantly lost from his overtaxed brain. Dodd recognised one man: Shakespeare, his fuzzy dome glinting in the candlelight above him. He had already folded. From the look of concentration on his face and the sideways manner he sat on his stool it was clear he was magnificently drunk. Next to him sat a short rotund man in a grey wool suit with a confiding way to him; Dodd couldn't remember his name. Another one, directly opposite the Courtier had a handsome slightly smug face, the kind of face that believes itself to be cleverer than any company, and very annoyingly often is, and a fine doublet of black velvet slashed in peach taffeta, almost as good as the Courtier's. Next to him was a pale man with a nose that had been broken once who Dodd vaguely thought was called Poley or Pool or something, and that took you to Robert Greene and the Courtier again. Dodd narrowed his eyes and sat down on a stool deferentially brought for him by Barnabus and decided that he could throw any one of them a lot further than he was prepared to trust them, and would on the whole prefer to throw them anyway.

'Will you join us, Sergeant?'

'Ah'd prefer to watch for a while, Sir Robert. I'm no' so well in practice with gleek.'

As Dodd knew perfectly well, they were playing primero and in fact he was in razor-sharp form for primero, for him.

The self-satisfied man in the pretty doublet raised his eyebrows at Dodd. 'Sergeant?' he asked. 'Are you a lawyer, sir?'

Was the man deliberately trying to insult him? 'Nay, sir, I'm a Land Sergeant.'

'Very important man, in Carlisle,' said the Courtier helpfully. 'Keeps an eye on some of the most important reivers' trails from Scotland into England. He has land and a tower in Gilsland.'

The reaction to this was glazed-over politeness.

'Fancy,' said pretty doublet, distantly.

'And ye, sir?' Dodd asked pretty doublet. 'What are ye yerself?'

Pretty doublet laughed. 'Oh, I'm a poet, a playwright, a scholar, a striver for the incomprehensible crystal reaches of the heavens.'

Dodd gave him a glazed look right back. 'Och, fancy.'

To his surprise pretty doublet grinned at him. 'Well, it's a more interesting trade than hammering shoes for a living.'

Carey coughed. 'Marlowe's being modest, which is extremely

114

unusual for him. Also he hasn't declared his points and I'm waiting to find out by how much I've beaten him.'

Marlowe leaned back, drank with an unnecessary flourish and said, 'Eighty-four, of course, like you.'

'I'm out,' said Poley or whatever his name was.

Shakespeare snapped his fingers at the potboy for more drink, which was there with a speed that surprised Dodd. The would-be poet and player looked as if he had a gigantic cloud of black melancholy hanging over his head, so black it was almost visible, and which was deepening by the minute as he drank. Dodd shook his head. Good God, he must be tired, he was coming over all fanciful.

There was a sudden snortle and an earthquake from the huddle on the bench, and Robert Greene lunged upright, his orange beard jutting like a preternatural carrot.

'Beer,' he roared. 'Where's the beer?' Somebody gave him a mug and he lifted it to the company. '*Holla, ye pampered jades of Arsia*,' he bellowed and drank it down. Marlowe rolled his eyes and stretched his lips briefly in a smile that said 'oh how witty, and only the hundredth time this week'. Greene had sunk most of his quart before he seemed to notice the taste of what he was drinking which he then spat out again onto the floor in a stream.

'For Christ's sake, Greene,' drawled Carey. 'It's only mild ale.'

'It's horsepiss,' roared Greene. 'You, boy, get me some proper booze. What the hell are you doing in London, Sir Robert? I thought you'd gone to wap the cows in Newcastle.'

'Carlisle,' said Carey. 'I'll see you, Marlowe.'

'York, Carlisle. Who cares? Somewhere ooop north.' Greene waved an arm expansively. 'I repeat. Why are you here?'

Marlowe put down four fives and Carey shook his head, sighed and threw in his cards. Marlowe smiled in his self-satisfied way and pulled what looked like a very tasty pot towards him.

Dodd tutted sympathetically. 'Your luck out today, sir?'

'I must be on the point of getting married, it's been so bad.' The man called Poley was dealing again and Greene waved a hand to be included.

'Don't waste your sympathy,' Greene slurred at Dodd. 'It's only justice because he won't tell me why he's in London and not up in your part of the world having fun hanging sheep-stealers.'

Carey picked up his cards, raised his eyebrows at Greene. 'You'd have heard about it by now if you hadn't been so stinking drunk when I found you.'

'A slight indisposition,' said Greene, wiggling his fingers generally at Carey. 'Nothing to be concerned about. I've been off colour since I overdid the eels and Rhenish wine last month.'

'No doubt,' said Carey. 'Shocking bad wine the Germans sell, isn't it?'

'On the contrary,' said Greene with dignity. 'I'm certain it was the eels that were off. Very dangerous to the health, bad eels.'

'So why are you back in London so soon, Sir Robert?' asked Marlowe, putting his new cards into a neat pile and laying them face down on the table. 'I thought Mr Bullard was after your blood.'

Greene sucked air in a whistle through his teeth and tutted with bogus sympathy.

'No, no,' said Carey nonchalantly. 'He's being paid off, he's perfectly reasonable.'

Poley laughed quietly at this and so did Greene, only more loudly. Marlowe nodded, grave as a parson.

'You'll be moving home to London then?'

'No, I like Carlisle. I'll be back there as soon as I can.'

'The Queen's in Oxford,' pursued Marlowe. 'Are you going to see her?'

Carey looked at him levelly and Dodd had the sudden feeling that this was a river with hidden whirlpools in it.

'Come on man, out with it,' roared Greene, who seemed unable to talk except in a bellow. 'We never thought we'd see you again, what with the creditors and King James and Lady Wi...er, the northern ladies and all.'

'Oh, don't be such an idiot, Greene,' said Carey, in the drawl he used when he was getting annoyed. 'You know perfectly well what I'm doing here, since my father's paying you to do the same.'

Greene opened his eyes wide in a parody of innocence. 'And that is, dear boy?'

'Look for my brother Edmund, who has somehow lost himself in London.'

'Ah yes,' said Greene. 'To be sure. Edmund. Fine chap.' There was a glugging noise as a mug of sherry-sack went down his throat. Dodd called for some himself, on the grounds that if the Courtier had decided to spend the night drinking and losing yet more money, who was he to differ? 'Drawn a blank, though. Nobody's seen him for weeks.'

'Maybe he's caught the plague and died of it,' said Dodd, surprising himself. 'There's plague in London, is there no'?'

'Nothing more than usual, is there?' asked Carey, looking concerned.

'No, no,' soothed Marlowe. 'Just the normal amount. Isn't that so, Will? You'd know if there was plague about?'

Shakespeare had said nothing so far, being more interested in drinking. He blinked owlishly at Marlowe, who was smiling at him. 'Plague?' he asked. 'Er...no, I don't...No.'

Good God, thought Dodd in disgust, it's true what Barnabus was saying, they're keeping it quiet for fear of losing business. He felt Barnabus staring at him desperately and wasn't sure what he could say next.

Greene had stopped in mid-drink and was scowling pop-eyed across the table at Shakespeare.

'You!' he hissed. 'What are *you* doing here?'

Shakespeare blinked at him. 'Drinking,' he said peaceably. 'Loshing...losing money at cards. What are you...er...doing?'

With an incoherent roar, Greene slammed both fists down on the table in front of him, causing it to jump. Both Marlowe and Carey immediately picked up their tankards, but before Dodd could do the same, Greene had surged to his feet, bellying the table over so that cards and coins and Dodd's full cup of sack went spraying in all directions. Like a charging bull, Greene waded past the table, grabbed Shakespeare round the neck. Momentum carried both of them up against the side of the stairs where Greene started banging Shakespeare's head against the bannisters while he throttled him.

There was a confusion of shouting. Carey tried to grab Greene round the oxlike shoulders and was shrugged off, Marlowe tried a simultaneous blow at the back of Greene's neck with his dagger pommel and was sent flying by a blow from the back of Greene's fist. Shakespeare's face was going purple and he was prodding ineffectually with his fists.

'Somebody had better stop him killing him.' The voice seemed to have only an academic interest in the matter, but Dodd had lost an expensive drink he'd been looking forward to and needed desperately, and he didn't like Greene in any case, while he felt sorry for the player. He picked up the stool he'd been sitting on, prodded the legs into Greene's meaty back, just where his kidneys should be, and heard the satisfying whoop of pain. He slammed the stool sideways into Greene's ribs, dropped it, got his left arm in a lock around Greene's bull neck from behind, leaned back, swivelled his hips and swept Greene's legs out from under him in a Cumbrian wrestling throw.

Greene's weight pulled him down, but he was expecting it and he fell on top of the man, bruising his elbow. Half crouching he got a knee up in the small of Greene's back and then said breathlessly, 'Will I break yer neck for ye?'

Greene heaved and made horrible noises, the cords on his neck expanding. Christ, he was strong, but Dodd was in much better condition and very angry.

'I'll do it, I'll break it and no' think twice. Stop still afore I hurt ye.'

Just to make his point, he levered up his elbow to lift Greene's chin and put more strain on his neck.

'I'd listen to him if I were you,' said Carey conversationally. 'So far Dodd's been quite gentle with you.'

There was that indefinable change of muscle tone beneath him that told Dodd the man was starting to think. He increased the pressure and felt the man surrender.

'Will ye behave yerself if I let ye up?'

'Hhhnnhh.'

After another jerk on his neck to remind him, Dodd let him go and stepped away smartly. Greene lay there whooping and gasping for several minutes before he staggered to his feet. He glowered at Dodd for a while, breathing hard.

'I want satisfaction from you,' he croaked at last.

'Are ye challenging me?' Dodd asked, almost laughing. 'Tae a duel?'

'Name your place and your weapons, sir.'

Behind him Dodd distinctly heard Carey say, 'Oh dear.'

'Ye want to fight *me*? With *weapons*?'

'Don't you speak English? Yes, I am, you northern yokel.'

'Och God, I would ha' thought ye'd want a rest after a' that booze and the battering I gave ye. But well enough. Let's dae it here.' Dodd drew his sword and dagger, crossed the blades in front of him in the *en garde* position and waited expectantly.

To his surprise Greene didn't draw his own blades. His jaw had dropped and he was staring at Dodd as if he didn't know what to do next.

'Come on, man, I havenae got all night. Let's get the mither done wi' and then I can get back tae ma drinkin'.'

In a voice overflowing with amusement, Carey translated this for Greene. Marlowe was standing next to Greene, whispering in his ear. Greene glared about under his bushy red eyebrows, but his hand made no move to his swordhilt.

'Do ye want tae fight, or no'?' Dodd asked, surprised at the delay.

Carey was on the other side of Greene now, whispering in his other ear. Greene was looking at the ground. He coughed.

'I withdraw the challenge.'

'Ay?'

'And the insult about northern yokels?' prompted Carey.

'I withdraw it,' growled Greene.

'Och, Ah dinna care what a drunken southerner wi' nae blood tae his liver thinks o' me,' said Dodd genially.

Carey translated this as acceptance of Greene's withdrawal of the insult.

Behind him Poley was setting the table upright again and arranging the stools round it. The innkeeper was standing nearby with arms folded, eyes narrowed and a large cudgel dangling from his wrist on a cord. The plump little man was sitting Shakespeare wheezing on the bench, dusting him down and handing him another cup of booze, which the player took with hands that shook like rivergrass.

'All right,' said Carey. 'Now shake on it, gentlemen.'

Dodd put his sword and dagger away, and held out his hand. After an almost insulting pause, Greene shook.

There was a universal coughing and the staccato laughs of released tension.

'Damn,' said Marlowe. 'I had ten shillings to put on Sergeant Dodd to win.'

'Yes, but nobody was going to take the bet, were they?' said Carey drily.

Greene slammed his bulky arse down on a stool and glowered. Dodd sat back down on the bench next to Shakespeare and accepted the drink brought for him by Poley. The primero circle reformed itself and the innkeeper stood watching for a few minutes more before he and two other large men with cudgels melted back into the loud shadows.

They were piss-poor, these southerners, Dodd thought to himself; if he could only get the remounts and a sufficiency of right reivers together, he could run the raid of all time down here.

Poley and the plump man, whose name was apparently Munday, were both down on the floor, scooping coins and cards out of the sawdust and complaining at Greene while they did it. Carey was watching Greene with narrow eyes and a very suspicious expression, making no move to help. Marlowe was watching as well. Greene seemed slightly deflated, though he was still knocking back the booze at a fearsome rate. Now Carey was talking to him quietly, to a response of shrugs and growls. Poley put the pack of cards on the table and bent again to pick up the coins. Some of them were gold crowns and angels, Dodd noted to his horror; it wasn't any wonder the Courtier was in hock to his eyeballs.

Shakespeare cleared his throat painfully next to Dodd.

'Um...thank you, Sergeant,' he whispered. 'Er...if you don't mind my asking, why did you...?'

'Och,' said Dodd, embarrassed. 'He knocked ma drink over when he sent the table flying.'

'Oh.'

'And he puked on ma boots earlier the day. I dinna take to loud drunks either. And I've had a long day.'

Shakespeare had a wide expanse of brow to wrinkle. 'Ah,' he said, evidently only understanding half of this, though Dodd tried to make his speech sound more like the Courtier's, which wasn't at all easy against the effects of the booze. You had to say this for London town, you could find good drink here. Even the aqua vitae tasted quite smooth, if fiery. He tasted some more of it.

'Ye've not had a good couple of days either, have ye?' Dodd said sympathetically. 'And what was it ye had me give to Mistress Bassano yesterday that made her so wild with ye?'

Shakespeare blinked gloomily at the sherry-dregs in the bottom of his mug. 'Sh...sonnets.'

'Ay,' said Dodd cautiously, not willing to reveal that he didn't know what a sonnet was.

The little bald player smiled wanly. 'Poems. Rhymes. In praise... in praise of Mistress Bassano.'

'They werenae lewd?'

'No, of course not. They were classical. I compared her to Helen of Troy, Aphrodite, Aurora goddess of the dawn, likened her hair to gold poured from an alchemist's flask, her eyes to sapphires...'

'But her hair's black and her eyes are brown.'

'It's poetic symbolism.'

'Ay. Does she ken that or does she think ye werenae thinking of her at all?' This produced an odd effect. Shakespeare stared at him for several minutes together with his mouth open, looking a complete simpleton. 'Only,' Dodd added, making a real effort to help the man, 'if I told my wife I loved her for her yellow hair, she'd hit me with a rolling pin in the certainty I was playing her false wi' a blonde. She's redhead,' he added, for completeness. 'An' I bought her a fine green velvet hat the day for twenty shillings.' He was now feeling quite proud of himself for spending so much money on a frippery for his woman, though Shakespeare either hadn't heard or was used to the stupid London prices. The player was now nodding to himself, seemingly oblivious to Dodd.

Across the table the Courtier appeared to have won a little

of his money back, since he was pulling in a reasonable pot. He raised his eyebrows.

'Dodd?'

Dodd shook his head. 'Yer stakes are too high fer me. I'm no' a rich man.'

Marlowe leaned over, smiling. 'I thought Sir Robert said you owned land.'

'I do. I'm rich in land and kin and kine, but no' in money,' Dodd explained. And yon Courtier's rich in nowt but kin, though that's never stopped him, he thought but didn't say.

'Come on, Sergeant,' said Poley with a little edge to his voice. 'Aren't you going to take the chance to enrich yourself? We could teach you if you don't know how to play.'

Just for a moment, Dodd was sorely tempted. He liked playing cards and he was a lot better at it than he had been.

In that moment, Barnabus brought another tray of drinks, leaned over the table to give them out and while his body was in the way, looked directly at Dodd and shook his head, mouthing a word silently several times. For a moment Dodd was annoyed and then realised that Barnabus was telling him the game was crooked.

'Nay, I willnae. Thank ye for the invitation,' he said politely, when Barnabus was out of the way again.

Greene belched disparagingly. 'Northerners,' he said. 'Mean as Scotsmen and not so friendly. You can't have spent all of Heneage's gold, surely?'

Through his instant anger at the fat drunk daring to compare him with a Scot, Dodd caught an infinitesimal twitch in Carey's expressive eyebrows and cooled immediately to ice. Yes, it was very interesting that Poley wanted him to play and Greene knew about Heneage's bribe, and now Poley was hiding what looked like fury at Greene blurting that out. It was even more interesting in view of the fact that Heneage's bribe or the Hampstead footpads' loot might have contained two forged angels. You could hang for uttering false coin, if you were caught.

'Nay, Mr Greene,' he said. 'It's no' meanness. It's only that I ken verra well ye're all fine card players with far more experience than me at such high stakes. I'm nobbut a fighting man, me.'

Greene tutted, then jumped and glared at Poley who had probably kicked him under the table. Marlowe smiled caressingly at Dodd.

'How quaint,' he said.

'Marlowe,' said Carey warningly.

Marlowe put his hands up placatingly. 'I only meant, how unusual to find someone who knows their limitations.'

Now he knew why these card-sharps wanted him to join the game, Dodd found he could watch their attempts to needle him into it with objectivity. It was even quite funny. 'Ay,' he said. 'What are yours, for instance?'

The cocky smile grew wider. 'Me? I have none. There is no limit on what a man may achieve, if his heart be bold and his spirit enterprising enough.'

'And he's ruthless enough,' said someone, who turned out unexpectedly to be Shakespeare, looking up from where he had been scribbling in a little notebook.

Marlowe nodded at him. 'Yes,' he agreed. 'It's important not to have any scruples.'

'Ha!' said Greene, in a shower of spit. 'Then why aren't you up in Scotland buggering King James?'

There was that tiny gap in the conversation while everyone waited to see how Marlowe would react.

'What a good idea,' he said silkily at last. 'I think I'll go. What do you think, Sir Robert? Do I stand a chance?'

Even Dodd knew that this was very dangerous talk, right here in London. As far as the Queen was concerned, making up to the King of Scots was tantamount to treason, even if he was her likely successor. And never mind that buggery was a deadly sin and officially a hanging crime.

Carey's eyes hooded themselves. 'Hm,' he said, coolly judicial. 'Classically educated. Playwright—His Majesty loves plays. Not too tall or broad—His Majesty doesn't like being towered over... Hmm. Yes, I think it's a good match.'

'Such a pity you don't like boys, isn't it, Sir Robert?' said Marlowe with sweet sympathy. 'You'd be running Scotland by now.'

Carey smiled lazily. 'Yes, I know. Her Majesty the Queen said the same. But I think Scotland might be very profitable for you, Kit. Why don't you go?'

Marlowe sighed and waved a tankard. 'So many entanglements in the south. Too many. Eh, Poley? What do you think Heneage would say if I went north?'

Poley's expression was peculiar. It combined knowingness and alertness with a kind of bewilderment. Before he could answer, Robert Greene butted in again.

'And what's Heneage up to, eh? What's all this I hear about alchemists? You know, Poley, don't you, you close-mouthed bastard, why don't you give us the gossip?'

Now Poley was looking worried. 'Isn't anybody going to play cards any more?' he asked. 'Or are you too busy talking treason?'

Marlowe clapped him on the shoulder. 'Come on, my dear,' he smiled sarcastically. 'Get your notebook out, write it all down before you forget, or Heneage will be cross with you.'

'You spell my name GREEN with an E,' bellowed Greene, dealing cards at expert speed.

Poley looked uneasy. 'I don't report private conversations,' he said unconvincingly and Marlowe put his arm over his shoulders.

'Sweetheart,' he said in a stage whisper. 'This *isn't* a private conversation.'

'Bloody Christ,' roared Greene, bug-eyed again at Marlowe. 'You're not a bugger too, are you, Poley?' Poley was concentrating on his cards and pretended not to hear. Greene shook his head. 'I don't know. What's the point? Once the Scotch king comes in all the buggers'll be dukes.'

Dodd wanted to escape from this horrible outrageous talk. He wanted to melt into the panelling and did the next best thing by sitting back as far as he could into the booth and sipping his drink quietly. The talk puttered along over the cards though it now seemed to be ranging across a vast range of classical allusion as Marlowe shamelessly explained that there was nothing whatever wrong with buggery.

Explain that to the hangman, Dodd thought. Greene thought the same and said so, loudly, incoherently and at length. Shakespeare had put away his little notebook, wiped his pen, stoppered his ink bottle and put them away neatly in a small leather case he had in his doublet-front. Now he smiled uncertainly at Dodd who finally asked the question he'd wanted to put all night.

'Why does yer man Greene hate ye so?'

Shakespeare looked depressed again. 'It's a long story.' His voice was hoarse and he rubbed his neck where the bruises were starting to show.

'Ay. Well, I'm no' playing primero wi' that bunch of perverts and card-sharps, so I've got time on ma hands.'

'None of them are cheating, are they?'

'Sir Robert only cheats when he thinks somebody else is at it.'

'Is he cheating?'

'Nay, did I say that?'

Shakespeare shook his head, evidently too drunk to deal with complexity.

'What's yer feud with Greene, then?'

Shakespeare sighed. 'A year ago he wrote a play for the troop of players I work for. The…the idea was good, about Henry VI, but the writing…' He shook his head.

'Bad, was it?'

'Hamfisted, cloth-eared. His prose is good—you should read his coney-catching pamphlets, but…er…his dialogue is terrible. Maybe it's the drink.'

'Ay?' Dodd looked over at Greene to see if he was eavesdropping any of this demolition, but he was in the middle of totting up his points again, one eye shut and breathing hard.

'Well, I'd been badgering Mr Burbage to let me try writing for them, but I was only a hired man, so…They said I'd be wasting my time. They said, what would a glover's son know about writing poetry?'

Will's mouth had turned down bitterly. Dodd felt sorry for him. Mistress Bassano hadn't liked his verse much either.

'But we needed a new play and the other ones we had were worse, so Mr Burbage said I could try my fist at reworking Greene's attempt. He's a very popular writer, very well-known, all the printers like him and they pay him…oh, several pounds a time for one of his books.'

'That much?' Dodd was shocked. Hats for twenty shillings was bad enough, but several pounds for mere words...? The Londoners were all mad. 'So did ye do it?'

'I did. I...er...sold up my horse-holding business, took three months off from playing and worked on it like a Trojan. I had it ready by March, and we put it on at the playhouse.' He sighed again and finished his drink, looked around blearily for more. Against his better judgement, but wanting to comfort the little man, Dodd poured him some.

'What happened? Did the groundlings no' like it?' Barnabus had told Dodd some of the things fellow-groundlings might do to plays they didn't like, in which eggs, rotten apples and stones featured largely.

'No, they loved it,' said Shakespeare gloomily. 'They cheered it. Burbage was cock-a-hoop, said I was nearly as good as Marlowe.'

Somewhere, he knew, Dodd had missed something important. Where was the problem?

'But, if they liked it...what's Greene got against ye?'

'He says he's an educated man, been to university, an experienced writer, he says the play was perfect before I meddled with it and ruined it.'

'But ye didnae?'

'No, of course I didn't. He's jealous because I've never been to university and I'm nothing but a common player and I can write a hundred times better than him.'

Dodd shook his head. Fighting over stolen sheep or a woman or even a drunken argument, that he could understand. But fighting over words? Why?

'So why do ye care what he thinks?'

'I don't. I care that he...er...he tries to kill me whenever we meet and he's told all the printers and booksellers to have nothing to do with me and he's half-convinced Burbage that the good bits in the play were his, not mine. The City shut our theatre the month before last and it's not opening until Michaelmas; Burbage fired me at the same time and I haven't been able to get another place as a hired man, not on any terms. Greene's making trouble for me any way he can. He knows the King of London, too. He keeps saying he'll arrange a little accident for me.'

'All because ye fixed up his play?'

'No,' said Shakespeare bitterly. 'Because I'm better than he is and he knows it.'

'Och,' said Dodd and poured them both some more aqua vitae. 'Why d'ye not go to be some rich man's gleeman, his house poet? Then ye'd be away fra London and Greene couldnae harm ye.'

Shakespeare nodded. 'I'd like that, I think. But the problem is… Every penniless university man who can string a couple of lines together wants the same and I've got no degree, no contacts, no… no nothing. I'd put out one of the poems I've written, dedicate it to someone likely, try getting a place that way, but the printers won't take it because they're scared of Greene, even Richard Field who I went to school with…he says he daren't.'

'Would ma Lord Hunsdon no' have ye?'

Will had an unfortunate propensity to blush. 'Not any more, I shouldn't think. It's only a matter of time before Mistress Bassano persuades him to fire me.'

'So ye're stuck.'

Shakespeare nodded dolefully. 'Stuck. I'll be in the Fleet by Christmas.'

Dodd nodded with him, full of oiled sympathy. You couldn't blame the man for wanting to break away from playing, it was no right work for a man.

'But could ye no' do some other line o' work? Like…er…ye said yer father's a glover? Could ye no' go back to that?'

To Dodd's horror, Shakespeare's eyes filled with tears. 'I'd like that,' he said. 'All I ever wanted to do when I was a boy was make beautiful gloves, but…I'm too clumsy. My fingers won't…You see the gloves Sir Robert's wearing, fine kid, embroidered in silk? It's very…very intricate, making top class gloves like them…My father did his best, but…It was no good. That's why he turned to drink, you see, because…because I was such a disappointment.'

Och, God, thought Dodd, he's turned maudlin.

'And I tried schoolmastering, and Christ, that's an awful job. No money in it. The children…I hate them. Ink down your gown. Nails in your seat. Crab apples through your windows. I've never been any good at anything, really...'

Dodd couldn't help it, his attention wandered. Marlowe had won again and the buggery argument was still rumbling on. Greene was quoting Leviticus on the subject and Marlowe laughed at him.

'Why should I live my life according to the notions of a starveling band of desert wanderers that were slaves in Egypt, slaves of the Assyrians, slaves of the Persians, slaves of the Macedonians and slaves of the Romans?' he asked.

'Because they were God's Chosen People,' said Poley sententiously and Marlowe laughed again.

'So they say. Which must have been a comfort to them. Surely God's Chosen would be a little more successful.'

Well, there it was, thought Dodd in an icy moment of clarity while Shakespeare droned on about his children and multiple failures beside him, if you wanted a reason for the plague hitting London, that was all you needed. Almighty God, they were doomed. They were drinking with an atheist and a pervert.

'That's enough, Kit,' said Carey very quietly. 'You've shocked us all, now be quiet.'

For a moment Dodd thought he might do as he was told, but then Greene had to stick his purple nose into the brew. 'God will repay,' he roared, wagging a finger. 'God repays the atheist and blasphemer. In the end, He repays!'

'*Your* God may rule by tyranny and injustice,' hissed Marlowe, leaning over the pile of gold on the table. 'You make a fat roaring idol in your own fat roaring image and you bow down before it and then you plume yourself on your stern Protestant virtue and nobility. God preserve me from such a god.'

'Playing I'm not bad at, but I'll never touch Alleyn or Richard Burbage,' Shakespeare was still talking, locked in the drunk's miserable obliviousness. 'I haven't got the size or the looks for it, though I'm not bad at character roles...'

'At least I'm no atheist,' spat Greene.

'I'm not an atheist, I'm a pagan,' said Marlowe composedly. 'The God who made the stars, the God who built the crystal spheres, the God of fire and ice and stone and wind, that God is worthy of my worship. But why should I bow down to books of gathered words from hundreds of years ago when with my own pen *I* can write such words *and better.*'

He's mad, thought Dodd in the horrified silence, clearly insane, not with the burbling drooling madness of men that talked with their shadows and shook their fists at the clouds, but a stranger more limpid madness that hid itself in elegance and urbanity. Even Shakespeare had stopped drivelling to gape at the speaker of such blasphemy.

To his surprise, it was Carey who answered Marlowe; not even Greene seemed to be able to find the words.

'Yes,' said Carey, still quietly. 'It's attractive to decide on what God is and worship that. How is what you do different from what you accuse Greene of doing?'

'If I must have a religion, what's wrong with rationality, science, justice?' said Marlowe in general, still leaning forwards as if he genuinely were trying to convert Carey to his strange brand of atheism. 'I could believe in those, not some fairytale designed to keep the people in awe.'

'No doubt,' said Carey. 'And kindness, wisdom, mercy? Where are these? Have you ever seen what happens in a land where the people are *not* in awe? Bloody feud and robbery, the strong against the weak, the children starving. Not everyone is as brilliant and powerful as you. Oh, and I'll raise you an angel.'

'And I'll see you, Sir Robert,' Marlowe didn't seem much abashed and nor was he ruffled when Carey proved to have a flush. He waved the gold coins farewell and called for a pipe of tobacco. Poley and Greene did the same.

'But poetry. I can do that.' Shakespeare was off again as the air around them filled with clouds of foul-smelling smoke. 'Maybe not the way Marlowe does it, but my way. My own way.' He caught Dodd's sleeve and breathed earnest booze-fumes in his face. 'I can *do* it. Do you understand?'

'Ay, ay, I understand.' Give him more aqua vitae, Dodd thought to himself, maybe he'll pass out and stop blathering at me.

'No, you don't, you couldn't. Plays, poems, anything. I looked at that pile of dung Greene produced, and I knew how to fix it, what it needed. And I sat down with as much paper as I could afford—it's awfully expensive you know, penny a sheet—and I started...It was as if something huge, God, something picked me up and carried me, like a spate-tide of words...You just open the tap and out it all flows, like...like there's this huge barrel of words inside you and you put the tap in and open and...whoosh.'

'Whoosh,' said Dodd, who was losing the will to live, what with mad atheism on one side of him and a barrel of words on the other.

Shakespeare nodded. 'Whoosh. The problem's stopping, really. I can't stop now, not now I've found what I can do, I can't. And that fat bastard, that lily-livered, carrot-bearded, word-mangling, purple-faced, pox-ridden tub of putrescent lard...I could kill him.' Shakespeare actually showed his teeth like a dog at Greene who was roaring across the table and betting an angel on whatever new cards he held in his paw.

Dodd patted the player's shoulder and poured some more aqua vitae for him. 'Kill him tomorrow,' he advised sagely. 'Too many wintes...witnish...people watching.'

Shakespeare drank it down in one and screwed up his eyes. 'Yersh,' he said. 'Tomorrow.' He swayed on the bench.

Quite quietly he folded his arms on the table, put his head on them and went to sleep. Thank God, thought Dodd, whatever that means hereabouts.

**

Many times in the days that followed Dodd wished he hadn't drunk so much that night so he could remember more of it. Occasional fragments would come back to him, wreathed in tobacco smoke: Carey and Marlowe locked in a crazy betting spiral over the cards, and he could not for the life of him remember who won; Poley coming back from the jakes and smiling; Greene scoffing a large plate of jellied eels; Marlowe trying to convince Carey that the Ancient Greeks were right and the love of men was far better than that of women and Carey laughing at him and saying he should try women some time, he might like them.

Late in the evening, when Carey had gone out to the jakes, Greene heaved his bulk up, took a gulp from a silver flask he kept in the front pocket of his doublet and then shook it disapprovingly next to his ear. He ordered more aqua vitae and refilled it carefully, breathing hard, one eye shut, stoppered it and put it back. He belched, farted, said something about eels always giving him the squits and went out into the yard.

Dodd wondered owlishly if he should go with the man, to make sure he didn't slip away, but somehow he didn't get round to it. Anyway, he thought, Carey would meet him. And then Carey was back and there was no sign of Greene. The Courtier was very annoyed, went trotting out into the street after him, but came back after a few minutes saying the bloody poet was nowhere to be seen. He glared at Dodd who was too drunk to do anything except shake his head regretfully.

'Oh, don't take on so,' said Marlowe. 'He's only gone home.'

'If you knew the trouble I had finding him and bringing him here...' Carey fumed and then sat down again on the bench and scowled. 'I'll see him tomorrow.'

At last they were the only ones left in the common room and the innkeeper came over and said hintingly that he had two rooms spare that night if the gentlemen needed somewhere to sleep.

Dodd had been wondering about that. Marlowe was whispering to Poley, one arm over his shoulder again, and Marlowe announced that since he was lodging in Holywell Street near the Strand and it would be a confounded nuisance to go back there with the city gates shut, he and Poley would take one of the rooms.

Trying to hide his disgust, Dodd tried to shake the player awake to ask him what he wanted to do. Shakespeare only snortled, muttered and slept on.

The innkeeper tried with a splash of water on the balding forehead and got no reaction at all. He sighed.

'Mr Shakespeare's no trouble,' he said. 'He can stop here on the bench until he's feeling better.' He and his son arranged the player on his side and even covered him up with the cloak that had warmed Greene, while Shakespeare slept peacefully through, not even snoring very much.

'Hardly seems worth going to bed,' Carey commented while Marlowe and Poley went upstairs arm in arm. 'It'll be dawn soon.'

'Och, God,' said Dodd, who could feel the father and mother of a hangover waiting for him somewhere in the future and wanted to be asleep when it hit. 'Ye please yerself, Courtier, I'm going tae my rest.'

He remembered the innkeeper giving him the key, he remembered climbing an infinity of stairs, he remembered being vaguely annoyed that Carey had somehow managed to remove and hang up on a nail the fashionable encumbrances of velvet doublet and hose, while Dodd was still struggling with his boots, he remembered being very much annoyed when Carey climbed into the best bed as of right without even tossing for who was going to sleep on the truckle. He hadn't the energy to argue, so he pulled it out from under the main bed and fell onto it full length as the room spun, settled, spun the other way and then stole itself into darkness.

SATURDAY, 2ND SEPTEMBER 1592,

EARLY MORNING

The morning came immediately and was as hideous as he had expected. Horrible full sunlight was shining into his eyes because some fool had opened the shutters, his bollocks were itching because he'd gone to sleep in his clothes, his stomach was tied protesting in a knot, his mouth and throat had clearly been roosted in by a fighting cock with the squitters, and his head...

'Auwwwgh,' he moaned in agony, rolled and put the pillow over his head.

'Good morning, Dodd,' said Carey's voice from somewhere over to his left. 'I think it's still morning. Or thereabouts.'

'Piss off.'

'Have some mild ale.'

'*Piss off.*'

There was the noise of chewing, swallowing, drinking, echoing as loud as trumpets in the huge beating drum of Dodd's head. I want to die, he thought, please God let me die. Vaguely he remembered treasonous table talk the night before. Fine. You can cut my head off, hang, draw and quarter me, just do it soon.

'Seriously, try and drink something,' said Carey's voice again, inhumanly cheerful and persistent.

Dodd wanted to tell him what he thought of people who were happy in the mornings in general, never mind what he thought of people who seemed immune to hangovers after a night spent drinking and gambling, but the effort was too great.

'Fuck off?' he pleaded.

'Well, Barnabus and I are going for a walk. There's a mug of mild ale next to your bed, don't knock it over. See you in an hour or so.'

Thank Christ, thought Dodd, as the door boomed like cannon fire, and he tried to sink back into beautiful black velvet sleep. But he couldn't because his head was hurting too much and he was dying for a piss.

He put it off for as long as he could and then hauled himself to a sitting position, got up and began searching tremblingly for the jordan.

It was on the windowsill, still full of the Courtier's water. Dodd emptied it out the window and used it which eased his pain somewhat. Some inconsiderate bastard was shouting in the street. Dodd leaned out of the window and screamed, 'Shut up or I'll kill ye.'

Whoever it was obediently shut up and Dodd went looking for something to drink, found the mug of ale just before he kicked it and swallowed it down.

Aggravatingly, the Courtier had been right. It did help a little. Dodd poured himself some more, looked for a moment at the bread and cheese Carey had left on the wooden trencher and dismissed the notion as mad.

Instead he lay down on the main bed, shut his eyes against the disgusting sunlight and went back to sleep.

The next time he woke, it was with the strange feeling that some-one small and smooth of hand was delving stealthily in his hose.

She was. When his eyes flicked open he stared full in the face of a pretty little creature with plump pink cheeks, blue eyes and bright golden hair, wearing a smock that had slipped down over her shoulders so that two plump and perky breasts were peering at him over the frills.

'Whuffle?' said Dodd, so stunned at this he almost forgot to feel his headache.

She tilted forwards and kissed him on the nose. 'Now now, my love, you're getting what you paid for.'

Hangover or no, Dodd was sure he hadn't hired anybody the night before. Almost sure. And Carey would…Maybe Carey had hired her? Yes, that must be it. The Courtier had paid for a woman to come and wake them up and then gone out and forgotten about it or mistaken the time? That made sense.

Or he was dreaming again. No, his headache was too bad. And she was tracking kisses down his chest, unbuckling his belt…Oh, what the hell?

Fumbling frantically at the stupid points to his hose, terrified in case the Courtier came back and spoiled everything by laying claim to his whore, Dodd caught the girl by the shoulders, pushed her gently back on the bed and climbed happily aboard.

She made such a squealing that Dodd actually paused to make sure there hadn't been some terrible mistake, but she reassured him by pulling him down and nibbling his ear before letting out another astonishing yell.

The thunder of Dodd's heart seemed to shake the room they were in, the door bounced against the latch, his mind went white, the girl squealed again, and the whole door crashed open as two men shouldered through it.

Too spent to do anything for a moment except lie on top of the girl's delightfully soft body and pant, while his headache clamped down over his eyeballs like some Papist torture machine, Dodd tried desperately to catch up with what was going on. It was clear he had visitors and that they were strangers. There was a portly man in fine silks and velvets with an expression of pompous and self-righteous rage on his face, and two other men with him in buff-coats, that had 'hired henchmen' all but written on them.

'Sir Robert Carey, what the devil are you doing with my wife, sir?' spluttered the portly gentleman, as if it wasn't perfectly obvious. 'What's your explanation, sir? You have committed fornication and adultery with a married woman, to wit, my wife...'

His heart was slowing down to only a triple-hammered pace. Dodd shook his head as the girl started eeling out from under him, her face twisted with fear.

'Oh no, no, my husband,' she gasped. 'I'm done for. All is lost!'

The two henchmen started forwards purposefully with their hands out to grab. Working purely on animal instinct, Dodd rolled the opposite way off the bed onto the floor beside it, landing with a crash that made his skull feel as if it had burst open, yanking desperately at his breeches. Where the hell had he put his weapons last night?

Next to the bed, of course, came the cool answer out of a growing rage. Those two henchmen should have at least cracked a smile at the sight of Dodd, breeches round his knees, draped bare-arsed across their master's wife. Dodd himself would have smiled at it. But neither of them had, their faces were grim and solemn, and that rang false, at least as false as the girl's wails and pleas for mercy.

There was plenty of room under the main bed and the two bullies were coming round it to grab for Dodd once more, so he rolled again until he was underneath, finally got his breeches fastened and belted, then reached out an arm and scooped up his sword belt.

One of them was bending down, flailing about under the tumbled blankets for Dodd. Dodd poked him in the face with the sword still in its scabbard, then emerged volcanically out the other side, kicked the truckle bed on its wheels into the portly gentleman and made for the door. It was locked and he couldn't open it, so he turned at bay with his sword and dagger out and snarled at them all,

'Get the hell oot o' my bed chamber!'

'Don't you realise who I am, Sir Robert?' said the portly gentleman. 'I am Sir Edward Fitzjohn and that's my wife you were attacking.'

Sheer outrage at this ridiculous claim stopped Dodd from roaring and charging at the man.

'What?'

'I am Sir Edward Fitzjohn and I will swear out a warrant against you in the church courts, sir, for fornication and adultery with my wife.'

'*What*?'

'Oh oh,' wailed the girl. 'Don't let them take you, they'll put you in prison, oh oh!'

'WHAT?'

'I have that right, as the offended party,' said Sir Edward Fitzjohn.

'Give him money, anything you've got, only don't let him take you away...'

Grinding headache and churning stomach notwithstanding, Dodd was now quite certain there was something very fishy going on here.

'What would it take to settle the matter?' he asked, only glancing at Sir Edward while he made sure he gave no opening for the two henchmen to grab him.

'Are you offering money?' spluttered Sir Edward. 'For my wife's honour? Damn you, sir...How much have you got?'

Dodd wanted to laugh, he could feel his mouth turning down with the effort to stay straight-faced.

'Ah dinna ken where ma purse is, Ah think it was lifted last night,' he said, which caused all four of them to wrinkle their brows, including the girl sitting prettily on her knees in front of her alleged husband with her smock still falling off. 'I wis robbed last night,' he explained, trying to speak slowly and clearly. 'I've no money left.'

Sir Edward's face went through a series of expressions— disbelief, disappointment and finally hard ruthlessness. 'We'll have to kill him then,' he said in quite a different voice, and the girl obediently started shrieking. 'Help, murder, oh oh!' while the two henchmen and Sir Edward himself attacked with their swords. The girl scurried on hands and knees under the bed and started pulling on her stays and petticoat, all the while shrieking,

'Murder, blood, help, oh save my husband, sirs, save him!' at the top of her voice.

In the flurry of ducking one sword while he parried desperately at two more, Dodd was never quite sure how soon it was before the door started juddering to somebody else's boot. The bolt ends came out of the door-jamb which was when Dodd realised it wasn't locked, just bolted top and bottom.

Carey appeared in the doorway, sword out, Barnabus next to him on the little landing with a throwing knife in each hand.

'Oh shit!' said the girl under the bed, crawling further under it and starting to pull on her boots. Dodd was in a corner by then, dagger and sword up and crossed, ducking as Sir Edward's rapier flicked for his eyes.

'What the hell is going on here?' demanded Carey's court drawl.

There was a bright glitter in the air and one of the little daggers was growing out of Sir Edward's arm. He yelped, grabbed it out and the henchmen stopped their attack to stare at Dodd's reinforcements. Dodd growled, rage truly flaming in him now for the ruination of one of the few pleasant awakenings of his life, aimed the point of his dagger and charged at Sir Edward's belly.

Sir Edward jumped back, bombast and wool bursting out of the wound in his doublet, the two henchmen exchanged glances, and all three of them suddenly broke for the door. There was a confused scuffle while Carey and Barnabus tried to stop them, but they had momentum and desperation on their side and all three sprinted down the stairs and out through the common room, followed by Dodd, still roaring.

They disappeared into the crowded street and Dodd had to stop chasing at the cross-roads because he couldn't see any of them. Also the Londoners were staring at him and Dodd realised that his shirt was open and his insecurely belted breeches were on the point of falling down.

He sidled back into the inn, up the stairs and found Carey leaning out of the window swiping at something there. Dodd peered over his shoulder to see the girl who had woken him up so well climbing briskly across the thatch, still in only her stays and petticoat. She flipped Carey the finger as she let herself down onto a balcony and he laughed and took his hat off to her.

Dodd slumped on the bed breathing hard, hung his head and moaned at the weight of his hangover.

'Threatened to sue you through the church courts for fornication and adultery, eh?' asked Carey, handing him another mug of mild ale.

'Ay,' said Dodd, rubbing his face. 'And then they tried to kill me when I said I had nae money.'

Barnabus tutted. 'I told you they'd 'ave another go,' he said. 'But you should never let on you're broke, not in London. 'S dangerous.'

Carey laughed. 'Somebody should have warned them about Dodd in the mornings. Bears with sore heads isn't in it.'

'Och. It wasnae so bad afore her husband bust in.'

'Husband!' Barnabus snorted. 'Molly Stone's never been wed in her life, 'cept to a bishop.'

'You couldn't pass the word, could you, Barnabus? Tell 'em to lay off?'

Barnabus shook his head. 'Nah, sorry, sir, I'm out of touch.'

'Give it a try, there's a good fellow. I'd be grateful.'

Barnabus shrugged. He didn't seem himself that morning, though it was hard to say what was wrong. He seemed subdued, depressed. Mind, it wasn't surprising, considering what had happened to his sister and her family.

'At least you're awake now, aren't you, Sergeant?'

'Ay, I suppose I am.'

'Excellent. Make yourself decent and let's go.' Carey had paced restlessly to the window and back again. He looked as spruce and tidy as ever: damn him, he must have gone to a barber's while he was out, his hair was shorter and his face was clean-shaven while he smelled daintily of lavender and spice and he had a new ruff on. It was obscene, that's what it was.

'Where now, sir?' Dodd moaned.

'Greene's lodgings.'

'Och, not him again, sir!'

'Yes, him again. I haven't talked to him properly yet and I'm bloody certain he knows more than he's letting on about my idiot brother Edmund, not to mention the false angels that Heneage slipped you, according to Barnabus.'

'I suppose ye want to catch him when he's sober,' said Dodd, dispiritedly dealing with his points and buttons and wishing there was a more sensible way of fastening your clothes. His head was still pounding and his eyes wouldn't focus properly.

'Good God, no,' said Carey. 'All we'd hear would be rubbish about snakes and spiders and demons attacking him. Catch him when he's only half-drunk, that's the best plan. Come on, Dodd, hurry up or we'll miss the golden moment.'

Dodd found his cap and jerkin, finished buckling on his sword and dagger and followed Carey's long stride out the door.

A thought struck him halfway down. 'Wait, Sir Robert, Ah've lost ma purse.'

'No, you haven't. You left it next to the bed and I took it with me this morning when I saw how dead to the world you were. Here you are. I haven't borrowed anything.'

He hadn't, as Dodd could tell by hefting it. Not for the first time since he met the Courtier, gratitude and annoyance warred in him.

'Not that it's any of my business,' said Carey after a tactful pause, 'but when did you hire yourself a trollop?'

'Me?' Dodd was outraged. 'Ah thocht she was yourn?'

One day Carey would hang for the way his eyebrows performed. One went up by itself and then the other joined it. 'What?'

'I thocht ye hired her, to wake us up like. Did ye no'?'

'No, I didn't.'

'Ye didnae?'

'No.'

Dodd shut his eyes tight and shook his head, trying to clear it, which was a mistake. 'But...but when I woke, she was already... at ma tackle, ye ken.'

'And so you...er...'

Dodd could feel himself getting red as a boy caught with his hands down a kitchen maid's stays. 'Ay,' he said truculently. 'Wouldn't ye?'

Carey grinned. 'Yes,' he admitted cheerfully. 'But didn't you wonder how she got there?'

'Ay, I did. Like I said, I thought she wis...'

'Mine.'

'So to speak.'

'Ah. So who the hell hired her? Barnabus?'

'No, sir. Why would I? You've never needed any help like that before.'

'Well, did you ask...?'

'I woke up with her hand rummaging ma privates and no, I didnae think tae ask her.'

'Hm. Now isn't that interesting. I wonder who the benefactor was?'

Dodd shrugged. 'Sir Edward Fitzjohn hisself?'

'Who?'

'The man in the pretty doublet that wanted all ma money or he'd put me through the church courts for adultery.'

Barnabus snorted. 'Sir Edward Fitzjohn, my arse. That was Nick the Gent.'

'Dodd, could I have a look at that false coin you had?'

'Ay.' Dodd fished it out and handed it over and Carey stopped to hold it up to the light and squint at the bite marks. 'It's very good, you know. It's an excellent forgery. I think it's pewter inside with a thin layer of gold, but the minting's perfect. And you got it where?'

'I think it was in Heneage's bribe. That he give me at yer dad's party.'

'Oh, that's when he did it, is it? Who was the...agent?'

'I dinna ken. The man give it me in the garden, all muffled with a cloak.'

'Hmm. Interesting.'

'Ay, well, he could have got me hanged for spending it.'

'So he could. Hmm. Can I keep it?'

'Ay. It's nae worth nothing now.'

'Hmm. You never know,' was all the Courtier would say while Dodd decided that the whyfores of forgery were more than he could handle with his present headache.

Oh God. Maybe it wasn't a hangover. Maybe it was plague. Was that a lump he felt in his armpit? Did he have a fever? He deserved God's wrath after such a sin of adultery and fornication, no matter how desperate the temptation. The Courtier might not be shocked but Dodd was, shocked at himself. Dear God, why had he done it? what if Janet found out? what if he'd taken the pox...?

In the common room they passed Shakespeare lying curled up on the bench with a cloak over his narrow shoulders. The only comfort was that Dodd felt quite certain Shakespeare would feel even worse when he woke up than Dodd did. Which served him right.

Carey strolled over to the innkeeper who was just opening and talking to him quietly—got nowhere, to judge by the sorrowful headshakings. And now the bastard Courtier was humming to himself as they walked along yet another stinking street, some tweedly-deedly court tune all prettified with fa-la-las. God, thought Dodd, I hate London and Carey both.

Very slowly, the exercise of walking through the noise and bustle of the London streets in the bright warm sunshine moved from being a torture to a pain to a mere misery. Very slowly the awful pounding in Dodd's head faded down to a mere hammerbeat. Maddened with thirst, he drank a quart of mild ale at a boozing ken's window and felt much better, though still more delicate than one of those fancy glass goblets from Italy the gentry set such store by. If you blew hard on him, he would break.

Greene's lodgings were over a cobbler's shop. Carey asked at the counter which produced hurried whisperings and a small skinny faded-looking woman hurried in from the back of the shop to be introduced as Joan Ball, Mr Greene's...ahem...common-law wife.

'He's not well, sir,' she explained. 'He's been ill all morning. Very, very ill.'

Carey made a dismissive *tch* noise. 'I know what he's suffering from. I'll see him anyway.'

'Well, I don't know, sir, he's very...It's not his usual illness, you know, sir. I'd get the doctor to him if there was any left in London.'

'It's no' plague, is it?' Dodd demanded, with another greasy thrill of horror down his back.

She rubbed her arms anxiously up and down her apron. 'Oh no, no. Nothing like that. Some kind of flux, I think. Or even poison. I don't know, sir. He says he's dying and he keeps calling for paper, says he's got to finish his swansong.'

Carey frowned with suspicion and disbelief. 'What? Let me see him, I'm his patron, damn it.'

'I'll ask,' whispered the woman and scurried upstairs.

'Ye never are,' said Dodd, staggered at this further evidence of financial insanity.

'Yes, I am. Or I was. I paid five pounds for a thing he wrote last year and dedicated to me.'

'What was it?'

'Er...can't remember, I only read the dedication.'

The woman came downstairs again, her face drawn and miserable. 'He's not making any sense, sir, and he particularly said he wasn't to be disturbed...' Carey slipped a sixpence into her hand and she shrugged. '...but you can go up if you want.'

They went up the narrow winding stairs at the back of the shop and into the room under the roof. It was almost filled by a small bed and a little carved and battered table next to it. Papers covered the elderly rushes on the floor, piled up in drifts and held down with leather bottles, plates, rock-hard lumps of bread and, in one instance, a withered half of a meatpie; there were books on the windowsill and books on the floor under the bed. In a nest of unspeakable blankets sat the barrel-like Robert Greene, wearing a shirt and nightcap he might have wiped his arse with, they were so revolting.

His skin was greyish pale under the purple network of burst veins, his face worked in pain. A full jordan teetered on a pile of books. Next to him on the table were a pile of papers covered in a truly villainous scrawl. With a book on his knees and a piece of paper resting on it, an inkpot teetering by his feet and a pen in his fist, Robert Greene was scribbling with the fixity of a madman.

'Mr Greene,' said Carey, marching in and bending over the man on the bed. 'I want to talk to you about my brother.'

Greene ignored him, breathing hoarsely through his mouth and sweat beading his face, the pen whispering across the page at an astonishing rate.

'Mr Greene!' bellowed Carey in his ear. 'My brother, Edmund. What have you found out?'

'I'm busy,' gasped Greene. 'Piss off.'

Carey sat on the bed and removed the ink bottle. The next time Greene tried to dip his pen, he discovered it gone, looked up and finally focused on Carey.

'Give it back,' he said hoarsely. 'Damn you, I'm dying, I must write my swansong...Oh, Christ.'

Seeing the man retch, Carey got up hastily and backed away. It was the one of the ugliest sights Dodd had ever seen in his life, to watch anyone vomit blood. There were meaty bits in it. When the paroxysms finished Greene was sweating and shaking.

'Joan,' he roared. 'Get these idiots out of my chamber and bring me another pot of ink.'

He doubled up again and grunted at whatever was going on inside him, a high whining noise through his nose with each return of breath.

'Edmund Carey,' shouted the Courtier mercilessly. 'Tell me what you found out about him?'

'Oh, for God's sake,' gasped Greene. 'Who cares? I'm dying, I know I am, I'm facing Judgement and what have I done, I've wasted my life, I've drunk away my gift, what have I ever done but write worthless plays, books full of obscenity, garbage the lot of it, I must write something good before I die, can't you see that, can't you understand?'

There were tears in the wretched man's eyes. On impulse Dodd took the ink bottle out of Carey's hand and put it back on the bed. With only a grunt of acknowledgement, Greene dipped his pen and started scribbling again. Carey didn't protest.

'Dear, oh dear,' said Barnabus from the stairs as Joan Ball pushed past him. 'What's wrong with him?'

'Why hasn't he seen a doctor?' Carey asked the woman.

'They've all run on account of the plague.' She was wiping sweat off Greene's face as he panted over his page.

'Plague? That's not plague.'

Not as far as you could tell, although Dodd felt it paid to be suspicious. But there was no sign of lumps disfiguring Greene's neck, no black spots. The smell in the room was unspeakably foul but more a muddle of unwashed clothes, old food, drink and an unemptied jordan plus the sour-sweet metallic smell of the splatter in the rushes by the bed. Plague had its own unmistakeable reek.

'No, sir, but there's plague hereabouts, and the doctors are always the first to know and the first to run for the country.'

Carey's eyes were narrowed.

'Have you heard about this, Barnabus?' he asked.

Barnabus coughed. 'There's always plague in London,' he said. 'It's like gaol-fever, comes and goes with the time of year.'

Greene had started whooping and bending over his belly, his face screwed up with pain.

Joan Ball scurried to the window with the disgusting pot, opened it wide, shrieked 'Gardyloo!' and emptied, before running to the bed. 'Get the apothecary.' She hissed, 'Get Mr Cheke.'

'The quality of the angels—there you see the cunning of the plot,' gasped the man in the bed. 'They're all in it, by God, who could doubt angels,...urrr...And where's Jenkins, eh? Answer me that?' His face contorted.

They tactfully left the room and Carey turned to Dodd. 'Go with Barnabus and see if you can find or kidnap a doctor or the apothecary,' he said. 'I've got to get some sense out of him or I've nowhere to start looking for my brother.'

Dodd was quite glad to get away from the place. As they went down again into the street he tapped Barnabus on the shoulder. 'Where's Simon?'

'Oh, he's back in Whitefriars, looking after Tamburlain the Great.'

'How is he?'

Barnabus didn't look up. 'He's fine. Let's try here.'

It was a barber's shop with its red and white pole outside. There was only one customer and he and the barber glared suspiciously at the two of them.

'What do you want?' demanded the barber.

'We're looking for a doctor.'

'Stay there. Don't come any closer. Why?'

'It's not for plague,' said Barnabus stoutly.

'So you say, mate, so you say.'

'I ain't lying. Will you come?'

'No.'

'Well, is there anyone who will?'

'Certainly not a doctor,' said the barber and sneered.

'What about Mr Cheke?' Dodd asked.

'The apothecary's round the corner. He's mad enough to try it.' The barber was snipping busily again. As he left the shop, Dodd heard one of them sneeze.

They went round the corner and found the right place with its rows of flasks in the windows and a pungent heady smell inside, and a counter with thousands of little drawers all labelled in a foreign language Dodd assumed was Latin. A boy peered over the top of the counter.

'Yes, sirs?'

'Where's the apothecary?'

'Out, in Pudding Lane.'

Philosophically they went back into the street, turned left and then right, and found themselves in a street where every door seemed to be marked with a red cross and a piece of paper, where there were already weeds growing in the silted up drain down the centre of the alley and what looked suspiciously like dead bodies lying in a row down one end.

Both Dodd and Barnabus stopped in their tracks and froze. Down the centre of the street a monster was pacing towards them. It was entirely covered in a thick cape of black canvas and where its face should be was an enormous three foot long beak of brass, perforated with holes. Above were two round eyes that flashed in the sun and from the holes in the beak came plumes of white smoke.

In the unnatural silence of the plague-stricken street, a plague demon paced towards them with a slow weary tread, a bag full of souls in one hand, and its head moved from side to side blindly, looking for more flesh to eat.

'Ahhh,' said Barnabus.

Dodd was already backing away, sword and dagger crossed before him. Would blades kill a plague demon? Maybe. Who cares? It'll not get me without a fight, he promised himself.

'Sirs,' said the demon, its voice muffled and echoing eerily from the beak, as it stopped and put up one white-gloved hand. 'Sirs, don't be afraid. I'm only a man.'

Holy water might stop it, Dodd remembered vaguely, or a crucifix; he'd heard that in the old days you could get crucifixes or little bottles of holy water blessed by the Pope to keep demons off, and neither of those things did he have with him. He had his amulet, but he couldn't touch it because his hands were occupied with weapons that he wasn't even sure could cut a demon and...

The demon took its face off and became indeed a tall pale man, with red-rimmed eyes and hollow cheeks. He coughed a couple of times.

'Ah,' said Barnabus. 'Would you be the apothecary for hereabouts?' All credit to him, thought Dodd, still shaking with the remnants of superstitious terror, I couldnae have said anything yet.

'Yes, I am,' said the man, giving a modest little bow before putting the beak and eyes back on and transforming himself into a monster again. 'Excuse me, please, until we are away from the plague miasmas of this place.'

That was sense. Dodd put his blades away and they left the street as fast as they could walk, trying not to breathe in the miasmas, with the demon-apothecary pacing behind them. Nobody else in the next street gave him a glance, though a few stones were thrown by some of the children playing by a midden with dead rats on it. At last they were back in his shop.

'Peter Cheke, sirs,' he said as he took the beak and eyes off again and carefully sprinkled his canvas robe with vinegar and herbs. He wiped his face with a sponge soaked in more vinegar and cleaned the beak with it, then opened one end and took out a posy of wormwood and rue and a small incense burner which had produced the smoke. Dodd watched fascinated.

'Does all that gear stop ye getting the plague?' he asked.

'It has so far, sir,' said Peter Cheke gravely. 'And I have attended many of the poor victims of the pestilence to bleed them and drain their buboes and give them what medicines I have.'

'Did ye cure any?'

Cheke shook his head. 'No, sirs, in all honesty, I think those that live do so by the blessing of God and a strong will.'

Without the sound-distorting beak his voice was unusually deep and rotund, speaking in a slow measured way. He seemed very weary.

'How may I help you, sirs?' he asked, blinking at them as if he was stoically preparing himself for more pleas for his puny help against the Sword of the Wrath of God.

'We don't think it's plague,' said Barnabus quickly. 'It's more like a flux or something. But he's puking blood and getting pains in his belly something awful.'

'Who is?'

'Robert Greene.'

Cheke frowned. 'Greene? When did he take sick?'

'He was well enough when he was playing primero last night,' said Dodd. 'Or he seemed like it. Will ye come look at him, Mr Cheke?'

The apothecary passed a hand over his face. 'Yes,' he said. 'I will, though I was up all night.'

'I dinna doubt it's all the booze,' said Dodd. 'Ye can rest after.'

Cheke smiled thinly. 'I very much doubt it, the way the plague is moving in these parts.'

'Spreading, is it?'

'With the heat, the miasmas are thickening and strengthening at every moment. I was called to three houses last night, and by the time I came to the third, every soul in it had died.'

'Och,' said Dodd. 'But it's plague, man. Why d'ye bother?'

Red-rimmed eyes held his for a moment and Cheke frowned. 'Do you know, I've no idea. I suppose I come in time to comfort some of them. Once I had some notion of finding the answer, of reading the riddle.'

'What riddle?'

'Why does plague happen? Why is one year a plague year and another year not? When London is full of stenches, why does one kind of miasma kill?'

'Och,' said Dodd shaking his head at the overweening madness of Londoners. 'Ye're wasting yer time, man. It's the Sword o' God's Wrath against the wickedness of London.'

'What?' snapped Barnabus. 'What's so wicked about London? Compared to Carlisle?'

'There isnae comparison,' said Dodd, quite shocked. 'London's a den of iniquity, full of cutpurses and trollops that try and blackmail ye oot o' yer hard won cash.'

'Carlisle's full of cattle thieves and blackrenters.'

'That's different. That's making a living.'

'So's cutting purses.'

'Gentlemen, gentlemen,' said the apothecary, putting on a skullcap. 'Shall we go?'

By the time they came back to the cobbler's shop, Joan Ball was back in the kitchen at the rear of the shop and Carey was leaning on the upstairs windowsill peering out.

Greene was putting a chased silver flask back under his revolting pillow, shuddering and coughing. He bent over a new piece of paper, still writing frantically. Next to him was the jordan full of something that looked like black soup. The stench was appalling.

Peter Cheke went in cautiously. Greene surged up in the bed, hands over his belly and started roaring with foam on his lips.

'You!' he shouted. 'You dare come in here...'

'Mr Greene, your friends...'

'I've got no friends and never you, Jenkins, never you, atheist, alchemist, necromancer...Get out, get out...!'

A book whizzed through the air and hit Peter Cheke on the head. He turned and walked down the stairs.

'I didna ken that Greene had a feud with ye as well,' said Dodd, hurrying after him. 'Why did ye not say, I wouldnae have wasted yer time.'

'If I had known, I would have mentioned it,' said Cheke. 'But we have never quarrelled before. It is clearly not plague that ails him, but nor does it seem to me a flux. For how long has he been purging blood?'

Dodd shrugged. 'All night according to his woman,' put in Carey as he came clattering down stairs. 'Is there anything you could give him that might bring him to his senses, calm him down? He won't do anything except write, and I need to talk to him.'

Peter Cheke thought for a moment. 'A lenitive might be lettuce juice and a decoction of willow bark. If you can get him to drink it and keep it down, he might sleep and give his body time to recover. Perhaps.'

'Aren't you going to examine him?' said Carey. 'Won't you cast a figure for him or taste his water or feel his pulses?'

'No, sir,' said Cheke gravely. 'I am not a doctor. I know very little of the humours and I have never studied at Padua. I have none of your right doctor's certainty. All I see in the many diseases of men is a great mystery. Besides, Mr Greene seems to think I am his enemy. I doubt he would let me examine him.'

'Try anyway.'

They trailed upstairs again and Dodd and Carey ignored frantic protests and held Greene down so Cheke could examine him. Greene fought like a madman and then stopped suddenly. 'You're not Jenkins,' he whispered like a bewildered child.

'No, you know my name is Cheke. May I use my poor skill to examine you, sir?'

Greene nodded, eyes darting from Carey to Dodd and back. Cheke listened at the chest and breath, felt neck and armpits, poked at Greene's stomach which produced a scream. At last he stepped back.

'It could be a flux, but such violence...I would suspect a poison.'

'What kind of poison?'

Cheke shrugged.

'You see!' roared Greene. 'I'm dying, I told you I was, the apothecary thinks so too.'

'Where is Edmund?' demanded Carey as soon as he caught a flicker of Greene's fleeting clarity. 'My father gave you five pounds to find him. Have you found him?'

'Repent or be damned, oh ye atheists of London!' bellowed Greene, picking up his pen and dipping. 'Find him yourself, I'm busy.'

'For God's sake, man...' said Carey, holding his shoulders. 'Tell me what you discovered about Edmund.'

Greene spat full in his face. 'I've got to finish,' he panted, shaking his head and swallowing hard. Back he went to his desperate scribbling, for all the world as if enough letters on a page could save him from hell.

Carey let go of him and wiped himself off distastefully with a handkerchief.

The apothecary was fishing in his bag, brought out a leather bottle. 'I have the calming draught here,' he said. 'If he could but take it and keep it down. Goodwife Ball,' he shouted down the stairs, 'will you come up?'

Greene's woman came up again, wiping her hands nervously.

She took the little cup of medicine and gently held it to Greene's grey lips. He swallowed, gagged, pushed her away and grabbed his flask from under the pillow to wash it down.

The apothecary put his bottle away, buckled his bag and shrugged the strap over his shoulder. 'I will go to my shop to fetch laudanum since I have none left, and you should fetch a priest, Goodwife,' he said as he left. 'Pray God that that will help the poor gentleman.'

For a while it seemed as if it did. Greene wrote faster and faster, shaking his head as sweat dripped down his face and off his nose, and then at last he seemed to finish for he signed the paper with a flourish, put the last piece on the pile beside him, stoppered his inkpot and wiped his pen on the sheets.

'Now,' said Carey firmly, turning away from the window where he had been getting a breath of fresh air. 'Will you please tell me what you found out about my brother?'

Greene had collapsed back on the pillows and was coughing. He seemed too exhausted even to talk. He whispered something indistinct and Carey bent close to make it out.

'Dying. I heard...Don't tell Heneage...where...Ohhh. Aaahhh!'

Something terrible was happening inside the poet, as if some kind of animal was trapped in Greene's bowels and was rending them, trying to escape. His eyes rolled up in his head and he jacknifed in the tangled blankets. Carey strode to the stairs and shouted for the woman again. Dodd turned his head away from the sight. 'Och, God,' he said, fighting not to vomit himself.

Even in his agony, Greene turned himself so as not to puke on his swansong and the bright red blood flooded amongst the sheets, pooled in the lumpy mattress, endless amounts of it. Dodd heard Barnabus dry-heaving behind him.

'Christ,' croaked Carey. 'Christ have mercy.' Then he did a thing which even Dodd found admirable. He picked his way back to the bed and gripped Robert Greene's shoulder, held onto him while death juddered through him, so he should know he was not alone while his soul battled clear of his flesh.

After several minutes Greene's eyes were staring and Dodd broke the paralysis that had clutched him, went to the window and opened it as wide as it would go, so Greene's ghost could fly free. Joan Ball was in the room, pushing past Carey to fling herself across her lover and wail.

Dodd looked down into the street, as full of people and noise as ever, breathed deep of the slightly less pungent air coming through the window. He heard a long shaky breath beside him and knew that Carey was standing there too.

'Wait...wait,' said Joan. 'I'll get it, darling, wait.'

They turned to see her running down the stairs and Barnabus standing by the twisted body on the bed, gingerly turning it on its back, shutting the eyes and putting pennies on them, to keep the demons out.

Will I die like that? Dodd wondered, alone with strangers, in my own blood. I deserve to, came the dispiriting answer, unless I'm lucky enough to hang or get my head blown off in a fight.

Clogs sounded on the stairs as Joan Ball came running back up, incongruously clutching a couple of sprigs of bayleaves from the kitchen. She twisted them together in a rough ring and then took the nightcap off, pushed them onto Greene's balding, carroty brow.

'There,' she said, kissing the bulbous chilling nose and wiping her hands in her apron again. 'That's what you wanted, my love.'

'What the hell...?' Dodd asked.

'It's a wreath of bays,' said Carey remotely. 'What they crowned dead poets with in Ancient Greece.'

There didn't seem anything to be said to that. In unspoken agreement they went down the stairs and out into the sunny street where nothing was any different. Barnabus emerged from the house too, a few moments later, blinking and looking shifty. Carey glanced at him and seemed to come to some decision.

'I need a drink,' he announced which showed he had some sense after all, and he led the way to the nearest house with red lattices.

They sat in a tiny booth and called for beer and aqua vitae. Carey lifted his little horn cup. 'To Robert Greene, may he rest in peace,' he said and knocked it back. Dodd and Barnabus followed suit gratefully.

The drink helped settle Dodd's stomach and scour the stench of sickness out of his nostrils. Before he had quite finished the beer,

Carey was up again, heading out the door.

'Where's the apothecary's shop?'

Barnabus led him there, and they met Peter Cheke hurrying into the street holding a bottle. Cheke stopped.

Carey shook his head.

'Dead?' asked the apothecary. 'Poor gentleman.'

'How much do I owe you?' asked Carey with strange politeness and Cheke put his bony hands out in front of him.

'I can hardly charge for such unsuccessful treatment as I attempted,' he said. 'Alas, sir, I am not a doctor.'

'I dinna think a doctor could hae done any mair,' said Dodd. 'There was death on him already.'

Cheke smiled wanly. 'As usual, I shall always be in doubt,' he said.

'Can we come in?' asked Carey and the apothecary ceremoniously ushered them into the pungent dimness of his shop, and then, on Carey's request for somewhere private, through a door into the kitchen at the back of the building. They sat at a scrubbed wooden table standing on painfully scrubbed flagstones; a womanless kitchen for the lack of strings of onions and flitches of bacon hanging from the rafters. Ranged like soldiers on shelves were a vast variety of cups and dishes and strange tortured things made out of glass. There was a bulbous-shaped oven instead of a fireplace.

'You said you thought it might be poison,' Carey asked, suddenly narrowing his eyes and sharpening up. 'Do you know what kind?'

Cheke shrugged. 'There are so many, sir, some masquerading under the name of physic. I only gave him a painkilling dose, but who knows...It could have been white arsenic. That attacks the gut although it generally works more slowly. It can make a man who abuses his belly with booze bleed to death.'

'That's Greene, all right. Is there any way you can be sure?'

Cheke shook his head. 'Arsenic has no taste or smell so it is a favourite of those who work with poisons. More than that I cannot say.'

Carey felt in his belt pouch and then produced the little twist of paper in which he had caught the beads of liquid metal in Edmund Carey's clothes chest. Very carefully he opened it.

'Do you know what this is?'

The apothecary looked at the bead of bright silver, his nostrils flaring a little. 'Certainly I do, sir,' he said. 'It is Mercury.'

'What?'

'In the art and science of alchemy we have various materials that partake of certain qualities: there is Venus, Mars, Saturn—and this is Mercury, the messenger and facilitator of the chemical wedding. It is a great mystery, for how can metal be a liquid? Some call it quicksilver. And so indeed it is, for after any reaction concerning it, you may find little dewdrops of it in your clothes, in your pockets, brought there too quickly to see.'

'Could Mercury have anything to do with the Philosopher's Stone?'

'Certainly it is one of the principals in the search. Do you have any understanding of the great quest, sir?'

Carey smiled. 'None at all. What can you tell me?'

'The Philosopher's Stone and also its liquid equivalent, the Elixir of Life, hath the great quality of turning that which is base—such as metal or flesh—into gold, the highest form matter can take. By means of repeatedly wedding Venus to Mars, with the intervention of Mercury, by the transitions through the many stages, it is certain that we shall achieve the transmutation of matter.'

'How d'ye do that then?' asked Dodd with interest. 'How can ye change a thing to gold?'

Cheke's eyes lit up. 'Change is unnatural and stability natural. Whatever changes is at a lower state than that which always remains the same. Yes? But change is itself not merely unnatural but also wearisome. Therefore, if we force base matter through enough changes it will eventually in exhaustion revert to its natural state, which is gold for metals. The Philosopher's Stone shortens the process much as bone ash aids in lead refining. It is actually a powder, of course, but I have seen such a powder, dissolved in boiling Mercury, change pewter to gold. I myself have seen it, with my own eyes.'

'Where?' asked Carey intently.

Cheke smiled. 'I am sorry, sir, I gave my word not to reveal where and exactly what I saw.'

'Who else was there?'

'The master alchemist that performed the reaction. Also a gentleman that was investing in the process.'

'What did he look like, this gentleman?'

'Reddish brown hair, a little the look of yourself, sir, but stockier.'

'What was his name?'

Cheke shook his head. 'We did not exchange names.'

'Who was the master alchemist?'

'A most worshipful gentleman, a Dr Jenkins, though not previously known to me.'

'How come you were there then?'

'As an assistant, to grind the powder and assist with firing the furnace. I am not one of the *cognoscenti*, you understand, I must study and work a great deal more.'

'No, I meant—who introduced you?'

'Why, a poet, a scholar from Cambridge.'

'Mr Greene?'

'No, a Mr Marlowe.'

Carey compressed his lips and leaned back a little on the bench. 'Hmm,' he said, his eyes narrow. 'How well do you know Marlowe?'

'Not well, but he too is a seeker after truth and the Stone.'

'Oh, is he?' muttered Barnabus. 'Well, fancy.'

'When did you see this demonstration, Mr Cheke?'

'It was a while ago. Last month. I was greatly inspired in my own labours by it—to see base pewter discs smeared with the Stone's matrix, and sealed in the pelican, heated in the furnace and then to see them come out transformed, transmutated into gold— wonderful. Truly wonderful. It seems to me that we are living in a new Golden Age, sir, when the mysteries of God's creation shall be unwound, when we shall truly understand how the world is made, what drives the crystal spheres, the nature of matter itself, all is within our grasp and from that wisdom we shall know the mind of God Himself.'

More mad blasphemy, thought Dodd, full of gloom, no doubt the apothecary would be dead of plague by tomorrow. And me too, perhaps, added the voice of terror inside, I've still got that headache.

'Then the reaction did not take place here?'

Cheke smiled again. 'I promised I would not tell where it happened. I brought some of my equipment, that's all, and some poor skill with the furnace.'

'What was the gentleman wearing?'

'He was very well-dressed, sir: black Lucca velvet embroidered with pearls and slashed with oyster satin.'

'And he looked like me?'

'A little, sir. Redder in the face as well as wider in the body.'

Carey nodded. 'Mr Cheke, you have been very kind and very helpful. Are you sure I cannot...er...pay you for your treatment?'

'With the Philosopher's Stone available, why would I need any gold in the world?' asked Cheke rhetorically and smiled like a child. Carey smiled back, rose and went into the shop. Barnabus hesitated and then spoke to the apothecary quietly and urgently.

Dodd came back to fetch him.

'I make no guarantees,' Cheke was saying. 'If I knew of anything that was sovereign against the plague, I would publish a book about it.'

Barnabus actually had hold of the man's sleeve. 'My sister's family got it and half of them are dead,' he hissed. 'Can't you give me anything? You could let my blood, couldn't you?'

'But I don't think it works.'

'Doctors do it against the plague.'

'If the doctors knew of a remedy, why would any of them catch it?'

Dodd thought the man had a good point there, but Barnabus wasn't paying attention.

'Listen,' he said. 'I'll pay you. But you've got to give me something, or do something.'

Cheke sighed. 'Sit down,' he said, digging in his bag again. 'I'll let your blood against infection and give you the best charms I can.'

Dodd waited patiently while Barnabus sat on a stool and proffered his left arm for Cheke to open a vein. The dark blood oozed out into the basin and Dodd wondered about it: men's bodies were filled with blood. When you let some of it out, how did you know which would be the bad stuff and which would be the good? It took only a short time, for Cheke refused to let more than three ounces, and he bandaged Barnabus's arm up again and carefully wiped off his knife with a cloth. 'Do you want to be treated too?' he asked Dodd while Barnabus put a silver shilling down on the table which the apothecary ignored.

'Nay,' said Dodd, thinking about it. 'Ah spend too much time trying to avoid losing blood.'

Cheke smiled. 'Both of you should take posies to counteract the miasmas.' He handed them more bunches of wormwood and rue and told them to put them inside their clothes.

'We'd best be getting along,' said Barnabus, rubbing his arm and looking pleased. 'My master was talking about going up to the Theatre or the Curtain to see a play this afternoon.'

'The playhouses should all be closed down until the plague has abated,' said the apothecary, putting his instruments back in his bag.

'What's the point of that?' demanded Barnabus. 'You'll be saying the cockpits and bull-baiting should be shut too, like the Corporation.'

'They should. Wherever men gather closely together the plague miasma forms and strikes.'

It was a horrible picture: Dodd could see it as a demon, now forever in his mind with a long brass beak, hovering over a crowd of men looking for places to strike. The thought made his bowels loosen just by itself.

'Bah,' sniffed Barnabus. 'Never heard such nonsense in my life. If that's true, why don't people get plague from going to church, eh? Or walking up and down St Paul's, eh? Come on, Sergeant, let's go or we'll be late.'

Perhaps only Dodd heard the alchemist answer Barnabus softly. 'But they do. St Paul's is where the plague always starts.'

SATURDAY, 2ND SEPTEMBER 1592, MIDDAY

Dodd's head was buzzing as Carey strode through the crowds, heading for the Mermaid tavern again. Carey talked at length with the innkeeper who had no idea how Sir Edward Fitzjohn, alias Nick the Gent, and his wife, alias Molly Stone, had managed to get into their chamber, and further could not tell where Kit Marlowe might be nor any of his cronies. Nobody knew anything, so far as Dodd could see, not even when Carey offered to pay them.

Shakespeare was still there, sitting in one of the booths, white and trembling and sipping mild ale very cautiously.

'Shouldn't you be getting back to Somerset House?' Carey asked him and he shook his head, then clutched it and muttered that my lord had told him to serve Sir Robert.

'Excellent. I want to find Mr Marlowe and ask him some questions. Do you know where he is, Will?'

'No, sir. Sorry, sir.' Shakespeare was staring into his beer, gloom lapping him round like a cloak. Carey sat himself down opposite.

'Did you know Robert Greene is dead, Will?' he asked cheerily.

Shakespeare shut his eyes for a moment. 'Oh,' he said, not seeming very happy at the news.

'That means I've got to start all over again, looking for my brother. Do you know anything about him?'

'No.' With a great effort Shakespeare looked up at Carey. 'I'm sorry, sir,' he croaked.

'Did you ever hear of an alchemist called Jenkins?'

'N...no, sir.'

'Are you sure?'

'Yes, sir.' Shakespeare was staring at his beer again. Carey watched him speculatively for a moment.

'I think you're lying to me, Will,' he said without heat. 'I'm not sure why. If you're afraid of anyone, it would be better to tell me so I can protect you.'

A tiny sliver of a smile passed over Shakespeare's face. 'I'm afraid of many things, sir,' he said, adenoidally honest. 'I doubt there's much you can do about any of them.'

Carey paused a moment longer, then clapped his hand on the table.

'Well, how do you feel? Ready for a bit of exercise?'

Shakespeare sighed deeply and sipped some more ale. 'Yes, sir,' he said dolefully.

'All right. You go back to Somerset House, you find my father's *valet de chambre* and ask him to find my second best suit, the one with lilies on the hose, and also the suit Sergeant Dodd here wore the other night for my father's supper party. Then you bring them both back here and we'll all go to see who we can find in Paul's Walk this afternoon.'

Shakespeare nodded, repeated his orders, swallowed his ale and hurried off. Carey watched him go, blue eyes narrow and considering. Barnabus coughed deprecatingly.

'Sir, I was wondering if I could go back to our lodgings, see how Tamburlain is getting on.'

'Who?'

'The cock, sir. My sister's fighting cock.'

'Oh. Yes. Well, it's a confounded nuisance. I want you to come with me to St Paul's.'

'Yes, sir. I could meet you there, sir.'

'Oh, very well. Hurry up.'

'Thank you, sir.'

Barnabus disappeared out the door, blinking and rubbing his forehead while Dodd watched him go doubtfully. Did he have plague? Maybe Dodd had plague too. As well as pox.

Carey was tapping his fingers on the blackened table top and frowning.

'Sir, why do you want to find Marlowe?' Dodd asked, feeling that the over-clever pervert was best left alone.

'Hm? Oh, he's in the middle of this tangle, somewhere. I know he is.'

'Well, but, what's he got to do with yer brother?'

'Look, Dodd, there's some kind of complicated plot going on here, something that Edmund's only incidental to.'

'Papist, d'ye mean, sir?'

'That's only one kind. My inclination is that Heneage is up to something.'

'Ay,' said Dodd, thinking back to the supper party. 'I didnae take to him, meself.'

'Father hates his guts. What the devil was he doing, inviting the bastard to supper?'

'Mebbe yer brother's at Chelsea, wi' Heneage?' suggested Dodd as he tucked into the bacon and pease pottage the boy put in front of him. Carey was staring at him, making him feel uncomfortable. 'Well, but ye said he could do the like to me, sir, could he not to yer brother?' Carey said nothing. Dodd chewed and swallowed, washing down the salty meat with more beer. 'That's how Richie Graham of Brackenhill runs it if ye're too strong to take on directly. Captures one o'yer relatives, puts him in ward somewhere he controls and threatens tae starve him to death if ye dinna pay up.'

'If Heneage tried something like that with my brother, my father would go directly to the Queen. Heneage knows that. The Queen doesn't think much of Edmund either, but she won't have her cousins mistreated.'

'Ay,' said Dodd, following a train of thought that twisted and turned like a hunted stag. 'But what if yer brother was up tae no good? Or what if Heneage knew he was dead or in gaol but wasnae sure where so he just let on to yer father he might have him but kept yer father in doot. Richie Graham does that too.'

Carey was scooping up pease pottage with a piece of bread. 'It's possible. If it's true, then Marlowe is the one who'll know what's really going on; he's one of Heneage's men.'

'He is? I wouldnae have placed him as a serving man.'

Carey laughed. 'No, he's a pursuivant. Been at it for years. Started working for Walsingham years ago, back before the Armada, and then when Walsingham died and Heneage took over, Marlowe went to work for him too.'

'What's a pursuivant?'

'A kind of spy. An intelligencer against the Catholics. An informer, a troublemaker.'

'I thought he was a poet.'

'Well, he's that as well but nobody can really make a living as a poet alone, unless he's got a rich patron, and not even Sir Walter Raleigh will take Marlowe on, he's too dangerous. You never know who he's working for, if he knows himself.'

'Och.' Dodd considered this while he sawed away at a tough bit of meat. 'I wouldnae have thought poets would make good spies.'

'On the contrary, my father says they're excellent. Literate, intelligent, good memory, practised liars.'

Dodd snorted, speared a chunk and started nibbling it off the end of his knife.

'And what's all this with alchemy?'

'Yes.' Carey was staring into space while he chewed at a bit of gristle. 'Just the sort of thing Edmund would get into, the idiot.'

'Ye dinna think it was really working?'

'I'd stake my fortune that it wasn't, if I had one.'

'Why?'

'One of the best pieces of advice I ever had was this: if something looks too good to be true, it probably isn't true. Alchemy as the road to enlightenment, possibly. Alchemy as the road to riches—no.'

'But Cheke said he'd seen it work.'

'I think he was mistaken, and so was my brother if he was the gentleman investing in it. I think he was involved in something a lot simpler and more dangerous.'

'What?'

Carey took the forged angel out of his sleeve pocket and spun it on the table where it glittered to a halt and fell over.

'Forgery. He was coining. That's where his purse of money came from that he showed Susannah.'

'Why would he need alchemy to do that? It's not so hard. The Graham's got his ain mint going at Brackenhill, making silver Scots shillings. Only, they're not silver, ye follow?'

'Has he? That's interesting. I was wondering why the Scots money was worth so little. Well, it's harder to forge gold coins. They're more carefully minted, you can't get the colour right with anything except gold...Hm. There's one way to find out and that's why I want us to look decent.'

'Mebbe Heneage was at the coining with this alchemy and yer brother caught him at it.'

'That's possible. If you look at it from Heneage's point of view, you could even see why he might think there was nothing wrong in it. The Queen never gives him enough money to do what he wants. She never gave Walsingham enough either, but he was willing to spend his own fortune on his intelligencing and Heneage doesn't fancy dying in debt like him. So along comes an alchemist who claims he's found the Philosopher's Stone and Heneage either believes it, or sees that it might work well enough to solve his money problems.'

Dodd shook his head sadly. 'Everyone needs more money,' he muttered. 'Where does it a' go?'

Carey looked irritated. 'We spend it, Dodd, where do you think? Besides, the Queen never likes her servants to be too rich, she thinks it might make us arrogant. That's why Father has to be so mean: if she heard how rich he really is, she'd send him to France as an ambassador or put him in command of the troops in Ireland or something ghastly like that.'

'Why would she hear of it?'

'The Queen is uncanny the way she finds things out. I've never known anybody successfully get something past her, except Walsingham's protégé Davison over the Queen of Scots. Anyway, Edmund's just the sort of man an ambitious alchemist would take his process to and if Heneage got to hear of it, which he would, then Heneage would want in on the deal. I think Edmund's precious alchemist transformed pewter blanks to gold which they then used to strike coins. Or at least that's what Edmund thought.'

Carey was turning the false angel in his long gloved fingers.

'And ye reckon it was all a load of rubbish?'

'Of course it was. Poor old Edmund. Always full of ways to make money, and each one is always the one that will finally make him richer than Father. He's the easiest mark for a coney-catcher I've ever met. Ingram Frizer took him for a hundred and seventy pounds on the old brocade-reselling trick.'

'Whit's that?'

'Oh, Edmund wanted to borrow more money off Frizer, but you're not supposed to charge interest to cover your risk. So Frizer gets Edmund to sign a bond for a hundred and seventy pounds, but Frizer gives him brocade instead of money, worth a little less than the amount Edmund is supposed to repay—theoretically. Then Edmund is supposed to sell the brocades to all his friends and get his money that way and if he makes more on the deal, he can keep it.'

Dodd screwed up his eyes to follow this. 'And the brocades was bad?' he asked. Carey smiled.

'Precisely. The dye wasn't fixed and the colours ran if you so much as sweated into them. The pile came out in the velvets and the silk weaving was atrocious. Edmund was shocked at it and Father nearly murdered him for being so stupid as to fall for such an ancient trick.'

'Ay.'

Shakespeare appeared in the doorway, still blinking and looking pale and sweaty. Maybe he had plague too. He was carrying two heavy bags over his shoulder and puffing slightly.

Dodd looked in dismay at the bag Shakespeare gave him. 'Och, sir, do I have to fancy up again?'

'Yes.'

Half an hour later, feeling sweaty and uncomfortable in Carey's tight cramoisie suit, Dodd was scouting Cheapside for bailiffs. Every jeweller's shop had at least two large men in buff coats standing guard at the door, but none of them looked like bailiffs so far as Dodd could tell. He nodded to Shakespeare, waiting next to the alley where Carey was skulking and a minute later Carey sauntered out with Shakespeare at his heels, looking every inch the court gallant in his blackberry-coloured velvet suit all crusted with pearls and embroidered lilies.

He went to the biggest and brightest jeweller's shop on the street under the sign of a golden cup and strolled past the heavy-set men on guard who, far from barring his path as they had Dodd's, actually bowed to him. One of them obsequiously opened the iron-bound door for him.

Inside, surrounded by gold and silver plate ranged on shelves all around the room, Dodd found his breath coming short. Look at it, he thought to himself, just look at it all. One gold dish, just one gold dish, that's all I need.

Carey drawled a request for the Master Goldsmith to the slender young man who came bowing and scraping up to them, and then hitched his pretty padded hose on the edge of the black velvet covered table and whistled through his teeth. Shakespeare stood blank-faced by the door, with his hands tucked behind his back and Dodd rested his itchy fingers on his sword belt and tried to think of something boring, like sheep-shearing.

'I suppose it's just as well Barnabus isn't here,' said Carey good-humouredly. 'I'd never be able to take my eyes off him.'

'Ay, sir,' croaked Dodd, whose throat had unaccountably gone dry.

The Master Goldsmith swept from his inner sanctum in a long velvet gown of black over a doublet and hose of gold and black brocade.

'Master van Emden?' said Carey with an infinitesimal bow. The goldsmith bowed back.

'Sir Robert. How very kind of you to grace my establishment.'

Was there just the faintest tinge of wariness in Master van Emden's voice?

'How may I help you, sir?'

'To be honest, Master van Emden, I'm not intending to buy today.'

And was that relief flitting across the Master Goldsmith's face? 'Oh?'

'No. I want some information about goldsmithing.'

One eyebrow twitched and the goldsmith's expression chilled further.

'Oh? What sort of information?'

'I'm not quite sure how to put it. Um...let's say you have something made of a base metal, such as pewter or silver, and you wanted to make it look like gold. How could you do that?'

'These are mysteries of the goldsmith's trade, Sir Robert. My guild-brothers would be very offended if I...'

'I think you can be sure that I have neither the skill nor the inclination to take up the goldsmith's art.'

'Nonetheless.'

'Well, is it possible?'

'Certainly.'

'Might the substance called Mercury or quicksilver have anything to do with it?'

Master van Emden's expression stiffened. 'It might,' he allowed. 'Quicksilver is an essential element in the parcel-gilding process.'

'Which means?'

'May I ask to what this is in reference, Sir Robert?'

Carey hesitated for a moment and then came to a decision. 'Master van Emden, I believe a coney-catcher calling himself an alchemist may have...'

'Not again,' sighed the goldsmith. 'I beg you, sir, have nothing to do with alchemists, they are either ignorant fools or thieves. May we be private?'

Carey bowed extravagantly and the goldsmith ushered him through into the room behind the shop. The slender young man moved up smoothly to bar Dodd's path. Dodd looked at him consideringly. It would be simplicity itself to knock the man down and then sweep as much gold as he could into a bag, but you had to reckon that the guards outside the door would hear the commotion and come in and you couldn't know who might be upstairs or in the back room with Carey and the master. No, Dodd thought regretfully, it's not worth it. You'd have all London to get through with a hue and cry behind you, and the long dusty road north. It simply wasn't possible.

The young man never took his eyes off either of them and you could swear he didn't blink either. Twenty minutes later Carey emerged from the back room, followed by the goldsmith, looking delighted with himself.

'Thank you, Master van Emden,' he said. 'You've helped me immensely. Perhaps I could suggest that my father come to you when he's thinking of Her Majesty's New Year's present?'

Now that pleased the goldsmith, you could see. His wary eyes brightened noticeably.

'My order books are almost full,' he murmured. 'But for your honourable father, naturally I will make the space. I have an excellent designer—possibly my lord Baron Hunsdon would care to see some of his sketches?'

'I'm sure he would. I'll tell him. Good afternoon.'

And Carey ambled out into the sunshine, just as if he had not a care in the world, although he looked round sharply at the passers-by once he was clear of the door.

'Where now, sir?' asked Dodd, sweating almost as hard as Shakespeare while Carey paced briskly westwards.

'St Paul's Walk.'

'Och, no, sir.'

'Why not? Most interesting place in London, best place for gossip, best for scandal and we're going to meet Barnabus there.'

'Och.'

'Don't worry. So long as you don't let anybody inveigle you into any little alleys, nobody is going to coney-catch you.'

'I dinna like the place, sir. It gives me the willies. And what about bailiffs?'

'There shouldn't be too much trouble with them, now Mr Bullard's been paid.'

'Why are ye watching out for yerself so carefully then?'

'Some of them may not have heard yet. Anyway, I'm looking for that clever bugger Marlowe.'

'Find him at St Paul's, will ye, sir? Praying, I expect.'

Carey looked amused. 'No, wandering up and down quoting Juvenal.'

St Paul's was as noisy and crowded as it had been last time, though there was no sign of Barnabus by the serving men's pillar. Carey glanced at the throngs, tutted to himself, bought an apple off a woman with enormous breasts, and slipped into the lurid parade in the aisle. Shakespeare stood still, hands tucked behind him again, staring hard. Dodd leaned against a pillar with his thumbs hitched on his swordbelt and watched, narrow-eyed in the shafts of sun striking down through the holes in the temporary roof. A pigeon strutted past, pecking at discarded piecrusts and trying to overawe its reflection in a brass set in another pillar. The resemblance to the young men at their posing was uncanny, you might even say poetical.

Carey was talking and laughing to people who seemed very anxious to fawn on him. None of them seemed able to help him and Dodd himself could see no sign of Marlowe nor any of his cronies. Carey swaggered all the way to the door by Duke Humphrey's tomb and then turned and swaggered all the way back trailing an eager group of hangers-on.

Just as he turned again to pace pointlessly back the way he had come, there was a stir and a swirl amongst the fashion-afflicted. Two men in buff-coats and green livery came in through the door, followed by a tall and languid exquisite in peach damask, festooned with pearls, and with a lovelock hanging over one shoulder.

The exquisite paused impressively at the first pillar and squinted down the aisle. His face lit up.

'By God, it's Carey!' he sang out. 'What the devil are you doing here, made Berwick too hot for you already?'

Carey stopped in one of the most mannered poses Dodd had ever seen in his life and flourished off a bow.

'My lord Earl,' he responded. 'What a wonderful surprise; my heart is overflowing with delight.'

Dodd stole a glance at Shakespeare to see if the player was as close to puking as he was. Carey was striding down the aisle, such happiness on his face you might think the peach-damask creature was a woman. God, surely he wasn't...No, whatever else he might be, Carey was not a pervert. And there was Shakespeare, face intent, hurrying to catch up with him.

Sighing, Dodd stood upright and followed.

Peach-damask was giving Carey a nice warm hug and Carey was returning it. Some of the other fashionable young men were staring at his back with faces twisted with envy. Shakespeare hesitated as they came close, but Carey clapped his back jovially.

'Now this is someone you should talk to, my lord,' he said. 'May I present Mr William Shakespeare, late of the Rose?'

Shakespeare's bow was a tidy model of deference.

Peach-damask put an elegantly gloved hand to his breast. '*Not* Mr Shakespeare who wrote *Henry VI*?'

The player bowed again, more deeply. 'I am more honoured than you can guess, my lord, that you should have remembered my name.'

Peach-damask seemed to like being flattered. 'Of course I do, best plays I've seen in years. *Oh, woman's heart, wrapped in a tiger's hide*. Eh? Eh? Wonderful stuff, Sir Robert, you remember?'

'Oh, indeed, my lord,' said Carey and Shakespeare murmured modestly.

Please don't introduce me to this prinked-up fancy-boy, Dodd was praying silently, I dinna want tae have to do any more bowing and scraping.

Peach-damask was absolutely full of good humour, you'd think he was drunk. He quoted more nonsensical lines that seemed to be from this wonderful play of Shakespeare's, then asked the player where on earth he got his ideas and how long it took him to write a play and then, while Carey and Shakespeare both laid on the flattery with a trowel, insisted that they all come back to Southampton House with him, since he was planning a little card-party for that evening. Carey accepted instantly, and as peach-damask took the time for a quick parade down the aisle and back again so everyone could admire his pretty suit, Dodd muttered desperately.

'I'd best be getting back to ma lodgings, sir, make sure Barnabus is...er...' Not coming down with plague, he nearly said, then stopped himself.

Carey didn't notice his hesitation. 'No, no,' he said at once. 'I'm sorry, Dodd, you've got to come with me. The earl will put us up.'

'Will ye no' be wantin' to be private wi' yer friend?' asked Dodd heavily and Carey drew a breath, stared for a moment, and then laughed.

'By God, you don't know me very well, do you?' he said. 'What the hell do you think you're talking about, private with my friend? Don't come it the Puritan preacher with me, Dodd, I don't like it. That's the Earl of Southampton, my lord of Essex's best friend, and if you think I'm snubbing him to keep your good opinion of me, you're sadly mistaken.'

'I ken I'm no' in my right company, sir,' said Dodd. 'I dinna care what ye do, but I'm no' a courtier, me, and I...'

'Oh, give it a rest, Dodd. Nobody's asking you to take up buggery for a living. Just come along quietly, and give me a bit of back-up, that's all I ask.'

'What about the alchemist and finding Marlowe or yer brother?'

'Marlowe's been paying court to Southampton for months now, he might well be at this supper party. As for the alchemist and my brother, they can wait.'

Arm in arm with the Earl, Carry led the way out of St Paul's to the churchyard where the Earl's horses were waiting, held by yet more men in livery. Carey was given a horse to ride, Dodd and Shakespeare left to walk with the other attendants. They made their own small procession around some fine lady's damask-curtained litter that joined the party at Ludgate. The Earl was on horseback, riding a magnificent chestnut animal that had Dodd sighing with envy, leaning back to chat to Carey occasionally. He wasn't a bad rider, if you liked that showy court-style of horsemanship, with one hand on the reins and one hand on the hip.

Southampton House stood in gardens surrounded by a moat in the fields to the north of Holborn at the top of Drury Lane. As they passed over the little bridge to the north of the house and rode round to the door, Shakespeare stopped in his tracks and went white.

Mistress Bassano was being handed down from her litter with immense ceremony by no less than the Earl himself. Her eyes skidded slightly as Carey made his bow to her, his face printed with naughty comprehension. To do the lady justice, she only checked for a second when she saw him, before curtseying almost as low to him as she had to the Earl.

As they followed the company indoors, Dodd distinctly heard Shakespeare moan softly to himself.

***

Supper at Southampton House involved more mysterious meats in pungent sauces, leaves doused in oil and vinegar decorated with orange nasturtium flowers, decorated pies, astonishingly smooth-tasting wines. It all gave Dodd a bellyache just looking at it being laid out on the sideboard by the servants who carried it in, and of course every bite of it was cold after the palaver of serving it up and displaying to the Earl and then passing it around. It seemed courtiers showed their importance by making even the simplest things pointlessly complicated. Did they have three servants to wipe their arse, Dodd wondered, once the wine had started to work on his empty stomach.

Shakespeare seemed to have latched onto him again and was sitting next to him at the second table in the parlour, continuing to explain something about how playing was in the way you moved and spoke, not just in gestures and rhetoric. For instance, if you were playing a learned man, it wasn't enough to wear spectacles, you had to look abstracted as well. Dodd nodded politely to all this unwanted information and tried not to yawn.

The Earl was laughing at something Mistress Bassano was telling him.

'Mr Shakespeare,' he called to them across the room. 'A fair lady has just made a serious complaint against you. What have you to say?'

Shakespeare paused in mid-analysis of the contribution clothes made to a play-part, swallowed what he had in his mouth whole, and stood up.

'What was her complaint, my lord Earl?' His voice had changed. It was clearer, less flat, less dull.

'She alleges that you used the fair muse of poetry to tell lies. I had heard better of you. Can it be true?'

Shakespeare paused, looking narrowly at Mistress Bassano who had a cruel expression on her face, rather like a cat torturing a mouse, and then at the Earl who was half laughing at him. Now that was an interesting sight to see, Dodd thought, because something inside the man shifted, you might almost say hardened. It was as if he came to some decision.

'My lord Earl,' said Shakespeare judiciously, his flat vowels filling the parlour full of overdressed people quite easily. 'I'm sorry to say that it is true, if she means the poor sonnets I sent her the other day.'

'So you admit the crime of corrupting the muse?'

'I do, my lord. The bill is foul. The sonnets I made to her praise should never have been sent.'

Mistress Bassano, who had clearly been expecting a pleasant few minutes of poet-baiting, now looked puzzled.

'Then you apologise to the lady?' pursued the Earl.

'I do, my lord. Unreservedly. I should never have said that her hair outrivalled the dawn nor that her voice put the birds to shame.'

'And what will you do for your penance, Mr Shakespeare?'

'Why, with the lady's permission, I'll read another of my poems.'

Perhaps because he was sitting right next to the man, only Dodd saw the tension in Shakespeare.

'Compounding your crime, Mr Shakespeare?' sneered the Earl.

Shakespeare smiled quite sweetly. 'No, my lord. Telling the truth.'

'A truthful poet. An oxymoron, to be sure?'

'Not necessarily.'

'Mistress Bassano? As Queen of the company, do you allow this?'

Creamy shoulders shrugged expressively. 'He may embarrass himself again, if he wishes,' she said.

The Earl waved a negligent hand to Shakespeare, who fumbled in the front of his doublet for his notebook, brought it out and opened it. The adenoidal voice filled the room.

'My mistress' eyes are nothing like the sun,
Coral is far more red than her lips' red:
If snow be white, why then her breasts are dun:
If hairs be wires, black wires grow on her head.'

Carey began by staring in shock, but then he smiled. The Earl laughed. Shakespeare let the titters pass round the room and continued.

'I have seen roses damask'd, red and white.
But no such roses see I in her cheeks:
And in some perfumes is there more delight
Than in the breath that from my mistress reeks.'

The whole room was laughing, except for Mistress Bassano who had locked her stare on Shakespeare. The player ignored her.

'I love to hear her speak, yet well I know
That music hath a far more pleasing sound;
I grant I never saw a goddess go,—
My mistress when she walks treads on the ground.'

You had to admire what the player was doing. He paused for long enough to let the laughter die down again. And then for the first time he looked Mistress Bassano full in the face, like a man taking aim with a loaded caliver, and gave the last two lines.

'And yet, by heaven, I think my love as rare
As any she belied by false compare.'

Even Dodd applauded with the rest of them. Shakespeare shut his notebook with a snap, sat down and finished his wine, studiously ignoring the way Mistress Bassano was staring at him. You could see she was angry but also that she knew better than to show it.

When the supper was done they walked in the moated garden amongst lavender and thyme and blossoming roses while pageboys of remarkable beauty scuttled between them with silver trays of jellied sweetmeats and wild strawberries dusted with pepper. Shakespeare was beckoned to the Earl's side, and walked respectfully amongst the box hedges talking to him, nodding his head in agreement, occasionally making him laugh.

'Enjoying yourself, Dodd?' Carey asked, his voice a little slurred with drink, interrupting Dodd's thoughts as he stood beneath a well-pruned tree and stared into the magnificent copper sunset.

'Nay, sir,' said Dodd. 'Why, are ye?'

Truth was a weapon it seemed these courtiers had no armour against. Carey blinked and his superior little smile slipped slightly, but he didn't answer, just strode off amongst the rose bushes, his left hand leaning on his sword hilt to tilt it away from catching on the flowers. Dodd folded his arms and leaned against the tree trunk. Away across the fields you could see the women folding up the linens that had been laid out on the grass and hedges to dry, before the dew came down to wet them again, and those gloriously fat London cows gathering at their gates ready to be brought in for milking. An old church poked its battered tower out of a small wood to the west.

'Whatever have you done to Will Shakespeare, Sergeant Dodd?' asked a throaty voice beside him and Dodd looked because he couldn't help it, to be rendered instantly dry-mouthed again at the soft bulge of woman-flesh against red velvet stays.

'What?' he asked, coughed and took a deep breath. 'I beg pardon, mistress, I dinnae understand ye.'

'Will says you gave him the best advice he ever had.'

Dodd wrinkled his brow and then shook his head. 'I cannae remember it. Might have been the other night when we were drunk.'

'Of course.'

He couldn't help it, he had to ask. 'Are ye no' angry with him, for his new sonnet?'

A maddening smile curved between Mistress Bassano's lightly powdered cheeks and her dark eyes sparkled. 'Oh, I am,' she purred. 'Enraged, infuriated.'

God, who could make head or tail of women? Dodd had no idea what to say.

'I wanted to speak to Robin again,' she continued. 'But I think he has gone to play primero with my lord Earl.'

'Ay, nae doot.'

'You can tell him for me. You can tell him not to trust Will, for he has been taking money from Mr Marlowe and providing information on my Lord Hunsdon in return.'

Dodd stared at her, trying to work out whether she was telling the truth or just trying to make trouble for the player. Both, perhaps? Mistress Bassano smiled again, rather complacently, and met his eyes without a tremor.

'Like many other poets, he has turned to spying to make money. He has a great desire for money, you know, Sergeant, great ambition, great passion. Even in bed he over-reaches himself, exhausts himself. And he is very jealous, consumed by it, I'm afraid. He hates my Lord Hunsdon, who is, of course, my lover, and he hates your master too. You should be very careful of him.'

Dodd felt his jaw drop. 'Ah thocht...' he gargled. 'I hadnae thought he was that kind of man.'

Mistress Bassano only smiled again and glided off into the garden. Dodd discovered he was one of the last remaining guests still out in the dusk and hurried back to the house. On the way he thought he glimpsed Mistress Bassano, locked in an embrace with somebody whose balding forehead gleamed in the last light of the west.

Carey was playing primero with the Earl and the other overdressed men of his affinity, cold and bright as a polished silver plate, calling his usual point-score of 'eighty-four' amid sarcastic groans. Dodd stood just inside the door and watched for a little while, trying not to think about what Shakespeare was getting up to in the shrubbery, nor what Mistress Bassano had said about him, nor the likelihood of Carey losing hundreds of pounds in this kind of company and in the mood he was in.

Christ, what do I care? Dodd demanded of himself; I'm not his mam.

'Are you joining us, Sergeant?' Carey called over to him, to Dodd's surprise, pulling in quite a respectable pot of gold coin.

'Och God, no,' Dodd said. 'Ye're all too good for me. Ye'd have the shirt off ma back, for what guid it would dae ye.'

'You disappoint me, Sergeant Dodd,' said the Earl, as hectic-eyed as Carey and even more drunk. 'I'd heard the men of Cumberland never turn down a challenge.'

'Nor we dinna,' said Dodd, thoroughly tired of being needled. 'Name yer place and yer weapons and I'm yer man.'

There was a moment of silence in the overcrowded, candle-heated room and Carey leaned sideways to whisper in the Earl's ear. The overdressed southern catamite smiled widely.

'Why, Sergeant, I think you misunderstood me. I only meant to challenge you to a card game.'

'Ay,' said Dodd, privately quite amused at this climbdown. 'Well, my lord, in that case there's nae shame in admitting ye'd have the mastery over me in any card game ye care tae mention. I've no' the experience nor the resources to meet ye on that field, eh, my lord?' He swallowed down a yawn. 'Ah'm nobbut a country farmer, me. An' wi' yer permission, my lord, Ah'll gang tae ma rest.'

After translation from Carey, the Earl waved negligently at one of the servants. 'Of course, Sergeant. Goodnight, pleasant dreams.'

'Ay, the same to ye, my lord.'

Dodd followed the servant through the carved and marbled rooms, feeling that if Carey didn't see some sense soon, he'd head north by himself.

**

Obviously, the Southampton household thought he must be Carey's henchman because the servant led him to a truckle bed in a very magnificent bedroom, painted with pictures that made you think you were looking at the sky filled with angels and fat cherubs and the bed hung around with tapestry curtains. Dodd took one look at it and decided he preferred the truckle bed anyway: how could you sleep with no air at all reaching you? He left the watchlight burning and slowly and carefully negotiated his way through the multiplicity of buttons and laces involved in dressing as befitted his station in London.

He woke already on his feet and his dagger in his hand because somebody was moving around in the room.

'It's only me, Henry,' came Carey's voice. 'Don't kill me.'

'Och,' moaned Dodd. 'What the hell are ye doing?' He scrubbed the heel of his palm in his eyes as Carey, with infinite care, transferred the watchcandle to a nest of candles in a corner next to a mirror and lit the room.

'I was...er...trying to find the pot,' said Carey in the slow painstaking way of the magnificently drunk. 'But it eluded me.'

Dodd blinked his eyes hard. 'It's in the fireplace. Dinna drop it,' he growled, not trying to hide the fact that he was staring at Carey's face where the clear print of a woman's hand was glowing red like the brand of Cain.

Carey swayed over to the fireplace and obeyed what was evidently a very peremptory call of nature, judging by the time it took him. Dodd sat down on the truckle bed again and rubbed his face with his hands, laying down to try and get some more sleep.

No, the bloody Courtier could not let him rest. Carey was next to the bed, reeking of aqua vitae and tobacco smoke.

'Very sorry, Henry,' he said. 'I'm afraid I'm...er...stuck.'

'What?'

'Can't get out of this suit without help. Irritating, but there you are. Fashion.'

'Och, Christ.'

'No Barnabus. No helpful woman. You...you're...you're it.'

Murder in his heart, but not sufficiently annoyed with Carey to make him sleep in his uncomfortable fancy clothes, Dodd got up again and followed his instructions as to which laces to untie.

All the back ones were inextricably knotted.

'What happened tae the woman?' Dodd asked as he picked away at them, the curiously neutral intimacy of helping another man undress giving him unwonted freedom to ask.

'Gone back to Father. In a litter. Very cross.'

'Is that so? What happened to your face?'

Carey took off his elegant kid gloves and fingered the weal with a nailless finger. 'All my fault,' he said. 'Tactless. Very.'

'Och, ay?'

'Advice for you, Henry. When you're...er...when you're making love to a woman, try and...er...remember who she is.'

With magnificent self-control, Dodd did not laugh. 'Och?'

'Yes. At a...sensitive moment. Called her Elizabeth.'

Dodd sucked air through his teeth, contemplating Janet's likely reaction to such a mistake.

'Pity really. Wonderful body.'

'Ay.'

'My...er...my child, I think. Not sure. Could be Father's.'

'Could be Will Shakespeare's?' Dodd asked, some small devil in him wanting to make trouble for Mistress Bassano.

Carey contemplated this in silence as the last laces finally gave way, releasing the back of his gorgeous doublet from the waistband of his lily-encrusted trunk-hose. He had been fumbling with buttons while Dodd worked on the laces and the doublet finally came off, revealing the padded waistcoat that held up his hose. He moved away, shaking his head.

'Thank you,' he said. 'Manage now.'

Dodd lay down again, properly awake by now but determined to go back to sleep, and turned his shoulder on Carey's continued troubles with his clothes. Serve him right for wearing such daft duds.

'Int'resting, what you say.' Carey was still talking, though by the smell he should have sloshed with every step. God, did the man never stop? 'The poet, eh? Thought so, wasn't sure. Said so. She denied it. Couldn't deny calling her Elizabeth. Rude of me. But...er...she'd no call to sneer at her for being provincial. Isn't. Anyway, what's wrong with provincial?'

'If ye're askin' me,' said Dodd wearily, 'Lady Widdrington is worth a thousand of Mistress Bassano, for all her pretty paps and all her conniving ways.'

'Father likes her. So does Will, it seems.'

'Then they can have her.'

'Yes, but…Elizabeth won't let me have her,' said Carey sadly. 'Won't. Tried everything. Won't let me bed her. 'S terrible. Never happened before. Can't think. Can't sleep. Can't bloody fuck another woman without…mistaking her. Terrible.'

Och God, thought Dodd in despair, any minute now the bastard'll be weeping on my shoulder. I want to go to sleep. I'm tired. I don't like London. I don't like all these fine houses and fine beds and fine courtiers. I want to go home.

'Go to bed,' he growled unsympathetically.

The magnificent four-poster creaked as Carey collapsed into it, with typical selfishness leaving the candelabrum in the corner still blazing with light. Sighing heavily, Dodd got up once more, snuffed the candles and left the watchlight in case Carey needed to find the pot again.

'Balls're bloody killing me,' moaned Carey as Dodd passed the fourposter. Firmly resisting the impulse to tell the Courtier what he thought of him, Dodd went back to bed.

SUNDAY, 3RD SEPTEMBER 1592,

EARLY MORNING

It gave Dodd inordinate pleasure, just for once, to be up before the Courtier, fully dressed even if it was in that nuisance of a suit, and having eaten his bread and cheese and drunk his morning small beer. He made no attempt to be quiet when he opened up the window and the shutters to let in the pale dawn and birdsong and nor did he keep his voice down when he told the manservant who brought in their breakfast to do something about the brimming pot by the fireplace.

Getting bored with listening to Carey's sawpit grunting, Dodd went out into the silent morning house, lost himself and ended up in the kitchen where the cook found him a sleepy pageboy to show him around. They inspected the stables and the mews and Dodd took a turn in the dew-soaked garden, marvelling at the trees and bushes there that had never ever been cut for firewood nor trampled over by raiders.

At last he wandered back to his and Carey's chamber where he found the Courtier sitting in his shirt on the bed, shakily drinking mild beer.

'Ah. Good morning, sir,' he said as loudly and cheerfully as he could. 'And how are ye feeling this fine morning?'

'Don't,' said Carey carefully. 'Don't bloody push it, Dodd.'

'Och,' said Dodd, enjoying himself. 'Is the light too bright for ye, sir? Will I shut the shutters for ye?' Perhaps he did bang them a bit hard but it was such fun to watch Carey wince. That'll learn ye to be happy in the morning, Dodd thought savagely.

Carey shut his eyes and sighed. 'All right,' he said. 'I'm not expecting sympathy.'

'That's lucky, sir. Ye never give me any. Now. What are we gonnae do about yer brother? Eh?'

'What do you care about Edmund?'

'Not a damned thing. Only I wantae go home and I can see we willnae leave this bastard city until we find yer brother, so let's get on wi' it.'

He picked up the outrageously pretty suit that Carey had left draped over the clothes chest and tossed it onto the bed beside him.

'Will I help ye dress, sir, or would ye like me to go fetch a manservant that kens how to dae it?'

Carey circled his long fingers in his temples, squeezed his eyes tight shut and opened them again. 'Let's not make a fuss. You help.'

'Ay, sir.'

They went through the stupidly complicated business in silence, except for curt instructions from Carey. At last he put on his hat and they went out into the passageway and down the stairs.

'Where's Shakespeare?' Carey wanted to know.

'I dinna ken. D'ye want him, though? Yon pretty woman said

he was spying on yer father.'

Carey's bloodshot eyes opened wide at that. 'Did she say that? Mistress Bassano?'

'Ay, sir, last night in the garden.'

Carey blinked contemplatively at a heraldic blaze of stained glass making pools of coloured light on the floorboards. 'It could be true. Marlowe's not the only poet who doubles as a spy.'

'Ay, sir.'

'On the other hand, she could be spying on my father herself and trying to put suspicion on Will to get back at him.'

'Ay.' The whole thing was too complicated for Dodd. He focused on the important thing. 'But it disnae matter in any case, since we have tae find yer brother. Or his corpse.'

Carey winced again. As they came into the wide marble entrance hall, he paused. 'We'll go and fetch Barnabus from the lodgings. Then we're going after this alchemist, Jenkins.'

That seemed reasonable enough. Carey took leave of Southampton's majordomo with some elaborately grateful phrases that sounded as if he picked them ready-made from the back of his mind, and only shuddered a little as they went out into the full sunlight. Dodd remembered to look round for bailiffs as they went out across the little bridge over the moat and round by country lanes full of dust heading eastwards, parallel to Holborn. There were a few men practising at the butts with their longbows in a field, puny little light bows and they weren't very good either, Dodd noted. Carey turned right down a broad lane that narrowed until it passed between high garden walls. A heavy sweet scent wafted across from the lefthand garden. Carey gestured.

'Ely Place Garden. Hatton makes a fortune from it.'

'Ay?' said Dodd, hefting himself up and peering over the wall at a sea of pink and red. 'Fancy? Fra flowers?'

'Rosewater,' explained Carey. 'Supplies the court.'

'Ay?'

Carey ducked down a little lane that passed by what looked like another monastery courtyard, and then into a wide crossroads by a square-towered church. He paused there and blinked cautiously around. He looked as if the effort of walking in his fancy doublet and padded waistcoat was making him sweat, and he didn't look very well. Could he have plague, perhaps? No, thought Dodd, all that ails him is drink and serve him right.

'That's Shoe Lane,' Carey croaked, swallowing a couple of times. 'You go down first and if you see anything you don't like, come back and tell me. It'll come out by the Fleet Street conduit. If you see a lot of well-dressed women there, not doing very much, come back and tell me. Off you go.'

He leaned elegantly in the shadow of the church porch, took off his hat and mopped his brow, while Dodd wandered down the lane between houses and garden walls, humming a ballad to himself. The conduit was running bright with water, but there were only a couple of maidservants with yokes on their shoulders busily chatting as they slowly filled their buckets. Dodd went back and waved a thumbs-up to Carey, who came upright with noticeable effort and followed.

They crossed Fleet Street at the wide point by the conduit, the girls staring to see a courtier up so early, and Carey nipped into an alley that gave onto a courtyard in front of a large handsome house where the servants were just opening the shutters. Dodd tensed when he saw a couple of men standing negligently in the doorway of one of the other houses. He nudged Carey, who glanced at them and shook his head.

'Heneage's men keeping an eye on the French ambassador.'

'Eh?'

Carey gestured at the big house. 'Salisbury House, French ambassador's lodgings.'

That was interesting, thought Dodd, squinting up at the bright diamond windows. Were there Frenchmen actually inside? What did they look like? He now knew they didn't actually have tails, but it stood to reason they must be different from Englishmen.

Carey was slipping into a narrow little wynd between houses and a garden wall, passed under a roof made of touching upper storeys and emerged onto one of the salty muddy lanes that gave onto the Thames. The tide was in—you could see water gleaming at the end to their left.

Looking at the river, Dodd lost track of Carey for a moment, but saw the small alley he must have gone into, like a rabbit into his hole. London was a warren and no mistake. How did anybody ever keep track of where he was?

Hurrying to the end of it, Dodd came out into a cloister court-yard he recognised, saw Carey's suit slipping into an alleyway at the other side of it, into the stair entrance under the figure of the woman tumbler standing on a rope with her head knocked off, and up the stairs all the way to the top.

On the last flight of stairs Dodd saw a sight that froze him in his tracks. It was a dead rat, black as sin, and swollen, lying out there in the open. Nameless dread filled Dodd and if Carey hadn't been ahead of him, he would have turned tail and run. But he wasn't a wean or a woman to be afeared of rats, though he was afraid of them, and he forced himself to go past, only to bump into Carey, standing stock still on the tiny landing.

Carey was staring, lips slightly parted, face ashen, at the door of their lodgings. There was a red cross branded there, the paint still wet, the latch sealed and a piece of paper nailed beside it. The plague-finders could only have left a few minutes before.

Dodd's legs felt weak and shaky. Simon Barnet and Barnabus Cooke were on the other side of that door, along with Tamburlain the Great, Barnabus's fighting cock. And Simon Barnet's family had been visited by God's wrath, and he must have gone in to say goodbye to his mam, must have done. You couldn't blame the lad, but that's how he had taken it and Barnabus must have taken it from him. Plague wasn't like a knife that you could see, it was mysterious, it struck where it wanted to.

As if there were no danger there, Carey went and hammered on the door. 'Barnabus! Simon!' he roared. For answer the cock crowed, and they could hear it flapping heavily about beyond the door. Nothing else. No sound of humanity at all.

Carey lifted his hand to break the seal on the latch, and that galvanised Dodd into action. He grabbed the Courtier's arm and pulled him back.

'Nay, sir. Ye willnae go in,' he growled.

'But...' There were tears standing in Carey's eyes. 'I can't leave them there.'

'Ye must. There's naething ye can do, save take the plague yersen.'

For a moment Carey resisted and something cold and calm inside Dodd got ready to hit him. 'I've seen plague, sir, back when I were a wean, when it hit us in Upper Tynedale. There's nothing ye can do, nothing. It gets in the air and if ye breathe near a man with the plague, ye get it yerself. Ye cannae go in.'

For a moment Carey stayed rigid by the door, Dodd still holding his arm, and then he relaxed, turned away and headed blindly down the stairs again.

We might have it already, Dodd thought as he followed, both of us might be just a day away from horrible pain and fever and death, you can never tell and Barnabus was with us yesterday when it might have been on him already, you can't tell with plague, there's no way of knowing until you get a headache or start sneezing and the black marks start rising on your neck and armpits and groin...

Carey was walking out of the cloister, across a little walled lane, to an elaborate gate. He tested it and found it opened, went through into a large walled garden full of big trees, so it was almost like a forest. Dodd could not get used to the way London ambushed you: five steps away from closepacked tumbled houses squatting in the ruins of a monastery and you came out in a cool green place, with grass and flowers as if you had escaped into the countryside by magic.

Carey didn't sit down under a tree, but leaned against the smooth trunk of an elm and blinked up at the blue sky between the leaves. Dodd hitched up the back of his hose and sat down on one of the roots. Neither of them said anything for a while, but they listened to the birds singing in the trees for all the world as if there were no such things as sickness and death.

'I didn't realise the plague was so bad in London,' Carey said, voice remote. 'Was that Barnabus's little secret?'

Dodd sighed, loath to explain what he knew. Best get on with it, he thought, and weather the storm.

He told Carey what had happened to Simon Barnet's family and Carey simply took in the information.

'Why didn't you tell me, Henry?'

KNIVES IN THE SOUTH

Dodd felt guilty. 'I'm sorry,' he said. 'I should have. But Barnabus begged me and so I didnae.'

'I see now why you're so anxious to leave London.'

'Ay, sir. Will we go and find your brother now?'

'It has got a bit more urgent, hasn't it?' drawled Carey. 'I mean, either one of us or both of us could be dead of plague tomorrow, couldn't we?'

'Ay, sir.'

'I wish you'd told me earlier.'

'Ay, sir. So do I.'

Carey shrugged. 'We'll try Peter Cheke again,' he said, and strode between trees to a small passageway running round the back of a magnificent hall facing a courtyard with a handsome round church in it. He went up the side of the church, past the railings, past some chickens and a small midden heap and came to another gate that gave onto Fleet Street. There he waited for Dodd to catch up, peered out onto Fleet Street and Dodd scouted ahead. The street was filling with people, handcarts, beggars, pigs going to market driven by children, and the shops opening up on either side. As far as you could tell with so many strangers, it seemed safe enough.

They had passed the conduit at the end of Shoe Lane, heading for Fleet Bridge, when it happened. Dodd was a little ahead of Carey, keeping his eyes peeled for men in buff coats, but unable to stop his mind wandering back to speculating on what was happening in their lodgings.

A man in a wool suit tapped his shoulder. 'Sir Robert Carey?'

'Nay,' said Dodd as loudly as he could. 'I'm not him.'

The man smiled cynically, and held Dodd's left arm above the elbow in a very painful grip. 'No, sir, of course you're not.'

'Will ye let me go?' Dodd demanded belligerently. Two other men smartly dressed in grey wool and lace trimmed falling-bands were suddenly on the other side of him. One of them had a cosh in his hand, the other had his sword drawn.

'Please sir, let's not make a scene,' said the man who had hold of Dodd's arm. 'Sir Robert Carey, I must hereby serve you with a warrant for a debt of four hundred and twenty pounds, five shillings.'

'Ye've made a mistake. Ah'm no' Sir Robert.'

The bailiff smiled kindly. 'Nice try, sir. We was warned you'd let on you was someone else.'

Dodd's hand was on his swordhilt, but a fourth heavyset man had joined the party surrounding him. This one briskly caught his right arm and twisted it up behind his back while the one who had first spoken to him held a knife under Dodd's chin and tucked the piece of paper he had read from into Dodd's doublet.

'I'm not Sir Robert Carey,' shouted Dodd, furiously. 'If ye want him he's over there.'

The bailiff looked casually over his shoulder in the direction Dodd was pointing and smiled again. 'Yes, sir. An old one but a good one. Please come along now. We don't want to 'ave to 'urt you.'

Admittedly there was absolutely no trace of Carey anywhere on the crowded street. The slimy toad must have run for it as soon as Dodd was surrounded, God damn him for a lily-livered sodomite...

Boiling with rage at such betrayal, Dodd let himself be hustled along in the direction he and Carey had been travelling, over Fleet Bridge, under the overgrown houses that made a vault above the alley, and up the lane beside the little stinking river to a large double gatehouse. The postern gate opened at once to the bailiff's knock and Dodd was hustled inside, blinking at the sudden darkness.

'Sir Robert Carey,' announced one of the bailiffs. 'On a warrant for debt, Mr Newton.'

A wide beetle-browed man with a heavily pock-marked face came hurrying out of the gatehouse lodgings, rubbing his hands and bowing lavishly.

'Sir Robert Carey, eh?' he said delightedly. 'Pleased to meet you at last, sir.'

'I tell ye,' growled Dodd, 'I am not Sir Robert Carey. I'm Henry Dodd, Land Sergeant of Gilsland, and I dinna owe onybody a penny.'

Mr Newton tutted gently. 'Dear me, sir, that won't wash 'ere, we know your little game. Now come along and let's do the paperwork, there's a good gentleman.'

'Ye've got the wrong man,' Dodd ground out between his teeth. 'I'm no' the one ye want. There's nae point in putting me in gaol, I'm no' Sir Robert...'

'So you say. But we was warned you'd come it the northerner once we caught you, so we know all about that. So why don't you give it up, eh? It's not dignified.'

Dodd gave a mighty heave and tried to trip the bailiff who was still wrenching his arm. Newton moved in close and rammed the end of his cosh into Dodd's stomach a couple of times. Dodd bent and whooped and saw stars for a few seconds. A horny thumb and forefinger gripped his ear.

'I don't want to have to give you a hiding, Sir Robert, I know the proper respect for me betters, but I will have order in my gaol, do you understand me? If I have to, I'll chain you, Queen's cousin or no, so don't make trouble. Now let's go and do the paperwork, eh? Get you settled in.'

Unable to do more than stay on his feet and wheeze, Dodd went where they pushed him into the guardchamber of the gatehouse.

***

It so happened that Nan was down on her hands and knees polishing one of the brasses, the one with the knight in armour and his lady wearing long flowing robes, when the handsome gentleman in the lily-embroidered trunk hose came sliding quickly and softly into the empty church, breathing a little hard. He paused as he shut the door to squint through the narrow gap for a minute, then let it close. He looked all around him at the brightly coloured tombs, the whitewashed walls that writhed with carved vine-leaves and fat bunches of grapes, the headless saints, and the high altar with its beautiful cloth and its empty candlesticks with no sanctuary lamp burning. He took a long stride to come up the aisle, but then paused as he remembered himself, took his hat off reverently. Nan began to warm to him, despite the lurid high fashion of his clothes, as she peered around one of the box pews, to see him walking up to the altar rails where he knelt, sighed and bent his chestnut head in prayer, although she was disappointed to see he didn't cross himself.

Her sight wasn't good enough to make out his face clearly, though he seemed a well-made gentleman, very tall and long-legged, but Nan felt she approved of him. She finished polishing the lady's face and thought about slipping out the sacristy door to find the vicar.

'Goodwife, I'd be grateful if you didn't fetch anybody. I won't be here long,' said the gentleman, without looking round.

She heaved herself up from the floor, folding her duster, and rubbing her creaking knees, then waddled round the box pew to curtsey to him.

He was standing by the altar rails now, bowed in return, smiled faintly down at her.

'I promise I'm not after the candlesticks, goodwife.'

'And much good they would do you if you were, sir,' she said tartly, 'since they're chained to the wall.'

'Ah.'

She blinked critically at him. He looked pale and there was a sheen of sweat on him which wasn't totally explained by his velvet doublet since the church was cool and dim. 'Can I help you, sir?' she asked, with another little curtsey.

'I very much doubt it.'

Nan shook her head. People always thought that because she was round, short and old, she was useless. 'Well, if you're here for a rest from the sun, which is certainly powerful for September, come into the pew and sit down, sir.'

He hesitated, then shrugged and let her open the door of the churchwarden's pew and usher him into it. His clothes were too fashionable to let him sit comfortably, so he leaned diagonally on the bench.

'Can I fetch you anything, sir?' she asked. 'Would you like some wine?'

'Communion wine?' he asked, sceptically. She grinned at him.

'I always replace it.'

'Ah.' He passed his tongue over his lower lip which did look dry. 'Well, why not?'

She trotted out into the aisle and went into the sacristy where she had a spare key to the locked cupboard where the vicar kept the wine. She came back with two plain silver goblets on a tray which held mixed water and wine since she believed in the curative properties of wine but could not afford to replace too much. 'The water is from St Bride's well itself,' she said, as she gave one of the goblets to the gentleman. 'It's clear and pure as dew, sir, and sovereign against all kinds of troubles: shingles, the falling sickness, leprosy, and scrofula too.'

'A pity I don't suffer from any of those things.'

'Now you never will, sir.'

He toasted her, and drank. 'How does it do against plague, cowardice and debt?'

She sat herself down on the bench with a sigh at the ache in her old bones, and drank from her own goblet.

'Oh, and idiocy,' added the gentleman.

'Who was chasing you, sir?' Nan asked. Well, if an old woman couldn't ask nosy questions, who could?

The gentleman shut his eyes briefly. Up close, Nan could see they were bright blue and also rather bloodshot. Something about his face was familiar, the beak of his nose, the high cheekbones, but she couldn't place it. She was quite sure she had never met him before.

'Bailiffs,' he said. 'Waving warrants for debt.' He sighed again, rubbed elegantly gloved fingers into his eyesockets. 'I let them arrest a friend of mine, one of the most decent and loyal men I've ever met, and I ran like a bloody rabbit to get away. Nice, eh?'

'And the plague?'

'My servants have it and my lodgings have been sealed.'

Nan tutted sympathetically and poured him more of the watered wine from the flagon. 'And the idiocy, sir? You don't look like an idiot.'

He raised winged eyebrows at this cheekiness and smiled shortly. 'I've been acting like a damned idiot ever since I got to London, goodwife. Looks aren't everything.'

'No indeed, sir. What will you do now?'

He puffed out a breath. 'I haven't the faintest bloody idea.'

She leaned forward and patted his arm. 'Please, sir,' she said. 'This is God's house. Don't swear.'

'Sorry.'

Despite her opportunities, Nan drank very little, preferring the life-giving water of the well. The wine was beginning to go to her head slightly and she waved her plump work-hardened hand at the church above and around them. 'I know it doesn't look like it any more,' she confided. 'You should have seen the church before the change in the boy-King's reign, when it was all painted with bright colours and the roof beams were gilded and stars painted there. Oh, it was beautiful, with the light through the glass. Noah's Ark was on that wall, before they whitewashed it, with elephants and striped horses too, and on this wall was the marriage at Cana and St Bride at the well, giving the child Jesus a drink. The same water from this very well, sir, Our Saviour drank from it, almost where we're standing.'

'When did Jesus Christ do that?' asked the gentleman.

'When he flew here as a child and got lost, and St Bride gave him her water and so he could fly back home to Our Lady in Palestine.'

The gentleman blinked a couple of times, but didn't laugh as one over-educated Divine had in the past. 'Oh?' he said.

'And certainly, if he didn't, he could have, so perhaps he did.'

'Ah. It's not mentioned in the Bible, though.'

'No, well, sir, if you read it, you'll find many things not mentioned there.'

The gentleman coughed. 'Er...yes.'

'The New World, for instance. Though I heard once that St Bride travelled there herself, in a silver boat.'

'Did she?'

She smiled sunnily at him. 'Perhaps. Perhaps not.'

He nodded abstractedly, clearly humouring her which was at least polite of him. His attention had wandered again, though; his wide shoulders were sagging with worry.

'Let me help, sir,' she coaxed, putting her hand on his velvet clad forearm. 'Tell me your troubles and perhaps you'll see a way through them.'

'I don't really see how you could...'

'Not me, sir,' she said simply. 'You. If you give yourself time to think, it's wonderful what notions God will put in your head.'

'He hasn't yet, and I can't say I blame Him, the way I've been behaving.'

She patted the arm, which felt very tense. 'We're all sinners, sir. If Our Saviour was walking in London town today, we would be the first he'd invite to dinner.'

Now that was better. What a charming smile the gentleman had to be sure.

'Well now, mother,' he said. 'That's certainly true.'

He stared at the high altar for a moment, his bright eyes flicking unseeingly between the wonderful painted glass of the workers in the vineyard and the scarred wooden saints of the altar-screen.

'Tell me. If only to pass the time while you wait for your enemies to give up.'

'It doesn't make sense,' he said to himself. 'I know he was wearing one of my old suits, but still...Mother, if you were looking for a popinjay courtier and you saw one man in a woollen suit and one man tricked out like me, which would you pick?'

Nan smiled and pointed at him.

'Quite. But I distinctly heard them address him as Sir Robert... by my name, and ignore his denials.'

'Perhaps a friend of yours pointed out the wrong man.'

'Yes, but...why? Why not have them arrest somebody completely different? Why Dodd? It doesn't make...' He stopped and stared at her without seeing her at all. 'I wonder. Would he do that? Why?'

Nan said nothing, only addressed an heretical prayer to St Bride and also St Jude to do something to help the young man. It seemed her prayer was answered for he suddenly smiled at her radiantly.

'I'm a fool. I've treed myself again. He's probably waiting outside with a good force of pursuivants. When is the Sunday Service?'

'In about an hour, at nine of the clock.'

'Excellent. Mother, would you run an errand for me?'

She smiled impishly. 'Walk, certainly. Run—no.'

***

Kit Marlowe waited for his henchmen, sitting perched languidly on the churchyard wall of St Bride's. He was annoyed with himself and with Carey. He hadn't thought the man so dense, had in fact considered him not far off his own intellectual equal, for all the Courtier's lack of the classics. And you could see what King James of Scotland saw in him; such a pity Carey only liked women.

Marlowe had one man to cover the side door and was himself

watching the main door. It was possible of course that the Courtier had found another way of escape, but Marlowe doubted it because his men were scattered strategically around the various alleys and he would have heard the noise if Carey tried to get past them.

Londoners dressed in their best clothes were arriving in the courtyard, the women gathering in bright knots to chatter, the men talking and nodding among themselves. Oh now, that was annoying. He had forgotten that Sunday Service would be starting soon, but it meant he couldn't search the place, even after his men had arrived. He should have gone straight in.

A little old woman came out of the church, trotted past with her hat on, as short and round as a chesspiece. He moved to block her path.

'Goodwife, a word please.'

'Yes, sir?' She curtseyed and smiled at him.

'I am looking for a Papist gentleman, very well dressed in cramoisie velvet, lilies on his hose, dark red hair, blue eyes, a little the look of Her Majesty the Queen. Have you seen such a man?'

Her round wrinkled face blinked up at him. 'A Papist gentleman, sir? Fancy!'

'Yes, a very dangerous man. Did he come into your church?'

'Why would a Papist go into our church?'

'To hide from me.'

'Oh, sir. I've not seen any dangerous Papists.'

'Where are you going?'

'To fetch vestments. Why, sir?' she said. 'Are you waiting for the service to begin?'

'Yes, goodwife,' he said shortly.

She nodded her head inanely. 'Isn't St Bride's beautiful in the sunshine?' she said. 'Isn't it a work of God to see it. We have a well of miraculous water, you know? Did you know that Our Lord drank from the well, our very own well?'

'Did He?'

'Oh, He did sir, it's quite certain.'

Marlowe rolled his eyes. 'Thank you, goodwife.'

'Then I'll see you at prayer, sir.'

'No doubt.'

189

'Well, God be with you, sir.'

Marlowe didn't give the normal reply, only turned his face and stared pointedly at the beheaded saints on the church wall. 'I very much doubt it,' he muttered, and ignored her curtsey as she trotted past.

The church was definitely filling up fast now, mothers with their children in clean caps, arguing and being threatened with beatings and bribes if they made as much noise as last time, elderly men with long beards and fine gowns...All of Fleet Street was there, and Fleet Lane and Ludgate Hill.

'There you are again, sir,' said a perky cracked voice beside him, and the cleaner was simpering up at him again, puffing hard with a heavy cloth bag in her hand. 'Well, would you care to see the vestments? Very beautiful, made of silk, you know, as beautiful as a rainbow.'

'No thank you, goodwife,' said Marlowe impatiently, watching hard for anyone going against the throng. If he was there, Carey would almost certainly wait through the Service and then try to slip out with the crowds of folk as cover—it was the obvious thing to do.

One of Marlowe's men came over for orders as the church cleaner went in at the sacristy door, and Marlowe disposed them as best he could. He was a hunter, and his fox had gone to earth. What he really needed were terriers and an ecclesiastical warrant. Unfortunately, it took at least three days to get one from the argumentative church courts. But Carey had to leave the church at some stage if he was going to do anything now he had no men to his back, and that's when Marlowe would nip him out. Then they could talk.

Marlowe sighed. Somebody had to go into the church, to be ready by the door, but not him. Carey knew his face too well.

Divine Service had never seemed so long before. Marlowe presumed the vicar was preaching the evils of atheism and the essential nature of God's church, with no doubt some lurid and dubious tales of Hell to keep the congregation in awe. It passed his understanding why anyone ever believed anything a priest said: how the Devil could anyone know what happened in Hell, since nobody was ever going to come back and describe it?

The church itself was nothing but a vast playhouse for instructing the people in subjection to their betters. He supposed it was good enough for the general run of men and for all women, of course, but anyone with a real brain must see through the mummery. However, hardly anyone did. They repeated meaningless words and yearned towards the void like the sheep they were.

At last the congregation was coming out. Marlowe stood straight and paid attention as the men took their leave of the vicar and the women started their ceaseless starling chatter again.

He waited, beginning to grow concerned. Leaving one man to watch the main door he went round to the side door but found it still locked. His man confirmed that none had come out.

He hurried back again and asked the man he had left there who had come out. An important family, some country bumpkins visiting London, another family, children, serving men.

'Any courtiers?'

'I'd have stopped him if I'd seen him, sir,' said the man, looking offended. 'I know what we're looking for. Tall, dark red hair, blue eyes, lilies on his hose. Right?'

'Nobody like that has come out?'

'No, sir. Nor anything even similar.'

The crowds were thinning; a few boys were being shouted at by their mother for tightrope-walking along the church wall. Marlowe folded his arms and his lips thinned with anger. Surely Carey hadn't given them the slip. His men weren't bright but their job involved watching carefully for men described to them and they were good at it. Also they were afraid of him and his power from Heneage. They wouldn't have missed Carey. He must still be skulking inside.

'Oh, the hell with this nonsense,' snapped Marlowe. 'We'll search the place.'

With his henchmen to back him, Marlowe went into the church and because he had to maintain some kind of respectability in front of his men, he took his hat off.

'Vicar,' he said to the portly man putting out the candles on the altar. 'I am going to search here for a Papist traitor I am seeking.

Please don't put me in the position of having to order my men to lay hands on you.'

The vicar stood stock still, and seemed on the verge of protesting. Then he took a deep breath and gritted his teeth. 'I protest, sir,' he said. 'And I will be writing to the bishop this very afternoon.'

'Do as you like,' said Marlowe and nodded to his men to quarter the church.

They did, very carefully, and then the sacristy and that was when one of them came hurrying out, triumphantly waving a lace with a glittering aiglet.

Marlowe took it between his fingers and held it up to the light. It was a beautiful piece of work: gold, with the sharp point of the aiglet formed in the shape of a stork's beak. Nobody except a courtier would bother with such elaboration. The lace had been snapped by someone in too much of a hurry to untie his doublet points properly.

There had been no naked men in the crowd. 'Devil take it,' growled Marlowe. 'He changed his clothes.'

He spun on his heel and barked at the vicar, still standing at his altar. 'What did he put on?'

'I beg your pardon?'

'Don't pretend to be any stupider than you are. What was he wearing when he slipped out?'

'Who?'

'The man I am looking for, on the Queen's business, Sir Robert Carey. The man who left this on your sacristy floor.'

The vicar looked at the pretty little thing in Marlowe's fist. 'I really don't know what you're talking about.'

'What was he wearing?' Marlowe was pacing across the church up to the altar, advancing on the vicar who shrank back at first and then seemed to find some courage somewhere in his windy fat body and faced him boldly.

'Sir, I was working on my sermon, putting last-minute touches to it, in my study. If there was a fugitive here, which I doubt, then to be sure he must have been wearing something. What it was, I have no idea.'

'The vestment bag. The old bitch coney-catched me,' said Marlowe to himself. 'Of course. Where's the old woman? A little short woman who burbled to me about St Bride?'

'Do you mean Nan? I'm sorry sir, she isn't here. She asked for the day off and I gave it to her and she's gone.'

'God damn it.'

'Will you stop taking the Lord's name in vain in my church?'

'No, I won't. It hasn't done me any harm yet and I doubt it will. I shall have words with my master, Mr Vice Chamberlain Heneage, I shall have you investigated thoroughly for Papistry and loyalty; if it lies within my power I shall have you in Chelsea and question you myself.'

'I'm sure you would,' said the vicar with a patronising smile. 'But my own Lord of Hosts will protect me, quite possibly through the agency of my lord the Earl of Essex who is my temporal good lord.'

Marlowe was outbid and he knew it. In the feverish scheming of the court, Essex was implacably opposed to Heneage and worse, Essex hated Marlowe, whereas the Queen loved Essex and generally did what he asked. And Essex was the ultimate object of all Marlowe's manoeuvring.

Marlowe wrestled with the urge to punch the fatuous old man.

'If the gentleman returns who changed his clothes very hurriedly in your sacristy, tell him that Kit Marlowe wants to speak to him. I'll be at the Mermaid.'

'Certainly sir. Goodbye.' As if trying to rouse Marlowe to an even worse fury, the vicar lifted his hand in the three fingered sign for benediction. 'The Lord bless you and keep you, the Lord make his countenance to shine upon you...'

The church door banged behind Marlowe before the old man had finished his superstitious prattling.

For a moment Marlowe stood in the courtyard, irresolute, his thoughts disordered by anger. Carey had somehow managed to give him the slip, probably by changing into his henchman's old homespun clothes. He was loose in London; probably he was already on his way to Somerset House to talk to his father, or possibly he was taking horse in St Giles in the Fields, to ride to Oxford.

He beckoned his men over and gave them orders for the search, then headed towards the Mermaid inn for an early dinner. He needed a drink badly and he needed to sit and consider how to rescue his plan.

***

Nan stood by the stairwell in Whitefriars over which there had once been a handsome figure of Our Lady standing on the globe, now defaced by Reformers. The young man she had taken rather a liking to came clattering down, now dressed in a well-made homespun russet suit a bit wide for him and short in the breeches, and a leather jerkin, with a blue statute cap on his head. He had done his best to hide the colour of his hair and the excellence of his boots with mud and dust and he had kept his sword which had anyway been an incongruously plain broadsword. There was no question but that he had been a great deal more fine when in his courtly clothes, but she liked him better now. Also he had pawned the whole beautiful suit he had been wearing and got an astonishing price for it, some of which he had given her, without her asking, which had pleased her greatly. And he had told her to call him Robin which also pleased her.

'Are you sure about this, mother?' he asked her with a worried frown on his face. 'When I wished I could find a nurse for my servants, I never...'

She tutted at him and pulled down her little ruff to show him the round scars on her neck. 'See?' she said. 'I had the plague years ago, when I was a maid. We all got it but I was spared. You never get it twice. That was why I went to the nunnery, you know: my family was dead, except my uncle and he didn't want me.'

'I didn't know you were a nun.'

She beamed up at him. 'Why should you? And I'm not any more, now I clean St Bride's church.'

'Don't you mind?'

Young men were so sweet, so worried about things that didn't matter. 'No, of course not. I can pray all the Offices whenever I want to.'

'Do you do that?' he sounded impressed.

She laughed. 'Generally I forget.' She took his arm. 'Now help me up all these stairs, I'm not as young as I was.'

The climb left her breathless, so she sat down on the top step just above the dead rat and fanned herself while Robin used his wonderfully enamelled little tinder box and lit the candle she had told him to bring.

As he put it back into the pocket of his jerkin, he paused and frowned, pulled the pocket inside out and looked closely at the seams, as if he was searching for nits. Nan couldn't make out what he had seen, but she saw his lips move. 'Mercury?' he asked and frowned in puzzlement, then shook his head and put the pocket back.

She was recovered by then so she heaved herself up and took her knife, heated it in the flame and carefully prised off the seals on the door, leaving them hanging by their cords.

Cautiously she opened the door while the young man stood back, looking worried, and then she braced herself and went in.

The smell was bad but mainly because of the magnificent fighting cock roosting on the bedhead. It took its head out from under its wing and crowed once, then settled down to watch her with the cold beadiness of all fowl. The place was a mess, the small chest was open and its contents flung on the floor, the main bed had been stripped and the mattress lifted, slashed open. The man in the truckle was obviously dead, but the boy lying on the straw pallet just inside the door was not. He was trussed like a boiling chicken and efficiently gagged and as soon as she came in his tear-swollen eyes flicked open and he started grunting at her frantically.

She put her head round the door. 'There's no plague here,' she said. 'Or not yet. Come and look.'

Carey came in after only a moment's hesitation and stood staring at the scene for one frozen second. His fists bunched and his blue eyes blazed with rage.

'God damn them to hell.'

Seconds later he had his knife out and was carefully cutting the boy free of the ropes, undoing the gag and helping him spit out the wad of cloth in his mouth. The boy was weeping and couldn't talk because his mouth was too dry. After shutting the door to stop the cock getting out, Nan gave him some of the wine posset she had brought with her, mopping it when he dribbled. Carey was rubbing his purple and swollen hands and feet.

'Don't talk for a bit,' he told the desperate boy. 'It's all right, Simon. Don't worry.'

Leaving Nan to give Simon more wine and help him use the pot, Carey went over to the truckle bed and stood looking down at the twisted body there, the sheets filthy with blood and muck. Nan came over to look.

'He died hard, God rest him,' she said objectively. 'Was he stabbed?'

Carey had tears running freely down his face. He checked the body carefully and shook his head. Then he went to the window, opened the shutters and flung them wide so the man's soul could fly. He stood there a while, his head bowed. Nan waddled over to give him her handkerchief so he could blow his nose, and then he went back to the boy who was still weeping, clasped him like a brother and patted his shoulder.

Whatever the little ferret-faced man on the bed had died of, it certainly wasn't plague. There were no swellings at his neck, nor was his face blackened. From the disgusting state of the blankets, she thought he must have died of a flux or bad food. She carefully shut his eyes and put pennies on them to hold them shut, then she drew up the least horrible blanket to cover his face.

'One minute, mother,' said the young man behind her, his voice still choked.

She stepped aside and watched as he gingerly felt about the little man's soiled doublet and then reached under the pillow. He drew out a worn silver flask that had once been nicely chased and enamelled. He looked at it carefully, then opened it and sniffed what was inside.

'Do you know what he died of?' she asked, seeing the enlightened expression on Carey's face.

'I think so,' he answered her gruffly. 'I saw a man die of the same thing yesterday morning.'

Nan tutted. 'It's no kind of plague I've ever seen. It isn't even the sweating sickness.'

Carey shook his head. 'I think it's not catching either,' he said.

196

'Except one way.'

He didn't explain any more, only went back to where Simon was sitting, tearing ravenously at the bread and cheese Nan had brought for her own meal. Carey squatted down in front of him.

'All right, Simon, what can you tell me?'

'It was awful, sir, it was terrible.' The boy was rubbing his cheek muscles and jaw hinges and wincing. His face was bruised and his lip was swollen from a cut but he was so desperate to talk that he was almost gabbling. 'Uncle Barney was sick in the night, he was up and down and then he was sick something horrible, and he wouldn't let me help, only said he thought it was something he'd eaten and he'd be better in the morning. So I went back to sleep, like he said, sir, I never meant him to...d... die...I never thought...'

'I don't think there was anything you could have done for him, Simon. Did he drink from this flask?'

'Oh, yes. He had it refilled at the boozing ken down the way, and drank that as well, said it was medicine, only it wasn't, it was aqua vitae, but that was before he took sick. He was scared because he had a headache and a fever like me, he was scared he had plague, see.'

'How's your head?'

'It's better, sir,' Simon sounded surprised. 'And me neck isn't stiff or anything. Do you think I won't get it, even though I kissed me mam goodbye?'

'You might not. Nobody knows why some people get it and some people don't.'

Simon was crying again. 'Me mam's dead now, in't she, sir? That's what Uncle Barney said. He said, if she was all covered in black spots, then she's as good as dead.'

Carey sighed. 'I don't know because I haven't seen her, but I'm afraid that is true.'

'Oh, sir. What am I going to do? Everybody's dead. 'Cept my sister and I don't like her.'

'Shh. Everybody has to die sometime.'

'Yes, but not all at once. Not like that.' He gestured at the shape on the truckle bed.

Carey sighed again. 'Tell me what happened. Your Uncle Barney was sick and you went back to sleep.'

'Yes, sir, 'cos I never knew how bad it was, he didn't tell me, he said I should...'

'Nobody's blaming you for sleeping. What happened? How did you come to be trussed up?'

'Oh, yes. Well, I went to sleep, like I said, sir. Next thing I knew, it was still night and they was banging on the door.'

'Who was?'

'They was. The men.'

'Who were they?'

'Didn't say, sir. I didn't want them to disturb Uncle Barney what had just dropped off, as I thought, so I went to open the door and tell them to be quiet and they just pushed it open and came in and one of them grabbed me and I tried to fight but he just clipped my ear and held me tighter and they searched the room. One of them looked at Uncle Barney and said, "Jesus", and then another one asked me questions.'

'What did they ask?'

'Where you were, sir, which I didn't know because Uncle Barney didn't tell me, and where your brother was, which I didn't know either and where some money was which I said you had and what we were doing in London which I said was looking for your brother...'

'Did they hurt you?'

'They knocked me about a bit, sir.'

'I can see that. Did they do anything...er...else?'

Simon shook his head. 'No, sir. Only they said they were going to tie me up and gag me because I was a bad boy and then they'd make sure nobody came in here at all until I was dead of thirst only they wouldn't if I'd tell them what they wanted to know, but I didn't know it, so I couldn't and Uncle Barney was dead so they couldn't ask him and they were worried in case it was plague, so they did what they said, they tied me up and...and...then they left me and then they scorched the cross on the door, I heard them, so I knew nobody would dare to come in and...and...'

Simon's shoulders hunched over and shook with sobs. Carey sat down next to him and let the boy howl into his shoulder. When the storm had died down a bit, he asked very softly, 'Did you know any of them, Simon? Had you ever seen any of them before?'

'Well they was four of them, but I couldn't see their faces because they had cloths muffled up to their noses and their hats pulled down.'

'Was there anything at all about them that you can remember?'

'They sounded like courtiers, sir, gents.'

'Hm. What were their hands like? Rough? Smooth? Did they have rings?'

'Well, the one that did the talking had two rings but I don't remember no more, sir, honest I don't, I was so frightened, what with Uncle Barney being dead and the men hissing at me, and I couldn't think what with getting my head slapped and everything...'

'It's all right, Simon,' said Carey. 'You did the best you could. None of it was your fault. Do you know what they were looking for?'

'No, only it was small from the way they searched.'

'Hm.' Carey stared straight ahead of himself, at the dented plaster of the wall. 'The men expected me to be here?'

'Oh yes, sir, when they came in they all had their swords drawn and one of them had a dag with the match lit.'

'Hm. Do you think you could walk?'

Simon sniffled and rubbed his hands. 'I dunno, sir. My feet are killing me wiv pins and needles.'

'Try. I want you out of here in case the men come back.'

'But where will I go, sir? What can I do? My Uncle Barney's dead and...and...'

'Simon, do you think I'm going to put you on the streets because Barnabus is dead? Do you think that's the kind of man I am?'

Simon gulped hard. 'No, sir.'

'You're not thinking straight. We need to get you somewhere safe. Now it'll be a lot easier if you could walk down Fleet Street to Somerset House, but if you really can't manage, I'll get you a litter.'

Simon shook his head and struggled to his feet, biting his lips and leaning on Carey's arm. Then he sat down again.

'It hurts. But I think I can. But I can't do my boots up, my hands is too sore.'

Nan came over with the boy's boots and between them, they

got them on. Then Carey took Nan to the window and looked out carefully.

'Mother,' he said looking straight in her eyes, so she found herself smiling and thinking what a pity it was she wasn't forty years younger. 'I want you to do me a great favour. Take this boy to Somerset House and ask to speak to my Lord Hunsdon. Tell him what we found here and what Simon told us and also tell him that Dodd's been arrested in mistake for me, God knows how. Can you do that?'

'My Lord Hunsdon?' she asked, very impressed. 'Is he your lord?'

'In a manner of speaking,' said the young man drily. 'Tell him Robin sent you and if he wants confirmation, you can tell him I said I'm at the reiving again, only for two-legged kine this time.'

'You're at the reiving again, for two-legged kine,' Nan repeated uncertainly.

'Don't be frightened if he laughs or shouts, that's just his way. Tell him Dodd's in the Fleet in mistake for me.'

'Will you not go with us?'

'No. I'll keep an eye on you, but my guess is that the men who did this might be watching the place and as it's me they want, I don't want them seeing me.'

'What if they stop us?'

'Play stupid but don't try anything with them, they're very dangerous.'

'I didn't take to the young man, your enemy.'

'No. I have a bone or two to pick with him.'

'And your servant?'

'Barnabus? He'll come to no harm here. I'll see he gets a decent burial when I can.'

'What about the fighting cock?'

Carey eyed the bird who stared back at him defiantly and decorated the ruined bed again. 'That's Tamburlain the Great. He's got water and he's got grain. I should think he'll be all right for the moment. I'll send someone with food and medicine to Simon's family as soon as I can.'

They helped Simon out onto the tiny landing and Nan used the candle very carefully to restick the seals. Carey had to carry the boy down the narrow winding stairs but once on the level Simon could shuffle along, holding tight to Nan's arm.

She walked down Fleet Street feeling heavy with fright, the boy sniffling beside her as he walked. The street was teeming with people, carts, large dangerous-looking men, women carrying buckets.

They passed the gauntlet of the beggars at Temple Bar and the ballad singer and the rat catcher with his strings of dead black rats slung across his back and onto the wide dusty Strand. When Simon showed her the gate to Somerset House she felt almost too frightened to try it, because it was so grand, but the boy insisted. They had to wait for a long time because the porter sent for the steward and when she said she had a message for my lord from Robin, this caused a flurry, before they were escorted into the magnificent marble entrance hall and then deep into the building. The steward's wife came to fetch Simon to her stillroom to dose him against plague and melancholy, which Nan found left her bereft since at least she had met the boy. This was so rich and brilliant a house, more elaborate than any church she had ever cleaned, it made her feel very small. They told her that my lord Baron Hunsdon was not at home, being out inspecting some properties, but was expected back that afternoon. They asked her if she wished to wait, or pass on her message, and she said conscientiously that she would wait.

***

Dodd had spent the morning trying to hang onto his temper. He had signed the Prison's logbook at the Deputy Gaoler's office in his own name, causing tuttings and sighings. Deputy Gaoler Newton wrote Sir Robert Carey's name next to it. Then two of Newton's bullyboys had held his arms while Newton personally searched his body, a process of nasty intimacy made worse by Newton's deliberate roughness. Triumphantly, he produced Dodd's purse and took one of the angels from it, biting it cautiously before he put it away. Ten shillings. Almost a week's wages.

'There's my garnish,' sneered Newton. 'Now, sir, the charge for the Knight's Commons is a shilling a night, or sixpence if you share a bed. The Eightpenny ward is eightpence a night or fourpence if you share.'

The charges were iniquitous. When Dodd had spent six months in ward at Jedburgh for one of his wife's relatives, the charge had only been a couple of pennies a day, though admittedly he had had to sleep on a bench instead of a bed and the food had been frightful.

'You'd better go in the Knight's Commons,' said Newton. 'Seeing as you're a knight.'

'I'm not a knight, thank God,' said Dodd. 'I'm the Land Sergeant of Gilsland.'

'Oh, really, sir, give over this nonsense. You'll go where I tell you and I say you're a gentleman, so you go in the Knight's Commons. Will you be wanting a bed on your own, sir?'

'Och, no, I'll share. I wouldna pay a shilling a night for the best inn in London.'

'Well, you would, sir, and more. But never mind. I take it kindly that you're willing to share, makes my job simpler. Now do I have your word as a gentleman that you won't cause trouble?'

'No, ye do not.'

'I'll have to chain you in that case.'

'Och. All right. I willna make trouble.'

'Your word on it, sir?'

'Ma word on it.'

Newton escorted him through the second gate and across the yard which boiled with people, men and women in all states of raggedness, most of them trading or working. There was a group of women gathered in the shade of an awning, sitting on the ground with their skirts spread out around them like brightly coloured pools, every white-capped head bent over some kind of linen stitchery and their fingers flashing.

Newton went over to one of the men playing cards in a doorway, sitting on boxes.

'Sir John,' he said. 'Here is Sir Robert Carey who is to be in your ward tonight.'

Sir John stood and bowed elaborately to Dodd who felt embarrassed at his imposture, despite it not being his fault. He did his best to bow back.

'Sir Robert is amusing himself by pretending to be a northerner,' said Newton sarcastically. 'See if you can bring him to his senses.'

Newton and his henchmen stumped off across the crowded courtyard and Dodd watched them go, wishing he could bring his kin all the way from Upper Tynedale and Gilsland, raid the man's house, lift his kine, take his insight and beat him to a pulp for insolence. He sighed. God, it was hard to be a foreigner.

Sir John was squinting at him curiously.

'Sir Robert,' said the man in charge of the Knight's Commons, whose doublet was velvet and his Venetians brocade but the whole outfit sadly worn. 'I'm sorry to see you in this state. How may I be of assistance, sir?'

Well, that was polite at least. What would Carey have said? Something witty about Sir John helping him by giving him four hundred pounds, no doubt. But that was not Dodd's style.

'Sir,' he said firmly, doing his best to copy the southern way of talking. 'There's been some kind of mistake. I am not Sir Robert. Ma right name is Henry Dodd an' I dinna owe anybody in this town a penny. But I canna persuade Newton of it.'

Sir John nodded noncommittally, evidently not believing him.

'That's all right, sir,' he said respectfully. 'I can see you're incognito.'

'But I'm not incognito, whatever that means. I am what I am. I dinna want tae make any pretence at being what I'm not. D'ye follow me, sir? I'm no mair a gentleman than Newton, thank God.'

Sir John nodded again. 'Well, sir,' he said. 'I myself have never met Sir Robert Carey before now, and so I cannot tell whether what you say is true or not. But Newton seems to think you are Carey and his word is law in this prison. So I suggest you go with what he says and be a gentleman until your friends can come and sort out the muddle.'

Dodd sighed again. It made him feel profoundly uneasy to have a gentleman calling him sir, it felt like he was sitting on top of a mountain and might fall off at any time. He couldn't enjoy being respected for something he was not.

'Is it right Newton can chain me if I make trouble, and me a gentleman an' all?'

'Oh yes, sir. I'm surprised he hasn't done it already; he usually does for the first week to encourage you to pay him garnish to strike them off. Then he chains you again until you run out of money.' Sir John gestured at one of the other primero players, a skinny man with a cavernous cough and an exhausted expression, whose damask doublet hung in folds on him and whose feet were chained.

'What else can he do?'

Sir John pointed at a group of ominous wooden shapes in the other corner of the courtyard; Dodd narrowed his eyes and saw they were a set of stocks, a pillory and a whipping post.

'Or,' added Sir John, 'he can throw you in the Hole which is six inches deep in water from the Fleet and has no light and not much air.'

'Ay,' said Dodd gloomily. 'Well, nae doot he must keep order.'

'He is heavily fined for escapes,' continued Sir John. 'And very vigilant since a notable and dangerous escape five years ago. If you spend a day in the pillory, you must spend a night in the Hole for he will not leave anyone out in the courtyard overnight as he did formerly. I beseech you sir, do not even consider escaping, no matter how unjust your imprisonment may seem; he has flogged gentlemen to the bone on a mere suspicion.'

'Och, Christ. I thought he couldna do that to a man of worship?'

'It is an iniquitous and barbarous tyranny, but as he has pointed out to me, he can see to it that a gentleman dies of ill usage, sickness and want before any suit can go to Star Chamber, and he will.'

'Och,' said Dodd, feeling more depressed by the minute. If being a gentleman couldn't protect you from a flogging, what the hell was the point of all the bowing and scraping involved? At least in Jedburgh there had been no question of that, since the Armstrongs would have taken any bad treatment against Dodd very personally.

There was a shouting and a bell-clanging, at which the gentlemen sighed and gathered up their cards and winnings.

'What's going on?'

'Sunday Service,' said Sir John. 'An excuse to muster the prisoners, in fact.'

Dodd followed and stood in a little group with the other inmates of the Knight's Ward, answered to the name of Sir Robert Carey with a growled 'If ye say so', and found himself being pointed out and stared at by many of the other prisoners. He scowled back at them.

The sermon was long, read aloud by a sweating little priest with a red bulbous nose, and dwelling on the iniquities of luxurious clothing and the wickedness of starch. Dodd couldn't quarrel with a word of it, but wished heartily it had been Carey listening to it instead of him. He still wasn't used to the way his smart woollen suit constricted his arms and legs and forced him to pull his shoulders back.

At last the priest wound reedily to a close, blessed them and trotted off already drinking from a flask he had in his sleeve pocket. Somebody tentatively touched Dodd's sleeve.

'Sir. There is a little time before dinner.' It was Sir John, smiling very friendlywise at him. 'Would you care to play primero with us?'

What was it with Londoners? Why did they all want him to play cards? Well, there was one obvious answer. Dodd was tempted. He knew he was a lot better than he had ever been before. Also that proved Sir John could not have met Sir Robert Carey, since no one who actually knew the man would think he was a good mark for a primero game.

'Ay. I'll play. Though I'm verra rusty and ye might need to remind me of the rules.'

Sir John exchanged glances with the skinny gentleman, who moved round so that Dodd could squat down in their circle. He looked around him at the four gentlemen who were playing and thought that he could definitely undertake to throw any one of them a great deal further than he would trust them. Carey's words paraded through his mind. 'Play very cautiously with people you don't know. If the odds are consistently wrong—whether you're winning or losing—then you can be absolutely certain somebody is cheating.' The odds were still something of a mystery to Dodd, though he had sweated to learn the numbers Carey told him were important. The Courtier had boiled it down by translating the numbers into fights: two to one against you, and you might fancy your chances, five to one and things were looking bleak, twenty to one and you might as well not bother. It had been a strange distraction against the griping misery of the Scotch flux but endless practice using pebbles for money had driven some of the ideas into his head.

An hour later he was pocketing a little pile of shillings and gloomily resisting the depressing certainty that the fine, if threadbare, gentlemen were clearly cheating, on Carey's definition. Dodd wasn't often lucky with the cards, which he supposed must mean Janet was a better wife than she sometimes seemed, but in that hour he had seen more flushes and choruses than he had seen before in all his adult life.

The bell went for dinner while he was wondering what to do about it and so he filed off with the others and his purse jingling, into the dining hall at one side of the courtyard, where the prisoners were carefully counted in by a gaol servant scowling with concentration.

The food wasn't too bad. Tough, of course, and mostly covered in a sort of brown sauce, but none of it actually stank. Compared to the garrison rations it was really quite tasty. Dodd was too busy filling his belly to look around at first, but after a while he realised that one of the women sitting at the other end of the table was looking at him curiously.

He looked back at her. There was nothing whatever remarkable about her, excepting that she had a child sitting on either side of her, but they weren't the only children in the hall, if a little better behaved than some. She was of middling height and quite slender build, she had brown hair neatly tucked under a cap and pleasant long-lashed brown eyes. Three needles were threaded through her bodice which was doublet-style and made of a dusky rose-coloured damask and she was squinting a little short-sightedly. Dodd felt as if Carey's fetch was sitting next to him and jogging his elbow; Carey would have tipped his hat to her and given her one of his most charming smiles, because that was the kind of man Carey was. Dodd, however, was different and proud of it. He preferred not to remember his sin of lust the previous morning, which was no doubt the cause of all his troubles since. Dodd was married. He looked firmly away from the woman and concentrated on his meat.

After they had filed out of the dining hall into the afternoon sunlight, there was Sir John at Dodd's elbow again, nagging him to play cards. This confirmed all Dodd's suspicions.

'Nay, I'll not chance it,' he said. 'I was lucky this morning but I'm not anywhere near as skilful as ye gentlemen.'

'The way to increase your skill is to play, surely?' said Sir John with a tight, rather desperate smile.

Barnabus's voice came to Dodd's memory. 'Wot you do is, you let the barnard win a bit and then you take it off him again and generally speaking, he'll play harder to try and get his winnings back which is when you skin him, so to speak.'

Sir John then suggested a restful game of dice and Dodd shook his head sadly. The card-playing circle were looking annoyed as well, which was a little worrying.

Somebody came up behind Dodd and said, 'Excuse me, sir?' He turned and saw the woman who had been staring at him during dinner. She curtseyed and he made his best bow which caused Sir John's eyes to narrow.

'Ay, mistress,' he said politely. 'Can I help ye?'

'Are you Sir Robert Carey?' Her voice trembled a little.

Dodd sighed. Was this another of Carey's multiplicity of women? How the devil did he find time for such a complicated private life?

'That's what Newton thinks,' he said.

Her brow furrowed and she looked about to burst into tears. 'Well, but do you know him?'

'Ay, I do.' No, of course it couldn't be one of Carey's trollops, what was he thinking of? She would hardly mistake him, would she? 'Though I dinna ken where he is, mind.'

She frowned again, obviously not understanding him.

'I don't know where he is,' Dodd said again, straining to speak in a southern way. 'But I do know him, mistress, ay.'

'Please, sir, will you come with me?'

'Why?' Dodd was suspicious now. Was this some means of inveigling him into a corner so Sir John and his cronies could take his purse?

'It's very important.'

'Nae doot. But what's it about?'

She beckoned him closer and when he bent towards her, stood

on tiptoe and whispered in his ear. 'His brother.'

'Och.' Dodd looked severely at her. Was it possible to be so lucky? 'What are ye saying?'

'Will you come?'

'Ay, I will, mistress.'

Newton had taken his sword when he was signed in, of course, but Dodd still had his dagger. He loosened it in its sheath and then followed the woman across the courtyard, past the sewing circle where the woman's children were sitting under the gimlet eye of an older woman, past a cobbler's stall and a general stall covered over with a dizzying array of objects for sale, and into the doorway of one of the oldest parts of the place, stone built and with a swaybacked roof.

They went down worn spiral steps. One of the gaol servants was standing there and after the woman had paid him a penny, he unlocked the heavy door. They went through into a dark stinking cellar, with a broad ribbed roof and small high windows that were barred and had no glass. The stone flags of the floor were slippery and there were puddles in the dips, the place stank of piss and mould and sickness to take your head off. There were still shapes lying huddled in the shadows, some of them in no more than their shirts, and there was no sound of talk, only harsh breathing, echoing coughs and the occasional moan.

'Och, God,' said Dodd, shaken. 'What's this place?'

'Bolton's Ward, sir, where Newton puts those who have no money left, the beggars' ward.'

'Why do they not leave?'

'They are chained, sir.'

'Jesus Christ.'

In his time Dodd had heard some fairly frightening sermons on the subject of Hell, but this was worse than any of them. Jedburgh itself hadn't been half so bad.

The woman went over to one of the huddled shapes in the corner. Dodd followed her, feeling sick with pity.

She bent down to the man who lay there and felt his forehead; he moved his head restlessly at her touch. For a moment, in the dimness, Dodd's belly clenched with superstitious fright because although the man was far skinnier than Carey, it could have been him, with the beaky nose and the high cheekbones. But the man's greasy hair was receding off his forehead into a widow's peak and there was a difference about the chin and mouth, and also he had a straggling beard. He was lying on a straw pallet with a bag of clothes for a pillow, wearing nothing but his shirt which was fine linen but ragged. The blanket hunched up over his shoulders was a stinking disgrace Dodd wouldn't have put on a horse.

'Do you know him, sir?' asked the woman.

'Is that Edmund Carey?' Dodd asked.

Her face relaxed a little. For the first time she smiled at him. 'Yes, it is.'

'But why did his father not find him?'

'He's in the book under another name, under Edward Morgan. He was kind to my children when he was first brought to the Fleet, in the beginning of August. Then he took a gaol-fever a week later. Newton was enraged with him for he said that all the garnish he had paid was forged and Newton himself was nearly arrested for it. He had no other money by then, and so Newton put him down here.' She looked down at her neatly clasped hands. 'I...um...I have been trying to nurse him. He told me his real name when he was delirious but then when he was in his right mind he begged me not to tell his family and...some other things...and so I did not, but I have been in a quandary to know what to do, sir, because I think the poor gentleman is not far off dying and he should be taken out of this place and looked after properly. I'm not even sure if I have done right bringing you here, sir,' added the woman, her voice dropping, 'because he was particularly anxious that his brother not be told; he kept begging me not to let little Robin see him in case he was frightened.'

Dodd kept his face solemn though in fact there was something funny as well as pathetic and idiotic at the idea of Sir Robert being 'little Robin' and at risk of fright at the sight of his brother brought so low. But then, he supposed, if he was in a like case and not quite in his right mind from fever, he might want to stop Red Sandy from seeing him. Old habits die hard and you could never stop being a big brother once you were one.

He squatted down and took the bony wrist which felt hot and dry. 'Och, puir man,' he said. 'How much would it take to move him somewhere better?'

'At least ten shillings, since he's in debt to Newton for the Knight's Ward charges as well. And another couple of shillings' garnish to unchain him.'

Dodd's lips tightened. He was beginning to take a considerable dislike to Newton.

'What's your name, mistress?'

'Julie Granville, sir.'

'Is your husband not about?'

She looked down. 'He was a sharer and officer in a ship bound for Muscovy, sir, and when the ship didn't return, and we had heard nothing of it for a year, our creditors arrested me for his debts.'

'But that's terrible, mistress. What about yer family?'

'I haven't any, sir. And my husband's family are...Well, his father was opposed to the voyage in the first place.'

Dodd shook his head. Impulsively he put his hand on her arm. 'I'm not Sir Robert, see ye, but I am his man, and I'm a man o' parts myself in ma ain country. Now dinna ye fret, Mistress Granville, I'll see it sorted.'

She obviously didn't understand much of what he had said, but she understood his tone of voice and she smiled. She took a cloth out of the bucket she had been carrying and began wiping Edmund Carey's face and hands. He woke a little more and began muttering. She shushed him and began feeding him spoonfuls of some kind of porridge she had brought in a wooden bowl.

Dodd stood, turned on his heel and strode to the door, banged on it and was let out of the hell of Bolton's Ward, up the stairs and into the courtyard. He was scowling with thought; God might move in mysterious ways, but this was a little too pat for his tastes. What a strange coincidence that he should be arrested in mistake for Carey, when Carey had been blazing about the streets with courtier branded on every inch of him, and brought to the one prison in London that also contained Carey's missing brother, for whom Greene had been searching before his death, and Carey as well. It didn't make sense, or rather it did and he didn't like the sense it made.

He was not at all surprised to find a familiar face in the courtyard when he came blinking out into the sunshine: Mistress Bassano's erstwhile servant, the balding poet.

Dodd strode over to the man, took his elbow between thumb and forefinger in a way which forbade argument, and propelled him into the shade of a corner between two buildings.

'Sergeant Dodd,' said Shakespeare, his voice shaking a little. 'I'm...er...I'm very glad I've found you.'

'Not half sae glad as I am to find you,' said Dodd, deliberately crowding him against the wall. 'Now, I ken ye work for Mr Vice Chamberlain and I dinna give a pig's turd why. But I'm sick and tired of being used as a fucking chesspiece in some fancy game o' yer master's, so now ye're gonnae tell me what the hell's going on here, or I willnae be responsible for what I do to ye. D'ye understand me or will I say it again more southern?'

Shakespeare was white-faced and trembling. 'I...er...I understand,' he panted.

'So.' Dodd leaned one arm against the wall in front of Shakespeare, blocking him with his body. 'I'm waiting.'

'Er...I really don't know...very much.'

'Och,' said Dodd with false sympathy. 'That's a terrible pity. I'll have to kill ye on general principles then.'

Dodd hadn't even bothered to draw his blade nor lay hands on Shakespeare, but for some reason the little poet believed him.

'I...I don't know where to start.'

'Ye're the man that told Heneage that Sir Robert was on his way south, ay?'

Shakespeare nodded. 'I told Marlowe, though.'

'When did he warn ye to do that?'

'About August, I think.'

'How did ye tell him? In person?'

'No, in writing, in code. I leave messages with a...a trustworthy person who passes them on.'

'Who is the person?'

Shakespeare shook his head. 'I can't tell you.'

Dodd considered beating the name out of him, but decided not to since he didn't want to draw attention to himself.

'What's Heneage's game? What's he trying to do?'

Shakespeare looked at the ground. 'I don't know. Why would he tell me?'

'All right. What's he told ye to find out?'

'He...er...I think he wants to know anything about my lord Baron Hunsdon that will discredit him with the Queen. He also wants to know where Edmund Carey is. That's quite urgent. He's been quartering London for the man.'

Dodd blinked and looked hard at Shakespeare, who was swallowing and trembling in front of him. He was not a fighting man and although he was a poet and must be good at lying, he didn't look as if he was lying now. In which case, what the hell was going on? Dodd had been convinced that Heneage had put Edmund Carey in the Fleet, possibly into Bolton's Ward as well. But if Heneage didn't know where he was...And wanted to find him...?

Dodd changed plan. 'What are ye here for?'

'To talk to you, find out if you needed anything.'

Dodd scowled deeper which made Shakespeare shrink back against the wall.

'Who sent ye?'

'I can't...er...tell you.'

'And why not?'

'B...because I...I'm more frightened of them than I am of you, sir,' said Shakespeare with a desperate glint of humour.

Against his will Dodd let out a short bark of laughter. 'Ay. Well, that's because ye dinna know me sae well.'

'I don't think so.'

'Bide there while I think what to do.'

Dodd looked around him for inspiration and scowled. The complexity of the situation was making his head hurt. His immediate impulse had been to send Shakespeare hotfoot to Somerset House to roust out Lord Hunsdon and bring him to the gaol to fetch his son. But the messenger was tainted. The likelihood was that a verbal message would go straight to Heneage or the mysterious person that scared the poet so much, and a written message the same. For a moment Dodd thought about codes but he didn't know any and besides, it stood to reason that experienced intriguers like Heneage or even Shakespeare would know more about secret writing than he did. He couldn't even tell Shakespeare simply to fetch Lord Hunsdon for the same reasons. He couldn't send the man to fetch Barnabus or Simon Barnet because they had the plague and were probably dead by now.

'I've got naething for ye to do, because I canna trust ye,' he said to Shakespeare, leaning towards him. The poet was trying to burrow backwards into the wall. 'If ye had a particle of decency in ye, ye'd go tell my Lord Hunsdon where I am and why, but as ye dinna, I willnae waste my breath asking ye to.'

'I...I'm sorry.'

Dodd drew back disgustedly. 'Och,' he said. 'Piss off. Ye're dirtying my nice clean gaol.'

Shakespeare sidled past him and into the courtyard, then scurried across it looking pinched about the mouth. Dodd spat in his wake.

For a moment Dodd thought of paying the money that would get Edmund Carey moved out of the stinking disgrace of the beggars' ward but then it occurred to him that any action like that would probably be reported to Heneage within the hour and Heneage would want to know why he was so solicitous of a stranger—might well make the connection.

It occurred to him that there was one thing he could do without giving away any secrets, since it would be expected of him. He went back into the courtyard and over to the table covered with a higgledy piggledy array of things, including a lump of rock covered in dust that the dog-eared notice by it claimed to be gold ore. There, after considerable haggling, he bought himself paper, pen and ink and sat down cross-legged with his back to a corner and a stone in front of him for a writing table. He hated paperwork. He knew his ability to write, which was rare among the Borderers, had helped him get his place in the Carlisle garrison as Sergeant, but he still hated it. The effort of making up words and then forming the letters for them always made his head hurt and his hand sweat. He avoided the labour as much as he could but this time there was no help for it.

***

Peter Cheke had gone to bed after another night of desperate labour against the plague, also ending in failure. He had slept the dreamless headlong sleep of exhaustion and woken very late in full daylight, feeling thirsty and still exhausted. He had even slept through the bells calling him to church. As he went to the window to look out into the street, he saw a tall man in ill-fitting homespun russet jogtrotting purposefully through the crowds, straight to his locked shop door.

The hammering resounded up the stairs and Cheke stood staring down at the statute cap of the man, overwhelmed with helpless misery. Yet another desperate father, begging for something, anything to save his babies, his wife, offering every penny he had for healing Cheke knew he could not give, as if salvation could be bought.

Eventually he put on his gown and hat, went down to open the door and tell the poor fool to begone.

At first he didn't recognise the man because of the conflicting signals of clothes and bearing and the fact that his hair and face were dirty. By the time he had worked it out, Carey had pushed his way into the shop and shut the door behind him.

'What...er...what can I do for you, sir?' he asked nervously.

'Mr Cheke,' said Carey. 'I've come to you because I have nowhere else to start. I must know where Dr Jenkins performed his alchemy.'

'Sir, I gave my word...'

'I know you did. But what if they were coney-catching? What if the process you saw was not alchemy at all, had nothing whatever to do with the Philosopher's Stone, but was a well-known goldsmithing mystery called parcel-gilding?'

'I am sure it was the true art, sir, as sure as my life.'

'Then let's prove it. Have you scales?'

'Yes.'

'Do you have any of the angels that were made?'

'I...I was given a fee, yes.'

'Excellent. I have here a true angel direct from Mr van Emden on Cheapside.' He took out a small yellow coin and tossed it, snapped it out of the air and showed it to Cheke, the Archangel Michael, battling the dragon, bright and fine upon it.

Angry at this bland certainty that Carey was right and he was wrong, Cheke led the way silently to the kitchen of the house, and brought out his scales. Then from a loose brick by the oven, he took one of the angels he had seen made and struck and brought it over.

Ten seconds later the last bastion of Cheke's world had fallen, for the pan with the true angel on it dipped much lower than the one he had been given by the worshipful Dr Jenkins.

He took the others out, checked them against Carey's coin.

'Yours is full of lead,' he said, desperately.

'No, Mr Cheke,' said Carey wearily. 'Lead weighs less than gold. Look how thin mine is, how much it weighs. You were coney-catched, Mr Cheke, like others before you, and like my brother, who was the gentleman investing in the project.'

'We weighed them at the...the place.'

'Who supplied the scales?'

'Dr Jenkins.' Cheke looked at the flagstones. 'But...'

'You know yourself it's not so very hard to alter the balance arm of a pair of scales so it's biased one way or the other.'

Cheke put his head in his hands and fought not to weep. Carey paused and then said quite softly, 'I am not claiming that the transmutation of matter, that the goal of alchemy, is impossible. I am only saying that you yourself have not yet seen it done.'

'You have no idea,' said Cheke, his voice muffled. 'You don't know how happy I was. I have spent most of my life seeking out the truth of matter, trying to understand God's mind therein. And to know it had been done, to know that someone had succeeded... It didn't matter to me that it was not I that did it, only that it had been done. That God had vouchsafed a little of his mystery...'

'Mr Cheke, I'm sorry. I must know. Where did the process take place? Where were the angels made?'

For a moment Cheke burned with rage and hatred for Carey and then the fire died inside him, to be replaced with a grey hopelessness.

'In the Blackfriars monastery, in the old kitchen where there is a fireplace we altered to be a furnace. The gentleman had a key.'

'Of course he did. And with the noise of hemp-beating in the Bridewell prison nobody would hear the sound of the coins being struck.'

'Yes, sir, that's right.'

Carey smiled at him. 'Come on, Mr Cheke. I want to see it.'

He hadn't the energy to resist any more. He stood and went with Carey. They threaded through the back streets of the city, behind Knightrider Street and St Peter's, alleys pockmarked with red painted crosses in some places and utterly normal in others.

Getting into the Blackfriars was made a little complicated by the fact that for some reason, Carey did not want to go through the gatehouse and the cloisters. Instead they went down St Andrew's Hill to Puddle Wharf and round the remains of the monastery walls that way, threading between the newly built houses to a much older, swaybacked stone building separate from the Blackfriar's hall.

Carey tried the door, but it was locked.

'The gentleman had a key to it,' offered Cheke.

Carey nodded. 'Yes, he would. I think my father owns this part too. Well, let's see.'

Carey padded restlessly round the whole building, disturbing a goat in its shed, craning his neck to look at the high windows and the massive chimney.

'Come on, where is it?' he said to himself.

'What?'

'I never saw a kitchen yet that only had one door. Where did the servants collect the food, where's the hatch?'

'Hatch?'

Carey looked across a tiny jakes-cluttered yard at the Blackfriar's hall, jutting above the rooftops with its buttressing, narrowed his eyes as he followed some invisible notional path and came up against the goat shed again.

'Must be,' he said, and barged into the shed where the goat bleated in fright. There were a couple of bangs and crashes. 'Come and give me a hand with this,' he ordered Cheke.

After sidling past the goat who stared with those unnervingly cold slit-eyes of hers, Cheke saw that Carey had managed to wrench two planks from the back wall of the lean-to shed and had uncovered what was obviously a serving hatch. They both tried to lift it, but it was stuck fast and so Carey simply picked up a stone that must have been used for milking and battered through the old wood. It gave in a shower of musty-smelling dust and Carey tutted.

'It's got dry-rot,' he said. 'We'll have to demolish it.' He climbed up onto the sill and pushed through the hole he'd made; Cheke followed him, borne along by Carey's certainty. The goat stuck her head through the gap after them, bleating with interest.

Very little daylight was filtering through the high glassed windows. A huge table stood in the middle of the flagged floor; the vast fireplace was empty except for its rusting fire-irons and spit. They had used the chimney from the smaller charcoal fireplace on the other wall because it was narrower than the great fireplace and the airflow was more easily controlled. Where the monks' food had been sinfully soused with complex spiced sauces, Peter Cheke had built a small closed-in furnace with stones and cement, sealed with clay. His own pair of bellows lay at one of the air-holes.

Carey hunted around until he found what he was looking for; a whole treetrunk made into a block, with a small neat round hole set into it. The mallet lay nearby.

'Now where are they?' he muttered to himself and began digging in the cupboards. In one he found a dusty academic gown and what Cheke at first took for a dead cat, until he picked it up and found it was a false beard such as players used at the theatre.

It was all too ridiculous for words. Cheke remembered his joy and pride at being present when Dr Jenkins produced the scrapings of the Philosopher's Stone, of actually admiring the curly dark beard, streaked with grey, that was now tangled with the noble doctor's gown. He started to snigger helplessly.

'What is it?' asked Carey, emerging from another cubbyhole, covered in dust.

Cheke couldn't stop. 'He...I think...this is all that's left of Dr Jenkins.'

Carey glanced at the gown and false beard. 'Of course it is.'

'Do you know who played the part?'

'I don't know. I suspect. Was the good doctor bald?'

'Yes.'

'Thought so. Well if the coin dies are here, I don't know where. Do you know?'

'I think that the gentleman had them. He told me he had bought them off a retired mint-master fallen on hard times who had kept a trussel and pile that should have been cancelled as an old design.'

'Hm. Are you convinced?'

'How was it done, sir?'

'Parcel-gilding—you dissolve ground-up gold in boiling mercury to make an amalgam. Then you spread the paste on your pewter rounds, fire it up in a furnace to drive off the mercury and out come your gilded coins.'

'So the Philosopher's Stone was only powdered gold?'

'That's right.'

Cheke shook his head. 'What a fool I've been.'

'Don't blame yourself. My brother was just as much a fool, if not worse.'

'Do you think Marlowe knew?'

'Of course he did. It was probably his idea.'

'What will you do now?'

Carey showed his teeth in an extremely unpleasant expression. 'I'm going to talk to him.'

SUNDAY, 3RD SEPTEMBER 1592, AFTERNOON

Marlowe waited at the Mermaid where the innkeeper was afraid of him as well as being an employee of sorts. He ate the ordinary which was a pheasant in a wine sauce with summer peas and a bag pudding to follow, and he drank the best wine they had which was always brought to him. As was only right the innkeeper refused his money.

He watched the people coming in and out of the common room, eating, drinking, talking, kissing their women. How could they think they were important, he wondered, since they lived like cattle in the narrow fields where they were born, according to the rules of their herd, and never looked up to the stars or out to the horizons? His father had lived like that, perfectly happy to make shoes all his life and taking an inordinate stupid pride in the smallness and evenness of his stitches and the good fit he produced. As a boy, Kit Marlowe could remember the boiling of angry boredom under his ribs while his father tried to explain how the strange curved shapes he cut out in leather would bend and be stitched together to form a solid boot. Once the silly man had tried his hand at sermonising: When it's flat, see how strange it looks, he had said, oddly tender, and then when it's made, see what a fit shape it was. Perhaps our lives are like that, Kit: strangely shaped when we are alive and then when we die, we see how the very strangeness made us better fit our Maker.

Even as a child I rebelled at being told I was God's shoe, Marlowe thought, and rightly.

'Sir,' said a low nervous voice beside him. Marlowe woke out of his thoughts and blinked at his man.

'Yes,' he said, not bothering to hide his impatience.

'A woman and a boy went into Somerset House,' said the man, sweating with his run up Fleet Street. 'We thought you'd better know.'

'A boy?'

'Yessir.'

'The same one?'

'Yessir.'

'Well, why didn't you stop them?'

'We weren't sure and anyway you never told us to.'

Marlowe rolled his eyes. 'I assume Carey wasn't with them.'

'Oh, no, sir, we never saw him.'

'You got the message that he's in disguise, wearing homespun?'

'Yessir. But we never saw him. We'd have stopped any man, just to be sure, but it was just an old woman and a boy.'

'A short old woman, built like a barrel?'

'Er...yessir.'

'Well, it's a pity you didn't stop them, but I don't suppose it matters that much. Off you go, keep your eyes open.'

The man pulled his forelock and sidled away. Marlowe tapped his fingers on the table and thought. Carey had evidently gone back to his lodgings despite the plague-cross on the door which Marlowe hadn't thought he would. He couldn't watch every place; he had the main roads out of the city covered; he had Somerset House under watch and the Fleet prison, but even with all the men at his disposal he couldn't cover everywhere. Perhaps he should have kept a man at Carey's lodgings, but then it had never crossed his mind that the Courtier would go into a plague house just for a couple of servants.

Damn him, where was he? Hadn't he worked it out yet? Was even Carey too bovine and stupid to understand what Marlowe was about? He ought to have enough information at his disposal by now, especially with the massive hint of Dodd's arrest. So where was he?

It occurred to Marlowe that perhaps Carey was lunatic enough to go to the Fleet to find his henchman. This was the trouble with real people as opposed to the shadows who danced in his head when he wrote plays: the real thing was so hard to predict.

Marlowe knew he should stay where he was and receive messages, Munday had told him often enough he was too impatient, but he was bored and worried and he could see the structure of his plan crumbling around him because of Carey who didn't know his proper place in it. Shakespeare hadn't come back from the Fleet yet either. He didn't think the ambitious little player had the imagination to know what was happening but he couldn't be sure.

'Damn it,' Marlowe said to himself and pushed away his half-finished ordinary, which was now as cold as a nobleman's dinner. He put on his hat and went and told the innkeeper to hold any messages for him until he came back and then went out into the sunlight, heading up Water Lane towards Ludgate and the Fleet prison.

Just as he passed through the old Blackfriar's Gateway, a tall fellow came up to him and pulled at his cap.

'Ah've a message for ye, sir,' came the guttural northern tones. Marlowe paused. 'Yes, what is it?'

The tall northerner moved up swiftly, caught his arm and twisted it up behind his back, rammed him bodily through the little door where the monks' porter had sat and into a dusty tiny room full of bits of padding, petticoats and sausages of cloth. Marlowe was shoved into a pile of the things, stinking of women and old linen; the grip on his arm shifted slightly but when he tried to struggle free, it was twisted and lifted so that pain lancing up through his shoulder joint made him gasp. He couldn't see, he could hardly breathe and now somebody's knee was in the small of his back, hurting him there and there was the cold scratch of a knife at the side of his throat.

'The message is,' came a familiar voice behind him, 'don't fucking play silly games with me, Marlowe, I'm tired of it.'

He'd been waiting, Marlowe realised dimly, bucking and gasping in an effort to find a way to breathe, and he's very angry. Half-suffocated and with lights beginning to flash in his eyes, Marlowe tried to say something, only to feel the knee dig harder into his back; the knife moved from his neck and Carey was fumbling for his other hand.

No, thought Marlowe, he's not going to tie me up. He grabbed desperately to move the bumrolls out from under his head, found the end of one and whipped it round as hard as he could left-handed in the direction of Carey's face. If you were willing to hurt yourself more, there was a way out of an armlock. Marlowe heaved convulsively to the left, felt Carey's weight slip, and punched still blind with his left hand for Carey's groin. He hit something, heard a gasp, scrambled out of the pile of underwear and got to a wall where he stood up and drew his sword.

Carey already had his sword and dagger drawn, crossed in front of him. Behind him the door was shut. The room was so small, their swords were already inches from each other's face.

'The Queen's going to be very angry when I get blood on her bumrolls,' said Carey conversationally. 'Why not surrender?'

'Do you really think you can kill me?' Marlowe asked, his heart beating hard with excitement and the fresh air in his lungs.

Carey grinned at him, looking much more like a wild northerner than the Queen's courtier Marlowe had known. 'Oh yes, if I want to.'

'But you don't want to, or you would have, already,' said Marlowe with absolute certainty.

'I want a few answers.'

'I'm sorry. I thought you knew them all.'

Marlowe was deliberately trying to annoy Carey into an attack. In such a small space his primitive broadsword was a positive liability against Marlowe's rapier. The glittering poignard was a much better weapon for close quarters, but that was in Carey's left hand.

To Marlowe's surprise and irritation, Carey laughed. He straightened slightly, though he kept his weapons *en garde*.

'You silly bugger,' he said, almost affectionately. 'You know you wanted to talk to me, tell me how clever you are. That's why you were hanging around in the Mermaid all morning, all on your lonely own. Do you think I don't know bait when I see it? So talk to me. Tell me your magnificent plan. Watch me gasp with admiration.'

'This wasn't how I'd intended to do it.'

'No, I'll bet it wasn't. Me in irons, no doubt, and you with the thumbscrews to aid my concentration.'

'Not quite like that,' murmured Marlowe, inspiration at his shoulder as it usually was in times like this. 'Is that what happened to you in Scotland?'

Carey had no gloves on since his own were no doubt far too fine to go with the baggy homespun he was wearing. Several of his fingernails were only half grown and Marlowe knew one thing that did that.

Carey's face tightened and lost some of its good humour. After a pause he answered, quite softly, 'Yes, it was.' The silence stretched a little and Marlowe suddenly found the look in Carey's eyes frightening.

'I didn't plan anything like that,' he said hesitantly. 'I promise you.'

'Oh really?' Carey's voice was still soft and inexplicably

terrifying. 'What about Heneage?'

'I'm not working for him at the moment.'

'You're commanding a lot of his men. I recognize them.'

'Well, he doesn't know that yet.'

Carey laughed, still quietly. 'What the devil are you up to, Marlowe? What do you want?'

Marlowe took a deep breath. 'I want to work for my lord Earl of Essex. Not Heneage.'

'What? Essex hates your guts.'

'I know that. I was hoping you might...er...intercede.'

Carey's eyebrows often seemed to have a life of their own. One went up, almost to his hairline. 'Me?'

'Yes. You're still his man, aren't you?'

'I am. So?'

'He'll listen to you; he has in the past.'

'He might.'

'You could at least get me an audience, so I can put my case.'

Carey barked a laugh. 'You don't know him very well, do you, Kit? And you haven't given me one reason yet why I should do a damned thing for you.'

'No,' Marlowe sighed, thought for a minute and decided to gamble that Carey hadn't been completely changed by his service in France and the North. He tossed his rapier onto the dusty floor and sat down on a pile of under-petticoats. Carey blinked, then smiled and sheathed his broadsword, squatting down peasant-style with his back against the door. He held his poignard in his right hand though, which Marlowe thought was probably fair enough.

'Heneage wants to be Lord Chamberlain,' Marlowe began. 'He wants the power over the Queen he believes your father has.'

'He's an idiot. The Queen...'

'The Queen's a woman and can be influenced.' Carey's eyebrows said he didn't think so, but Marlowe continued. 'In any case, it doesn't matter what's true, it matters what Heneage believes. Heneage has been trying very hard to find a way to discredit your father in her eyes, but it's difficult. Your father's so bloody honest, so far he's just ignored all the attempts Heneage has made.' Carey grinned. 'Or the Queen has. Now this summer Heneage ran some kind of operation involving your brother Edmund—I'm not clear what, since I wasn't involved then—which should have got your brother arrested on a capital charge, probably treason, thus giving Heneage the lever he's always wanted against your father. But just before the net closed, your brother disappeared, and when he did, he had some evidence that would have got Heneage into trouble. So the Vice Chamberlain has been combing London for your brother, just as your father has. When he sent for you to come back from Newcastle...'

'Carlisle,' corrected Carey.

'Wherever, Heneage decided that one son was as good as another and besides, if he had you, Edmund might come out of hiding. So he made sure that the bailiffs knew you were coming...'

'Did you kill Michael?'

'Who?'

'The servant my father sent to warn me off?'

'Oh, him. No, that was a mistake. Heneage wanted the footpads to stop him, not kill him.'

'He should have been more specific. And perhaps if he hadn't paid them with forged money, they might not have been so anxious to jump us,' said Carey in the soft tone of voice Marlowe found so worrying. 'Michael left a wife and children, you know?'

Marlowe shrugged. What was he supposed to do, weep for the man? 'The next thing Heneage decided was that perhaps we could take your henchman and use him to trap you...'

'Who, Dodd?'

'The northerner.'

'*Take* him?' Carey sounded very amused. 'What happened?'

'We didn't succeed.' Marlowe was annoyed. 'He got away from us.'

'Was the trollop and Nick the Gent you as well?'

Marlowe nodded. 'It wasn't a very good idea, but Heneage was getting impatient.'

'Why the hell didn't he just arrest me, Dodd, the lot of us? Why be so complicated?'

'How could he possibly arrest *you* on a charge of treason? The Queen would have hysterics. He wanted you imprisoned, but he didn't want to do it himself.'

'What's Shakespeare's part in all this?'

'Who? Oh, him.' Marlowe waved a dismissive hand, 'He's my informer in your father's house. He was supposed to keep an eye on you and report back. He's not much good.'

'He played the part of Dr Jenkins the alchemist well enough.' Marlowe eyed Carey unhappily. 'Oh?'

'Come on, Marlowe, don't try doling out your story like bloody ship's rations. You were there at the time, you organised the whole rigmarole with little Mr Shakespeare dressed up in a gown and a false beard to be an alchemist.'

Marlowe smiled reminiscently. 'He was really very convincing. I almost believed it myself.' He caught himself at the expression on Carey's face. 'I'm sorry. It was one of the things that made me decide to quit Heneage's service.'

'Oh, was it, indeed?' Carey's voice was soft. 'I wish I could believe that.'

Marlowe coughed. 'Why would I lie about it?'

'Why? I don't know. I think you've got so used to plotting and making people dance like puppets, you don't know what reality is any more. What about Greene? Did you poison him?'

Marlowe shook his head. 'Of course not, I wanted to know what he'd found out as well. We were sure he'd discovered something but the way he was drinking…Well, you saw him yourself. Nobody could get any sense out of him.'

'So how did he come to be poisoned?'

'I've no idea. I'm not the Devil, I'm not responsible for everything bad that happens.' Marlowe was sneering. 'Anyway, by this time, I'd decided that whatever Heneage was up to, I didn't like it. So when the order came to set the bailiffs on you again, I made sure they arrested the wrong man.'

'And put Dodd where?'

'In the Fleet, of course; it's the debtor's prison for this area. Also, I think your brother's there but I haven't been able to find him. He's not in the book and he's not visible.'

'Why do you think Edmund's in the Fleet?'

'Because Newton tried to spend some of the forged angels.'

'Ah.' Carey tossed his poignard from one hand to the other, making the jewels glitter. 'Does Heneage know that yet?'

'No.'

'And my servants?'

Marlowe sighed. 'That was Heneage again. He'd decided to take you himself and see what he could get out of you or...'

'Make me confess to?'

'Yes. It's how he thinks. I was with him when we broke into your lodgings, and all we found was your man dead of something that wasn't plague and the boy who was too stupid to tell us anything useful.'

'You left him tied up.'

'Heneage is planning to go back this evening when he's had time to think and...'

'And get thirsty and hungry and cramped? And terrified?'

'Well, yes. And then persuade him to tell us where you were and what you were up to, perhaps other things.'

Carey's eyes had become chips of ice. 'Confess to Papistry? Say I've been hiding Jesuits?'

Marlowe shrugged.

'You went along with this?'

'Heneage has done worse,' said Marlowe defensively. 'He's not like Walsingham.'

'No.'

'I've been trying to find you, have a meeting with you, all day... All I wanted was to explain...'

'You're a fool, Marlowe,' Carey said. 'Why didn't you just go to my father and tell him all this?'

'How could I possibly go into Somerset House with Shakespeare hanging around there?'

'Written him a letter?'

'You don't know much about how Heneage works, do you?'

'The other night, at the Mermaid?'

'With Poley there?'

Carey sighed. 'No,' he said. 'I think you enjoy the play too much, I think you like making people dance.'

Marlowe shrugged. 'I've talked to you now,' he said. 'What are you going to do?'

Carey told him.

***

Dodd had finished his letter, sealed it, and after careful enquiry among the stallholders had given it to the gaol servant who normally carried messages, along with a shilling to encourage him to deliver it. Obviously, it would be opened and read before it left the prison, but he had written it with an eye to that fact.

He sat in the sun and watched the activity around him, the children playing games in the dust, the women sewing, some of the men gambling or training rats or trying to press their suit with the women, some of whom were suspiciously well-dressed and vivacious. Apart from the glowering gaol servants and the men who were dragging chains around with them, it could have been a busy marketplace.

Dodd was just thinking wistfully of Janet and what she would make of him in his fine suit when three of the largest gaol servants came up to him, holding clubs. They looked worryingly purposeful and Dodd scrambled to his feet and looked for somewhere to run. Only there wasn't anywhere, of course: that was the whole point of a gaol.

Two of them grabbed him and twisted his arms behind him.

'What the hell is it now?' he growled. 'Why can ye no' leave me alone?'

'Sorry, Sir Robert,' said the third, sounding pleased. 'Orders.'

They started hustling him across the courtyard, causing the other prisoners to stare, into the gatehouse office, through another door and into what were obviously Newton's living quarters. There were four other men standing waiting for him. The one in the middle, dressed in dark brocade and a fur-trimmed velvet gown, looked familiar with his smug moon-face and small pink lips. His expression wasn't smug, however. It had started that way but as soon as it caught sight of Dodd it changed, ran through puzzlement, incredulity, horror and ended in rage. Then it went blank.

'I told you to fetch Sir Robert Carey,' he snapped.

'Yessir,' said the gaol servant who had spoken before. 'This is him, sir.'

227

Under the plumpness, jaw-muscles clenched. 'No, it isn't, you fool. It's his henchman, Cod or Pod, or whatever his name is.'

'Dodd, sir. Sergeant Henry Dodd, o' Gilsland. Mr Heneage, is it no'?'

'Where's your master?'

'Och,' said Dodd sadly, his heart thumping hard. 'I wish I knew that maself, sir. Only I don't. I wis arrested in mistake for him and that's the last I saw of him.'

'You? In mistake for him?' Heneage's face was incredulous again.

'Ay, sir,' said Dodd. 'It's a puzzle to me too, sir. I dinna look anything like him, but there it is.'

'Where's Carey gone then?'

'I told ye, sir, I dinna ken.'

'Don't try that half-witted northerner game with me, Dodd, I know you know.'

'I dinna, sir. Sorry.'

The blow when it came was open-handed to the side of Dodd's head, and hard enough to make his teeth rattle. It hurt, but Dodd had been hit much worse than that in his life, many times, and that wasn't what he found frightening: it was the considering expression on Heneage's face, the sort of expression boys wear when they take the wings off flies to see what they do. Heneage hadn't been angry, hadn't lashed out in a rage like most men. He had taken a cold considered decision to strike Dodd, to see how he would react.

If he could, Dodd would have hit him back, beaten him to pulp, Queen's Vice Chamberlain or not, but he was being held too tightly by men who knew how to do it.

'We'll take him anyway,' said Heneage to someone who was standing behind Dodd.

'Would you sign the book, please, sir?' said Newton, his face twisted with deference. 'Only the trustees get...'

'This man isn't the one I wanted.'

'Yes, well, would you sign it anyway, sir? Seeing as it's not my fault?'

Heneage tutted and clicked his fingers. Newton brought the

logbook over, held the inkpot while Heneage wrote swiftly in the space next to Dodd's name.

'Are you bailing him, sir?'

'No, I'm transferring him.'

'The warrant...'

'This is the Queen's business, Newton, don't interfere.'

Dodd knew that phrase; Carey had told it to him. 'I'm no' a Papist,' he said. 'And I'm no' a traitor, neither.'

Heneage looked at him fishily. 'I think you're lying,' he said conversationally. 'We'll go to Chelsea where we can talk, as I suggested a few days ago, remember?'

And Carey had told him what that meant. Dodd felt cold.

'What d'ye want from me?' he asked.

'I want the whereabouts of your master or his brother. It's quite simple. When you've told me, I'll have no further interest in you.'

Dodd drew a long shaky breath and thought quite seriously for several seconds about simply telling him that Edmund Carey was sick near to death a few yards away in Bolton's Ward, in the name of Edward Morgan. He thought about it, part of him wanted desperately to do it, but he couldn't. He couldn't give a sick man to Heneage to save his skin, even if it hadn't been Carey's own brother. Not that he particularly liked the blasted Courtier or his family, it had very little to do with them, only something inside Dodd set hard into an obstinate rock and wouldn't allow it.

Heneage was watching him very shrewdly. 'Yes,' he said, mainly to himself. 'You do know something. Well, that's good.' He smiled. 'Come along, now, we haven't got all day.'

Dodd was not at all surprised to find his arms being manacled behind him by one of Heneage's men who then prodded him in the back. Heneage swept out of the Fleet prison with Dodd in the middle of his entourage and out into Fleet Lane where a carriage stood, drawn by four horses. Somebody opened the door, somebody else shoved Dodd up the steps and into the dimness, forced him to sit on a leather-covered bench. The carriage creaked sideways on its leather straps as Heneage and another man got in and sat down on the bench facing him.

'Lie down,' said Heneage.

'What?'

The other man's gauntleted hand cracked across Dodd's face. 'Do as you're told.'

Slowly, staring at Heneage all the time, Dodd laid himself awkwardly down, sideways on the padded leather, sniffling at the annoying blood trickling out of his nose. Heneage's subordinate put a blanket over his head, something that must have been used for horses in the past because the smell of them was pungent. Dodd found it comforting, it reminded him of home. What would Janet do when she heard she was a widow? Marry again, certainly, being the heiress she was; probably she would forget him since she hadn't even a bairn to remember him by. The men of his troop might drink to his memory a couple of times, Red Sandy would remember him, but in a few years he would fade as others had. Even Long George had left more of a mark than he would.

Would he go to heaven? Privately he doubted it, especially after his sin of venery with the whore, so that was no comfort either. When he was dead, he would face an angry God who would know exactly how many of his bills were foul.

The carriage jerked and bounced along the streets, its iron-shod wheels clattering and scraping where the way was paved and then rumbling and squeaking and bouncing even worse where the road was dusty and rock hard from the sun. Dodd didn't know which way it was going since he didn't know where Chelsea was and the movement and the stifling darkness of the blanket were making him feel sick.

Should he tell Heneage about Edmund Carey? Would it help? No, he decided it wouldn't, because if Heneage was like Richie Graham of Brackenhill, admitting that much would only convince him Dodd must know more and that would make everything worse, not better.

There wasn't anything he could do except hope that the Courtier, who had run like a rabbit from the bailiffs that morning, would find a way of helping him. Would he? The Carey that Dodd knew in Carlisle would, he thought, certainly. The Carey Dodd had seen in London—he wasn't sure. He didn't know the man so well. Liked him even less.

The coldness Dodd felt inside wasn't helping him against the heat of the day and the blanket, and the wool suit didn't help either. Drops of sweat were trickling down his back and chest under his shirt and his left arm was going to sleep because he was lying on it. He tried to move into a more comfortable position and was kicked in the shins. He sighed. There wasn't any point in frightening himself even more by imagining all the things that might happen to him and at the moment there wasn't anything else he could think of. All he could do was wait. Luckily, he was good at that.

Dodd relaxed and did what he always did when he was lying in ambush. He thought back to when he was a boy in Upper Tynedale, an unimportant middle son in a string of them that made his father proud, a cheeky bright lad that his mother insisted on sending to school to the Reverend Gilpin when he was in the area. When he wasn't learning his letters and listening to the Reverend tell him of the hellfire that waited for reivers, he was running about the hills, herding cattle or sheep, potting the occasional rabbit with his sling, fishing in the Tyne, fighting his brothers, playing football. His mother as he remembered her then was plump and almost always either suckling a babe or round-bellied with another one, plodding in stately fashion after the particular hen she had decided to kill for the pot. She would corner it against the wooden wall of their pele and then squat down and wait patiently for the stupid creature to stop fluttering, calm down and start scratching, at which point she would grab, pull and twist and the hen would be dead. Dodd smiled fondly under his blanket; she had told him once when he had asked her in childish awe if she had a special charm for chickens, that people always wasted a lot of effort chasing after something that would come to them if they waited.

The rocking and jolting stopped and Heneage pulled the blanket off his captive, only to find him fast asleep and smiling. It faded the smug expression on his face more effectively than any defiance and he punched and slapped Dodd awake like a schoolboy.

Dodd, who always hated being woken, reared up and tried to headbutt him, only to be stopped by his henchman after a confused scuffle.

'Och, whit the hell d'ye want?' he demanded.

'Edmund Carey's whereabouts,' said Heneage, straightening his gown and dusting himself off fastidiously. 'Or his brother's.'

'Piss off. Ah dinna ken where they are.'

Heneage sighed and shook his head with theatrical regret and waved at the henchman. 'Keep clear of his face,' he said. 'And don't kill him.' He went down the carriage steps, making it lean and creak again, and at his nod another heavyset man went up them, holding a short cosh in his hand, and shut the carriage door behind him.

There was a short silence and then Heneage heard the northerner's voice, sullen and contemptuous. 'Och, get on wi' it then.'

That was followed by a crash and a series of thumps and grunts that made the carriage rock. Heneage looked about him. They were parked in a corner of Salisbury Court, where the noise of the carpenter's yard next door in Hanging Sword Court would disguise most of the noise. The people passing through the court were mainly Frenchmen, servants of the French ambassador, and the rest were men who worked for Heneage, watching the Papists' coming and going. He had decided against going to Chelsea immediately simply because it was a long way and took several hours in a coach and he wanted to be able to get back to Whitefriars before the London gates shut officially. He had driven around the lanes and streets for a while to see if the motion of the coach would upset the northerner's stomach, but that had been a failure. The blasted yokel had gone to sleep.

It was always a difficult balance to strike. Given enough time, Heneage could guarantee to crack any man, usually without even having to damage him too much, so he could be executed without the fickle London mob feeling too sorry for him. He had found that lack of sleep, hunger and thirst would do the job more effectively than Topcliffe and all his ingenuity. But Heneage had a strong feeling that he didn't have very much time. He was walking on a thin crust over a quicksand and there were too many things he didn't know: Marlowe was supposed to arrest Sir Robert Carey, Marlowe knew him well, and Marlowe had managed to arrest this useless northern bumpkin instead. How was it possible? Marlowe was usually far more reliable than that. Had he betrayed Heneage?

Surely not, surely he wouldn't dare.

As a result, Carey was still loose in London and had been for several hours when Heneage had thought he was safely caught. What had he been doing? Had he managed to reach his father, despite the cordon of watchers around Somerset House? Surely he hadn't worked out what was going on? Had he found his brother? Had Edmund Carey come out of hiding and met him? There were so many perplexities, the whole thing depended now on Heneage finding Edmund Carey first, damn the man for an unreliable drunk and a thief.

The rocking carriage had settled down to a steady rhythm. Heneage watched, thinking of ways and means. After a while, he banged the flat of his hand on the carriage door.

'That's enough, open up,' he ordered. After his henchman had swung down from the carriage, he climbed the steps and looked at the northerner who was on his knees on the narrow floor, hunched in a ball and making the soft pants and moans men make when they think they're being stoically silent.

'Get him on the bench, I want to talk to him again.'

Heneage's man kicked the northerner. 'Get up.'

The northerner stayed where he was, probably hadn't heard. 'You'll have to help him.'

In the end it took both of them to heave the northerner back onto the bench, where he sat still hunched and wheezing.

'You're being very foolish, you know,' Heneage said sadly. 'I'd always thought Borderers were sensible folk who know when something is quite hopeless.'

The man lifted his head and made a coughing noise which Heneage realised was actually a breathless chuckle. He said something indistinct. Heneage reached across, took a handful of hair and lifted his head a bit more.

'What did you say?'

'Ah said...ye dinna ken any of us then.'

'Edmund Carey,' said Heneage. 'Where is he? I know you know where he is. Tell me and this will stop.'

The Borderer showed his teeth in a grin and spat as copiously as he could in Heneage's face.

***

Mistress Julie Granville had been sewing ruffs for a long time and quite enjoyed the work. Sitting in the shade of an awning with the other respectable women in the gaol, her fingers flew as she hemmed the narrow twelve yards of linen that would eventually decorate somebody's neck. She didn't even need to look at what she was doing any more: her fingers worked automatically making a very soft rhythmic sound, of the prick as the needle went in and out, the tap of her thimble pushing it, the drawing sound as the thread passed through. She was sitting where she could watch the gatehouse to see the return of the man who had promised to help her unfortunate gentleman in Bolton's Ward. She was worried about him. The gaol servants had grabbed him in the way they used when they were about to give someone a beating. For all she knew he might be in the Hole already, though generally Newton made a big production of it when he was ill-treating some poor creature: he would make sure everyone knew so they would fear him more.

Some people were at the gate, haggling with the guard there over the garnish he wanted to let them in to visit their friends, as they said. It was only about an hour after the northerner had been taken away, but her ears caught the different sound and rhythm from one of the servingmen, the same sound Henry Dodd's voice had had.

She looked at him, hoping it was Dodd. It wasn't. This was somebody taller, dressed country-style in a completely fashionless suit that didn't fit him properly and a leather jerkin, somebody with wavy dark red hair. She blinked and squinted, catching her breath: he looked so like Edmund when he first came to the gaol, only younger and less stocky, so much the same swagger in his walk, the same humorous smile, the same...She knew she had gone pale and then flushed. Of course she had been lonely in the summer and she knew how wrong was the heady rush of feelings that had struck her like a summer storm when she talked to Edmund that first time, after her son had accidentally hit him with a flung stone meant for a rat...But he had been rueful and sympathetic, allowing her to bandage his ear where the stone had clipped it, even interceding to save the little boy from her anger. When he looked at her she felt he looked at her as if she were another man, not just a woman to be seduced or ignored. No, that was wrong: not another man, but as if she were his equal, as if he thought of her as a person and was prepared to like her. He had been gentlemanly, he had made none of the usual suggestions that the men in the gaol routinely tried on all the women not over the age of sixty nor deformed, he had been respectable and friendly. It had been the most seductive experience of her life. In her heart she had fallen into sin at once, without any coaxing from Edmund.

Now here it was again, unmistakeable: the same energy, the same flamboyance, though subtly different. After Edmund took sick with the gaol-fever and she had nursed him, he had raved in delirium about himself, his brothers, his father, his mother, as men do when they don't know what they're saying. That was when she had learned his true name and begged him to write to his father to bail him out and he had adamantly refused. He had spoken of his younger brother with a wistful, envious admiration and then as the fever disordered his brain more and more, with a touching concern, begging her not to let Robin or Philly see him in such a state...

Julie Granville put down her sewing carefully on the piece of canvas she used to wrap it in when she wasn't working. Then she stood up, dusted off her skirt, adjusted her cap and ruff and walked across the courtyard to where Edmund's brother was squatting, talking gently to some of the children playing knuckle bones in the dust.

'...a man in a blackberry-coloured suit, a bit shorter than me and stronger-built with a very glum face and funny way o' talking like this? Have you seen anyone like that? I might pay as much as a shilling to someone who could tell me about him...'

'Yes, I seen 'im, sir,' said one of the urchins. ''E was the one wot Mr Gaoler Newton's men was going to give a leatherin' to, they took 'im out of the courtyard an hour ago.'

'Where did they take him?'

'Mr Newton's lodgings, and there was strangers here, a fat man in brocade and velvet wiv lots of servants...'

Ceremoniously Edmund's brother handed over a sixpence. 'I'll give you the other half of the shilling if it turns out you're telling the truth. Now have any of you seen another man, a gentleman who looks like me...'

She shouldn't address him as Sir Robert. He was wearing a country farmer's clothing and his face and hands were dirty, he must be in disguise, though his boots fitted him far too well to belong to a farmer. She coughed and held her hands tightly together over her apron. He looked up at her cautiously, smiled, stood, took off his hat and just stopped himself at the beginning of what would surely have been a very magnificent court bow.

'Are you...are you called Robin?' she asked.

The intensity of his blue gaze shook her. 'What of it, mistress?' he asked with a strong northern sound in his voice.

She must be careful. What if he was one of Edmund's enemies, one of the men he was hiding from? Just because he looked so like Edmund didn't necessarily mean they were brothers, and perhaps there was some other urgent reason why Edmund didn't want his family told. Family members could hate each other more bitterly than mere enemies, as she knew to her cost.

How could she check? Inspiration came from one of the many nights she had spent sitting next to Edmund as he fought and raved, trying to cool him down with Thames water, fanning him with her apron.

'Goodman, can you tell me who taught you to ride?' she asked.

Blue eyes narrowed, the man frowned. 'It was my brother, mistress, why?'

'What was his name?'

'Edmund.'

'Can you tell me what...how you treated him at the first lesson?'

The frown got heavier. Oh God, what if she was wrong? What if this was Heneage's man...

'Why?'

'Please, bear with me.'

'Well...' he grinned infectiously. 'I'm afraid I bit him. I'd fallen off and he was making me get back on again, so I bit his ear. Drew blood too.'

'What happened?'

'No, you tell *me* what happened.'

She smiled, pleased that he had good sense. 'He shouted, the pony bolted and you both got into trouble because it broke into a garden and ate the peas.'

He had caught her arms, was leaning down to stare into her eyes and she caught a faint spicy lavender smell from him, under the normal musk that no man produced naturally, which confirmed her opinion that he was not wearing his own clothes.

'Where is he, mistress? Yes, my name's Robin, I'm his brother. Can you take me to him? Did he send you?'

It was the shadow of desire to feel Edmund's brother's hands on her and she flushed, stepped back. He let go at once.

'Please, mistress, I've been combing London for him…Is he all right? Is he still alive?'

For answer she turned, led him across the courtyard to the steps down, paid an ill-afforded penny to the gaol servant who was dozing there on a stool to let them in. Robin looked up and around at the darkness and stink of Bolton's Ward, his nostrils flaring. She went across towards where Edmund lay, and saw him move feebly, trying to turn away, hide his face. Robin spotted him too, lengthened his stride and was there first, kneeling on the slimy stones, bending, catching his brother's shoulders, lifting him, embracing him. She smiled to see it, then turned away so they could have some privacy.

When she approached, Robin had sat back on his haunches.

'What the hell were you playing at?' he was demanding in a furious whisper. 'Father's been searching for you for weeks, why the devil didn't you send a message? Why in hell did you stay in this shit hole, you could have died…You can't mess around with gaol-fever, it nearly killed me and I had the two best nurses in the world looking after me, for Christ's sake…'

His rage convinced her more than his affection had, but it was distressing Edmund who was lying back on his grubby pillow, panting.

She touched Robin's shoulder and he whipped round, glaring at her. 'Mistress, why didn't you…'

'He begged me not to, sir,' she said firmly. 'I tried my best to get him to write to your father, but he wouldn't, even when he was lucid. And most of this time he has been too ill to do anything.'

'You might have done it on your own, got him out of this filthy place.'

His anger shook her, though she knew it was really a diffuse fury that wasn't aimed at her.

'S…sir, I didn't know what to do. I didn't dare reveal who he was or contact your father because he was so desperate that I shouldn't. How could I go against what he said? He pleaded with me not to betray him, said if I sent any message to my lord, the spy in his household would make sure Heneage found him first… And he was so afraid of Heneage. And in any case, I think he was ashamed. He said many times he wanted to die.'

'Oh Christ.'

'He very nearly did, sir, and is still not recovered. This is the most dangerous time with gaol-fever; if he strains himself too much now, it will come back and probably kill him. Please be gentle with him.'

It was touching and made Julie want to smile at them. Although Robin was still fuming, Edmund's frail hand had crept out from under the blankets and into his brother's. They were holding hands like children and neither of them had noticed.

'Yes, you're right,' Robin said eventually. 'I'm sorry, Ned, I should have thought. I suppose it probably was right to lie low, but…for God's sake, why in this place? Why not the Eightpenny Ward?'

'Most of his money was counterfeit and somebody stole the rest,' Julie explained.

'Bastards.'

Edmund said something with a faint smile.

'No, you're damned right nobody would have thought to look for you in here. I didn't. How could you possibly bear it? It's worse than below decks in a ship. It's like…it's like a circle of hell.'

Again Edmund whispered something to his brother with a look at her that Julie knew meant she was the subject. She could feel herself flushing.

Robin listened for a moment. 'One question,' he said. 'When did you understand Heneage's game?'

'When I...paid my tailor with the gold we made...I thought we'd made...and he weighed it and threw it back in my face for a forgery...I suddenly saw it...' came Edmund's creaking breathless voice, '...saw how it used me against Father. All I could think of was to hide and the only place I thought they might not look at first was in gaol, especially...in a different name. I made a deal with the man to arrest me for the debt in mother's name, as Edward Morgan.'

Robin nodded. Edmund lay back and panted, white with exhaustion. Very gently, Robin released his brother's hand, put it under the blankets, tucked him up like a child and then stood, dusting his fingers and his legs.

'Mistress Granville,' he said quietly to her. 'I don't think we have much time. I want you to go to the courtyard and find a man there, by the name of Kit Marlowe. He's almost as tall as I am, velvet peascod doublet slashed with peach taffeta, but he looks like a cocky smug bastard and that's exactly what he is. When you find him, tell him...tell him to go to my father and fetch reinforcements.'

Edmund was plucking at the blanket, the cords of his neck straining to lift his head. Robin saw and patted him. 'I know, I know, Marlowe's Heneage's man. He says he wants my help to get him in with Essex and just for the moment, I believe him. All right?'

Edmund let his head fall back and closed his eyes. They looked sunken and his colour was bad. Robin looked down at him with a worried frown and then at her.

'Please, mistress, hurry,' he said. 'I'm staying with Ned. If a plump-looking man in a fine marten-trimmed gown asks you where he is, even if he says he's Mr Thomas Heneage, the Queen's Vice Chancellor, lie.'

She nodded, frightened at the large stakes these men were playing for...Defying the Queen's official? Well, she could do it for Edmund.

**

In the end, it was lucky that Heneage had brought no thumbscrews with him because he had expected to be able to capture Sir Robert Carey and put the next part of his plan into operation. It meant he had to send one of his men to fetch some to use on his prisoner. While he waited, he decided to see if painting word pictures of some of the effects and refinements of thumbscrews would have any effect on the yokel. He had been talking for ten minutes when he realised that the blasted man had somehow managed to doze off again, lying sideways on the carriage bench.

His first impulse was to use his dagger on the man's eyeballs, see if that would keep him awake, but he controlled himself.

He was absolutely certain the northerner knew where Edmund Carey was hiding. The spittle he had carefully scrubbed off his face before snatching his henchman's cosh and using it for five satisfying minutes on the bastard northerner's kidneys, that infuriating childish gesture confirmed his instinct that he was dealing with defiance and not ignorance.

He was planning how to use the thumbscrews to break Carey's man quickly, considering other places you could use them than merely fingers, when it occurred to him to wonder how it was a northerner could know where Edmund Carey was when nobody else did.

The answer came to him from God, as simply as the sun rising. He actually laughed, because it was so obvious.

He leaned out of the carriage and called his second in command over to him, told his driver to whip up the horses again. He called to where his henchmen were standing in a group, sharing a leather bottle of beer and practising knife throwing at the swollen corpse of a rat lying in a gutter. Then he kicked the northerner's shins to wake him up.

'Edmund Carey's in the Fleet, isn't he?' he said, and saw the telltale change in the man's eyes. 'You really should have told me before, it would have saved you some pain. And you would have told me in the end, you know; people always do. Probably after we'd crushed one or both of your balls.'

'Ay,' croaked the man. 'Ay, he's in the Fleet. Deid and buried, wi' gaol fever.'

Heneage laughed at this nonsense. 'Oh, really,' he remonstrated. 'If that was true, you'd have told me at once, you're not mad.'

'Mr Heneage,' said the man, breathing carefully. 'I wouldnae willingly tell ye where yer ain arsehole was, not if yer catamite begged me to.'

Heneage blinked at him. 'When I've finished with Edmund Carey and his interfering brother, I will take you apart, piece by piece.'

The carriage jolted into motion, causing the northerner to whine through his teeth very satisfactorily as he fell helplessly off the bench and in a huddle onto the narrow floor. Heneage left him there, so he could get the benefit of the bone-jolting movement of the coach. Generally anybody but an invalid or a woman would prefer to ride but for some purposes, such as privately transporting prisoners, a carriage was unimproveable.

***

Julie Granville heard the hammering on the prison gate and went to look, along with a crowd of children. When Newton opened the postern a plump man was standing there, four square in fur-trimmed velvet and at his back at least eight hard-faced men-at-arms.

He stood with his arms folded while Newton bowed and scraped and tried to argue in a wheedling tone of voice about his authority and his position and his properly paid-for office.

One of the men-at-arms stepped forward and cuffed Newton. 'Don't delay Mr Vice Chancellor,' he said. 'This is in the name of the Queen.'

Newton cringed and stepped back. The men-at-arms filed through with the Vice Chancellor in the middle.

Julie picked up her skirts and ran across the courtyard, down the steps to Bolton's Ward. The gaol servant now sitting there was an odious man she had had dealings with before who leered at her bodice and told her he didn't want a penny for garnish, but a nice loving kiss. For a moment she couldn't think what to do, whether she should let him or not, but her guts revolted at the thought. She could hear the sounds of the upper parts of the gaol being searched while the prisoners were harried into groups according to ward in the courtyard. Her children would be frightened without her, but one of her gossips would look after them, she knew. Meanwhile she didn't have time to argue with a lecherous gaoler.

She went up close to him, putting up her mouth as if yielding, and when he reached for her she kneed him as hard as she could in the balls. He made a pleasing *oof* noise and reeled against the wall, and she took the keys off his belt, opened the heavy door with it.

Her eyes took a few minutes to adjust to the dimness, but she could see Robin Carey over near his brother, sitting cross-legged, talking quietly to him. He looked up as the door opened, saw her and came instantly to his feet.

'What is it, mistress?'

'The Vice Chancellor…Mr Heneage…he's searching the gaol.'

For a moment Robin looked astonished.

'But he's only had Dodd for a couple of hours…' he said to himself in a voice of bewilderment. Then he stood absolutely still and she had no idea what he was thinking because his face had gone stiff like a mask.

He looked at her, considering. 'Mistress,' he said, quite conversationally. 'Will you help me?'

She hesitated. What would happen to her, to her children? Could she, dare she trust him? His family were important and rich, perhaps they might help her? Or perhaps they would simply use her and forget her. She didn't know.

She saw Edmund was raising his head again, looking at her. His eyes were less vividly blue than his brother's, more of a sea-grey colour, but the memory of the kindness and laughter in them steadied her.

Her heart was thumping hard. She came in, shut the door behind her and locked it with the key, then came across to him.

'That won't hold them very long, I'm afraid. Newton has the master keys,' she said.

'Do you have the key for his ankle chain?'

'Probably.'

They tried a couple, found the right one and unlocked it, revealing a wide bracelet of ulcers on the bony ankle. Robin bit his lip when he saw it, then raised his head and looked around. Some of the other beggars and sick men in the ward were looking up; a couple of them were moving anxiously as far away from the brothers as they could, being tethered.

'Over there,' Robin said, pointing at an alcove under one of the high semi-circular barred windows that were at the ground level of the courtyard. 'I'll carry Edmund, you bring his bedding.'

Edmund was trying to struggle upright, but his brother simply picked him up in his arms and straightened his knees.

'Oh, shut up, Ned,' Robin told him. 'You don't weigh anything like as much as several of the women I've carried into my bed.'

Julie scooped up the straw pallet that had cost her sixpence, trying not to think about its likely population of lice and fleas, took the pillow and the blanket and followed as Robin carried his brother briskly over to the alcove, apologising politely as he stepped over prone bodies and cursing once when he nearly slipped on a turd. Julie put down the pallet and Robin laid Edmund gently down on it, arranged the blanket and pillow and then stood and leaned his arm on the pillar of the arch. There was a querulous tone in Edmund's voice, though Julie couldn't quite make out the words.

'Ned, you're a prize idiot. Heneage isn't going to get you and nor are you going to hang for coining. I'm going to hang you myself for causing me so much trouble. Mistress Granville,' Robin added gently to her. 'I really think you ought to leave.'

'I don't want to,' she blurted out, cut to the quick that he would dismiss her like that.

'Mistress, life might get a little tense in here for a while. Those other poor sods can't escape but you can.'

She sniffed at him, turned her shoulder and went resolutely, holding her breath when necessary, to unlock all the other ankle chains in the room. Some of the beggars were too far gone to move, but those that could instantly crawled or staggered out of the way to the stone benches at the side of room. Robin watched her without further comment. She came back and sat down on the stone floor next to Edmund, spread out her skirts and put her knife in her lap. Then she took Edmund's hand in her own and stroked it.

'You know he's married, mistress,' she heard Robin's voice above her. He was looking down, not unkindly.

'So am I, sir,' she said.

Whether Edmund's brother would have been tactless enough to ask the question he must have been wondering about, she never found out. Somebody tried the door, found it locked, hammered a couple of times and then there was a sequence of shouts as others were sent scuttling off to find the gaoler and Mr Vice Chancellor.

'Oh, bollocks,' Robin said, mainly to himself, drawing his sword and stepping out a little to block the alcove's opening with his body. She heard him muttering to himself and thought he might be praying, hoped fervently that the Lord God of Hosts would hear and perhaps send a few angels to help, then smiled at herself for being childish. It was odd she could do it. Her heart was thumping so hard and her hands had gone cold.

The gaoler's keys scraped and clattered in the lock, it was flung open and two men-at-arms came in, clubs in their hands. They stopped when they saw Robin standing there, waiting for them, sword bare.

'Good afternoon, gentlemen,' he said, and Julie could hear that he was smiling.

The Vice Chancellor pushed past and stood between his two henchmen, his little mouth pursed and pouched with anger.

'What do you think you're doing, Carey?' he demanded. 'Your brother is guilty of forgery, which is a hanging offence, witchcraft which is a burning offence, and treason which is a...'

'Hanging, drawing and quartering offence,' drawled Robin. 'Yes, I know.'

'Are you going to hand him over to me in a sensible fashion or are you going to be stupid?' demanded Heneage.

'Oh, normally I'd instantly decide to be stupid,' said Robin. 'But first I want to know who you're after.'

'Your brother, Edmund Carey. He stole property which is mine and he...'

'Edmund Carey? That's not him. That's Edward Morgan. Didn't you check the book?'

'I know your mother's maiden name as well as you do, Carey, if that's what she was and...'

'You know, if you insult my mother I'll simply have to kill you, which I could do, right now, if I wanted to. And then it would all be very inconvenient, I'd hang for it if I lived, which might upset my father, but you would be dead and facing God Almighty and all the poor souls you've destroyed with torture and ill-treatment. And then you would go to hell for the rest of eternity. So don't you think you ought to try to be polite, hm?'

'The sick man that you are standing in front of is Edmund Carey and I want him,' said Heneage impatiently. 'I'm going to take him, so get out of my way. I won't tell you twice.'

'You're going to take him, are you? Who? You personally? I don't think so. You haven't the stomach and you haven't the strength for it. So who's going to do it?' Again Julie could hear the smile in his voice as he moved his head to look lazily round at the men-at-arms crowding the stinking cellar and making it even more airless. 'Are you?' he asked the nearest one. 'Or you? Or you, over there? Or the two of you? I think that's all you could get in on me at once, given the way this cellar's built. Such inconvenient pillars, aren't they? Whyever did they build it like that? So you see, it isn't really very easy for your men, Heneage. They've got clubs and knives and I've got a sword and I'm sure they'll knock me down eventually, but in the process I should be able to kill at least one, maybe even two of them. Maybe I'll maim a few more of them, you never know. This is a broadsword: it's not perfect for close-quarters work but it's quite sharp and it has two edges as well as a point and I'm in excellent practice with it.'

He looked round again, balancing on his toes and looking quite relaxed. 'So who's it to be? Which of your men love you, Heneage, which ones would follow you into battle?'

You could feel the tension in the air and also the way uncertainty spread among the men around Heneage. They were looking at each other, assessing Robin's stance, deciding whether he was telling the truth, wondering why he was talking so much. Julie knew. He was acting, playing for time. Edmund's bony fingers were gripping hers tight enough to hurt.

'Maybe we could just fight it out, Heneage, eh?' Robin was moving now, waving his sword in elaborate arcs and making it flash hypnotically in the sunlight filtering down through the window, shifting his feet like a tennis player. 'You and me, sword to sword, or knife to knife. That would be fun, very chivalric, very old-fashioned. Or use guns. I can see you're not a fighting man, more of a desk man really, aren't you? Standing back while other men do your dirty work, get themselves killed in your service? But you could probably fire a gun, couldn't you, something light like a dag, only weighs a couple of pounds, you could do that. Maybe you could even aim it straight? I'm not as good a shot as I should be, you'd have a chance.'

Heneage's mouth tightened. 'Don't be ridiculous. In the name of the Queen I order...'

'Don't drag my cousin into this,' said Carey pointedly and Julie had to hide a smile because of the expression on some of the men-at-arms' faces.

'Webster, Oat, arrest that man.'

Two of the men-at-arms moved forward uncertainly. Heneage seemed to expand with rage like a pigeon's neck. 'And you, Potter, get him out of there.'

The men-at-arms were advancing in a circle on Carey who had stopped his little dance and taken up a fighting crouch, the open *en garde* with sword and poignard recommended for more than one opponent. He was grinning at them, showing his teeth like a fox at bay.

'I'll give twenty-five shillings to the man who subdues him,' said Heneage. Carey laughed.

'Christ, Heneage, you're cheap. The Borderers are offering ten pounds sterling for my head.'

That was when everything got confused. Julie noticed that the men-at-arms at the back of Bolton's Ward were distracted, they were looking over their shoulders. Heneage was listening to one who was whispering in his ear, there was the sound of boots on the stairs, shouts. Meanwhile the men at the front hadn't realised anything was happening, they were focused on Carey and nerving themselves. Suddenly they made their rush, two of them from either side with their clubs high. One swung down, one swung sideways, Carey blocked the higher one with his blade, leaped sideways to avoid the worst of the sideswipe, used his poignard to stab for the man's face when his sword got stuck in the cudgel's wood and the man fell backwards away from Carey's stab while the other two tried to hit him as he tried to shake the cudgel off his sword. Julie flung herself forwards trying to catch the boots of one of them as Carey took a blow on the shoulder and faltered; she caught them and got a kick in the face though she brought the man down.

There was another man-at-arms in the fight; Carey had dropped his sword, dodged a club, kicked someone in the kneecap and then somebody had caught his arm, he was hit again, shrewdly with the thrusting end of a cudgel in the belly and he doubled over. One man-at-arms lifted his club high to bring it down on Carey's head and finish the fight. It bounced off the sturdy haft of a halberd thrust out by a broad elderly man in black velvet and brocade. There was a sweep of tawny satin and flame-red velvet gown as the elderly man whirled, punched the man-at-arms and knocked him down.

Carey was upright again but obviously couldn't see properly, hadn't realised he could stop fighting now, he was lunging towards the newcomer with his poignard. Julie put her hand to her mouth, but the old gentleman stood his ground with the halberd held in defence across his body and roared, 'ROBIN.'

It was almost comical to see Carey stop almost in mid-air, skidding on the slimy floor, fighting for balance. One of the new men-at-arms in a blazing livery of black and yellow put out a hand and stopped him from falling over.

'F...Father,' he wheezed as his sight cleared, looking round him at his father's men, some of whom were grinning. 'Where the...hell have you been?' He sheathed his poignard carefully at the back of his belt, and leaned against the wall, tenderly cradled his midriff, easing his shoulder and wincing, shaking his head to clear it.

Lord Hunsdon looked at his son for a moment, obviously assessing him for serious damage, and then he turned to Heneage who had suddenly seemed to shrink in size and had drawn back. The place was so full of men now it was hard to move, every one of Heneage's men countered with one of Hunsdon's.

Hunsdon stared coldly at Heneage for several seconds. 'Mr Vice Chamberlain, I'll deal with you later,' he said. 'Where's Ned?'

Carey gestured wordlessly, still working on catching his breath. Julie picked herself up from where she had been nursing her painfully bruised cheek, curtseyed as low as she safely could to Lord Hunsdon.

'He's here, my lord,' she said. 'Be careful, don't go near him if you've never had gaol-fever. He's been terribly ill with...'

Quite gently Hunsdon put her aside, went over to his son and embraced him. Only Julie heard what he said which was, 'There now, poor boy, you bloody idiot, there now.'

The next moment Hunsdon had turned round and was giving a dizzying series of orders which cleared Bolton's Ward as if by magic, Heneage standing blank-faced in a corner under guard, his men-at-arms told they'd get in no trouble if they went and stood quietly in a corner of the gaol courtyard, some of Hunsdon's men sent running to find and hire a litter, no bloody new-fangled carriages mind, they could ignore the useless contraption standing in Fleet Lane.

Hunsdon went over and clasped his youngest son to him as well. Carey was recovering quickly now, bright eyed and rather pleased with himself until something occurred to him and his face clouded.

'Where's Sergeant Dodd, Father?' he asked anxiously. 'Have you found him?'

Heneage's second-in-command scooped up Carey's sword, pulled the cudgel off the blade and gave it to him, hilt first. 'If you mean the northerner, sir, he's in the carriage.'

Carey turned and ran out of Bolton's Ward, up the stairs. Hunsdon nodded at two of his men to go with him. Heneage looked down at his boots.

Another of Hunsdon's men came trotting in to report that the litter was ready in the courtyard. Hunsdon took his magnificent gown off and wrapped it around his son before two of the men picked him up carefully under the knees and armpits and carried him up the stairs.

Hunsdon nodded to Julie and offered her his arm. They were all at the door of Bolton's Ward, ready to leave, when Carey came back down the stairs two at a time, went over to Heneage and, without preamble, lashed out with his fist. Heneage fell back grabbing at his nose and Carey followed up, quite silent, white to the lips, crowding him against the wall, punching him with a blinding flurry of short cruel blows. Heneage cringed, wailing, 'I didn't touch him, he didn't tell me, I worked it out, I never hurt...' The words ended in a gargle as Carey put his hands round the man's neck and started to squeeze.

'Stop him,' ordered Hunsdon wearily and it took three of his men to do it because Carey was deaf and blind to anything except killing Heneage. Julie had never seen a gentleman go berserk before and she found it very ugly and frightening. Edmund would not have lost all control like that, used such barbarous violence.

Hunsdon went close to his son who was still struggling white-faced.

'Is your man dead?' he asked. He asked the question several times before his son could be sane enough to answer him.

'No, I...no, he's not.'

'Is he crippled?'

Carey's eyelids fluttered as he thought. 'I don't...think so.'

'Well, thank God for that. You've a good man there. Now you know you can't throttle the Queen's Vice Chancellor, she wouldn't like it.'

Robin was breathing hard and shakily. 'One of...one of Heneage's servants was there, with thumbscrews.'

'But they hadn't been used.'

Robin shook his head.

'Well, thank God for that too,' rumbled Hunsdon, putting his hand on his son's shoulder and shaking him gently back and forth. 'Thank God.'

Heneage was pinching at the bridge of his nose, bent over to keep the blood away from his fine clothes, his handkerchief darkening.

'I'll see you in Star Chamber for this,' he said huskily. 'How dare you...'

'How dare you touch my man?!' roared Carey, swinging round to him and making his father's men grab at him again to stop his lunge. 'If he dies I'll make sure you follow him, you'll swing for it or I'll kill you myself, you fucking piece of...'

'ROBIN!' bellowed Hunsdon, nose to nose with Carey. 'Do I have to hit you to calm you down?'

Carey was breathing heavily through his nose again but he was trying to regain his self-control. Julie saw him trembling all over like a nervous horse with the effort.

Heneage was still muttering sulkily and stupidly about lawsuits for battery and assault. Hunsdon looked over at him contemptuously.

'Be quiet,' he ordered. 'This is unseemly. We shall discuss these matters somewhere more private.'

That reminded Julie of the secret Edmund had given her to hold. She turned aside to lift up her kirtle and take it out of the pocket of her petticoat where it had been weighing her down for weeks. She held the heavy little package out to Lord Hunsdon.

'My lord,' she said. 'Ned...Mr Carey gave me this to hold for him.'

Hunsdon took it, looking puzzled. Carey reached out his hand. 'My lord, may I?' Hunsdon gave it to him, he opened it, glanced at it and nodded. Heneage watched and for the second time Julie saw real fear in his face. Carey held one of the little round lumps of metal up to the light and squinted.

'The Tower mark,' he said. 'I thought so.' He smiled so cruelly at Heneage that Julie decided she didn't like him at all. 'We can destroy you now, Mr Vice, you know that don't you?'

Heneage didn't answer.

***

In a manner that brooked no argument, Lord Hunsdon took over the gaoler's lodgings. Julie felt that perhaps she should withdraw now, go and see to her children who were staring at her from behind the skirts of the woman who ran the ruff-making circle. But Hunsdon insisted that she stay with him even after Edmund had been loaded barely conscious into the horse litter and sent off at a sedate walk down Fleet Lane towards Somerset House, past the row of tethered horses that had brought Lord Hunsdon and his men to the Fleet. Another litter was being fetched for Robin's henchman, who was sitting in the sunlight on the steps of the carriage, bent like an old man and looking putty-coloured and ill. Obstinately he insisted in his guttural, almost incomprehensible, voice that if they would just get him a decent horse he could ride, for God's sake, what did he want wi' a litter like a woman, he was nae sae bad, he'd been worse, dinna fuss, and forebye he didnae want to go back to Somerset House until he knew what the hell had been going on...In the end, to stop his complaints, two of Hunsdon's men helped him into Newton's living room and sat him on the best padded chair, with a cushion to ease his back.

There Carey paced up and down in front of his father who had taken the only other chair and was sitting behind Newton's table like a judge.

'As you know, my lord, Mr Heneage wants to be Lord Chamberlain and have control over the Queen's courtiers, her security arrangements and her mind, if possible.'

Hunsdon grunted at this in a way which indicated he was neither surprised nor shocked nor very impressed. Carey answered the comment with a smile.

'I know, my lord, it's pathetic, isn't it? But still. He wants to remove you, and since you won't oblige him by committing treason, raping a maid of honour or going to Mass, he's been looking for some way to blackmail you into resigning your office.'

'I protest at these outrageous accusations. I have never been so insulted...'

'Oh, be quiet,' growled Hunsdon. 'Let the boy...let my son tell his tale.'

'Under protest, be it noted.'

'Noted, noted. Yes, Robin?'

'Dodd pointed out to me the similarity with some of the gangsters we have in the north. If a man is too strong to attack directly, they kidnap one of his near relatives and apply pressure that way. King James does something similar when he takes noble hostages off his Border lords.'

'Dirty business.'

'Effective, though, my lord. If Mr Heneage had succeeded and taken Edmund into the Tower on some trumped up but believable charge, you might have been willing to exchange the office of Lord Chamberlain for him.'

'Certainly not,' said Hunsdon, and glared at Heneage.

Carey didn't comment but continued. 'This summer Edmund was inveigled into a project by two men who called themselves alchemists. The plan as presented to him was to use the Philosopher's Stone they claimed to have discovered to create a large quantity of gold blanks. They wanted him to lay his hands on a set of Tower coin dies: that way, they said, what they did would not be forgery. The blanks would be gold, the coin dies would be genuine, so the coins they struck would be no different from the Queen's money in any way.'

Hunsdon sighed heavily at this. 'He fell for it?'

'I'm afraid he did, my lord. Of course they needed some seed-gold to work the transformation, which Edmund got for them somehow. And the coin dies—well, by a remarkable coincidence, Edmund knew a man who had just retired from being one of the Deputy Mint-masters at the Tower and who had kept a pair of dies that should have been cancelled because they were an old design.'

'Heneage's man?'

Carey smiled. 'Of course. Edmund bribed the man to get the dies. He witnessed the transformation, which he found very impressive since he knew nothing at all about the goldsmith's art. What he saw was a method called parcel-gilding. According to the goldsmith I talked to, it's a very simple thing to do if you know how to control a furnace and the main problem is to keep the mercury fumes from escaping so you can resublimate it and reuse it. An alchemist's pelican does the job perfectly.'

'At the end of it he actually had a pile of parcel-gilt pewter blanks, but he thought they were genuinely gold?'

'Yes, my lord.'

'Why in the name of God didn't he weigh them himself to make sure?'

Carey waved an arm. 'I don't know, my lord.'

Hunsdon rolled his eyes and sighed heavily. 'Go on.'

'Well, then they struck coins from the blanks using the Tower dies and of course the coins looked perfect. Edmund believed that the whole operation was nearly official; one of the alchemists had a warrant from Heneage and the idea was that the coins would be used to help pay for the expenses of his intelligencing which the Queen will never give him enough money to run properly. Edmund took a fee for his part in getting the seed gold and finding the coin dies.'

'And then he tried to spend it and found...'

'Quite so. They were straightforward forgeries. His tailor weighed them and told him what they were.'

Hunsdon was staring coldly at Heneage. 'Of course uttering false coin is a hanging offence.'

'Which the Queen takes very seriously.'

'Very seriously indeed. She would be enraged,' said Hunsdon. 'The most I could have done would have been to beseech the mercy of the axe for Edmund. She might also have been suspicious of me.'

'Precisely, my lord.'

Hunsdon nodded. 'Well, it's clever, you have to give him that,' he rumbled. 'It might have worked.'

'I think Heneage planned that Edmund would be arrested for coining. He would then offer to you the services of his pursuivants to find the alchemists responsible, in exchange for your resignation from the Lord Chamberlainship. Possibly he might even have found somebody to take the blame.'

Hunsdon nodded again. 'Under such circumstances...Hm.'

'Only at last, Edmund started to use his brain. When the tailor accused him, he worked out what had been going on, what the whole elaborate coney-catching operation was about. He isn't stupid, he's...'

'He has no common sense. Whatsoever.'

Carey coughed. 'At that point he panicked. He knew Heneage must be behind the business because of the warrant. All he could think of was to lie low somehow. It seemed to him that he might be safer in gaol than out of it, so he struck a deal with the tailor to be arrested in a false name.'

'But why the devil didn't he come to me?'

'He was afraid of your anger, my lord, and also…He was ashamed. He knew how stupid he'd been.'

'Urrrh.'

'Also, in the summer you were on Progress with the Queen and very hard to contact. Gaol might not have been such a bad idea, as a temporary measure, until you came back. Unfortunately, within a week of coming here to the Fleet, he had caught a gaol-fever, his true money had been stolen or, more likely, he had gambled it away, and Newton, who didn't know who he was, had slung him in Bolton's Ward. There he might have died had not Mrs Granville here nursed him and supported him.'

In his pacing, Carey had come close to where Julie stood, drawing her forward. He smiled encouragingly at her, but she looked down, not liking him any more.

She curtseyed to Lord Hunsdon.

'Is this true, mistress?'

'Yes, my lord.'

'You kept my son alive through a gaol-fever in that pesthole he was lying in?'

'Er…that was God's Will, my lord, I only nursed him.'

'Why?'

'Well…er…' she knew she was flushing and she hoped Edmund's father would just think she was shy. 'He was kind to my children, sir, and very patient when Johnnie accidentally hit him with a stone on the ear, and…er…' Edmund's father had a look of amused understanding on his face. 'We are both married, my lord,' she added hurriedly. 'There was nothing improper…'

'You weren't working for Mr Heneage?'

That angered her. 'No, sir, certainly not.'

'I hardly think so, my lord,' drawled Carey. 'Since she saved my skin as well just before you arrived, by bringing down one of Heneage's men when they attacked. She also kept safe the packet of coin-dies and the warrant which Edmund gave her, which she would undoubtedly have given back to Mr Heneage if she had been working for him, since that was one reason why he was searching for Edmund.'

'Mistress Granville,' said Lord Hunsdon, with a little bow from his chair, 'I apologise for suspecting you. I am deeply in your debt and unlike most of my sons, I pay my debts.'

She didn't know what to do except curtsey again.

After a pause to glare at his father for the covert jibe, Carey continued. 'So Edmund had disappeared and with him the Tower coin-dies and the warrant which incriminated Mr Heneage, since he had access to them and Edmund didn't. Heneage was looking for him, you were looking for him...Incidentally, my lord, why did you employ Robert Greene about the business?'

Hunsdon harumphed. 'I thought Edmund might have gone on a binge and you set a drunken gambler to find a drunken gambler. Greene has investigated for me in the past; he's good at it, when he's sober, or nearly.'

'I see,' said Carey in a tone that skirted very close to being an insult. 'Well, after he had also drawn a blank, you sent for me, very inconveniently, from Carlisle.'

'How was I to know how many warrants for debt you had waiting for you? None of you idiot boys will ever tell me how bad your position is.'

You could see Carey didn't like being called a boy by his father, Julie thought, and also this clearly was a sore point. Carey scowled. 'We fear your wrath, sir.'

'Oh, do you, by God?' growled Hunsdon, scowling back. 'Well, spend less then. Or engage in some halfway sane investments.'

Just for a moment there looked to be the fascinating prospect of father and son leaping into battle against each other. Somebody cleared his throat.

'Ay,' droned a doleful northern voice. 'But how was it yer man Michael got hisself strung up on the Hampstead Hanging Elm?'

Carey looked thoughtfully at Sergeant Dodd. 'It was a mistake. One of Heneage's men paid the footpads that infest the Heath to stop him and wasn't specific enough about how, so they shot him. They didn't have time to bury him so they strung him up so that if our horses spooked at the smell, we wouldn't wonder at it.'

He looked back at his father who was shaking his head regretfully. 'Poor Michael,' Hunsdon said. 'His wife's taken it very hard. Presumably Mr Heneage wanted you, so he could use you to winkle out Edmund.'

'Precisely, sir. I think you know most of the rest of the story.'

That obviously wasn't true if Hunsdon's expression was any guide, but Julie saw him take the hint. He swung round on Heneage.

'Mr Heneage. Have you anything to say?'

Heneage put away the blood-soaked handkerchief he had been using on his nose. 'This is not a court of law, my lord,' he said thinly. 'But I will say this. Every word of Sir Robert's ridiculous tale is a lie. I have nothing but respect for you, my lord, and for your family, nor would I ever engage in such preposterous plots against you.'

Carey's hand had gone to the hilt of his sword. 'How dare...?' he began through his teeth. Hunsdon waved him down.

'Mr Heneage, do you want my son to call you out?'

'I would not accept the challenge, my lord, since duelling is against the law and the clearly expressed will of Her Majesty the Queen. I will however consult my lawyers in case there is a suit for slander that can be pursued, in addition to the charges of assault, battery and false imprisonment for which I have a cast-iron case.'

'How do you explain the Tower Mint coin-dies?'

Heneage shrugged. 'I can't, my lord. Nor do I intend to try. Doubtless you or Sir Robert best know what happened. Neither they nor the warrant amount to evidence because a warrant can be forged and the coin-dies might have been come by in a number of ways.'

There was a frustrated silence before Sergeant Dodd spoke up again.

'Ay, well, sir,' he said, his voice compressed. 'I dinna ken what all yon fine courtiers and cousins to the Queen can do agin ye, Mr Heneage, but I think I have as good a case agin ye for assault, battery and false imprisonment and better. And I'm sure my lord Hunsdon will see me right wi' a good lawyer to take the case.'

'With pleasure,' said Hunsdon.

'Possibly I made an unfortunate mistake with you, Dodd...'

'Och, did ye now?' said Dodd, sitting forward with a wince.

'Did ye, by Christ? I was slung in gaol in mistake for Sir Robert and ye came along and took me oot on nae warrant whatever, pit me in yer foul contraption of a carriage, and had yer men beat the hell out of me on the suspicion I knew where Sir Robert's brother was. Ye threatened me wi' torture. Ye beat the hell out of me yersen, sir, d'ye recall, personally, wi' a cosh? It's no' gentlemanlike to get yer hands dirty, but ye did and since ma kith and kin are hundreds o' miles away and I canna raid ye and burn yer house down about yer ears, I'll go the southern way to ma satisfaction, and I'll see you in court, sir.'

'I might be...er...willing to pay compensation to you, Dodd, for a very unfortunate...'

Outrage burned in Dodd's face, propelled him out of his chair.

'By God Almighty!' he bellowed, fists on the table. 'I am the Land Sergeant of Gilsland and I have had enough of yer disrespect, Mr Heneage. Ye can call me Sergeant if ye wish tae address me.'

Heneage looked taken aback. 'Er...Sergeant.'

'Incidentally, I think the offer of compensation is rather close to an admission here,' said Carey drily. 'Which was witnessed. Do you still want to take me to court, Mr Heneage?'

Heneage's mouth was pinched. 'Possibly we could come to some arrangement.'

Dodd sat down again in the chair quite suddenly. 'Jesus,' he muttered and rubbed at his lower back.

Hunsdon leaned forward and put his forearms on the table. 'We are going to come to this arrangement. You will drop any and all lawsuits against my sons, rescind any warrants you have sworn out regarding them, and in all ways hold them harmless for the events of these past few weeks. In return we will drop any and all lawsuits against you and I will use my best endeavours to persuade Sergeant Dodd of Gilsland to be merciful to you in the matter of his own lawsuit, which is of course a separate issue.'

Heneage sneered. 'I wish to consult my lawyers...'

'Why?' snapped Hunsdon. 'Be your own lawyer in this case.'

'And if I refuse?'

'Mr Heneage, you know me. I prefer a quiet life now I'm old. But if I'm stirred to it, I like a fight as well as any man. I think I have the resources and the friends to tie you up with parchment and paper from one end of Westminster Hall to the other.'

'And the Queen?'

'I will not lie to my sovereign. But she'll hear none of this affair unless she asks me about it, so you had better hope she doesn't ask.'

'So had you,' said Heneage venomously. 'She hates coiners.'

Hunsdon tilted his head noncommittally.

Heneage gestured at the warrant and the Tower Mint dies, holding his hand out for them. Hunsdon's eyes half-hooded themselves and he passed them to Sir Robert.

'I want the coin-dies,' said Heneage. 'And the warrant.'

'You admit they were originally yours?' asked Carey.

'No, Sir Robert. I want to suppress false evidence.'

'If they're false, then they can do you no harm,' growled Hunsdon. 'If they're true, then you should certainly not have them since the coin-dies may tempt you to trespass again. I'll keep them safe for you.'

Heneage departed in his carriage, his men jogging along beside it, heading west for his house in Chelsea. Hunsdon's men mounted up in a flurry of circling horses while Hunsdon conferred with the lawyers he had summoned as back-up to the brute force of his henchmen. They conferred at length with Gaoler Newton who proved obstinate now he had the real Sir Robert Carey physically in his power. Eventually, he agreed to release both Carey and Mrs Julie Granville and her children on bonds of a thousand pounds each. Lord Hunsdon uncomplainingly wrote out bankers' drafts for both sums which Gaoler Newton sent straight round to the Exchange to be checked, before putting them in his strongbox.

Mulishly, Sergeant Dodd rejected the expensively hired litter and climbed slowly aboard a quiet-paced mare, where he sat grimly staring ahead of him. Julie refused Sir Robert's courteous offer that she should ride pillion behind him, but accepted the same offer from Lord Hunsdon. Her children came tumbling and squeaking with excitement out of the gate and John her eldest instantly agreed to go up in front of Sir Robert.

The cavalcade trotted sedately down Fleet Lane, over the little bridge and down Fleet Street, threading out to single file at

Temple Bar and then going straight in at the main gate of Somerset House. Until that moment, when Lord Hunsdon handed her down with immense ceremony to his waiting steward, Julie had not been able to let herself believe this was anything other than a dream. She looked around at the courtyard with its fine diamond windows shining with sunset, at the strapwork in the brick and the wonderfully elaborate chimneys and she found herself clasping her children as they jumped down or were lifted from the horses and laughing at the madness of it all.

SUNDAY, 3RD SEPTEMBER 1592,

LATE EVENING

Hunsdon's stately Portuguese physician had prescribed bed rest and cold cloths to be applied to Dodd's belly and lower back. The surgeon had been ordered to let eight ounces of blood from Dodd's left arm to prevent infection. The doctor had also prescribed the drinking of tobacco smoke to ease his kidneys, which were very painful. Dodd had pissed some blood when the doctor asked to see his water, which had terrified the life out of him, until Dr Nunez explained that as it was dark and not bright, that meant it was corrupt blood being expelled rather than healthy blood, which was a good sign, generally speaking. He had left, leaving a long list of dietary orders, such as forbidding beer and recommending watered wine, and settled an astonishing bill with the steward which included a very large fee for going on to visit Barnabus's relatives in the City.

Carey was lounging on a chair sharing the long clay pipe with Dodd. He had changed out of Dodd's homespun clothes into an old doublet and hose he used for fowling, and which he had been pleased to find was now a bit loose in the waist and tight on the shoulders.

He blew smoke expertly out of his nose and frowned. 'Smells

a bit funny, not like the usual tobacco.'

'Ay,' said Dodd, taking the pipe and sucking smoke cautiously into his lungs. If he did it too fast it made him cough, which hurt. 'The doctor mixed some Moroccan herbs and incense with it, said it added the element of earth to the smoke, or some such.'

'Is it helping?'

'Ay,' Dodd admitted reluctantly. 'It is. Ay.'

'Hm. I think my shoulder's feeling better too.' They both watched blue smoke curl up in ribbons through the last rays of the sun, an elegant and calming sight. Dodd leaned back on a pile of pillows and sighed. Being bled had left him feeling as weak as a kitten, never mind the aftermath of Heneage's persuasions, and the pipesmoke was making his head feel quite light, as if he was mildly drunk.

'All right,' he said. 'Did yer dad hear any more about yer man Michael?'

Carey gave an eloquent lift of his shoulder. 'Apparently somebody turned up yesterday to claim his money and blame it all on the footpads we killed. It might well have been them, after all.'

'Ay.'

'Interestingly, the man insisted on being paid in silver, not gold.'

'Hm.' Dodd chuckled a little at that, and wondered at himself. Really, this tobacco-smoke drinking wasn't so bad; if only it weren't so expensive he might take more of the medicine. 'How did ye ken it was the little bald poet that playacted Dr Jenkins?'

'Well, he is a player, after all. But there was another thing. Do you remember Cheke explaining how dewdrops of Mercury transfer themselves into your clothes during the reaction?'

'Ay.'

'That's how there were beads of the stuff in Edmund's clothes chest, of course. But there was also Mercury in the inside pocket of your leather jerkin.'

'Eh?'

'Of course, I knew you couldn't have been there for the coining. But you carried Mr Shakespeare's *billet doux* to Mistress Bassano and there might have been Mercury on that from Shakespeare's best suit. It was the only connection I could think of.'

Dodd tilted his head in acknowledgement that this made sense. 'And was it him that killed Robert Greene, then?' he asked.

Carey smiled lazily. 'How do you make that out?'

'It's nobbut a guess. The apothecary said he died o' poison and d'ye mind ye left Shakespeare guarding him the day we found him drunk. Maybe he put poison in his meat or beer then.'

'What makes you think he'd want to?'

'Och God, he was telling and telling me all about how Robert Greene was stopping him at his poetry-writing and how he hated his guts. I think I may even have advised him to...er...kill the man.'

Carey reached into the breast pocket of his doublet and pulled out a chased silver flask. 'Remember this?' he said. 'Robert Greene's flask. He had it on him when we found him and he was drinking from it most of the night. He got it refilled by the tapster with aqua vitae and no doubt drank some more on his way home and for a nightcap before he went to bed. The next morning he sickened and died.'

'Ay but it could ha' been the eels,' Dodd pointed out from sheer perversity while Carey smoked.

'Could have been,' said Carey and sighed. 'Only it wasn't. Barnabus and Simon didn't have plague. Heneage sent men to capture me and found only Simon, with Barnabus already dead the same way as Greene.'

'How d'ye ken that?'

'I broke into my lodgings.'

Dodd winced at this plain admission of madness. 'But are ye sure it wisnae plague?' he asked on a rising note of panic.

'Certain. We found Simon trussed up like a chicken with Tamburlain roosting on the bed and Barnabus...Well, it was easily recognisable, what he'd died of. And under Barnabus's pillow, I found this flask.'

Dodd narrowed his eyes. It took him a while, thanks to his wooziness, but he worked it out. 'Och, Barnabus and his light fingers.'

'Precisely,' said Carey giving him back the pipe. 'I've told him thousands of times that his habit of thieving whatever didn't belong to me and wasn't nailed down would kill him in the end, and it did. But it's certain there was poison in the flask, for there was nothing wrong with Barnabus before and he didn't have plague.'

'So yon Shakespeare killed both Robert Greene and Barnabus?'

'I think so.'

'Can ye prove it?'

Carey shook his head. 'I've nothing but suspicion. Shakespeare had the chance to put poison in Greene's flask—that doesn't prove he did it. And he can't have known in advance what Barnabus would do, so he's hardly to blame there.'

'Will ye ask him?'

'I got hold of him while the doctor and the surgeon were seeing to you and Edmund. I think hearing he'd killed Barnabus by accident shook him a bit, but then he denied everything, the whole boiling lot and challenged me to arrest him for it.'

'Ay, well, he would.'

'Of course he would.'

'Och.' Dodd was shaking his head, more in amusement than disapproval, 'I've allus said ye cannae trust poets.'

A MURDER OF CROWS

To Barbara Peters and Robert Rosenwald,
who got Carey and Dodd
back in the saddle again.

PROLOGUE

A hunchback and a poet met in the glorious gardens belonging to the hunchback's father. The poet was dusty and tired, having ridden up from London to report to his new employer on the sensational events in and around the Fleet Prison the previous Sunday.

The hunchback preferred to sit in the shade, dressed in his customary black damask and white falling band, his lean handsome face tilted slightly sideways to listen more carefully. Beside him, since he liked to make notes, was pen, ink and the very best, most expensive paper, smoothed with pumice so that his pen nib never caught nor spattered. The poet stared at the sheets hungrily, knowing they cost as much as tuppence each and wishing he could afford such a pile. The bench was carved to look as if it had grown from the ground and faced across a labyrinth made of low-clipped box-trees, filled in with scented flowers, some of which were making a valiant last flowering in the autumn light. The Queen had often walked in these very gardens and still occasionally did. When the hunchback's father chose to inspect his plantings, he would normally travel around the carefully raked and weeded paths on the back of a small donkey since he was now crippled by gout.

The hunchback generally walked the paths when he was thinking, at a fast pace and with hardly a limp despite the bandy legs of a childhood trampled by rickets.

The poet prided himself on his memory and never wasted precious paper on mere notes. He had been a player and hoped to be one again, used to being presented with a part the night before its first afternoon performance with only one rehearsal in the morning. He could read pages twice and know them by heart. His memory was just as good for what he heard: once he had written out in full a sermon that had lasted three hours for the benefit of his then-employer who suspected the preacher of subversive puritanism.

Naturally the hunchback had chosen a bench where the trees behind it would give him shade but the sun would shine direct on the poet's face. He was glad he had done that. The poet's tale was very nearly incredible. Yet there had been reports from Carlisle which were almost as insane but which came from different and unimpeachible sources.

'Are you telling me that Mr. Vice Chamberlain Heneage organised a plot to implicate one of Lord Chamberlain Baron Hunsdon's sons...'

'Edmund Carey,' put in the poet quietly.

'Yes, whichever one, in the forging of gold angels by alchemical means?' The poet nodded. 'That when he saw the trap closing, Edmund Carey then took cover, as it were, under the nose of the cat and that his brother Sir Robert, whilst disguised as a north country man, later caused a riot there, and ended by breaking Mr. Heneage's nose because Mr. Heneage had taken and beaten a man of his from Carlisle?'

'Yes, your honour,' said the poet promptly. 'He also...'

The hunchback put up a long pale hand, leaning back as far as he could. 'Mr. Heneage was trying to oust my lord Baron Hunsdon from his place as Lord Chamberlain?'

'Yes, your honour.'

The hunchback smiled, making his face immediately charming and attractive, never mind the weakness of his body. 'Good Lord!' he said. 'Who would have thought it?'

The poet considered answering this question, but decided it was rhetorical.

The hunchback sprang to his feet and began pacing. 'Sir Robert's antics are not so surprising,' he said, more to himself than to the poet, who stood patiently with his hands tucked behind his back. 'God knows, he was dangerously bored the last time I saw him at Court and was as badly in debt as he was a couple of years ago when he walked to Newcastle in ten days.'

The poet blinked a little at this. The hunchback smiled ruefully. 'I lost several hundred pounds on that bet, blast him, and so did a lot of his friends. He made about £3000. It didn't do him any good at all, of course. Once a spendthrift, always a spendthrift.'

The poet looked down discreetly.

'That's why I recommended to Her Majesty that she appoint him Deputy Warden of the West March instead of that corrupt fool, Lowther, and also for...good and sufficient reasons.'

The poet narrowed his eyes but was far too sensible to ask what they were.

'It's Heneage's behaviour that I find extraordinary,' said the hunchback, sitting restlessly back down on the bench and leaning forward now in a confiding way. 'What do you think of his proceedings?'

'Ah...' The poet thought very carefully, since he had been working for Heneage at the time. 'I felt...unhappy.' Unhappy didn't really cover the poet's incandescent rage when he understood just how dangerously he had been set up by the Vice Chamberlain, a man he had trusted. Having played the part of the alchemist, he realised he would have been perfect meat for the hangman if the scheme had worked the way it was supposed to. It still made his innards quake to think about it.

'How about that rival of yours, Marlowe?'

'I wouldn't describe him as a rival,' murmured the poet. 'I would describe him as a friend and...and teacher.'

'Really?'

'For all his faults, Kit Marlowe is a wonderful poet.'

The hunchback shrugged. 'Nevertheless he's still working for Heneage, as far as anyone can make out.'

The poet struggled with his conscience for a moment, and then lost. 'I had heard...I believe that he may be trying to use Sir Robert as a means of entering the Earl of Essex's service.'

There was a considering silence while the hunchback thought about this. The poet wondered if he had done right telling him.

'Interesting,' was all the hunchback said. 'So he's unhappy with Heneage too?'

'I imagine so.'

'As unhappy as you were when you realised that the delightful Mistress Emilia Bassano was not only Baron Hunsdon's official mistress but was also having an affair with his son?' The hunchback was watching intently for the reaction to this prod.

The poet's ears went pink which was unfortunate because he didn't have much hair to hide it.

'I understand the lady is now in bed with the Earl of Southampton,' he said smoothly. 'Clearly love blinded me to her unchastity.'

'Quite over it?'

The poet bowed. 'Of course.'

'Good. And what's your opinion of this Carlisle henchman of Carey's?'

The poet paused. 'Sergeant Dodd?'

'That's his name. He seems to be...ah...the wild card in the game.'

'He appears to be no more than a typical Borderer, very proud of being headman of his little patch of country and holding a tower there...'

'Gilsland in fact controls one of the routes from Scotland into northern England,' said the hunchback, who had been reading ancient reports and squinting at maps prepared by his father's agents in 1583.

The poet bowed a little. '...as well as serving in the Carlisle Castle guard under Carey. He looks and behaves like a mere stupid soldier, useful on horseback, and with any weapons but especially with a sword and his fists...'

'But?'

'I think there's more to him than that,' said the poet. 'Sir Robert certainly thinks so. And I like him.'

The hunchback's smile was sunny. 'Excellent,' he said. 'His lawsuit against Mr. Heneage?'

The poet shrugged. 'He wants compensation, of course.'

'And if he doesn't get it?'

'I think he'll look for another kind of compensation.'

With one of his typically sudden movements, the hunchback threw a small full leather purse and the poet just caught it. The hunchback's face was impossible to read for sure but it seemed that somewhere in what he had said, the poet had told him something of value. He bowed again.

The hunchback rose and held out his hand to shake friendliwise.

The poet took it and found his fingers were gripped with surprising strength.

'Thank you very much, Mr. Shakespeare,' said the hunchback. 'It seems we will do well together.'

'I hope so, sir,' said the poet.

'Keep me informed.' The hunchback stood. 'I will be back in London by tomorrow.' He turned his bent shoulders and walked quickly towards the rows of hazel trees that shielded a raised lawn full of sculptures of minotaurs and fauns and mermaids and other fantastical creatures. The bees browsed on frantically in the late flowers and Shakespeare headed back to the stables and London town.

Monday 11th September 1592, Morning

'Nothing like an execution, eh Sergeant?' Sir Robert Carey was lounging elegantly against the fence that kept the groundlings in their places, one kid-gloved hand tipped on the pommel of his sword, the other playing with the beginnings of a new Court goatee.

Dodd looked at him gravely for a moment and then turned his attention back to the bloody mess on the Tyburn scaffold. On the other side of the scaffold he noticed a man with a badly pock-marked face who was staring transfixed at the priest. Suddenly, the man turned aside and vomited on the ground. The goings-on didn't upset Dodd's stomach as much—for all the smell of roast meat—since there had been no screaming. They had actually burnt the priest's balls in front of him, a detail Dodd had not expected, though at least they'd done it after cutting them off and before they slit the priest's belly to pull out his guts.

The priest hadn't been screaming because the hangman had given him a good drop off the ladder and had let him hang until his face was purple, eyes set and popping and his tongue cramming his gag in the ludicrous mask of a judicial death. Evidently a kind or well-paid hangman. In fact, the man had been unconscious on the hurdle as he was dragged along the Oxford Road, grey-faced and hollow-eyed. He had seemed only half aware of what was happening when the hangman had put the noose over his neck, though there had been something like a smile around the corners of his exhausted eyes. Impossible to tell with the gag forcing his lips into a grimace, but he had looked confidently up at the sky before stepping off the ladder. The hangman hadn't needed to push him.

Now they were quartering him efficiently with cleavers, working like the butchers at the Shambles. Quartering a man was not so very different from butchering a pig and Dodd had killed and colloped his own pig every November since he'd been a married man and knew something about it.

No sausage-making here, though. Nobody had caught the blood in buckets to make black pudding nor pulled out and washed the bladder to be a bouncy toy for children.

That thought did make his stomach turn so he was glad that Carey was speaking again.

'Eh?' said Dodd.

'I said, he'd been one of Heneage's guests at Chelsea,' Carey nodded at the man's wrist which was flopping from the nearly severed arm not far from them. It had a thick swollen bracelet of flesh around it and the fingers were tight-skinned and swollen as well.

Dodd saw that Carey was rubbing his gloved left hand where two of his fingers were still slightly bent. The rings for those fingers were still at the jeweller's to be resized since they no longer fit, and Carey was wearing kid gloves all the time not only because it was fashionable and they were extremely fine embroidered ones, but also to hide his very ugly bare nailbeds while he waited for the fingernails to regrow. All in all he had recovered well from the mysterious damage that had been done to him at the Scottish court. As to body, at least. As to mind and spirit…Only time would tell. He was being irritatingly breezy now.

'Priest was he not?' Dodd squinted slightly as one of the men working on the scaffold held up the peaceful head.

'So perish all traitors to Her Majesty!' shouted the hangman.

'Allegedly,' murmured Carey. 'Hoorah!' he added at a bellow, and clapped. The crowd cheered and clapped as well, with some wit about the priest's equipment.

'Ay,' Dodd had tired of fencing games. 'So why did ye bring me here, sir? Ah've seen men hang afore now. Hanged a couple mesen under Lowther's orders while he was Deputy Warden…'

Carey's eyebrows went up and he made a little courtier-like shrug with his shoulders. 'Thought you might be interested to see a real hanging, drawing, and quartering, they don't happen so often.'

'Ay. Nae ither reason?'

Dodd knew his face was dark with suspicion and ill-humour and didn't care. Why shouldn't he be miserable? He was still stuck in this hellhole of London, still wearing uncomfortable hot tight clothes loaned him by Carey so he could look the part of his natural station in life. He knew what and who he was and he didn't care whether the bloody southerners knew or not so long as they left him alone, so he didn't see the point of the play.

Today, for the first time in his life, he had been to a London barber and had had his hair trimmed, washed, oiled, combed, and his beard trimmed back to a neat pawky thing on the end of his chin. One of the things that was making him bad-tempered was the fact that he had caught himself enjoying it. If he wasn't careful he'd go back to Janet and his tower in Gilsland as soft and wet as any southerner and Janet's geese would eat him alive, never mind Janet herself.

Dodd glanced again at the scaffold where they were sweeping sawdust into clumps and bringing up mops and buckets. The bits of human meat were slung into a cart to be taken to the gates of London for display and the head to London Bridge to join the priest's colleagues.

Carey was already heading off through the crowd and Dodd followed him until he found a little house with red lattices and reasonably clean tables on the Oxford Road near to Tyburn. By some magic known only to him, Carey immediately snared a potboy to take his order and quickly settled down to a quart of double beer and a small cup of brandy. Dodd took mild ale, mindful of what the Portuguese physician had advised about his bruised kidneys.

'Obviously I want you to know what manner of man you're dealing with,' Carey said in a random way, blinking into his cup of brandy before swallowing all of it.

'Thank ye, sir,' said Dodd in a careful tone of voice. 'But Ah ken verra fine what manner o'man he is, seeing he laid about mah tripes wi' a cosh and me wi' ma hands chained and ye had at him yersen, sir, an hour later and he never drew blade nor struck ye back nor sent his man to arrange a time and a place.'

Dodd would never forget what had happened on that Sunday, particularly Carey finding him still curled up and half-conscious on the floor of Heneage's thrice-bedamned foreign coach after a thorough beating from Heneage and his henchmen. Those lumps had been intended only as a preliminary to further interrogation and one of the henchmen had just come back with thumbscrews to help. Dodd had not personally seen but had heard from several witnesses that Carey had then gone straight for Heneage with his bare fists, being without his sword at the time, until unfortunately restrained by his father. It hadn't been very gentlemanly of Sir Robert, but it had given Dodd some pleasure to see Heneage with a swollen nose, two black eyes, and a doublet and gown ruined by blood a little later.

And Heneage hadn't even called Carey out over it, which just showed what a strilpit wee nyaff he was. Well, lawsuits to be sure would be multiplying like rats, but that was a different matter. Dodd had never heard of a gentleman hitting another gentlemen right in the nose with his fist and not having to at least talk about a duel afterwards. For form's sake. Dodd himself didn't plan to take Heneage's demeaning beating of him as if he was some poor peasant with no surname to back him. He planned revenge.

As well as lawsuits.

Carey coughed. 'I want you to remember how powerful and ruthless he is. If you take him on, there's no going back nor crying quarter.'

Dodd squinted in puzzlement at Carey. 'Ah dinnae understand ye, sir,' he said. 'Are ye suggesting Ah should beg his honour's pardon for damaging his cosh wi' ma kidneys?'

Carey grinned. 'No, Sergeant, it's just he's not some Border reiver like Wee Colin Elliot or Richie Graham of Brackenhill. He's the Queen's Vice Chamberlain, he came this close...' Carey held up his gloved forefinger and thumb an inch apart, '...to outplotting and removing my father, he's wealthy, he's clever and he likes hurting people. He has many of Walsingham's old pursuivants working for him, though none of them like him, and he has taken over Walsingham's old network of spies and informers, although unfortunately not his shrewdness. He's highly dangerous and... well...my father says he'll back you but...'

Dodd breathed hard through his nose: a few months ago he might have been offended enough to call Carey out on it, but now he was prepared to give the Courtier benefit of doubt although it came hard to him. After all, Heneage's nosebleed had been very messy.

'Ay sir,' he said. 'Ay, Ah ken what he is.' For a moment, Dodd considered explaining to Carey some of the things he'd done in the course of his family's bloodfeud with the Elliots, then thought better of it. Wouldn't do to shock the Courtier, now would it? The corners of Dodd's mouth twitched briefly at the thought.

'But?' asked Carey, waving for more beer.

'Ah dinna think Heneage kens what I am.'

There was a pause.

'You won't take his offer?'

It had been paltry, offered the previous Wednesday by a defensively written letter carried by a servant. A mere apology and ten pounds. Where was the satisfaction in that? Dodd hadn't bothered to answer it.

'Nay sir. I've talked tae yer dad about it and he says he'll gie me whatever lawyers I want, all the paper in London for ma powder and shot...'

'Yes, father's very irritated at what happened to Edmund,' said Carey with his usual breezy understatement.

'Ay sir,' said Dodd, 'And I'm verra irritated at what happened tae me.' Dodd was trying to match Carey with understatement. 'Irritated' didn't really describe the dull thunderous rage settled permanently in Dodd's bowels.

Carey nodded, looked away, opened his mouth, shut it, rubbed his fingers again, coughed, took a gulp of his new cup of brandy, coughed again.

'I feel I owe you an apology over that, Sergeant,' said the Courtier, finally getting to the point of what had been making him so annoying for the last couple of days. He wasn't looking at Dodd now, he was staring at the sawdust-scattered floorboards of the boozing ken.

'Ah dinna recall ye ever striking me,' Dodd said slowly.

'You know what I mean. I used you as a decoy which is why you ended up in the Fleet instead of me and why Heneage got his paws on you in the first place.'

Dodd nodded. 'Ay, Ah ken that. So?'

'So it's my fault you got involved...'

While a penitent Carey was both an amusing and a rare sight, Dodd thought he was talking nonsense. Besides which it was done now and Dodd had a feud with one of the most powerful men in the kingdom. It wasn't a bloodfeud yet but it probably would be by the end. Which reminded him, he needed some information about the size of Heneage's surname. But first he had to clear away Carey's daft scruples.

'So it would ha' bin better if thon teuchter had taken ye instead? Got what he wanted right off, eh?'

Carey frowned. 'Well, no...'

'Listen, Sir Robert,' said Dodd, leaning forward and setting his tankard down very firmly, 'I've done ma time as surety in Jedburgh jail for nae better reason than I wis Janet's husband and the Armstrong headman could spare me for it.' And Janet had been very angry with him at the time, of course, a detail he left out. 'It wisnae exactly fun but it was fair enough. Same here. Ye used what ye had and what ye had wis me—there's nae offence in that, ye follow? Ah might take offence if ye go on greetin' about what a fearful fellow Heneage is and all, but at the moment Ah'm lettin ye off since ye dinna really ken me either or ma kin.'

Carey frowned. 'You're not accepting my apology?'

Dodd reached for patience. 'Nay sir, I'll accept it. It's just I dinna see a reason for it in the first place.'

Carey smiled sunnily at him and stripped off the glove on his right hand. Dodd had to squash his automatic wince at the thought of touching the nasty-looking nailbeds so he could shake hands with good grace.

'Now, sir,' he added, 'since ye've not had the advantage of partakin' in a feud before, will ye be guided by me?'

Dodd was trying hard to talk like a Courtier, his best ever impersonation of Carey's drawl, and Carey sniggered at the mangled vowels.

'Good God, Ah niver sound like that, do I?' he asked in his Berwick voice, which almost had Dodd smiling back since it sounded so utterly out of place coming from the creature in the elaborately slashed cramoisie velvet doublet and black damask trunk hose.

'Ay, ye do, sir. But nae matter. It's nae yer fault, is it?'

Carey made the harumph noise he had got from his father, thumped his tankard down and stood up.

***

Lawyers being the scum they were, most of them tended to clog together in the shambolic clusters of houses and crumbling monastery buildings around the old Templar Church. Nearby were the Inns of Court, new a-building out of the ruins of the Whitefriars abbey. In the long time the Dominicans had been gone, bribed, evicted, or burned at the stake in the Forties, the reign of the much-married Henry VIII, something like what happens to a treetrunk had happened to the old abbey. Small creatures taking up residence, large ones raising broods there, huts and houses like fungus erupting in elaborate ramparts that ate the old walls to build themselves. There was a long area of weedy waste ground stretching down to the river and inevitably filling with the huts, vegetable gardens, chickens, pigs, goats and dirty children of the endless thousands of peasants flooding into London to make their fortune. They were not impressed by the lawyers' writs of eviction. However, the writing they didn't know how to read was very clearly on the wall for them in the shape of scaffolding, sawdust, wagons full of blocks of stone, and builders finishing the two magnificent halls for the rich lawyers to take their Commons.

Dodd had almost enjoyed the short walk of a couple of miles along the Oxford Road from Tyburn to the Whitefriars liberties where Carey was more comfortable even though his father had (yet again) paid his creditors. Most of them. The ones he could remember or who had served him with writs at any rate.

He had to admit, it was interesting to see the different styles of working in London and the numberless throngs in the streets and the settled solidity of the overhanging houses. He also had to admit that despite the pathetic lack of decent walls or fortifications, London was impressive. Dodd was still tinkering with his plans for the greatest raid of all time, even though he knew it was hopeless. Where would you sell that much gold and insight? How would you even carry it all back to the Debateable Land?

Very near the round Temple church with its wonderful coloured glass, Carey swung off down an alleyway and up some stairs into a luxurious set of chambers, lined with leatherbound books and with painted cloths of Nimrod the Hunter on the walls. Two haughty-looking clerks surrounded by piles of paper and books looked up briefly as they came in, announced by a spotty page boy with a headcold.

There was a pause. The clerks continued to write away. Carey looked mildly surprised and then leaned on the mantel over the luxury of a small fireplace and hummed a tune. Dodd put his hands behind his back and waited stolidly.

Nothing happened. Surprisingly, Carey cracked first. 'Is Mr. Fleetwood available?' he asked coldly, and the haughtiest clerk ignored the magnificence of his embroidered trunk-hose and raised a withering eyebrow.

'Do you have an appointment, Mr...er...' intoned the clerk down his nose. The pageboy had announced them correctly and clearly.

Carey's eyebrow headed for his hairline as well. Dodd leaned back slightly and prepared to watch the fun: would the two pairs of eyebrows fight a little duel, perhaps?

'Robert Carey,' he drawled, '*Sir* Robert Carey.'

The clerk held his ground. 'Do you have an appointment, Sir Robert?'

'I believe my worshipful father, m'lord Baron Hunsdon, mentioned that we might be coming here this afternoon.' Carey paused. 'To see Fleetwood. Your master.' He added as to a child, 'About a legal matter.'

'Ah yes,' sneered the clerk, 'The assault at Fleet Prison.'

The other clerk glanced up nervously from his copying, then down again. The page boy was hiding on the landing, listening busily.

'And unlawful imprisonment of my man, Sergeant Dodd,' said Carey, 'and sundry other matters of a legal nature.'

The clerk sprang his trap. 'Mr. Fleetwood is *not* available.'

One Carey eyebrow climbed, the other dropped. Did he know he was doing it, wondered Dodd who was not in the slightest bit surprised at what was happening. It seemed from his face that Carey was surprised. Now the left eyebrow was mounting Carey's forehead again to join his brother in chilly wonder. Did he practise? In front of a mirror?

'How unfortunate,' said Carey. 'Perhaps tomorrow...'

'Mr. Fleetwood is very busy,' said the clerk with magnificent contempt, 'for the foreseeable future. A year at least.'

'My lord Hunsdon had assured me that Mr. Fleetwood could represent Sergeant Dodd in this matter.' Carey was losing ground here.

'My lord was mistaken. Mr. Fleetwood had not first consulted me,' sniffed the clerk. 'His daybook is full.'

'Hm,' said Carey, eyebrows now down in a frown.

Dodd stepped forward and leaned his hands not too threateningly on the clerk's desk. 'Is Mr. Vice Chamberlain Heneage payin' ye?'

The clerk quivered slightly and then answered with fake indignation, 'Of course not, Sergeant, the very idea is outrageous.'

Dodd looked around at the other clerk, industriously copying, and nodded. 'Ay, so he's threatened ye.'

It was satisfying to see the haughty clerk now reading very carefully in Mr. Fleetwood's daybook which seemed to be empty as far as Dodd could see. Nobody said anything.

'Thank ye,' said Dodd, remembering a little late some of Carey's lectures about London manners. 'Nae doubt it's just as well, Ah wouldna want a man wi' nae blood tae his liver standing up for me in court.'

He clattered down the stairs followed by a Carey who was smiling now.

'Well, I never saw that before,' he mused. 'A lawyer turning down a fat fee. Amazing.'

'I have,' said Dodd.

Carey wanted to try other lawyers he knew of, Dodd said it wasn't worth the bother. They had an argument about it in the arched old cloister next to the round church.

'See ye,' Dodd said, 'if it ha' been nobbut a bribe, then maybe, but if Heneage is threatening 'em, he's threatened the lot of them. Threats are cheap.'

'I know that, Sergeant,' said Carey. 'I just want to check.'

Sighing Dodd followed Carey on his route through the dens of lawyers and found he was right. No serjeant, utter barrister, attorney, nor even humble solicitor would touch Dodd's case on the end of a polearm. Not that any one of them could have lifted such a weapon.

Frustrated, they sat on a bench facing a small duck pond next to the other shiny new hall, still having its windows installed. Carey had to lean awkwardly with his legs out because of the idiocy of his clothes and their tight fashionable fit.

He pulled out the long clay pipe and started filling it with the mixture of tobacco and expensive Moroccan resin that Dr. Nunez had prescribed for them the previous week. Carey liked it enough to have made enquiries about importing some to Carlisle but it was eyewateringly expensive.

Despite the fact that the practise of drinking herbal smoke was a highly fashionable London vice, Dodd rather liked it too. He took the pipe and drew some of the aromatic white smoke into his lungs and after a moment was blinking peacefully at the tumble of huts going down to the water.

Carey chuckled. 'It's a mess, isn't it? Last time I saw him, Sir Robert Cecil was talking about planting gardens down to the river. Of course you'd have to get the riffraff thrown out first.'

'What? The lawyers?' Dodd said deadpan, and Carey grinned.

'Good idea, as they won't bloody work for us.'

'Ye canna blame them. Heneage will have said to a few of them, tsk tsk, d'ye think the Careys'll take care of yer kine and yer tower while you're lawyering for that Dodd, tsk tsk, and the word will have gone round,' Dodd said knowledgeably.

'Metaphorically speaking, but yes. Shortage of Readerships, strange famine of appointments to the serjeantcy, etcetera, etcetera. Quod erat demonstrandum.'

'Ay. So. Will we do it ourselves?'

'What, go to court? Certainly not.'

'Why not? It canna be so hard if lawyers can do it.'

Carey snorted with giggles and Dodd almost giggled as well, feeling pleasantly drunk from the smoke.

'Sergeant, you've run wood. How long does it normally take you to draft one bill? An afternoon? And I'm certainly not studying the law at my age.'

'Other young gentlemen study at the Inns of Court,' Dodd pointed out. One of the young gentlemen happened to be standing nearby wrapped in his black cloth robe, very like a crow, blinking at the ducks on the pond. For a moment Dodd thought he was familiar, but couldn't place him at all.

Carey took the pipe back from Dodd who had forgotten he was holding it. 'Not me. I went to France and wapped a lot of French ladies,' said Carey coarsely. 'We need a lawyer.'

'All Heneage has done is reive our horses,' Dodd said.

'Metaphorically speaking,' Carey corrected, waggling the end of the pipe at him.

'So then we go after him on foot. We do it ourselves. Ay, so it's slower but...'

Carey shook his head and passed the pipe back to Dodd. 'I keep telling you, this is not a Border feud, we do things differently in London. Perhaps Father could twist some arms, raise the fees... Maybe one of the Bacon brothers would take it pro bono if I asked nicely.'

Dodd shook his head firmly and opened his mouth to argue but there was a soft cough which interrupted him.

'Excuse me, sirs, but I couldn't help hearing your discourse.'

It was the young man in the lawyer's robe. As the man made his bow, Dodd stared at him suspiciously, assuming this must be one of Heneage's spies you heard so much about. The young man was average height, narrow built, with sandy hair under one of the newly fashionable beaver hats. Sharp blue eyes peered out of a face ruined by smallpox, worse even than Barnabus. His attempt at a friendly smile was actually twisted by the scarring. There was a shocking pit right next to his mouth, the size of a farthing.

'Is it true that you are in need of a lawyer?'

'Possibly,' said Carey, eyeing the man.

He bowed again to both of them, making Dodd feel uncomfortable. 'I am James Enys, at your service, sirs, barrister-at-law.'

'And yer daybook is no' full?' asked Dodd cynically.

'Empty, sirs.' The man laughed without humour and spread his soft white hands. One of the fingers was dented by a ring newly taken off. 'I have just hocked my last ring, sirs, and turned off my clerk.'

'Are ye no' rich then?' Dodd asked curiously, 'I thought all lawyers was rich.'

'Potentially, yes. But generally not when they start, and especially not if Mr. Vice Chancellor Heneage has taken a dislike to them.'

This was too pat for either Carey or Dodd's liking. They exchanged glances.

Enys coughed and held up one hand.

'Gentlemen, I know you are trying to launch a civil suit for damages and a criminal charge of assault, battery, and false imprisonment against Mr. Vice, and that Mr. Vice has forestalled you by frightening off all the courageous men of law in this place.'

'Ay,' said Dodd, putting his elbows on his knees and leaning forwards, despite the damage this made his chokingly high collar do to his adam's apple. 'But whit can ye dae to show us ye're no' one o' his kinship come tae trap us in ambush?'

Carey coughed as Enys frowned in puzzlement. 'My friend is from Cumberland,' he explained, and translated Dodd's challenge.

Enys inclined his head slightly. 'Quite right, Sergeant,' he said, 'you have a point there. Yet the same could be said of any lawyer you hired—if not already a spy, turned into one the minute Heneage found out who he was.'

'So?'

Enys shrugged. 'Make enquiries, sir. Ask about me. You will find I am a little notorious. I still have chambers in my lord of Essex's court. My...um...my sister keeps house for me there although she does not...um like to keep company. You may find me there any time from ten in the morning.'

'Not at Westminster Hall?' Carey asked.

Again the stiff smile. 'Frequently, in hopes of a brief. However, Mr. Vice has made it clear that he prefers my room to my company there and the Court officials often oblige him. Please—at least consider my offer.'

'Do you know who I am?' Carey was crossing his legs at the ankle, leaning back and tapping his gloved fingers on his teeth.

Dodd nipped the pipe from his other hand and smoked the last of the tobacco in the bowl, then tapped it out, his head spinning. Not only did the smoke ease his kidneys, it also seemed to do something to the dull ball of rage in his gut against Heneage.

'I believe you are the son of my lord Baron Hunsdon.'

'How did you find out?'

'When I heard you enquiring of one of my brothers-at-law, I asked him and he told me. Also, sir, with respect, you and your family are not entirely unknown to the legal profession.'

Carey ignored that. 'Well, you'll know then that I'm the youngest and utterly penniless at the moment, so it's my worshipful Father you must convince, not me. He'll be paying you.'

Enys bowed. 'I should be delighted at the chance to try.'

'Hm,' said Carey again, 'Very well, come to Somerset House tomorrow afternoon.'

The young man bowed again and his robe swirled as he walked away, whistling softly to himself. Dodd watched him go. 'I dinna trust him.'

'Quite right too,' said Carey, putting the pipe away again. 'Even if he's not Heneage's spy, he's still a bloody lawyer.'

***

When they got back to Somerset House they found that Hunsdon was not there. He had gone upriver to Whitehall Palace in a matter for the Queen and required his son and his son's henchman to join him there immediately.

They got into one of the Hunsdon boats, still munching some hurried bread and cheese. Dodd leaned back and idly watched the flapping standard at the prow. Certainly there were aspects to being a gentleman he could well get used to—such as not being one of the men in blinding yellow and black livery sweating to propel them to Westminster against the tide. Carey sat opposite, upright, tapping his fingers on the gunwale and looking thoughtfully into the distance.

Dodd had nothing against boats and found himself quite enjoying the crowded river, full of vessels crossing in all directions;

a red-sailed Thames lugger headed straight for them at one point causing the men on the larboard side to back water in order to avoid it. Derisive shouts echoed over the water from the larger boat. The water was brown but not too bad-smelling, all things considered. Somerset House had its own well and in any case Dodd was sticking firmly to mild ale because it was good for his kidneys. He saw no need to take the suicidal risk of drinking expensive Thames water which was so full of ill humours and mud, although he was quite happy to eat the salmon from it when he wanted a cheap meal. The standard flapped in the breeze on the water.

'What are you smiling at, Sergeant?' asked Carey, who seemed to be worried about something. Dodd realised he had indeed been smiling; he must still be a little drunk from the tobacco.

'Nowt.' Dodd hastily averted his eyes from the thing.

'Come on, it's Father's badge, isn't it?'

It had been. Dodd had been wondering, why did the Queen's Lord Chamberlain, one of the richest and most powerful men in the kingdom, choose as his badge the figure of what looked like a rabid duck?

Carey stuck his lower lip out. 'It's a Swan Rampant.'

'Ay?'

'It's in honour of my Lady Mother, if you're interested.'

'Ay?' Dodd was very interested, but tried hard not to let it show. 'Is she still alive then, yer...ah...Lady Mother?'

'Oh yes,' said Carey, not explaining any more. Dodd wondered where Hunsdon kept her as there was no sign of a wife at Somerset House. Perhaps she was tired: Dodd would have thought she would be after birthing the full Carey brood of eight living children, and possibly more pregnancies depending how many babes she might have lost.

'So...ah...where is she?' asked Dodd in what he hoped was a tactful voice. After all, there was an official mistress at Hunsdon's residence. 'Prefers the countryside?'

'You could say that,' answered Carey. 'She has no interest in the Court and would have to attend the Queen if she lived in London, so...er...she doesn't. She was here in '88 though.'

'Wise lady,' said Dodd, feeling sorry for her. It could be no easy thing to be married to the likes of lord Baron Hunsdon nor mother to his reckless sons. He pictured the lady in a manor house somewhere, living a dull but respectable life, embroidering linen and doing whatever else ladies did, whilst her husband philandered through the fleshpots of London.

Carey nodded, still looking worried. Just once he cast a glance over his shoulder where the ship-forest of the Pool of London, on the other side of the Bridge, was disappearing round the bend.

'I thought I saw...No,' he said to himself, 'can't be.'

Dodd peered at the bridge himself but the crowded houses gave up no clue and nor did the carrion crows and buzzards squabbling over the new head there. He saw a flight of fourteen crows swoop up and attack the buzzards together, driving them away from the delicacy. He blinked for a moment. Did birds have surnames to back them? Crows all lived together in rookeries, of course, but did they foray out together against other birds like men? It was fascinating. He knew that the proper thing to call such an avian group was a 'murder' of crows because of their liking for newborn lambs.

More of Hunsdon's liverymen were waiting for them at the Westminster steps. Carey and Dodd were led briskly not into the palace but to a small stone chapel tucked into the side of Westminster Hall, then down into the cool crypt. From the stairs Dodd smelled death, and so did Carey for his nostrils flared.

A bloated corpse lay on a trestle table between the various tombs and monuments of the crypt. The body was surrounded by candles to burn out the bad airs. They were not doing a good job. Hunsdon stood before the corpse, hands on his sword belt, his Chamberlain's staff under his arm.

Carey bowed and so did Dodd. 'My lord,' said Carey, 'I was hoping that your business at the palace would be more pleasant.'

Hunsdon scowled at his son. 'Eh? What are you talking about?'

Carey looked annoyed and uncomfortable. 'I was hoping you might have been...ah...mentioning my unpaid fee to Her Majesty and...'

'Oh, for God's sake, Robin,' growled Hunsdon, 'she'll pay it when she's good and ready and not before. Meanwhile, look at this.'

Unwillingly, they looked.

'Besides she's still in Oxford with the court or possibly heading back by now if she takes one of her notions. Odd this.'

Hunsdon gestured at the corpse. It was a man wearing a good linen shirt, skin waterlogged and flaking away, eyes and other soft parts already eaten by fish, stomach swollen and pregnant with gas.

'Who is he?' asked Carey, taking a handkerchief out of his sleeve pocket and holding it to his nose.

'Nobody knows his name and he's in my jurisdiction, blast him.'

Dodd wanted to ask why but didn't. However, Hunsdon swung on him and said, 'As Lord Chamberlain to her Majesty I am *de officio* President of the Board of Greencloth with a remit over any murder done within the Virge of the Court, that is, within two miles of Her Majesy's sacred person or her palaces. The blighter washed up against the Queen's own Privy Steps, so he's my responsibility.'

With a lurch in his gut, Dodd realised the man had no feet. Carey was approaching the corpse, handkerchief still over his mouth and nose, looking carefully all over it and turning the swollen hands over. Dodd knew Carey had been spending time with Mr. Fenwick the Carlisle undertaker and he seemed to have got a strong stomach from it. The man's left index finger was missing a top joint.

Dodd found that the close air in the crypt with its musty smell of the long dead and the gassy fecal stench reeking from the corpse was on the verge of embarassing him. He didn't have a hanky, so he put his hand over his nose and swallowed hard.

Carey smiled at him. 'Look here, Sergeant,' he said, 'see? It's interesting, isn't it?' Carey was holding up the flaccid swollen fingers. By the guttering light of the candles Dodd could see they were scarred with burns in a couple of places, but also that there was a clerk's callus on the middle finger of his right hand. Yet the palms had the calluses you got from using a spade, not a sword.

He frowned. Yes, it was interesting. What manner of man was it? A gentleman wouldn't have spade calluses on his palms and a commoner wouldn't have a clerk's bump from holding a pen.

'Ay,' he said, 'He wis wearing a ring too.' He pointed gingerly at the mark on the little finger left by a ring.

Carey carefully lifted the other hand. 'No other rings, the same marks though.'

'And what happened to his feet?' said Hunsdon, watching his son with his head on one side and a look of baffled pride on his face.

Carey moved to that end, past a pair of knobbly knees, and blinked down at the exposed ankle joints. 'It looks like they were torn off after the man was dead,' he said thoughtfully. 'Hmm.' He bent closer to look and Dodd peered as well, brought one of the watchlights over.

The bone seemed to have been ground by something hard leaving little grains of red there. Perhaps flakes of rust?

'Hm,' said Carey again and went to the head end. 'I wonder...'

To Dodd's disgust, he took out his poinard and levered open the man's mouth with it. A trickle of brown came out. Carey placed his gloved hand flat on the man's chest and pressed. More brown water came out of the mouth.

'There's no wound in the body, is there?'

'Stab wound in the back,' said Hunsdon, now holding a pomander to his nose, 'probably to the kidneys.'

'Ah,' nodded Carey, taking refuge in his hanky again. Dodd was desperately trying not to cough. 'I wonder if...'

At that moment the corpse shifted and farted, as if some horrible wall had been breached. All three of them were at the door in unspoken terror before the air filled with a stench so foul they were coughing and gagging as they ran up the stairs, leaving the watchcandles flickering blue behind them.

'Christ,' gasped Hunsdon as they tumbled out into the street with very little dignity, 'I hate these cases. Bloody man will have to be embalmed until we can hold an inquest for him.' He gestured irritably at three of his men who were standing around holding a large tarpaulin and after an unhappy pause, they went down into the crypt to cover the corpse up again.

By unspoken agreement, all three of them went up the street and into a nearby Westminster boozing ken, a wooden hut but very nicely painted hard by the Court gate, with the traditional red lattices. Its battered patriotic sign bore the Tudor Rose, painted over a carving that looked as if it was of a boar or a pig of some kind.

The barman knew Hunsdon immediately and was obsequious, bowing him into a private alcove away from the feverishly gaming young courtiers. Their brandies came from a different barrel under the counter and when Dodd gulped it, he wished he hadn't for it was very much better than the aqua vitae he normally drank when pressed. At least, he thought gloomily, he had held his water and hadn't vomited, though it had been a close thing when the corpse moved...To be sure it was no more than the gas in it and Dodd had seen it happen before, but in a small space and in the light of the candles...As Carey's father had said, Christ!

His heartbeat was settling again. Two more of Hunsdon's men, Turner and Catchpole, stood around nearby. Now Dodd had to suppress another moment of happy smugness. Normally it would be him standing by walls, watching his betters drinking, bored and waiting for an order from Lowther or Scrope, not sitting down and doing the drinking. He had done the same duty for his wife's uncle, the Armstrong headman, Kinmont Willie Armstrong, although on those occasions he hadn't been bored at all because he was waiting for the fight to begin. So this gentlemanning around London was a pleasant change and it worried him that he was getting used to it.

His face settled back into its normal glum scowl and he sipped more carefully at the aqua vitae so he could actually taste the stuff.

'Good isn't it,' said Carey, whose face was not quite so pale now. 'It's a French aqua vitae, made from cider.'

'Ay?' Dodd was interested. 'What's normal brandy made of then?'

'Wine usually.'

'Is that the same as brandywine?'

'No, that's wine mixed with brandy and usually some spices and sugar. Very good it is too...'

Carey caught the potboy's eye, established that the boozing ken was high-class enough to have brandywine, and a few minutes later Dodd was sipping that as well. Carey hadn't even asked the price—that was what having a rich father did to you, thought Dodd.

'I've already told the Board to convene tomorrow, damn and

blast it,' said Hunsdon, knocking back his own aqua vitae. 'God, I hate council meetings.'

'When exactly was he found?'

'Low tide, yesterday,' said Hunsdon. 'Gave one of the Queen's favourite chamberers a nasty turn.'

'So probably carried downriver by the current, not up by the tide.'

'Probably.'

'Hm.' Carey was looking thoughtfully into his wine.

'Any ideas, Robin?'

Carey smiled cynically. 'I think you should procure six witnesses to swear that they saw him going to Heneage's house in Chelsea and the inquest should find him unlawfully killed by person or persons unknown and...'

Hunsdon rolled his eyes. 'There's no sign he was one of Heneage's.'

Carey shrugged. 'And?'

Hunsdon shook his head. 'Come on, what could you see from the corpse?'

'Not the face of his killer in his eyes,' said Carey. 'And I don't know whether he was a commoner or a clerk or a gentleman. But I do know that the stab to his back didn't kill him for he was put in the river still breathing since his lungs were full of water. I suspect that what killed him was the weight of iron chains on his feet pulling him to the bottom from the rust flakes on his ankle bones.'

Dodd nodded at this. 'Ay, and when his flesh rotted enough, his feet broke off in the currents and the body could fetch up at the steps.'

'How long ago was he put in the river?' rumbled Hunsdon.

'Perhaps ten days, two weeks ago? I don't know, it's hard to tell with water.'

'Any more of Walsingham's tricks?'

Carey shook his head. 'Nothing that would give us his name, my lord, but I expect that's why he had only his shirt on—his doublet would give too much away.'

Dodd sat still, transfixed with a sudden thought. If the man was stripped, why *did* they leave his shirt on? Modesty? Not very likely. Och God, he thought, I'll have to go back into that pest pit again.

Fortified by brandy he leaned forward. 'Ay, so what's under his shirt?'

Carey frowned and was clearly thinking the same as Dodd. He sighed and stood up. 'We'll have to look.'

They walked back down the street, took several deep breaths of relatively clean London air, and then went down the stairs and past the guard. The tarpaulin was heavy and the ragged remains of the man's shirt sticky with…something. Carey pulled it back. Dodd and he stared, looking for anything of interest. Nothing, if you ignored the damage done by fishes, except for a small knife scar on the ribs and a recognisable healed swordslash across the chest.

They looked at each other and Dodd's gorge rose. He swallowed hard and held his breath.

Fearful of causing another corpsely fart, they hefted the man onto his left side very carefully. Dodd brought the flickering candle as close to the man's back as he could. And there, at last, they found something interesting—little arrow-shaped scratches scattered at random across the water-swollen skin of his back. There were more grouped near the shoulders, as if the dead man had rolled in a bramble patch. Nothing else—the scars were mostly white and old, although a few seemed more recent.

Neither spoke as they let him down again, saving their breath. They pulled the tarpaulin back and hurried up the stairs.

Dodd was panting from lack of air and both of them were sweating. His head spun. He had to stop and sit on a wall for a moment because of the memories from when he was very little and still in his skirts: the bodies of people he knew, dead from plague, lying unburied around the village, and what had happened to them.

'I hope that was worth it,' said Carey. 'I wonder what made those scratches. I know I've never seen it before but there's something niggling me about it.'

'Ay,' croaked Dodd, very ready for more brandywine now, 'but he wisnae actually flogged, that's for sure.'

Carey nodded, gazing into space intently as if he was trying to read the answer written on the clouds.

They rejoined Hunsdon at the boozing ken who had got in more brandy for them and mild ale for Dodd.

'Just some odd little scratches on his back, and a couple of healed cuts' Carey answered his sire's eyebrows. 'They don't help identify him. No tattoos or birthmarks that I could see, although you could cry the fact that his left index finger is missing its top joint.'

Hunsdon sighed heavily again and drank. 'It's worth looking at the warrants Mr. Heneage has sworn out over the past month just in case the man's one of his, but it's unlikely we'll match them up. We need a proper identification. I'll have the town criers in Westminster and the City cry the news, and bills printed up with his description. All I can do, unfortunately.'

'Meanwhile Mr. Recorder Fleetwood's bloody nephew refuses point blank to act for me,' said Carey.

'Damn and blast,' said his father, sounding no more than wearily irritated, certainly not surprised. 'I thought that might happen.'

'Is it no' possible to proceed then?' Dodd asked mournfully.

'Of course it is. I'll ask Cecil what he suggests. Or one of the Bacons...'

'Perhaps my lord earl of Essex could help?' Carey put in.

'Possibly. He's back in her Majesty's favour again at least,' said Hunsdon and Dodd thought he heard something cautious in his tone.

'The Bacons won't deal with a mere case of assault...'

'They might know someone who will.'

'He'll no' come to trial will he, my lord,' Dodd said. 'Heneage, I mean. He's too important.'

'Criminal trial? We can make the attempt though I agree, I doubt it. It's the civil case for damages that I'm interested in.' Hunsdon let out a tight little smile.

'And will the Queen no' take his side? Seeing he's her henchman?'

'There's no telling what Her Majesty the Queen my cousin might take it into her head to do.'

Dodd knew about this. Hunsdon was indeed cousin to the Queen through his mother Mary Boleyn, the sister of the more famous Anne.

Dodd looked hopeful. 'Untouchable, are ye, sir?'

'Good God, no,' said Hunsdon with a bluff laugh, 'nobody's untouchable. If Heneage could convince the Queen that I've turned traitor, I'd go to the block just like anybody else. Quite right too if the bill was foul and I was guilty.'

That was worrying. If somebody like Hunsdon came down, so would anyone associated with him. Hunsdon slapped Dodd on the back.

'Don't look so worried, Sergeant, the Queen's a lot more difficult to fool than Heneage thinks she is.'

Dodd nodded.

They sat in the back of the boat while Hunsdon sat in the front. Carey was looking annoyed, possibly because a boat full of musicians was following the Hunsdon boat, playing for all they were worth. Dodd couldn't hear a word of what Carey was muttering.

'Eh sir?' he shouted. Carey tried again but couldn't whisper loud enough. 'What are they following us for?' Dodd wanted to know, wishing he'd brought a crossbow, especially for the viol player.

'Father's in charge of the Queen's entertainments at Court,' Carey explained. 'They're hoping he'll give them a job.'

'Och.' Dodd shook his head at such folly. 'Whit were ye saying...'

'I was saying that I was hoping to start for Carlisle soon.'

'Afore ye've seen the Queen?' Dodd was surprised.

'She's at Oxford which is on the way.'

'Ah.' Dodd felt the corners of his mouth turning down sourly. Typical Carey, no consideration for anyone else.

'I'm surprised you're not delighted, Sergeant.'

Dodd scowled at him for his ignorance. 'Nay sir, I'm in nae hurry.'

'I thought you hated London.'

'Ay sir, I do.'

'And there's plague about.'

'Ay sir.' Both of them were quiet for a moment remembering Carey's servant Barnabus and his family. Hunsdon had indicated he would take Barnabus' niece into his household until she could be found a good husband, and young Simon, his nephew, was already lording it over the other boys in the stables where he was a great deal more use than he was as Carey's page.

'So? Why don't you want to go home?'

'I havenae had my satisfaction fra Heneage yet.'

Carey barked with laughter. Dodd was annoyed again. He wagged a finger at Carey.

'Say what ye like about Richie Graham of Brackenhill, but he'd know better than to treat a Dodd like that. Wee Colin Elliot might treat me like that if he got the chance, but he wouldnae have the insolence to leave me alive after.'

Carey grinned. 'Jock of the Peartree did something similar to me a few months ago and I'm not planning vengeance.'

'Ay sir, but ye was spying out his tower and forebye it was in the way of battle and retaliation for the lumps ye gave him yersen. That's fair, is that, and ye both know it.'

Carey nodded. Dodd leaned back with his hands on his thighs.

'So. I canna leave London until I've given Heneage back what he gave me.'

'With interest?'

'Ay. Wi' interest.'

'Trouble is, it might take a while and I really want to talk to the Queen and my lord of Essex.'

Dodd sighed and looked him in the eye. Carey winced, probably at the horribly sour but valiant viol-scraping in the boat that was now closing on them rapidly.

'Sir,' said Dodd, 'do ye not ken that the Dodds have a bloodfeud wi' the Elliots that goes back tae the Rough Wooing of Henry VIII, over sixty years? If it takes a while, then it takes a while. Or if he dies afore I'm satisfied, then I'll do the same to his son.'

'I don't think Heneage has a family.'

Dodd shrugged. 'If he dies wi'out issue, then I'll take it to his cousins or his nephews.' He'd been wondering if Heneage had family to back him as well as the Queen. It was good news that he didn't.

Even so, Carey seemed worried.

Dodd tapped his knee. 'Dinna be concerned, sir. It's no' a blood feud, only a feud. It might be composed if he offers enough to me or I can burn his tower or the like.'

'Ah,' said Carey. 'Good. I need you back in Carlisle this autumn.'

'As yer father tells it, I can leave the court case with my lawyer once I've made my statements and he'll take it on for me until he needs me again. Once it's well begun I'll come back wi'ye to Carlisle and happy to do it.' Dodd thought wistfully of Janet. He would never have guessed how much he missed her visits to him on market days and his visits back to her in Gilsland when he could.

'How much would you take to compose your feud?'

Dodd thought carefully. 'Ah dinna ken, sir. Whit would be the London price for twenty kine and ten sheep and five good horses.'

At that moment they heard a muttered 'God's truth!' from Hunsdon in the prow. He stood and gestured so that the rowers backed water. Then he beckoned the boatful of importunate musicians even closer.

'How much for your viol?' he roared across to them.

The musicians elbowed each other and there was a fierce argument. 'He doesn't want to sell, my lord,' shouted a harpist with long hair.

Hunsdon fished out a purse of silver and hefted it. 'This much?'

There was a scuffle in the boat and one of the flautists brandished the viol in the air while the drummer sat on the viol player. Hunsdon gently threw the purse of silver into the boat and, despite wild protests from the viol player, the instrument was lobbed spinning across the water to be caught by Hunsdon's man Turner. He handed it to Hunsdon, who took the instrument by the neck and smashed it to pieces against the side of the boat. Carey looked mildly pained, then shrugged.

'That's better,' shouted Hunsdon, 'and don't for God's sake let the man buy another bloody instrument.'

The Hunsdon liverymen bent grinning to their oars again and they left the musicians well behind.

Carey and his father were uncharacteristically quiet as the boat sped downriver, helped by the current. As they rounded the bend and came in sight of Somerset House, both men gasped and stood up in the boat, nearly upsetting it.

Another boat was tied up at Somerset steps, a long gig from a ship, also sporting the Swan Rampant that was Hunsdon's badge. Men were standing on the boatlanding who were clearly not Londoners, being barrel-shaped, mainly red-haired and short, and sporting long pigtails down their backs.

Dodd stared with interest at the play of expressions on Carey's face—absolute horror predominating. Strangely Hunsdon was grinning with delight from ear to ear and let out a bellow of laughter.

'Good God, it can't be,' groaned Carey.

'It is!' laughed Hunsdon, slapping his son on the back and taking him unawares so he nearly went in the Thames. 'I'd recognise that crew of Cornish wreckers and pirates anywhere. Ho, Trevasker!'

The most evil-looking of the men touched his cap to Hunsdon and said something to one of the others.

'Oh Jesus, this is all I need,' said Carey, sitting down and putting his head in his hands.

His father stayed standing all the way to the steps and jumped off onto the jetty before the boat was even tied up. The crew of Cornish wreckers and pirates touched their foreheads respectfully to Hunsdon as he hurried past them, through the gate in the wall, and up through the gardens. Carey followed nearly as quickly with a face of thunder while Dodd scrambled after, near to dying of curiosity. He caught up with Carey in the orchard.

'Is it one o' yer creditors?'

'No, much worse. You saw the badge, didn't you? It's much, much worse.'

Dodd shook his head, loosened his sword just in case Carey wasn't exaggerating again, and followed up to the house which was blazing with candles in the grey afternoon.

In the magnificent entrance hall stood more short, broad, pigtailed men with hands like hams and a strong smell of the sea on them. Hunsdon hurried through to the parlour where a smallish woman in her sixties with very bright blue eyes was just taking off a large sealskin cloak and handing it to a pink-cheeked girl.

She turned, smiled, and curtseyed to Lord Hunsdon who bowed formally, then opened his arms and bellowed 'Annie!' as he scooped her up and swung her round in a delighted hug.

'Put me down, Harry, you old fool!' shouted the woman as she hugged him back with just as much violence, laughing with an infectious gurgle in her throat. 'You'll knock my hat off.'

Although she otherwise spoke like Hunsdon there was a strong flavour in her voice. It was the sound of the Cornish sailors who plied up and down the Irish Sea in appalling weather, trading tin, hides, wood, and contraband in all directions.

Hunsdon put her down gently and she straightened her smart French hood and smiled lovingly at Carey. 'Where's my little man to, then, eh?' she demanded.

Real pain crossed Carey's face. Dodd's mouth dropped open as he finally worked out who he was looking at. Carey stepped past him, swept a very fine Court bow, and bent over the lady's hand with unimpeachable respect.

'My lady mother,' murmured Carey in a resigned tone of voice. 'What a delightful surprise.'

She laughed a gravelly laugh and thumped him in the ribs. 'No it ain't, Robin.' she said, 'Don't try that Court soft soap with me. You're shaking in your fine boots.'

Carey smiled wanly.

'Er...'

'You're worried I know what you've been at, boy, and you're right. I do.'

'Ah...'

'Meanwhile, who's this henchman of yours?'

Guts cramping, ribs aching, and his face stiff with the effort not to laugh, Dodd stepped forward and made the best bow he could manage.

'Ma'am, may I present Land-Sergeant Henry Dodd of Gilsland, presently serving under me in Carlisle,' said Carey in the tones of one going to his execution.

Dodd found himself being looked sharply up and down.

'Hm. So you're the Dodd headman that came out for my son with your kin when he got himself in trouble at Netherby,' she said.

'Ay, my lady. Wi' the English Armstrongs o' course.'

'And as I heard it, you convinced the Johnston to back you and ran a nice little ambush on the Maxwell to bring the handguns back from Dumfries in the summer.'

Dodd could only nod. How the hell could she know so much? Carey had his eyes shut and his hands clasped firmly behind his back like a boy reciting a lesson.

Lady Hunsdon swung on her husband. 'I take a little trip to Dumfries in summer with Captain Trevasker and the *Judith of Penryn* in Irish whiskey and some vittles for the Scottish court and what do I hear? My youngest son's doings all over the town although the King's gone back to Edinburgh and his mangy pack of lordlings with him.'

'Did you sell the cargo?' asked Hunsdon.

'Of course I did, husband, that's why I went. I knew the Court would have eaten and drunk the place bare. Triple prices for the whisky from my Lord Maxwell, no less.'

She was advancing on Carey now who backed before her with his shoulders up like a boy expecting to have his ears boxed for scrumping apples. Dodd held his breath in mingled hope and fascination.

'Now one of the things I heard was not at all to my liking,' she said, prodding Carey in his well-velveted chest which was as high as she could reach. He flinched. 'Not at all. What's this about Lord Spynie and Sir Henry Widdrington, eh?'

Carey smiled placatingly and spread his hands. 'I couldn't possibly say, ma'am, are they in bed together?'

'All but.' Pouncing like a cat, Lady Hunsdon grabbed her son's left hand and pulled off his embroidered glove. After a moment when it seemed Carey would snatch his hand away and possibly run for it, he stood and let her look, towering over her and yet somehow gangling like the lad he must have been fifteen years before.

In silence Lady Hunsdon reached for his other hand. Carey sighed and pulled the glove off for her. More thunderous silence. Dodd saw tears rising to Lady Hunsdon's eyes and suddenly she pulled Carey to her and hugged him.

'Mother!' protested the muffled voice of Carey. She let go at once and turned to her husband.

'We shall set a price of five thousand crowns on Spynie's head and the same on Widdrington's,' she said coldly.

'Er...no, my lady,' said Hunsdon, 'I think not. Spynie's still the King's Minion, though there are hopes of Robert Kerr, and John needs the Widdrington surname to help him rule the East March.'

Their eyes locked and Dodd could see the tussle and then the agreement between them flying clear as a bird. 'At least, not yet,' amended his lordship.

'Of course, my lord,' said Lady Hunsdon with the dangerous meekness Dodd had learned to fear in Janet.

Carey was pulling his gloves back on with fingers that trembled slightly.

'Have you seen Edmund?' Hunsdon asked to break the silence. 'Doctor Nunez is very pleased with him.'

Lady Hunsdon sat herself down in a carved chair as Hunsdon sat as well. 'I talked to him while I was waiting for you, my lord.'

At Hunsdon's gesture, Carey and Dodd sat on a bench. Hunsdon's majordomo was bringing in a light supper and spiced wine for them. Carey spoke quietly to him and Dodd saw a small cup of brandy brought and added to his wine. He looked like he needed it and drank gratefully while Dodd helped himself to a mutton pasty.

'Did you plan to put a price on Heneage's head as well, wife?' asked Hunsdon teasingly as he carved a plump breast of duck with a sauce of raspberries and laid it on her plate. Lady Hunsdon sniffed and pulled the dish of sallet herbs towards her.

'Your sister wouldn't like it.'

'She wouldn't,' agreed Hunsdon.

'He mistreated you too, Sergeant Dodd?' Lady Hunsdon said suddenly to Dodd, who had to swallow quickly.

'Ay, my lady.'

'What are you going to do about it?'

'Ay well, milady, if I was at home the bell'd be ringing and the Dodds and Armstrongs would be riding and the man would ha' lost a few flocks of sheep and herds of cattle and some horses if we could find them and likely a tower or two burned.'

Lady Hunsdon nodded. 'Of course. Powerful long way for your surname to come though, isn't it?'

'Ay, it is. Your good lord has offered to back a court case for me but...ah...'

'The lawyers won't take the brief, ma'am,' explained Carey. 'None of them will.'

Lady Hunsdon nodded at this.

'Except that pocky young man we met the day,' put in Dodd. 'He said he'd dae it since Heneage disnae like him in any case.'

'What's his name?' asked Hunsdon.

298

'James...Enys?'

'Enys?' said Lady Hunsdon, 'That's a Cornish name. Where's he from?'

'No idea. We were worried he might be Heneage's man so we asked him to come here tomorrow so you could look at him, my lord.' Lord and Lady Hunsdon both nodded.

'Heneage isn't going to give up just because his last attempt blew up in his face,' said Hunsdon, 'and Edmund...'

'...has horse-clabber for brains,' snapped Lady Hunsdon. 'At least you did well there, Robin, from what he said.'

Carey inclined his head politely while still studying the floor.

Dodd watched as Lady Hunsdon polished off her wine and nodded at the Steward to replenish it. 'So what I'm hearing from you, my lord, is that there's not a thing we can do to pay back Spynie and Widdrington, and Heneage is more than likely going to have another try at pulling you down just as soon as he can think of something twisted enough.'

Hunsdon inclined his head in a gesture just like his son's.

'God damn the lot of them,' swore Lady Hunsdon, tapping her fragile Venetian wine glass decisively. 'Do you need money, Robin?'

Carey coloured. 'Ah...well...'

'Of course you do, look at your fancy duds. Cost a couple of farms just for your hose, I shouldn't wonder. Well, I had a lucky voyage coming up the Channel, so here you are...'

She threw a bulging leather purse at Carey who caught it and whistled soundlessly when he looked inside.

'Pieces of eight?'

Lady Hunsdon smiled and wiggled her fingers. 'We caught a Flemish trader off the Carrick Roads as we came out of Penryn. And you're not to spend it on clothes,' she added, setting off another near-hernia in Dodd's abused diaphragm. 'Sergeant, don't you let him go near that devil Bullard and his doublets.'

'No, milady,' Dodd managed somehow.

'Invest it, Robin,' said Lady Hunsdon. 'As I've told you before, George Cumberland has the right idea...'

Hunsdon was standing again, leaning over to his wife and proffering his arm.

'My lady wife,' he said softly. Lady Hunsdon swallowed the last of her spiced wine, put her hand on her husband's arm, and allowed him to help her up. Then she stood on tiptoe and kissed Lord Hunsdon's ear as they turned towards the door to the stairs.

Carey put his fists on his knees, stood up and hurried after his parents, caught up with his mother at the foot of the stairs and started whispering to her urgently. Dodd followed them. He didn't need to hear Carey's question as he knew exactly what it would be about—the woman Carey was disastrously in love with. She was still married to Sir Henry Widdrington, a jealous husband who had clearly seized the chance to mistreat Carey in Dumfries.

'Mother, how is Elizabeth Widdrington?' asked Carey, 'I'm anxious for her. Sir Henry might...'

'I think she's well enough, all things considered,' said Lady Hunsdon with a worried frown. 'She's very strong. Sybilla's still furious with me for the ill match I made for her daughter.'

Carey's inaudible next murmur sounded angry and Lady Hunsdon put up her hand to his shoulder and gripped. 'Robin,' she said, 'I know, I know. You must be patient.' Carey's response was a characteristic growl. Lady Hunsdon smiled fondly at him, pulled his chestnut head down to hers and kissed his cheek. This time Carey didn't bridle like a youth but kissed her back and put his arm around her shoulders.

They parted as Hunsdon led his lady up the stairs. Carey avoided Dodd's eye as they made for their respective bedchambers.

'Now you see why my Lady Mother doesn't often come to Court,' he said. 'She prefers to stay in Cornwall with her sister Sybilla Trevannion and her friends the Killigrews.'

'Ay,' said Dodd.

'It wasn't my mother's fault that I first met my cousin Elizabeth when I went to Scotland with the message for King James from the Queen about his mother's execution,' added Carey. 'Which was after she had been married off to Sir Henry.'

'Ay,' said Dodd, not much interested in the complicated tale of Carey's love-life. If the woman was willing and her husband odious, why did Carey not simply gather a nice raiding party, hit the man's tower by surprise, kill him and take the woman? Dodd would be perfectly happy to be best man at that rough wedding and it would at least end Carey's perpetual mooning over her, alternating with an occasional seduction of some even more dangerous female. 'Ah...Does yer mam hold a letter of marque from the Queen?'

Carey's gaze was cold. 'Of course she does, she's not a pirate. Father got it for her after she happened to help sink a Flemish pirate off the Lizard.' Dodd was proud of himself for not letting a flicker across his countenance.

'Ay?'

'What the Devil do you expect her to do all day, sit at home and embroider?' Carey slammed into his chamber, shouting for the ever absent Simon Barnet to see to his points.

Dodd went to his own chamber and could laugh at last. The wild cherubs over the mantelpiece seemed to laugh back as he carefully worked through all his buttons and laces and folded his suit before climbing into bed in his shirt. As he went to sleep, he thought happily that he now had all the explanation he needed for Carey's wild streak. By God, the Careys were an entertaining bunch. For a while, Dodd felt pierced with loneliness that he didn't have Janet in bed beside him to talk about it. He rather thought Janet and Lady Hunsdon would get on very well.

TUESDAY 12TH SEPTEMBER 1592,

EARLY MORNING

Just after daybreak Dodd was enjoying bread and beer in his chamber at his good vantage point at the window where he could watch the doings in the street. What a pleasure it was to be able to look through a window quilted with diamonds like the jack of an Englishman, so the glass kept the wind out but let the light in.

Nobody ever bothered with glass in the Borders because it broke too easily, although Dodd thought he had heard that Richie Graham had a couple of windows of the stuff for his wife's chamber which were removeable in the case of a siege. Here in wealthy London, every window glittered like water with it.

The knock on his door was nothing like Carey's hammering. When he opened it he found a square young man with red hair and freckles clad in the Hunsdon livery of black and yellow stripes. The youngster opened his mouth and spoke words that might as well have been French for the sense Dodd could make of them, although he knew the sound from the sailors that came into Dumfries and took copper out of Whitehaven.

'What?' Dodd asked irritably. Why could nobody in the south speak proper English like him? It was worse than Scotch because he could speak that if he had to.

The man tried again, frowning with the effort. 'M'loidy wants ee.'

'Ma lady Hunsdon? Wants me?'

More brow-wrinkling. 'Ay, she do.'

Dodd picked up his new hat and washed down the last of his manchet bread. It was a little tasteless for all its fine crumb, he thought to himself; he really preferred normal bread with the nutty taste from the unsieved flour and the ale in it and the little gritty bits from milling. There was something very weak and namby pamby about all this luxury.

He clattered down the stairs after the red-haired lad, trailing his fingers along the wonderful carved balustrade as he went. In the hall were two other wide, pig-tailed Cornish sailors, Will Shakespeare looking neat but a little less doleful than he had the week before, and the fresh-faced, cream-skinned girl in neat dark blue wool.

'What's up, Will?' Dodd asked the ex-player and would-be poet. 'Ah thocht ye were well in with the Earl of Southampton?'

Shakespeare shrugged. 'These things can take a little time. My lord had to post to Oxford to meet her Majesty. He...er...he took Mistress Emilia with him.'

Dodd nodded tactfully. 'Ay? And what are we doing now?'

'My lady Hunsdon has a fancy to go into town to do some shopping,' Shakespeare explained.

Dodd's brow wrinkled this time. 'Why?'

'My lady is a woman and women go shopping,' Shakespeare explained patiently, 'especially when they are in London in Michaelmas term with the Queen's New Year's present to consider.'

'Ay, Ah ken that, but why wi' me?'

'For conversation?' offered Shakespeare with just enough of a twitch in his eyebrows for Dodd to get the message.

The horses were outside in the courtyard, nice-looking animals and one stout gelding with a pillion seat trimmed in velvet.

'Ah, Sergeant Dodd,' came the ringing voice tinged with the West Country from the other doorway, 'I have a fancy to spend some of my gains in Cheapside and require a man to manage my horse as I shall ride pillion.'

Dodd knew perfectly well that there were grooms aplenty in Hunsdon's stables who could have done the job. He sighed. Then he bowed to Lady Hunsdon who was standing on the steps with a wicked grin on her face, wearing a very fine kirtle of dark red velvet with a forepart of brocade. She had a smart matching feathered hat on her head over her white cap. It looked similar to the green one Dodd had bought at outrageous expense for Janet and which was now sitting packed with hay in its wicker box in his chamber.

'Ah, I havenae done the office before, m'lady,' he said nervously. 'Ah dinna...'

'Good Lord, how does Mrs. Dodd travel then?'

Dodd couldn't help grimacing a little at Janet's likely reaction to the suggestion that she should ride pillion. 'On her ain mare, m'lady,' he replied, and said nothing about the mare's origins.

Lady Hunsdon nodded, making the feather bounce. 'Ah yes, I used to hunt when I was young, though never as well as Her Majesty. There's nothing to it. All you have to do is ride, which I am sure you can do very well, and keep me company.'

Shakespeare glanced meaningfully at Dodd and mounted the other gelding which had a less decorated pillion seat behind the saddle. Lady Hunsdon was busy handing out staves to the two Cornishmen so the pretty round-faced girl hoisted her skirts, climbed the mounting block, put a pretty little boot on the pillion saddle's footrest and, while Shakespeare held one of her hands, one of the grooms lifted her up and sat her on the seat behind him. The girl whispered something in Shakespeare's ear and he smiled over his shoulder at her. Dodd narrowed his eyes. All right. He could do that.

He went up to the gelding and patted his neck, let the long face and inquisitive nose have a delve in his doublet, eased the cheekpiece a little which might chafe. Then he checked the girth, gave the horse a look that warned it not to dare anything, put one hand on the withers and vaulted up to the saddle the way he always did. He shifted the animal over to the block and while he waited for her ladyship, he lengthened the stirrups to his liking.

She came up to the mounting block, puffing a little, and it took the two sturdy Cornishmen to lift her onto the pillion seat, where she settled down, sitting sideways. The gelding sighed and cocked a hoof.

'Would ye no' prefer a litter, m'lady?' asked Dodd.

There was a loud pshaw noise in his ear. 'I hate the things,' snapped Lady Hunsdon, 'Disgusting stinking contraptions. Only thing worse is a bloody coach. Now then, off we go.'

Two of Hunsdon's men ahead, one Cornishman on each side of the two horses in the middle, a packpony with empty panniers led by a boy, with a footman to follow as well—a fine raiding party for the pillaging of London's shops. They waited for the gate to be opened for them and clattered out and into the noise and dust of the Strand.

'It's my poor knees,' explained Lady Hunsdon, behind him. 'And my hip, alas. I much prefer ships. Of course, it's a nuisance to get aboard in the first place...' Dodd was suddenly transfixed by the idea of Lady Hunsdon shinning up a rope ladder. '...but once you're there, that's it. Off you go and you can go anywhere in the world. Wonderful.' Presumably she used a gang-plank or they somehow winched her up?

'Ay but...' Dodd was struggling with a truly terrible urge to ask what that noted courtier of the Queen, Lord Baron Hunsdon, thought about his wife gallivanting about the oceans. After all, he could guess what the lady's youngest son thought of it.

'Out with it, Sergeant.'

'Ahhh...does me lord no' mind if ye...'

Lady Hunsdon's laugh was a throaty gurgle. 'I'm sure he would have played merry hell about it once upon a time. But it was after darling Robin went off to court and Philadelphia's match with Scrope was made and my lord was busy at Court as usual. I was sitting about with nothing whatever to do and a perfectly good steward to run the estates. Once I was tired of embroidering everything that didn't move, I went to visit my sister Sybilla at Caerhays in Cornwall. Ever been to Cornwall, Sergeant?'

They were pushing through the constant jam of people being pestered by stinking sore-ridden beggars at Temple Bar, some of whom had spotted the great lady and her party and were fighting to get through the crowds and do some serious begging.

Dodd could see the prick of his gelding's ears and feel the neck begin to arch at the smell and the noise. He patted the neck again, shook his head to answer Lady Hunsdon. He fixed one of the scabby beggars with his eye and moved the toe of his boot suggestively.

'It's quite beautiful there. But again, very little to do and so I went visiting the Killigrews at Arwenack by the Fal estuary and Kate was fitting out a privateer to be captained by my cousin Henry Morgan, and so naturally, I took a share and went along with her and we caught a pirate out of Antwerp, in the mist just by St Anthony's Point and sank her.'

Dodd's mind reeled at the idea of these two stout mothers taking a whim to go privateering. It was truly terrifying.

'Poor Morgan was killed in the melee, so after my lord got me the letter of marque—half in jest, I'm afraid, poor dear—I decided to go into it properly, fitted out my own little ship the *Judith* with Captain Trevasker, and paid for the whole thing and more with our first Spanish merchant full of sugar and timber that we caught in the Channel.' She laughed throatily again. 'You should have seen the faces of the crew when they saw who had caught them. "Bruja," they called me, which is Spanish for witch, and other less flattering names.'

'Ay?'

'Of course it's all a terrible gamble, but not if you have good intelligence and watchers along the coast and a good haven for the ships and to land the prizes. And Cornishmen to sail your ship, of course. Penryn is at the neck of one of the finest natural harbours in the world, according to dear Sir Francis Drake. Kate agrees with him—her windows in Arwenack House near Pendennis Fort have stunning views across to St Mawes—and she's used her spoils to buy up most of the land around the bay that the Killigrews don't already own. It's expensive, land-prices in Cornwall are ridiculously high, despite being very poor for anything but pasture or tin-mining.'

There was a scuffle as the beggars tried to dodge past their escort. One of the Cornishmen caught a particularly cheeky beggar right in the forehead with his fist. The other shook his cudgel and growled something incomprehensibly Cornish and most of the beggars fell back.

Lady Hunsdon was oblivious to the excitement and didn't seem to need any prompt to carry on talking as Dodd urged the horse on through the crowds.

'Of course, the real reason I go privateering is that it's very entertaining—you never know what might happen or where you might find a fat prize. My lord says that if I were younger and a little more spry, he could see me boarding with the sailors and laying about me with a belaying pin—which is a cruel thing to say since I would naturally use a sword or a pistol.'

Dodd winched his jaw shut and managed a neutral, 'Ay?'

Lady Hunsdon laughed again. 'Which of course I wouldn't either because my hands are too small and my wrists far too weak for a pistol or a sword. And anyway, the last thing the sailors need is another fighter, Sergeant. What they do need is a cool head and an eye for merchandise. That was how we sank the pirate. The sailors were so furious the Flemish had been sinking their fishing boats, they didn't even notice how they were manoevring us into a very dangerous position. Fortunately I did, and we were able to trap them, board them, free some prisoners, and take the ship into Penryn as a prize. We took some very fine jewels as well. I hadn't had such fun since I used to hunt with my lord husband and Her Majesty the Queen.'

· She leaned against him and put a hand on his belt while she rearranged her skirts with her other hand. 'And since then, of course, I've done well enough at the privateering that my lord is quite happy with me. He's planning to begin rebuilding the Blackfriars with my latest spoils, very pleased he doesn't need to go to Sir Horatio Palavicino for a loan after all. Ha!'

Lady Hunsdon subsided into a sudden thoughtful silence. They were ambling up Ludgate hill and into the city, past the huge Belle Sauvage carter's inn where the players were parading around with drums to announce a terrible and savage and improving tragedy of Dr. Faustus. As they pressed on past St. Paul's churchyard, Lady Hunsdon called out in a voice clearly more used to a full gale,

'Letty, my bird, I need writing paper, ink, pens ready cut, sealing wax, and a new shaker. Off you go now and don't pay more than a penny a sheet for the paper.'

Dodd watched carefully how Shakespeare gave Letty his hand again and braced himself to take her weight as she hopped down and headed towards one of the stationer's stalls in the Churchyard. They waited while she went and spoke earnestly to one of the better-dressed stallmen. He had a brightly-painted and lurid sign over his head of a pen dripping red blood. A pile of the popular though scandalous coneycatching pamphlets decorated his stall as well and a crowd of people were buying them. Despite being busy, he and his wife came over personally with the package to make their bows to Lady Hunsdon. One of the Cornishmen stowed it in the pack pony's basket and Shakespeare and the other man helped Letty back to her seat.

They carried on into Cheapside with the pack pony mouthing his bit and looking sulky. Cheapside was jammed with litters and men on horseback and part-blocked by a cart that was unloading. Lady Hunsdon ignored the bedlam, passed by many fine windows, and stopped at the sign of a Golden Cup beside some barred windows that blazed with assorted gold plate—nothing so common as silver to be seen.

Letty hopped down first and spoke to the scarfaced man in a worn jack standing at the door. Dodd eyed him with automatic interest since he was different from the one who had been there a week or so before. The man's jack was Scottish with its square quilting and some of the details made him think of the East March surnames. The man nodded and turned to shout inside.

Moments later the handsome willowy young man came out with a mounting block for Lady Hunsdon to use, followed by Master Van Emden in his fine brown velvet gown, bowing low to Lady Hunsdon.

Dodd looked over his shoulder at her to see that she had magically transformed into a very haughty court lady. She held out her hand imperiously to him and he took it, braced, and managed not to grunt at the effort of helping her step down to the block where she took the young man's proffered arm to step to the pavement. A page swept the flagstones before her clean of mud and some hazelnut shells from the people idly snacking as they gawped at the goldsmiths' windows. Lady Hunsdon was already in full flow, her voice quite without the Cornish rounding it had when she was relaxed.

'Master Van Emden, I have heard all about your shop from my dear son. You recall that you were kind enough to advise Sir Robert regarding the goldsmith's art a week or two ago and he was very complimentary about the beauty and fineness of your work. I desire you to make the Queen's New Year presents both for myself and for my husband, Lord Chamberlain Baron Hunsdon...'

The play of expressions on Van Emden's grey-bearded face was very funny. It started with understandable wariness at mention of Carey, then continued with delighted surprise to be finished off by a look of quite frightening greed. He settled into an ecstasy of respect as Lady Hunsdon paraded into the shop, followed by one of her Cornishmen, trailing clouds of wealth.

Shakespeare settled back in his saddle, took a small notebook from his sleeve and a small stick of graphite from his penner, and started scribbling. Dodd contented himself with looking about for half an hour, enjoying the sightseeing and idly planning his Great Raid. There were three or four of the goldsmiths' windows which looked worth the trouble of breaking the bars for their contents and they would have to remember to bring a crowbar. Master Van Emden's windows were perhaps the best, but the bars looked too solid to bother with. Dodd had decided that all the insight would need to be taken in a single morning before the City fathers could call out their trained bands to stop Dodd and his gang of men...

A little later when Dodd was starting to think seriously about beer, Lady Hunsdon emerged, followed by Letty holding a velvet bag that clanked, Master Van Emden, his young man and his page all bowing in unison.

'By the end of the week, I has sketches for your ladyship,' the Master was saying, mangling his foreign English in his excitement. 'Young Piers shall to Somerset House for your inspection the plans bring.'

'Splendid,' said Lady Hunsdon with great satisfaction, 'I will look forward to it.'

The process of setting the ladies back on their pillion saddles was very hard on your back since you had to help lift with your shoulders twisted round. Dodd darkly reckoned Shakespeare had about half as much work to do with Letty as he had with Lady Hunsdon, who was no taller than her maid.

They carried on to an inn next to the Royal Exchange. Looking perky and happy as usual, Letty went in followed by a Cornishman. There was a pause and then she came out, frowning.

'He's not there, my lady,' she said.

Lady Hunsdon frowned. 'Is he not? Are you sure? Ask the landlord if he's gone out?'

Letty went back in and returned a moment later. 'Landlord said he's gone, he's not here any more.'

Lady Hunsdon held her hand out to Dodd who swung her down and then, on an impulse, jumped down from the horse himself, gave the reins to one of the henchmen to hold, and followed her into the inn's commonroom to back her up if she needed it.

She didn't really. The landlord was hunched and hand-washing with anxiety but he stuck to his guns.

'A thousand pardons, your ladyship, but e's gone. I dunno where, just gone. That's all I know.'

'We arranged to meet at this very inn this very day, oh...several weeks ago,' rapped out Lady Hunsdon. 'Of course he isn't gone.'

'He's gone, your ladyship, or rather, I don't know what's happened to him and his bill not paid and he left his riding cloak and some duds here when he went.'

Lady Hunsdon's eyes narrowed. 'That's ridiculous. Let me see his room.'

'I can't your ladyship, beggin' your pardon, but I let it again and I sold his duds to pay his bill wot he hadn't, see.'

'When did you last see him?'

'More'n a week ago, ladyship, honest,' said the innkeeper. 'He saw his lawyer and then he went out to a dice game, he said, and that's the last I seen of him.'

'Didn't you look for him?'

The landlord shrugged. ''Course I did, 'e hadn't paid his bill had he, but I couldn't find him.'

Dodd's eyes were narrowed too. There was something radically wrong here.

Lady Hunsdon made a harumph noise like both her husband and her son. Behind her, Letty was snivelling into her sleeve. The landlord invited them to a drink on the house and Lady Hunsdon agreed, sharp as a needle. They were shown to a back parlour with some ugly painted cloths hanging on the walls where Lady Hunsdon drank brandywine with a large spoonful of sugar, Letty drank mild, and Dodd had a quart of some of the worst beer he had ever tasted: thin, sour, over-hopped and not very strong. Lady Hunsdon said nothing, gazing beadily at Letty who was trembling and clearly trying not to cry.

Before they left, Lady Hunsdon beckoned the landlord and spoke quietly in his ear. A gold angel passed from the lady to the landlord and his demeanour changed.

'Sergeant Dodd,' she said, 'would you be so good as to go upstairs with mine host and search the bedroom used by Mr. Tregian?'

'Ay m'lady,' said Dodd, not sorry to be leaving his beer unfinished.

He followed the landlord who seemed nervous. The private room was better than the common run, reasonably well-furnished with a half-testered bed, a truckle for the servant, and a couple of straw palliasses for pageboys or henchmen, a chest with a lock and a table and chairs. The jordan was under the bed, not only empty but clean. So the room hadn't been let.

Dodd couldn't slit the mattresses with the landlord watching but he could and did search methodically and carefully, working from one side to the other, like a maiden doing the cleaning. All he found was an old book of martyr stories on a shelf which was a little loose. Dodd jiggled it a couple of times and then looked at the join it made with the wall. It was definitely loose at one end. He peered at it from underneath and saw something folded and wedged up behind the wood of the shelf. With the tip of his dagger he teased it out and found two blank sheets of paper. Presumably they'd been put there to stop the shelf wiggling and he was about to throw them in the fireplace when he caught a faint scent of oranges from the papers. It was an expensive way of fixing a shelf after all.

He folded them carefully and put them in his belt pouch, then went on down the stairs. The ladies were ready to go so Dodd went ahead. Out of habit, he checked under his saddle and his girth, mounted then bent to hand Lady Hunsdon up behind him.

'London Bridge,' she ordered.

They carried on, shoving through the crowds, all of whom seemed to be heading for the Bridge, which was hard on the temper.

'Powerful lot of folk here,' said Dodd as he pushed on through an argument between three men and a donkey stopped in the middle of the path and all four braying furiously.

'Have you never been on London Bridge, Sergeant?' asked Lady Hunsdon with a naughty sparkle. 'Or did you cross several times and simply not notice that the best drapers, haberdashers, and headtiring shops in the world are there?'

'Ay,' Dodd admitted, 'that'd be it.'

They were coming to the gate towers with their fringe of traitors' heads, where you could hear the rush and creak of the newly installed waterwheels, the crowd nearly solid as they passed through the narrow entrance. The gate gave onto the street over the Bridge which was enclosed by the shops and houses built right on it and dim enough to need lanterns at the shop doors. Suddenly there was a gasp behind them as if somebody had been stabbed. Dodd jerked round to see Letty staring up at the row of spikes along the top of the gatehouse. A crow was flapping heavily away from the newest of the heads there, arrived from Tyburn the day before. Letty seemed struck to stone by the sight of the bearded and now eyeless face. Her hands flew to her mouth, she breathed deep, and then she screamed like a pig at the slaughter.

Dodd's gelding took severe offence and, despite the weight of two people on his back, tried to pirouette, then backed frantically into a group of stout women with baskets who all shouted angrily. Letty was still screaming which had thoroughly spooked the mare she was sitting on. Shakespeare was frantically sawing at the reins as the animal lunged sideways, snorting and kicking and starting to crow-hop to get rid of her burden. A gap opened in the frightened crowd and she looked ready to take off for the far hills.

Dodd felt Lady Hunsdon's arms clasp tight around his waist and her hands lock together.

'Help them, Sergeant,' came the firm cool voice behind him.

Dodd brought his whip down brutally on his gelding's side, which got the beast's attention. Then Dodd turned him around and drove him after Shakespeare's and Letty's mount, knocking pedestrians and one Cornishman aside. He came alongside the bucking, frantic nag, grabbed the bridle, and leaned over to put his sleeve across the silly creature's eyes. Being a horse, she immediately stood still because she couldn't see and Dodd muttered in her ear, telling her gently how he would have her guts for haggis casing and feed her rump to the nearest pack of hunting dogs he could find. It didn't matter what you said to the animal, so long as your voice was right. At least Letty's screaming had stopped, though a glance over his shoulder showed this was because Shakespeare had a hand firmly on her mouth.

Shakespeare's face was white and there were hot tears boiling down Letty's cheeks, little cries still coming from behind Shakespeare's palm.

'God's truth, mistress, did ye wantae die…?' he snarled.

'Shhh,' said Lady Hunsdon behind him in a voice that was an odd mixture of fury and sadness. 'She's seen something that upset her. We'll go back to Somerset House now.'

'Ay m'lady,' said Dodd, and turned both the horses. 'Will ye bide quiet now, lass?' he asked Letty who was trembling as much as her mare. She nodded so Shakespeare took his hand away, after which she dropped her face into her hands and started to cry.

Dodd was sweating from all the drama, which was made much worse by the stares and sniggers of the Londoners standing back unhelpfully to watch the show. The Cornishmen were helping Hunsdon's henchmen to pick up and dust down a couple of annoyed lawsuit-threatening Londoners who hadn't moved away fast enough.

Dodd jerked his head at Shakespeare and they closed up the distance between the horses. A Cornishman cudgelled an urchin who had his hand in the heaviest pannier on the packpony as Dodd swatted away a small bunch of child-beggars with their hands up and their sores exposed. Their party formed a tighter group and headed back for the other side of the City as fast as they could.

'M'lady, what the...'

'She's just seen her father's head on a spike at London Bridge,' said Lady Hunsdon drily into his ear. 'I think that's a reason to be upset, don't you?'

Dodd craned his neck to see. The only recognisable head was the priest's that he and Carey had seen hacked off the day before. His mouth went dry.

'But m'lady...?'

'Be quiet.'

'But...but Ah thought Papist priests couldnae wed...?'

'Precisely. We'll discuss this in private.'

***

A war council of the Hunsdon family convened at dinnertime, with Sir Robert, Lord and Lady Hunsdon, and Sergeant Dodd staring at each other over some marvellous venison and more of the mutton pasties. When the second cover was served and Dodd could wonder at the jellies and custards that were laid out for no more than a normal meal, the servingmen were sent out of the room. Letty had been put to bed with a strong posset and a girl to watch her, while Dr. Nunez and his barber surgeon had been sent for to bleed her against the shock.

'You are quite certain it is Richard Tregian, my lady?' rumbled

Lord Hunsdon, staring at his clasped hands.

'I am, my lord,' said his lady soberly. 'He had a scar by his mouth from a hunting accident a few years ago and his beard was still red. I knew him at once even on a...at that distance.'

'No priest then,' said Hunsdon.

Lady Hunsdon snorted. 'Hardly. He was a Papist though.'

'He was the man you were in London to meet?'

'Yes, my lord. I wanted to find out more before I broke the matter with you, but events are now ahead of me. I discovered from my sister's husband that there have been some very dubious land-deals happening in Cornwall and Richard Tregian was up to his neck in them. He was in desperate need of money to pay his recusancy fines, to be sure, but there was more to it than that. There was Court money involved. The land around the Fal has tripled in price in the last three years, but additonally there have been some very surprising purchases further north in the tin-mining areas near Redruth. I would have gone to Sir Walter Raleigh as President of the Stannary when I had consulted you, my lord, but Sir Walter is in the Tower for venery, I find. I wanted to warn Richard away from whatever deals he was doing and I brought Letty up to town with me in the *Judith* to talk some sense into him.'

'Was there any question of treason involved, my lady?'

Lady Hunsdon bowed her head. 'Letty says not, but I simply don't know.'

Lord Hunsdon sighed heavily. 'Sir Robert?' he said formally to his son.

Carey looked at Dodd briefly, then at his mother, before he answered his father quietly. 'We watched Richard Tregian die yesterday under the name of Fr. Jackson. He was gagged and had been tortured. The hangman gave him a good drop so he was quite dead by the time they came to draw and quarter him.'

Lady Hunsdon nodded. 'Thank God for that at least.'

'How do you know he was tortured?' asked Lord Hunsdon.

'His wrists were swollen and showed the print of bindings with swelling above and below. I would say the rack or the manacles.' Carey's voice was remote.

There was a long moment of silence. 'What statute was he

sentenced under?' asked Lord Hunsdon.

'Henry VIII's Praemunire.'

'Nothing more?'

'Now that I think about it, the announcement was very short.'

'He made no sign?'

'He was in no state to do it before he was hanged and moreover he was gagged.' More silence. 'I wonder whose authority was on the warrant?' Sir Robert added softly.

'It will have been genuine and the authority unexceptionable or Her Majesty would not have signed it.'

'Heneage?'

Hunsdon shook his head. 'Not necessarily. Sir Robert Cecil or Lord Burghley himself could have been involved, or even my lord the Earl of Essex. Someone of lesser rank could also have originated the warrant, such as the Recorder of London or the Constable of the Tower. Of course, I could do so if I needed to.'

'Was yer man not tried?'

After a pause Lord Hunsdon said reluctantly, 'Obviously not, Sergeant.'

'So what was Richard Tregian actually doing?' asked Sir Robert, leaning his elbows on the table. Nobody had touched any of the elaborate sweet dishes, but Dodd, who had a less delicate stomach, reached for a pippin and started munching it. He liked apples and you didn't get many of them on the Borders because raiders kept cutting or burning orchards down. 'Buying land from cash-strapped fellow-Papists and then selling them on to a courtier or two? Or informing on Papists and getting a cut from the lands when they were confiscated?'

Lady Hunsdon shook her head. 'I don't see Richard informing— and even if he did, he wouldn't last very long in Cornwall. They don't like blabbermouths there. I would say it was the first. He may even have been an agent, using his principal's money and then taking a cut.'

'Well there's nothing treasonous about that,' boomed Lord Hunsdon. 'Perfectly legitimate thing to do, I use agents myself. Keeps the prices down a bit.'

'My lord, I dinna understand,' Dodd put in. Lord Hunsdon

KNIVES IN THE SOUTH

looked enquiringly at him. 'Only, this land was to be sold? To somebody wi' plenty o' money at court?'

'Probably. That's where the money tends to be.'

'Ay, so why would they buy it? Cornwall's a powerful long way and...'

'It might be the tin. It's quite a fashion at Court now to start mining works and similar on your land if there's anything there to be mined.'

'Is tin worth so much?'

'Not really,' put in Lady Hunsdon, 'There's more of it in Spain and easier to get at.'

Something Dodd had heard in a long drinking session with a miner from Keswick tickled his memory. 'There's tin, so is there gold as well?' The Hunsdons were watching him thoughtfully. 'Only that would make sense of poor land being worth buying on the quiet until ye could take the gold out.'

'If there is it would belong to the Crown anyway,' said Hunsdon. 'You'd need a license.'

'All the more reason for keeping it quiet until ye could take out the gold for yersen.'

'Hmm.'

'Well the obvious candidate for his principal is Heneage,' pointed out Sir Robert, 'and that would explain his ending up on a scaffold if Heneage didn't want to pay him.'

'I doubt it,' said Hunsdon. 'Heneage could simply have delayed payment until Richard Tregian got tired of asking or went to jail. There would be no need to kill the man.'

'And why did he do it like that?' Dodd asked, which was the main question on his mind. 'Why be so complicated? Even in London it canna be hard for a man wi' Heneage's power to slit his throat and drop him in the Thames and nae questions asked?'

Nobody said anything.

The steward knocked on the door, came in, and whispered in Lord Hunsdon's ear.

'Oh. Ah. Yes, of course. We will see him in the large parlour. I believe your lawyer has arrived, Sergeant.'

'Ay.'

'In the meantime,' Hunsdon summed up with weary distaste, 'we shall keep this matter as quiet as possible until we can discover what really happened. The final decision on any action to be taken will, of course, be mine although I may be forced to take the matter to my sister.' There was a warning tone in his voice and yes, he was glaring directly at his wife.

'Of course my lord,' she said, 'Naturally.'

Carey closed his eyes briefly and seemed to be praying while Dodd fought down the urge to snicker. After all, it was hardly a laughing matter. Still, the blandly respectful look on Lady Hunsdon's face as she lowered her eyes to her meekly clasped hands was very, very funny to Dodd. Lord Baron Hunsdon seemed quite satisfied and nodded approvingly. 'I knew you would understand, my love.'

Carey caught Dodd's eye and one eyebrow flicked infinitesimally upwards. However, Dodd was ready for it and his mouth drew down and his face settled in its normal scowl.

Tuesday 12th September 1592, afternoon

With Hunsdon leading his wife out, they processed to the large parlour where Lord and Lady Hunsdon were seated on two well-carved arm chairs that teetered on the edge of being presumptuous thrones. Hunsdon's bore the lions of England carved into the wood while his lady's was padded with tawny velvet. They had stopped short of a cloth of estate, though.

Following Carey's lead, Dodd sat down on a bench at the side of the room and watched as James Enys came in, wearing a good if out-of-fashion green wool suit and his Utter Barrister's monkish black cloth robe hanging from his shoulders. He took off his velvet cap and bowed low to both the Hunsdons. He was already sweating with nerves. Lady Hunsdon made a noise that sounded a little like 'Tchah!' and stared down her nose at the lawyer.

'Mr. Vaughan, good of you to come,' said Hunsdon, who was

politely elbowed by his wife, and coughed. 'Enys, yes, of course.'

Enys bowed again.

'I understand you are willing to take the brief on behalf of Sergeant Henry Dodd of Gilsland here against his honour Mr. Vice Chamberlain Sir Thomas Heneage?'

'Ah…yes m'lord.' Enys's voice was quite light but firm and pleasant to listen to. It carried easily. Dodd noticed he was holding the lapels of his gown with his thumbs under the material in a way which made him look combative but was probably designed to stop his hands shaking.

'Despite Mr. Vice Chamberlain having frightened off all of your legal brethren?'

A faint smile crossed Enys's ugly face. 'Ah…yes m'lord.'

'Why?' asked Hunsdon bluntly. 'Have you no wish for preferment?'

'There is no chance whatsoever that Mr. Vice will ever offer it to me. Whereas you, my lord Chamberlain, have a reputation for dealing justly and I have no doubt but that you will be my good lord, whatever the result of the litigation.'

It was prettily put and Lord Hunsdon beamed and expanded slightly. Lady Hunsdon leaned forward.

'We can't help you if you end in Chelsea with that devil Topcliffe questioning you.'

Enys shrugged. 'I am a good loyal subject of Her Gracious Majesty, I attend Divine service every Sunday, and my brother fought and was wounded in the Netherlands.'

'If you go against Mr. Heneage as things are at the moment you may find that these things do not protect you,' put in Carey.

Enys shrugged again. 'I may die of plague tomorrow if God wills it.'

'Hm.' Hunsdon leaned an elbow on the arm of his chair and tapped his teeth. Lady Hunsdon had fixed Enys with a gimlet blue stare which would certainly have had Dodd sweating. However, the young man seemed to have calmed somewhat. He took a breath to speak.

'My lord, my lady, may I be quite frank with you?'

Hunsdon nodded while his lady only narrowed her eyes.

'Obviously, you will be wondering if I am in fact Heneage's man.'

Hunsdon smiled; his lady remained grim.

'Also, obviously, there is very little I can do to convince you that this is not the case since any test of my truthfulness you could think of, Mr. Heneage could circumvent. Here is my tale. Immediately after I was called to the Bar and whilst I was still in pupillage a year ago, I was approached by a man of business, a solicitor of some fame, and asked if I would take some cases in King's Bench dealing with forfeitures of Papist land and other property dealings. Knowing no more than that Mr. Vice Chamberlain was the principal and that he was high in the counsels of our most worshipful Sovereign Lady, I naturally agreed. I took the cases, drafted the pleadings, and appeared in the initial hearings.'

He sighed. 'At this point I found that all was not as it seemed and that I could not appear for Mr. Heneage without lying to the court and going utterly against mine honour.'

The Hunsdons exchanged glances and then both scowled at Enys. It was quite admirable that he stayed steady and continued with his rhetorical story.

'I withdrew, charging no fee, and Mr. Heneage offered me a higher fee to remain, then a cut of the proceeds plus many further tempting blandishments. I still refused and he said he would destroy me since he would not be denied by anyone, especially not a stripling lawyer. He has gone some way to achieving his threat as I have had practically no cases in the past six months and will soon lose my chamber as well. I have no profession but the law and have no family other than my brother...um and sister...to help me, nor any good lord.'

'So?' asked Lady Hunsdon.

'So, my lady,' answered Enys, 'When I heard two gentlemen discussing their problems regarding Mr. Vice and realised from his speech that one of them must be your son, I thanked Providence that I had stopped by the pool instead of going to sell my cloak, and made haste to offer them my services.'

Hanging in the air was the wonder of such a stroke of luck. Lady Hunsdon summed it all up by sniffing eloquently.

Hunsdon smiled on the young man. 'Mr. Enys, it could be dangerous to act for Sergeant Dodd. Mr. Heneage has a tendency to attack the smaller fry in a dispute. You could easily wind up in the Tower confessing to Papistry.'

Enys smiled back bitterly. 'The man is a scandal and a tyrant, m'lord. Yes, I could. But I may do so in any case since he is mine enemy in which case…'

'In which case, Mr. Enys?'

'In which case I might as well take the fight to the enemy first.'

Dodd nodded at this piece of good sense. Hunsdon laced his fingers together.

'Mr. Enys, I shall naturally make enquiries about you. What were the cases?'

'Matters relating to the estates of Mr. Robert Boscoba, Mr. John Veryan, and Sir Piran Mawes of Trenever.'

'Cornish lands? You're Cornish, aren't you?'

'Yes, your ladyship. My father was from Penryn and came up to London after Glasney College was put down. My sister…' Enys paused. '…My sister was wed to a Cornishman until the smallpox widowed her.'

Lady Hunsdon nodded intently. 'Do you know a Mr. Richard Tregian who would have come up to London about two or three weeks ago?'

'No, my lady,' said Enys, his eyes narrowing, 'I have never met him.'

'Assuming my enquiries are satisfactory,' said Hunsdon, 'I shall retain you for the amount of a guinea per week plus refreshers for court appearances.'

The lawyer bowed low. 'My lord is very generous,'

Lady Hunsdon leaned forward confidingly. 'Mr. Enys,' she said coaxingly, 'what were the cases you withdrew from about?'

Enys's eyelids fluttered. 'I cannot tell you more, m'lady, I'm very sorry. Client confidentiality.'

'You withdrew from the cases,' Hunsdon pointed out.

'I did, m'lord, because they would have gone against my honour.' There was a pause whilst Enys nerved himself. 'It would also go against my honour to babble about them like a woman at the conduit to anyone who asked.' Hunsdon nodded.

'How soon can you draft and lodge the pleadings on Sergeant Dodd's behalf?'

'Once I am fee'd and briefed, m'lord, by tomorrow.'

'Any ideas on the conduct?'

'Yes, m'lord.' The young man took a deep breath and clasped the lapels of his gown tightly. 'I would recommend a writ of *pillatus* against Mr. Heneage for the criminal assault and wrongful imprisonment, to be served immediately.'

Both Hunsdon and his lady stared at the young man for a second, transfixed, before Hunsdon bellowed with laughter and his lady gurgled. Carey too had a wicked grin on his face. 'What's that?' hissed Dodd to him, knowing he was missing something important here.

'He's saying we should get a warrant to arrest Heneage immediately on the criminal charges,' whispered Carey, still grinning.

'He'll surely wriggle out...'

'Of course he will, but he'll spend at least a night in prison if we time it right.'

Dodd's lips parted in delight. 'Och,' he said, 'I like this lawyer.'

'While he's in prison,' added Enys, 'we should serve writs of subpoena on all potential witnesses and put any that are... frightened...into protective custody.'

Hunsdon let out another bark. Dodd understood this. 'Mr. Enys,' he called across the tiled floor, 'one o'them's the Gaoler o'the Fleet.'

Enys's pock-marked brow wrinkled. 'Then I think he needs to be named on the originating warrant as a confederate and also arrested, or he'll never testify.'

***

Barnabus Cooke's funeral was later that afternoon and a respectable affair, attended naturally by Carey, Dodd, and the young Simon Barnet, though not Barnabus' sister's family which was still locked up in their house with plague. No more of them had died apart from the mother. Hunsdon had paid for Barnabus's coffin and the burial fees and also four pauper mourners, one of whom seemed to be genuinely upset. The Church of St Bride's was convenient and the vicar glad of the shroud money, but had the sense to keep his eulogy of Barnabus short and tactful. Carey had pointedly invited Shakespeare to come as well, but had received an elegantly phrased letter of regret. Apart from a remarkable number of upright men who turned up hoping to be paid mourners too, there were several women in veils and striped petticoats and a round-faced man in a fine wool suit with a snowy falling band whom Dodd felt he had seen somewhere before. Carey seemed to know him and once the small coffin had been lowered into the plot in the crowded graveyard, strode over to greet him.

'Mr. Hughes,' he said, 'how kind of you to attend.'

The man took his hat off and bowed. 'Thank you, sir,' he said easily, 'I try to attend them as gets away.'

Carey smiled. 'Still smarting?'

Hughes smiled back. 'No sir, though I'll allow as I had a rope measured and properly stretched for him. I'm also here to bring the compliments of my brother-in-law and his thanks to your worshipful father for his support of Barnabus Cooke's family.'

Carey seemed surprised by this for he paused, and then bowed shallowly. 'My father is proud of his good lordship and feels it is the least he could do.'

'Nonetheless, sir, there's not many would bother nowadays. My brother-in-law would like you to know that he is obliged to your honours and at your father's service.'

With a dignified tip of his hat, Mr. Hughes moved quietly away and through the gate. Carey blinked after him. 'Well well,' he said, 'that's interesting.'

Dodd was irritated that again he didn't know what was going on here. 'Ay?' he complained.

Carey smiled and led the way to a boozing ken on Fleet Street, filled with a raucous flock of hard-drinking black-robed lawyers and their pamphlet-writing hangers on.

'That, Sergeant,' he said as he drank brandywine with

satisfaction, 'is the London hangman. You saw him performing his office yesterday.'

'Jesu,' said Dodd, feeling slightly queasy.

'He is also, and this is where it gets interesting, the brother-in-law of the King of London, Mr. Laurence Pickering himself. Who has just as good as offered an alliance to my father for some reason.'

'The King of London?'

'Mr. Laurence Pickering, King of the London thieves, chief controller of the London footpads and upright men, main profiter by the labours of the London whores, coming second only to his Grace the Bishop of Winchester who collects their rents.'

'Ay,' said Dodd with respect. 'Is there only the one King of London, then?'

'Oh yes,' said Carey drily, 'Only the one. Now.'

WEDNESDAY 13TH SEPTEMBER 1592,

MORNING

At dawn the next day, itching in tight wool and with a new highcrowned beaver hat on his head, Dodd went with Carey to take a boat at Temple steps with Enys for Westminster Hall. Enys was carrying a sheaf of papers in a blue brocade bag and looked tired with bags under his eyes. He pulled his black robe around him and held his hat tight to his head. It was hard to tell the expression on his face, so thick were the scars from the smallpox, but he looked tense.

'Sir Robert, is your father providing bailiffs to back up the court staff?' he asked Carey.

Carey was busy smiling and taking his hat off to a boatload of attractive women heading downstream for London Bridge.

'Hm? Oh yes, the steward's arranging for it and they'll meet us at Westminster once you have the warrant.'

'Ay, but we'll niver arrest him, will we?' Dodd said, thinking of Richie Graham of Brackenhill's likely reaction to any such attempt, never mind Jock o'the Peartree's. Jock would still be roaring with laughter at the joke as he slit your throat.

The Hunsdon boat was butting up against the boat landing. Carey and Dodd hopped in, while Enys seemed very nervous of the water and nearly fell as he stepped across. He sat himself down and gripped the seat hard with his hands, swallowing.

'I rather think we will, Sergeant,' said Enys, 'although I'm sure not for long. And as there is no doubt at all that as soon as he's bailed he'll be trying to intimidate the witnesses, I have drafted a writ against him for maintenance to keep in reserve.'

Carey blinked as if puzzled for a moment and then shouted with laughter. 'That old Statute against henchmen?'

'Old and from Her Majesty's grandfather's time, but still on the books. It's not the oldest statute I shall be citing.'

'What is?' asked Dodd fascinated, although he had no idea that henchmen were illegal.

'Edward III 1368,' said Enys. Dodd used his fingers to work it out.

'It's two hundred and twenty-four years old,' he said. 'What good is that?'

'It's a highly important principle,' said Enys, looking annoyed. 'You might say it is the foundation of our English liberty. It says that no man may be put to the question or tortured privily without trial or warrant. In effect, habeas corpus.'

Once again Dodd struggled with foreign language. He supposed they meant something about dead bodies.

'I don't recall Mr. Secretary Walsingham paying that much attention to the statute when he was questioning some Papist,' Carey pointed out.

Enys looked at him distantly. 'Sir Robert, it is a fact that a man who murders another for his money may pay no attention to the statutes against murder. It is in the nature of sinful men that they break the law. It is a very different thing to hold that there is no such law to be broken, which Heneage does by his actions.'

'And if the law be changed in parliament?' asked Carey.

'If it be changed, then we must abide by the new law,' said Enys. 'But this law has not been changed nor repealed. It was excluded from matters of treason and the Henry VIII statute of Praemunire made many religious matters into treason. Therefore Mr. Secretary Walsingham could and did rightly ignore the statute since he was seeking out Papist traitors against Her Majesty and the Commonweal of England.'

Carey nodded while Dodd stared in fascination to hear such a young man speak in such long and complicated sentences, using such pompous words. Now the lawyer lifted one finger in a lecturing manner. 'However, this is not a matter of treason at all. Sergeant Dodd was neither guilty of nor accused of any crime whatsoever when Mr. Vice falsely imprisoned and assaulted him. There was a fortiori no trial and no warrant. I have seldom heard of such a clear case.'

'Ay,' said Dodd, catching up with most of the last part of the speech, 'that's right.' His head was buzzing with the legal talk.

'Perhaps Mr. Vice will simply claim that he was looking for me and laid hold of my henchman to track me down,' said Carey.

'I'm sure he will,' said Enys. 'However the fact remains that you were not accused of treason either, Sir Robert. Even your brother was accused only of coining, which may indeed come under the treason laws as petty treason...'

Dodd stretched his eyes at that. Was coining treason? Did Richie Graham with his busy unofficial mint know about it? Did he care?

'...but it is not a direct attack upon her Majesty nor upon the Commonweal of England. And in point of fact, if what you have told me is correct, I believe that Mr. Heneage may be vulnerable to a charge of coining and uttering false coin himself, with your brother and the apothecary Mr. Cheke as witnesses against him.'

Carey whistled through his teeth. 'I thought we couldn't prove that?'

Enys shrugged. 'Heneage will bring oath-swearers to disagree but it will depend on the judge. It's arguable. At this stage it doesn't have to be provable.'

They came to Westminster steps and jumped out—Enys seemed

clumsy again and hesitant as he stepped onto the boat landing at just the wrong time. He might have wound up in the Thames without a quick shove from Dodd.

'Thank you, sir,' he muttered, looking embarassed. 'I am still weakened by my sickness.'

'Ay, but your face is healed?' said Dodd, immediately worried because he had never had smallpox in his life.

'Oh it is, I am no longer sick of it. But the pocks attacked my eyes as well, and my sight and balance are not what they were,' said the man, rubbing his hand on his face and jaw. Dodd could see the pits on the backs of his hands going up his wrist. Jesu, that was an ugly disease as well, worse than plague in some ways. Of course you were far more likely to die of the plague, but that was relatively quick and if your buboes burst you'd probably get better with no more than a couple of scars on your neck and groin and never be afraid of getting it again. You weren't going to be hideous for the rest of your life. As for pocks on your eyes...Jesus God. At least there wasn't much smallpox on the Borders, though Dodd had had a terrible fright when he was nine when his hands had got blistered from a cow with a blistered udder. Both his parents were alive then; it hadn't been anything, and the blisters on both him and the cow got better soon enough.

They walked up through the muddy crowded alleys to the great old Hall of Westminster, hard by the Cathedral. The place was teeming with a flock in black robes, some wearing silk with soft flat square hats on their heads and followed by large numbers of young men carrying bags and papers.

'Lord above,' murmured Carey, 'It gets worse every year. Michaelmas term hasn't even started yet and look at them.'

Enys took a deep breath at the doorway into Westminster Hall, gripped his sword hilt lefthanded, and forged ahead into the crowd of lawyers around a desk who were shouting at the listing officers.

He came threading out again, his hat sideways. Just in time he grabbed it and clamped it back on his head.

'Sirs, we shall go before Mr. Justice Whitehead in an hour to swear out the pleadings and have the warrant granted.'

Dodd nodded as if this were all quite normal but he thought

that it surely couldn't be so simple. Normally it took months for a bill to be heard in Carlisle and years if it was a Border matter. Hunsdon had handed Carey a purseful of silver that morning to be sure the matter was well up the list which he had passed to Enys. Perhaps that had worked.

They ventured into Westminster Hall which was split into a dozen smaller sections by wooden partitions while the old-fashioned ceiling full of angels and stone icicles echoed with the noise. You couldn't see the floor at all because it was covered in straw and dung from the streets. Dodd rubbed with his boot and saw some pretty tiles under the muck.

It was indescribably noisy. Not all the partitions had judges sitting behind a wooden bench, but in the ones that did, red-faced men in black gowns were shouting at each other and waving papers. Bailiffs and court servants shouted at each other for the next cases to come to whichever court. There was a hurrying to and fro and an arguing and shouting between lawyers, between litigants, between lawyers and litigants. At every pillar it seemed, there was a huddle of mainly black-robed men engaged in some kind of argument at the top of their voices. It was exactly like a rookery.

Dodd was already starting to get a headache. Although lacking the clang of metal and the snort of horses, the row was as loud as a battlefield, or even louder.

Enys seemed to have spotted his judge and was beckoning them over to stand next to him by the partition.

'I wanted to see what kind of mood his honour is in.'

Dodd peered around the high wooden boards. The judge, sitting with his coif on his head and a pen in his fist, pince nez perched on his nose, was scowling at a shivering young lawyer in a rather new stuff gown.

This judge seemed a little different from the others: an astonishingly luxuriant but carefully barbered grey beard decorated his face and his grey eyes glittered with wintry distaste.

'Mr. Burnett,' he was saying witheringly, 'have you in fact read your brief?'

The young lawyer facing him trembled like a leaf and gulped. Judge Whitehead threw his pen down.

'This matter, Mr. Burnett, clearly comes under the purview of the Court of Requests, not King's Bench. Why you have seen fit to plead it in front of me is a mystery. Well?'

The young lawyer seemed to be choking on his words while behind him his clients looked at each other anxiously.

'God's truth,' said the judge wearily, 'Get out of my court and go and redraft your pleadings, paying due attention to the cases of Bray v. Kirk and the matter of the Abbot of Litchfield v. Habakkuk. Adjourned.'

The young lawyer scurried off, trembling. An older lawyer warily approached the bench, trailing his own clients. 'Yes, Mr. Irvine, what is it now?' said the judge in a voice as devoid of welcome as a winter maypole.

Dodd glanced at Enys to see how this was affecting him. To his surprise he saw Enys was smiling quietly and his brown eyes sparkling.

'Disnae sound verra happy the day,' said Dodd, tilting his head at the judge who could be heard berating the unfortunate Mr. Irvine from the other side of the partition, his weary voice cutting through the hubbub like a knife.

'Shh,' warned Enys, with his pocked finger on his pitted lips, 'Mr. Justice Whitehead has very good hearing.'

'Ay.'

'Mind you, he may not be able to understand you for all that.'

Dodd sniffed, offended. It was southerners who spoke funny, not him. Meanwhile Enys was listening to the judge's comments with his head tilted as if listening to music. At one piece which seemed to be entirely in foreign, he chuckled quietly.

'Whit language are they speakin'?' Dodd wanted to know.

'Norman French,' said Enys. 'Generally most cases are heard partly in English nowadays, but a great deal of the precedent is in Latin or French.'

'Jesu. And what's sae funny?'

'His honour just made a rather learned pun.'

'Ay?'

Enys chuckled again in the aggravating way of someone enjoying a private joke. Carey had found a pillar he could lean languidly against and had crossed his arms while he surveyed the passing throngs through half-shut eyes.

'D'ye think he'll be on my side?'

'Sergeant, his honour will find what is correct in law, you can be sure of that.'

'Ay, but will he be on ma side?'

'My father was wondering if a gift...?' said Carey delicately.

Enys shook his head. 'Asolutely not, sir...It would guarantee the opposite decision.'

Carey looked surprised and worried. 'Yes, but if we can't buy him...'

'If we *could* buy him, then so could Mr. Vice—it would become not a court case but an auction,' said Enys. 'I had rather deal with someone that gives justice without fear or favour.'

Carey's eyebrows went up further. 'I hadn't thought that any judges did that.'

'Remarkably, sir, there are a few. In fact, I am in some hopes that Mr. Vice might make the mistake that we will not.'

Dodd was listening to the learned judge asking Mr. Irvine if he had ever heard of the relevant law and precedents to this case, and if he had, why had he quoted the wrong ones? Enys had an appreciative grin on his face.

'He sounds a terror,' said Dodd.

The bailiff gave mournful tongue with their names five minutes later as Irvine and his clients fled with their case adjourned until the lawyer could learn to read.

With a spring in his step and an expression on his face that looked remarkably like Carey's before he launched into some insane battle or gamble, Enys led the way into the little booth and bowed to the judge. Watching Carey out of the corner of his eye and seeing him uncover and bow, Dodd scrambled to do likewise, dropped his new beaver hat on the disgusting floor, and had to grovel to pick it up again before somebody stood on it.

'Mr. Enys,' growled the judge, 'I had heard you had thought better of the law and gone back to Cornwall?'

'No, my lord,' said Enys surprised. 'Who told you that?'

'Evidently a fool,' snorted the judge. 'Well?'

Enys handed over the sheaf of pleadings and the warrant written in a fine clear secretary hand. The judge paused as he saw who was named as the Respondent and shot a piercing grey stare over his spectacles at Enys who stared straight back, not a muscle moving in his face. Not that you could have told if it had, thanks to the scarring, thought Dodd. That lawyer would be a nightmare opponent at primero.

The judge turned to the warrant. Very briefly, something like the ghost of a smile hovered near his mouth.

'You have started proceedings in the Old Bailey?'

'Yes, your honour. Not wishing to waste any time, I briefed a solicitor to file the necessary criminal indictment about an hour ago. We are here because although the crimes were committed in the City, Mr. Vice Chamberlain Heneage is in fact resident at Chelsea which is for our purposes in the borough of Westminster.'

Another small smile. The judge turned to Dodd. 'Mr. Dodd...'

Dodd coughed hard with nervousness, but he was not going to go down in the record as anything other than what he was and what he was came to more than a mere mister.

'*Sergeant* Dodd, my lord,' said Dodd. 'Beggin' your pardon.'

'You're not a lawyer, surely?' said the judge, his brow wrinkling.

Crushing his immediate impulse to challenge the man to a duel over the insult, Dodd coughed again.

'Nay sir, Ah'm Land-Sergeant o'Gilsland, in Cumberland. On the Borders, sir.'

The judge's lips moved as he worked this out. 'Really? My apologies. How do you come to be in London, then, Sergeant?'

'Ah come with Sir Robert Carey, my lord.'

The judge transferred his attention to Carey who stepped forward and swept him another Courtier's bow.

'*Carey*? Is my lord Baron Hunsdon involved in this matter, Sir Robert?'

'Yes, your honour,' explained Carey with a face so open and innocent, Dodd felt the judge was bound to get suspicious. 'My most worshipful father is outraged that Mr. Vice Chamberlain Heneage should have falsely imprisoned and assaulted Sergeant

Dodd who serves under me in the Carlisle Castle Guard where I am Deputy Warden under my Lord Warden of the West March. My father is very kindly helping Sergeant Dodd seek redress for his injuries and the insult.'

Even Carey shifted slightly under the impact of the judge's skewering glare and silence. 'Is this a matter of Court faction, Sir Robert?' he asked at last.

'No your honour, of course not. It is a matter of seeking justice for an abhorrent and illegal assault and...'

'Yes, yes, Sir Robert, thank you,' sniffed Judge Whitehead. 'Mr. Enys, I suppose you had better open these pleadings.'

This Enys did with verve and in detail, not seeming to need to shout to be heard quite clearly in the court, quoting various laws in parliament against which Heneage had offended and various legal precedents establishing the same. More than half of what he said was in Norman French but Carey, who spoke French, whispered a translation for Dodd. Enys came to the end and Dodd was surprised to find he had understood most of what had been said that wasn't actually in foreign.

'Sergeant Dodd,' said Judge Whitehead, 'are those the facts as Mr. Enys has related them? You were arrested in error instead of Sir Robert on a warrant of debt and not believed as to your true identity. You were shortly after removed from the Fleet by Mr. Heneage who was fully aware that you were not in fact Sir Robert Carey since he complained of it. You were then falsely imprisoned by him in his coach and interrogated by him therein, during which time he himself as well as his servants and agents laid violent hands upon you?'

'Ay, my lord.' Dodd felt himself flushing with anger, enraged again at being beaten like a boy or a peasant of no account and not able to fight back.

'Mr. Heneage produced no warrant and did not accuse you of any crime?'

'No, my lord.'

'What religion are you, Sergeant?'

Dodd blinked a little at this although Carey had prepared him for it. 'My lord...eh...I am a good English Protestant and attend church whenever my duties at Carlisle permit it.' Dodd had practised saying this. It wasn't strictly true—like most English Borderers, Dodd worshipped where and how he was told to and concentrated on avoiding the attention of a God who was so terrifyingly unpredictable. It was only powerful Scottish lords like the Maxwell who could afford to go in for actual religions such as being a Catholic.

'No dealings with Papist priests?'

'No, my lord,' Dodd said, then ventured, 'I might have arrested one once, a couple of years back. For horse-theft.' He had never been quite sure whether the man had been a priest or a spy or indeed, both. Lowther had been doing a favour for Sir John Forster.

Carey coughed, Enys blinked, and the judge looked down at the papers for a moment.

'I see, thank you, Sergeant.' The judge was rereading the papers in front of him. He snorted.

More silence. Dodd stole a glance at Enys to see if he was going to say anything, but he wasn't. He was watching the judge carefully.

'On the face of the case and on the facts here presented to me, Mr. Enys, we have here a quite shocking incident. Ergo...' The words degenerated to foreign again.

Enys's face split in a delighted grin.

'You may take two of the Court bailiffs when you go to execute the warrant, Mr. Enys.'

Enys bowed low. 'Your lordship is most kind, thank you.'

The judge scribbled a note on the warrant and passed the pleadings to his clerk who was looking alarmed. 'I shall look forward to seeing you again, Mr. Enys,' said the judge in a chilly tone of voice. 'You have been admirably succinct.'

A flush went up Enys's neck as he bowed again, muttered more thanks and then led the way out of the court. As he threaded at speed through the shouting crowds, Carey called,

'And now?'

'Time to arrest him.'

WEDNESDAY 13TH SEPTEMBER 1592,

LATE MORNING

The Court bailiffs were two stolid looking men who took the warrant and went down to the Westminster steps where two of Hunsdon's boats were waiting. The second was low in the water with the weight of some large and ugly Borderers. Among them Dodd recognised jacks from the Chisholms and the Fenwicks which reminded him that Hunsdon was also the East March Warden. The Berwick tones were now pleasantly familiar to him, mingled with the rounded sounds of the incomprehensible Cornish who made up the other half of the party in the first boat.

Dodd, Carey, Enys, and the bailiffs got in the first boat and they headed upriver, past leafier banks, straining against the flow, to the oak spinneys of Chelsea where Heneage maintained his secluded house on the river frontage.

Dodd's heart started beating harder as they came near. He looked about him to spy out the approaches to what he couldn't help thinking of as Heneage's Tower. There was a boatlanding and a clear path heading up through market gardens and orchards. Not bad cover, no walls to speak of, no sign of watchers on the approaches. He jumped onto the boatlanding with the rest of the men, loosening his sword, then felt Carey touch his elbow and draw him aside.

Some of the men went round the back of the house while the bailiffs strode up to the main door, surrounded by the largest of Hunsdon's men.

'You and I stay out of this,' said Carey to Dodd.

'Ay sir. I wantae see his face when...'

'You'll see it but from a distance. I don't want any risk of a counter-suit if you whack him on the nose. And you're definitely not allowed to kill him.'

'I know that,' said Dodd with dignity. 'This isnae a bloodfeud yet. But...'

'No. It's bad enough that I lost temper and hit him myself after I found you. I don't want to give him any more ammunition.'

'Och sir,' moaned Dodd rebelliously. It was typical of Carey that he let some bunch of Berwickmen have all the fun.

The bailiff was speaking to Heneage's steward whose expression was one of astonishment and horror. Not only, explained the bailiff, was there a warrant for Mr. Heneage's arrest, there was also a warrant to search the house for him if he didn't come out, which warrant they were minded to execute immediately.

The steward was objecting that Mr. Vice Chamberlain was not there, had gone out, had never been there and...The bailiffs shouldered past him, followed by Mr. Enys, who was wearing an oddly fixed and intent expression.

There was a sound of shouting and feet thundering on stairs. Carey's face clouded. 'Hang on,' he said, 'that's not right.'

He headed for the door and brushed past the still-protesting steward, followed by Dodd who was pleased to be in at the kill.

The house was expensively oak panelled and diamond-paned, there was an extremely fine cupboard with its carved doors shut, and the steps going down to the cellar truly reeked.

The bailiffs had fanned out and were checking all the doors. Enys had hurried down the stairs and into the arched cellar where there were a few barrels of wine and a central pillar. Barred windows level with the courtyard paving let in some light. Bolted to the pillar about eight foot off the ground was a pair of iron manacles. Somebody had dug a pit in the earth underneath them which was soiled with turds. The manacles were darkened and rusty with blood.

Carey paused, took a deep breath and then went forward to where Enys was opening both of the smaller doors that gave onto two further cellars that were tiny, damp, and had not been cleaned since last there were prisoners there. However, they were otherwise empty and Enys turned away, the shadows making his face hard to read, though Dodd could have sworn he saw a glint of something on the man's face.

'Who were you looking for?' Carey said quietly, his hand on Enys's narrow shoulder.

'No one...' Enys looked down. 'My brother. I heard...I was afraid...Heneage might have taken him.'

'So you used me and my father...'

'No sir,' said Enys, looking straight at him. 'It's clear that Heneage was warned to be away from here by someone, probably the clerk of the court. But we had to make the attempt to begin the case.'

Carey nodded. 'And? Is Cecil involved in this? Raleigh?'

Enys shook his head. 'Not to my knowledge, sir, only I had to try. My brother has been missing for over two weeks. We should leave immediately so we can...'

Carey took his hand away from his sword. 'Oh not so fast,' he drawled. 'I think we should check more carefully for Mr. Vice. Now we're here.'

Starting at the top of the house, moving from one room to the other while the Cornishmen stood around the steward and the couple of valets busied themselves with the horses in the stables, Carey searched the place methodically. In one room that had a writing desk and a number of books in it, he found a pile of papers newly ciphered which he swept into a convenient post bag. In a chest he found another stack of rolled parchment, one of which he opened. He whistled.

'Mother would be interested by these,' he said. 'It seems our Mr. Vice has been busy buying lands in Cornwall—look.'

Dodd looked, squinted, and sighed because the damned thing was not only in a cramped secretary hand but was clearly in some form of foreign.

'You can see it's a deed—see the word "Dedo" which means I give, and that says "Comitatis Cornwallensis"—which means Cornwall. We'll just borrow this one, I think.' Carey dropped it in the bag.

There was a book on the desk, much thumbed, which Carey looked at and which turned out to be Foxe's Book of Martyrs.

Dodd had been attending to the cupboard with the carved doors. Eventually the lock broke and he opened it. There was a nice haul of silver.

'Jesu, Sergeant, put that back,' Carey said behind him, 'we're not here for the man's insight.'

Dodd was puzzled. 'Are we no'? I thocht that was what we were about. Can I no' nip out that fine gelding in the stables then, the one wi' the white sock?'

Carey grinned. 'We're not raiding the man, we're searching his house for evidence of wrongdoing and I'm certainly not losing my reputation for the sake of a second-rate collection of silver plate and one nag with the spavins. The man has no taste at all.' Dodd scowled. Who cared what the silver plate looked like since it was going to be melted down? And the gelding certainly did not have the spavins and was in fact a very nice piece of horseflesh, as Dodd knew, and probably Carey did as well.

At the foot of the stairs Enys was anxiously waiting for them. 'I had no intention of taking Mr. Vice Chamberlain's papers...' he began.

'Of course not,' said Carey breezily. 'We came to arrest Heneage but in the course of our search for him we came upon some papers which might possibly relate to treason and which my Lord Chamberlain, as his superior, would naturally wish to know about. We'll give them back as soon as we can find Heneage himself.'

He led the way out of the door and along the path to the boat-landing. To the steward he gave a shilling to pay for the damage to the cupboard and to convey his compliments to Mr. Vice Chamberlain—he was sure they would meet soon.

***

It seemed a very long row back to Somerset House steps, even though Dodd wasn't rowing and the current was helping the men sweating at the oars in the warm afternoon sun. Enys remained silent, staring into space, and Dodd had nothing much to say either. Carey watched Enys for a while before remarking, seemingly at venture, 'Have you truly seen nothing of your brother for more than two weeks?'

Enys turned his gargoyle's face to Carey's. 'Nothing. And he would be back by now. He...he was concerned in something dangerous connected with Heneage, something to do with land, but that's all I know.'

Carey handed over the deed he had taken. 'Is it real?'

Enys squinted his eyes, read the deed, and nodded. 'Yes, quite in order, a few hides of farmland near Helston. In Cornwall they call them "wheals."'

'Are these anything to do with the cases you withdrew from?'

Enys shook his head. 'Not this piece of land, no. Were there other deeds there?'

'Plenty of them.'

Enys smiled bitterly. 'It's a popular game. Arrest a man for non-payment of recusancy fines, offer to release him in exchange for some land sold at a very low price, and then release or don't release him, depending how much land you think his family have left. There is nothing, alas, illegal about it.'

'But you find it dishonourable?'

Enys shrugged.

'Are you a Papist?' Carey demanded, voice harsh with suspicion.

'No sir,' Enys said with a sigh, 'but my family were church-Papists and I find it hard to cheat their friends and neighbours.'

'Are they still Papists?'

'No sir, all of them are buried in good Protestant graves. My brother is my only living relative apart from my sister.'

'Was?'

Enys lifted his hands, palms up. 'What else can I think?'

Dodd nudged Carey's foot with his boot. 'D'ye think...?'

Carey sighed. 'We can but try.'

***

The men were very happy to stop off at Westminster steps and have ale and bread and cheese bought for them for their labours. Carey, Dodd, and Enys hurried to the crypt of the little chapel by the court.

The undertakers had been and the smell was less appalling since the entrails had been taken out and the cavity packed with salt and saltpetre. Now the corpse was wrapped in a cerecloth. Carey lit the candles with a spill from the watchlight.

Enys swallowed hard, took a deep breath. He had his hands clasped together at his waist as he went forward and Dodd peeled the waxed cloth from the dead man's face. He looked intently for a few moments and then let his breath puff out in a sigh of relief.

'This is not my brother, sir,' said Enys. 'Poor soul.' His gaze travelled down the body and he made a jerky movement with his right hand, then looked down.

Dodd grunted and put the waxed cloth back as carefully as he could. There was a sound behind him and he saw a small, fragile, very pregnant girl coming down the steps being carefully helped by a large man wearing a buff coat. With them was one of Hunsdon's liverymen.

'Yerss,' said the large man to the liveryman, 'it's Briscoe, Timothy Briscoe. And this is my wife, Ellie.'

Carey stepped back from the corpse and so did Dodd. Enys was already in the shadows.

'Only she 'eard about a corpse being found wiv a bit of 'is finger missing,' Briscoe continued, 'and she was scared it was 'er big bruvver who she 'asn't seen for years and so I brung 'er so she wouldn't worry 'erself and upset the baby.'

Dodd thought that if anything was likely to bring the baby on, it was the sight and smell of a corpse that had been in water for a while. The girl was shaking like a leaf and gripping tight to Briscoe's arm. He looked a dangerous bruiser but his square face was full of concern and the girl crept close to the corpse and peered at the man's left hand. There was a gasp and a gulp.

'Ellie, my love,' Briscoe rumbled. 'You mustn't...

'I've got to know,' trembled Ellie. Carey stepped forward and lifted the cerecloth from the man's face. He was watching the girl carefully. She stood on tiptoe and stared, gulped again and again, and the tears started flowing down her face.

She turned her face to her husband's shoulder quite quietly. 'I'm not sure,' she whispered, ''is face is different, but it might be Harry. It could be.'

Carey was good with distressed women, Dodd thought. He beckoned Briscoe and his wife up the steps and into the sunlight, gestured for them to sit down on a bench. He sat next to her and offered Mrs. Briscoe a sip from his silver flask of aqua vitae which she took gratefully.

'Mrs. Briscoe,' he said gently to her, 'if you haven't seen your brother Harry...What was his surname?'

'Dowling,' Briscoe said and his wife sniffled, fumbled out a hankerchief and blew her nose. 'Harold Dowling was his name.'

'If you haven't seen him for so long, why did you think it might be him?'

She gulped again with her hand resting on her proud belly. Thank God it didn't look as if the babe had been brought on by shock yet. 'I thought I saw 'im in the street a few weeks ago, only he wouldn't talk to me. I was so sure it was him and I was so pleased but he wouldn't stop and he wouldn't speak.'

'Where did you see him?'

'Seething Lane, near Sir Francis Walsingham's old house.'

'How was he dressed?'

'He looked like a gentleman which is what he always wanted to be, you see. He went off to Germany after he had a big fight wiv my dad and went for a miner, but we never heard nuffing more from him and my dad said he'd probably died in a mine and good riddance.' She sniffled. 'He was always in trouble, Harry, so maybe he was soldiering as well. It's a good thing my mam never saw what he come to after she spent all that money to put him to school.'

Carey nodded. 'But you're not sure it's him?'

She shook her head. 'It might be because of the finger, that's why I came. When I heard the crier say that about the body. He lost the tip of it when he was a boy and he caught it in a gate and the barber cut it off cos it went bad.'

She stopped, frowned and blinked at him. 'Who are you, sir?'

'I'm Sir Robert Carey. My father asked me to try and find out why this man ended in the Thames with a knife wound in him.'

She gasped again. 'I don't know about that. He was a lovely bruvver,' she said, "e took to me to Bartalmew's Fair when I was little and every year after and he was such fun, always laughing and full of ideas for making money. He was certain he'd end as a gentleman.'

'I believe the inquest will be tomorrow...' said Carey, looking for confirmation at Hunsdon's man who nodded, 'in front of the Board of Greencloth. Afterwards you'll be able to claim the body to bury.'

The girl nodded again and blew her nose again. 'Thank you, sir.'

'May we help you to your home? I have a boat waiting for me.' Carey was watching the girl with concern.

Briscoe coughed. 'Thank you kindly, sir, but we don't live far from here and my wife prefers to walk, don't you, Ellie?' The girl nodded as she heaved herself off the bench. 'I've been walking a lot today, haven't I, Tim?' she said with a watery smile. 'It's easier than sitting, to be honest, sir. And I don't know if I could get in a boat at the moment, I'm so clumsy.'

'I see,' said Carey and smiled at her. 'Well, God's blessing on your time, mistress, I hope all goes well for you.' Ellie Briscoe went pink and dropped him a clumsy curtsey as she waddled off with her husband's arm around her into the molten light that the sun was pouring into the Thames like a beekeeper measuring honey. Enys headed with his shoulders bowed towards the boatlanding.

'Will you not take a quart of ale, sir?' said Carey.

'If we do not presently round up the witnesses to Mr. Heneage's assault on Sergeant Dodd, be very sure we will never find them,' said Enys in an oddly strangled voice. 'Since he himself has given us the slip, I'm sure the lesser fry can and will.'

'Ay but surely they'll be feared for their kin,' said Dodd who deeply doubted there was any point in finding the witnesses at all. Unpaid ones, anyway. 'They'll no' testify, naebody would.' He'd thought that their only chance of persuading anyone to do it was being able to say 'and Mr. Heneage is locked up now, what do you say to that?' while persuasively bouncing heads off walls. He'd assumed that was what they were about.

'You have a point,' said Carey regretfully as he followed the lawyer, gestured to the oarsmen and bailiffs who were sitting in the sun by the red lattices of the alehouse, and headed to the boat again.

Enys had a list of witnesses that Dodd had drawn up. Most of them were in Heneage's pay. And Dodd had been looking forward to wetting his whistle which was starting to go dry, which was his own fault.

Scowling he got back in the damned boat again and sat there watching as Enys fumbled and wobbled his way to the seat. Carey stepped across and sat down at the prow, trailing his finger in the water and looking thoughtful.

'It's a pity Mrs. Grenville's a woman so she can't testify,' he said. 'All the rest are Heneage's men, apart from Mr. Cheke.'

Enys frowned. 'Nobody else?'

'The Gaoler and the gaol servants.'

'Hmm. Sergeant, you were marked in the register as Sir Robert.'

'Ay, but I writ me own name in the book, clear as ye like,' said Dodd proudly, 'not me mark but me name and office as well.' It was almost worth the missed football games and beatings from the Reverend Gilpin to be able to say that to the hoity toity London lawyer.

Surprisingly, Enys didn't seem impressed by Dodd's clerkly ability but he did look pleased.

'So under whose name were you removed from the gaol? Yours or Sir Robert's?'

Dodd thought he'd been through this with Enys the night before. 'Well, it couldnae have been Sir Robert's name because Heneage knew fine Ah wisae him for he was angry about it.'

'Did he say anything?'

'Ay, he did.'

'In front of the Keeper and the gaol servants?'

'Ay, he was furious. So he kenned verrah well who I wis and called me *Mr.* Dodd forbye. Like ye said to the judge.'

'I believe we should pay a visit to the Fleet and arrest the Keeper,' Enys said to Carey. 'It's possible he has not been warned by Heneage and putting him in gaol might help to flush out the Vice Chamberlain.'

'He'll get bail,' Carey said.

'I expect so,' said Enys placidly, 'but the point will have been made. And with luck we will be able to establish something very damaging to Mr. Vice in the process.'

Dodd leaned forward. 'Ay, but surely Heneage will get away wi'' it in the end,' he said, realising as he spoke that that was why he had been in a dump since they left Heneage's house in Chelsea. Jesu, the man had his own personal dungeons and torture chamber. He was going up against someone more dangerous than the Grahams, that was sure. He couldn't bring himself to admit it but it had been the blood on the manacles bolted high on the pillar in the cellar that had sent him queasy. Him. A Dodd from Upper Tynedale. At the age of sixteen he had taken a fine and bloody revenge for his father's murder by the Elliots and...

No, he wouldn't take the insult from anybody...but was law the right way to go about it? For all Carey's father's fine talk about paper weapons and lawyers as men-at-arms and champions.

'On the criminal charge, yes, he'll likely compose with a fine which you should accept. On the civil...' Enys shrugged. 'If we are before Mr. Justice Whitehead and any of the witnesses agree with you...Again it will be in the nature of a fine.'

Dodd grunted. It all came down to money for these folk, didn't it? Well, was money what he really wanted? And since Heneage was still at large, would they find he had called out his affinity and descended on Somerset House while they were away? Och God, was that where he was?

He was about to mention the possibility to Sir Robert when Enys interrupted.

'It is certainly worth subpoena'ing the henchmen to testify that Heneage laid hands on you himself. Was he the only one?'

Dodd blinked at him. 'Nay, they all had in wi' a boot or a fist, tho...' Dodd paused and brightened. 'Ay, but they might not mind admitting that Heneage laid into me wi' a cosh if I said that he was the only one. Ay, I'll say that.'

Enys coughed and looked at the bottom of the boat. 'If we are in front of Mr. Justice Whitehead, may I urge you to tell the truth at all times. His honour is most perspicacious.'

Dodd didn't care how much he sweated, he wanted to know how to get the judge on his side and keep him there. If telling the truth was what it took, then so be it. He sighed. 'Ay, so it were all of them with Heneage in the lead.'

'How are you now, Sergeant?'

Dodd shrugged. 'Ah've had worse, I think.' He couldn't recall exactly when, mind, certainly since he'd learned to fight, but he had woken up hungover and aching as badly on more than one occasion.

'Did you see a surgeon?'

'Ay, better than that, my lord had his ain physician tend to me.'

'Would he testify as to your injuries?'

'He might,' said Carey, 'for a fee.'

'He give me this stuff for medicine, which is very fine indeed,' said Dodd taking out the clay pipe and the henbane of Peru again. Once he'd got it lit he took a good lungful of smoke which was tasting better and no longer made his head whirl so badly. He liked the odd sensation of mild drunkenness without the rage that booze normally uncovered in him, and it definitely helped with aches and pains. He offered the pipe to Carey first, who shook his head, and then to Enys.

'I've never drunk tobacco,' said Enys.

'Ay? I thought all the students at the Inns of Court were terrible for it.'

'Oh they are,' said Enys ruefully, 'drinking, gambling, fighting. It never appealed to me, drinking smoke. What are chimneys for?'

Nonetheless Enys took the pipe and cautiously sucked some smoke. Then he burst into a mighty coughing and wheezing, handing the pipe back to Dodd just before he would have dropped it.

'Ay, it takes you that way first,' Dodd agreed, smiling wisely as the medicine took hold. 'I thought my head would fall off with the phlegm. It's better now. You wouldnae think it wis medicine at all since it disnae make you purge.'

Still coughing, Enys nodded and mopped his eyes. That henbane of Peru surely did blast the phlegm out of you, though Dodd was hazy as to how that might help your kidneys.

They went first to Mr. Cheke's apothecary shop, but did not even knock on the door. The windows were shuttered and on the door was the painted red cross and the printed warrant saying that the house was under quarantine.

Dodd felt sick. Poor man. Of all the physicians and apothecaries in the city, he had at least tried to fight the plague…Which was probably why he had caught it himself, despite all his terrifying precautions.

Ignoring the danger of infection, Carey shouted up to the

shuttered windows. 'Mr. Cheke!' he roared, 'Mr. Cheke! Can you hear me? Do you need food or water?'

There was no answer, no sound, no movement. Carey stood for a moment with his head bowed and then turned wordlessly, heading away from the stricken shop.

In a methodical manner, they went round making sure the bailiffs delivered subpoenas to all the names on Dodd's list after dumping the bag of Heneage's papers at the Somerset House gate. One more witness was dead of plague. The Gaoler of the Fleet was quite upset to see them again, even more upset to be served with court papers, and positively horrified when Enys impounded the register as vital evidence. Slightly to Dodd's surprise, there still witten in it as clear as day was the Gaoler's wobbly painful letters which read 'Sr Rbt Carey Knt' and next to it 'Sgt Henry Dod' in Dodd's own hand. Dodd thought he'd written it quite tidily, if large.

WEDNESDAY 13TH SEPTEMBER 1592,

LATE AFTERNOON

Inevitably they ended up in the Mermaid again where Marlowe was playing primero with Poley and Munday and some obvious barnards as if nothing at all had happened. Marlowe stood up as they came in and bowed elaborately. 'Ave, vos moriture saluto,' he said.

Carey returned the courtesy with a lordly nod, sat himself down on a bench, stretched out his legs and crossed them at the ankles. Then he smiled and said, 'If that means what I think it does, we're not going to die yet.'

'Of course you are, gentlemen,' said Marlowe, waving at the potboy, 'but it will have been worth it. You've tried to put the honourable Mr. Vice Chamberlain into gaol. Wonderful idea. What would you like to drink?'

The two barnards looked in horror from Carey to Marlowe and back again, gathered what was left of their money, and practically ran out the door. Munday tutted quietly.

'Aqua vitae from the barrel under the counter and sherry sack,' said Carey promptly. 'Did Heneage pay you your wages at last then, Kit?'

Marlowe smiled and kissed his fingers at Carey.

'I'll have a quart of double, if ye're buying,' said Dodd suspiciously. 'This here is Mr. Enys, he's our lawyer.'

'Better and better,' said Marlowe becoming more dramatic by the minute. 'Mr. Enys if you were the man who had the balls to draft the pleadings, please do join us.'

Enys coloured slightly and smiled. 'Mild for me, thank you,' he said, sitting himself down nervously on a stool with his robe wrapped around him.

'Many- tongu'd Rumour is rampaging up and down Whitefriars and the Temple,' declaimed Marlowe, who had clearly been drinking all day, flinging out an arm as if to introduce her. 'Is it true Mr. Vice tried to escape and was stopped by Sergeant Dodd here leaping on board the coach, wrestling the driver to the ground, running across the backs of the horses, and halting the coach just before it should tragically fall into a ravine with Heneage in it, at which Mr. Vice ran into the woods and escaped?'

'No,' said Carey dampeningly, 'he wasn't there.'

Marlowe struck his forehead with the heel of his palm. 'Such a pity, another wonderful story sadly exploded by prosaic reality.'

'Somebody must have warned him what was afoot.'

'Ah yes, the clerk of the court. As always, a useful purchase. What will you do tomorrow?'

'I have other matters to pursue,' said Carey, 'but I expect I shall go to court again. What's the book?'

Marlowe produced a small notebook from his sleeve. 'Here we are. Five to one on that the Sergeant composes the criminal assault with Heneage and makes a deal for the civil damages. Ditto that it's taken out of Whitehead's court on account of his notorious honesty. Ten to one on and no takers that you're both in the Tower for treason by the end of the month.' Carey smiled faintly. 'Are you in?' asked Marlowe, reaching for his pen.

'Probably,' said Carey, 'I'll have to think about it. I'll put in a noble on myself to stay out of the Tower.'

Dodd gulped. Six shillings and eightpence wasn't much of a bet in Carey's scheme of things. Plus he hadn't said 'myself and Dodd.'

'Your father's backing this, isn't he?' asked Poley suddenly as he added some coins to the primero pot and took another card.

Carey had his eyes shut and had not been dealt into the game. 'Obviously.'

'Why? I mean why is he backing it?'

'Oh, high spirits and a love of justice, I expect.'

Poley had a pale oblong face with eyes that seemed not to blink very much. Dodd considered that he would certainly not buy a horse from the man. 'Surely he's taking revenge for what happened to your brother?'

'Of course not,' said Carey, still smiling with his eyes shut.

'Must be,' said Poley, relentlessly. 'He wouldn't want to leave it lie.'

'Whatever you wish, Mr. Poley,' said Carey, which made Dodd blink at his unaccustomed soft-spokenness.

'They've never got on, have they, the Lord Chamberlain and Vice Chamberlain?' Poley continued to poke, 'And your father wouldn't like...'

'Mr. Poley, I can't imagine why you think I'm going to discuss my father's plans with the likes of you,' said Carey. 'If I wanted to tell it all to Heneage I'd write a letter and get Marlowe to deliver it which would probably be quicker.' Marlowe had been over by the barman, talking quietly to him.

Poley coloured slightly. 'I don't...'

'Oh tut tut,' said Marlowe silkily, coming back, picking up and laying down his new cards, 'Chorus. Mine I think. If you want my lord Baron Hunsdon to employ you when Heneage goes you'll have to do better than that, my dear...'

Poley gave Marlowe an ugly look. 'I...'

'Crows white, noonday night, hills flying, pigs roosting in the trees,' murmured Carey seemingly apropos of nothing.

'Eh?' Poley paused in a blindingly deft shuffle of the cards.

'He means,' Marlowe told him patronisingly, 'that these things will happen before Hunsdon employs you. Very poetic I'm sure, Sir Robert, since you've nipped it straight out of a Border ballad.'

'I don't know why I'm being insulted,' sniffed Poley as Marlowe took the cards from him to shuffle again.

'Tell me about the body in the Thames,' said Carey.

'Which one?'

Carey's eyebrows went up. 'A gentleman or seeming like one, dark hair, sallow complexion, marks of burns and stains on his hands, top joint of his left forefinger missing.'

It was the merest flicker, but Poley looked uncertainly at Marlowe and then quickly back at his cards. Meanwhile Marlowe had paused infinitesimally as he dealt Carey in. Dodd shook his head and stayed out of it. So did Enys who was sitting quietly on his stool, sipping his small beer and watching everything. From the corner of his eye Dodd saw the potboy trot through the commonroom and out the door into the street where he speeded to a run.

'No idea,' said Marlowe glibly, 'Where was he found?'

'Washed up against the Queen's Privy Steps.'

Marlowe raised his eyebrows, very Carey-like. 'So?'

'In the jurisdiction of the Board of Greencloth. My father wants me to investigate. He also wants me to look into rumours of crooked land dealings in Cornwall.'

Marlowe shrugged. 'It's all the rage at court, I believe. Bald Will was talking about how the Earl of Southampton is buying himself a sheaf of godforsaken Cornish hills.'

Carey nodded, picked up his cards, glanced at them, put them down, leaned forwards and put his chin on his clasped hands. 'And?'

Marlowe shrugged again. 'I don't know. I'm certainly not about to buy some dubious marshy fields somewhere I am never likely to go. No matter what they might have under them. And even if I had the money.'

Carey murmured something to Enys who had been blinking at Marlowe as if tranced like a chicken. Enys started, coloured, and fished in his satchel of papers and brought out a stiff piece of paper, written and sealed. Carey took it and handed it to Marlowe who took it absent-mindedly while adding his bet to the pot, glanced at it, and then scowled.

'Damn it, Sir Robert.'

'You've been served, Christopher Marlowe. I'm calling you as a witness to Heneage's dealings with my brother and the incident with Sergeant Dodd here.'

Dodd's spirits lifted slightly. That had been nicely done. Marlowe's face was a picture and no mistake.

Marlowe screwed up the paper furiously. 'You tricked me!'

Carey shrugged.

'I can't appear in open court against Heneage.'

'Yes you can,' said Carey. 'Until it's time to testify you can stay at Somerset House and we'll organise you a boat to take you to Westminster.'

'I can't appear,' said Marlowe through his teeth. 'I was not a witness. I wasn't there. I was in Southwark.'

'Were you now?' said Carey easily, not seeming ruffled by this abject lie. Poley's eyes darted from Marlowe to Carey and back. 'Any corroboration, any witnesses to that?'

'Oh yes. Mr. Poley here for one.'

Poley didn't look happy at this. 'That's right,' he said, 'I was with Mr. Marlowe on...ah...the day in question and he was in Southwark.'

'Was he?' Carey's eyes were half-hooded. 'You sure about that, Kit?'

'Yes,' Marlowe was giving Carey back stare for stare.

'Despite all the witnesses I have to you sitting in the Mermaid waiting for me on the day in question?' Carey was smiling. 'Come on, I know Heneage is powerful and wealthy but so is my father and he likes poets for some reason. He'll protect you.'

Marlowe finished his brandywine, checked his cards again, and folded. 'Does your father employ Richard Topcliffe?' Now where had Dodd heard that name before?

'No. Who's that?' From the look in Carey's eyes, Dodd suspected he did know but wasn't admitting it.

'You've never met him?'

Carey shrugged.'No.'

'Consider yourself lucky,' said Marlowe. 'Topcliffe is...well he's ingenious and he's very good at his job which he likes very much.'

'Really?'

'He's a freelance inquisitor. He often works for Heneage. He has the breaking of most of the Papist priests we...the pursuivants catch. He's at the Tower working on one called Robert Southwell at the moment. That's why you haven't seen him and why he wasn't at Chelsea.'

'And?'

'And? I don't want him after me. Because he's completely insane and kills for fun and Heneage protects him, gives him completely free rein.'

Dodd nodded, struck by a memory. 'Ay, Shakespeare was saying there was someone he was more affeared of than me...Which was a surprise to me, ye follow.'

Marlowe blinked at Dodd as if he'd forgotten his existence and then nodded. 'That will be Topcliffe.'

'Come on, Marlowe,' said Carey comfortably, 'this isn't like you. Where's the student of the lofty spheres...'

'The student of the lofty spheres prefers to keep his own fleshly spheres away from Topcliffe who likes playing games with men's stones. I mean it, Carey, I'm not testifying against Heneage.'

'I heard Topcliffe buys the bawdy-house boys that get poxed and nobody ever sees them again,' put in Poley.

'How does he get away with it?'

'The Queen protects him because she's been told he's useful. He's mad, of course. Bedlam mad. He'll tell anyone who listens the dreams he has of the Queen where he...Well, you'd expect her to hang him if she'd heard what he says, so I assume she hasn't. And he has other friends at court, powerful friends. And although he's old now, he's a very good pursuivant.' Marlowe lifted his hands palms up. 'I'm not doing it.'

'Isn't anyone going to play primero?' said Poley. Enys shook his head and pushed the cards he'd been dealt back towards Marlowe, who picked them up with his eyebrows raised. 'Mr. Enys, I'm surprised, I thought all Gray's Inn men were shocking gamblers.'

Enys smiled faintly. 'Not me, sir. Or rather I am a shocking gambler as I generally lose. I lost so much last Christmas that I have sworn to my sister that I will have no more to do with play.'

Marlowe nodded but said nothing more. 'Sir Robert?'

'Oh eighty-five points,' said Carey languidly, dropping a sixpenny stake into the pot. Dodd shook his head as well, filled a pipe, and lit it. Once again the aromatic herb and incense mixture made him feel as if some tight knot in his stomach was being slowly unwound. He passed the pipe to Enys who took some and hardly coughed at all this time. As the pipe went round, Dodd considered that there were London vices he would be sorry to leave behind him and he'd have to buy in a good stock of the doctor's medicine before he went north.

Although Dodd hadn't drunk very much by the end of the long evening he was feeling peaceful and light in the head as he left the Mermaid and all three of them headed up past the Blackfriars monastery wall. They were heading for Ludgate and Fleet Street to pass onto the Strand and Hunsdon's palace of a place. Only a madman tried to cut through the Whitefriars liberties at night after curfew and they were no longer using the little tenement Hunsdon had given them earlier in the month. He and Carey had felt that if they were taking on Vice Chamberlain Heneage in the courts they were better off somewhere with walls and a large number of serving men. Dodd was thoroughly enjoying the luxury of Somerset House, now he had got over his shock at having an entire chamber to himself. He was even starting to get used to the ridiculous hot tight clothes Carey insisted he wear.

There was a movement of something too large to be a cat in a shadowed alley. The hair on Dodd's neck stood up straight. Automatically he loosened his sword and took a quick glance behind him under cover of a coughing fit. A large shape moved into shadow in the corner of his eye. Heart thundering and his head still swimming with the tobacco, Dodd paused and then turned left into the nearest alleyway, feeling for his codpiece laces. He needed a piss anyway.

'Och, Sir Robert,' he called, 'Will ye look at this?' and pretended to be squinting into the alley.

Carey had been trying to persuade Enys to sing 'A Shepherd to His Love' in harmony with him, to Enys's giggly but steadfast insistence he had no voice. Now Carey swung back and Enys trailed after them, still sniggering.

Dodd shook his head violently, trying to clear it. 'S' a place here looks a lot like Tarras Moss,' he slurred. 'Would ye credit it?'

Carey sauntered over, whistling happily. For a moment Dodd thought he hadn't got the reference until he saw Carey's hand go stealthily to the poinard dagger hanging at the small of his back.

Dodd looked down, annoyed. Sheer tension meant he could not actually piss.

'Och damn it,' he moaned, wishing he hadn't had the beer. Carey was leaning one arm against the wall, singing softly and pretending to fumble at his own lacings.

'How many?' he muttered very quietly.

'Ah've seen two,' Dodd muttered back, quickly tying again, 'so I'd bet on five or more.'

'Me too. Break for the Temple, not Somerset House.'

'Ay sir,' said Dodd. 'Will we charge 'em now?'

'Not exactly,' said Carey with a smile, 'Let's see if we can avoid a trial for murder, shall we?'

He drew sword and dagger and crossed them. Dodd drew his sword and faced the other way. Enys was leaning against a wall, still giggling.

Carey stepped out a little so that a public-spirited torch, in a sconce on one of the linen shops, showed him up in the blackness.

'Gentlemen, I know you're there. Shall we talk?'

There was a pause and then a heavyset man moved from the shadows of an alley and another came out of the bulk of Temple Bar itself where he must have been pretending to be a carved saint. Dodd strained his eyes to penetrate the other shadows and thought he caught a glimpse of metal as someone drew a dagger. Three visible, so a possible six in total.

Seeing Enys still leaning against the wall giggling from the tobacco fumes, he kicked the man on the ankle. 'Ow,' said Enys aggrievedly, 'Why...?'

'Will ye draw, ye fool?' Dodd hissed furiously.

'Wha'?' Enys tried to stand upright and blinked about himself. Yes, definitely a fourth man visible next to the huge permanent dungheap a little way from Temple Bar. Probably that was where the ambush had been planned for. Dodd squinted hard looking for the fifth and sixth whilst Enys hiccupped and fumbled at his sword hilt. No help there then, damn it, typical soft southerner.

'Talk?' said the large man in a jack who seemed to be the leader. 'Wo' abaht?' His voice was as full of glottal stops as Barnabus' had been, very hard to understand.

'Oh nothing much,' said Carey, doing a couple of showy juggling tricks with his dagger and sword, swapping them over and then back again. 'Just talk. What a pleasant night it's been. How you gentlemen must be tired of waiting for us. Who's paying you. That sort of thing.'

'Nuffink to talk about.'

Dodd saw what Carey was doing. He was deliberately drawing attention to himself, aiming to draw the attackers out so they'd show themselves. Presumably it would then be up to Dodd to kill them...Except what was that the Courtier had said about avoiding a trial for murder in London?

There was a scrape behind Dodd, he spun, saw a large moon-face looming near him with a veney stick raised over his head, and slashed sideways with his sword. He heard a yelp and smelled blood as the man reeled backwards, clutching a spurting arm. Dodd heard a cry behind him and saw Enys clumsily trying to block with his sword against a man battering down on him with a club.

Another club? No blades? Ay, the Courtier's right, Dodd thought in a sudden slow moment of icy clarity, this is to get us all arrested for murder.

Furious at the man who had hired roaring boys and set them deliberately against fighters who could kill them, Dodd ran up behind the man who was so intent on Enys, his prey, that he had no defence against Dodd's powerful boot in the arse which sent him sprawling.

Enys had dropped his sword and had his hands over his face as he crouched in a corner, moaning. Jesus, thought Dodd as he went past the ninny, what a pathetic sight. What's wrong with him?

Dodd grabbed the club-wielder who was just trying to climb to his feet, picked him up bodily and crashed him backwards over a stone conduit filled with slimy horse-slobbered water. Dodd shoved the man's head deep into the water and held him there while he clawed at Dodd's arm. Meantime Dodd looked around cannily for more attackers. Something complicated was going on down Fleet Street, involving Carey and the big man-at-arms, but the other two men, if they existed, were still waiting their moment, or possibly had run.

Dodd let the man with the club crow in some air, and then had him blowing bubbles again.

'Wh...what are you doing?' came a slurred voice behind him. Dodd glanced over his shoulder and saw the soft southerner staggering over, trailing his sword in his left hand and twisting his right as if it pained him. Perhaps he'd sprained it somehow. He was panting and wild-eyed.

'Ah'm drowning this pig's turd,' Dodd explained casually, letting the man up for a second so he could hear.

Enys watched the renewed bubbles and then jumped at a further clang and ting down Fleet Street followed by Carey's customary bellow of 'T'il y est haut!'

'What about Sir Robert? Won't you help him?' trembled the soft lawyer.

Dodd leaned an ear expertly in the direction of the clanging.

'Neither o' them are trying to kill each other,' he said. 'And yon Courtier nearly held Andy Nixon to a draw for three minutes in the summer, he'll be well enough while I make sure of this loon. Will ye fetch his dagger?'

The loon's hands were flailing more feebly now, so Dodd let the man up to breathe while Enys gingerly fished the dagger from its sheath. What was it doing still there, Dodd wanted to know.

'Now then,' Dodd said to the man, who was coughing and spluttering fit to bust his lungs, 'who was it set ye on tae *me* wi' nobbut a stick and a knife, eh?'

'Heeh...heh...'

Dodd said it again patiently, only more southern. He hoped.

'Hur...ha...he said you was only a farmer, and not a gentleman.'

'Ay,' said Dodd, 'I am certainly no' a gentleman and I am a farmer, did he tell ye where I farm?'

The man shook his head, spattering slime everywhere. Dodd told him.

'I have boys that scare crows for me that are better fighters than ye, ye soft southern git, so who was it that tried to get ye killed? Eh?'

The man gasped for breath then said the name. Dodd sighed and dunked him again until the flailing had stopped, then hefted him out and laid him on his side on the filthy cobbles to puke and cough his way back to consciousness. On a thought, he picked up a nice piece of brick from a nearby pile of rubble. He realised with irritation that his sleeves were wet to the elbow and hoped they wouldn't shrink too much.

Then he sauntered over to where Carey was seemingly playing a veney with the large man who had been first to show himself. The man was now backing up carefully, probably trying for one of the many alleys off Fleet Street that led into the liberties without actually turning his back on Carey. The Courtier was quite breathless by now but clearly enjoying himself, fencing like a sword instructor and never trying to come to close quarters with the lethal twenty inch long poinard in his left hand.

'If ye can leave off playin' yer veney wi' yon catamite,' called Dodd as southern as he could, 'we might catch Marlowe afore he runs for it.'

Carey missed a beat and nearly lost the tip of his nose before coming back to the attack with more purpose. 'Oh for God's sake,' he groaned in disgust.

'Ay,' said Dodd, narrowed his eyes and threw the brick hard at the man-at-arms' chest. It caught him in the rib cage, giving Carey the chance to beat past the man's blade and smash him in the face left-handed with the pommel of his poinard. The man went down like a sack of flour.

Carey pounced on him at once, bashed him a couple more times with the dagger hilt, then straightened and caught his breath for a moment. He started dragging the large man over to his mate who was still heaving and coughing by the conduit. Dodd glanced at Enys who was staring at the swordsman as the blood came gouting out of his nose and down his face from the nasty cut on his forehead caused by one of the jewels in Carey's poinard hilt. So that's what they were for, eh? That made sense of why anyone

354

would want a pretty dagger hilt.

Dodd sheathed his sword which was still clean and gave the puffing Carey a hand to carry the man to his mate and lay him down in a suggestive position behind Dodd's victim. Carey grinned and pulled off both men's belts, then tied them tightly together with the swordsman's wrists in front of Dodd's man and that man's hands belted behind him as far around the bulk of the swordsman as his arms would go. The swordsman started to struggle and mutter so Carey bashed him a couple more times, while Dodd tied their feet in a tangle.

It was a cosy sight and would give the Fleet Street wives a good laugh when they came to fetch water at the conduit in the morning.

'Ay,' said Dodd, deeply satisfied at justice done. He unbuttoned his sleeve cuffs because they felt tight.

Enys still seemed upset for some reason and was saying nothing. Dodd took his sword from his unresisting left hand and put it back in his scabbard, then examined the man's wrist which was unusually thin and seemed mildly sprained.

'Caught a blow awkwardly, did ye?' he asked with not much sympathy. Enys nodded. It was hard to tell colour in the flickering light from the Gatehouse Inn torch and the one on the linen shop, but it looked as if Enys had gone beetroot-cheeked and so he should.

'Sergeant, I apologise, I'm...well...I'm no good as a swordsman. I only wear one because the Inn regulations say I have to.'

'Ay.' Dodd nodded with dignity at this apology, 'When yer wrist is well, would ye like me to teach ye a few moves?'

Enys blinked rapidly. 'Ah...yes...if you don't mind.'

'Ah dinna care one way or the other, I just dinnae want the trouble of finding a new lawyer to take my case. Why did ye no' kick him in the cods, he was open for it?

Enys smiled shakily. 'I didn't think of it.'

Dodd sucked his teeth. 'Ye've never fought before?'

'My brother.'

Dodd nodded sourly. 'Ay but he wasnae trying to kill ye. Generally.'

'Come on, gentlemen!' called Carey from up the street where he was heading briskly towards the Blackfriars again. 'He's an arrogant bugger is Marlowe, there's a chance he might still be there.'

Dodd speeded to a sprint to catch up with Carey, followed slowly by Enys who seemed to run in a lumbering fashion that boded ill for his sword-fighting. He seemed remarkably tired by the short sprint of a few hundred yards as well. He walked behind them, hunched, breathing hard, and pressing at his ribcage.

'You should consider going to your home, Mr. Enys?' Carey said to him, 'This might get nasty.'

Enys shook his head. 'I'm afraid I shall be...no use to you gentlemen...at all,' he panted, 'but I would prefer to stay with you, if I may.'

Carey raised his brows at Dodd for his opinion and Dodd shrugged.

'If it a' goes wrong, we wilnae protect ye,' he warned Enys. Looking at Carey he thought it was quite likely to go wrong. Carey's lips were compressed in a thin line and the light of battle gleamed in his eye.

'D'ye think he'll be there?' Dodd asked.

'Oh yes. He'll want to know what happened. His calculation will be either...'

'We got a beating and think better of it, or we kill someone and wind up in gaol wi' yer friend Hughes measuring a rope for us,' said Dodd.

'Or, in my case, sharpening an axe, of course,' pointed out Carey the aristocrat. 'I am more sick than I can say of Marlowe's stupid plotting...bloody idiot. What does he think he's playing at?'

'Trying hard to get back in Heneage's good opinion.'

'A week ago he convinced me that he wanted to switch to my lord of Essex's affinity.'

'Ay, but that was a week ago. He's changed his mind, nae doubt.'

'Though I did have his head buried in a pile of the Queen's old bumrolls at the time so he may not have been telling me the whole truth.'

Dodd hid a smile at the picture this presented. 'Did ye now?' he said still glum, 'Why did ye not slit his throat then and save us all trouble?'

'Didn't want to get her Majesty's linen all dirty,' said Carey very prim. 'Also, despite his faults, Marlowe's a remarkably fine poet and it would be a pity...'

Dodd shook his head at such an irrelevance.

WEDNESDAY 13TH SEPTEMBER 1592, NIGHT

Carey paused as he turned towards the Mermaid Inn, checking round the corner. 'God, I wish Barnabus was here,' he said, 'this is the perfect job for him.'

Dodd said nothing, never having much liked Carey's thieving manservant. Before they came to the Mermaid, Carey ducked into an alley that wound its way between the old walls of the monastery and the new shacks of incomers, to the sturdy wall at the back of the inn's yard. An unmistakeable reek of malt came from it. Carey looked thoughtful then climbed up on a shed roof and thence to a wall. Dodd boosted Enys onto the shed, then climbed up himself. Carey was peering down into the courtyard which was empty apart from a couple of goats tethered near a wall.

'Stay here,' he whispered, and climbed quietly down from the wall, using a hen house as a step.

There were sounds of activity in the common room and the noise of somebody playing a lute much less expertly than he thought he could.

'Mr. Enys,' breathed Dodd in his ear, 'can ye understand me?' Enys nodded. 'If it a' goes wrong I want ye to leg it for Somerset House fast as ye can. Dinna fight, dinna stop to wait for us, get to Somerset House and roust out my lord Hunsdon's kin. D'ye follow?'

Enys took a breath, possibly to argue, then nodded firmly. 'How will I know?' he whispered. Dodd thought.

'Ye'll know if ye hear fighting or me yowling like a cat as a signal.'

In Tynedale they gave a yell but Dodd didn't want to give too much away. Meanwhile Carey had crossed the yard without waking the chickens or the goats and got to the horn-paned window of the scullery. He knocked on it. Out came the sleepy-eyed potboy with wet hands red raw from lye. After quiet conversation and the transfer of a coin in the normal direction—away from Carey—the boy ducked back inside and a few minutes later, the innkeeper came out. He was carrying an empty barrel. Another quiet conversation and another transfer of coin.

Meanwhile Dodd had been thinking and none of what he thought pleased him at all. Even he was wishing for Barnabus now who would have been the ideal man for what he needed done.

The innkeeper went back inside, Carey crossed the yard again and used the henhouse to climb back up onto the wall. This time the hens inside clucked anxiously.

'The innkeeper tells me Marlowe is on his own and I've bribed him to get Marlowe out into the yard and...'

'Nay sir,' said Dodd, coming to a decision. 'I dinna think so.'

'I beg your pardon, Sergeant?' Carey's voice was cold. He always hated being contradicted. No help for it, Dodd was not about to stand by and watch Carey run headfirst into an ambush again.

'Sir, did ye never run a raid on someone wi' but a few men and have the rest lying out in a valley to ambush them when they rode in on the hot trod?' It was so obvious, it was painful.

'This isn't the Borders, Sergeant,' sniffed Carey, 'and I've seen that...'

'Sir, ye've seen nothing, ye've been told.' With decision, Dodd moved to the end of the wall and climbed quietly down into the alley again, helping Enys down as he went. 'It's a' too bloody convenient,' he muttered to himself.

'Where are you going Sergeant?' hissed Carey from the wall.

'I'm gonnae see for meself,' Dodd told him, trotting quietly down the alley and then into another one on a sudden thought. Aggravatingly the alley suddenly twisted on itself and ended up at some riversteps, so Dodd moved along the bank to another alley and then jogged along it back to the main road.

There he saw exactly what he had suspected: a large group of large men in jacks carrying loaded crossbows. They were filing down the alley he had just accidentally avoided coming out of.

'Och,' thought Dodd with fury, 'Will I niver get to ma bed?'

He opened his mouth and let out what he thought was quite a good caterwaul, heard running feet stumbling down Fleet Street for the Strand. Two urchins who had been asleep on a dungheap for its warmth were sitting up and staring at him. Dodd nodded at them and beckoned them over, gave each of them sixpence which was all he could bear to part with, and told them what they were to do.

There was no sign of alarm from the men-at-arms who had paused at Dodd's imitation cat. Moving quietly and deftly through the shadows, Dodd came round by a different direction to the front of the Mermaid where the sign hung over a coach waiting outside, with the horses half asleep, their hooves tipped. Dodd recognised the damned thing, and crept up to it on the other side with his heart thundering.

The coach itself was empty. Dodd peered round and saw one man standing by the door to the tavern, who was probably the coachman, looking in with interest.

Suddenly there was a shouting and yelling followed by the loud twang of a discharged crossbow. Then a grumble of voices.

Dodd sighed. Instead of waiting for Dodd to come back with his report, the daft Courtier had got himself captured and he hoped that he hadn't got in the way of that crossbow bolt.

'Thish ish an outrage!' came Carey's voice at its loudest and most affected. 'How dare you, shir, unhand me!'

Dodd nearly smiled, it was all so theatrical. Had he done it on purpose, perhaps? Peeping around the coach he could see Carey through the diamond-paned windows, lit up by candles and menaced by several crossbows, dusting mud off his hat.

Dodd skulked back behind the coach and very quietly, using the point of his dagger and a fingernail which broke, pulled out two of the axle pins in the coach wheels. He then went back down the alleys, past the two urchins who were bent over a tinderbox, and climbed onto the wall of the courtyard again. The goats were up, giving occasional excited bleats, the chickens were complaining to each other but not daring to come out of their hutch, which in any case was bolted against alleycats. With infinite care, Dodd climbed down from the wall and crossed the yard. In front of him was the usual shamble of kitchen sheds and storesheds and the entrance of the cellar. A gabble of talk came from the commonroom.

Holding his breath, Dodd tried the back door to the kitchen which was latched on the inside. Very carefully he put his dagger through the hole and jiggled. For a wonder the bar was not pegged and came up. He went into the scullery where the pots and pans were piled up and into the kitchen where the boy was fast asleep by the fire, wrapped in his cloak with the spit dog huddled in his arms.

A loud growling came from the spit dog. In any case, Dodd needed to talk to the boy. He went over, gripped the dog's nose with one hand and clamped the other one over the boy's mouth. The boy woke and squeaked with fright.

'Can ye understand me?' Dodd said patiently, and told the boy what he had come to say. The boy shivered and stared at him, so Dodd hoped he had got the message, tapped the dog on the nose, and padded on to the serving passage, closing the door behind him as he went. He heard a scramble of feet and excited yipping.

There was a second door to the commonroom and Dodd put his ear to it.

'I have no idea what you're talking about,' came Carey's pained tones, 'Jusht...on my way home from an evening'sh cardplay with my friendsh and I am shurrounded...shurrounded, sir!...by Smithfield bullyboys who threaten me with croshbows and make me come in here, no idea why, sure it's illegal. Eh?'

There was a quiet ugly murmer which Dodd could not make out. He was sure it didn't come from Marlowe, being too deep and not nearly cocky enough. It contained rather a dull certainty. The owner of the coach, then? But Heneage's voice was lighter than that.

'Yesh, I wash, marrer of fact, wiv him, your friend and mine, Mr. Kit Marlowe, playwright. Got lorsht.'

More muttering. 'Mr. Topcliffe,' said Carey's voice with magnificent boozy arrogance, 'my friendsh have all gone home and I would like to ash well. What...ish the problem?'

More murmering. Carey laughed theatrically. 'Don't be ridiculoush,' he said, 'I can't turn Papist. I'm the Queen'sh bloody nephew. And her coush...cousin. If I so much as think about it, which I wouldn't because it'sh evil and treashon as well, I'd already be in the Tower with my head chopped off. So to shpeak.'

Dodd risked a peek round the door. Carey had sat himself down on one of the settles by the fading fire with his right leg propped on his left knee and a mannered right hand placed just so on it. Standing nearby with a strange expression of mixed fear and amusement on his face was Marlowe. In front of Carey at an angle from the door, arms folded, dark gown with hanging sleeves trailing off his shoulders and men behind him, was an old man with a sword. At odds with the lines on his face was his hair and beard which was a sooty black colour. Dodd didn't know him.

Marlowe was staring straight at Dodd and must have seen him. Infinitesimally he moved his head to right and left at Dodd, then lifted his brows and his gaze went over Dodd's shoulder. He turned back to the black-bearded man.

Dodd's stomach froze twice. First when he knew Marlowe had seen him, once again when he realised what Marlowe was urgently trying to tell him.

A click of the safety hook coming off a crossbow trigger. Dodd sighed softly, let the door shut, and turned with his hands up.

One of the henchmen was standing there grinning gaptoothed, a beer mug in one hand and a crossbow in the other. That was the nuisance of crossbows. Unlike firearms you couldn't hear them because there was no match to hiss.

'Ha ha!' said the henchman, 'Got yer.' He took a pull of beer from his mug and waved the crossbow slightly. 'Wotchoo doin 'ere, yor sposed to be watchin ve coach.'

Dodd paused for a moment, completely mystified then said as near to London-talk as he could get, 'Ah wis 'opin to find booze.'

It didn't work. The man's eyes narrowed so Dodd gave up on subtlety and kicked him as hard as he could in balls, hoping he wasn't aiming the crossbow straight. The man's eyes crossed, he slowly started to crumple up. Dodd's hand closed on the crossbow and took it off him to find the thing wasn't properly loaded and the bolt had stuck fast. There were too many men backing the black-bearded man in the common room, so Dodd changed his plan.

He ran back through the kitchen where the kitchen boy was methodically helping himself to meat hanging up in a larder while the spit dog yipped excitedly. He grabbed the boy by the ear. 'Ah tellt ye to run, now run!' he growled and propelled the boy out the door in front of him, followed by the spit dog, still yelping.

The boy ran across the courtyard, slammed open the gate, and disappeared into the alley. The tied-up goats set up a loud bleating and the chickens clucked. Dodd sprinted round the side of the lean-to, found a water barrel, and climbed up it onto the slippery wooden-shingled roof.

He watched with interest, counting under his breath, as a stream of broad men in jacks came rushing into the yard, across it and through the gate, followed by the black-bearded man who was pointing with his sword and shouting furiously as he hobbled after.

Wishing again, pointlessly, for Barnabus who would have been very useful with his throwing daggers, Dodd stayed as flat as he could and listened for the sounds to die down. Then he climbed up a little to a balcony, hearing the whispering and giggling of the urchins down in the yard.

It was a struggle to get over the rail thanks to the stupid stuffed hose he was wearing. He tried the door to the best bedroom but it was locked. He used his dagger to attack the hinges of the window shutters where the wood was old and a moment later after some stealthy cracking, managed to lever the shutter back and off, leaving a space large enough for him to climb through and into the empty bedroom. He hoped. He held the useless crossbow out and waited for the shout and scrape of steel but there was no sound of breathing in the room.

The corridor was also empty. Dodd clattered down the stairs with his sword in his right and the crossbow in his left, and came upon a fascinating picture.

Two men must have been left to guard Carey but they were both in crumpled heaps on the floor. Marlowe and Carey were standing over them. Carey looked up as Dodd came down the stairs, slightly breathless no doubt because of the tightness of his doublet.

Carey beamed at Dodd. 'Excellent, Sergeant, I told Kit you wouldn't be long.'

Dodd crushed the impulse to grin back like some court ninny. They were very far from being safe and in fact he could smell smoke already. He went over and checked the men on the floor and was happy to find a pouch of quarrels on one of them, which he took. He then carefully discharged the crossbow in his hands which popped the bent bolt out onto the floor, put his toe in the stirrup, rebent the bow and hooked it so he could slot in a new bolt. Much happier, he shook his head at Carey and Marlowe's move for the kitchen and instead went straight for the main entrance to the inn where the coachman was sitting on the coach driving seat, looking worried.

Dodd pointed the crossbow at him and he froze and sat back down again.

'Ay,' said Dodd. 'Ye didna see nothing.'

The coachman nodded wildly. Carey and Marlowe looked at each other.

'Shall we steal the coach?' asked Marlowe, giggling slightly.

Dodd sighed. This was a serious business, not a boy's escapade. 'Ah wouldnae advise it,' he said coldly.

Carey looked over his shoulder. 'Somerset House,' he said.

They bunched together and headed up to Ludgate and then left into Fleet Street over the Fleet Bridge that stank to high heaven. Dodd's eyes were itching with tiredness.

Behind them were heavy running feet and shouts. After one glance to see the black-bearded man's henchmen coming after them in a close-packed crowd and several crossbows being raised, all three of them picked up their heels and sprinted along the Fleet, running like hell for Somerset House or one of the little alleys leading into the Whitefriars if necessary. After about half a minute of serious running, Dodd was starting to feel breathless and tightchested. A crossbow twanged and he ducked instinctively, was outraged to see Marlowe drawing ahead of him as they pounded up the cobbles and wondered, in some cranny of his skull which was not in a panic, what had happened to his wind?

There was the rumble of coach wheels on the cobbles behind him, changing to scraping as they came onto the rutted muddy disgrace of the Strand. He risked a glance over his shoulder to see the black coach hammering after them, the horses nearly at the gallop, then the sound of clattering as it turned to avoid the margins of the dungheap. There was a crack and an ear-jangling crunch and crash as the wheels on one side of the coach tilted inwards and fell off. The coach toppled over sideways in a heap as the coachman leaped desperately for safety and landed on a soft pile of rotten marrows. Now that was a highly satisfying sound. Dodd had taken a great dislike to that coach and he risked another glance to see it in its splintered ruin, half on the dungheap with the coachman climbing groggily out from the muck. The horses had come to a stop with their traces trailing and were eating a London wife's herbal windowsill.

Then he heard another cry and squinted ahead and his heart sank: up ahead was another large body of men jogging towards them, torches held high. Dodd immediately swerved left to the awning of the Cock Tavern and eyed the red-painted shutters with a view to climbing them for a good vantage on the roof. Marlowe too dodged behind a stone conduit. Carey however picked up speed and kept running forward.

'Mr. Bellamy!' he yelled. 'Don't shoot...'

There was a shout and the group of men stopped, Carey was among them, and Dodd heard his voice carolling, 'How very good to see you.'

'Likewise sir,' said Bellamy, and Dodd recognised the voice of Hunsdon's deputy steward.

Men in Berwick jacks and black-and-yellow livery were fanning out into the street to block it. They raised an interesting variety of weapons. The black-bearded man's henchmen came to a halt and the two parties stared at each other across a gap of a hundred yards.

Dodd decided he fancied some height, so despite his lack of breath, he swung himself up on the lattices and hoisted himself to the join with another shingled roof, prayed devoutly that it wouldn't collapse nor slip, and eased himself to a squatting position at the corner. Trying to control his ridiculous puffing, he aimed his crossbow carefully for the black-bearded man. Am I ill, Dodd wondered anxiously, och God, I must be. His heart was pounding, his breath so short that his hands wobbled on the stock of the bow, and he couldn't get a clean shot. Ah Jesu, maybe it was plague?

Marlowe had broken from the shelter of his conduit for the Hunsdon liverymen, and he and Carey were now invisible in the mass of them. There was a thud of hooves on the mud behind the Hunsdon party and two horses skidded to a halt. The foremost was being ridden by a broad grey-haired man in clothes that glinted with gold brocade.

The black-bearded pursuivant was staring in rage and horror, himself panting and leaning on his sword. His mob of bullyboys were close-packed and yet he had a gap around him Dodd noted, which would be helpful for a killing shot if only his own breathing would quiet.

Lord Hunsdon sent his horse through his men who parted for him and up alongside the black-bearded man. He had his white staff of office as the Queen's Chamberlain under his arm.

'What the devil do you think you're playing at, Mr. Topcliffe? What is the meaning of this outrage?' rumbled Carey's father.

Topcliffe's face drained of blood, making his face and beard more like a balladsheet woodcut than ever. He had forgotten to dye his eyebrows which were grey. The mouth moved but no words came out. Dodd squinted in the darkness and saw that the rider of the second horse was his puny lawyer, riding a little better than he ran at least.

'I am...arresting...some notable Papist priests,' panted Topcliffe's voice in a blustering tone.

'You were attempting to arrest *me*, Mr. Topcliffe, with no warrant,' called Carey's voice reproachfully.

'If you had nothing to hide, why did you run?' said Topcliffe insinuatingly. 'My lord, it's a wise father that knows all his son may...'

'I had a fancy to keep my balls,' called Carey, 'I've got more use for 'em than Papist priests do. Or you.'

'My lord, the Queen's grace must be protected from the Jesuitical plots...'

'Good God almighty,' said Hunsdon in disgust. 'Mr. Topcliffe, shut up. You may not be aware of it but my youngest son is possibly the least likely candidate for the Roman Catholic priesthood since the death of my revered and worshipful natural father, King Henry the Eighth of that name. And my half-sister, Her Majesty the Queen, knows it and has a considerable liking to him.'

There was a silence in which Dodd could actually hear Topcliffe swallowing stickily.

'A...a...mistake, my lord,' stammered Topcliffe, 'A case of... mistaken identity. We are seeking one Father Gerard who is... well-known...to go about dressed as a gentleman.'

'Is he?' said Hunsdon, heavily. 'My lord Burghley told me the man was in Worcestershire.'

'Quite so,' said Topcliffe, 'We had the word of an informant... clearly wrong.'

'Clearly.'

'I shall reprimand him. Many...many apologies, my lord, Sir Robert,' gabbled Topcliffe, 'I...I shall continue the search.'

'Excellent.'

Out of sight there was a loud clanging of a bell and the shout of fire at the Mermaid. Dodd winced. He had forgotten about that. Ah well, it would teach the innkeeper better manners than to help set up ambushes for his regulars.

Topcliffe turned and walked with some dignity towards Ludgate Hill, past the wreckage of Heneage's expensive coach. His men gathered round him but the coachman seemed to have run.

Carey was at his father's stirrup, talking fast, Marlowe not far behind. Dodd saw the flash of Hunsdon's teeth as he sat back in the saddle and grinned.

'Sergeant Dodd?' called Lord Hunsdon, looking around him. The City Watch shambled into view at last, with their lanterns, rattle, and bells, cautiously peering around to make sure that the trouble was truly over. One of them went over to the coach and picked up a broken bit of door, tutting.

'Ay,' said Dodd, raising an arm, 'up here, my lord.'

Hunsdon contemplated him for a second, taking in the crossbow in his right hand.

'There you are, of course,' he said. 'By God, I do like having a Dodd on my side again.'

He nodded at Carey who came over with a self-satisfied look

on his face to help Dodd down from his narrow perch.

***

The Watch wandered away again with a couple of shillings each to help them forget all about the exciting events they had just missed and Hunsdon's small war party went back in the direction of Somerset House. The local urchins, whores, and beggars were already gathered around the coach looting it for firewood, saleable bits of metal, cushions, and leather. By the morning it would probably be completely gone. Dodd allowed himself a satisfied smile. One to me, he thought.

'Your mother was furious when Mr. Enys brought the news,' Hunsdon said conversationally as Carey walked at his stirrup.

'Oh Jesu.'

Hunsdon was thoughtful. 'Very sharp-tempered she is at the moment, my lady wife,' he rumbled. 'Took a lot to stop her coming out with me along with her entire crew of Cornish cut-throats.'

'Thank you, sir,' said Carey with feeling.

'Don't thank me, lad, I can't have your mother loose in London in the temper she's in. Richard Tregian is still...unaccounted for.'

Dodd heard the intake of breath from the lawyer whose horse was right behind him and gave the man a sharp look. Enys caught this and smiled a sickly smile.

Somerset House was ablaze with torches, intense activity on the boat-landing at the end of the gardens. Lady Hunsdon was standing in the doorway to the marbled hall, fists on her hips and two Cornishmen on either side of her with torches. She looked terrifying.

Carey stepped up to her swiftly and bowed. 'Madam,' he began, but his mother stood on her tiptoes and boxed his ears violently.

'That's for falling into a trap as clear as the nose on your face,' shouted Lady Hunsdon while Carey scuttled crabwise away from the backswing. 'What were you using for brains, boy?'

'Mother!' he roared, ducking another blow. Lord Hunsdon had dismounted and was very busy thanking and dismissing his men, half of whom were trying not to grin.

Lady Hunsdon swung on Marlowe who was watching the scene between mother and son with a supercilious expression. 'As for you, you goddamn sodomite, how dare you come into my lord's house after what you...'

Carey had edged closer to his enraged mother, caught her elbow, and was whispering urgently into her ear. Lady Hunsdon listened and her jaw set.

'Is that a fact?' she sniffed, 'Well, I'll leave it for now if my son says you helped him, but you watch out, boy.' This was snarled at Marlowe. 'If you try one of your games, I'll have you. I don't like you nor I don't trust you.'

Marlowe bowed in his superior way. 'Likewise, madame, I'm sure.'

Lady Hunsdon paused and like a witch shape-shifting was suddenly the haughty Court lady again. 'Oh, very smart, aren't we, young Mr. Marlowe, who spied for Walsingham all those years for money and a crumb of silence about his boy punks and now thinks Heneage and Topcliffe are his friends. Pah!'

She turned her back on him with the finality of an offended lioness and hooked her arm through Hunsdon's.

'Mr. Bellamy, see to Mr. Marlowe and Mr. Enys, they will be our guests...' said Hunsdon.

Enys was pale again and came anxiously up to Hunsdon. 'Sir, my lord, I...I must get back to my chambers in case...'

'Nobody is leaving Somerset House until the morning,' said Hunsdon flatly. 'As for your chambers, Mr. Enys, I think you can assume that they will be ransacked tonight and there is nothing whatever you could do about it even if you were there. Best not to be there.'

Enys looked horrified. 'But...'

'Mr. Enys,' said Lady Hunsdon, 'You are, I fear, in a war with Heneage and his men. If you weren't prepared for it, you shouldn't have got into it.'

Enys said nothing as the Hunsdons processed stately fashion up the stairs, lit on their way by servants carrying candles.

***

Enys had gone meekly to his bedchamber and Carey and Dodd were sitting up in the Lesser Parlour over a flagon of brandywine and a pile of papers, the contents of the bag Carey had raided out of Heneage's house earlier. Carey had set up as clerk with clean paper and an ink bottle and pens, plus a large candelabra of expensive wax candles.

'Walsingham had me taught something of this art by Thomas Phelippes when I was in Scotland with him all those years ago,' said Carey picking up a piece of paper covered in code and putting it neatly to one side. 'Of course, at the time I had no idea why...' He laughed softly for a while as if recalling a very great joke. Another piece of paper, this time mostly in ordinary writing, went to a different pile. A third piece, all over with numbers except for a sequence of letters at the top, and a third pile begun.

Dodd watched the piles grow with Carey setting a few letters aside, wondering what was nagging him, why he was sure he had forgotten something.

'Now then,' said Carey, picking up the first of the letters in clear and taking a gulp of brandywine. He held it up against the light of the candles, shook his head and then put it back in the bag. Several more letters followed.

'What are ye looking for, sir?' Dodd asked at last, thinking about another pipe but then deciding against it. He didn't like the way his chest had felt tight when he ran and it couldn't be blamed on his doublet because he had undone the buttons in what Carey called the melancholik style. He poured himself brandywine instead.

'Oh...I'm not sure. Something to do with Cornwall. Something about Richard Tregian or Harry Dowling or whoever the poor soul in the Thames may be.'

'Ay sir, but they're both dead. What's the point?'

'Good question.' Carey had taken off his kid gloves the better to handle the papers, and he now put up an elegant but nailless finger. 'Imprimis, Richard Tregian was judicially killed in the place of another man—the Jesuit called Fr. Jackson. It's certainly an alias. So where is Fr. Jackson? Did he escape? Did he turn his coat and then get released? In which case why go through all the palaver of having Tregian hanged, drawn, and quartered in his place? Normally when a Jesuit turns, the Cecils trumpet it abroad so why hide this one so lethally? And why Tregian? He's a respectable gentleman, even if he is Cornish. If you were going to murder the man, you would be better advised to slit his throat in an alley and blame it on a footpad, as you pointed out before. It's not as though there's a shortage of them in London.'

'Ay sir, though I've not been troubled recently.'

Carey grinned. 'No, Dodd, good news like you gets out quickly.'

'Ay,' said Dodd, wondering if this was a compliment.

'Secundus, we have a corpse from the Thames that might be Mrs. Briscoe's brother or not, yet nobody else has claimed yet despite my father having had the announcement cried at Westminster and in the City and offering a reward for information.'

Dodd nodded.

'There's something odd about the corpse though I can't place it.' Carey frowned and stared into the fire in the fireplace for a moment. 'Very irritating.'

'Ay,' said Dodd.

'Tertius, and possibly not connected at all with any of this, we have Enys who mysteriously turns up and offers to be our lawyer just when we need one. He has a Cornish name. His brother, he says, has disappeared and must have gone at roughly the same time as the corpse wound up in the Thames, but he says the dead man isn't his brother.'

Dodd thought back to that. 'Ay sir, but he didnae say he didn't know the man.'

Carey nodded. 'No, he didn't, did he? Hm.' He paused and put up a fourth finger, this one still with its nail. 'And item, we have mysterious land-deals happening in Cornwall, a Godforsaken place good for nothing but tin-mining, wrecking, and piracy. My mother likes it there, but I do not see the likes of the Earl of Southampton going and farming sheep or mining tin for that matter. It's too far from London. Riding post and hoping not to be waylaid on Bodmin Moor, you'd feel pleased if it only took you three days to get there. If they had post houses in Cornwall, which they haven't. A ship is a better option, frankly. More comfortable, the Cornish probably won't rob you or wreck you if you're sailing in an English ship, and it only takes a week.'

He paused thoughtfully and put up the thumb. 'And item, of course, we have my esteemed lady mother's interest in the whole matter which I frankly find very worrying. As does my father. The connection to our family of Richard Tregian is close enough to be dangerous under the wrong circumstances. Also the connection to my Lady Widdrington's family—her father is the Trevannion who holds Caerhays Castle.'

Dodd nodded politely. It always got back to Lady Widdrington somehow.

Carey blinked at his spread fingers, then closed them into a fist. 'Topcliffe running about the city with an armed band of men. My father here instead of going back to Oxford where the Queen still is—though she ought to be coming back to London in October despite the plague. She'll probably stay in one of the outer palaces like Nonesuch or Greenwich, well away from the city.'

'Why did the judge ask about court faction?' Dodd asked from idle curiosity. It had been like the question a sensible juror would ask on the Borders—is there a feud here? And then take tactfully sick if there was.

'Good question. Why did he? What's he heard about, or been told.'

He looked down at the pile of papers. 'We'll have to give these back at some stage and I don't have time to copy them all out.'

For some reason that was the thing that tripped Dodd's memory. He fumbled in his belt pouch and brought out the folded pieces of paper he had found wedged behind the bookshelf in Tregian's chamber at the inn. He explained where it had come from as Carey passed the paper under his nose, smiled, and held it near the candle. Soon the brown numbers appeared written in orange juice and Carey had Dodd calling them out while he copied them out carefully. All were numbers except for a letter at the bottom which Dodd read out as a letter A, upside down.

As Carey dipped his pen and wrote them down, he paused. 'Hang on,' he said, and pulled one of the other papers towards him. Two of them were also covered with groups of numbers and the same letter at the top. An A, upside down.

Immediately he dipped his pen and started copying them out as well, ending with three sheets of paper entirely covered with groups of numbers.

'D'ye know what they say, sir?' Dodd asked, fascinated.

'No, not yet. But I know how they've been coded,' said Carey with satisfaction, wiping off his pen and sharpening the nib.

'Ay?' said Dodd, very unwilling to admit how little he knew about codes and ciphers.

'Well, you see, these are just number substitution codes—where you write out the alphabet and then replace each letter with a number. There's two ways of doing it. Either you do it in a pattern—say call A a 1, B 2 and so on, or you do it at hazard where A is 23 and B is 4 or whatever. Follow me?'

'Ay,' said Dodd cautiously. It seemed a lot of work to be sure nobody could read what you wrote—why write it down at all then?

'Of course the random one is better than the one in a pattern because believe me, someone skilled in the art like Mr. Phelippes or Mr. Anriques can find a pattern like that in a matter of minutes and then they can read all the correspondance you think is so secret—that's what happened with the Queen of Scots.'

'Ay,' said Dodd, who felt he was now on more familiar ground. Hadn't he gone into town with his father and all his brothers and sisters to have a good gawk at her while she was being kept at Carlisle? Carey had told him before how Walsingham had trapped her, twenty years ago.

'Now if you do it randomly, of course, you have to make sure everyone you write to has the key. That's dangerous as well—you could lose it or your enemies could capture it. A good codebreaker can break that one as well if you've written enough or been careless.'

Dodd looked at the uncommunicative numbers. Surely Carey couldn't do something like that?

'I know some of the common patterns used so when I have the time I can try a few out on it. And we can try and find a code book. Do you think you could go back and search Tregian's room again?'

'Nay sir, I dinna think so. It's likely got a new man in it.'

'Hm. It might be worth going and charming mine host for it. Failing a code book I'm just going to have to try and break the bloody thing.' Carey puffed a sigh out. 'God, I wish I'd paid more attention to my lessons with Mr. Phelippes instead of chasing Scottish ladies.'

Dodd grunted. That was no surprise.

Dodd looked again at the numbers and at the letters at the start. 'A,' he said. 'Is that the codebook?'

'Could be. And of course the really interesting point is what is a ciphered letter in invisible ink which comes from either Topcliffe or Heneage—or perhaps is intended for them—doing in Richard Tregian's chamber? Especially if he's going to end up being executed by them.'

Carey blinked at the copies and yawned cavernously. 'We'll have a try at possibilities tomorrow,' he said, 'I'm going to bed.'

THURSDAY 14TH SEPTEMBER 1592, DAWN

Dodd was woken by a hammering on the door. He woke up fully to find himself at the door in his shirt with his sword drawn and raised to strike whoever it was had just ruined a very fine dream about Janet. Carey's voice rang out.

'Come on, Sergeant Dodd, get your arse out of bed, the sun's nearly up...'

From the sound of it Carey too was in a temper and as usual full of energy and enterprise at a time when more decent folk were still asleep. The London sky had barely started to pale. Dodd lowered his sword regretfully, unbolted the door, put the sword on the bed and started assembling the daft confection of cloth he had to wear in this Godforsaken hell hole. He refused to let a man help him with it which was why it always took him so long, especially with it happening in the morning and all. He looked longingly at his nice comfy homespun suit Janet had woven for him and that he had been so proud of when he first came to London. At least he had to admit that he was the target of a lot fewer London coney-catchers when he wasn't wearing it.

There was another bang of fist on panelling. Shrugging the braces over his shoulders and bending to pull his boots on, he called, 'It's no' locked,' and Carey burst through the door looking furious.

'That bloody lawyer's bolted,' he snarled at Dodd, who just sighed.

'Ay, o'course.'

'Why of course?'

'Anybody could see he wis hiding something.'

'Course he was, he's a lawyer, but why'd he bolt?' Dodd said nothing and Carey started to pace up and down after finding that the wine flagon was empty. 'Steward says he went to his bedchamber last night and this morning there's no sign of him at all.'

Dodd was struggling into his doublet. 'Nae doot of it, he's out of London and heading for his ain country,' he said wistfully because it was what he would have done.

'May I remind you, Sergeant, that we have to appear in Court this morning in order to swear out a bill against Heneage in his absence. For that we need a lawyer and Enys is the only one we've got.'

Dodd sighed again, fumbling with his multiple buttons. Carey came over impatiently and twitched it into place on Dodd's shoulders, then briskly started rebuttoning. He was, inevitably, immaculate in black velvet and brocade, though his breath was as bad as a dog's.

'So let's get over to the Temple and see if we can find the blasted man before he leaves.'

'He'd go back there first would he?' Dodd said, wondering if even a lawyer could be so stupid.

'Course he would, you could see how upset he was about it being ransacked. Probably got a little treasure trove of fees and bribes there.'

'Ay sir, but I wouldnae...'

'He's an idiot. That's where he'll be,' said Carey looking distinctly furtive as he stepped into the corridor.'Come on, hurry up before my lady mother wakes and insists on coming too.'

Despite not having had any breakfast or small beer to wake him up, Dodd's mouth turned down with the effort of not laughing at Carey's tone of voice when speaking of his mother. Dodd rather liked the old lady, but he could see how she was a terrible trial to her sons.

The steward had orders that Carey was not to stir without a bodyguard—no doubt by order of Lady Hunsdon, and equally doubtless to keep him from leaping into trouble as well as protecting him in case trouble should come to find him.

After considerable argument they went out with two Berwickmen in buff coats and Shakespeare. According to him Marlowe wasn't up yet which was perfectly normal. Or had he shinned out of the window too, Dodd wondered?

'His window overlooks the courtyard and his door is locked,' Shakespeare said primly in answer to Carey's suspicious look. 'I have seen to it that he has paper, pens and ink, food, booze, and tobacco any time he cares to call for them. He'll be no trouble, trust me. He will know that Topcliffe will wait until he shows his nose and then arrest him for thwarting the ambush in the Mermaid at Sir Robert's urging.'

Which Marlowe himself had set up by sending the potboy to Topcliffe and paying the roaring boys earlier to make their feint attack on Fleet Street. What a fool the poet was, Dodd thought. Heneage must have ordered him to do it as soon as the clerk of the court warned him to avoid Carey's arrest. Mind, it must have been fun to watch him, he would have been enraged. Perhaps that was why Marlowe had gone along with it.

They found Enys' chambers by asking around. It was at the very top of a tottering building facing a dilapidated courtyard that had apparently just been bought by the Earl of Essex. They left Shakespeare and the Berwickmen in the courtyard and went up. At the top of the rickety stairs was a door that had plainly been broken into and then set back carefully in place later. Carey started by knocking politely. After a long wait there was a sound from inside. Carey hammered on the wall next to it.

'Mr. Enys,' he bellowed. 'Enys, God damn your eyes, open up!'

'One moment,' came the cry. They waited. Dodd went to the

small window on the landing and peered out at the Berwickmen who were standing around looking bored. Shakespeare was sitting on a mounting block scribbling in his notebook. At last there was the sound of furniture being scraped back and a broken panel was pulled away. A woman peered through the gap. In the dim light they could see there was something wrong with her face as well as her eyes being swollen with tears.

'Is Mr. Enys within, mistress?' asked Carey, moderating his tone a little.

The woman sniffled and shook her head. 'He was away from home last night and he came back in a hurry very early this morning and then was away again, he said, to see that Mr. Heneage's bill was fouled in his absence as quickly as possible.'

Carey looked taken aback. 'Oh. Westminster?'

'So he said.'

'Well, Mrs. Enys...'

'No sir, Mr. Enys is my brother. My name is Mrs. Morgan.'

Carey paused. 'Ah? Really? My mother's family name is Morgan...I wonder if there's a connection.'

'I don't know, sir. My husband's cousin Henry Morgan was a well-known...er...sea trader.'

'Can we come in?'

For answer the woman started removing a piece of door. Dodd and Carey helped her and entered Enys' chambers.

There were two rooms visible. In the light from the small window they could see that the smallpox had made as bad a mess of her face as it had of her brother's. She was quite a tall woman, a little stooped, in a plain grey wool kirtle and doublet bodice, with her hair covered by a linen cap that was crooked. Carey bowed to her and she curtseyed.

'I'm sorry not to be able to offer you anything, sir, but...you can see...'

She waved a hand helplessly. Carey took a deep breath.

'Mrs. Morgan, I am Sir Robert Carey, and this is Sergeant Henry Dodd, your brother's client.'

'Yes, my brother has told me about you.'

'Can you tell us what happened, mistress?'

Mrs. Morgan bit her lip and shut her eyes tight. 'They came and battered the door in and they said if I stood facing the wall and did not scream they wouldn't hurt me.'

'They kept their promise?'

She shrugged. 'Yes sir.'

It was easy to recognise the handiwork of pursuivants. Every chest had been upended, every book opened and dropped on the floor, the great bed and the truckle in the bedroom with the curtains ripped and the mattress slashed so that wadding bled out of it.

Carey sighed. 'Did they get all the papers?'

'I expect so, sir,' said Mrs. Morgan. 'They took every piece of paper they could find, even things that were nothing to do with your case.'

'Who were they?'

'They had their cloaks muffled over their faces and their hats pulled down. I didn't know them. My brother said he needed to consult some books at his Inn and then he felt he could apply for a judgement immediately. Is there anything else I may help you with, sir, as I have a great deal to do?'

It was a clear, though polite, invitation to leave. Carey looked at the woman seriously, not seeming put off as Dodd was by the pock scars disfiguring her face.

'I now understand why Enys was reluctant to stay at my father's house last night. He should have mentioned you.'

The woman said nothing and curtseyed.

'Would you feel safer in Somerset House under my father's shelter and protection, mistress?'

Mrs. Morgan curtseyed again.

'I would prefer to stay here. There's…a lot to do.' She coloured under Carey's gaze and stepped away from the light.

'Are you sure?'

'Yes sir. Thank you for your offer.'

Carey shook his head. 'As you wish, mistress. If you change your mind simply come to my father's house on the Strand and tell the porter that I sent you.'

She nodded and looked at the ground until they left.

They went in silence down to the Temple steps and waited an

unconscionable time for a boat. Just as one finally rowed languidly towards the boat landing where Carey was pacing up and down impatiently checking the sun and the tide every minute, there was a clatter of boots behind them and Enys appeared, running down the steps towards them, holding his sword awkwardly up and away from his legs.

'Ah, Mr. Enys,' said Carey, 'there was I thinking you might have left town?'

Enys was puffing and wheezing alarmingly. He shook his head, unable to speak.

They all got in the boat with the Berwickers and Shakespeare looking as if they were prepared for a boring day. Soon the boatman and his son were rowing upstream to Westminster. Once Enys had got his breath back, Carey looked at him consideringly.

'Why didn't you mention Mrs. Morgan to us last night?' he asked.

'Um...' Enys looked panicky.

'Mr. Enys,' said Carey pompously, 'what my mother said is true. We are in a war with Heneage and Topcliffe, but luckily my father has the capacity to protect his counsellors and servants and friends at the moment. He would have sent men to guard your chambers or bring your sister to safety if you had said something...'

Enys coloured red. 'I know, sir. I am afraid I was in a panic. I... my sister is very shy and prefers not to be seen in public, or at all.'

'She has Lady Sidney's malady.'

'I beg your pardon?'

'My Lady Sidney—Sir Philip's sister, you know—caught the smallpox whilst nursing the Queen when she had it and took it very much worse than Her Majesty. She was a very beautiful lady before but now considers herself hideous and never comes to Court. She meets with poets and writers at her house which she refuses to leave. And yet, we would all delight to see her at Court for there never was a kinder nor wittier lady. Even the Queen, who dislikes any kind of ugliness, has often said how she misses her.'

Enys was an even darker red.

'I...'

'No one can convince Lady Sidney that nobody is laughing at

her and that if anyone should dare to laugh an hundred swords would be drawn in her defence, including mine. I have told her so myself but she only smiles sadly and shakes her head,' said Carey, tilting into the romantic flourishing speech of the court. 'And so we are deprived of the company of the finest jewel that could adorn any court, saving the Queen's blessed Majesty, a woman of intellect and discretion and wit, all because she fancies a few scars make her hideous.'

Enys seemed unable to speak. He coughed a couple of times and mopped his face with his hankerchief. Shakespeare was staring at him with interest but he seemed not to notice.

'I'm afraid, sir, my sister is not of so high blood as my lady Sidney,' he said at last, his voice husky. 'And all...er...all she ever wanted was to marry her sweetheart and bear his children.'

Carey nodded. Enys stared out over the river.

'Three years ago I heard that my best friend that had married my sister had taken the smallpox,' he was almost whispering as if he had difficulty getting breath to speak even slowly. 'He...I posted down to Cornwall when I heard and found him dead and buried and his two children sickening. After they died my sister took sick and so I nursed her for I would not bring any other into that house of ill fortune to do it. Then when she recovered, I took sick of it as well and so turn and turnabout she nursed me. We lived, barely, hence we have such similar scars, but my sister says...No one cares how ugly a man be, so he be rich enough and kindly, but for a woman to lose her complexion and her looks is an end to all marrying. And so, since her jointure was small and her husband's land reverted to his brother on the death of his issue, we shut up the house in Cornwall and came to London together to try if the law would make our fortunes.'

Carey nodded. 'Her Majesty says that Lady Sidney's scars are as much honours of battle as any gallant's sword cuts. And so I think yours and your sister's must be too.'

Enys inclined his head at the compliment, then turned aside to stare over the water again. 'My apologies, sir, but I hate to remember that year.'

Carey and Dodd left him to it. The tale was common enough,

Dodd thought, but hit each person it happened to as rawly as if no one else had ever caught smallpox. He might catch it himself and die with his face turned to a great clot of blood as the blisters burst—though they said that when the blisters came out you were on the mend so long as none of the blisters turned sick. That was why they tied your hands to the bedposts so you wouldn't scratch.

Dodd shuddered and trailed his fingers in the waters. Fish rose to him from the depths and he wished vaguely for a fishing rod.

Westminster steps was again clotted with lawyers in their black robes; Enys dug his own robe out of a drawstring bag of fashionable blue brocade and slung it round his shoulders. At once the transformation happened; he seemed to relax and settle as if he had put on a jack and helmet and was waiting for the fight to begin.

'Did they get all the papers?' Carey asked him.

Enys smiled for the first time, even if lopsidedly. 'No sir, not all.' He scrambled to get out of the boat and nearly fell in the Thames again when his sword got between his legs. Dodd rolled his eyes regretfully. God preserve him from ever having to take Enys into a real fight.

In the din and confusion of Westminster Hall they found no trace of Heneage appearing to answer their plea.

'Calling Mr. Enys in the matter of Sergeant Dodd versus Mr. Vice Chamberlain Heneage et aliter,' shouted one of the court staff.

Once again they lined up in front of Mr. Justice Whitehead who scowled at them from under his coif.

'Mr. Enys?'

'Yes, my lord.'

'I regret to inform you,' said the judge in English, leafing through the papers before him with the expression of one skinning decayed rats, 'that Mr. Heneage's case has been transferred under the Queen's Prerogative to the court of one of my brother justices and has been adjourned sine die. He has seen fit to rescind all warrants of pillatus on Mr. Heneage and all and any co-defendants.'

Enys sighed.

'What?!' shouted Carey. 'God damn it!'

Dodd's hand went to his swordhilt and his face set into what his men would have recognised as his killing face.

'Mr. Enys' snapped the judge, 'be so good as to inform your clients that if I hear any more blasphemous disrespect from them, I shall have them committed for contempt of court.'

Both Carey and Dodd subsided. It seemed that the only one who was unsurprised was Enys who was looking exceedingly cynical.

'Which honourable judge was it?'

'Mr. Justice Howell,' said the judge with a sour expression.

Enys nodded. 'Thank you, my lord,'

'By the way,' said the judge, 'for completeness, I have had copies made of the papers filed this morning under the Queen's prerogative by a Mr. Evesham. I believe he is the clerk to Sir Robert Cecil.' He leaned over and gave a sheaf of papers to Enys who took them with an expression of cautious surprise. Carey's lips were formed into a soundless whistle.

'My lord,' he said. 'Sir Robert Cecil, Privy Councillor?'

'Yes,' said the judge, glaring at Carey over his spectacles. Carey swept a magnificent bow.

'Then my apologies to you, my lord,' he said, 'for having unintentionally misled you yesterday. It seems that this *is* a matter of Court faction, a complication of which I was unaware.'

The judge nodded and rubbed the margin of his beard with his thumb. 'Quite so, Sir Robert.'

'Thank you very much, my lord,' said Carey, and led all three of them from the Hall. Behind them they heard Judge Whitehead's weary voice. 'You again, Mr. Irvine. I hope you have the correct pleadings this time...'

Once again they needed a drink with even Enys accepting a small cup of aqua vitae. He was reading the papers he had been given very carefully, eyes narrowed, his lips moving as he reread some of the words.

Carey was cutting into a large steak and kidney pudding which was the ordinary for that day. 'Well?' he said.

'The case has been adjourned sine die, which means indefinitely, for reasons good and sufficient to the Queen's Prerogative. That means both the civil and the criminal case. We can apply for a new court date but this will set the proceedings back by weeks...'

'Does the Queen no' like my case, then?' asked Dodd, wondering if he should leave the country immediately. Then he thought of something. 'Ay, but how does she know about it? Is she no' still at Oxford?'

Carey looked thoughtful. 'Yes, we only tried to arrest Heneage yesterday. I suppose he could have sent a message the forty odd miles to Oxford and back in the time, but the man would have had to ride post and ride through the night as well.'

'Eighty miles. Ay,' said Dodd, 'ye could dae it if ye could see the Queen immediately...'

'No, the Queen will not have heard anything about it. These papers are from Sir Robert Cecil acting for Lord Burghley who, as Lord Chancellor and Lord Privy Seal, may wield the Queen's Prerogative during pleasure.'

Carey nodded. 'Hm. Interesting. I wonder...Hm. Must ask my father.'

'Can I no' sue Heneage then?'

'You can continue with the litigation by requiring reasons for the adjournment and you can make representations to the Privy Council asking for the case to be heard in a different court,' said Enys, narrowing his eyes. 'Obviously it would be ridiculous to take it in front of Mr. Justice Howell who is notoriously corrupt.'

'So I get nae satisfaction?' said Dodd mournfully.

'Well, you might...' began Enys.

'I think I should go and talk to Her Majesty about this,' said Carey, through a mouthful of kidney.

Dodd grunted and pushed away the rest of his pudding. He hadn't expected much justice, but he had allowed himself to hope he would get some down here in the foreign south. Ah well, serve him right for being a silly wee bairn about it. His face lengthened as he considered the matter.

Carey washed down the last of his meal with the reasonable beer and leaned back with his fingers drumming on the front of his doublet. 'I wonder what the surnames are up to at the moment?' he said to Dodd.

Dodd shrugged. Early autumn, the horses and cattle fat, bad weather not set in yet, but the nights not long enough. The planning would be feverish.

'It's October and November they'll start at the reiving,' he said, 'when they've killed their pigs and calves. We've time yet.'

'Wouldn't want to miss the fun,' agreed Carey, who probably meant it, the idiot. 'Well then, I think I'll find out about that corpse which annoyed my father. The inquest might not have happened yet—shall we go to the Board of Greencloth?'

The Board of Greencloth was held in a meeting room at the business end of the Palace of Whitehall, a short walk from Westminster Hall. Carey spoke gravely to the yeoman of the guard at the entrance and they were all three admitted to a wood-panelled room whose dusty glass windows let in very little light. The corpse itself was not present for which Dodd heartily thanked God, but there were several women there. One of them was Mrs. Briscoe, as round and pregnant as a bomb. Mr. Briscoe stood behind her looking nervous as if ready to catch her when she fell. Another was a grave looking lady in a dark cramoisie woollen kirtle with a doublet-bodice and small falling band. She had grey hair peeking under a white linen cap and black beaver hat, and a very firm jaw. Behind her stood a pale-faced young woman in dove grey furnished with a modest white ruff.

The men who served on the board filed into the room, led by Hunsdon who already looked bored and was carrying his white staff of office. The others were pouchy faced and dully dressed, men of business who ran the complex administration of the palace. A couple of them were distinctly green about the gills which might have been because they had gone to the crypt to view the body in question. Or it might have been the green baize cloth that covered the trestle table boards in front of them, a cloth which made some sense of the name of the Board. All of those waiting bowed to the members of the Board who sat down. One drank some of the wine in a flagon before him and took a little colour from it.

'We are here,' intoned Hunsdon, 'to enquire as to the probable identity and cause of death of the corpse found by Mistress Wentworth, Queen's Chamberer, at the Queen's Privy Steps. Have we all viewed it?'

Everyone nodded, one swallowed again. 'I have had the body

cried three times in the cities of Westminster and London. Has anyone any...'

The grey-haired woman stepped forward and curtseyed to Hunsdon. 'My lord, I am here to claim the body which I have identified as Mr. John Jackson who went missing in London some three weeks ago.'

Hunsdon's bushy eyebrows climbed his forehead. 'Indeed, mistress. And you are?'

Carey was staring at the woman with his lips parted in a half-smile and his eyes narrowed. 'Hm,' he said, in a tone of great interest.

'His cousin, sir, Mrs. Sophia Merry, gentlewoman.'

'Ah.'

Mrs. Briscoe had a puzzled expression on her face, mixed with some relief. Hunsdon looked shrewdly at her. 'And you, mistress? Have you anything to say?'

'Oh, ah.' Mrs. Briscoe seemed confused at being addressed so courteously. 'Um...I thought it was my bruvver, but I wasn't sure.'

'You are willing to yield the body to Mrs. Merry?'

'Oh yes, my lord, if she's sure. I'm not, see. His face...Might not have been him.' She looked down and frowned.

Mr. Briscoe put his arm across her shoulders and whispered in her ear. 'My lord, may I sit down?' she asked in a whisper.

'Of course, mistress,' said Hunsdon, no more eager to have her go into labour there and then than any man would be. One of the court attendants brought up a stool for her to sit on.

The rest of the inquest went quickly. No mention was made of the man's missing feet, all the attention was on the dagger-wound in the back and the missing joint of his finger. The Board of Greencloth found that Mr. John Jackson had been unlawfully killed or murdered by person or persons unknown and released the corpse into the keeping of his cousin Mrs. Sophia Merry.

They all bowed, the Board filed out of the room, and moments later they were in the little alley behind Scotland Yard where were the kilns that fired the staggering quantities of earthenware the palace kitchens used.

'Why did Poley say, which corpse?' Dodd asked, the thought

having just struck him. 'Do a lot of deid men wind up in the Thames?'

'Of course, it's very convenient if you don't care about the dead person coming back to haunt you—no questions and no shroud money. Dead children too, dead babies. He could have been joking.'

'Or he could have known of more than one that he'd heard tell of or had to dae with.'

'He could. I think I should ask the watermen.' He stopped and frowned. 'Except I can't because I haven't got Barnabus, damn it. They wouldn't talk to me and if they did they'd lie.'

'Whit about the hangman?'

Carey smiled. 'Hughes? Hm. I don't know if the watermen would talk to him, but I wonder if...'

He immediately changed direction and headed northwards. Dodd sighed and followed, whilst Enys looked bewildered.

'Verrah impulsive gentleman, is Sir Robert,' said Dodd to the lawyer. 'If ye'd like to tag along, I doot he'll notice now he's got a notion in his heid.'

Enys nodded, rammed his robe and the papers back into his brocade bag, slung it over his shoulder, and hurried after them.

Mr. Hughes lived near his normal workplace at Tyburn, in a pretty cottage surrounded by the shanties of the poor. He had his doublet off and his sleeves up and was working in his garden, carefully bedding out winter cabbage.

Carey stood by the garden wall watching with interest. After a while Hughes looked up and took his statute cap off.

'Well sir,' he said.

'Mr. Hughes, what would you say if I told you that the man you executed on Monday was the wrong one?'

'I'd say, they're all innocent if you listen to...'

'No, I meant, genuinely was the wrong man.'

Hughes put his cap back on again slowly, narrowing his eyes.

'I'd be very surprised, sir.' Something about his eyes said he wouldn't.

'You never get substitutions?

'Never, sir, though I suppose it could happen.'

'What about the priest? Fr. Jackson?'

KNIVES IN THE SOUTH

'What of him?' Now the eyes were wary although the mouth was innocent.

'It wasn't a priest, in fact it was a friend of my mother's called Richard Tregian.'

Hughes came to the gate of the garden and opened it. 'Come inside, sir,' he said, with a bow. 'Try some of my fruit wines.'

The main room of the cottage was clean and swept though bare. They sat at the small wooden table that had a bench beside it and one stool and Hughes bustled into the storeroom to bring out a pottery flagon with a powerful smell of raspberries. He poured them a measure into horn cups, then sat down on his stool and braced his hands on his knees.

'Mr. Topcliffe brought him on the day. I had not seen him before to weigh him and calculate the drop, but Mr. Topcliffe said it was no matter, he was to be dead before he was drawn and gave me a purse for it as well.'

'Did he speak?'

'No sir, he was in…er…no condition to speak, he had been given the manacles and then he had been waked for a while and could hardly hold his head up nor see straight.'

'Waked?' asked Carey.

Hughes studied the floor. 'He had been stopped from sleeping for many days, sir. It sends a man mad and kills him quicker than starving. Topcliffe prefers…other methods, but waking is a speciality of Mr. Vice Chamberlain.'

Carey had a look of disgust on his face. 'And what was the purpose of this waking?'

'Dunno sir, usually it's to make him talk so they'll let him sleep, but sometimes all they get is nonsense and vapours of the brain from the poisonous humours, sir.'

There was a penetrating silence.

'And it don't show, sir,' Hughes added, still staring at the floor, 'So the mob don't get too sympathetic.' More silence. Dodd realised that Carey was using it as a weapon. 'See, if it's a Papist priest, I wouldn't mind sir, not since they sent the Armada—I heard tell they tried again this summer too, sir, only God saved us again. But this…I was worried, see, sir, cos he didn't look like a priest.'

Carey blinked. 'How could you tell?'

Hughes looked up with enthusiasm for the first time. 'Oh it's remarkable what you can tell from a man's body and his clothes, if you know what to look for. See, your papish priest is always doing some sort of penance, see, and it shows. Like most of them have knobbly knees, see, from kneeling at their prayers.'

Carey shook his head. 'Could mean he's a courtier, I've got knobbly knees myself from kneeling in the Queen's presence and I'm no priest.'

'True, sir. But it all goes together, you see. Or if he's been wearing a hair shirt, even if it's been taken from him, he's usually got a rash in the shape of a shirt on his body and often a lot of lice cos they don't take them off at all, sir. Or if he's been using the discipline—that's a little scourge with wires on it—you've got the marks of that—sort of criss-crossing scratches as if he's been rolling in a bramble bush, more on the shoulders 'cos they're easier to reach...'

Carey's head had gone up, as had Dodd's. They exchanged satisfied glances. Enys was staring at Hughes in some kind of mute horror.

'So you could see none of that on Richard Tregian?' asked Carey.

'No sir, nor he didn't say nothing except gibberish, but still Mr. Topcliffe would have him gagged—in case he made some kind of Papist sermon which Topcliffe couldn't allow, so he said.'

'What kind of gibberish, Mr. Hughes?' asked Enys.

'Ahh...Funny words like Trenever and Lanner and Kergilliak, couldn't make head nor tale of them. Bedlam he was, far as I could tell. Slept like a baby while he was being dragged on a hurdle to Tyburn which is something you don't often see and gave the mob a bit of a turn, too.'

Carey nodded.

'Course it's not my place to ask the likes of Richard Topcliffe the wheres and whyfores but I...I was troubled, sir.'

'Why?'

''Cos I asked to see the warrant and it was for Fr. Jackson right enough but it didn't look right.'

'Why not?'

'The ink, sir. The warrant was nicely done in Secretary hand, but the places where Fr. Jackson's name went and the date, the ink was darker there, like they'd put it in later. They're not supposed to do that. Each death warrant is for each person, it's not respectful otherwise. You can't just have a general warrant with spaces to fill in to hang anyone you fancy...'

'No, indeed. Is there anything else you can tell us about Richard Topcliffe?'

'I don't like him, sir. Bring him to me when I'm working with a proper warrant for him and I won't charge you a penny for the rope nor nothing for my services.'

'Do you often have cases like this?' Hughes paused, took breath to speak, paused again with reluctance.

'Not often, no sir,' he admitted. 'Mr. Secretary Walsingham did it a couple of times, but this year...'

Carey was scratching the patch on his chin where his goatee beard was regrowing. 'More?' he asked.

Hughes seemed to remember something and stopped suddenly, gulped. 'Couldn't say, sir,' he mumbled.

Dodd sipped his raspberry wine and was stunned. He had never tasted anything so delicious in his life. He drank a little more and then finished the cup. Perhaps Janet was right in her planting of fruit bushes. He wondered if the blackberry wine Janet made for her gossips to drink and which he had always disdained as fit only for weak women was anything like this wonderful stuff. He had to concentrate to pay attention to what was going on.

Carey leaned across to Hughes. 'Mr. Hughes,' he said, 'thank you, you've been very helpful. Would you mention to your brother-in-law that I appreciated his compliment and so did my father?'

Hughes nodded and stopped looking so frightened. 'I'll mention it. He...er...he was wondering if you would be interested in a primero game at Three Cranes in the Vintry on Thursday evenings—he had heard you were quite a player.'

Carey coughed modestly. 'Oh, I wouldn't say that, Mr. Hughes, Her Majesty and Sir Walter Raleigh regularly beat me hollow.'

Hughes' gaze was steady. 'Perhaps you should try your luck at the Three Cranes, sir.'

Carey smiled. 'Perhaps I shall. Thank you, Mr. Hughes.'

***

Now nothing would do but that they must walk south to Westminster to the crypt by the palace to take another look at the mysterious corpse with no feet, to see as Carey said if his knees were knobbly or not. When they arrived they found the crypt empty and no sign of a corpse, embalmed or stinking. Carey was annoyed.

'She collected the body already?' he demanded. 'That's smart work.'

'Gentleman's cousin, since the Board of Greencloth concluded killing by person or persons unknown. She collected him wiv a litter, sir, for immediate private burial,' said the churchwarden in charge of the crypt. 'I have her name in the book here, sir.' He was pointedly not opening the pages and finally Carey got the point in question and handed over a penny. The name and address at the sign of the Crowing Cock were neatly written there, and the woman had made her mark as well.

They took a boat to the Bridge and walked to the street by London Wall where there was no house with the sign of the Crowing Cock and nor had any of the neighbours ever heard of a Mrs. Sophia Merry.

Sitting on a bench at yet another alehouse, drinking beer, Carey was scowling with thought. Enys had said nothing whatever the whole time but finally Carey noticed him again.

'Mr. Enys,' he said irritably, 'have you no cases to attend to?'

'No sir,' said Enys humbly, 'I told you. Mr. Heneage has seen to it my practice is almost extinct.'

'Why are you tagging along?'

'I might be of some assistance...'

Dodd snorted. 'It's allus better to let the women clear up after a raid on their own, otherwise they start sharpening their tongues on you for letting it happen.'

Enys coloured up. 'I had no intention of...'

'Did I say it was ye? I was speaking in general.'

Enys steepled his fingers. 'I will of course be on my way, as you are quite right, my sister has much to do. But I have been wondering about this matter.'

Carey lifted his brows forbiddingly. 'Oh yes?'

'The gentleman from the river was...not unknown to me. I told you, I think, that my family were church Papists. We went to church when we had to but in our hearts...in my parents' hearts we still considered ourselves Catholics.'

'What do you consider yourself now?'

'A good obedient subject of the Queen who worships where I am told,' said Enys without a tremor. 'I have no interest in the ambitions of any Bishop of Rome nor Spanish king to take this land under the colour of a crusade, except to do whatever I can to stop it.'

Carey nodded approvingly. 'And the man from the river?'

'I don't recall his name. I saw him a few years ago when he first came to Cornwall as a stranger and he was a man of many accomplishments. He was an alchemist and metal assayer and a mining engineer. He could devise wind pumps to take the water out of the tin workings that went deep. He was strong for the Catholic faith and I am not surprised if he was indeed a priest although I am surprised he should end in London for he said he hated the place.' Carey waited but Enys spread his hands. 'That's all I know, sir.'

'The words that Tregian was babbling are place-names in Cornwall aren't they?'

'Yes, they are. None of them are in the tin-mining areas though as far as I know.'

'Could there be gold there?'

Enys shrugged. 'I...doubt it. They say gold breeds out of tin in some places so perhaps there is. I know there is gold in some places in Cornwall though never very much, not as much as in Wales or Ireland.'

'Would this metal assayer be able to tell if there was gold?'

'Oh yes, sir, he could, and he knew how to take the gold out of the ore as well.'

'Ah hah!' Carey looked pleased with himself.

'In the meantime, sirs, please excuse me. Sergeant Dodd has touched my conscience, I should not leave all to my sister who has no gossips in London to help her.'

He rose, finished his beer, bowed to both of them, and walked away. Carey grinned at Dodd.

'Christ, I thought he'd never go. Now then, let's take a look at St Paul's.'

Expecting Carey to spend the rest of the afternoon parading up and down Paul's Walk with other overdressed, overbred, underworked Court ninnies, Dodd was surprised and suspicious when Carey went to the Churchwarden's office instead and asked to see a register of churches in London both old and new. He studied it carefully for so long that Dodd got bored and began peering at the Cathedral treasure chest and wondering if it was full and if it was, would it be hard to get the lid off? It certainly looked securely locked and the iron strapping looked strong as well. Which argued that there was some good plate inside. It didn't move when he accidentally toed it with his boot.

They did go into the cathedral, but Carey went to the serving-man's pillar where the men who wanted work stood about near their notices pinned on the stone arch. He went straight up to the largest of them and asked him a question, only to receive a firm shake of the head. He asked all of them, all seemed to say no, and Carey rejoined Dodd looking irritated.

'Blast it,' he said, 'word's gone round obviously. None of them want to work for me.'

Dodd thought it showed there was some sense amongst the servingmen of London.

'Or at least, none of them want to work for me in Carlisle,' Carey amended, proving that Londoners were idiots.

Carey was now hurrying out of the main door and heading north across the city. Dodd hurried after him and noted that despite the rebuff of the servingmen, Carey was wearing an expression as smug as a bridegroom. On general principles, he loosened his sword.

They came to a very small lane not far from London Wall. It was one of the poorer places and was full of houses that seemed to have been patched together from pieces of something larger, some of them still clinging to the foundations made of large granite blocks.

People were passing up and down the street, and occasionally one of them would turn seemingly on impulse and head down an alleyway. Carey watched for a while and then headed for the alleyway himself. On the corner a crowing cockerel was chalked on the wall.

Dodd followed him full of forboding. The alleyway seemed to end, but in one corner were steps leading down and a boy sitting there. Carey smiled at him, spoke for a moment, and then beckoned Dodd to go down the steps with him.

It was a small crypt with an arched ceiling and thick plain pillars. At one end was a table laid with linens and six black candles about the coffin and a large number of people were standing about, talking quietly. In an alcove was a worn chipped figure of a man fighting what looked like a bull—perhaps some Papistical saint? Carey looked about him and took his hat off, so Dodd did the same.

'I don't like the looks of this,' Carey said quietly to him. 'I was expecting something quieter.'

Dodd didn't like it either. He hated being in a place that only had one exit and he certainly was not planning to listen to a Papist mass which would be in solid foreign from start to finish and even more boring than a proper church service. Besides being treason outright. He saw that there was a door in the side of the opposite wall which was some comfort but...

There were some young men near the front with worryingly holy expressions, praying hard for something. Dodd didn't like the looks of that either. He threaded through the crowd, some of whom were praying rosaries of all dangerous treasonable things, and squinted at the door. Was it clear? He tested it gently but it didn't move.

Shaking his head, he went back up the steps and hurried round the corner to where he calculated the door should come out. It too was down some steps, but when he went to look at it, he realised it had been nailed shut and the nailheads were still shiny.

Dodd's spine froze. Carey was in a stopped earth and so were all the other people. He looked about the street. He couldn't actually see Heneage's men but he knew they were there. If they had nailed this exit, probably they wouldn't be very interested in it, although there would be someone checking it soon to make sure. Somebody must have been following the grey-haired woman when she collected the body.

He leaned against the wall by the entrance and felt for his pipe, started filling the bowl with fingers that shook slightly. How

Carey had found himself a secret Papist requiem mass he wasn't quite sure, but he was certain that it would be raided once it had properly got going and Carey would be the biggest prize.

Of course there was one possible option for Dodd. He could simply walk away, head for the Great North Road, and keep going until he got to his own tower where, by God, he would stay.

He puffed angrily. He wouldn't do it. Couldn't do it. Any more than he could have given Heneage the name he had wanted so badly the week before. Damn it, there was something wrong with his brains, that was sure.

He leaned against the door and looked about him at suspiciously little activity for a London alley and there were no plague-marked houses hereabouts to provide an excuse. Any minute now Heneage or Topcliffe and their human terriers would arrive and go into the stopped earth and...

Dodd smiled toothily, tapped out his pipe which was a pity because he hadn't finished it, spat in the bowl to cool it, and put it away in his belt pouch. He looked about casually again; nothing, not even someone visible at a window across the street. Ay well, no help for it then.

He hammered with his fist on the nailed-shut door in the slow, fear-inspiring way he had seen Lowther use on farmers who hadn't paid up their blackmail money.

'Open up,' he roared, imitating a London voice as well as he could. 'Open in the name of the Queen.'

He banged again, roared again, and waited. There was absolute silence inside. As he sauntered around to the front alley again, he saw a couple of men in travelling cloaks, then a group of women talking merrily, then the young men who had been praying, then a mother with children. Everybody was walking as calmly and normally as if they had not just been about to commit treason.

'What the hell are you doing still here, Dodd,' hissed a voice at his elbow. Dodd turned and saw Carey emerging from amongst the women with a pale and anxious-faced Letty Tregian clinging to his arm. Her brown hair was trailing from under her hat and she seemed to be on the point of collapse. 'Heneage and his...'

'Ay well,' said Dodd. 'That were me.'

Carey's eyes turned to points of ice. 'If that was your idea of a joke...'

'Nay sir, I saw the escape door had been nailed shut and I thocht I'd get ahead of them a bit.'

Carey frowned for a moment before his face split in a broad grin. He cupped his hand over Letty's confiding paw, slowed and backed under an awning so he could turn to look over his shoulder. A large contingent of buff-coated men were heading for the steps down to the crypt, at the back of them Topcliffe with his matt-black hair and jerky gestures. Dodd allowed a brief smile at the heart-warming sight before hurrying on in Carey's wake.

'They certainly know what to do in a crisis, these Papists,' said Carey as they sat down again in yet another boozing ken where Carey had already called for brandy to restore some colour to Letty's cheeks. 'Never seen anything like it. You banging on the door and shouting the way you did, everybody stops what they're doing—the priest had just arrived and was setting out his Papist trash on the altar. Next thing, everything on the altar is cleared away, the priest has disappeared, the candles are gone, the altar has turned into a mere table, and the people are nearly gone as well. Nothing but the coffin and a bad smell. Only Letty here was upset and some women were helping her and when I told them I was a son of her mistress, they insisted on bringing us both out amongst them. A most delightful escape.'

He laughed with the kind of boyish delight that particularly annoyed Dodd. 'Best of all I got to see Topcliffe and his men going in to roust out an empty earth. Wonderful.'

He turned to Letty and smiled at her. 'And I managed to fish you out of a muddy puddle that would have been a difficulty even for my redoubtable lady mother. So, my dear, what were you doing in there?'

Letty started trembling again, cupped her hands around her mouth, and as the tears spilled out of her brown eyes, Carey whipped out a large white hankerchief from his padded sleeve's pocket and handed it over to her. She buried her face in it, sobbing.

Carey leaned back, crossed his ankles, lifted one finger to the potboy and ordered more booze by no more than a nod, then sighed tolerantly. Dodd, who was not at all accustomed to maidens who wept so openly and freely, being bred amongst much less delicate women, was staring at Letty with pure horror.

'It's all right, Sergeant, no point hurrying her,' said Carey. 'Doctor Nunez explained it to me once. Something about a maiden's womb being not so securely fixed as a woman's and apt to rise and wander up to her head, causing hysterics, fits of tears and fainting, and so on. They really can't help it. Best you can do is wait for the storm to pass.'

For some reason this kindly explanation caused Letty to sob even harder. Dodd considered chancing the theory on a Carlisle damsel one day when she was in a mood and decided that he simply didn't have the bollocks—and even if he did, he wouldn't keep them. He was reaching for his pipe again when he stopped and scowled. He had better get used to doing without the London vice as he was certainly not planning to stay there, nor ever come there again.

'Now then, Letty,' said Carey to the girl as she blew her nose. 'How did you know the Mass was happening?'

'I got a message to say they were saying a mass for my f..f... father's soul and where it was and if I liked I could come if I brought the message to show. So I did. I didn't know it was a requiem. Who was it in the coffin? I thought he was...he was...'

'Show me the message.'

She handed over a scrap of paper which was neatly written in the Secretary script used by half the clerks in London. It gave clear instructions to reach the place.

'Who brought you this?'

'Just Will, you know, Bald Will who everyone says is a poet. He said it had been left with the gatekeeper.'

'And it was addressed to you?'

'Yes, to Lettice Tregian, which is what everyone calls me in Cornwall though your mother calls me Letitia which I think is French.'

'Latin.'

'Oh. And I just thought it was nice of them to invite me so I went.'

'But you're alone. What would my mother...'

'She said I could. I asked if I could go to church and she said I could.'

'You didn't tell her what kind of church? Or why?'

Letty shook her head. Her eyes filled up with tears again. 'Oh what will she say to me?'

'She'll say you have horse-clabber for brains, probably,' said Carey, 'because you clearly do. Don't you know how dangerous it is to go to a Papist mass? Never mind the danger to your soul, it's the danger to you of getting into Topcliffe's hands and what my mother would have to do to get you out again.'

Dodd felt this was a bit rich coming from the man who blithely stuck his head in any noose that happened to be handy, but said nothing.

'But we g...g...go in Cornwall and nothing happens,' sniffled the girl.

'This isn't Cornwall,' said Carey, scratching his patch of beard. 'Listen, Letty, you must promise me faithfully not to do it again.'

She nodded vigorously. 'I was so frightened.'

'Rightly so. God's teeth, I was frightened when Dodd roared out like that.'

'I saw you half-draw your long thin dagger,' said Letty.

Carey nodded seriously. 'That's what I do when I'm frightened. It's lucky I was there at all and I certainly didn't expect to see you there.'

'I had to go,' explained Letty, finally making a start on her pork pie with her very pretty little pearl-handled eating knife. 'That's why I came up to London with my Lady Hunsdon, you see. I had to bring Fr. Jackson's survey with me. My father had a copy and he was going to meet Fr. Jackson and talk about it with him and then talk to...to the lawyers and other people for he said there was some great land piracy afoot in Cornwall and he wouldn't have it because of what it was doing to the common folk and the tinners.'

'And what was this land piracy?' asked Carey with a tone of indulgent disbelief. 'I'm sure there was nothing wrong going on.'

'That's what I said, but he said something about gold and how the Cornish wouldn't be able to live on their own lands and half of them weren't even recusants, just foolish. And then off he went, only he sent a message to my Lady Hunsdon saying he was going and she was in such a taking about it when she came back from visiting Mrs. O'Malley in Ireland and sailing the whisky up to Dumfries that we went straight to the *Judith* and sailed out of Penryn and up the coast. That's where we caught the Spaniard, you know.'

'So my mother said,' Carey answered drily. 'So Mr. Tregian was part of whatever this was.'

'And it wasn't treason, I know it wasn't. It was just boring old buying and selling of land.'

'Yes,' said Carey, staring into space. 'And what's in this survey?'

'I don't know,' said Letty, rolling big tragic eyes at them, 'I haven't got it. That's what I went to tell them. I don't know where it went. I had it when we went to meet my father and then when I...when I...' She clutched the hankerchief and gulped hard. Dodd had to admit that seeing her father's head on London Bridge must have been a shock to her just as seeing his father dead with an Elliot lance through his chest had been a shock to him. 'When I saw my father was dead I...well, I don't know what happened to it.'

Dodd had the satisfaction of seeing Carey momentarily lost for words. His mouth opened and then he shut it again.

'You lost it?'

'I think so. I can't find it anywhere. It was in my purse, you see, and something funny happened to my purse because the cord was cut and it was proper safe under my kirtle you know and I didn't notice nothing and then when I got home I realised it was gone.'

Dodd and Carey exchanged looks. 'Your purse was cut and this survey was in it, yes?'

Letty nodded brightly. 'Yes. I even said to my lady, oh I don't know where my purse is to, lucky I didn't have any money in it, and we both laughed, sort of in the middle of crying about my father, you see.'

Carey sighed again. 'What was in the survey?'

Letty shook her brown curls at him. 'Oh sir, you are funny. I can't read. My dad wouldn't have my brains roiled up with it, he said it was bad enough he'd had to learn and him not even a priest.'

Dodd nodded at this wisdom. You couldn't argue with that,

reading was nothing to do with women.

'That's a pity,' said Carey, very strangely, 'because if you could read there are all sorts of good books I could recommend you to read to help you get away from your Papish superstition...'

Letty's brow wrinkled. 'I heard the heretics *are* always abusing their brains with reading, even the Queen herself, poor soul, but luckily I don't need to for Fr. Jackson tells me everything I need to know.'

Carey shook his head. 'Was...er...is he in London too?'

'Oh yes, my father came up to town to talk to him. Fr. Jackson went a month or two ago. He was very cross about it, said he hated London and was only going because he had to prevent a crime and a scandal and if he didn't come back I was always to be a good girl and do what my father told me and pray to Our Lady and obey my husband.' Letty beamed at them. 'Which I will,' she added in tones of great piety, sounding just like a very self-righteous little girl.

Neither Carey nor Dodd had the courage to tell Letty what they thought might have happened to Fr. Jackson in case of reopening the floodgates. Dodd was frowning and blinking at the sunlight trying to remember what had happened when they made Lady Hunsdon's abortive shopping expedition and when exactly Letty's purse might have been cut. Just after she saw her father's head and screamed and the horses bolted? Perhaps? Did the cutpurse know what he had or had he perhaps dumped the survey somewhere?

'Ah,' said Carey gravely, 'excellent. Though of course you should pray to God, not Our Lady.'

Letty shook her curls again with great good humour. 'Oh no, I'm only a silly maid so He wouldn't be interested. Our Lady is much kinder.'

Carey blinked and then seemed to give up his attempt at theology. 'And what can you tell me about Fr. Jackson?'

That opened another kind of floodgate entirely. Fr. Jackson was, apparently, the most perfect specimen of manhood alive on this sorry world of sinners. He was not only handsome and well-built, he was very very clever and could tell gold-bearing rock from the other kind with his strange waters and his touchstone, and he knew how to build things as well which he had learned in Germany. And then he became a priest for he heard God calling him, which was something that happened to men who were going to be priests, and all he wanted was to be a good priest to the people in Cornwall.

Carey sighed again which Letty didn't notice. Fr. Jackson came to Cornwall as a priest from the Jesuit seminary in Rheims, but he wasn't evil or a traitor. He travelled around helping people and advising them how to pay their recusancy fines and which bits of land to sell because of course nobody wants to sell land and usually the land he sold for them was poor or fit only for pasture and...

'Fr. Jackson would sell land for people?'

'Not exactly,' said Letty, 'It was only because he was clever and knew some people in London. My father did as well, I think. So when somebody had a terrible lot of fines to pay—because they changed the magistrates a year ago and now they're much more strict—he would write to his friends and sometimes someone would buy the land in exchange for the fines so there wouldn't be any more fines or bailiffs or court cases but the person in London owned the land, you see?'

'Hm. Yes, I do. What else did Fr. Jackson do?'

'He said Mass of course, like priests do, you know and he would hear your confession...' Letty went very pink at that and Dodd wondered why. '...and he was very kind though I once had to say a whole rosary a day for a week which was a bit much.... And he would catechise and baptise and marry and all that. He was very busy.'

Carey nodded. Letty smiled. 'I know he's a priest and everything and I know a priest is dedicated to God and can never marry like the heretic priests do...Sorry, the Church of England priests do, so...well...I...but I was thinking I might go beyond the seas to be a nun which would be...um...almost as good.'

Carey raised his brows. 'Oh, I wouldn't advise that,' he said. 'Did you know nuns have to cut all their hair off and never talk to anybody again except other nuns?'

Letty stared. 'Cut all their hair off?'

'Yes. Very short. I used to see nuns when I was in France and they had everything except their faces covered up but a…a friend of mine told me they have to keep their hair very short or even shave it all off.'

There was a silence. 'Oh. But I'm sure they're quite beautiful.'

'I didn't see a beautiful nun all the time I was there. They all looked cross and disagreeable,' said Carey blandly.

Another silence. 'Well,' said Letty.

'I'm sure my mother will help you find a good husband when you're old enough,' said Carey kindly, 'if you ask her.'

Letty brightened at that, then her face fell again. 'I suppose…' she said sadly. '…I was hoping to see Fr. Jackson again. They did say the priest might hear confessions after Mass and I was going to tell him what happened to my father—in private when I made my confession, you know—and ask his advice. But the priest wasn't him at all and then Sergeant Dodd shouted and…Do you think we'll see Fr. Jackson?'

'Oh I doubt it,' said Carey easily. 'I don't think he's even in London any more. Not if he has any sense.'

The blue glare warned Dodd but Dodd was in no hurry to cause another waterfall. In fact he was spending a good half of his attention on not taking another pipe of tobacco. What was wrong with him now? It wasn't as if he was hungry, he had had a pork pie with a few winter sallet roots and some pickled onions and bread and was quite full. Yet, there it was. He wanted a pipe.

He growled and pulled it out, cleaned the bowl, filled it and lit it and sighed with satisfaction. He would have to try and buy some before they left, that was all there was to it. He wondered if it was possible to grow the herb in Gilsland and if he would be able to persuade Janet to do it if he could get the seeds.

'What now?' he asked as Carey stared into the distance while Letty engulfed her pie. 'Are we going to take Letty back to Somerset House?'

'Letty, didn't my mother send someone with you?' Carey asked after a moment.

Letty went pink. 'Yes, she did, it was Will but I…er…I lost him.'

Carey's eyebrows went up.

Letty's shoulders hunched and dropped. 'I didn't want him

following me around with his calf eyes trying to be witty and everything and besides...er...I wanted to go to my father's Mass by myself and he would have told my lady and...umm...' Her face squinched in the middle. 'Oh, Sir Robert, do you think your lady mother will beat me?'

Carey spread his hands. 'Ahhh...possibly, she's never hesitated to box my ears any time she thought I needed it. But she soon forgets all about it. So where did you dump poor old Shakespeare?'

'I left him in Paul's Churchyard and just speeded up when he started reading something off a stall because once he does that he has no idea what's going on around him and he once had his purse taken out of his cod-piece without even noticing.'

'Perfect,' said Carey, smiling at the picture this made. He piled money on the table in an amount Dodd was beginning to get used to. 'Come on, if we get back there quickly enough he may not notice you ever left.'

Letty immediately brightened and she swallowed the rest of her meal in two large gulps, brushed crumbs off her chin and small ruff.

'That's a wonderful idea, sir...'

'I'll still have to tell my mother, mind you, but at least you won't be embarassed in front of Bald Will.'

They hurried through the crowds with Carey offering Letty his arm so she wouldn't fall off her pattens on the muddiest parts—though London was less muddy than Dodd expected, considering the horses clattering through and the pigs, goats, and chickens wandering around the place. However, crowds of urchins fought each other to shovel up the dungpiles on street corners and several little stalls offered it for sale to those who had gardens. The king's share was picked up early in the morning by the nightsoil men and taken out to Essex. Dodd had learned to sleep through their shouts, their clattering and banging every morning. In London everything had a price. Water was more expensive than beer, for instance, if you had it from one of the men with barrels on their backs, and it tasted far worse.

Paul's Walk was thronged as usual and the churchyard filled with people reading books in a hurry next to the various stationers' stalls. Shakespeare was deep in discussion with the printer who had served Lady Hunsdon when they found him and blinked at Letty in bemusement. He had clearly forgotten all about her.

Carey dusted off his hands as she departed, chatting happily about watching the young courtiers in St Paul's and how there was one in tawny velvet and lime green satin who seemed to be having a contest with another one in cramoisie and tangerine as to who could cause the worst headache. Carey had pointed them out as they passed through the huge old cathedral.

'Now where?' moaned Dodd, as Carey immediately headed purposefully for Ludgate.

'I want to know precisely what lands in Cornwall were sold and who bought 'em. Particularly who bought them. I'm beginning to wonder if it matters which lands.'

'Eh?' said Dodd.

Carey shook his head. 'Lands in exchange for recusancy fines. That's quite an old system for getting rich. Anthony Munday's been at it as hard as he can for years. But what was it about them that brought those two up to London and then both of them wind up dead—one as a substitute for the other as well?'

'What system? I dinna ken nowt about land buying and selling.'

Carey had the grace to look a little ashamed. 'Well...if a Catholic landowner continues to be foolish and obstinate and go to Mass, he gets fined for it. After a while, if he doesn't pay the fines, he could be arrested on a warrant for debt. Now if someone...er... with influence could buy the warrant, he could then exchange it... ahem...for the deeds to some of the man's land and it would... er...be perfectly legal.'

From the way Carey was avoiding Dodd's eye, he assumed Carey had either dabbled in this system or his father had. More likely his father; Dodd didn't see Carey having the sense or the ready funds.

'Ay,' he said, 'it's like when the Grahams first came south to the Border Country.'

'Is it?'

'Ay, in King Henry's time. The brothers—that'd be Richie of Brackenhill's grandad, Richie and his great-uncles, Jock and Hutchin Graham. They decided they liked the look o' the place and they had some men with them. So they took the land for theirselves and kicked the Storeys off it and naebody did nothing about it for the King of Scotland had just hanged Johnny Johnstone.'

'It's not like that at all.'

'Ay, it is, but wi' warrants, not torches and fists and swords,' said Dodd firmly.

'You're not seriously suggesting that Papists should be allowed to simply...be Papists.'

Dodd shrugged. 'I dinna care one way or the other,' he said, 'so they dinna bring in the King o' Spain—now that's not right. Nor try to harm the Queen. That's terrible treason, and who wants to end up like the Scots, forever killing their kings?'

'Quite.'

'Still, when ye take a man's land wi'oot paying him fairly for it, I dinna see the difference whether ye come in wi' your kith and kin and boot him off to lie in a ditch and greet, or do it all nice and tidy wi' bits o' paper.'

Unusually, Carey said nothing.

They came to the Temple and climbed up the stairs to the top of the rickety building where James Enys had his chambers.

Carey knocked on the new door. 'Hello? Anyone there?' he called.

There was a pause and Mrs. Morgan's face looked out. Just for a moment in the semi-darkness at the top of the staircase, Dodd thought it was Enys himself, so close was the resemblance, but the polite matron's white linen cap and small ruff disabused him.

Her brother was not there and had gone out. No, she did not know where. No, she didn't know why. She had spent all day clearing the mess left by the pursuivants and had had to buy a new door which she could ill-afford, even if her brother was about to be paid by Lord Hunsdon.

'It's your other brother's papers I came for?' said Carey. 'The one who disappeared?'

There was a long pause. Then, 'Yes?'

'The lands he was selling in Cornwall. Does Mr. Enys still have any papers connected to that?'

'I don't know, sir, you must ask him when he returns.'

She shut the door on them. Carey stood there a while with

his head cocked as if listening and Dodd thought he could hear a stealthy sniffle.

Finally Carey banged his hand on the wall with frustration and led the way back down the stairs and into the courtyard where two lawyers in their black robes stood conferring together. Carey went straight up to them with a shallow bow. 'Your pardon, sirs, do you know a man called James Enys?'

One looked at the other and smiled. 'Oh yes,' he said, 'a fine lawyer when he pleases, but I think Mr. Heneage doesn't like him.'

'Do you know where he is now?'

The other shrugged. 'In his chambers...There he is coming out of the door.'

Carey spun on his heel to see Enys coming towards them looking tired and anxious.

'Can I help you sirs?' he asked, nodding to his brother lawyers who tactfully moved away, one of them suppressing a laugh.

'I need to see the documents about the land sales in Cornwall, Mr. Enys,' said Carey, his eyes narrowed. 'I think they were not taken by the pursuivants though I'm sure that's what they were after. I think you have them somewhere safe.'

Enys swallowed convulsively and seemed to be thinking. 'Very well, Sir Robert,' he said. 'I have them in a safe place and I can fetch them for you, but you cannot go into it. Can you not ask me what you want to know about them?'

Carey hooked his thumbs in his swordbelt. 'I want to know who bought them, Mr. Enys.'

Enys paused. 'Ah,' he said. 'Worshipful gentlemen at the Queen's Court...'

'No sir, I want the names.'

'Of the sellers?'

'No, of the buyers. Was my father among them?'

Enys looked at the ground. 'Er...no.'

'The sales were secret, yes? But at high prices?'

'Yes.'

'Who bought them?'

'I...I cannot say, sir.'

'Cannot? Will not?'

'Dare not, sir. They were mainly proxies for a very...noble gentleman who would be...offended if his name were linked with the matter.'

'Hm. Burghley?'

'I really cannot say, sir.'

Carey showed his teeth in a grimace of frustration. 'If you should change your mind, Mr. Enys,' he said evenly, 'please let me know.'

They both turned to go but Enys called after them, 'Sergeant Dodd.'

Dodd turned. 'Ay?'

'Would you like me to continue the civil suit?'

Carey's father was paying for it after all and it would likely annoy Heneage even if nothing came of it. 'Ay,' said Dodd, 'see what ye can get.'

Enys nodded. 'You may be surprised, Sergeant.'

'I will be if aught comes of it,' said Dodd, and continued with Carey out onto Fleet Street.

Naturally the Cock Tavern was beckoning and they were soon sitting in one of the booths inside, drinking ale. Dodd crushed the impulse to reach for his pipe.

'Well for what it's worth, here's what I think,' said Carey. 'Last year the magistrates changed in Cornwall and the recusants started getting squeezed. A couple of them had to sell some land and whoever bought the land went to look at it. He found some interesting-looking rocks and had an assayer who happened to be in the area—Fr. Jackson—check it for gold.'

'D'ye think they found it?'

Carey paused significantly. 'I think they did. Perhaps quite a lot. Everyone knows that gold comes from base metals which are forced to change and change again until the true principal metal emerges. There's tin in Cornwall, and where there's tin there's lead usually, and sometimes silver. It would be strange if there weren't gold, in fact.'

Dodd nodded. 'Ay.'

'Of course they didn't want to let out that there was gold, because then it would belong to the Crown, and in any case the price of the land would go up. So they kept it quiet and started buying more and more land, probably using Richard Tregian as their agent. They want to start getting the gold out of the ground—probably covered by tin mining so they get the Papist priest Jackson to come up to London to talk to him and for some reason he turns difficult, he threatens to spread the word or perhaps just demands more money for his silence. They don't need him any more as there are plenty of mining engineers in Cornwall, so they kill him and dump him in the Thames. Who does it is difficult to say, but I would suspect Mr. Enys's mysterious brother who has so conveniently disappeared. Or, more likely, there is no brother and Mr. Enys did it himself.' Carey leaned back looking triumphant. 'Which is why he keeps following us around and also won't tell us who was buying the land.'

Dodd didn't think Enys would be able to kill anyone, but knew there was no point arguing with Carey in the grip of a pretty idea. 'And Richard Tregian?'

'Heneage or Topcliffe are after Fr. Jackson and instead of catching him, they catch his friend Tregian. They need to produce a priest and so they use him.'

'Ay well then,' said Dodd, thinking this was distinctly thin and far-fetched, puffing on the pipe he had just lit, 'all we need to do is grab Enys and get him to tell us he did it. Ah dinna think he would take much thumping.'

Carey gazed wearily on him. 'Dodd, that's simply not the way I do things.'

Dodd shrugged. It was the way most people did things and it generally seemed to work for Lowther.

'And it doesn't work,' Carey insisted, 'if you're beating someone up for information, either he'll spit in your eye and say nothing as you did to Heneage, or he'll tell you whatever he thinks you want to hear, whether it's true or not. It's a complete waste of time.'

Dodd shrugged again. 'Worth trying on Enys though.'

'Well, do you want him to work for you as your lawyer?'

Dodd sighed through his teeth. On the whole he did, so grabbing him and beating him was not the way to go. On the other hand...

'Why can we not go home now, sir? The criminal case is lost and the civil will take far longer than I wantae stay in this place.'

Carey scowled. 'My parents want me to find out what happened to Richard Tregian, particularly my mother. Until I've done that, we're stuck here, so you might as well help me.'

'Ay, but why do they care? Somebody stabs a priest in the back and dumps him in the Thames. Ye might think Heneage would be pleased about it. Heneage then hangs, draws, and quarters Richard Tregian in his place. It's all done wi' and the men'll not be back again. What's the point of your parents sending ye hither and yon in London to find out about it?'

Carey started to answer and then stopped. He leaned back with his eyes half-hooded and a lazy smile on his face. 'As ever, Sergeant, you ask the right question. Why indeed? Hmm.'

'D'ye think your...eh...lady mother might have bought some of the lands in Cornwall? She said the prices were high.'

'She might have. She has to do something with what she gets from her privateering.'

'And she came up to London to talk wi' Tregian as well, she said so when we went to find him at his inn and he wasnae there, on account of being on a pike on London Bridge instead,' said Dodd thoughtfully. 'She was no' best pleased when Letty said he wasnae there and she had me go and search his bedchamber.'

'That was where you found the paper with the cipher on it?'

'Ay, tucked in behind a shelf.'

'Did you show it to her?'

Dodd opened his mouth to speak, then paused. 'Ah, no, it slipped me mind, what with the heid on a pike and Letty screaming, ye ken.'

Carey was looking thoughtful. 'Well, we've read the invisible ink now and it shows, but we haven't cracked the cipher so we've no way of telling who it was addressed to. I wonder if...'

'Ay,' said Dodd who was well ahead of him. 'We should try giving it to her. Only I might get in trouble for not giving it to her before.'

'She won't be very pleased, but at least she won't box your ears and call you clabber-brained,' said Carey with some edge.

Dodd hid a smile. Carey stood and went out the back to the jakes. He came back with a small purse of gold that he must have been keeping in his codpiece, gave it quietly to Dodd.

'I've taken half out of it and I want you to look after it for me and not give me any of it, understand?' said Carey very seriously. 'If we're going to play in the King of London's game, I want still to be solvent afterwards.'

'We're gonnae go there, are we?'

Carey blinked at him. 'Of course. I've been before but we were very clearly invited tonight and I'm going. Only...' He spread his hands and shrugged.

'Will they be cheating?'

'Oddly enough, they won't. Laurence Pickering, the King of London, guarantees his game against all pricksters, card-sharps, and highmen and lowmen, and kicks out anyone who breaks that rule. Which makes it more difficult for me because if I'm playing against crooked players, I can usually guarantee to win whereas if I'm merely playing against good players, I can't be so certain.'

THURSDAY 14TH SEPTEMBER 1592, EVENING

According to Carey, Pickering's game moved around a lot so you could only find it if you were invited. When the sun started to go down they walked into the city and along the busy wharves until they came to Three Cranes in the Vintry. There the men inside the great treadmills that worked the three enormous cranes were just finishing and jumping down to drink their beer and be paid for a day's work. The last of the barrels of Rhenish and Gascon wine were being hurried on handcarts into warehouses to be locked up, watched by the Tunnage and Poundage men who put the Queen's seal on the locks.

Other brightly dressed young men were standing around in casual ways, so Carey and Dodd took their ease on a bench by the water and Dodd kept his hands away from his tobacco pouch. They saw the lad in cramoisie and tangerine, large ruff, haughty nose, highly coloured, acned and with a target all but pinned to his back.

Once the Tunnage and Poundage men had gone off in their boat, things changed. At the back of one of the securely sealed warehouses, a part of the wall slid aside and two imposing men in buff coats came to stand stolidly by the opening. Dodd recognised one of them but Carey held Dodd back from going in at once.

'Let's see who's there,' he said, and watched the other well-dressed courtiers and merchants who went in by the entrance after a muttered conversation with one of the men in buff coats.

At last Carey stood and followed them, trailed by Dodd. At the door he nodded at one of the men. 'How's your wife, Mr. Briscoe?'

Briscoe smiled and nodded back. 'Near her time, Sir Robert,' he said. 'It's a worry. She says she'll stop wearing herself out about her brother now she knows it was a man called Jackson and it wasn't him. Which is a relief, you know.'

Carey smiled. 'By the way, did you happen to hear about the veney I played the other night with some Smithfield brawlers working for Topcliffe?'

Briscoe's broad face broke into a grin. 'Nearly split my sides, sir. And what came after. I heard it was that mad poet Marlowe wot hired 'em and he'd better be careful if he goes near Smiffield again, cos none of 'em are 'appy about it.'

Carey laughed. 'Well if you should happen to hear anything else about it, I'd be grateful if you'd pass it on.'

'I will, sir.'

'Anything else going on?'

Briscoe's brow creased. 'Well, Mr. Pickering's very worried by the plague in the city, though none of the City Aldermen is bovvered. It's in the Bridewell now, you know?'

Carey grimaced. 'Thanks for the warning.'

'And I heard tell one of the bearwardens was sick of it yesterday and died and one of his bears run wild for sorrow.'

'Not Harry Hunks?'

'No sir, he's retired now. Gone back to the Kent herds to sire more bears. That was Big John and they 'ad to shoot him in the end.'

Carey shook his head as he handed over the price of entry in gold. 'The city fathers think all they have to do is shut the theatres and the plague will disappear, even though it never does.'

Dodd was thinking of what that poor apothecary had said a couple of weeks before—that the plague always started in St Paul's, not the playhouses. He resolved not to go near the place again, never mind the rats in the crypt gnawing on only God knew what remains from two hundred years before.

Briscoe tipped his hat and they climbed the wooden stairs to an upper room lit with ranks of candles and glass windows, with fair rush mats on the floors and painted cloths on the walls. It all seemed very wealthy and respectable until you looked more carefully at the cloths which were covered with pictures of shockingly naked people wearing leafy hats and playing cards and dice and drinking. Some of them seemed to be doing...what they shouldn't have been. Dodd's eyes stretched as he took in the details. Somewhere at the back of his mind he wondered if he and Janet..? He gulped and turned away, hoping his face hadn't gone guiltily red.

Carey had put on the Courtier again and was also wearing a suspiciously knowing look. Dodd was beginning to suspect that the real article was the Berwick man who showed up occasionally when Carey was under pressure, but Carey as Courtier never failed to irritate him with his breeziness and arrogance. As the Courtier sauntered into a group of glaringly-dressed young men and greeted them affably, Dodd found a padded bench to park his padded hose on and felt for his pipe.

A small bullet-headed man with a smiling face sat down next to him and offered him a light so Dodd passed him the pipe.

'You're the northerner, ain't you,' said the small man, puffing away appreciatively, 'what's come sarf wiv Sir Robert?'

'Ay,' said Dodd, taking the pipe back.

'I've 'ad the word out to leave you be and not try to tip you any more lays.'

Dodd nodded politely at this because he had no idea what the small man was talking about.

'Fing is,' said the man, 'I can't be seen talking to Sir Robert in public and he knows it, 'cos that cove over there is one of Cecil's boys...'

Dodd followed the man's glance and saw the pale oblong face of Poley.

'So when you see 'im go in the back, I want you to go wiv 'im. Understand?'

Dodd bridled slightly at being told what to do but simply nodded. 'Ay,' he said.

The small man smiled, held out his hand. ''Course, I can see you don't know me. I'm Laurence Pickering.'

Dodd shook. 'Ah...Henry Dodd, sir. Sergeant of Gilsland.' He blinked. Was this the King of London in dark brocades and furs, his balding head bare? Brother-in-law to the London hangman and master of the thieves of the City? He looked like a very prosperous merchant. Which in a way he was, just as Richie Graham of Brackenhill was very much the lord of his manor, never mind where his family came from nor how they got there.

Pickering winked at him, jumped up, and headed into the throng of players in the corner. The way everyone parted for him told Dodd a lot more than the man's compact size and modest manner.

Carey was deep in a game of primero, with the boy in cramoisie and tangerine clearly set out before him like a peacock ready for carving. He drank and smiled and laughed and shouted eighty-five points as he always did and casually tossed an angel—a genuine gold angel this time—into the pot.

Dodd, shuddering at the idea of a week's wages being where you started in this game, stood up and wandered over to the dice players. They were playing with very fine ivory dice with gold pips—perhaps to make them more difficult to palm and swap which had been one of Barnabus' specialities—the women cheering as one of them threw two sixes and scooped the pot. It was all shillings and crowns there and as Dodd generally played dice for fractions of a penny, he didn't fancy that game either.

He hid a yawn. He could have spent the time gazing at the naked women all over the painted cloths, but didn't want to risk being tempted by one of the girls with her tits peeping over the lace edging of her stays. Although there were musicians in the corner, they were playing quite complicated music on lutes with no drums at all which was boring to listen to. He had thought that rich folks in London somehow had more fun but as far as he could make out, they did the same things as poor folks only their boredom was more expensive and complicated and took a lot longer. In fact it was worse because with horse-racing you had the excitement of reiving the nags first.

He could see there were special arrangements to make sure none of the games were crooked. For a start the floormats were clean and white and obviously changed often, while the light from the banks of candles made the room quite bright if very warm. There were no handy shadows where you could hide things or drop inconvenient cards. Young men in tight jerkins with tight sleeves moved about, picking up packs of cards and dice between games and inspecting them. One player had his cards taken and then he was grabbed by three of the burly men standing near the door. Two of them upended him while the other searched him and pulled out several high-ranking cards. He was removed, squawking, down the stairs and some of the gamers peered out the window to wait for the splash as he was thrown in the Thames. There were cheers and catcalls and Pickering leaned out of a window.

'Don't come back. If you do, I'll give you to my brother-in-law.'

Much obsequious clapping from the young men in jerkins and the women in very low-cut bodices. That was when Dodd spotted him. He frowned. What was Enys doing here—he didn't gamble? Or he said he didn't. As casually as he could, Dodd got up and sauntered over to the table where he had seen the heavily pock-marked lawyer.

They were playing primero, the play tense and close and the pot large. Dodd couldn't quite make out Enys's face because he was sitting well back in a corner so he waited until the man had lost and got up to get a drink.

'Mr. Enys,' said Dodd as breezy as he could, 'fancy meeting you here...'

The man seemed to jump, but then bowed shallowly. 'I'm sorry, sir,' he said, 'I fear you mistake me, my name is Vent, not Enys.' Dodd blinked at him, puzzled. Certainly the voice was different, but the face...The face was definitely familiar though not really Enys's.

'Ay?' said Dodd, 'ye're nocht ma lawyer?'

'Er...no,' said the man, Vent, 'though I have heard I have a double practising law in the Temple at the moment.' He coughed or perhaps hid a laugh. 'Possibly I should sue him for defamation of character.'

'Good Lord, Ah'm sorry, sir, I was sure it was ye.'

'No matter,' said Vent, 'Perhaps you would give your lawyer my compliments, and tell him I would be delighted to meet him over a hand of cards.'

'I will,' Dodd answered, now feeling awkward. After all, he never liked it when people thought he was the legal type of Serjeant as opposed to a Land-Sergeant. They bowed to each other and Dodd turned back to watch Carey at his game. Several others were watching the game, including Pickering and three of his bully-boys.

Carey nodded and laid his cards down. 'Prime,' he said. The boy in cramoisie and tangerine stared fixedly and then laid his own cards facedown without another word. Carey smiled sweetly at the lad and pulled the pot towards him. As he pocketed his haul, two of Pickering's men came and stood behind him, one murmured in his ear. Carey looked surprised and then stood up, headed for the door at the back of the room.

After a moment of concern, Dodd quietly followed them and into a small parlour with a bright fireplace where Laurence Pickering was standing blinking at the flames.

'Well, Sir Robert?'

Carey smiled. 'Well, Mr. Pickering?'

'How's 'e doing it? Young Mr. Newton?'

'He's not cheating in any way I can see,' said Carey thoughtfully, 'although he's not as good a player as he thinks he is.'

'So why does he win?'

'I'm not sure,' said Carey spreading his hands. 'He might simply be lucky.'

'Or 'e's got a magic ring.'

Carey's eyebrows went up. 'Hm. I've heard of them and a number of astrologers and magicians and whatnot have tried to sell them to me but I've never heard of one that actually worked. It's like alchemy. It's always going to work, or it would have worked if you hadn't scratched your nose at that particular moment, or tomorrow when the stars are conjunct with Jupiter it will work, but today, right now, when you want them to, in my experience, they never work.'

Pickering had his head on one side, exactly like a blackbird eyeing up a worm. He looked sceptical. Carey smiled his sunny, lazy smile. 'Besides, if you had a ring like that which actually did work, would you sell it?'

Pickering hesitated and then burst into laughter, slapping his knee. He poured Carey brandywine and offered some to Dodd who shook his head. He wanted to keep a clear head for whatever was going on here. That was why he hadn't had another pipe since the first one he had shared with Pickering.

'So that's a relief,' said Pickering. 'None of my boys could understand it. We actually let him win a night wiv Desiree de Paris so we could check his clothes properly, but nothing. 'E's just lucky and one day 'is luck will run out.'

'I expect so,' said Carey easily. 'Comes to us all, I'm afraid.'

''Course the only ovver one I've known win so often wivvout cheating, is you, Sir Robert.'

Carey bowed a little. 'Since my love-life is a catastrophe, this is only to be expected.'

Pickering smiled shortly. 'All right, then, you've done what I asked. Now. How can I help you, Sir Robert? Or your worshipful father, of course?'

'Both really. Firstly information about Heneage.'

'Hmf.' Pickering was rubbing his lower lip. 'What do you want to know?'

'Anything you feel may be of interest, Mr. Pickering.'

'He's short of money,'

Carey's eyes went up. 'You'd think with all his loot from catching Catholics and so on that he'd be rich.'

'Well, he's short enough that he's wanting me to pay him rental for him leaving me and my people alone.'

'Oh really?'

Dodd was surprised. Heneage claiming blackmail money from someone like Pickering? Was the man mad?

Pickering's lips thinned. 'Yes, really.'

'You had an arrangement with Mr. Secretary Walsingham...'

'Yes I did, Sir Robert. He left me in peace. I made sure that there was reasonable peace in London and if he needed to know anything, he knew it, no questions asked.'

'And Heneage...?'

'Wants paying.'

Carey tutted quietly.

'And sends Topcliffe to collect.' Pickering spat deliberately into the fire.

'Dear oh dear. He certainly seems in a hurry at the moment, Mr. Pickering. Are you aware of the problems my father and brother had with him a week or two ago?'

'I'd 'eard somefing,' said Pickering cautiously. 'You was in a good stand-off in the Fleet's Beggar's Ward, I 'eard all about that.'

'Mm. And you'll be aware that Sergeant Dodd here has been trying to bring Heneage to court over his maltreatment.'

Pickering snorted quietly at this, an opinion Dodd shared.

'Now there's something afoot over Cornish land,' Carey said. 'I asked your brother-in-law about the hanging, drawing, and quartering of a purported priest named Fr. Jackson.' Pickering's small bright eyes narrowed and sharpened at that. 'The man whose head ended up on London Bridge was in fact a Mr. Richard Tregian, a respected Cornish gentleman and a...an acquaintance of my mother's.'

Pickering nodded.

'He had been involved in the selling of Cornish lands that had gold in them, working with a surveyor and assayer, who was the priest Fr. Jackson under whose name Tregian ended being executed—if that was actually the man's name. In fact my mother came up to town herself to talk to him—although I don't yet know why. His daughter is in my mother's service and came with her—bringing a copy of a survey of the areas in question.'

Carey paused to take a drink of brandywine. 'She had it in her purse under her kirtle—she's a Cornish girl and nobody there would steal it from her so she had no idea...Anyway, she comes up to town with my mother in the *Judith of Penryn*, she cannot find her father where he is supposed to be lodging, she goes with my mother shopping on London Bridge, and there she sees her father's head on a spike.'

Now it was Pickering's turn to tut.

'Understandably she screamed the place down, spooked her horse and gave Sergeant Dodd here some trouble to control the nag. In the flurry she thinks her purse with the survey in it was stolen, or at any rate, she didn't have it any more when she got home and the cord had been cut.'

Pickering nodded. 'If it was any of my people wot nipped that bung, I'll have the survey back in your hands by tomorrow, Sir Robert,' he said in measured tones. 'There's no chance she might of sold the survey and then...'

Carey smiled and shook his head.

'Who would she sell it to? She knows no one in London, she's only a country maid. Besides she has been with my mother the whole time she's spent in London.'

'Hm.'

'And one other matter. A corpse fetched up against the Queen's Privy Stair a few days ago, but in a state that showed it had been in the water considerably longer. The man had been stabbed but died of drowning—perhaps because he was wearing leg-irons at the time he fell in the Thames. It fell into my father's jurisdiction, and at the inquest today a woman turned up calling herself Mrs. Sophia Merry, claimed the body as Mr. Jackson, and then almost held an illegal Requiem Mass for him this same afternoon. I want to know if any of the watermen saw him going into the water? He had the top joint missing from his left index finger.'

Pickering nodded again. 'They might know. I'll ask around, Sir Robert. Now. If...ah...if any of these Cornish lands was to be offered to me, just for argument's sake, what would you advise?'

'Mr. Pickering,' said Carey with a shrewd look, 'I would advise you not to touch it with a boathook.'

'Not even as an investment? In case...ahem...there was gold?'

'And what if there were? It's Crown prerogative in any case. You would have to dig it up, refine it, and then share anything you made with the Queen's Majesty. Or do it in secret and risk having the whole thing confiscated. And the land is in Cornwall, for the Lord's sake, Mr. Pickering. What do you know about Cornwall? You wouldn't even be able to understand what they said to you, nor they you. It's at five day's ride from London and there are no posthouses beyond Plymouth.'

'I could take ship...'

'Mr. Pickering, if you have bought any of these lands, I advise you to sell as soon as you can and buy any land at all you can lay hands on around the Blackfriars.'

'Oh yes?' Pickering's beady little eyes were wide open. 'I fort your father owned the lot.'

'Not all of it. And he's not selling. Nor can I tell you what his plans are with my elder brother, however...At least if it's in London you can go and look at the place.' Carey smiled confidingly. 'Please don't tell my father I mentioned it, though.'

Pickering nodded, eyes shrewd. 'Well, that's interesting. Thank you, Sir Robert. Can I offer you gennlemen any...ah...further entertainment?'

Carey hesitated and then regretfully shook his head. 'I think I should return to Somerset House, Mr. Pickering, especially as my lady mother is in town and has...er...sources of her own.'

Dodd had to hide a smile at this one, as did Pickering from the slight clamping of his teeth. Both Carey and he stood to leave.

'I'll send a couple of my boys wiv you, Sir Robert,' said Pickering with a wink. 'We don't want no more veneys in Fleet Street, now do we?'

'Indeed not,' said Carey primly. 'Thank you.'

In fact, they took a boat, which turned up the minute Mr. Briscoe roared 'Oars!' from the wharf, and got out at Somerset House steps, a highly convenient way of travelling. On the way, Carey seemed thoughtful.

'How is it that ye're sae friendly wi' the King o' the London thieves?' Dodd asked for pure nosiness. 'Ah wouldnae have thought...'

'Oh, it's a long story, Sergeant. Long time ago too. When I was first at Court, before I went to Scotland, I...ah...somewhat over-reached myself at a London primero game...'

'Ay?'

Carey's expression was rueful. 'Yes. Lost my shirt, actually. Literally.'

Dodd's mouth turned down. 'Ay?'

'Well, I wasn't going to let that bother me so I was heading for my lodgings as I...ah...was...'

'Wi'out yer shirt?'

'Nothing but my underbreeches, I'm afraid. It gave a couple of punks a terrible turn, I think. Anyway, Mr. Pickering caught up with me and gave me back my cloak which was kind of him. He said he liked the way I'd carried it off and as he had suspicions about the cards, he would take it as a compliment if I would allow him to buy me some temporary duds at a pawnshop he knew on a loan so as not to...er...frighten anybody.'

Dodd was enchanted at this picture. 'Ay.'

'Of course, he wasn't the King then, he was working for the man who was. We got talking over a few quarts of beer and I told him if he wanted to draw in the courtiers with money, he should set up a game which was absolutely clean, no cheating at all, guarantee it and charge for entrance. And make sure it was somewhere comfortable.'

Carey took his hat off to a lady wearing a velvet mask as she went past in another boat. She turned away haughtily.

'And whit was it about that boy in the terrible get up?' Dodd asked.

'Occasionally, if Mr. Pickering has a player in who wins too much but he can't work out how, he asks me to check up on him,' Carey said casually.

'And was he cheating?'

Carey gave Dodd a warning look. 'No, or I would have said so,' he said, 'He was simply counting cards and playing by the odds. It isn't cheating but it does give you an advantage. There's an Italian book explains how to do it and I expect he's read it. That's what I've been teaching you to do, by the way.'

Dodd remembered about the Italian book and its notions about numbers. 'Why did ye no' tell Pickering about that?'

Carey looked amused. 'What, and have him work out how I do it myself? I don't think so.'

***

Back at Somerset House Dodd was hoping for his bed. But no, it seemed, despite both of them being weary and the hour a ridiculously late eleven o'clock, Carey had to speak to his parents if they were still up.

They were companionably playing cards together in the little parlour in the corner of the courtyard, with wax candles on the table and a little dish of wafers to dip in their spiced evening wine.

Carey bowed to his parents and his mother immediately stood up and hugged him, and then to Dodd's horror, gave Dodd a hug as well.

'Letty told me how you helped her when she was such a fool,' said Lady Hunsdon. 'What with Sergeant Dodd spotting the trap and giving warning and you helping her leave so quickly...She said you were both wonderful. Lord alone knows what trouble there would have been if she had been taken by that evil bastard Topcliffe. She isn't really a Papist, she's just a silly maid that's been wrongly taught, but in Topcliffe's hands...'

Hunsdon smiled fondly at his wife. One of the footmen standing by the wall came forward and brought up another small table while more wafers and wine arrived so that Dodd could do something at least about his aching belly. The pork pie he had had in the afternoon was long gone and Carey, being Carey, hadn't stopped since then.

'Well Robin?' said his father as Carey leaned back in his chair, crossed his legs at the ankle, and took a long draught of wine.

'The Devil of it is,' he said, seemingly at random while his mother frowned at him for swearing, 'there's a pattern here and I know there is, but I can't seem to see it.'

He told the whole tale of their very busy day from start to finish, with no embellishments at all.

'How did you know where the memorial service was to?' asked Lady Hunsdon. 'Letty said she couldn't imagine.'

'Oh that.' Carey smiled faintly. 'The Papists themselves told me. It was in the book at the crypt—the woman who claimed the priest's body gave a false address and called herself Mrs. Sophia Merry.'

'Never heard of her.'

'Of course not, my lord, it's a false name as well. But it told where the service would be—at the site of the old church of St Mary Wisdom.'

Hunsdon gave a shout of laughter. 'Ha! I didn't realise you'd actually managed to learn some Greek as a boy, between reiving cows and playing football.'

Carey smiled ruefully. 'I didn't, my lord, I'm afraid. But while I was in Paris I...er...knew a lady whose name was Sophia who told me often that her name meant wisdom and very proud of it she was too although she was as feather-brained as a duck.'

Lord Hunsdon seemed to find this very funny whereas Lady Hunsdon only smiled briefly.

He finished with his account of Pickering's game, then wet his whistle and waited for his parents' reactions. They were a time coming. Lady Hunsdon in particular seemed very interested in her cards.

After a moment, Carey said gently, 'I find it alarming, my lady, that Pickering seems to have bought some of these Cornish lands on the grounds that there's gold in them.'

Lady Hunsdon said nothing. She was dipping a wafer in the wine.

'I advised him to sell immediately,' Carey added, 'on the grounds that even if there was gold, he would get no good of it since it was so far away and well out of his manor.'

There was more thundering silence.

'My lady mother?' said Carey, even more softly. Lady Hunsdon refused to meet his eyes. He sighed. 'Well then, my lord, I don't know what more I can do. Perhaps it would be best if I went north again...'

'Not yet,' said Lady Hunsdon sharply.

'No,' said Lord Hunsdon at exactly the same time. The two of them looked at each other while Carey watched the pair of them with hooded eyes and a cynical expression.

Dodd had woken up to the fact that there was something complicated going on between Carey and his parents and indeed between Lord and Lady Hunsdon, but he wasn't sure what it might be. His own parents had been very much less complicated and furthermore were both long dead. Inside the silence there seemed to be some kind of three-way battle going on.

In the end Carey broke it by uncrossing his legs and planting his boots firmly on the black and white tiles of the floor.

He stood up and then went formally on one knee to his parents.

'My lord father, my lady mother,' he said quietly, 'I am urgently needed in Carlisle before the autumn reiving starts. I will not investigate this matter any further until I have a true accounting of the background to it from both of you.' His eyes were on his mother as he spoke. Then he stood, bowed gracefully to both, backed three steps as if from royalty, turned and left the parlour.

'I told you Robin would...' Hunsdon began but his wife slammed her cards down, stood and marched out of the parlour, her cheeks flaming as if she had painted them. Hunsdon followed her, leaving Dodd sitting at a cardtable all alone except for the servingman standing by the door, seemingly dozing where he stood.

Dodd finished the spiced wine, which was very good, crushed immediately the impulse to steal the silver cups and the candelabra, and headed for his own bed. To his disgust he found Carey sitting by the small fire in the luxurious fireplace, busy mulling the wine which was normally left for him in a flagon on a table by the wall. Dodd's eyelids felt as if they were lined with lead and sand.

'Och,' he moaned.

'God damn it,' snarled Carey in general, ramming the poker back among the coals as if stabbing someone. 'She still thinks I'm a boy that can't see the nose on his face because his head's too full of football, she thinks I still can't add it up. What the hell does she think she's playing at?'

Bewildered, Dodd sat on the edge of his bed since Carey had his chair.

'Ay?'

'As for my father...Why the devil doesn't he keep her under control? Privateering at her age. Dodgy land-deals with God knows what bloody Papists. He should bloody well assert his authority and make her behave!'

Dodd was open-mouthed at this notion as he rather thought Hunsdon would be. He decided not to say anything since Carey was evidently spoiling for a fight with someone, and if he didn't dare fight his parents combined, might well pick on Dodd. Who hadn't the energy for it.

Carey drank some wine and then seemed to remember his

manners, poured another gobletfull and handed it to Dodd, who had really drunk enough but didn't feel like arguing either. Would he never get to his bed?

'Don't you understand, Sergeant?' Carey said more quietly. 'My mother doesn't like the Court and doesn't really know how it works. You know my father is the Queen's half-brother through Mary Boleyn, Anne Boleyn's older sister? Who was King Henry's official mistress before Anne.'

Dodd had heard something about it, but discounted it as the usual overblown nonsense. His eyes stretched but he nodded once.

'Now if King Henry had married Mary instead of Anne, my father would have been king and I would have been a Prince of the Blood Royal.' He shuddered briefly. 'And my ghastly elder brother would have been the heir to the throne, Heaven help us. But the bastardy means that can't ever happen, thank God, which means my father is her Majesty's closest kin and also her most trusted man at court. As Lord Chamberlain he runs the entire *domus providenciae* of the Court. The...ah...I suppose you'd translate it "the House of Supplies" which is to say, the servants, supplies, kitchens, laundries, and what-have-you. Courtiers are generally part of the *domus magnificenciae*, the House of Magnificence, and very much worse treated. My father also guards her Majesty against assassinations. Everyone thinks of him as no more than a knight of the carpet, a courtier and patron, never mind what he did during the Northern Earls rebellion. And never mind that he's kept the Queen safe all this time. Heneage wants to destroy him and take his job—he thinks he could have enormous influence with the Queen which my father, on the whole, rarely uses.'

Dodd nodded again, still not sure where this was going.

'That means that if my mother has been indulging in some half-baked scheme involving Cornish lands and Papist priests and Heneage gets wind of it and goes to the Queen, my father could be in the Tower on a charge of treason by the end of the year.'

'Ay,' said Dodd, wondering if it was too late to steal a horse from Hunsdon's stable and head north as fast as he could.

'That's the thing about the Court. Nothing is steady, nothing is certain. People plot and lie and scheme for power. My father has never been very interested in political power which is one reason why the Queen trusts him. He's also seen to it that she stays alive, with God's help. But if Heneage can convince her he's turning Papist or has been dealing with them in some way, no matter how ridiculous the charge would be, the Queen would turn on my father. And her anger can be as terrible as my grandfather's.'

'Ay.'

'And as lethal.'

'Ay.'

'Then there's the fact that the Cecils have intervened on Heneage's behalf. Generally speaking they're at loggerheads because Sir Robert Cecil wants to run Walsingham's legacy instead of Heneage. So why would he organize the adjournment of our case for Heneage? Either it's some kind of trick to lull him along or Heneage blackmailed him. Or Cecil's after something else entirely and this is just byplay...' Carey's voice trailed off leaving Dodd feeling he was a very small pawn on a very large chessboard full of extremely dangerous, heavily armed chessmen. Carey had a wary, calculating look on his face. After a moment he began again.

'My father wants me to find out what's going on, in case my mother hasn't told him everything. Meanwhile my mother wants me to find out how Richard Tregian was swapped for a priest and what happened to the priest—although I think we know—and how. And in all of it I must ask questions, but if I don't know what they're up to, how can I be sure to ask the right questions and still protect them?'

'Ay.'

'So that's it. I'm not doing any more. I think I'll go hawking tomorrow.'

Carey smiled tightly and finally, thanks be to God, headed for the door. He paused.

'We'll probably be on the road north in a day or two,' he said.

It was while Dodd was fighting his way out of his suit that he found it. A piece of paper which had been slipped into the little pocket in his sleeve. When he opened it, he found a short and imperious note.

'Please be so good as to meet me in the main courtyard at dawn.'

The thing was signed with Lady Hunsdon's initials. Dodd groaned aloud. Dawn? It was past midnight now. He'd get hardly any sleep at all.

Feeling hard-used, he shucked the rest of his stupid clothes, dumped them on the chest, and climbed into bed, closing the curtains around him against the foul ague-producing airs of the Thames.

FRIDAY 15TH SEPTEMBER 1592, DAWN

Dawn found the courtyard full of horses. It seemed that when Carey went hawking near London, he couldn't possibly do it the way he did near Carlisle, which was to ride out with only Dodd or another man of the castle guard and a tercel falcon on his fist, a couple of dogs at the heels of his horse. That was fun.

This kind of hawking involved the dog-boy and the Master of the Kennels plus two or three dogs including the lugubrious lymer that had hurt his paw but was much better now, half a dozen mounted servingmen, the Baron's Falconer, and at least five birds with their hoods on and a couple of boys to climb trees for the falcons in case they didn't come back. Dodd saw Marlowe for the first time in days: he was looking out of a second-storey window smoking a long clay pipe while everyone mounted up and lengthened stirrup leathers and argued. They were seemingly headed for Farringdon Fields.

Carey raised his hand in salute to Dodd as the whole cavalcade clenched and gathered itself around him and waited for the main gate to be opened to let them pass.

'Off we go now,' said a firm voice at Dodd's elbow, and he looked down to see Lady Hunsdon in a respectable but ordinary tawny woollen kirtle, holding a walking stick and wearing a very determined expression.

'Ah...' Dodd began.

'We'll take a boat and you can explain it all to me,' she said.

Dodd looked about for her normal gang of Cornish wreckers and found only the wide and freckled Captain Trevasker standing behind her, looking highly amused.

'Ay m'lady,' said Dodd, since there was evidently no help for it.

They walked down through the gardens with their polite boxtree knot designs and orchard at the end, hedged with raspberry and gooseberry bushes and a row of hazels. Lady Hunsdon didn't lean much on her walking stick since she had her hand laced into the crook of Dodd's elbow, not quite a jailer. They got to the boatlanding, where Dodd found that Captain Trevasker had already hopped into the smaller of the two Hunsdon boats, and handed Lady Hunsdon down to the cushioned seat at the end. The rowers were waiting there in their headache-producing black-and-yellow stripes. Once Lady Hunsdon was settled and had nodded to the chief of them, they set off.

In the middle of the river, Lady Hunsdon leaned over and tapped him on the knee.

'Now then, Sergeant Dodd,' she said, and her eyes had a roguish twinkle in them which went some way to explaining why the bastard son of Henry VIII had married a West Country maiden with only a small dowry. 'Let's find out what that scallywag son of mine has been up to. Tell me everything you've been doing.'

Dodd coughed, thought hard and then decided that the unvarnished truth was easier to remember than any improvement of the story. He started at the beginning, went through the middle, and ended with Pickering. He left out his discussion with Carey the night before.

'Hmm,' said Lady Hunsdon. 'Well then, let's go and see that young lawyer, shall we?'

It was only a little way along the Thames bank to Temple steps where Trevasker hopped out first and handed the Lady up while Dodd helped make fast and jumped out onto the small boatlanding.

A group of lawyers in their sinister black robes were clattering down the steps and tried to get into the Hunsdon boat. Trevasker moved in front of them and growled that it was a private craft. One of them had the grace to bow in apology for the mistake to

Lady Hunsdon while the others started bellowing 'Oars!' None of the Thames boatmen seemed in a hurry to take them anywhere, probably because they were students at one of the Inns and law students were notoriously almost as bad as apprentices for not paying tips and being sick in the back of the boat on the way home.

Lady Hunsdon climbed the steps and then headed in the direction of the Temple. Dodd led the way to the ramshackle buildings where Enys had his chambers. Lady Hunsdon looked narrow-eyed at the steep uneven stairs and sat herself down on a nearby pile of flagstones.

'Ask Mr. Enys if he will come down to meet an old lady,' she said. 'I doubt my poor old knees will take me to the top of that lot. Off you go Sergeant. Captain Trevasker shall bear me company.'

Dodd headed up the stairs. Halfway there he heard shouting and speeded up, taking them two at a time until he came out on to the landing where the pieces of Enys's door were stacked in a corner, the new raw wood of its replacement wide open and two men standing facing each other in the still half-wrecked sitting room. There was a curtain across the gap to the second room.

One was Enys pale-faced and furious, the other was Shakespeare, hat off, bald head gleaming in the light from the small window, and a certain smug look on his face. They had obviously stopped their quarrel when they heard Dodd's boots on the stairs.

Shakespeare peered out of the window and smiled. 'I see my lady has come to see you as well,' he murmured. 'I shall leave you to consider matters.'

With a bow to Dodd he left and trotted down to the courtyard, humming some ditty to himself. Dodd glared after him. If they had been on the Borders, he would have been certain the man was putting the bite on for protection...Mr. Ritchie Graham of Brackenhill is willing to protect your barn from burning while it has such a wonderful quantity of hay in it, but will need his expenses paying...That kind of thing. It was the expression on the face. That smugness. Dodd scowled. Having once felt sorry for Shakespeare for being a poet, he no longer did. The man was nothing but trouble.

'Sergeant,' said Enys, sounding tense again, 'Can I help you?'

'That poet,' said Dodd, 'what did he want?'

Enys paused, frowned, took breath, then let it out again and smiled cynically. 'Nothing good, you may be sure. However, it is confidential.'

'Ay,' said Dodd, being rather tired of the word and the general atmosphere in London of people not telling other people things they needed to be told. 'Milady Hunsdon wants tae know if ye'll be kind enough to come down to her...'

'Of course,' said Enys, putting on his hat.

Down in the shade of an old almond tree perhaps planted by one of the Knights Templar, Lady Hunsdon looked Enys sharply up and down. 'What did that poet want?'

Enys bowed. 'Unfortunately,' he said, 'I am not at liberty...'

'He's not one of your clients, is he?'

'Not exactly. However...'

'Well then, what's he up to? I know he spies for somebody, probably Heneage.'

Enys blinked and tried unsuccessfully to hide his surprise. Then there was another cynical smile pulling his face. 'I cannot say I'm surprised, ma'am, but the matter is still confidential.'

'Indeed?' said Lady Hunsdon, very chilly. 'When you change your mind you may speak to me about it. Now then. Mr. Vice Chamberlain Heneage. How far have you got with your case for Sergeant Dodd?'

Enys gave her the situation pretty much as Dodd had described it, only in legal-talk. Dodd might have been offended a month or two earlier, but he knew that this was simply the way Carey proceeded and no doubt he had learned it from someone.

'Attend upon me at Somerset House tomorrow,' milady ordered. 'I shall have the steward make you a payment and I may have a little more work for you. My son tells me he was impressed by your abilities in court.'

Enys coloured at that, bowed to her.

'We shall see how you are at drafting. Do you have a clerk?'

'No milady, but I myself can write a fair Secretary or Italic, as needed.'

Lady Hunsdon nodded and wiggled her fingers at him. 'Off

you go then, Mr. Enys. Oh by the way, are you any kin to the Enys twins from the farm near Penryn?'

Enys paused, breathed carefully. 'Cousins, my lady,' he said. 'There are only two of them but three in my family.'

'Hm. Interesting. I didn't know that old Bryn Enys had a brother?'

'Perhaps second cousins?'

'Hm.'

Enys bowed and turned back to his chamber. 'Sergeant, may I ask you something.' Dodd went with him up the stairs again. 'I was wondering if you meant what you said about teaching me to fight?'

Dodd rubbed his chin. 'Ay, I did. I dinna want tae be put to the trouble o' finding another lawyer. And it's a pity for a man to wear a sword and not know how to use it.'

Enys nodded and swallowed hard.

'Is it a duel,' Dodd asked nosily, unable to help himself. 'Wi' Shakespeare?'

'Er...no, only...Ah. I think you're right. I mean about not knowing how to use my sword properly.'

'Ay. Where's yer sword?' Enys picked it up out of the corner and handed it to Dodd. 'And is yer wrist better?'

'A little sore still but...'

'Ay. Draw yer sword then.'

'But...um...surely we cannot practise in such a small space...'

'No, we're no' practising. I wantae see something.'

Enys obediently drew his sword from the scabbard with some effort and stood there holding it like the lump of iron it was.

'Ay, I thocht so,' said Dodd, holding Enys's wrist and lifting his arm up to squint along the blade. 'It's too big for ye and too heavy. When would ye like a lesson? I cannae do it now for I'm attending on her ladyship.'

'Perhaps this afternoon? Should I buy a new sword?'

'Not wi'out me there or they'll cheat ye again wi' too much weapon for ye.' Of course, in London you could simply go to an armourer's and buy a sword instead of having to get it made for you by a blacksmith. He kept forgetting how easy life was here.

Dodd tipped his hat to Enys and trotted down the stairs again to Lady Hunsdon who smiled at him.

'What did he want?' she asked as they set off again.

'Swordschooling fra me.'

'A very good idea. I'm sure you would be an excellent teacher, sergeant, if unorthodox.'

'Ay,' He might as well agree with the hinny, even though he didn't know for sure what unorthodox meant.

'Try and find out what Shakespeare was about for me, will you?' added Lady Hunsdon. 'I'm sure it's important.'

'Ay milady.'

'Now then. About the documents that Robin has been keeping from me.'

Dodd said nothing. There was that roguish twinkle again. She tapped his knee as well. He suddenly realised where Carey got some of his more annoying habits. 'Come along, Sergeant, the pair of you managed to raid Heneage's house a few days ago and my son could no more keep his hands off any interesting bits of paper he found there than turn down the chance of bedding some willing, married, and halfway attractive Frenchwoman. Also you searched Richard Tregian's room for me but didn't tell me what you found there—quite understandable in the circumstances but no longer acceptable.' She smiled at him, dimples in her rosy cheeks.

Dodd leaned back on the seat and sighed, wishing for his pipe. 'They're in his room,' he said, deciding to save time. 'I dinna think he had decoded them yet, but...'

'He might not tell you if he had.' She nodded.

The boat was heading back to Somerset House steps where they climbed out—Lady Hunsdon was lifted bodily up to the boatlanding by Captain Trevasker without noticeable strain, something that impressed Dodd.

He went with her back to the house and followed her up the stairs and along the main corridor into the chambers that Carey had been given, along with Hunsdon's second valet to help with the perenniel labour of his clothes. Dodd felt awkward, snooping about in another man's property, but Lady Hunsdon marched in and looked about her.

'At least he has grown out of dropping his clothes in heaps on the floor,' she said, 'now he's learned the cost of them.'

Dodd considered that it was hardly thrift that had cured Carey of dropping his clothes, much more likely it was vanity and the training that serving the Queen at court had given him.

She went over to the desk Carey had been using and looked at the pile of papers there. Her eyebrows went up. 'Well well, are these the ones?'

Dodd recognised the copy of the paper he had found in Tregian's rooms and the paper itself, still smelling faintly of oranges. Lady Hunsdon was frowning down at it.

'Ay,' said Dodd, wondering why Carey hadn't hidden them. Presumably he hadn't bothered to lock his door because he knew his mother would have the key but...He stole a look at Lady Hunsdon.

'Hm.' She went to the fireplace, picked up the poker, and stirred the ashes. There was a mixture of charred wood and the remains of one of the withered oranges that cost outrageous prices in the street until the new crop arrived from Spain nearer Christmas. Also there was a lot of feathery bits of burnt paper. She bent and picked up a charred fragment and peered at it closely.

'Sergeant, my eyes are not what they were. Can you make this out?'

Dodd came over and looked at the burnt paper—there were letters on it in Carey's handwriting but that was all he could see.

'Ah canna read it, but it's Sir Robert's hand right enough.'

'I thought so.' Lady Hunsdon glared at the fragment, then went to the chest in the corner where Carey kept some of his books and started sorting through them.

Dodd checked the desk and found a pile of books, including two bibles, poetry, a romance, and a prayerbook. He also found a cancelled pawn ticket which he quietly picked up and put in his beltpouch.

Lady Hunsdon sighed, closed the chest, and sat on it.

'I think Robin has managed to decode the two letters,' she said. 'But I don't understand why he burnt his translations yet kept the coded copies. Damn it. I shall have to ask him when he comes back from hawking this evening, although no doubt he will be very full of himself. Walsingham trained him well when he was in Scotland.'

Dodd was thinking about going out into the courtyard and filling his pipe since he hadn't had one today yet when he realised Lady Hunsdon was looking at him beadily again.

'I wonder what that big-headed sodomite has been up to all this time,' she said. 'Shakespeare says he's quite happy, writing a play and drinking our cellars dry. Would you go and see him, Sergeant?'

At least with Marlowe he could get a pipe of tobacco. Dodd stood up in something of an unseemly hurry and Lady Hunsdon followed him out of the room, bending to lock it with one of the keys she was wearing on her belt. When in her husband's house, it seemed, she was the lady of the house and no other. Emilia Bassano seemed to have moved permanently to the household of the Earl of Southampton which was tactful of her. Although it left unsettled a number of problems, including the question of who was the father of her unborn babe.

Dodd bowed to milady and then went to the back of the huge house, where the second floor guest chambers overlooked the courtyard. Sitting by the door to one of the lesser rooms was one of Hunsdon's servingmen who gave Dodd a cautious look and forebore to stand up.

'I've come tae speak tae Marlowe,' Dodd explained.

The servingman waved at the door. 'He's got it locked from the inside,' he said. 'My lord says he can go out any time he likes but I have to go with him. So far he hasn't.'

Dodd went to the door and knocked on it.

'Go away,' came a slurred voice.

He knocked again. Not loudly, he just kept knocking. There was an explosion of swearing and the sound of a chair being pushed back, then a bolt being shot. Marlowe's unshaven face looked round the door, eyes frighteningly bloodshot and a reek of tobacco and booze blending into a fog around him.

'Oh, it's you,' he said ungraciously. 'What do you want?'

'I want tae speak to ye, Mr. Marlowe,' said Dodd as politely as he could. 'Can we share a pipe o' tobacco?'

'No we can't because I've bloody run out and that boy hasn't come back yet.'

'Ah could go and buy ye some?'

Marlowe grunted.

'Or ye could come wi' me and...'

'Look,' said Marlowe through his stained teeth, 'I'm busy, understand? I'm writing a play that will never be performed and it's the best play I've ever written. I don't care what you want to talk to me about and I don't care what Sir Robert wants but if you'll fetch me a pouch of Nunez's New Spanish mix, I'll be grateful.'

Dodd shook his head regretfully at the insanity of writers, along with the servingman, and trotted off down the stairs. The gateman opened for him with a smile and he headed for Fleet Street where the tobacconist was in his shiny new shop with printed papers and ballads of the wildmen of New Spain. That was where you went if you wanted gold or silver, over the sea to the New World, everyone knew that. Not marshy Cornwall.

On impulse, once he had the tobacco he went into the pawnbroker's at the end of Fleet Bridge where an old skinny man in a skullcap and long foreign-looking robe sat reading a book back to front.

'Ah,' said Dodd, not sure how to start, 'are ye the master here?'

The foreigner unfolded himself and came to the counter where he smiled. 'Senhor Gomes,' he said with a bow and a strong sound of foreign in his voice. 'At your service, senhor.'

'Ay,' said Dodd, pulling out the cancelled ticket. 'D'ye ken...Ah, do you recall if Sir Robert Carey redeemed anything here today?'

Senhor Gomes took the ticket. He smiled at once. 'Ah, milord Robert, of course, senhor. He said you might enquire. He has repaid his loan on his court suit, the doublet with lilies and pearls upon velvet, and a cloak he had pawned before.'

'When did he do this?'

'Yesterday, very late. He woke me up to do it, he said it was very urgent.'

'Ay?' Dodd was puzzled. Why would Carey need his court clothes urgently to go hawking? In any case, he had left for Finsbury Fields wearing his hunting gear, the forest green and nut-brown doublet and hose that was now a little ill-fitting, or so he complained proudly. 'Did he pawn anything else?'

'No, Senhor. Forgive me, but can you tell me your wife's full name?'

'What?'

'Your wife? Her full name?'

Dodd's eyes narrowed and his neck prickled. Once again he caught the scent of deception and intrigue where nobody can be trusted simply by their face. And why on earth would Carey want his Court clothes? 'Janet Armstrong,' he said with a gulp.

Senhor Gomes reached under the counter and brought out a letter addressed to Sergeant Dodd and sealed with Carey's carved emerald ring—the Swan Rampant again. Dodd broke the seal, opened the letter and read a short note: 'Sergeant, I have decided to go to Court to discuss recent events with my liege Her Majesty the Queen. Please reassure my parents if necessary. Use my funds as you see fit to solve the problem. I will look forward to seeing you in Oxford or at Court if the Queen decides to move.' The letter was signed with Carey's full signature.

Pure rage practically lifted Dodd from the ground. He could feel his neck going purple and his teeth grinding. The bastard. The ill-begotten limp-cocked, selfish popinjay of a...

Senhor Gomes was backing away from the counter and quietly reaching down for a veney stick behind him. Dodd folded the paper, his fingers clumsy with the urge to throttle the man for betraying him and leaving him in the complicated, confusing pit of iniquity that was London. Unfortunately, Carey was not immediately available so he stuffed the letter in his belt-pouch. Then he stood for a full minute, fists quivering, breathing hard through his teeth until he had calmed down enough to talk and act like a normal man.

'Ay,' he said. 'Is that all?'

'Yes, senhor.'

Dodd walked out of the shop and stared up at the awning unseeingly. God damn it. God damn it to hell. On a thought he turned back. 'Er...Thank you, Senhor Gomes,' he said. The old foreigner was again reading his book back to front and raised his hand slightly in acknowledgement. Poor old man, not knowing which way round you read a book. Even Dodd knew that.

He hurried up the street, keeping a weather-eye out for attacks as always, and came to Somerset House without a single person claiming him as their cousin. It must have been true what Pickering had said, that he had ordered his people not to try anything with Dodd.

Marlowe opened his door a crack and reached for the pouch, but Dodd held it out of reach and scowled at him meaningfully. Marlowe scowled back, his hand dropping to where his sword would have been if he had been wearing it. Dodd dropped his hand to where his own sword actually was and showed his teeth in as pleasant a smile as he could muster. In the temper he was in, he was half-hoping that Marlowe would try something on with him so he could have the satisfaction of beating somebody up.

Marlowe cursed and opened the door so Dodd could come in. He almost fell over a tangled heap of shirts by the door and then had to wade through screwed up papers, bits of pen, drifts of hazelnut shells and mounds of apple cores, and several books lying on the rush mats face down. The bed looked as if a pack of bears had played there and the desk was piled high with paper and more pens. The place reeked of aqua vitae, beer, wine, and pipe smoke, and someone who has been cooped up indoors for too long. At least there were no old turds in the fireplace, although the jordan under the bed badly needed emptying.

Marlowe was standing by the flickering fire with his arms folded across his embroidered waistcoat. He had his doublet off, presumably lost somewhere in the junk on the floor—no, for a wonder it was hanging on a peg—and his shirtsleeves rolled up and stained with ink. There were bags under his red eyes big enough to hide a pig in and his voice was hoarse with smoking.

'Well?' he demanded. 'What's so important that you're bothering me with it?'

'Have ye been in here all this time?' asked Dodd, tucking the tobacco into his sleeve again.

From the contempt on Marlowe's face it was obvious he thought this was a very stupid question. 'Yes, of course I have. Where else would I be? I'm writing a play.'

'What's it about?'

'Edward II, a King of England who loved boys and was not ashamed to show it,' snapped Marlowe.

'Like the Scottish king?'

Something in Marlowe's face softened slightly. 'Perhaps.'

'Ay,' said Dodd. 'And what happened to him?'

'First his favourite and minion Piers Gaveston was murdered by his lords as happened in Scotland with the Duke of Albany. Then the King was murdered at the orders of the Earl of Mortimer. It is said, by a red-hot poker up the arse.'

'Ay,' said Dodd after a moment's assessment to see if the poet was joking. It seemed he wasn't. 'Verra...poetic.'

Marlowe frowned. 'It depends on your definition of poetic. Do you mean appropriate?'

Dodd coughed. He did, but wasn't going to admit it.

'That was done so there would be no mark on the body, you know.' Marlowe explained in a distant tone of voice. 'Since he was a king they wanted it to seem that he died of natural causes. However, his screams gave them away.'

He spoke in a disinterested way as if what he was describing was not quite enough to turn your stomach. He then took a sip from a cup of aqua vitae and Dodd realised that he was actually drunk. Not staggering drunk, nor fighting drunk, just thoroughly pickled. It surprised Dodd that anyone could write anything at all in that condition, but then Robert Greene had been able to scribble away when he was just minutes from death.

Marlowe sat down again at his desk, picked up his pen, and dipped it.

'Go away,' he said. 'I'm busy. Leave the tobacco on the mantelpiece.'

God, the man was rude. Dodd considered simply hitting him and seeing what happened. No, he had to talk first. 'I bought it because I wanted tae ask ye about a matter of spying as there's naebody else I can think of.'

'Why not ask Will?'

'Ah dinna think he'd tell me. If he knows.'

Marlowe grunted, dipped, and wrote. It was amazing how fast he did it as well, all the letters flowing out of the tip of his pen as if he didn't need to think about it at all and the pen not even catching a little, it was so well cut, just sliding smoothly across the paper. Incredible. Dodd enjoyed watching a craftsman at his trade. He noticed that Marlowe didn't hold the pen the way he did, in a clenched fist that soon became dank with sweat, but lightly, as if it were a woodcarver's awl.

'There's code I need to work out. Ah need tae find out how to break a code? How do you work it out?'

Marlowe grunted again.

'Well?'

'Well what? Are you still there?' He was counting something under his breath. 'Why don't you go away?'

Dodd reached for patience. 'Ah wis askin ye...'

'About codes. Why should I care? I only worked for Heneage because he has been known to pay well for it and I don't want to go on working for him which is why I'm here, as well as the fact that this is the first time I've had the peace and quiet to write my play since I drank the money the Burbages paid me for it...'

Dodd sighed. Why did Marlowe always have to be difficult? The man was as spiky and arrogant as if he had his own tower and a large family.

'Is this your play?' Dodd asked idly, putting a finger on the pile of paper in front of Marlowe.

'Yes it is and you can leave it alone...'

Dodd picked up the pile of papers and wandered over to the fire with it. He crumpled up the first page and fed it into the flames, which made Marlowe jump from his stool with a yelp of horror.

'What the hell...?'

'Ah wanted yer attention, Mr. Marlowe,' said Dodd, judiciously feeding the next page into the flames. 'Have I got it?'

'You can't burn my play...I...'

'Ah can,' said Dodd, puzzled at this irrationality, 'And Ah am.' Another curled into red and yellow and fell to ash.

'I'll kill you.'

'Nay, I dinna think so,' said Dodd, smiling with genuine enjoyment at the humour of this idea. 'Besides, there's nae need. All I wantae know is how ye work out a code.'

'What code?' Marlowe was staring at the pile of papers in Dodd's hand, particularly the fourth page which he already had near the fire. He knew enough not to dump the whole lot onto the flames at once because that would put them out. In any case, this method worked better.

'A code made of numbers. Ah ken that Carey worked it out and I wantae know what he found but I've nae experience of spying.' Dodd shook his head. 'It's verra annoying.'

Marlowe was actually trembling, although whether it was with fear or anger only time would tell. 'And how the hell do you think I would know? Is it one of Heneage's codes?'

'Ah dinna ken, one paper wis in his office when we searched it, the other was…ah…in another place.' Dodd stopped himself just in time. He didn't think Marlowe ought to learn anything he didn't already know about Richard Tregian and the mysterious Father Jackson.

'And do you know what kind of code it is?'

'Sir Robert said it might be one that used a pattern to change letters to numbers or that changed them at hazard and he'd need a codebook. There's been nae codebook found so he must have worked it out but I dinna ken what pattern it could have been and I havenae the time to puzzle ma heid over it.' Dodd grunted with sour humour. 'Nor the talent forebye. Ah'm no' a clerk, me.'

Marlowe's eyes were narrowed. 'There are other kinds of code. I doubt Carey could puzzle out either kind of numerical cypher by himself either. If he managed to work it out that means it must be tolerably obvious and simple because the man isn't nearly as clever as he thinks he is.'

'Nor are ye, Mr. Marlowe,' said Dodd pointedly, moving the pile of paper in his hands.

Marlowe paused and then added grudgingly, 'There's a simpler kind of code which is where you use a very common well-known book as the key and refer to particular words by page number, line, and word number in a sentence. Then all you need to do is tell your correspondents which book it is and they can do the rest. The system has the benefit that you can use different codings for common words like 'and' and 'but' which makes it harder to crack.

You also don't have a written key lying around which always looks suspicious. In some ways it's very secure, but simple to work out if you can guess the book being used.'

Dodd thought about this. That made sense. 'How d'ye find out what book it was?'

'Usually there's a symbol or name in another code which sets it out.'

'Could that be an upside down A?'

Marlowe shrugged. 'Could be, yes. You have to use that, then get the correct book, decode some of what's written, and see if it makes any sense at all. Generally you use a book that has been commonly printed but isn't obvious. For instance, nobody uses the Bible because it's too obvious. Why don't you ask Carey when he comes home from his hawking?'

Dodd wasn't about to answer that question. 'Ah wantae surprise him.'

'I'm sure you will. Now can I have my play back?'

Dodd showed his teeth. He would probably never get a better opportunity to find out what Marlowe had been up to. 'Not sae fast, Mr. Marlowe.' It was interesting to watch him: he folded his arms, his eyes half-closed and he leaned back slightly.

'If this is to be an inquisition, Sergeant, would you object if I got myself a cup of aqua vitae to wet my whistle?'

A rare smile lit Dodd's face. 'Well now,' he said, 'On the one hand I *would* object, for a cup of aqua vitae's a fine thing to throw in a man's face when ye're about tae try and stab him and I'll thank ye to take yer hand fra yer eating knife, Mr. Marlowe.'

Marlowe scowled and uncrossed his arms.

'There again,' Dodd continued thoughtfully, 'On the ither hand, Ah wouldnae object for I'm in a bad enough temper that Ah'd be fair grateful to ye if ye gave me the excuse to give ye the beatin' of yer life.'

Marlowe looked sour. 'What is it you want to know, Sergeant?'

'Ah wantae know what the hell ye've been up tae these past few weeks, Mr. Marlowe,' said Dodd, 'I know Sir Robert thinks he's got it worked out but fer me, it's a' a mystery.'

Marlowe said nothing. To encourage him, Dodd put another

sheet, taken at random from the middle of the pile, into the fire. The poet winced.

'I'll tell you what I can,' he said sulkily, 'If I know myself.'

'All I wantae know whit were ye thinkin' of, setting a pack of roaring boys on us the ither night? Eh? And then bringin' in Topcliffe tae ambush us all? Ah take that as unfriendly, Mr. Marlowe, I surely do.'

Marlowe was squinting slightly and Dodd realised he was talking too northern again. But before Dodd could try and repeat it more southern, Marlowe began to speak.

'Heneage was furious when you raided his house. He got the word from the clerk of the lists when he went to see how another case of his was progressing and instead of going to his house in Chelsea, he called upon me instead. He blamed me for...for arresting you instead of Sir Robert and for destroying his fine plan against my lord Hunsdon. He reckoned the whole mess was my fault and threatened me with a treason trial and Topcliffe, everything.'

'Speakin' of which, why *did* ye arrange for me to be arrested?'

Marlowe shrugged. 'It's not important, I made a mistake. I thought Carey and you would have changed clothes when I sent the men in to take you.'

'Did ye tell Heneage this?'

'I did. He didn't believe me. He said I was working with Carey and accused me of betraying him.'

'Ay?'

'He offered me the chance to redeem myself if both of you ended up either in the Fleet or dead. I warned him that if he killed Sir Robert, Lord Hunsdon would cease to be a Knight of the Carpet and become again what he was when he defeated Dacre in the Rebellion of the Northern Earls. And that his lady would be even more dangerous. We had an argument about it. At last he said I had to work with Topcliffe, who was with him, as it happened.'

'Ay?'

'So Topcliffe and I laid a plan. I hired some roaring boys in Smithfield that I had used before, to lie in wait for you in Fleet Street that night in case you didn't come to the Mermaid. I told them you were not to be killed and if they were asked who had paid them, to make a show of resisting and then give my name. I thought that might bring Sir Robert into the Mermaid where Topcliffe could take him.'

Dodd grunted. So he hadn't needed to get his sleeves wet half-drowning the man, he could have just asked him. That was annoying.

'Meanwhile Topcliffe went to gather his men and waited with them at another boozing ken near the Mermaid. I sent for him as soon as you arrived but he wasn't there—he had been called to the Tower on another matter. You had left by the time he came back and he was threatening me with the rack though it was all his fault. So when the boy told me there was a gentleman in the back yard asking questions, I near as damn it praised the Lord for it. Topcliffe sent for all his men and we took Carey easily enough, playing drunk, but you weren't with him and that worried us. We were right. Once Topcliffe had gone chasing after you into the night, Carey said something to me which...well, which made me reconsider. I wanted sanctuary, that was all. So...I helped him by knocking out one of the guards Topcliffe left behind and Carey dealt with the other one. Then you turned up and you know the rest.'

Dodd nodded. Most of this fitted quite well. He would have to think it through very carefully before he trusted it, but just for the moment he would accept it.

Marlowe had crossed his arms again. 'So, Sergeant? Are you satisfied?'

'Mebbe,' Dodd allowed. 'It isnae an obvious lie.'

Marlowe gritted his teeth, obviously working hard to be civil. 'Will you give me my play back now?'

Dodd put his head on one side, assessing Marlowe's temper. He remembered that the man had actually been arraigned for murder once, but got away with it on grounds of self-defence and probably Walsingham's pull and good lordship on behalf of his pursuivant.

'Nay sir, Ah've too much respect for ye. I'll take it wi' me, and leave it by the door when I'm done.'

'But...'

Another page edged closer to the flames and Marlowe withdrew again, took his hand off his dagger hilt. Dodd tilted his head at the part of the room on the other side of the bed. 'Ah want ye to stand ower behind the bed where I can see ye.'

Marlowe went there with ill-grace.

'Ay, now lie on the floor wi' yer legs in the air against the wall where I can see them.'

'What?'

'Ye heard me, Mr. Marlowe.' Dodd screwed up some pages at random from the pile and put them in the flames where they flared and the iron salts in the ink which thickly coated the paper turned the flames red. As always there was a feeling of relief to see something burn when he was angry. Marlowe made a choking sound in his throat. He lay down slowly, and put his legs up against the wall. Dodd thought of pinning him down with the clothes chest but then decided it was too much trouble.

He put the wad of paper under his arm, grabbed a handful of tobacco out of the packet he had brought and tucked it in his own pouch, then went very quietly to the door, opened it and slid into the passage. There he left Marlowe's precious play about boy-lovers, as he'd promised, although the play had made a good hostage and he didn't think he'd ever get any co-operation again from Marlowe. And it wasn't as if anybody would ever actually want to watch the thing in a playhouse. Not even London could be that full of buggers.

Dodd walked back to Carey's chambers—Carey had a bedroom and a parlour as well, which was twice the size of the little hut where Dodd had come to manhood after the Elliots burnt them out. Ridiculous—what would anyone want with all that echoing space? He tried to go in, but then stopped. Damn it. Lady Hunsdon had locked the door.

A low groan came from his lips. But Carey had clearly wanted him to solve the conundrum of the man who wasn't a priest being executed, and the man who was, dying in the Thames. Therefore... Dodd felt along the top of the doorframe and along the edge of the panelling by the tiled floor. There was a chest with a silver candlestick on it which caught Dodd's eye, so he went and picked it up and found a key tucked up in the base. He snorted, took the key, put the candlestick down, opened Carey's chamber door, went in and locked the door behind him.

He sat down and stared at the papers with the upside down

As at the top, looked at the books. None of them began with the letter A, nor were they about anyone whose name began with A, nor were they by men whose names began with A. Yet Carey had worked the thing out and as Marlowe had said, he wasn't that clever, bloody sprig of a courtier that he was. Nor did he have magical powers, God damn him, unless you counted overweaning self-confidence and the luck of the devil.

Dodd wandered around the room again, looked in the chest, and nodded. Carey had taken his dags with him, somehow, and his sword. He must have sent someone to meet him in Finsbury Fields with a remount and packpony.

A thought occurred to Dodd. He carefully locked up behind him, went back to his own chamber, found the wickerwork box stuffed with hay in which was Janet Armstrong's highly valuable new green velvet hat, and picked it up. Another thought occurred as he saw his old homespun doublet and hose hanging on a hook at the back of the door. Time to do something about them, so he took out some of the hay and stuffed the clothes and his old hemp shirt and a few other things into the box. Then he wandered down to the kitchens off the back courtyard where he had a quiet word with the undercook and appropriated a bag of sacking that had contained pot-herbs. This he shook out carefully and wrapped around the package with string, wrote a label addressing it to Mr. Alexander Dodd, the Guardroom, Carlisle Castle in his best handwriting. He thought a moment and added a note to say that he, Sergeant Dodd, would pay back the man that paid the carriage on it.

Then with a bellyful of good brown bread, cheese, and pickled cabbage, and a quart of remarkably good ale that he had cadged as well, Dodd went out the gate of Somerset House and carried the whole surprisingly heavy thing all the way to the Belle Sauvage Inn on Ludgate. It took him half an hour to find a carter who was heading for York and knew another one that made the round as far north as Carlisle, carrying supplies for the Castle. He paid an eyewatering amount for a deposit to the carter, plus more for the man who would take it on from York, and hoped that his brother Sandy would be kind enough to stump up the money if it got to Carlisle. He could imagine the stir when the thing arrived, especially if his men were nosy enough to open it, and was quite cheered up by the thought of their mystification.

He walked back a little quicker and went down an alleyway into the dens of lawyers that clustered around the Inns of Court, found Enys's chamber, and knocked on the door.

Enys put his head out immediately. 'One minute,' he said. Dodd heard his voice murmuring and then another higher pitched voice— it seemed he was urging his sister to greet Sergeant Dodd but she adamantly refused.

Then Enys was on the landing, hat on his head and his too-heavy sword at his side.

'Where will we get a new sword?' Enys asked as he locked the door.

'We'll go to an armourer's I saw near Cheapside,' said Dodd. 'Sir Robert said they made good weapons there.'

In fact Carey had been trying to persuade Dodd to buy a gimcrack unchancy foreign-style rapier with a curly handguard and a velvet scabbard to replace his friendly, balanced, and extremely sharp broadsword that had been made for him by the Dodd surname's own blacksmith and fitted his body like a glove. Dodd had sniffed at all Carey's reasons why rapiers were the coming thing and then smashed the entire argument to bits by enquiring why, if rapiers were so wonderful, Carey was now bearing a broadsword himself.

'You know my rapier broke last summer when I hit that Elliot who was wearing a jack...' Carey had said incautiously.

'Ay,' said Dodd, feeling his point had been made for him. Carey grinned and started campaigning for Dodd to buy a twenty-inch duelling poinard instead until Dodd had lost his temper and asked if Carey was working on commission for the armourer.

Enys nodded and trotted down the stairs and out into the sunlight. The year was tilting into winter right enough, with the orchards full of fruit and nuts and the hedges and gardens full of birds stealing the fruit, and angry wasps.

They walked up Ludgate, past St Paul's, and Dodd found the armourer's shop he wanted. It was not at all showy and didn't have parts of tournament armour and wonderfully elaborate foreign pig-stickers hanging outside in advertisement of the weaponsmith's abilities. On the other hand, his barred windows were of glass and the swords hanging there seemed nicely balanced.

They went in, Enys hesitating on the threshold and looking around in wonder.

'Ay,' said Dodd, 'it's odd not to have yer sword made for ye, but...' He shrugged.

The armourer remembered Dodd as having come with Carey since he was wearing the same unnaturally smart woollen doublet. Soon there were several swords laid out on the counter with the armourer excitedly pointing out the beauty of the prettier sword. Dodd picked up one of the others, with a plain hilt, a grip of sharkskin and curled quillions. He felt the weight, drew it, sighted along the blade, flexed the blade, sniffed it, balanced it on his finger, then handed it to Enys who nearly dropped it.

Enys swung it a few times experimentally while Dodd and the armourer retreated behind a display post with breastplates mounted on it. Enys smiled.

'That's much better, much easier.'

'Ay,' sniffed Dodd, 'I thocht so, Mr. Enys. The one ye've got is a couple of pounds heavier.'

He turned to the armourer and asked if he would do a part-exchange while Enys eagerly fumbled his sword belt off and handed it over for inspection. The armourer frowned when he saw it, looked hard at Enys, then shook his head.

'You're right, sir,' he said, 'this is the wrong sword for you. May I ask where you got it?'

'It's mine. My brother gave it to me.'

'Ah. I see, sir. And I expect your brother is a couple of inches taller and wider-shouldered? Well, I can certainly make a part-exchange. Shall we allow an angel for the old sword and thus I will require fifteen shillings.'

Dodd thought that was very reasonable for a ready-made sword and so Enys handed over the greater part of what Hunsdon had paid him for his court work to date, buckled on the new weapon, and went to admire his fractured reflection in the window glass.

'Sir, I should tell you that I've seen this sword before,' said the armourer quietly to Dodd. 'Seeing as you're Sir Robert's man.'

'Ay?' said Dodd.

'I sold it to a man who called himself James Enys but who was not that man.'

Dodd found his eyebrows lifting. 'Ay?' he said, rubbing his lower lip.

'Taller, broader-shouldered, something similar in the face and just as badly marked with smallpox.'

'Hm.'

'Also, he was wearing the exact same suit. But it wasn't him, sir, I'd stake my life on it.'

Dodd quietly handed over sixpence, ignoring the small voice at the back of his head that protested at this outrage. 'Thank ye, Mr. Armourer,' he said, quite lordly-fashion, 'That's verra interesting.'

He went out into the sunny street where Enys was waiting for him and gave the lawyer a considering stare.

'Now where shall we practise?' asked Enys. 'Will you teach me to disarm people?'

'Ah'm no' gonnae teach ye nothing special,' said Dodd with a shudder. 'Just the basics.'

On a thought he went back into the shop and came back out with two veney sticks the armourer had sold for a shilling—he liked them because they had hilts and grips like swords but were still sticks. They made adequate clubs, but were best for sword practise with someone who was unchancy and ignorant.

As they made their way to Smithfield, Dodd was thinking hard. There had always been something not quite right about Enys and it seemed Shakespeare had found it out. Perhaps Enys had killed his brother and taken his place and then pretended to look for him afterwards? Perhaps Enys's brother was still in the Thames as the priest had been?

Or perhaps he was playing cards at Pickering's? The man Dodd had thought was Enys—what was his name, Vent?—fitted the armourer's description exactly. And what about the sister? Where was she? He'd heard her voice but…Why had Enys locked the door of his chambers when his sister was within? Was she his prisoner?

Eyes narrowing, Dodd led the way to a corner of the Smithfield market that was not already occupied by large men loudly practising their sword skills, generally sword-and-buckler work which was the most popular fighting-style. Some of them watched him cautiously out of the corners of their eyes. In another corner were better-dressed men doing what looked like an elaborate dance composed of circles and triangles and waving long thin rapiers. Foreigners, no doubt, doing mad foreign things.

Dodd gave Enys one of the veney sticks and decided to see if the man was faking his cack-handedness. He took him through the en garde position for a sword with no shield or buckler, with his right leg and right arm forward as defence, and showed him the various positions. They went through a slow and careful veney using the main attacks and defences that Dodd's father had first taught him when he was eight. Dodd's face drew down longer and sour at that thought.

Once Enys had corrected his feeble grip and got out of the habit of putting his left hand on the hilt for the cross-stroke, as if he were wielding an old-fashioned bastard sword, Dodd bowed to him, saluted, and attacked.

Enys struggled to do what he'd been shown but that was not in fact the problem. He defended slightly better now, but even when Dodd spread his hands, lowered his veney stick and stood there completely unguarded, Enys still did not attack. Dodd scowled at him ferociously.

'Och?' he said, 'whit's wrong wi' ye, ye puir wee catamite of a mannikin? Want yer mother? She's no'here, she's down the road lookin' for trade.'

Enys stopped and blinked at him with his veney stick trailing in the mud. Dodd, who had never seen anything so ridiculous in his life, lifted his own veney stick and hit Enys hard across the chest with it. Enys yelped, staggered back clutching the place, and nearly dropped his stick.

'It's ay hopeless,' said Dodd disgustedly. 'If ye willnae attack me when I'm open nor when I strike ye...'

For a moment he thought there were tears in Enys's eyes, but then at last the man made a kind of low moaning growl and came into the attack properly. Dodd actually had to parry a couple of times and even dodge sideways away from a very good strike to his head.

There was a flurry when Enys came charging in close trying for a knee in Dodd's groin and Dodd trapped his arm, shifted his weight, and dropped the man on his back on the hard-trampled ground in a Cumbrian wrestling throw he hadn't used for ten years because everyone in Carlisle knew it too well. Enys was still struggling, mouth clamped, face white, so Dodd twisted his arm until he yelped again.

'Will ye bide still so I dinna have to hurt ye?' shouted Dodd in his ear, and Enys gradually stopped. He was heaving for breath and even Dodd was a little breathless, which annoyed him. 'Now then. That was a lot better. Ye had some nice blows in there and ye came at me wi' yer knee when ye couldnae touch me wi' yer weapon, that's a good thing to see. Ah like a man that isnae hampered by foolish notions.'

'What?' Enys was still gasping.

'Ye'll need tae watch yer temper,' added Dodd, helping the man up and dusting him down. 'Ye cannae lose it just because ye got thumped on the chest.'

'You deliberately made me lose my temper?'

'Ay. Ah cannae teach nothing to a man that willnae attack and if ye've the bollocks to attack when Ah touch ye up, then there's something to work wi'? Ye follow?'

Dodd was aware that Enys's eyes were squinting slightly as he tried to follow this and so Dodd said it again, less Cumbrian. He was getting better at that, he thought. Enys laughed shortly.

'So should I get angry or not?' he asked, still rubbing the bruise on his chest. 'Lose my temper or not?'

Dodd shrugged and took the en garde position again. 'It depends. If ye cannae kill wi'out losing yer temper, then lose it. But if ye can get angry and stay cold enough to think—that's the best for a fighting man. Not that ye're a fighting man, ye're a lawyer, but still...There's nae harm in being able to kill if ye need to.'

Enys nodded, and guarded himself. Dodd attacked again. He was still as careful as he could be and pulled most of his blows, but Enys was at least taking a shot at him every so often, even if he generally missed or was stopped. He lost his stick half a dozen times before he learnt not to get into a lock against the hilt since he wasn't strong enough for it. And on one glorious occasion, he caught Dodd on the hip with a nice combination of feint and thrust. Dodd put his hand up at the hit and grinned.

'Ay,' he said, 'that's it. Well done.'

Dodd decided to stop when he saw that Enys was alarmingly red in the face and puffing for breath again, even though they had only been practising for an hour or two. Dodd had taken his doublet off and was in his shirtsleeves, but Enys seemed too shy to do it.

He seemed relieved when Dodd lifted his stick in salute. 'Ah'm for a quart of ale,' he said. 'Will ye bear me company, Mr. Enys?'

'God, yes.'

Over two quarts of ale at the Cock Inn, hard by the Smithfield stock market so rank with the smell of livestock, and a very fine fish pie and pickles, Dodd lifted his tankard to Enys with an approving nod.

'Ye're a lot better than ye were,' he said, 'though I'd not fight any duels yet.'

Enys smiled and flushed. 'I never thought I could be able to fight.'

'But did ye no' fight any battles wi' yer friends when ye were breeched and got yer ain dagger?' Dodd asked with curiosity. He remembered with clarity the great day when he had been given his first pair of breeches made for him by his mother and his dad strapped his very own dagger round his waist. He must have been about six or seven and very relieved to get away from baby's petticoats and being bullied into playing house all the time with his sisters' friends. After that he spent most of his time play-fighting with his brothers, cousins, and friends when he wasn't having to go to the Reverend for schooling. Within months he had lost a front tooth in a fistfight over football and got a birching from Reverend Gilpin and several thick ears from other outraged adults for damaging things by carving them with his dagger. He still liked to whittle when he could.

Enys looked down modestly. 'I was a sickly child,' he said. 'I don't think I did.'

The ale tasted wonderful when you were so dry, Dodd finished his quart in one and called for more. He shook his head. 'Well, if ye keep on wi' it and hire yerself a good swordmaster, there's nae reason ye couldna fight yer corner if need be.'

'It's interesting,' said Enys after he'd found a bone in a large lump of herring from the pie. 'The manner of thinking for a fight that you explained to me is very similar to that needed for a courtroom—being angry without losing your temper, so you can think. Only in the case of a courtroom, of course, the weapons are words.'

'Ay?' Dodd thought Carey had said something similar about legal battles. 'Surely ye need to be verra patient as well.'

'That too,' Enys agreed, 'and also well-organised and thorough. But there is very little to equal the joy of disputing with a fellow lawyer and beating him to win the point. I used to greatly enjoy mooting at Gray's Inn.'

'Ah.' The second quart was going down a treat and all Dodd's worries about what would happen that evening started to fade away. Not his fury with Carey, though. That still nested in his gut. He could find out what mooting was later. 'A man I met the day said I should give ye his compliments—he had very much the look of ye and I thocht he was ye at first, but his voice is deeper, and he's taller and broader as well.' Enys had stopped chewing and was staring at Dodd. 'Could it be yer brother that ye thought Heneage had taken?'

Enys swallowed the piece of pie whole and nodded vigorously. 'Yes sir, it could indeed. May I ask where you met him?'

'He denied his name was Enys, said it was Vent, James Vent.'

Enys smiled at that. 'Even so. Where was he?'

'He were at Pickering's game, playing cards and losing.'

Enys banged his tankard down. 'Almost certainly it was my brother,' he said. 'I never met a man who was worse at cards nor more addicted to playing.'

Dodd nodded. 'Would ye like to meet him? Ah ken where Pickering's game is at the moment and Vent said he'd welcome a meeting wi' the man that wis insulting him by impersonating him to be a lawyer.'

To Dodd's surprise Enys laughed. 'That's my brother. Yes, I would. Thank God he's not dead. I had given him up and thought he was surely at the bottom of the Thames like poor Jackson whose corpse you showed me.'

'Ay.'

'How much had he lost and was he playing for notes of debt?'

'Nay, Pickering willnae allow it, he was playing for good coin and a lot of it.'

'Oh,' Enys frowned. 'How unusual for my brother.'

He looked thoughtful and pushed away the remains of his pie so Dodd polished it off and washed it down with the rest of his ale. He checked the sky for the time.

'It's too early for Pickering's game to start. I wantae go back to Somerset House now to...ah...do something. I can meet ye at sunset by Temple steps and we'll take a boat?'

Enys put down the money for his part of the bill and Dodd put down his. They went companionably enough out of the alehouse and headed across London. Enys went down one of the little alleys off Fleet Street to his chambers whilst Dodd ambled along Fleet Street to the Strand, thinking hard about the damnable book code that Carey must have broken the night before. It was the only thing that explained his actions today. And Dodd didn't have much time to solve the thing either. He had to be out of Somerset House before the trouble started.

What had Marlowe said? A commonly printed book but not predictable, therefore not the Bible. Obviously to make a code from it, you had to have it to hand...Now what was the book that Richard Tregian had had on the shelf where Dodd found the paper? Something quite common, as Dodd recalled, but a little surprising. What the hell had it been? He couldn't quite remember it.

Not realising he was scowling so fiercely that people were taking a wide path around him as he walked down through the crowds on Fleet Street, Dodd stopped and stared unseeingly at an inn sign for the Fox & Hounds, a few doors up from the Cock Tavern where he and Carey usually went out of habit. He'd looked at the book, recognised it, and dismissed it as uninteresting. Damn it to hell. It had been...

The inn sign was particularly badly painted, mainly out of over-ambition on the part of the sign painter, with the fox running as it were towards the sign and the hounds in the distance behind him, so it looked as if his head made the shape of a capital letter A upside down...

The backs of Dodd's legs actually went cold as he realised what the answer was. He blinked up at the inn sign which may have inspired the original code and almost certainly had inspired Carey to guess what it was. He cursed under his breath. Next thing he had loped along Fleet Street, past Temple Bar, knocking the beggars flying, along the Strand, and in at the gate of Somerset House which was quiet that afternoon. He went up the stairs two at a time to Carey's chambers and sat himself down sweating and puffing slightly at Carey's desk where he pulled Foxe's Book of Martyrs towards himself and set to the first coded letter.

It took him a long time and at the end of the hard labour he realised he actually had one and a half letters: one was from Fr. Jackson to somebody he addressed as 'your honour' explaining that the trap was ready to be sprung as most of the lands were now held by the one called Icarus. The other was from Richard Tregian and also addressed to somebody he called 'your honour' explaining that he had found out why certain lands were being sold for inflated prices as full of gold ore and good sites for gold mines. He was horrified and alarmed at it and was about to...The letter was unfinished.

Dodd leaned back and stretched his aching ink-splattered fingers. He stared into space for five minutes and then gathered up his translations and the original letters, folded them all and put them in his belt-pouch along with Carey's infuriating message. Hearing the cacophony of hounds and horses returning to the courtyard by the main gate, he stood up quickly and ran down the passageway to his own chamber where he collected his cloak and his new beaver hat that Carey had bought him a week before as a celebration of Carey's deliverance from his creditors.

He clattered down the back stairs and into the kitchen where he quietly grabbed half a loaf of bread and a large lump of cheese, then put them back because he had nowhere to stowe them since he wasn't on a horse and wasn't wearing a loose comfy doublet.

In the rear courtyard that led to the kitchen garden, the cobbles were covered in hunting dogs, very happy to be home and already gathering around their dog boy, tails wagging, tongues hanging, waiting to be fed.

'Sergeant Dodd, have you heard...' sang out the dog boy excitedly, but Dodd just waved a hand at him, slipped through the gate into the main garden, and headed down for the orchard and the boatlanding.

All the way there he was quietly praying there would be a boat waiting for him. There wasn't, of course. Still, Temple steps wasn't very far away, so Dodd climbed from the boat landing to the narrow strip of land between the orchard wall and the Strand itself, then eased himself along until he came to a fence which he climbed over, followed along until he came to the other fence, climbed over that, and continued through a narrow alley that led to a secret set of steps hidden by a curve in the river. That wasn't the one so he struggled along the top of a sea wall and then to another alley that passed through a shanty town full of hungry looking children in nothing but their shirts and dogs scuffing hopefully through the mud.

Finally he was at Temple steps, his ears itching in anticipation of the hue and cry that would be made for him once Lord and Lady Hunsdon realised who was missing. Enys was standing there, wrapped in cloak and hat, his expression a strange combination of hope and fear.

'Ay,' said Dodd, not explaining why he was arriving by climbing out of a tiny handkerchief of herb garden, guarded by a ginger tomcat.

Enys raised his arm and yelled 'Oars!' A Thames boat arrived quickly, the boatman looking very hopeful—ah yes, of course, the taste of students at the Inns for the fleshpots and dissipations of the South bank.

'Three Cranes in the Vintry,' Dodd ordered, practically vaulting aboard. As usual Enys dithered over stepping in and nearly fell in the Thames again before he sat down.

'Are you sure, sir?' said the boatman. 'I heard there's a good game at Paris Garden tonight...'

'Ye heard what Ah said,' snarled Dodd. The boatman shrugged and started rowing the hard way.

They came up against the wharf which was quiet and Dodd paid the man and jumped out. Jesu he was getting as high-handed with his cash as Carey was—mind, it wasn't his cash, it was Carey's. That gave him a warm cosy feeling in the place where the rage was still packed tight.

As before there were a few well-dressed exquisites and one or two prosperous merchants hanging around not doing very much, including the boy in the tangerine paned hose and cramoisie doublet, a walking headache everywhere he went.

Mr. Briscoe was on the door as before, looking haggard with bags under his eyes. He touched his hat sadly to Dodd before stepping forward to stop Enys.

'Do I know you, sir?' he asked very politely.

'Ah, Sir Robert asked me tae bring him to meet Mr. Pickering.' Dodd tried. Briscoe hesitated. 'It's Mr. Enys, my lord Baron Hunsdon's lawyer. He wis at the inquest, ye recall?'

Briscoe allowed them past and they climbed the steps to the gambling chamber with its banks of candles and white mats. Enys seemed quite open-mouthed at the women standing about there, with their strangely cut stays that cupped their white breasts but left them bare so the nipples were visible peeking over the lacy edge of their shifts like naughty eyes, prinking and pinking in the draught from the door.

Dodd dragged his eyes away and swallowed hard. It seemed his kidneys were recovering. Then he stopped one of the comely boys running past with trays of booze, and asked if Mr. Vent was there.

'No sir,' said the boy. 'Shall I tell Mr. Pickering you're here? He has some information for you.'

'Ay.'

Dodd took two cups from the tray as the boy turned to go and gave one to Enys who was bright red again. Dodd knew how he felt. All those round plump tits just begging to be cupped and fondled and licked...

He took a large gulp of brandywine and tried to look at something less entrancing. But the walls were hung with the cloths painted with completely naked people doing lewd things with swans and bulls and such. It was impossible to concentrate, which no doubt was half the intention.

'Mr. Pickering will see you gents now,' said the boy at his elbow, so he tapped Enys on the shoulder and followed the boy into the back room where Pickering sat by the fire with a large plump man in a dark brocade doublet and snowy white starched falling band.

Pickering smiled as they came in and Dodd made his bow to include both of them, reckoning that a bit of respect to a headman on his own ground never did any harm and might do some good. Enys sensibly bowed too, rather more gracefully.

'Welcome back, Sergeant Dodd,' said Pickering. 'Sir Horatio was 'oping to meet Sir Robert. Is 'e here?'

'Ah. No,' said Dodd, hoping he wouldn't have to explain further.

'Is 'e on 'is way?'

'Ah. No,' said Dodd.

Pickering frowned and so did Sir Horatio. 'I'm sorry to hear that. I hope I haven't offended him in...'

'Nay sir, nothing like that. He...ah...he found he had urgent business at court.'

The plump man stood up and turned out to be as tall as Carey. He held out a hand to Dodd who shook it.

'Sergeant,' he said in a smooth, deep, slightly foreign sounding voice, 'I was hoping to discuss the question of the Cornish lands with your Captain, Sir Robert. I am Sir Horatio Palavicino, Her most gracious Majesty's advisor on matters financial and fiduciary.'

Dodd wasn't quite sure what that meant.

''e's the Queen's banker, Sergeant,' said Pickering, spotting Dodd's confusion. 'He sorts out the Queen's money.'

Dodd's mouth went dry. 'Ah,' he said. Oh God, had the Queen bought some of the worthless Cornish lands? Was it too late to steal a horse and head north?

Yes it was. Much too late.

'Sit down, Sergeant, and you, Mr. Enys.'

They sat on stools noticeably lower than the chairs seating Pickering and Sir Horatio. Sir Horatio smiled genially.

'I assume that Sir Robert has gone to Court to apprise the Queen of what he knows?' Dodd was relieved to be asked something he could answer with confidence.

'Ay sir,' he said, 'he couldnae do it safely by letter so he went tae speak to the Queen hisself.'

Sir Horatio smiled and nodded. 'As ever,' he said, 'Sir Robert is precipitate but correct.'

From flushing an unbecoming shade of red as a result of the ladies outside, Enys had now gone an equally ugly pale yellow.

'Sirs,' he said, leaning forward, 'excuse my interruption, but is it true that the Queen does not know of this...ah...this land fraud?'

Sir Horatio sighed. 'As far as I know, she does not.'

'Ay she does now,' said Dodd with confidence, 'Sir Robert will have left this morning when he gave the huntsmen and falconers the slip and it's ainly forty miles. He'll be at court for sure by now.'

'It may take him some time to gain audience with Her Majesty,' said Sir Horatio. 'But yes, correctly put. She *did* not know, Mr. Enys.'

'Ah hope she hasnae bought none?' Dodd asked, voicing his main worry.

Sir Horatio laughed kindly. 'Why would she need to,' he asked, 'since if there were gold there, she would own it in any case through Crown prerogative?'

Dodd nodded. 'Ay,' he said. 'That's a relief.'

Sir Horatio seemed highly amused by this. 'Indeed it is.'

'But...sir...' Enys was frowning with puzzlement, 'I drafted many of the bills of sales and the deeds of transfer and I told Mr. Vice Chancellor Heneage that I thought the thing was not what it seemed. I told him that I knew many of the places had been assayed for tin many times and found to be barren of all metals including gold. It was why he dismissed me as his lawyer and then took steps to destroy my practice because he would not have what he called the falsity told abroad. But I assumed he had told Her Majesty at least.'

There was a silence at this. Mr. Pickering seemed the least surprised at it, and in fact had a cynical smile. Sir Horatio turned and stared at Enys with an expression of mixed anger and calculation while Dodd groaned softly under his breath.

'When did you tell him this, Mr. Enys?'

'Months ago. He was very angry. I think because he had bought some.'

'Hm. He was not the only one,' said Sir Horatio. 'Mr. Enys, I understand that you were in contact with the assayer, a Mr. Jackson.'

Enys lifted his head. 'No sir,' he said, 'that was not me, that was my brother whom I came here to find. And it was Father Jackson SJ.'

'Society of Jesus.'

Enys nodded.

'The man that was hanged, drawn, and quartered by Mr. Hughes?' said Pickering with a puzzled frown.

'Nay sir, that wasnae him. It was one Richard Tregian.' Dodd corrected him. 'Mr. Topcliffe substituted him for the Cornish gentleman.'

Palavicino was leaning forward, his face full of bewilderment. 'Substituted him?'

'Ay sir, and Fr. Jackson seemingly ended up in the Thames wi' a knife in his back but we dinna ken how or why.'

Enys drew a deep breath. 'Sir, my brother has been calling himself James Vent. Do you know where he is? Sergeant Dodd said he thought he had seen him here?'

'Vent?' Pickering's glittering little eyes had gone hard. 'He was here but he ran out of money. Said he was going to the Netherlands again to make his fortune and headed for a ship he knew of in the Pool of London.'

'Do you know which ship, sir?'

'The *Judith of Penryn*,'

The name didn't seem to mean much to Enys but Dodd recognised it. Och God, he had to get back to Somerset House after all.

'Thank you, sir,' Enys was saying. 'Will you excuse me, gentlemen. I must try and track down my brother and speak to him urgently.' Sir Horatio was looking very thoughtful while Pickering was scowling.

Enys was already bowing to Pickering in thanks and heading for the door, no doubt to find a boat to chase his brother. For a moment Dodd wondered about telling him who owned the ship, then decided he would find out soon enough. As the lawyer clattered down the stair, Dodd had a thought about the now-decoded letters.

He had been wondering about it but now he made a decision. If Palavicino was the Queen's banker, perhaps he was the best way for Dodd to get the information safely out of his keeping and into the Queen's. It clearly all hinged on whoever Icarus might be a codename for and he had no idea, although he suspected Carey did. Icarus had been in normal letters, not numbers, so he supposed it was doubly important. He pulled out the coded letters and his laborious translations and handed them to Palavicino.

'That one,' he said, tapping it, 'I found hidden in Richard Tregian's chamber. The ither one...' He coughed, not sure how this would be received. '...ah, the ither one we found when we had a warrant to arrest Mr. Heneage for assault in my case and we were searching his house for him.'

It seemed both Pickering and Palavicino knew about that because they both smiled.

'As usual, ingenious and appropriate,' said Palavicino, not making a lot of sense as far as Dodd was concerned. 'And what have we here?'

'The translation's there,' said Dodd, quite proud of what he had done in only an afternoon. Sir Horatio looked hard at the writing and his lips moved as he read it. Then he looked up and nodded.

'Sergeant, thank you,' he said. 'I shall see the Queen receives this at once.'

'Ay,' said Dodd, thinking it might be about time to be going. Pickering stopped him. 'Just a word before we go, Sergeant, about Sir Robert's enquiry,' said Pickering quietly. 'I've asked around and I will lay my life on it that not one of my people 'as lifted that survey out of the Cornish maid's purse.'

'Eh?' said Dodd, then remembered. 'Ay?' He was surprised. 'Are ye sure?'

'Certain. I'd've 'ad it in my 'ands by yesterday night if any nip-purse or foist or any of their friends 'ad it, believe me.'

Dodd nodded. That left only one place the survey could have gone to, and now he thought about it, that made perfect sense.

'As for what the watermen think about whoever did in the Papist priest...It's only a rumour but they say 'e was escaping from Topcliffe's place in south bank marshes when it happened.

I haven't found the man who rowed the boat for them so I can't say for sure. Unfortunately, he disappeared a couple of days ago.'

'Thank ye, Mr. Pickering,' said Dodd, thinking he knew what had happened to the poor boatman. 'If ye hear any...'

There was a thunderous banging on the doors downstairs. Pickering jumped to his feet and stood there with his fists clenching and unclenching.

'What the 'ell...?' he said.

'Open in the name of the Queen!' came the roar from below. Dodd moved to the window and peered out. The area around the warehouse was full of large men in buff coats, another boat pulling up with more men in it. Out of it stepped Mr. Vice Chancellor Heneage with a very prim and satisfied expression on his plump prissy face. Dodd had forgotten how much he disliked the man. At least he was still sporting green and purple around his eyes and his nose was swollen.

Poor Enys had obviously walked straight into an ambush as he left to find his brother. He was being held with his arms twisted behind him by two men who looked pleased with themselves. Enys looked as if he might be sick and was still struggling.

'Och,' said Dodd, cursing himself for a fool. He looked at Sir Horatio who was still frowning at the letters.

'Get him out o' here, Mr. Pickering,' he said to the King of London who seemed too shocked to react. 'Have ye no' a bolthole?'

Pickering blinked, shook himself and moved. ''Course I do. Come along, Sir Horatio.'

He went to the corner of the small room and rolled back one of the mats. Dodd lifted the trapdoor, revealing stairs leading down. To his surprise, Pickering did not go down the steps but motioned to Sir Horatio.

'At the bottom is a door into a basement, it's a bit wet but don't worry. Open the door and go along the passage and you'll be in the warehouse over by the third crane, see?'

Palavicino looked out the window and nodded. 'Now Sir Horatio,' gravelled Pickering, making the two words sound like 'sratio', ''ere's the key to the door of the warehouse. The seals is fake and you can put them back. Bring me the key when you can.'

Palavicino nodded, took a candle from the mantlepiece, shook hands with Pickering, and then went down the stairs, moving remarkably quietly for so large a man.

There was more thundering and a banging downstairs and Heneage ordering the door to be opened in the name of the Queen. Pickering, short sturdy and bullet headed, looked at the door, pursed his lips, sucked his teeth, and squared his shoulders. From a mere wealthy merchant he had become something much more dangerous.

'I'm going to welcome in our visitors. I think you should slip away as well as I'm quite sure 'e's got a warrant for you.'

Dodd quietly loosened his sword despite what Pickering had said, then followed the man through the gambling room where the players and the half-clad women were staring through the windows. 'Mary,' said Pickering to one of them, 'put 'em away, luv,' and the women started pulling their shifts up and relacing their stays so as to look a little bit more respectable. 'Start moving out, girls,' he added as he went past, quite quietly. The girls started ushering all the wealthy players to the back room where the trapdoor and secret tunnel were.

Dodd went down the polished stairs. Briscoe and the other henchman were standing on the inside of the barred and locked door as it shuddered to the blows of a battering ram.

'Yerss,' said Pickering, 'plenty of time, gentlemen, these doors was put in by the Tunnage and Poundage. The girls are still busy upstairs. Meantime...What would you do if some jumped-up court clerk did this to you in your own country, Sergeant Dodd?'

Dodd was amazed Pickering needed to ask. 'If it were the Queen herself as did it, then I'd do nowt,' he said, heavily, 'but if it were aye one o' her men, then I'd have the Border alight in two hours, Mr. Pickering, the bells would a' be ringin' and the men would a' be riding. But Ah'm nobbut the Land-Sergeant of Gilsland and Ah could ainly call on the Dodds and the Armstrongs there and mebbe the Bells and the Storeys, four hundred men at best. If it were Richie Graham of Brackenhill that had his tower burned, by God, Mr. Pickering, there'd be fifteen hundred men i'the saddle by daybreak and Carlisle in flames the day after.'

The King of London smiled briefly. 'Hm,' he said, 'it ain't quite like that here in London, mind, but I agree wiv you, I will not be treated like this and I won't 'ave my men treated like this either. So, Sergeant, wot do you reckon?'

'Me? There's a man I'd like to talk to first and then...I wantae talk to the owner o' the *Judith of Penryn* and find this man Vent. And then, Mr. Pickering, Ah'm at yer disposal.'

Pickering looked consideringly at his men. ' Mr. Briscoe,' he said quietly as the battering ram hammered home again, 'would you do me the kindness to come and speak with me...'

To Dodd's surprise the man called Briscoe suddenly looked hunted and made for the stairs. His mate caught hold of him firmly by the neck and held him there.

Pickering went up to him. 'Easy way or hard way?' he said softly through his teeth.

Briscoe licked his lips and started to cry. 'Only, 'e took my Ellie, my missus, what's gonna have a baby, he took 'er down to his house and he said to me, 'e'd have 'er belly cut open to get the baby out and then 'e'd make me watch while 'e...'

'Heneage?'

Briscoe shook his head 'Topcliffe.'

'And?'

'And so I told 'im where the game would be and that we was waiting for Sir Robert to come back and...I told 'im.'

'Topcliffe still got yer mort?'

Briscoe nodded, then hid his face in his hands. 'I signalled when I saw the Sergeant,' he whispered, his voice muffled.

Pickering shook his head. 'Tim,' he said in a low voice, 'Why didn't yer come and tell me?'

''e said 'e'd know if I did and 'e'd kill 'er right away.'

Bang went the battering ram again. You had to admire the way the doors were standing up to it, thought Dodd. Surely Heneage would try gunpowder next?

Pickering nodded once. 'I'm 'urt Tim,' he said thoughtfully, 'I'm 'urt you didn't find a way to tell me what was going on,'

'I know, Mr. Pickering, I'm ever so sorry, I couldn't fink 'ow to do it.'

'Well, the damage is done now. What do you fink I should do about you?'

Briscoe studied the ground, and sniffled. He muttered something Dodd couldn't make out.

Pickering smiled. ''Course I'm going to kill you, Tim, but what should happen first?' He put his hand up on Briscoe's burly shoulder. ''Ave a fink about it, tell me later. Meanwhile, see Sergeant Dodd here?' Briscoe nodded. ''e needs a man at 'is back if 'e's to get away and do somfink about yer mort and yer kinchin. Will yer do that? Wivvout tipping 'im no lays?'

Briscoe nodded convulsively and looked up at Dodd who was now halfway up the stairs.

'Come on,' Dodd grunted, and Briscoe followed him up to the room where the girls were just staggering down the steps carrying large bags of money, but still leaving some scattered about the tables. Dodd approved of that—the money would slow the searchers down considerably. The girl called Mary stood waiting by the trapdoor and a couple of the younger ones were bunched around her, looking angry and frightened.

'You're slow,' she snapped. 'I've got to lock it. Hurry up, we ain't got all night.'

She looked somehow familiar but Dodd couldn't think where he might have seen her before. He went down the steps, followed by Briscoe, a long way down, to a passage that was dripping and evil-smelling but quite wide and well-flagged. It looked to have been built a long time ago. The trapdoor shut and locked behind them and there was a scraping sound of furniture going over it.

'Wait,' said Briscoe, and paused by a grating. Dodd stood next to him and peered through the bars.

They were at foot-level. Like giants the men with the battering ram ran past them, hit the door…And went straight through, landing with shouts and crashing on the other side of it. Stepping over their legs, delicately, came Laurence Pickering, the King of London.

'Good evening, your honour,' he said to the Vice Chamberlain of the Queen's Court with a perky bow. 'How may I serve Her Majesty?'

Heneage brandished a paper at Pickering. 'I have here a warrant to search for ill-doers and malefactors engaged in unGodly gambling and whoring within the bounds of the City of London and I have here one warrant for the arrest of one James Enys for assisting in the escape of a prisoner of Her Majesty and a further warrant for the arrest of Henry Dodd for high treason.'

The pursuivants were already in the building, thundering and crashing around; Palavicino and the girls carrying the coin were somewhere ahead of them but Dodd couldn't tear himself away. From the odd angle, he could just make out Enys who was now standing very still between the two bullyboys who had hold of him, his face as white as his falling band. From the way he was part-hunched over, Dodd assumed somebody had kneed him or punched him in the gut.

Soon the men in buff coats started bringing out the girls who had been left behind and there was a gull-like clamour of furious argument, insult, and insinuation from them.

Heneage gave a smile of triumph. 'You are James Enys, member of Gray's Inn, Utter Barrister?' said Heneage to Enys who hesitated for a moment and then nodded convulsively. Heneage struck him across the face as he had once struck Dodd: an experiment, to see what reaction he would get.

'Answer me properly,' he said.

'Yes, I am now,' said Enys softly, his eyelids fluttering. 'God help me.'

Heneage slapped him again. 'You say, Yes I am, *your honour*,' he corrected with a spiteful smile. Enys looked him gravely in the face and managed a lopsided smile in return.

'Your honour is of course, most wise and just,' he said in his court-voice. 'I am most grateful for your honour's elucidation in this matter.'

Heneage's lips thinned and he raised his hand again. However, for no good reason, he seemed to think better of it.

Dodd found his hand gripped so hard on his swordhilt, it hurt. He forced himself to relax and take his hand away. No point drawing a sword in a little tunnel, there was no room to wield it. He thought he had most of the whole mess worked out now, but not all of it, and he stared at Heneage as if the simple pressure of

462

his gaze could damage the bastard.

'Your honour,' came Enys's low voice. 'Who was it saw me...'

'The boatman you hired. Did you think I wouldn't find him?'

Enys nodded, looking at the ground. The print of Heneage's hand was bright red against the pockmarks.

At last Heneage turned away from Enys to shout at the pursuivants who were crashing and ripping through Pickering's gambling room to bring any money to him. The girls were being loaded into one of the boats, still arguing and cursing and complaining that the Bridewell was becoming a pesthouse.

'Well, Mr. Heneage, ain't you going to arrest me too?' asked Pickering conversationally.

A muscle twitched in Heneage's cheek. 'Later,' he said. Pickering chuckled quietly.

'Queen's Warrant still in force then?' he said. Heneage said nothing.

That was interesting but Dodd heard another loud banging and crashing above. They had better get on. He hurried along the passage and then paused at a side turning.

'Whit is this place?'

'Smuggler's passage,' said Briscoe, 'to get the wine in and out of the bonded warehouse.'

'Ay then, there'll be a door ontae the river to get to the Pool.'

Dodd scratched with his dagger on the corner and then went down it. The passage tilted downwards and came to a grill that seemed to be locked. There had to be a mechanism or a lever or...

Briscoe had leaned down and pulled and the grill came up. They ducked under it and he let it go down again. A wooden door that was part rotten from the damp was a little further on. When they peered around the door, they found watersteps washed by the river.

As always the Thames was busy in the twilight. Dodd put his fingers between his teeth and whistled sharply. A boatman paused, changed direction, and came up to the steps. 'Where to, masters?'

'Pool o' London, the *Judith of Penryn*.'

'No chance, mate, I'm not shooting the bridge now. I'll take you to the bridge and you can walk.'

Dodd shrugged and stepped into the boat, followed by Briscoe, who sat down in the back—no, the stern—his face working.

'Never seen no one take a boat at them steps before,' said the boatman. 'What are they from?'

'Ah, a private house. Of a merchant,' lied Dodd, even though Pickering would probably never use the place again and the Tunnage and Poundage men would have lost a useful source of income.

'Hm. Shows you never can tell. I thought I knew every set of watersteps on the river. I was telling my lord of Southampton just the other night that...'

Dodd was thinking as hard as he could. If Heneage truly did have a warrant against him for treason, then the only possible sensible place to hide was the *Judith*. And he hoped that the man who called himself Vent would be there as well. But now he had the time to think, he realised that there was someone else he urgently needed to talk to first. He tapped the boatman on the shoulder as he prosed on and on about the Earl of Essex who seemed to be a very fine fellow and said, 'Ah've changed ma mind, I wantae go to the Blackfriars.'

The boatman tutted and rolled his eyes. 'Well that's double, with the tide as it is. Are you sure?'

'Ay,' said Dodd. He was too. He glanced at Briscoe in the back... stern of the boat but the man was too hangdog and miserable to say anything about the change of plan. He had better not try any signalling. Still Dodd was annoyed with himself about that: he had noticed the man was hollow-eyed but he had done nothing about it.

On impulse he leaned over and touched the man's shoulder. 'Mr. Briscoe,' he said, 'Ah need tae find a man by the name o' Will Shakespeare and Ah cannae spare much time for it. He could be at Somerset House, he could be at the Earl o' Southampton's place, or he could be...'

He didn't want to risk Somerset House just yet, if ever, and the Earl of Southampton had gone to the court according to Carey. That left two places.

Ordering the boatman to wait, Dodd ran up the steps and down an alley. The Mermaid Inn was half-empty, the landlord looking as if he was staring ruin in the face now Marlowe was drinking somewhere else. A greasy damp smell of fire came from the half-burned kitchen at the back. Only Anthony Munday sat alone by the bar, scribbling into a notebook and looking very dapper in a pale grey woollen doublet and hose.

'Nobody's here,' said Munday dolefully. 'Have you seen Marlowe? He owes me ten shillings.'

'Ay?' said Dodd, 'I dinna ken where he is the day. Have ye seen Shakespeare?'

'No,' said Munday viciously. 'With a bit of luck he's got plague and died of it.'

'Ay,' said Dodd, having almost forgotten about the plague that was running round the city still.

One place left to try, but Dodd decided to swing through the Temple and quietly check on one of his ideas for solving the mess in front of him. He found Essex's court and climbed the stairs to Enys's chamber where he had locked the door as he left. Dodd hammered on the door.

'Mrs. Morgan,' he roared, 'are ye there?' Silence. No sound of fire, no sound of breathing, nothing.

Dodd pulled out his dagger, levered the hinges of the new door with it, and then used one of the bits of the old door to prise into the crack and break the door open. He'd pay for it after, if it came to that, but above all he needed information. The room was dim in the dusk now, so he used the tongs to pick a coal out of the fireplace and lit a tallow dip with it. The smoke was choking, but it gave just enough light.

The place was completely empty. Dodd went through into the second room where there was a bed and a trundle under it, which bore no signs of having been slept in for some time. Somebody had put back the remains of the mattress and there was the clear print of one body in it. The jordan was emptied, most of the mess of the pursuivants' search had been swept away. In no place was there any sign of Mrs. Morgan, Enys' unfortunately pock-marked sister.

'Ay,' said Dodd, putting the tallow dip in its sconce on the mantleshelf. He was fully satisfied he had it right. There were not three siblings, there were two. And if one brother was now calling himself Vent and hiding out on the *Judith of Penryn* in the Pool of London then that left...

'What are you doing here?' It was Shakespeare's voice, nasal flattened vowels and doleful tone again.

Dodd drew his dagger, strode across the floor, grabbed Shakespeare by the front of his doublet and slammed him against the cracked wood panelling with the dagger threatening to split his nose. Shakespeare looked down at it cross-eyed.

'Ah'm lookin' for Mrs. Morgan or Mr. Enys, depending,' Dodd growled. 'Ah'm also searching for the land-survey that Lady Hunsdon's maidservant brought up from London and which ye stole, ye bastard.'

Shakespeare's eyelids fluttered. 'I...I...'

'Who'd ye give it tae?' Dodd bounced Shakespeare against the wall, 'Eh? Mr. Heneage?' Bounce. 'Mr. Topcliffe?' Harder bounce.

Shakespeare was breathless with fright and what he said came out as a hiss. Dodd nearly slit his nose for him before he realised what Shakespeare was trying to tell him.

'The Cecils?'

'Sir Robert Cecil, my lord Burghley's second son, the hunchback.'

Dodd stopped banging the man against the wall and stared into his bland face. 'That who ye serve and spy on the Hunsdons for?'

Shakespeare flushed and nodded. 'I cut young Letty's purse while you were busy calming the horse,' he explained. 'And then I took the survey to Cecil myself because...well, I thought it might interest him even though it said there was no gold. And he said that he needed to keep it secret before the matter could be revealed.'

'Was he surprised or shocked at it?'

Shakespeare's very large brow wrinkled slightly. 'No, he wasn't. In fact he seemed amused to hear that my lady Hunsdon had come up to London specially to put a stop to the dealings in lands she knew to be worthless.'

'Whit did he say?'

Shakespeare shrugged. 'Only that the horse had bolted and there was nothing she could do.'

Dodd let go of the man's doublet front and smoothed it out for him. 'Ah'm glad I saw ye,' he said. 'Why did ye come here?'

'I...ah...was hoping to have an answer from Mr...er...Enys,'

'And whit answer was that? How much ye wanted payin' to keep quiet about what ye knew?'

'No,' said Shakespeare warily, 'I wasn't going to ask her for money, only for assistance, advice.'

Dodd paused, speechless. Her? He had assumed that Mrs. Morgan was Mr. Enys in disguise, not...

'*Her?*'

'You must have realised what I did: she had no adam's apple, her feet were small, and her doublet had been taken in at the shoulders whilst her hose had been let out.'

'Ye saw that, did ye?' Dodd was starting to recover a little.

'Of course. In the theatre we go to a lot of trouble to turn boys into passable girls and women. Once I had noticed one hint, it was easy to put the others together. I think she may have been passing as a man for a while though, she does it very well.'

'Ay, though she canna fight.' A thought struck Dodd. 'That's whit she wanted me tae teach her swordplay for, she was gonnae have a try at killing ye, Mr. Shakespeare.'

'Why would she want to do that?'

'Mebbe she didnae like givin' ye the *assistance* ye wanted.' Dodd's sneer made it clear what kind he thought that probably was. To his surprise and disbelief Shakespeare shook his head vigorously.

'No, not at all. I wanted her advice.'

'Ay?'

'Really and truly! I thought it was marvellous what she had done, quite extraordinary. Here she is, a woman alone in London, whose brother has disappeared mysteriously, and she puts on his clothes and sword, appears in court before a judge, and sets about finding out what happened to him. A mere weak woman to do all that and even show enough learning at the law not to be discovered.'

Dodd hadn't thought of that part of it though he had to admit it was clever of her. He was only thoroughly annoyed with himself for not seeing through the game quicker. There had been plenty of clues, after all. Had Carey worked it out, he wondered? Shakespeare was pacing up and down now.

'I wanted her to advise me on the law and describe her feelings as she went from woman to man and I was hoping to write her story as a play and put it upon the stage at the Blackfriars when the hall is ready for plays. *Justicia or The Woman at Law*. How could I possibly miss such a chance?'

Perhaps he had been unfair to the poet. 'Ay well, ye'd best be quick for Mr. Heneage has arrested her...him...Enys the lawyer for helping the escape of a prisoner of state. Ah didnae ken fully until I saw that and then I did.'

'Arrested?' Shakespeare had gone pale.

'Ay. Heneage raided Pickering's game this evening. Ah came here to be sure I was right about Enys and then I'm gaunae roust out Carey's kin and fetch her and Mrs. Briscoe away from Heneage.'

Shakespeare's jaw dropped. 'You can't do that.'

'Can I no'?' asked Dodd, full of interest. 'Watch me.' At the very least they could ransom her before Topcliffe got started on him...her—had they discovered Enys's sex yet, he wondered? He looked at Shakespeare who seemed genuinely concerned and upset and something inside him said it could do no harm to bring Cecil's man along. So he took Shakespeare's elbow and hustled him out of the chambers and down the stairs, down through the Temple to the river where he found Mr. Briscoe still there with the mutinous-looking boatman who was lighting his stern lamp.

'Thank ye,' he said, in a lordly fashion, giving the boatman some more of Carey's money. 'Ah'll double that if ye'll take us tae the Pool of London right now.'

The boatman looked at the pile of silver in his palm and then at Dodd. 'All three of you?' he asked and Dodd said 'Ay.' Briscoe was looking at the planks, Shakespeare licked his lips, but neither of them disagreed. 'Sure? In the dark, with the tide on the ebb?'

'Ay,' said Dodd.

The boatman laughed a little, leaned over, and put his hand in the inky waters. 'Well the flow's not too vicious for the bridge, but it'll be fast.'

'Good,' said Dodd, wondering why he didn't get on with it.

'I've never done it at night,' said the boatman with a grin, tossing the coin and catching it on the back of his hand. The Queen's head shone bright silver from the sixpence in the light from the rising moon. 'Well, we'll see if the old girl likes us or not, eh?' With a little dip of his head, he tossed the coin again and deliberately let it fall into the river. Next minute he had shoved off from the Blackfriar's steps and rowed the boat round to point down stream at the bridge.

'You'd best hold on tight,' shouted the boatman. 'Hold onto yer 'ats, gentlemen.'

It certainly was fast. The boatman rowed out into mid-stream, well away from likely eddies and whirlpools around the sandspits near the bank. You couldn't tell easily in the darkness, but the faint ruby lights to their left seemed to be speeding past.

The tide being on the ebb with the flow of the river doubled the speed. The boatman was rowing hard to keep the prow aimed straight. His only guide was the torches hanging on the sides of London Bridge which were not easy to see. As they bounced and slid nearer and nearer the noise of the water against the starlings and the grind and clank of the waterwheels still working at the ends were enough to take your head off.

Suddenly, at a horrible speed they were approaching the dark arches with their single lanterns hung over the two central ones. The wet bricks swooped towards them like mouths of sea monsters intent on eating them. Next second they were under the echoing arch with the dripping brickwork and the great beams going across to brace them, the roar of the waters battering their ears and brains far worse than thunder, nearly as bad as cannon. For a second, Dodd saw eyes peering at them from the narrow ledges and realised there were creatures so poor that they tried to sleep in that awful place. The second after that they had shot across the churning white water and out into the relative peace of the Pool of London with its waterborne forest of ships, each showing its sternlight and mainmast light.

The boatman backed water and caught his breath. 'Done it!' he crowed. 'Nobody of my lodge ever did that, ha! Old Noah'll be proud!'

He reached over and shook Dodd's hand, laughing with delight at himself. Dodd gave him a golden angel since it wasn't actually his money and the man had done well by them. He didn't plan to shoot the Bridge on the ebb ever again, night or day, but it had been...exciting.

They were coming close to the *Judith of Penryn*, a long slender ship with three masts crowded on the deck. There were cannon ports along the side and movement on deck. Dodd saw more lanterns being lit.

He blinked across the dark waters and had to shut his eyes and refocus carefully: a small rotund figure in the stern was aiming a pistol at him, he could clearly see the match burning.

'Mr. Briscoe, Mr. Shakespeare,' he said quietly, raising his hands. 'Lie down.'

They stared at him, followed his gaze, saw the pistol in Lady Hunsdon's steady hands, and ducked immediately. Briscoe drew his dagger and convinced the boatman to keep rowing. Carefully, slowly, Dodd stood up and balanced. There wasn't a lot of chance she could hit him at that range, but you never knew.

'My lady Hunsdon, can Ah talk wi' yer ladyship?'

'If you have any information on my son who went missing whilst hawking in Finsbury Fields, Sergeant, yes.'

'He's gaun tae Court. Naebody's taken him, he went off by hisself. I didnae ken until this afternoon.'

'How do you know for sure, Sergeant?' That gun was still pointing at him, steady as a rock except for a gentle movement to allow for the rocking of the ship.

'He used yer money to get his Court duds out o' pawn, my lady,' said Dodd, coming up with the only piece of evidence that would have convinced Janet. 'And he left me a letter wi' Senhor Gomes.' There was a thoughtful pause.

'Explain why I should believe a word of this considering I think that you are the most likely man to have betrayed him.'

'It's the truth!' shouted Dodd, outraged to have his word doubted. The match glowed brighter as she blew on it and settled the dag on her forearm to aim better. 'Ah, if ye let me on yer boat wi'out my weapons, my lady, ye can kill me wi' a dagger if ye're not convinced. Which will save ye the recoil on the pistol.'

The pistol was still steady. After a very long time, she simply nodded. The boatman rowed carefully up to the tall wooden side of the ship. Dodd unbelted his sword, looked at the ropeladder, and climbed it as fast as he could so he wouldn't have time to think

470

about it. At the top as he climbed puffing over the rail, Captain Trevasker steadied him, a long carved stick in his left fist, and then walked him up some steps to the rearcastle where Lady Hunsdon was waiting. She looked magnificent and was wearing a steel gorget as the Queen had been rumoured to do when the Armada came. Captain Trevasker drew his long knife.

Dodd ignored this and pulled the crumpled sheet of Carey's letter to him out of his pouch, gave it to Lady Hunsdon. Some of the lines of fury on Lady Hunsdon's face relaxed as she read in the light of her lantern. 'Well, Sergeant?' she said and so he told her what had been going on. After a little more time, she pinched out the dag's match with her gloved fingers and laid it down. As the tale went on she began to get angry again.

'Is the man completely without common sense?' she asked haughtily at the news of Heneage's raid on Laurence Pickering, 'What a wittol, eh Captain?'

Dodd added the facts on James Enys' true nature, expecting surprise, and found that Lady Hunsdon simply shook her head.

'Of course I knew that, Sergeant, I knew they were twins and there was no spare brother. I also could see for myself that Enys had no adam's apple and walked like a woman when she wasn't concentrating. I didn't see any need to talk about it.'

Bitterly Dodd wondered if he was the only one to be taken in.

'Well Heneage has got her and he's got Mr. Briscoe's wife forbye to use for anither hostage.'

There was a moment's silence. Lady Hunsdon had her chin on her chest in thought.

'And Laurence Pickering's got some plans, but he didnae tell me what they were,' added Dodd. 'He said he'd find out where they were keeping her.'

'Who else is in the boat with you?' Lady Hunsdon asked.

'Tim Briscoe, Pickering's man and...er...Bald Will,' said Dodd.

'Any idea who he's working for now?'

'Ay milady, he told me he stole the survey Letty had and giv it tae Sir Robert Cecil.'

Her very bright eyes glittered slightly at this, but all she said was 'At least that's an improvement. Why did you come to the *Judith*?'

'Ah had a mind tae speak wi' this Vent, who I think is the real James Enys. He disappeared in the last two or three weeks which makes me wonder what he's been at. Heneage arrested Enys for helping the escape of a state prisoner.'

'If he hasn't jumped off, he's on board now. The bo'sun's a cousin of his.'

Dodd nodded at the sense this made. Naturally if you were on the run in a foreign city like London, you'd take refuge on a ship from your own county so you could get back there eventually. Also they might be less likely to betray you. He'd do the same. In fact it might be worth finding out if there were any Newcastle coasters in the Pool since it was a long way by sea to Carlisle.

There was a clattering. First Shakespeare's head appeared and he climbed over the rail to be followed by Briscoe, who had evidently been pushing him.

Dodd realised he had scuffed his knuckles and made a hole in his hose which thoroughly annoyed him. Still, what could you expect from fancy, expensive, but delicate duds? How the devil did the elderly and stout Lady Hunsdon get aboard?

Briscoe and Shakespeare were looking around themselves nervously at the short, mostly red-headed men bustling about in the lantern light with ropes and barrels.

A man was brought up from below through a hatch, dressed in workman's clothes, but with soft hands and a pocky face that might have been good-looking once. It was definitely Vent the card-player. Dodd squinted at him in the flickering light and there was indeed a resemblance to Enys the lawyer. He was a little taller and broader in the shoulder, but the hair colour was the same and the general cast of the features very similar. His voice was deeper and rougher though.

Lady Hunsdon sat herself down on a cushioned seachest with Trevasker beside her, and rested her hands on the top of a silver and ebony cane and her chin on her hands. Bright beady eyes raked Enys like gunfire.

'Well, James Enys, I want a full accounting of yourself.'

The man bowed nervously. 'My lady, I asked for refuge on your ship being a Cornishman because I am a little entangled in gambling debts and I...'

'Pfui. You are on the run and your sister has taken your place as a man of law. Heneage arrested her in place of you not an hour ago for assisting the escape of a state prisoner. Well?'

The man paused carefully. 'I don't understand...' He sounded as if his breath was short with shock.

'Och, my lady, this canna be the man,' said Dodd sourly. 'I heard fra his sister while I thought her to be a man that she had sae loving a brother he came and nursed her while she was sick of the smallpox and her husband and children had died, and then caught it himself.'

'Who are you?' said the man.

'Sergeant Dodd, Sir Robert Carey's man. I saw the woman calling herself James Enys taken by Heneage. He slapped her about a bit, mind, but what he and Topcliffe will do to her when they find she's a woman, I darenae think.' He paused. 'And they'll find it oot as soon as they strip her for the rack.'

The man swallowed convulsively.

There was a pause broken by shouts and an occasional long creak as the ship swayed at her mooring.

'My lady, I...perhaps I should speak in private...'

'You can speak here, now. This is all tangled up with the coney-catching practice about Cornish lands, isn't it?'

Enys nodded.

'And the killing of Fr. Jackson,' added Dodd, since he thought he might as well. 'It was ye killed him, was it no'?'

Suddenly Enys sat down on a coil of rope and put his face in his hands. 'I couldn't think what else to do...'

'Shh,' said Lady Hunsdon kindly. 'Nobody minds you killing a Papist priest. We haven't much time. Oh, while I remember...Mr. Shakespeare!' The bellow could have cut through a full gale. After a moment, Shakespeare appeared at the top of the companionway to the rear castle, looking frightened.

'Go and find your master Sir Robert Cecil immediately and tell him I want to speak to him here on the *Judith*.'

Shakespeare's mouth opened. 'But milady...'

'Don't argue. Go and fetch him immediately.'

'But what if he won't come?'

Lady Hunsdon's eyes narrowed. 'He'll come.' Shakespeare bowed.

A man came running up to Trevasker and whispered in his ear. Dodd noticed the ship moving and creaking more and seeming to move at its anchorage. Lady Hunsdon nodded. 'Good, the tide will turn in an hour,' she said to Trevasker. 'Will you have the men get ready for a cutting-out expedition?'

The imperturbable Trevasker's jaw dropped slightly and he stared. 'Where'd that be to, milady?'

'Oh, somewhere around here.' She turned her head, looked straight at Dodd and winked. Dodd almost snorted with amusement.

Then she rapped with the cane on the deck. 'Come along, come along, James,' she said. 'Just spill it all out, you'll feel so much better. When did your sister—Portia isn't it? I remember that. Her mother named her after a little fishing village in Cornwall for some reason. When did Portia start playing at being a man?' No answer. 'Do you want me to ask Dodd to encourage you a little? Just to salve your pride with a black eye, or something?'

Not for the first time, Dodd's ribs were hurting with the effort of not laughing. James's face reappeared from behind his hands and scowled at Lady Hunsdon.

'Ah'll dae it and glad to,' said Dodd, wishing he had leather gloves on to protect his scabbed knuckles. 'It might be safer for him if ye have a man holding him though.'

'That's not necessary,' growled the real James Enys.

'Och,' said Dodd, quite relieved, but did his best to look disappointed.

'It started after we both came up to London from Cornwall, after it seemed everybody we had in the world had died of smallpox. I went back to Gray's Inn to continue my legal studies which I had broken to try my fortune in the Netherlands. I had no enthusiasm for it any more, after...after the smallpox. Portia came with me to keep house for me and because she had nowhere else and we always agreed very well so it seemed the best idea. I found that...I was falling behind and so she would help with my studies and write briefs for my moots. The first time she wore my clothes and pretended to be me was a day when I had a terrible megrim and fever...'

'I expect you were hungover, weren't you? Distempered of drink?' came Lady Hunsdon's scalpel-like voice.

James looked at the deck. 'Yes, my lady, I was. She went and mooted for me and did immensely well, carrying her point and utterly destroying my opponent that I had been afraid of. She came back in the best spirits I had seen her in since the death of her children and husband and the next time I had to moot, she went on my behalf again as I never liked doing it.'

'Ehm...milady, what's a moot?'

'As it were a practice court case for the law students at the Inns of Court, like a veney with words,' said Lady Hunsdon. 'Often on very foolish subjects.'

'Whiteacre and Greenacre arguing over a square yard of land upon which is an easement and a flying freehold, generally,' said James incomprehensibly. 'Utterly tedious. But Portia enjoyed it and was much better at talking Norman French, so I...well, it seemed kinder to...'

'You were very relieved at not having to do the work yourself and let her do it.'

'Yes. She studied and began taking some clerk work to support us and even began being approached for some court paperwork. When it came time for me to be called to the Bar...She was in the hall, not I, and it was she that was properly called. It seemed only just.'

Lady Hunsdon nodded. 'Had she no wish to marry again?'

'My sister is convinced that no man will look twice at her since her complexion is now so hideous.'

Lady Hunsdon nodded sympathetically.

'And she has no inheritance for all her husband's land went to his brother with the death of his issue and very little jointure, nor no dowry from me neither. A man would have to take her in her smock or not at all.'

Lady Hunsdon nodded again.

'In the meantime, as she says, she must eat and as it seems she has an ability and an understanding for the law—which to be sure, I have not—then she will carry on being a man to do it for as long as she can.'

Enys sighed, spread his hands on his knees. 'I have been a

very ill brother to her. I did find some clerkwork for Heneage but that went wrong too. For him I drafted many of the deeds for the Cornish lands that were supposed to have gold. They were all being sold by a Mr. Jackson—a man I only knew as a correspondent in Cornwall. I didn't realise he was a Papist priest. I even found him new buyers. It became quite the fashion at Court and many of the lands have been conveyed at higher prices—so much that I began to wonder at it. I was sure most of the lands I was dealing with bore no gold. To be sure there was gold in Cornwall—there are a couple of places near Camborne where there were gold mines in the olden days, but they are all worked out now.

'Then suddenly Jackson came up to London and...I had never met him face to face and he was being elusive. So I spoke to a lady who had lent him a chamber in her house. It turned out he was a Jesuit.'

'You are not a Catholic, Mr. Enys, are you?'

Enys coloured and stared hard at the deck. 'Not really, my lady, not a proper Catholic. My parents were and tried their best with me but...I attend church service when I should and...' He shrugged. 'It seems very unimportant to me what exact flavour of religion we should follow, when it's most likely that we are simply howling into the void and mistaking the echoes for divinity.'

There was silence at this shocking statement and Trevasker crossed himself and fingered an amulet. Dodd felt for his own; just because it was probably true didn't mean you should go shouting about it like Marlowe and offending...Something.

'It was the children,' said Lady Hunsdon gently although she had frowned at first. 'Seeing the children die of so evil a pestilence as smallpox?'

Enys nodded, gulped again, and continued in a rush. 'Suddenly, somehow, everything went wrong and Heneage arrested Jackson.'

'How did you find out?'

'I...heard about it. Then I was in terror it would be me next for being with him—after all, once they put him to the question mine would be a name he would give. I was hiding at the Belle Sauvage under another name. Then I recognised Richard Tregian when he came to town—God, I was pleased to see him. I asked his advice and he warned me off the Cornish goldmines himself. He said he had been sent up to London by you to warn the authorities and that you would bring his daughter with a true survey of the lands in question to prove they had no gold-bearing ore in them.'

'So who was it ordered you to help Fr. Jackson escape from Heneage?'

'From Topcliffe in fact, Jackson was being held at one of his private properties upriver in Chelsea so Heneage could deny knowing about...what was happening.'

Lady Hunsdon leaned forwards and spoke very clearly. 'Who ordered you to break him out?'

Enys licked his lips. 'Sir Robert Cecil.'

Lady Hunsdon sat back with a triumphant smile on her face. 'I thought so,' she said smugly, 'No wonder Robin bolted for the Court.'

'I had gone to him to ask for an audience for Richard Tregian and when I explained why, he just smiled. Then he asked me if I would do a dangerous job for him for fifty pounds and I said yes. I was desperate for money to go abroad in any case, it seemed to me that the Netherlands was the only hope I had of ever being able to find my sister a husband.

'Cecil gave me a map to show where he thought Fr. Jackson would be kept and a password and key for the dungeon. I went there at a time when Heneage was overpressed with business to do with another matter, and I managed to fetch Fr. Jackson out of Topcliffe's hands before he had been badly hurt.

'I had him in the boat with me, in his shirt, crowing with triumph, boasting of how he had destroyed the Queen's best men through their own greed. And I had trusted him and recommended him and found buyers for his lands and...'

'And had bought some yourself, I'm sure.'

'Yes, my lady, I had. And he told me that none of it was true, it was all a lay to coney-catch the great men at Court, there was no gold or hardly any, but that he had turned many worthless Cornish wheals into money and freedom for Catholic families.'

'And so?'

'I had taken his manacles off, but not the chains on his feet. I stabbed him in the back and heaved him into the Thames.'

'Where?'

'Upstream of Whitehall. Near Chelsea. And then I realised that if Cecil had ordered me to break him out then they must have known what he was doing and so...and so...'

'It was all a great deal more complicated than you thought. What did you do then?'

'I lay low. I tried to win some money to take me to the Netherlands but I couldn't and Heneage was looking for me. Pickering was willing to help.'

'And then?'

'Heneage arrested Richard Tregian.'

Silence.

'Why didn't you rescue him?'

'I was sure it was a trap to catch me. And...I didn't dare. I got drunk.'

Lady Hunsdon nodded. 'You were probably right,' she said. 'It doubtless was a trap to take someone they knew to be your friend. Why did Cecil not help?'

'I tried to see him and talk to him, but I couldn't get an audience.'

'I see.'

'And then came the news that Fr. Jackson would be executed at Tyburn and I wondered how it could possibly be. So I went to observe—and found they had substituted Mr. Tregian. I think you were there too, were you not, Sergeant? With Sir Robert?'

Dodd didn't answer.

'And then?'

'I...er...lay low again. I couldn't understand why they would do that—the poor man was only trying to stop people being fooled by Jackson's con-trick. I was even more afraid and didn't dare go back to my sister or my chambers. I tried to get a message to her, but it failed. I was beginning to think I might be safe when Sergeant Dodd saw me at Pickering's game and knew me.'

Dodd nodded. Enys had carried it off well.

One of the ship's boys came and doffed his cap to Lady Hunsdon. 'We'm all ready, my lady,' he said. 'Where's the battle to, then?'

She smiled at him and beckoned both Dodd and Enys closer.

'Gentlemen, I have a mind to break your sister Portia Morgan out of Topcliffe's clutches and also poor Mr. Briscoe's wife. I am very certain of the illegality of his whole proceeding from start to finish. Mr. Enys, do you recall where you released Fr. Jackson?' Enys nodded. 'Do you still have the key and the password?'

'The password is likely to be different.'

Lady Hunsdon grinned roguishly. 'I don't think you'll be needing the password, really, except for the purposes of confusion. You will accompany Sergeant Dodd and Mr. Janner Trevasker and give them whatever aid and assistance they need.'

It looked for a moment as if Enys was contemplating refusing to help, but although he hesitated, he then seemed to remember what was likely to happen to his sister—might have been happening at that moment—and his jaw firmed.

'Madam, I have no sword, I left mine with my sister since she must wear it when she dines in Hall.'

'I'm sure Captain Trevasker can find you one.' Enys followed the boy down the deck where a motley crew of red-heads and wreckers were arming themselves with long knives, belaying pins, and a few with grenados hanging from their belts. Among them was Mr. Briscoe, looking considerably happier than he had earlier that evening.

Lady Hunsdon beckoned Dodd to lean in closer. 'Mr. Janner Trevasker is Captain Trevasker's brother and he generally commands our cutting-out expeditions since these are his men. He is very experienced on the sea, less so on land. And so I would value your help,' she said. 'I have asked him to accept you as an advisor for I feel you may well have done something like this before.'

Dodd rubbed his chin. 'Ye'll no' be commanding us yersen, milady?' he asked, very straight-faced.

She beamed at him. 'Of course, I should love to but alas I'm too old and stout for it and would slow you down to protect me. Like the Queen, I must ask brave young men to do my fighting for me, and very well they do it, too.'

Dodd found himself bowing as if he were Carey. 'It's an honour, my lady.'

'Prettily said, Sergeant, my son must be teaching you his naughty ways.'

'Ay.' Dodd thought that must be the reason. 'Ah, is this place a tower or a house?'

'As I understand it, this is a private house on the south bank quite a long way up river, well past Lambeth Palace. It will take you at least a couple of hours to reach it, even with the tide in your favour. However, there may be a tower of some kind. The house is one of several owned by Mr. Heneage and let to Topcliffe for his disgusting pastimes and used by both of them when what they are doing is shadier than usual. I am quite sure Mr. Pickering knows its location as well.'

'How many men does he have?'

Lady Hunsdon shook her head. 'I have no idea, I'm afraid. It could be only a couple, it could a couple of dozen. You have the two gigs and ten men in each. You are not to use guns if you can avoid it, and you are to try not to kill.'

Dodd snorted. A full assault on a defended house? No killing? Lady Hunsdon grimaced. 'I'm skirting the borders of the law myself—my husband can probably smooth it over, but if it's a blood-bath...'

'My lady, why are you doing this for Mr. En...for Portia Morgan and Mrs. Briscoe? They're not your kin, are they?'

'Mrs. Briscoe isn't, but Mr. Briscoe looks a useful man in a fight and he'll be wanting to rescue his wife. Portia Morgan...well, I knew her family of course though not herself and her brother. She was in my service when she was taken, therefore she is my responsibility for good lordship. And also...' she leaned towards Dodd confidingly, '...I'm fair delighted at the chance to give Heneage a bloody nose for the way he treated my sons.' She sat back again and rapped her cane on the deck. 'Something I thought you might enjoy too.'

Dodd smiled at her. 'Ay, my lady. Whit about yer man Cecil?'

'What about him? I shall offer him my full hospitality, whether he likes it or not, until you come back with the women. We shall discuss many things. Off you go, Sergeant. Please conduct the raid as you see fit.'

***

It was pitch black night as the two gigs slid away from the ship and across the inky Thames. Even with the tide behind them again, they would have to row hard to get past the roaring leaping water at the bridge and into the relatively more peaceful upper part of the Thames. Going with Mr. Trevasker in the lead gig was the heavily bribed Thames waterman who had left his badge behind so as not to be blamed. Dodd took no part in it since he had no skill at boats at all, apart from the occasional fishing expedition in the Solway. They had no lanterns, relying on their nightsight and the fact that so long after sunset there would hardly be many boats ferrying across the river.

Even the lights in the city were gone out now, and their way only lit by starlight. The moon was at the quarter and not very bright. It was a harvest moon you needed for a good raid, silver-yellow light that turned the world to faery.

Dodd was sitting wishing very much for his comfy old clothes and jack and helmet. It seemed all wrong to be going into a fight wearing his fancy tight clothes, no smell of oiled leather and steel. At least he had his sword back. Perhaps he should have bought that poinard dagger after all. Briscoe was in the other boat. They had no guns since there was very little point in trying to keep the thing secret if they were going to be firing them—although their opponents might well have guns and would certainly shoot. The worst of guns was the notice they gave with the hissing and light of matches in the dark—and the *Judith* had no guns with snaphaunce or wheel locks because they hadn't penetrated to Cornwall yet. Their only real hope was surprise.

Enys was next to Dodd at the back of the boat and Dodd looked him over cautiously. He kept licking his lips but other than that seemed steady enough. Still, you never knew with a man until you'd seen him fight and even then, you still never knew. Please God he was better at it than his extraordinary sister.

Enys claimed to know a small muddy beach where there was a path that led to Topcliffe's house—it couldn't be helped but they had to use the path as the house was on a small knoll in the middle of the Lambeth marshes.

They were at the Bridge, the slender pointed gigs pointing straight into what seemed a vast pile of foam where the tide and the river current came to blows. The White Tower gleamed a little in grey starlight. There were some incomprehensible shouts from boat to boat. They slowed, steadied, took aim and then the men started leaning into the stroke while Mr. Trevasker and one of the second mates, Ted Gunn, called the time.

With the creak of oars in the rollocks and the bellowing of the waters, Dodd found himself ducking down as low as he could to avoid the spray. The turbulence was appalling where incoming tide met the river flow, slow as it was from the summer. For a moment they held, trembling on the foam, the oars moving rhythmically. Even Dodd could tell that if the Cornish weakened or made a mistake in their rowing, the gigs would be turned sideways by the pounding waters and probably turn over and wreck. It was a ridiculous thing to do, as ridiculous as the salmon swimming upstream. Could they do it? Would they all die of drowning? Dodd knew he was holding his breath in fear of the boat sinking.

The vast wet starlings were moving, passing by as the oars speeded their rhythm. Gradually they seemed almost to climb up a mountain of water, battered one way and the other, under the arches with their echoing roar, under the bracing beams, and then out into the quiet of the broad reach of the Thames where the turbulence was less. Dodd heard the rasping of the men's breath as they eased their stroke. They had to keep rowing or the current would take them down under the bridge again but they were panting like men who had been in battle—which they had been. Without the tide behind them, the thing would have been impossible, and they still had three miles to go.

They settled into a steady rhythm after they had caught their breath and Dodd felt guilty for not helping—but this was no time for apprentices at rowing.

'How far do we go fra the river's edge to the house?' Dodd asked.

'Half a mile perhaps,' said Enys. 'The path is muddy but passable. It's narrow though. If they have anyone watching it, they might warn the house and they could lock the place up or even cut some throats.'

'Ay,' said Dodd, 'We need to catch them unawares. Two men to go up the path on the quiet and cut any guards' throats...'

Enys coughed meaningfully.

'Oh ay, ehm...Capture them or something. About five more behind to get into the house and the rest to follow on if there's trouble. Are there stables?'

'Yes, at the back. But there was only me and everyone was asleep, so when I got in I just passed as one of them, taking the priest off for more interrogation.'

'Why did ye kill him, really? It wasnae the coney-catching, was it?'

Enys said nothing.

'Hm,' There was something Enys had said earlier that was niggling Dodd. He tried to track down what was worrying him. 'Ye had the password, did ye?'

'Yes. And it worked. I must say, I was surprised.'

'Cecil gave it ye?'

'Yes.'

'And the men slept through?'

'Well neither Heneage nor Topcliffe was there, but yes...'

Dodd sniffed. 'Ay well then, Cecil's got a man there and he drugged their beer.'

Enys was silent and Dodd saw his teeth flash in a rueful grin. 'And there was I congratulating myself on how cunning I had been.'

No, it was still all wrong. It felt wrong. You took on a job to fetch a man out of imprisonment and then straight away you stabbed him in the back and heaved him in the river? It made no sense. Far better and far less effort to just stab him where he was in the prison and leave in a hurry. If that was your intent, of course. Perhaps Enys had intended to rescue him after all. But why had Cecil organised his escape in any case? Why couldn't Cecil simply ask his father Lord Burghley to order Heneage to release him? From what Carey said, Burghley might have been old, but he was the chief man of the kingdom and the most trusted of all by the Queen...

Had Cecil ordered the killing then? But why didn't Enys say so? And if Cecil had ordered it, why did Enys feel he must run? And why use Enys at all instead of whoever it was he had working for

him inside the house? Why make it so complicated?

Dodd stared into the darkness, sucked his teeth, and listened to the steady rhythm of the oars as the powerful Cornishmen shoved the boat upriver against the flow. What was he getting into? Was that where they would have taken the women? How did Lady Hunsdon know for sure? What about Pickering?

'Did ye know Jackson well?' Dodd asked, fishing for some kind of clue, somewhere.

'No, I didn't. Only by correspondance.' Enys's answer was curt.

'Ah thocht ye came from a Papist family?'

'I do. I was in the Netherlands in the Eighties.'

It was there, just out of reach, somewhere in the darkness. If he'd been paid to kill Jackson, why would he have broken him out of jail first? Had he been paid at all…?

Dodd stopped breathing for a moment. Enys had certainly been paid in advance—he'd had money to gamble with at Pickering's game which never allowed any kind of credit. Or…he had been given money at any rate, perhaps with the promise of more. Then he had been given careful instructions and he had followed them and successfully freed his man. And then, while in the boat on the Thames, no doubt heading for the Pool of London to take ship and escape, seemingly on a whim, Enys had put a knife in the back of the man he had just rescued at considerable risk and dumped him over the side with his feet still in chains to weight him down.

Dodd tried to imagine doing that kind of a job and what might make him put a knife in someone at the end of it. After all, you never really wanted to do it, did you? Killing someone in cold blood like that? No matter how many men you might have killed in battle or a fight or even on somebody else's instructions, you never wanted to do something like that at such close quarters, especially not in a boat. He might spot what you were doing and certainly would resist, you might fall in or be stabbed yourself. Unconsciously, Dodd shook his head. You wouldn't do it just because the man had coneycatched a lot of people, though you might disapprove of it. And you certainly wouldn't do it if the son of the most powerful man in the kingdom had just paid you to help the prisoner escape.

In Dodd's mind there was only one reason why he might put

a knife in someone he had just rescued like that. He cleared his throat to ask Enys if that was the reason, then paused. All right. The only way the thing would work is if you realised that the man you had just rescued was going to try and kill you. Then it would make sense to put your knife in him first.

Why? Why would a priest who had just been rescued by Enys on behalf of...probably Cecil, possibly someone else...for what reason might he want to kill his rescuer? Well, they were alone in the boat apart from the boatman who had been well-bribed. One man goes upriver in a boat. A prisoner disappears from a safe-house. One man comes back, gets on a ship, and leaves England using the same name. And one man who knows too much about the scheme ends at the bottom of the Thames with a hole in him.

But you wouldn't expect a priest to behave like that, even a Jesuit. Also, how did Enys know for sure? His own voice came to him. 'You were from a Papist family.' Fr. Jackson was also a Papist—but what if Enys knew he wasn't what he claimed? Didn't all the Papists in a place tend to know each other?

Once again the backs of Dodd's legs went cold. Even the sounds of the oars faded to nothing as his mind slewed round to the new idea. Good God. Maybe? Perhaps little Mrs. Briscoe had been right and the corpse really had been her brother Harry Dowling, always in trouble, greedy for money. Perhaps the stern-looking Catholic lady who was not called Mrs. Sophia Merry was also right and the corpse was Fr. Jackson SJ. Perhaps they were the same man? In fact, thinking about what Ellie Briscoe had said of her brother and how he had refused to know her when she saw him in London, perhaps Harry Dowling was more of a coney-catcher than a priest. Perhaps he was working all the time for someone else...Such as Heneage? Or maybe Sir Robert Cecil? And both Harry Dowling and James Enys had been in the Netherlands where Englishmen tended to bunch together in places like Flushing or under the same captains. It was more than likely Enys and Dowling/Jackson had met.

So when he finally saw the man, Enys must have realised Jackson wasn't a priest at all. In fact, Cecil's involvement made it almost certain he was someone who had been spying for Cecil's steadily growing secret service. Cecil's involvement in helping him escape also suggested that he was someone who was valuable and knew too much to be left in Heneage's hands for too long. Enys had worked this out quickly because he knew the priest was lying, realised he himself knew too much to be allowed to live, and that the most likely way of getting rid of him was in the middle of a rescue.

But it had gone wrong for Cecil. Enys had fought in the Netherlands and he had struck first. The so-called Fr. Jackson went into the Thames still breathing and drowned—a nasty death, probably worse than the one Richard Tregian had suffered since Tregian had been hanged until he was dead. And Richard Tregian had died because Heneage assumed he was Cecil's man, so took him and put him to death publicly as a warning to Cecil. Enys had to lie low with what he had been given as a downpayment and being what he was had tried to gamble it into a nest egg and lost the lot. So he couldn't even pay his passage out of the country.

What had he done next? Gone to Cecil? Hardly, the man had tried to have him killed. Gone to...Well, obviously he had gone to Heneage who was the other side of the war he had stumbled into. He had gone to Heneage, spilled everything he knew. Probably he was trying to broker some kind of deal but of course Heneage had realised how that gave him a weapon. The taking of Briscoe's wife had been a side-game and a tidying up of loose ends in order to take Pickering's game. Heneage had arrested Portia Morgan to keep James Enys obedient and Portia Morgan would also be the bait that would draw the chivalrous and impulsive Carey into a trap, and alongside him that thorn in Heneage's side, Sergeant Henry Dodd. Enys was the stone that would kill two birds at once. You could hardly blame Heneage for not resisting the temptation. He had overegged the pudding when he ransacked Pickering's gaming chamber, but that was his habit as well.

However, Carey had run to Court to speak to the Queen so he conveniently wasn't here to stick his neck in another noose.

What had Enys said ... 'It was all a lie to coney catch great men at court.'

Dodd's own voice came back to him. 'Ye know nowt,' he had said to Carey about another ambush. 'Ye've been told.'

Two boats? Sergeant Dodd as advisor, in command with Mr.

Trevasker? Did Lady Hunsdon suspect something? He realised that he had sweat trickling down his back under his shirt, his stomach was crunched up, hiding under his ribs. This was far more frightening than a mere battle. He had been sixteen the last time he was this frightened. He looked across at the other boat which might as well have been on the other bank for all the talking he dared do. He couldn't even signal with a lantern for fear of being seen, and he certainly couldn't shout.

All right then. So they took Portia Morgan and had taken Briscoe's wife to make sure of Briscoe's help. It was provocative, an invitation to an attack. If there was to be an ambush there would be an alluring trail. And there was. Enys right there on the *Judith* where Carey would likely go to keep his father out of it, with the story of the house in the marshes, how he knew the path, how he had the key...

Dodd shook his head. This was all too complicated. It was simpler to think about it as if the Elliots had taken Janet and, say, Lady Widdrington.

No, perhaps not. Carey would be in the game then and make it complicated again. So. The Elliots have taken Janet. You think they've gone to their chief tower, but it could be one of the others. What do you do?

You hit the one with the less obvious trail and hope they haven't double-bluffed you. In fact, you hit both towers, but you personally, Henry Dodd, you go to the less obvious one and make damned sure it's taken quickly before they can cut Janet's throat.

Which is less obvious? Lady Hunsdon had said 'properties' so there were more than one. There was Heneage's large house in Chelsea and the one Enys had been talking about in the marshes on the south side of the river. Both houses accessible by boat, one on the north and one on the south of the river. One approachable through orchards and gardens, in the village of Chelsea where there are witnesses. The other out in the empty marshes along a single muddy path which you could mine, lay an ambush along, or simply wait until your attackers are in the house and then... say...blow it up. And which one has the more attractive trail?

Dodd showed his teeth to the night and relaxed. He leaned

over and tapped Ted Gunn on the arm. 'Can ye bring the boats together?' he asked. 'I wantae talk to Mr. Trevasker?'

Gunn nodded and called in a foreign language across the water. It sounded a bit like the funny jargon you sometimes heard from Welshmen or Irish kerns. The other boat came cautiously closer.

'Mr. Trevasker,' said Dodd, 'I've a mind tae talk to Mr. Pickering.'

Trevasker looked blank so Dodd repeated it as southern as he could and added 'The King of London.' Trevasker nodded hesitantly.

How and where could he find Pickering? Well, he was a headman who was also presumably about to go to war. He would have men placed on his borders to watch for him and tonight they would be awake.

'Take me to the nearest set of steps on the north bank,' Dodd said, 'Wait there for me,' Mr. Trevasker was frowning slightly but eventually he nodded and the gig that Dodd was in began cutting north towards Blackfriars steps again. The other gig backed water well out from the bank.

Dodd was impatient to meet Pickering. He climbed out as noisily as he could, went up the steps a little way, then turned suddenly and laid hands on the two beggars quietly following him. They choked because he was holding both of them by the neck.

'I havetae talk to Mr. Pickering at once,' he hissed. 'You go tell him, you stay here wi' me.'

Bare feet sprinted into the distance and Dodd settled down to wait. Pickering announced his presence by the unmistakeable pressure of a knife against Dodd's side and the smell of feet and sores. That was one of his henchman who had come up very silently next to Dodd despite the fact that he had his back firmly pressed to a wall from the old Whitefriar's monastery. In front of Dodd was the interesting sight of the King of London wearing rags and almost silent turnshoes.

Dodd grinned, knowing his teeth would show in the paltry moonlight.

'Well, Sergeant?' came Pickering's voice, steady in the greys and blues.

Dodd told him everything he knew, had worked out, and

thought he knew. At the end of it, Pickering was silent for two beats of Dodd's heart, and then he chuckled. Dodd nearly chuckled back because there was nothing more satisfying when you were on a raid than to know there was an ambush and where it was.

'I got some news for you too, Sar'nt. The prisoners ain't in Chelsea, nor the marshes,' Pickering said., 'And they ain't at the Tower neither. They come off their boats at the Bridge. My bet is Southwark or the Bridewell.'

'Ay,' said Dodd, rubbing his chin. 'But which?'

'We'll know in a minute or two, I've got young Gabriel watching the Southwark house for me. One of Topcliffe's places, but outside the City so 'e can play 'is games.'

'Can Ah go and tell my lady Hunsdon's men whit's in the wind?' said Dodd.

'Eh? Lady Hunsdon?'

'Ay, there's two boatloads of Cornish pirates that brought me here.'

Dodd saw Pickering's eyes glint with mischief. 'Well well, who'd ha' thought it. I know my Lord Hunsdon left Somerset House this evening heading up the Oxford road at the clappers.'

Dodd almost smiled back. Careys on the move, eh? Ay well, the Dodd headman was on the move too. He nodded and went down the steps to where the gig was tied up with a large Cornishman standing on the boatlanding looking nervous. Dodd saw Enys still sitting in the boat, waiting patiently, his tense face giving back moonlight. Dodd beckoned Enys to him and the man climbed out of the boat and came over. Dodd clapped him on the shoulder.

'There's a change of plan, Mr. Enys,' he said. 'We're gaunae...' Then he punched the man as hard as he could in the gut, caught his shoulders, steadied him and put his knee into Enys's groin. It was very satisfying and the man went down with little more than a whine. Ted Gunn was staring at him. He listened while Dodd carefully explained what was going on as southern as he could, and then climbed out of the boat, tied Enys's arms behind him, and stuffed a bit of rope in his mouth. He and another Cornishman lifted him into the gig and laid him down along the length of it. Then Gunn raised his arm and whistled like a curlew across the water. Dodd could hear the rhythm of the oars as the gig came in to the boatlanding. He explained again to Mr. Trevasker who also grinned happily. Then he tensed and one of his men raised a crossbow.

Dodd spun on his heel to see Pickering with a couple of ugly mugs and a remarkably handsome young blond man beside him. 'Gabriel 'ere says it's the Southwark house, but the Bridge is guarded,' explained the King, 'Not seriously, just someone watching. 'E also saw your boats climbing the Bridge rapids and the watermen says it was well-done but you was lucky not to die, and one of them lost ten shillings on it.'

'Ay,' agreed Dodd. 'Will yer man lead us across the flow tae Southwark?'

'Course 'e will.'

'Are there horses at the house?'

The blond man nodded. 'Three of them for dispatch riders to Dover,' he said in a deep voice.

'And where are the women?'

'Cellars of course,' said Gabriel. 'We 'eard 'em crying, couldn't see them.'

'Crying?' asked Dodd, his blood chilling.

'Yer, screaming one of them was, like she was being tortured.' The young man's face didn't change when he said it. 'Or flogged,' he added thoughtfully, 'she was a bit breathless.'

Dodd set his jaw. 'Mr. Pickering, what would you suggest?'

Pickering sucked his teeth. 'Gabriel tells me the house is locked up tight, no open winders, no outhouses to climb on. Front door's locked, o'course. There's a courtyard onto Upper Ground wiv men in it and dogs and one of the horses is there ready to take a message.'

It was a pity Heneage wasn't sloppy nor completely stupid. No doubt the house in the marshes was mined and the house in Chelsea well-defended. Southwark would have the fewest men, but there'd be enough to defend against a sneak attack or a frontal assault just in case. Well then, what you needed was distraction.

Dodd squatted down with Pickering, Gabriel, Mr. Trevasker, and Ted Gunn and laid out what he thought would make a good plan. At the end of it there was a moment of shocked silence.

'Well, Sar'nt,' said Pickering eventually, 'You can go back to Newcastle...'

'Carlisle,' Dodd corrected automatically.

'...the north, but I've got to live in London. This is my manor, you might say. And I've never done anyfink like that.'

'Ay, and anither man has put a brave upon ye. If ye dinna hit him back wi' more and worse, ye'll no' be a headman for long,' said Dodd with finality. 'But if ye can think of another way intae a house that's defended and has hostages of yourn, I'll be glad to hear of it and take the news back tae the north country.'

More silence. Finally Dodd recognised Gabriel's gruff voice. ''e's right, master,' it said, 'and that 'ouse is in a garden and right on the river.'

There was the sound of teeth being sucked. 'All right,' said Pickering, 'But we do it my way. We've got a bit of time to spare.'

Ted Gunn was delighted with his part in the business and kept quietly snickering to himself.

Pickering, Gabriel, and a couple of his upright men climbed into the gigs and the waterman who had piloted them through the bridge went with Ted Gunn to direct them going upstream against the difficult flow of the Thames without being sucked into any of the whirlpools or grounded on a sandbank. Both gigs were low in the water, but one crossed the current to the South Bank while the other with Ted Gunn and the still-sleeping Enys in it continued upstream towards Chelsea.

SATURDAY 16TH SEPTEMBER 1592,

DARK BEFORE DAWN

The boat kissed the boatlanding a little upstream of Heneage's house so Pickering, Dodd, Gabriel, Briscoe, and a couple of upright men that had fought in the Netherlands could get out. The boat carried on softly to the steps that led up to the garden of the house. There would be a wall and an iron grill, of course, but the Cornish had brought crowbars. It was at least an hour after midnight, maybe two, and Southwark was asleep, although the bakers would probably be stirring in an hour or so to light their ovens. There were lights from some of the bawdy houses to be sure, but Gabriel popped his head in one of them and spoke to the Madam who came out to curtsey to Pickering. The Bishop of Winchester may have been her landlord, if what Carey said was right, but Pickering was her real lord. She listened to what he had to say and then nodded, went indoors and started shouting at the girls. A little later all of them who weren't with clients came slinking out in their striped petticoats and elaborate hats and dangerously lowcut bodices. There was one striking redhead there with a cheeky grin and perfect white rounded tits that Dodd remembered from somewhere or other. He had to swallow hard and pull his eyes away. He had always liked red-heads and the fact that the girl had a couple of freckles low down only made her more interesting...

Pickering elbowed him in the ribs. 'If this lot works, Sar'nt, you only 'ave to say the word and she's yours.'

Dodd coughed. 'Ay, but Ah'm a married man.'

'So what?'

'Ah, ma wife's got some...eh...powerful relatives.'

'Oh. Well, never mind, they probably don't come to London.'

That was true enough to be quite tempting. Dodd thought about it for a moment and then decided he'd better concentrate. The girls went with them as they quietly walked towards Heneage's house, led by Gabriel. It was indeed closed—the door locked, the windows shuttered tight. At the back was a walled courtyard but there was nobody visibly keeping a watch. From the house came a series of howls and screams which then bubbled away.

'Jesu,' said Dodd, horrified. Nobody else took any notice. The girls fanned out and went and knocked on the doors of the nearby houses whilst Dodd and Pickering took a couple of the grenadoes that Trevasker had brought, lit them from a slow match that Trevasker had kept in a pot, and went round the back of the house.

Dodd hefted the heavy pottery ball filled with serpentine gunpowder and sawdust with the fuse coming out of the top. He hated grenadoes, always felt sick when he lit one because you never knew how long you had to throw it...Or whether someone brave might throw it back. But for setting fire to a roof, they couldn't be bettered.

Dodd threw the grenado overarm onto the thatch of Heneage's house where there was a dip between eaves. It landed, rolled, it was going to roll off the roof...And then it exploded—not as loudly nor as destructively as a petard which was the same thing made of iron rather than pottery—but well enough. A hole was blown in the thatch and the drier thatch inside caught alight immediately. Pickering's lob went neatly onto the roof, but then fell off and landed and exploded in the courtyard where there was an immediate squealing of pigs and a dog started barking manically.

Dodd went to the gate at the front of the house. Somebody fired at him with a pistol which missed, of course, and an arrow clattered against the shutter next to him. Another arrow followed it. He left a grenado there and took cover until that exploded too. Then he ran up to it and kicked it in as fast as he could while arrows and bullets clattered into the ground a yard behind him. They were shite, really. Quite clearly they knew nothing about defending a place, their angles of fire were all wrong.

Behind him he felt Briscoe, who was completely silent with a veney stick in one hand and a poinard in the other, behind Briscoe the other upright men, and then Pickering and Gabriel. He charged his shoulder into the remnants of the door, found himself facing a boy with his mouth open and an empty crossbow in his hands, and knocked him down with his stave. There was a mill in the part of the courtyard penned off for pigs and the two dogs on chains were barking themselves hoarse at it. An older man came at Dodd, who dodged and knocked him sideways. Briscoe took a man with a bow who was aiming at Dodd. Pickering and Gabriel were already across the yard and at the front door of the house itself. Gabriel knelt down at it as if he was praying while Pickering stood in front of him with a throwing dagger in each hand and an intent expression on his face.

Dodd's mouth turned down mournfully as he swapped blows with a swordsman, knocked the weapon aside, and sliced down through his shoulder. No jack. Was the man mad? On the other hand, Dodd had no jack on either and didn't think a fancy doublet could do much to protect him from a better-wielded sword. Somebody else came running at him and without thinking he kicked the men's legs from under him and knocked him out. Jesu, he'd never fought so gently in his life.

Gabriel was kneeling beside the lock with a hooked piece of wire in his fist and a grin on his face. Pickering opened the door, Dodd shouldered past him and spitted the man waiting with a raised sword.

Outside the harlots were helping to ring the firebell and shout fire. The next-door-neighbours were already forming a bucket chain from the Thames. Nobody had time to worry about the pitched battle around the house as the Cornish broke through the barred gate and into the garden.

Dodd knew he was in a dangerous state. The smell of the fire seemed to unroll the black rage in his belly and turn it into something like pleasure. He walked swiftly into the hall of the house which was already starting to fill with smoke, saw somebody start up from their sleep next to the fire, and hit him with his veney stick. It seemed a waste not to kill him, but Dodd was trying to do things the way Lady Hunsdon wanted them. There was somebody on the stairs so Dodd held his breath, burrowed through the smoke, grabbed him by the doublet front and threw him downstairs where Gabriel or Pickering coshed him.

There was a knot of them at the top of the stairs, two or three men, getting in each others' way as Briscoe fought his way up. Dodd pulled a painted cloth off the wall, threw it over their heads, and then beat everything round he could see with his cosh before throwing them down the stairs one after another. Gabriel laughed behind him as he stepped over one of the bodies.

Breathing as little as he could in the acrid smoke, Dodd slammed through several doors. Somebody shot a pistol at him again and by sheer luck the ball went into the wall not a foot from his face. Dodd's mouth drew down as he kicked through the door where the man with the pistol lodged, dodged the downswing of the ball of iron on the pistol's stock, knocked the arm aside, grabbed the front of the man's doublet, and headbutted him right on the nose. The man dropped his pistol and fell back clutching his flattened nose and mewing so Dodd kicked his legs out from under him and stamped on his hand. Behind him was Portia Morgan with her hands tied to a bedpost, her doublet off and her trunk hose half pulled down. What he could see of her arse was as marred with pockmarks as the rest of her, though nicely shaped.

Dodd looked at her face with the bloody nose and the black eye and the split lip and something told him what to say as he sawed through the rope around her hands.

'Ay, Mr. Enys, can ye fight?'

She paused, gulped, nodded. 'Where's my sword?' She was making her voice deliberately deep. She was hitching her braces back over her shoulders, rebuckling her belt, coughing hard in the smoke. With shaking hands she caught up her doublet from the floor and slung it on, doing up the buttons quickly. Now he knew what to look for of course it was obvious; her hands may have been pock-marked but they were smaller than a man's and very deft.

'Take this,' said Dodd, giving her his veney stick. 'Where's Mrs. Briscoe?'

'She's in the cellar. Can't you hear her?'

Another earsplitting scream sliced through the building. Enys bent down to the man Dodd had flattened, who was trying to get up again. She pulled his eating knife from his belt and went to stab him in the chest with it.

'Better slit his throat,' Dodd said, 'It's easier.'

Enys snarled, caught the man's hair in her fist and pulled his head back.

'Mind the blood,' Dodd said to her, deliberately turning away. He felt she had the right. He still heard the soft sound of blade on flesh and the suck of air into a slit windpipe. Then he heard her being sick. The smell of the fire was gaining on him, the rage in him and the smell of blood: he wasn't angry exactly for there was none of the red mist of it, but he was far out the other side of the particular black rage that took him in situations like this and made him cold and ruthless and evil. He knew he was evil, but it couldn't be helped.

'Sar'nt,' growled Briscoe from the door, 'they're hooking the thatch off.'

Outside the street was full of purposeful activity as men with long hooks pulled down the burning thatch and poured Thames water over it. In the courtyard at the front the pig was squalling so loudly and the dog was barking himself hoarse, you couldn't hear what was going on in the cellar—except there was something loud still happening there too.

'Mr. Pickering wants you downstairs, Sar'nt,' said Gabriel.

Dodd was panting for air as not enough of it came through the holes in the roof, and he hadn't the breath to argue, so he turned, clattered down the stairs, followed by a still-retching and swallowing Portia Morgan, through the hall and another door. Somebody erupted from a closet door behind him and found Enys in the way. She managed somehow to back-hand the man in the face with her stick. There was an audible crack as his jaw broke. He fell back as she kicked him hard in the knee and when he went down she grabbed his dagger from his belt and went to cut his throat as well. Dodd grabbed her arm and stopped her with regret.

'Mr. Enys,' he shouted, 'Milady wants us no' to kill tae many o' them.'

She blinked, shook her head and—typical woman—said, 'Why?'

Dodd didn't have breath nor time to tell her. He just shrugged, broke the man's knee properly with the hilt of his sword so he couldn't make trouble after, and carried on down into the cellars which stank badly of blood and shit. Pickering was standing in the middle of the place looking horrified, the heavy iron-bound door had been smashed in and when Dodd braced himself to look through into the straw-scattered little cell, he understood why.

A sigh puffed out of him. There was young Mrs. Briscoe on her hands and knees in the straw squawking and howling. Portia Morgan blinked, took a long shaky breath, blinked again. Then she dropped her veney stick, went over, bent and stroked the girl's shoulder. 'It's all right, it's coming.'

Another horrendous shriek came from the girl as her belly moved. Enys saw Dodd standing staring, stood up, and came to him.

'Sergeant, can you get me two stools or blocks of wood this high, a big bowl of hot water or some aqua vitae, linen strips and a clean knife.' The girl was howling again, calling for her mum.

'Now hush,' said Portia Morgan. 'You're not going to die, it's only a baby. Sergeant!'

She was lifting the girl's petticoats to look and Dodd turned quickly and ran up the stairs. Pickering came with him.

'God's truth,' he said as Dodd stripped off one of the stunned men's doublet and hauled his shirt off over his head, then moved to the corner where there was a wood-basket and a promising looking small barrel. Dodd tapped some into a mug, tried it. The aqua vitae was cheap but drinkable, so he drank that to steady him, poured another one and gave it to Pickering to sustain him, and then put the barrel under one arm, picked up the woodbasket after slinging the man's eating knife into it along with his shirt, and carried the lot down the cellar steps to where Portia Morgan had her hand under the girl's petticoats and a look of concentration on her face.

'If you could find a real midwife, Sergeant,' she said, 'that would help, I'm having to try and remember what the woman did for...er...my sister.'

'Ah've helped ewes at lambing and dogs wi' whelping,' Dodd offered. 'It's no' sae different.'

At that point the girl squealed angrily again and started to cry. Portia Morgan turned again and looked under the blood-splattered petticoats. 'It's coming, I can see it,' she cried, and dug into the wood basket to pull out two large blocks of wood which she set on the floor. 'Come on, Ellie, sit on these.'

Dodd lent a hand to heave the girl off her hands and knees and sit her down with her legs spread, a buttock to each block, while Portia shoved the petticoats back and the girl grabbed her head and howled. Something black and bloody was showing between her legs. Suddenly he decided this was a lot more frightening than a lambing and ran up the stairs.

'It's coming,' he said in explanation to Pickering who was sitting on the master's seat in the kitchen with his feet on the table, drinking from another barrel he seemed to have found. Dodd helped himself. 'We canna move her until her wean's born now.'

'I could see that, Sar'nt,' said Pickering. There was a thundering about upstairs and the firebell had stopped ringing. 'Fire's out, fank goodness. I've got Briscoe to check for any remaining cinders, keep his mind off things. I'll blame the fire on you.'

Dodd shrugged. What did he care what a lot of Londoners thought of him? His cold black rage had gone now, he felt as happy and relaxed as if he had...well, as if he had just had a pipe of Moroccan incense and tobacco.

At that moment there was a distant boom and all the shutters rattled. Dodd cocked an ear to it. The shriek from the cellars had almost drowned the noise.

'So it *was* mined,' he said.

'Yer,' said Pickering. 'I wonder if that bloke Vent survived.'

'Best not talk about it,' Dodd said, 'Whit do the neighbours say?'

'Oh they're all right. They know I'll pay 'em for their trouble. And the roof is off and the fire's out and Gabriel's tying up the men here in one of the bedrooms. There was only twenty of them and only a couple of dead.'

'So the maist o' them will be at Chelsea or the marshes.'

'Yer,' said Pickering, 'waiting for us with not the faintest idea.' He laughed. 'Until now, mind.'

He laughed again and lifted his cup of wine in a toast to them.

***

Perhaps an hour later there was a clattering of a boat at the watersteps, a challenge from the Cornishmen. And then there were mutterings and Mr. Trevasker saying 'milady' and 'your honour.' Pickering took his feet off the table and sat up warily.

Into the looted kitchen walked the small sprightly figure of Lady Hunsdon, pink-cheeked and happy. Beside her, dark and lean and bowed over sideways and forwards by the curve of his back, was a man in sober black damask and a white falling band, a fashionable black beaver hat shading a long face. And behind him trotted Shakespeare.

Dodd came to his feet and so did Pickering.

'Sergeant, my compliments on a very neat piece of work,' said Lady Hunsdon, with her wonderful roguish smile that had caught Lord Hunsdon, the King's bastard, in a permanent web. 'Sir Robert Cecil, Privy Councillor, asked to meet you at once.'

Dodd bowed to her and inclined his head to the second son of the most powerful man in the Kingdom. From things Carey had told him, he thought that Burghley, Cecil's father, and Carey's lord, the Earl of Essex were at some kind of courtly feud. So why was Cecil so friendly with Carey's mam, eh?

'Ay,' said Dodd, 'Ehm...' How did you do it properly? 'Ah, milady, may I present Mr. Pickering, the...eh...'

Pickering stepped forward quickly, bowed to Lady Hunsdon and Cecil and took his hat off. 'Laurence Pickering, milady, your honour,' he said. 'Merchant of London.'

From the half-closed eyelids and the faint smile, Dodd felt that Cecil knew perfectly well who this was. From the expression on Lady Hunsdon's face it seemed that she wasn't entirely sure.

'Ah...Mr. Pickering helped wi' the raid,' Dodd finished slightly lamely, hoping he hadn't offended or insulted anyone. 'He's... ah...a friend of Sir Robert's.'

'An honour to be of service to you, milady, yer honour,' said Pickering, staring hard at Cecil.

'Mr. Pickering,' said the hunchback, inclining his body slightly, 'I've heard a great deal about you from my mentor and friend, Sir Francis Walsingham, God rest his soul. I believe there was an... understanding between you?'

'Yes there was, yer honour,' said Pickering, 'I 'ad the...ah.. the honour of 'elping Sir Francis on several occasions. Though never as...ah.. dramatic as this time.'

'Quite so.' Sir Robert Cecil smiled and his dark face instantly transformed into a handsome and charming man. 'I understand you run the only game that's worth visiting in London and that Heneage had the impudence to raid it?'

'Yerss, yer honour, that's right.'

'Outrageous. I hope you will be continuing with it...'

'Of course, yer honour. When I get it set up again, shall I send your honour word of its whereabouts?'

'How kind, Mr. Pickering,' said Cecil. 'I would be delighted to learn to play properly.'

Pickering bowed. Dodd could almost see the implied handshake between them. 'Wiv yer honour's permission, I think I'll take my... friends...away now.'

'Do so, with my thanks,' said Cecil.

'And mine, of course, Mr. Pickering,' said Lady Hunsdon. 'How wonderful to meet another of my son's more interesting friends.'

'Yersss, milady,' said Pickering, rocking gently on the balls of his feet with his thumbs in his belt.'Your son has some very good friends.' He turned to Dodd, winked, and left the kitchen, whistling through his teeth.

Cecil came forwards into the kitchen while Lady Hunsdon went and sat down in the chair with arms. She still had her silver and ebony cane which she leaned on. Cecil sat beside her on a bench, leaned his elbows on his bowed legs, and winced slightly. Shakespeare took up his unobtrusive position with his back to the wall near the door, his hands behind his back, the perfect servingman, listening for all he was worth.

'Well, Sergeant Dodd,' Cecil said, 'why not tell me the story.'

Dodd told him. He told it as short as he could, not including the tangle over the Enys twins. There was no more shrieking from the cellar but nothing much seemed to be happening there. Dodd really hoped that nobody had died. Somewhere a cat was miaowing.

At the end of it Cecil smiled his shockingly charming smile again.

'I will elucidate a couple of points for you, Sergeant, since it seems you have worked out most of it.'

Dodd tilted his head and prepared to be lied to.

'The Cornish lands that were hawked about London by Fr. Jackson, were of course, nearly worthless. Certainly there was no gold. Unfortunately...Very unfortunately many courtiers were taken in by his plausibility and bought them. Fr. Jackson was a Jesuit in that he had studied briefly at Rheims—long enough to counterfeit a Catholic priest—but his real name was Harry Dowling, as you surmised. He had offered to work for me against the Catholics but I naturally turned him down as he was not to be trusted.'

Lady Hunsdon let out a small sniff of disbelief at this. Long practise allowed Dodd to keep his face completely straight. So did Cecil. By God, Burghley's second son would be very dangerous at primero.

'Among the spectators was Heneage. Being deeply implicated, he arrested Jackson to find out who he was working for. I engaged James Enys to free him and all did indeed fall out as you said. I heard no more from Enys. Heneage did not know what had happened to Jackson nor his rescuer. Heneage was also desperate to keep the secret of the lands he had bought being worth nothing much so that he could sell them to other innocent barnards. Hence he arrested Richard Tregian and after torture had revealed no information as to the whereabouts of Jackson nor to the source of the lay because of course the whole game was due to Jackson's greed, substituted him for the priest so that no one would ask questions about the priest.'

Dodd inclined his head. That was more or less true. Except that he was even more sure that Cecil was the one who had set Jackson on to sell the lands. That coded letter had said most of the wheals were owned by Icarus—presumably Cecil's target. It still made sense that way. God, the man was twisty.

'And then you come into the mix and Heneage begins to panic. He knows he has no defence in law to your suits, and so he resorts to force against you.' Cecil smiled and chuckled. 'A very foolish man. He should have made you a respectable offer.'

'Ay,' said Dodd. Perhaps he would have taken it.

'And it ends here, does it not?' Cecil continued. 'Unfortunately it seems that some ill-affected Papists have blown up another property owned by Heneage and that there has been a riot here between the rabble and scum Heneage chose to employ. You fortunately happened to be nearby with my Lady Hunsdon's men and you were able to quell the riot and out the fire—oh, and rescue a young lawyer and Mr. Briscoe's wife. You have not been able to kill Topcliffe?'

'He wisnae here,' Dodd said. It had been a disappointment, that.

'How unfortunate,' said Cecil with that charming smile again. 'So both myself and my worshipful father owe you thanks for preventing worse bloodshed here. I shall be writing a report to him to that end and quite possibly, Her Majesty may choose to reward you as well.'

From Carey's constant complaints on the subject, Dodd suspected that he would find a nest high in a tree that was full of suckling pigs before that happened, but still it was a nice thought. And it meant he was free to go?

'Ay, sir,' he said, 'Ah…I heard Mr. Heneage had a warrant for me on a charge of high treason.'

Cecil tutted. 'I am quite sure that is not the case, or if it was, in the heat of the moment, it will no longer be the case after I have spoken to the gentleman. Which I intend to do immediately at his home in Chelsea.'

Dodd stood as Cecil levered himself to his feet and so did Lady Hunsdon. 'Ay,' said Dodd, feeling inadequate to the task of taking his leave properly from Carey's amazing mother. 'Yer Cornishmen are fine fighters,' he said lamely. 'And…ah…it wis an honour to serve ye, my lady.'

Lady Hunsdon beamed and held out her hand to him. Dodd knew what he was supposed to do, frantically thought back to what Carey normally did, dismissed it as impossibly complicated, and just took her hand and bowed over it.

He found her arms around him in a surprisingly fierce hug. 'Sergeant,' she said as she let him go, 'like my husband, I'm honoured to have you with me. Give Robin my love when you see him.' She paused and her dimples showed again. 'If you can, my handsome.'

Dodd coughed, 'Ay. Thank ye yer honour. God speed, my lady.'

***

Dodd wandered out to the grey courtyard where he found a wounded and bleeding pig lying exhausted in its blood while the dog barked hoarsely on the end of his chain. Thoughtfully Dodd stepped up behind the pig and slit its throat quickly to put it out of its pain, then found a bone in the trough which he threw to the dog. In the way of dogs, the animal barked a couple more times and then starting gnawing on the bone.

There was something kicking and pounding at the stable door and neighing in panic, so Dodd went to the stable door and opened it, dodged the wild-eyed head that immediately tried to bite him, then looked hard at the animal. It was the nice one with the white sock he'd noticed at Chelsea, one of the regular dispatch horses no doubt which meant he'd be fast and probably quite strong.

Dodd unbolted the bottom door and slid into the stall quickly, then up close to the horse and spoke to him in his ear, stroking his neck and shoulder, gently fending off the teeth. 'It's all done wi', ye stupid jade,' he said since it didn't matter what he said, 'And ye're coming with me,'

The saddle was hanging up and the bridle with it, so Dodd spent a little longer gentling the animal until it snorted and lowered its head for him, and then he brushed the coat down with a whisp of hay and put the bridle on and the saddle. Both were very nice, good leather and not too fierce a bit.

He had forty miles at least and wanted to be able to go quickly, so he checked the other stalls and found another perfectly good horse, not a gelding this time, but a chestnut mare also upset and relieved to see a man who patted her neck and called her a bastard in a soft and friendly voice. He put her bridle on as well and took the reins forward over her head, then led both horses out into the courtyard.

Gabriel was standing there, watching with interest. 'Where are you going?'

'Och,' said Dodd, 'Mr. Pickering's a man o' parts here, but Ah'm not and I dinna wantae be in London when Heneage finds out whit happened.'

'S'all right,' said Gabriel looking offended. 'There won't be any witnesses. Mr. Pickering and his honour said so.'

'My lady Hunsdon said she didnae want killing.'

'No, they just won't remember. Any of 'em.'

'Ay, well. Ah'm tired o' London and now Ah've had ma satisfaction for the insult Heneage put on me, Ah've nae reason to stay.'

'I'd stay for Molly, she likes you.'

'Molly?'

'The mort wiv the big tits wot gave you the eye,' said Gabriel, grinning. 'She says her and Nick the Gent tried to tip you the marrying lay a few weeks back but it went wrong. She says you was fun, though.'

Dodd could feel his face prickling with embarrassment. So that's where he'd seen her before. 'Ay, but that woman were blonde,' was all he could say.

Gabriel sniggered. 'Well, you never know what colour her 'air's going to be, so it's best to look at 'er tits, innit?'

'Tell her she can find me at Carlisle castle if she wants,' Dodd told Gabriel with dignity. 'Ah'm a married man.'

Gabriel spread his hands in mock despair and turned away. 'Gi' my respects to Mr. Pickering,' Dodd shouted after him, 'and ma thanks for coming out for me.' He put his hand on the horse's withers and jumped up into the saddle and immediately felt happy and at home.

'It's been a pleasure,' said Pickering's voice from the kitchen door, ''av a good journey norf now, Sar'nt.'

Dodd nodded, took his hat off to Pickering, and was interested to see Pickering lifting his statute cap in return. Gabriel had already opened the courtyard gate.

Dodd came out of the gate with his remount trotting behind him and turned right to head west along Upper Ground to the horse-ferry for Westminster where he could pick up the Edgeware Road that led to Oxford. There was no point trying to cross London Bridge before the dawn broke when they would open the gates on the north side, and there was another hour to go at least.

Behind him he could now hear the outraged bawling of the new baby which was one of the happiest sounds in the world, he thought, even if it wasn't his. That ball of rage had been cleared from his stomach by arranging for the blowing up of one of Heneage's houses, the burning and raiding of another, and reiving two good horses from him. Who knew what the court case might bring or what Sir Robert Cecil might do? So he laughed out loud, put his heels in, and cantered west along the south bank of the

Thames, past the round wooden structure of the bear baiting and the scaffolding around another round building that was going up right next to it. Londoners were always building something new.

Behind him the sun rose.

AN AIR OF TREASON

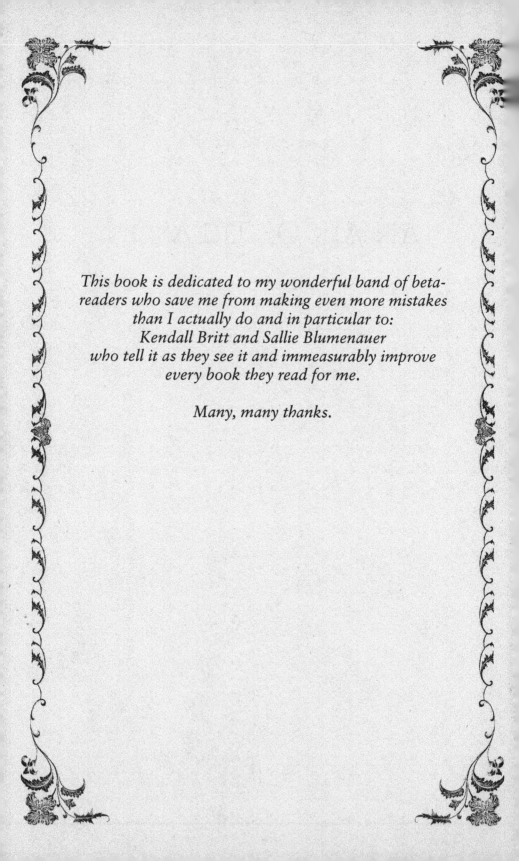

This book is dedicated to my wonderful band of beta-readers who save me from making even more mistakes than I actually do and in particular to:
Kendall Britt and Sallie Blumenauer
who tell it as they see it and immeasurably improve every book they read for me.

Many, many thanks.

SATURDAY 16TH SEPTEMBER 1592, MORNING

It was the devil's own job, it truly was, thought Hughie Tyndale. How the hell had he agreed to it? Why had he agreed to it?

The internal voice that never missed a chance to jeer at him was quick with an answer. So ye wouldna hang, it said, why else?

'I'll hang if I manage it,' Hugh said back to the jeering voice.

The jeering voice said nothing because this was plainly true. If you got caught killing someone, you generally hanged. All the more if they found out why you were killing him, which they probably would if they used the boot or the pinniwinks or whatever it was the English authorities used when they urgently wanted to find out something. And killing a cousin of the Queen would most certainly draw their attention.

He'd tried before to get close to the man he was to kill and failed miserably. Several times. That time in St. Paul's Walk by Duke Humfrey's tomb. The place had been crowded despite the plague running through London. It was full of ugly men in worn jacks, while Carey the Courtier, the man he was supposed to kill, had wandered by dressed in many farms' worth of velvet and pearls, deep in conversation only a yard away.

Of course he hadn't been intending to do the killing out in public. The first part of the plan was to go to work for the man, find out everything about him and pass it on to Scotland. How? He didn't know, but someone would tell him, apparently. Then he would do the killing and if he could get away in time, he'd be free as a bird. That was according to the mysterious man who said he worked for the Earl of Bothwell. When the funeral had been held, Hughie could visit a certain goldsmith in London town and receive a pile of gold. Allegedly.

Hughie shifted his weight and consciously straightened his back. He'd do it, of course he would. He wouldn't hang; he'd be rich. So now he wondered how he could be sure he stood out among all the mob of unemployed servingmen under the Cornmarket roof—without being so obvious about it that he tipped off the Courtier. Bothwell's man had warned him, the Courtier is a lot cleverer than he looks or sounds.

Oxford Cornmarket, with its smart lead roof held up on round pillars down the centre of the street, was packed with men and quite a few women, people having come to the hiring fair from villages and towns for miles around. The Queen and all her Court and baggage and hangers-on were at last only seven days away. The city fathers and the university were in the last contentious stages of setting up the elaborate expensive pageantry of welcome. No doubt most of them were in meetings, speechifying at each other.

The whole of Oxford seemed to be armoured with scaffolding. The streets were clean for the first time in twenty-four years, and some of them were being newly paved, some boarded over.

A college steward was standing on a box, shouting aloud from a list.

'I want eight carpenters, four plumbers, five limners, eight labourers for college of Trinity,' he bellowed. 'Thruppence a day until the Queen leaves, a bonus from my Lord Chamberlain if all work is done before the Queen arrives, another bonus if nothing is amiss when she leaves.'

Those were good terms. Some of the men standing around Hughie shifted toward the steward, even though several of them didn't look like skilled men but like simple bruisers.

A few of the girls were surrounding a stout woman on another box, roaring her needs—laundresses, sempstresses, confectioners, cleaners. An entire new city was foisting itself awkwardly on the scholarly city of Oxford, like an eagle on a blackbird's nest.

Hughie backed a little to the wooden pillars of the smart merchant's house next to the church. Most of the men there were quite a bit smaller than him and a few looked at him sideways.

His quarry would come, of course he would. The Courtier needed at least one henchman and Hughie would be perfect for him. Where else was he going to find so cheap a servingman with Hughie's abilities?

Hughie scanned the better-dressed men walking around

amongst the people for hire. Most were stewards and college bursars, narrow-eyed, tight-pursed. A few were clearly harbingers for the Queen or the greater lords.

Hughie knew the Courtier was in town for sure, and would probably leave again on Sunday afternoon. Possibly earlier. He had arrived late on Friday night, dressed in hunting green with one spare mount and a lathered pony heavy-laden with packs. That was quite impressive, Hughie had to admit. It was more than forty miles from London to Oxford and he hadn't really been expected so early—Hughie had been carefully buttering up Lord Chamberlain's steward and making himself pleasant to the minor officials of his household on the assumption the quarry would travel with his father.

No, according to the horseboy Hughie had been paying on retainer at the main carter's inn near Christ Church, the man had arrived Friday night, both horses and the pony exhausted, at around seven o'clock. Forty miles in a day—despite the heavy cart and pack horse traffic on the Oxford Road—meant he must have been using the higher causeway reserved for the Queen's messengers, and galloping at least half the time. The man himself was tired but quite alert enough to make sure Hughie's helper carried the heavy packs up to his room and then was tipped a sixpence to guard the door. The Courtier saw the host, paid for the room, and ate the ordinary for his dinner.

He had no henchmen with him, not one. Not even the surly-looking borderer who had been shadowing him in London. So it stood to reason that he would be in need of at least one follower. At least one.

Hughie peered through the shadowed forest of humanity again. He had to be there, where else would he find a servingman? He had to come.

'What's your name?' came a snappy voice beside him.

It wasn't the Courtier. Hughie looked as nervous and as thick as he could. 'Oh ah, Hughie, an' it please yer honour, Ah'm a...'

The steward tutted and passed on immediately. It was Hughie's accent, he knew that. Not only was it a harsh voice, like a corncrake, but you could easily hear in it that his first language was Scotch not English. And although cheap, the Scotch were notoriously dangerous employees.

Someone who had been leisurely buying a pie from a nicely shaped girl under the portico opposite spun round to look at him.

God above, it was him! Hughie did his best not to stare, modestly looking at the ground. The man was well built, tall, chestnut hair under his hat and a goatee beard that needed trimming, extremely bright blue eyes and beaky nose, and a breezy manner that breathed of what he was and what he thought of himself.

Carey the Courtier was first cousin to the Queen in two different directions, one of them firmly on the wrong side of the blanket, according to Bothwell's man's clerk. His father's coat of arms said so proudly, boasted of it in fact, blazoned with three Tudor roses. You couldn't hardly put it plainer, the clerk had sneered, and the English heralds had allowed it, the scandalous Papistic perverts.

This was the man he had to kill: Sir Robert Carey, youngest son of the Lord Chamberlain, Baron Hunsdon, connected by blood and marriage with half the Court as well as the Queen. Carey was currently a controversial deputy warden on the English West March, where he was interfering in things that didn't concern him.

Mind, he hadn't looked quite so full of himself the time he'd been pointed out to Hughie at the Scottish Court, but that had been in the summer and he'd had a stressful few days there.

Carey did seem a little worried and he hadn't seen a barber for a couple of days either. Would he remember the disastrous last time Hughie had made a play to work for him? That was the point. God, those musicians had been angry.

Carey had come over and was standing in front of Hughie, looking him up and down.

'Quhair are ye fra?' he asked in passable Scotch.

That shouldn't have been a surprise to Hughie, yet it was. He stuttered.

'Ay...ah...Edinburgh.'

'Quhat are ye at sae far fra yer ain country?'

'Ah'm trying to get maself home, sir,' said Hughie, getting ahold of himself, switching to English and straightening his spine.

'Oh?' One of the man's eyebrows had gone straight up his forehead.

'Ah come south on a ship wi' a merchant, but we had a falling out and Ah'm heading north now.'

Carey came closer and looked Hughie up and down again, carefully. He stood still for it, feeling a blush coming up his neck.

'What's yer trade?'

'Ma dad wis a tailor, sir, I prenticed tae him but it didna suit me well....' That had been his uncle Jemmy, not his dad but no matter, near enough.

The other eyebrow went up and Carey crossed his arms and started stroking his goatee thoughtfully. 'Did you grow too tall to sit sewing all day?'

Och thank God, thought Hughie, excitement rising in him. Is it working? Is it really working?

'Ay, sir.' It was quite true he had got too tall. Sitting cross-legged all day had cramped him something dreadful, though not as much as frowsting about indoors all the time. 'Once Ah grew and got my size, I couldnae stick the tailoring, so I prenticed wi' a barber for a while and then after I got...ah...intae a wee spot of bother...I hired on as a merchant's henchman to come south, sir.'

Carey beckoned Hughie to turn his head and lift his hair. Ah, yes, looking for a ragged ear from having it nailed to the Edinburgh pillory for thieving. No, Hughie's ears were still the shape God had given them.

'What was the spot of bother?'

This was the lie absolute, the only one completely adrift from the truth.

'It wis a riot, sir, in Edinburgh, after a football match. Ah killed a man and the procurator banished me from Edinburgh for a year and a day.'

'Hmm. How did you kill the man?'

Hughie improvised. 'Ah hit him on the head with an inn table, sir.'

Carey nodded, looking cynical. It struck Hughie that lying about it was actually fine, so long as he could come up with a more believably serious killing-method when he needed it. Only not as serious as it had actually been, of course. Carey wouldn't hire him if he boasted about killing his uncle.

Hughie knew he was too saturnine and large to be able to look innocent and so he settled for looking hopeful. Come on, man, Hughie begged silently, thinking of the pile of gold that would be his when he'd done the job. I'm what you need. Come on.

The man had his head on one side, appraising Hughie with his eyes narrowed. 'Do you know who I am?' he asked.

'Ah, no, sir. Sorry, sir.'

'What's your name?'

'Hughie Tyndale.'

'Like the translator of the Bible in King Henry's reign?'

'Ah...maybe, sir?'

Who the hell was that? Hughie thought. He used the name Tyndale because he wasn't inclined to tell them his right surname and that was where his family came from originally. 'Ah dinna ken...'

'No matter. So you're looking for a master who might take you north?'

'Ay, sir.' He risked it. 'And disnae mind ma voice.'

Carey nodded absently. He seemed to be thinking, appraising Hughie again. There was a faint frown on his face. 'Have I ever met you before? I was in Edinburgh as a young man.'

'Ah...' Oh God, oh God, he'd remembered. 'Ah...when was it, sir?'

'Oh, about ten years ago now.'

'Och, Ah wisnae mair than a lad...'

'Yes, of course. Or perhaps one of your family?'

'Perhaps, sir.'

Hughie's stomach was getting tighter and tighter. This might work. The Courtier hadn't turned away. It might work. Please God, let it work.

The man in front of him, in the mud-splashed hunting green and long boots, laughed and slapped his fine gloves on the palm of his hand.

'So you know how to tailor and barber and you can fight?'

'Ay, sir. That I can.'

'Fourpence a day, all lodging and food found. Will that do you?'

'Ay, sir?' Hughie heard his voice tremble. It wasn't riches, but it wasn't bad, a whole penny a day better than labouring, which he'd done before and didn't like. 'Ah, sir, that'd be fourpence a day English?'

Carey laughed again. 'Oh, yes. I might even be able to get you some livery if my father's feeling generous.'

'Ay, sir?' It was working. 'Ay, that's verra…ah…very good, sir.'

Carey stripped off his right glove and his right hand came down on Hughie's right shoulder and gripped. Hughie looked down at it, with the bright golden ring on it and a couple of nails almost regrown.

'Excellent! Do you, Hughie Tyndale of Edinburgh town, swear to serve me faithfully according to my commands within Her Majesty's law and your right honour, so help you God?'

'Ay, sir, I do.'

'Then I, Robert Carey, knight and deputy warden of Carlisle, swear to be your good lord as long as you serve me well, so help me God.'

They spat on their palms and shook hands. It was the old-fashioned way, the way of Hughie's grandfather, when the duties had gone in both directions from man to master and back again. Hughie felt a vast golden bubble of relief escaping from his lungs. No matter that he'd sworn fealty to the man he was to spy on and, in due course, kill. He'd sort it out with God later. God would surely understand that he had no choice.

SATURDAY 16TH SEPTEMBER 1592, NOON

The first thing that Hughie Tyndale found after becoming Sir Robert's henchman was that he hadn't been walking fast enough. He kept getting left behind as Carey forged through the crowds of the hiring fair to the desk at the centre where the master of the fair kept his register. Carey signed his name and paid the tax, Hughie made his mark. He could in fact write but he had decided long ago not to make too much of that.

'Can you read?' Carey asked him when he saw the mark.

'Ay, sir,' Hughie said. 'Ma dad put me tae the Dominie to learn ma letters.'

'Good, read that,' said Carey pointing at the words of the indenture the clerk was writing up three times. Hughie struggled through the easier words despite some of it being in some kind of foreign.

'Hmm, creditable,' said Carey as the clerk tore the indenture in three, gave Carey one part, Hughie himself the other part, and kept the third. It was for a year and a day from the hiring fair, plenty long enough to do what Hughie had to. On the other hand, making it official in the modern way as well meant that killing Carey would be petty treason and he might burn for it. If he got caught, of course, which he wouldn't.

Gulping slightly he half-trotted after Carey's long stride, out from under the roof and into the alehouse on Carfax opposite the tower, where Carey bought ale for both of them and they toasted each other, sitting in the window.

'Whit will ye have me do, sir?' Hughie asked, then stopped himself because you should really wait for the master to speak first.

Carey didn't seem to mind. 'I lost my body servant to...well, to a flux in London,' he said, drinking deep and looking surprisingly sad. 'That's why I hired you, so I hope you really did prentice with a tailor for a while. I urgently need someone to make sure my Court suit fits me properly.'

'Och,' Hughie frowned, 'Ah dinna ken much about English Court fashion, sir.'

'You don't need to, I know plenty. You only need to be able to sew.'

'Ay.'

'If you can't do it, I'll have to find a tailor for the work, but I hope you can as there's a dreadful dearth of tailors in the town at the moment.'

'Ay, sir. I hear the Queen's coming.'

'Indeed she is and I want to make sure she likes me well enough to pay me my fee and confirm my warrant as deputy warden,' said Carey. 'Meantime, where are you staying?'

The money he'd been given by Bothwell's man to take him south had run through his fingers with dreadful speed. Hughie had slept under a haystack the night before. He'd had nightmares that the stone mushrooms holding the base of the huge stack of hay off the ground were shortening so he'd be crushed and he kept waking, covered in sweat to find rats using him as a convenient ladder to get up into the hay. He'd scrambled out into the grey dawn feeling horrible.

'Ehm...'

'No matter. There'll be a truckle bed or a pallet for you somewhere. Can you ride?'

'Ay, sir, well enough.' He'd ridden before he could walk of course, but he'd also been in Edinburgh learning to sew at the time when most lads got their mastery on horseback.

'You've used a pike, I expect. Sword and buckler work?'

'Ay, sir, a little. Wi' the Edinburgh trained band.'

He'd loved the trained band as a lad, rushing off to the musters like an arrow from the bow to work off his pent-up energy, while his uncle complained at the loss of time. His uncle had been a hard man....Too bad he'd—well, no reason to think about that. It hadn't been his fault.

'Of course. We'll play a veney or two when we get to Rycote,' said Carey. 'Come along. You can have my spare horse and we'll be going. They should have recovered enough from getting here and we'll take an easy pace now.'

They had been heading all the while to the stables of the inn where two smart-looking horses stood ready, saddled and bridled, and the pack pony dozed stoically with one broad hoof tipped, the packs very badly stowed.

Carey saw this, narrowed his eyes, and checked them. 'Nothing stolen,' he said, opening a very fine leather pistol case. Hughie glimpsed two matched dags inside and his mouth almost watered at them. Were they snaphaunce locks? Wheel-locks? Would Carey let him fire one?

Hughie and Carey between them took all the packs off and

re-stowed them with a better balance. Naturally, Hughie got the smaller mount, but he was used to his legs dangling a bit. Carey was a tall man, too; Hughie wasn't used to looking straight at anyone.

Carey mounted in a way Hughie hadn't seen since his childhood—hands on the saddlebow and leaping straight up, not touching the stirrups until he was seated. He looked pleased with himself at the trick. 'Hmf,' he said, as he found the stirrups. 'Come on Hughie, up you get.'

Hughie tightened the girth a little to allow for his weight and climbed into the saddle the less showy way. Lack of practice made heavy weather of getting his leg over the beast's back. He'd learnt the other way, but hadn't done it for a long time and wasn't about to risk landing on his back in the straw and dung of the inn stable.

Carey nodded and clicked to his horse, took the pack pony's leading rein and led the way forward into the High Street and eastward, over Magdalen Bridge and into the countryside.

Carey put his heels in. 'We're going to Rycote, which is where the herald I talked to says she is at the moment. It belongs to Lord Norris, poor chap. I want to talk to my own lord, the Earl of Essex, very urgently so if you see anyone in tangerine-and-white livery, shout out to me. Same if you see anyone in black and yellow.'

They went up to a canter as soon as they were clear of the large herd of pigs being brought into the city as components of porkpies, sausages, and spit roasts for the arrival of the Court. The smell was acrid, catching at the back of Hughie's throat, and several of the pigs seemed up for a fight.

Past them they were still heading upstream into a steady current of farm carts laden with fodder and wheat and apples and late raspberries and chickens in cages and, on one occasion, a cart laden with barrels of water that smelled horrible, probably containing crayfish for the Queen's table. It was a flood tide of food, drawn in by the whirlpool of the Queen's promised arrival.

Saturday 16th September 1592, noon

As he crested the brow of the hill, Sergeant Henry Dodd of Gilsland and Carlisle Castle blinked and yawned. He had been up and very busy all the night before, getting even with Sir Thomas Heneage, and now he had been in the saddle since dawn. He thought he'd made good progress though the Oxford Road was terrible in some parts, great potholes where the winter rains had tunnelled between the rough stones laid by monks, laying bare the orderly even-sized cobbles that were the hallmark of the ancient giants that built the border wall as well. Or were they faeries? There were different tales that gave both possibilities and it stood to reason it couldn't be both of them.

The Courtier had insisted it was all done by ordinary men called Romans who spoke Latin like the Papists, and had come over with Brutus thousands of years ago. That made some sense of the slabs of stone you sometimes found with well-carved letters in foreign, though Dodd doubted that grinding them up and drinking them in wine would cure you of gout.

He knew he had to stop because he urgently needed to find a bush. Unfortunately the road was very straight and the brush had been recently cleared back from the verges. He also had to water his horses at some stage. Straight roads were giants' work as well, or Romans'. He wondered how they had done it so far across country.

Bushes had been rare among the great broad fields northwest of London, though he was coming into enclosed land now. At last he'd spotted a handy-looking small copse well back from the road a little way ahead.

Dodd shifted in the saddle and hoped he hadn't caught a flux in London. He was riding the soft-mouthed mare and leading the horse he had decided to name Whitesock, on the grounds that he had the one white sock on him. The mare had a nice gentle pace to her but something made him prefer Whitesock for his sturdy determined canter and lack of nonsense. You didn't often meet a sensible horse, especially here in the South where so many of them had been ruined by overbreeding. Dodd clicked his tongue and moved the horses closer to the bushes. The mare pulled a little and her trot got choppy while Whitesock blew out his nostrils.

Hmm. Dodd peered between the leaves to see if anyone was waiting there, sniffed hard, couldn't smell anything except previous travellers' leavings. And he couldn't wait much longer, damn it.

So he loosened his sword, pushed into the bushes, which were luckily not entirely composed of thorns, saw nothing too worrying, and hitched the horses to the sturdiest branch. Then he found a bare patch, dug a hole with his boot heel, and started undoing the stupid multiple points of his stupid gentleman's doublet so he could get his stupid gentleman's fine woollen breeks down to do his business.

Just as he was about to drop them, he heard a stealthy movement behind him and turned around with his hand on his sword.

A bony creature was standing there in rags, holding out a rusty knife.

'Giss yer money!' hissed the creature that didn't seem to have many teeth.

Dodd blinked at him in puzzlement for a moment.

'Whit?' he asked.

'Giss yer money.'

'Whit?' Dodd genuinely couldn't work out what the creature was saying because the idea that something so pathetic might want to rob him was simply too unbelievable.

The creature came closer with his dull knife high. 'Money!'

'Och,' said Dodd, pulling the breeks down, hoicking his shirt up and squatting anyway because he couldn't wait any longer. 'Whit d'ye want tae do that for?'

'I don't want yer 'osses, just yer money.'

Dodd looked down and shook his head.

'Yer interfering with me opening ma bowels,' he growled. 'Could ye no' ha' the decency tae wait?'

'What?' asked the creature, frowning with puzzlement and lowering the knife.

'Wait!' snarled Dodd as the little grove of bushes filled with London's fumes. The creature stepped back and lowered the knife a little more.

'Now,' said Dodd, looking about for non-nettle leaves or even a stone so long as it was smooth, 'Ah'll gi' ye a chance. If ye go now and pit yer silly dull blade awa' Ah'll no' kill ye. Right? D'ye hear me?'

'Money, I want yer money!' insisted the creature.

'Och no, awa' wi' ye, Ah've better uses for it. I'm givin' ye a chance, see ye?' Dodd was trying to be peaceful and gentlemanly, and it just wasn't working.

The creature was clearly deranged because he suddenly lunged closer.

'I'll cut yer then!' he shouted, 'Giss yer money or...'.

'Och,' sighed Dodd as he shifted his body slightly, straightened his knees, and punched the creature in the face with a nice smooth stone he'd just picked up.

The poor creature was clearly a Southern weakling, for he folded up at once. Dodd picked up the rusty blade and threw it in the bushes, finished his business, covered up his leavings and went through the stupidly complicated fuss of the retying of points that gentlemen had to suffer every single time.

Then he left a penny beside the man bleeding gently from the mouth, on the grounds it was gentlemanly and, in any case, Carey's money not his. He shoved back out of the ill-starred bushes to find the horses watching gravely and chewing on some leaves. He mounted Whitesock for the next stage, took up the mare's reins and put his heels in.

Whitesock changed smoothly and started pounding stolidly along, followed in a scramble by the mare. Dodd laughed for a moment, a rare indulgence as no one was looking.

It seemed all the terrible tales you heard about southern footpads and sturdy beggars were just those—tall tales to frighten southron weans. The rest of the journey would be easy, even though his head had that oddly fixed metallic feeling in it of not having slept.

He could be in Oxford by the evening if he pushed it, he thought, but what was the point of that? He could use some more of Carey's money to stay at a proper inn, get some sleep, and then come into Oxford city nice and leisurely on Sunday morning. That would get him out of having to go to church with the Courtier and listening to some boring sermon about turning the other cheek. That thought made him laugh again.

He slowed down to a walk and looked about him, taking in the sunshine and berries in the hedges and the peaceful fields being cropped by fat cows before the autumn ploughing for winter wheat or barley. There was no hurry. He was enjoying himself.

SATURDAY 16TH SEPTEMBER 1592, NOON

As Carey the Courtier and his new servant Hughie Tyndale trotted along the rutted road that led to Rycote, he was keeping his eyes open for the unmistakeable signs of the Queen's progress.

He saw some on the other side of a hill where men were busy mending the disgraceful road, trundling wheelbarrows full of rocks to fill in the potholes and hammering down a corduroy of logs into the slopes to give the Queen's carts somewhere to grip in the soft earth they would soon turn to slurry.

He took a turn off the main road that led in that direction and rose in the stirrups to peer over the hedges—not a lot of stock in the fields, where a boy was leading the cows in.

As they came alongside the road menders, he found the master who was sitting on a rock, criticising.

'Which way is the Queen's Court?' He got a laconic thumb pointing further along the road.

He shifted the pack pony to the middle, so Hughie was behind and he was in front. You could think of the Queen's Court as a kind of army or a very large and disorderly herd of sheep with some sheepdogs in the centre and a few wolves around the outside. Generally, as with armies, the further out you were, the more disorderly it got.

There had clearly been some riders crossing hillsides, presumably the Queen's regular messengers taking shortcuts to avoid the no doubt thoroughly overwhelmed village of Rycote. Lord Norris was entertaining Her Majesty for a few days while she prepared to descend on the university city itself.

They followed the muddy track across pasture covered in

molehills until they crested a hill and looked down into the valley of Rycote.

Carey could see at once that not all of the Court was there. He supposed some of them must still be packing up at Sudley or unpacking at Woodstock and a lot of them would have gone straight on to Oxford to grab the best camping and sleeping places. That suited him.

Carey was sure that his father's household would be setting up in one of the colleges. He could probably have found out where if he'd bothered to ask, but he didn't want to have to explain to anyone why he had bolted from London on Friday morning. Firstly he had to find his own lord, Robert Devereux, Earl of Essex, who would certainly be in Rycote Manor and as close to the Queen's majesty as he could get. Therefore, to find his lord, all he had to do was find the Queen.

Carey stared down at the swollen village, frowning with worry. He had deliberately escaped from his parents, particularly his mother, leaving the best of his men, Sergeant Henry Dodd, behind him in a very ticklish situation. On Friday morning he had faked a large hawking expedition after redeeming his Court suit from pawn at Snr Gomes' shop. The plan had worked brilliantly and he had been away from the falconers and beaters and dogs by an hour after dawn on Friday, thundering along at a messenger's pace as he had done so often before, changing horses regularly. He enjoyed doing that, loved the sense of distance destroyed by his horse's legs. Even having to keep to a slower pace because of the pack pony, he'd made good enough time to get to Oxford by evening.

However, he had, no doubt, severely annoyed his father and infuriated his mother, quite apart from leaving Dodd in the lurch. He had done it because he had put together in his mind what had really been going on with the sale of Cornish lands and the Jesuit priest. And it had made a picture that appalled him.

The clue that had given him the whole plot had been that code name 'Icarus.' If he was right about who Icarus really was...if... That was why he was here.

Unfortunately, he didn't think the Earl would want to hear what he had to say, and if he did listen would probably be extremely angry as well. Carey sighed. And that would mean the Queen would be angry with him and so he'd have very little chance of coming away with his warrant or his fee. Particularly not the fee.

Carey scowled at his horse's ears and pulled again at his regrown goatee as they carried on down the winding road to the village.

There had been a whole host of excellent reasons why he had grabbed at the chance to become deputy warden of the West March under his brother-in-law, Lord Scrope. One reason could be summed up as the *problem* of the Earl of Essex.

Robert Devereux, Earl of Essex, was his second cousin via the scandalous and outrageous Lettice Knollys, the earl's mother and his Aunt Katherine's daughter. Carey was related to an awful lot of the Queen's Court where the ties of blood were both useful and dangerous. With Robert Devereux it wasn't just about family.

He had liked and admired the man. He still did. There was something about him. But what was it? Time and again the Earl had done something, said something so outrageously stupid or hotheaded that Carey had been on the verge of turning his back on his cousin. Always in the past he had kept faith with the man. But it was becoming more and more difficult.

Take the summer of 1591 for instance. The Earl of Essex had insisted on taking men to France to help the King of Navarre win the throne of France. Carey, up to his eyes in debt again, had gone with him, the first time since the Armada that he had gone to war.

There in the pinched, muddy, and ugly campaign with Henri of Navarre, he had found out many things about himself. One of them was that he was actually good at war. He had found that he was a good commander and could keep his men both alive and at his side. His desertion rate was half anybody else's. He had hit it off well with Navarre, who was a very canny fighter indeed and had offered him a permanent place at his side.

Robert Devereux looked every inch the perfect leader—large, loud, magnificent, very good at hand-to-hand combat, chivalrous, honourable...

He was useless. He was sloppy. He didn't send out scouts. He didn't understand anything about artillery. He didn't pay attention to the lie of the land. He didn't see the lie of the man either—how the King of Navarre never really committed himself to the alliance. Sure enough, in the end, Navarre left Essex and the English to hold Sluys and then went off and raided fat countryside while they guarded his back.

Carey didn't blame the man; he was doing what princes do, but why hadn't Essex seen what was going to happen when Carey could so easily? They had all missed out on good plunder and got bogged down in the damp flux-ridden misery of a siege.

He shook his head and glanced back past the pack pony to young Hughie. The man must have been gangling a few years ago but had now filled out and probably didn't realise how dangerous he looked with his broad shoulders, big limbs, and saturnine face. Like most Scots he always looked as if he was nursing a grievance until you spoke to him and then his face opened out with a smile and was almost pleasant. It remained to be seen if he knew one end of a needle from the other and Carey would wait a while before he trusted his face to the man's razor.

Hughie was looking up the road past Carey. 'Whit's that?' He pointed, then blushed and added, 'sir?'

It was a mummer's cart, brightly decorated and full of costumes and scenery with a tent on top. At first Carey thought it was stuck, but then he caught sight of a very small personage in bright gold-and-black brocade with farthingale sleeves, sitting on a white pony looking very annoyed. Her tiny size and childish face made her anger funny. However, Carey knew that it would be most unwise to laugh at the Queen's Senior Fool and muliercula, Thomasina de Paris. She had two women with her and two men in the livery of the Master of the Revels. They were all some way back from the cart.

There was a boy driving the cart, looking very hangdog.

'If you don't know who I am,' shouted the tiny creature, 'then I've got no further use for you. And in any case I heard you left one of your company behind in London, sick with plague.'

Carey reined in at once. An old man was climbing up clumsily from the depths of the cart, sweating heavily in the sudden sunlight, his face pale. He had a rash on the middle of his forehead, spreading down his nose.

Thomasina instantly backed her pony away from the cart. 'Stay there!' she shouted. 'No nearer.'

Carey opened his pistol case.

The old man got down unsteadily from the cart and stood there, holding onto it with one hand. He coughed.

'How long since you left London?'

'A few days...' started the hangdog boy.

'Last spring,' shouted the man hoarsely. 'We've not been in London since...April.'

'And where's your Fool?'

The boy started to cry. 'Left us!' shouted the man. 'Went his own way.'

'How dare you!' shrieked Thomasina. 'How dare you bring plague near the Queen's Court? Get away! Go back to London at once and stay there until you've got better or died.' The high voice was tinged with the London stews and the mummer stepped back at her fury.

The old mummer swayed by his cart, his mouth opening and shutting, bright blood on his lips.

Carey began loading his pistol. Sometimes men went crazy in the first onset of plague, as their fever rose and they became delirious. That's why they had to be shut up in their houses, cruel though it was, because if you came within ten feet of them you could catch it and die and all your family with you. Half the purpose of the Queen's summer progresses was to get her out of London and away from the plague.

'We've got no money,' sniffled the boy. 'He said we had to come because we haven't got no money what with the theatres all shut and Mr. Byrd wanted singers.'

Thomasina pulled a small purse from her saddlebag and threw it to the boy. 'Get yourselves back to London,' she said to him more gently. 'Keep away from people. If any of you are alive in six weeks' time, you may apply to the Master of the Revels again.'

The old man was shouting hoarsely again, making no sense at all, about how he was owed money and he had a new play and the rest would catch up with them. The boy started crying again. Neither of the Master of the Revels' men had firearms and were standing there looking as if they were about to bolt.

Carey rode up beside Thomasina and aimed his pistol at the man. It was a long shot and he hadn't wound his other dag, so he rested the gun's barrel on his left wrist and breathed out to steady his pounding heart. With those death-tokens on him, shooting the old man would be doing him a kindness.

Another lad, with bandages round his neck, climbed trembling out of the cart and persuaded the old man back into it. Thomasina had acknowledged Carey's backing with a quick glance and a lift of her shoulder. He saw she had a throwing knife in her right hand, from the sheaf she kept under her wide sleeves. Although she was only three-and-a-half-foot tall, her childlike round face had a few lines on it. She could still pass as a child if she wanted to, and perhaps she did. She had begun as a tumbler at Paris Garden and was as good with throwing knives as Carey's previous servant, Barnabus.

They took their mounts widely around the stricken cart, Carey keeping his pistol pointed at the mummers all the way. One of the Master of the Revels' men stayed on the road to be sure the mummers didn't try coming into Rycote again. No doubt all of them would die out there in the field.

Thomasina was shaking her head and puffing out her breath as she slipped her knife back under her brocade sleeve. Once they had put some distance between themselves and the plague, Carey bowed to Thomasina from the saddle. 'Mistress Thomasina,' he said to her, 'what an unexpected pleasure!'

'Ha! You're not sickening for anyfing yourself, are you?' she snapped at him, 'I heard your servant got plague and died of it.'

'Mistress,' said Carey reproachfully, 'do you think I would be coming to Court if I had knowingly been near the plague? That wasn't what he died of.' And how the devil did she know that?

'What about *him*? Is that Sergeant Henry Dodd that I hear so much about?'

Hughie's mount pecked suddenly. 'Er...no, that's Hughie Tyndale, my new manservant.'

Hughie's mouth was half-open and he looked shocked. Perhaps he was recovering from his new master treating someone who looked like an overdressed little girl with such respect. Or maybe he was frightened by the plague.

'Oh, 'e got plague then?' asked Thomasina.

'Not as far as I know, mistress. There hasn't been plague at Court, surely?'

She shook her head. 'We've been on progress since before it started to spread in London. If I had my way, I'd let nobody come near the Queen what hadn't been in quarantine at least forty days and scrubbed with vinegar as well.'

'Surely with the Court around her...'

'It's the idiot players and musicians all coming up from London to make their fortunes. As if there weren't enough of them in Oxford already.' Her voice was changing back to the way courtiers spoke but she turned and fixed him with gimlet eyes. 'So what are you doing here?'

Carey almost coughed but stopped himself. 'Really I'm on my way north for the raiding season after my father very inconveniently ordered me south,' he said. 'I want to speak to my lord Earl of Essex urgently. After that I'll be on my...'

Thomasina snorted. 'So you won't want to talk to the Queen?'

'Of course,' Carey continued smoothly, 'I would be utterly delighted if you could arrange an audience for me, Mistress Thomasina, but I know what it's like on progress and...'

Thomasina's brown eyes were narrowed. 'Hmm. Well, there might be something you could do for me. I can't promise, but...'

Heart hammering again with the hope that he might actually be able to talk to the Queen directly and even (please God!) get his wardenry fee and warrant, Carey took off his hat, held it against his heart and bowed low in the saddle.

'Mistress, if you can bring me to the Queen, I will forever be in your debt...'

'Yes, yes, Sir Robert, I know all about you and your debts, no need to add to them. You can do me a small service first and then we'll see, eh?'

'Whatever you want, mistress.'

He couldn't leave his dag shotted and wound when he put it back in the case and he didn't like the thought of trying to unload it while riding—always a ticklish business which could take your hand off if the powder exploded at the wrong moment. He aimed at a crow sitting on a branch ahead and pulled the trigger.

He missed. The crow flew off the branch in a puff of feathers and the other crows rose up into the sky cawing and diving. Thomasina's pony skittered, the pack pony came to a dead stop, and Hughie's horse pirouetted for a moment before he got it under control again. Carey's own horse was a hunter and not at all concerned. Thomasina's two women were walking and one of them jumped and clutched the other, while the Master of the Revels' man looked near fainting. He smiled at the thought of what Dodd would likely think of such jumpiness at gunfire.

'Where are you planning to stay?' Thomasina wanted to know. 'With your elder brother? Your father's already in Oxford, I think.'

'Er...no.'

'Suing him, are you?'

'No, that's my brother Henry who stole my legacy. But George thinks he can still order me around.'

'You won't find space with his grace the Earl of Essex. He's just sent most of his men ahead to find a good place for his pavilions at Oxford, so he's in the manor house with the Queen and Lord Norris.'

'I would very much like to see him...'

'Don't push it, Sir Robert. I have no pull at all with Essex.' Her face was wry with distaste. 'How's your reverend father?'

'Very well, mistress, thank you...in good health.'

She smiled then. 'Now he's a good lord, keeps the old-fashioned ways.' Once upon a time, Thomasina had been one of his creatures on display at Paris Garden stews, bought from Gypsies. She had learned her tumbling there and Lord Hunsdon had been the person who showed her to the Queen at a masque.

'In trouble with him again, are you?' she asked, seeing through him as usual.

'Er...possibly.'

'Well, try the Master of the Revels then.' She tapped the white palfrey onward with a whip decorated with crystal beads that flashed in the sun. 'You could make yourself useful there.'

'How? My tumbling is middling to poor and my acting...'

She sniffed at his sarcasm. 'You can sing, Sir Robert, and he now has a desperate need for good tenors 'cos one of 'em's dead of plague and the other's dying on that cart. I'll find you later.'

She gestured for Carey to go past her and so he went to a canter up the path.

SATURDAY 16TH SEPTEMBER 1592,

AFTERNOON

They had to rein in well before they got to the church, the place was such a bedlam of tents, carts, fashionable carriages bogged in the mud, servingmen, people generally. You could hardly move at all. No women under the age of thirty were visible, but boys were running about everywhere because this was the Queen's Court, not the King of Scotland's, and propriety was usually observed.

All the main barns were guarded by the Queen's Gentlemen Pensioners in the red-and-black livery from her father's Court that they wore on ordinary days, no doubt because the harbingers and heralds would have stockpiled food in them for the progress, bought on treasury tickets in advance. They were oases of order.

The rest of the village was essentially a fair. At the back of the church some large makeshift clay ovens stood surrounded by faggots of wood with more being brought in on the backs of trudging peasants.

Carey took one look at the only alehouse in the place, where a skinny middle-aged woman with a hectic look in her eyes was raking in cash. He didn't fancy his chances with the queue.

Still, the smell of pies was making his mouth water. He'd eaten the pie he was buying when he heard Hughie's Scotch accent; he'd had bread and ale as usual when he got up but that was all. Now he was starving. So he did what he often did on progress, and come to think of it, at war. He turned his horse to the left and rode slowly around the mass of humanity.

At last he saw what he was looking for—the Earl of Cumberland's blue-and-yellow-chequered flags around a small cottage surround by a mushroom ring of tents.

Carey immediately rode toward the cluster, followed by Hughie, who was looking nervous, and by the pony which was busily taking mouthfuls of everything green and poisonous it could find in its path.

A large henchman in a Clifford jack barred his way.

'What's yer name and what's yer business?' he demanded, his voice from the Clifford lands in Chester.

'Sir Robert Carey, come to see my lord, one follower, two horses, and a pack pony,' said Carey, looking around for the Earl. There was a table set up in a muddy orchard behind the cottage and sitting there was definitely none other than Sir George Clifford, third Earl of Cumberland, known as the Pirate Earl. Only now he was standing up and playing a veney with his opponent, a man in the buff coat of a master at arms.

A yell announced a hit by the earl on his opponent. They saluted each other, then dropped their veney sticks and sat down at the table again. Carey wasn't sure what was on the table, but it didn't look like playing cards.

The henchman had sent a lad to talk to the earl. Carey watched with a smile.

Next moment, Cumberland had bounced to his feet and was striding across what remained of the vegetable garden to where Carey was waiting. He slid down from the saddle, prodded Hughie to do the same, and bowed as Cumberland came up to them, wreathed in smiles.

'My Lord Earl,' Carey said formally.

'By God, Sir Robert,' laughed Cumberland, 'where the devil have you been? How's Carell Castle treating you? What's this I hear about the Grahams and the King of Scotland and...?'

Cumberland pumped his hand and clapped him round the shoulders.

'My new servingman, Hughie Tyndale,' Carey said. Hughie managed a reasonable bow, then reconsidered and went on one knee to the Earl.

'Tyndale? Are you from there?' the Earl asked with interest, waving him up again.

'Ah...ma family...is...was...m'lord,' Hughie stuttered, 'I think...'

'Ran away to Edinburgh, did they?' asked Cumberland. 'What's your trade then?'

'Ay sir, Ah wis prenticed tae a tailor sir but it didnae suit and...'

Cumberland bellowed with laughter.

'Don't tell me you've got yourself the perfect combination at last?' he shouted. 'I thought that was your little thief Barnabus. Where's he gone?'

'I'm afraid he died of the flux in London.' No point in going into details.

'Not plague?'

'What do you take me for, my lord?'

'Well, I'm sorry to hear it. I was hoping he could teach me knife-throwing one of these days. Speaking of which, come and look at this.'

Carey told Hughie to find somewhere to put the horses and fetch some food for them, and to make sure the baggage stayed with them and not to unload the pony until they were under cover. Then he went over to the orchard with Cumberland.

'Now then. D'ye see what we're doing here?'

The master at arms was standing four square by the table, arms folded. Carey looked down at the very nicely carved ivory and ebony chess set on a gold and silver board that Cumberland had robbed out of a Spanish ship a season before. It looked as if Cumberland was losing as usual, but Carey thought he could see some useful opportunities for the queen, possibly.

'Now then...' said Cumberland, his dark face beaming. He was sporting a gold earring in his right earlobe like the Spanish grandee he took it from, and Carey thought it looked better on him than on Sir Walter Raleigh. None of his portraits showed that he had a piratical crooked smile with a tooth missing that somehow caused devastation among the ladies of the Queen's bedchamber and worse than that amongst the Maids of Honour. However, like Carey himself, Cumberland had the sense to leave the maids strictly alone, for all their sighing and fluttering. He wouldn't risk joining Sir Walter in the Tower for marrying a Maid of Honour in a hurry. Anyway, he was already married to the formidable Margaret Clifford.

'Mr. Simmonds, would you mind if we went back a move?'

The master at arms nodded and Cumberland replaced two pawns, which were in position to take.

'Now then, see here. Chess is a dreadfully dull game, in my opinion, but this makes it fun. Normally with two pieces of equal power we'd throw a die or a coin to decide which wins the fight.'

'Yes,' said Carey who actually preferred the newfangled way of doing it where the first that was in place took, regardless of power. That removed chance from the game and made it a matter of pure skill which suited him better. 'And you're fighting a veney instead?'

'Exactly! First hit wins the piece.'

Carey laughed. Cumberland was a very good fighter. 'What an excellent martial exercise.'

'Of course. I think I'm doing better with this game than the last one, Mr. Simmonds.'

'Yes, my lord,' said Simmonds tactfully and Carey smiled knowingly at him because it was obvious to him from the board that in the long term, the Earl would lose no matter how good his veneys.

'Are you playing a puissant queen?' Carey asked.

'Oh yes, compliment to Her Majesty and all that. Makes it a better game anyway. We should play a game, Sir Robert.'

'I'd be delighted, my lord,' said Carey, quite truthfully with a little tickle of excitement under his ribs at the idea he suddenly had for some side bets on himself to win.

'So, what are you doing here anyway?' asked Cumberland later as they sat on a couple of stools and Carey munched the heel of a game pie from the Earl's table. 'Lowther already kicked you out of Carell?'

'Not yet, though it's a tricky situation.' Carey explained as much as he was willing of the tricky situation, then changed the subject. 'I'm really here to talk to the Queen about my warrant and get my fee...'

'Hah! Good luck. She's in a terrible mood at the moment.'

'Why? She's usually happy on progress.'

'No idea. Everything was fine until just after we got to Rycote and then suddenly...clouds! Thunder! Kaboom! Zap! Poor Devereux didn't know what had hit him....'

'How much trouble is he in?'

Cumberland smiled. 'On Friday Devereux was driven from the presence in a hail of shoes, muffs, and one surprised lapdog, and today is out hunting to recover his spirits and bring Her Majesty some suitable trophy to calm her down...ideally venison.'

'So what did he do?'

The elegant tawny shoulders shrugged. 'Nothing. For once he's been angelic. He's starting to get the benefit of the customs farm of sweet wines though he hasn't found anyone to manage it for him yet. He's recovered financially from his forays into France, more or less, though there are the usual rumours that he's done something stupid with his money again.'

Carey said nothing to this despite Cumberland's expectant look. He also didn't mention that the Earl of Cumberland himself was famous as the man who was taking good fertile land and pouring it into the sea as he fitted out one privateer after another in hopes of taking a big enough prize to recoup himself. The Royal Spanish treasure fleet probably wouldn't be enough by now.

'So you don't know the reason for Her Majesty's ill humour?'

'No, it's probably just the wind changing in her internal weather, that's all. What do you expect if you call her Astraea?'

'Do you know where my lord of Essex is hunting?'

'No idea. He's ignoring me at the moment. It's all Cromwell and Mountjoy and his other cronies. Maybe tonight at my ball— poor Norris asked me to arrange it so the Queen won't be bored.'

They looked around at the destroyed hedges, foraged apple trees, dung heaps, and escaped dogs that made a ragged new perimeter to the village. Every landowner dreaded the arrival of the Queen and all her Court on progress, and many had been known to fake absence so as to avoid the honour.

'My Lord Norris was saying he'll have to remit all the rents for the next five years until the place recovers,' Cumberland commented as he went back to his chess-veney game. 'Thank God I live too far north for her to turn up at my place.'

Carey laughed. 'Your wife would love it.'

'She wouldn't. She's not a fool. What about you? My Lord Hunsdon found you a juicy little heiress yet?' Carey shook his head. Cumberland looked comically appalled. 'Oh, for God's sake, Carey, you're not still mooning after Lady Widdrington?'

Carey's expression chilled and he cocked his head as his hand dropped to his sword hilt. The Earl put his hands up, palms out placatingly.

'All right, all right, let's not fight about it, I completely agree that your cousin Elizabeth is a wonderful, sagacious, virtuous, and beautiful woman and a perfect match for you, but for pity's sake...'

'Yes?' growled Carey.

'She's poor!'

'So what?'

'And she's married. I heard something about your last run-in with her husband. But even once he's dead, how can you ever afford to marry her? It's just not practical.'

Carey's expression was mulish. 'I love her,' he said.

Cumberland shook his head at his friend's lunacy. 'What does your father say?'

'He married for love, too.'

'Maniacs, the lot of you. I blame the Royal blood. Come on then, which way should I go here?'

Carey blinked down at the board. Simmonds' face was carefully neutral so Carey looked for a trap. There were two obvious moves that would lead to a very nice ambush, but there was one move that wasn't obvious at all. Carey was willing to bet that Cumberland hadn't noticed it. Damn it, what his friend said was perfectly true and only what all his friends had been telling him for the last five years, but...

He didn't care. He was a landless younger son and common sense dictated he must marry money or land. But he had to have Elizabeth. There was simply no alternative.

'You could move your puissant queen from here to here,' he said. Simmonds' granite face shifted infinitesimally to sadness. 'Sorry, Mr. Simmonds,' Carey added, because he had just destroyed a very nice march on the king.

Cumberland stared, frowned, stared again. 'By God, Carey, how do you see these things? Amazing! Right.' He moved the carved ivory queen. 'Check, I think.'

Carey was sitting down, playing Mr. Simmonds at the new style of chess with no veneys, dice, or coins plus the puissant queen who shook everything up so well, when he heard a caressingly familiar voice beside him.

'*Alors, M. le Deputé,*' came the Italianate French. '*Je suis vraiment enchanté de vous voir autrefois.*'

Carey shot to his feet. There was a tiny pause during which he checked to make sure that it was indeed none other than Signora Emilia Bonnetti, looking amused. Cumberland had a very unattractive smirk on his handsome face.

'Emilia!' he said, bowing to hide the fact that his memory was in an uproar. 'Signora Bonnetti, I, too, am utterly delighted to find you here in such an unworthy setting.' He said it in English because that was a dig at Cumberland who was clearly playing his very own puissant queen. Anyway, it would be rude to speak French in front of the earl who was no linguist.

Emilia smiled again, with her head tilted perkily. This time instead of a feathered mask and crimson silk gown and dancing slippers, Signora Bonnetti was modestly dressed in a black *devoré* velvet slashed with grey satin in a Parisian style and was wearing small but determined hobnail boots. Her black hair was modestly tucked under a white linen cap, but she wore a crazily tilted little black hat with a feather in it, making every other woman in the world look unforgivably dowdy.

'Hey, less of the unworthy, Sir Robert,' boomed Cumberland, putting his arm around Emilia's waist. 'Signor Bonnetti is helping me find good wines from Italy for my household and his delightful wife has been...advising me.'

Carey nodded, cynically wondering how far the advice had gone. He found himself looking at the place just below the modest neckline of her bodice where, a month or two ago, he had bitten her very gently on a summer night in a rose garden. She brushed the place with her hand, which made him smile.

Signora Bonnetti wound her arm into Cumberland's elbow and looked up at him, smiled back.

'So you do know each other?' Cumberland asked, very smug.

It wouldn't be the first time he and Cumberland had collided over a woman, but he thought the Earl was making a point here about his romantic notions. And, uncomfortably for him, it was a good one. He wondered exactly how much the fascinating Signora might have told her new lover about Carey's disastrous plottings at the King of Scotland's Court. Emilia was watching him carefully, her black eyes full of amusement and something else—he wasn't sure what.

'Yes,' he said, deciding to push his luck a little, 'we met at the King's Court in Dumfries.'

'Ah,' said Cumberland, 'so that was before your unfortunate journey to Ireland and your problems there, my dear.'

Emilia Bonnetti, who must know by now exactly who had caused those potentially lethal problems, laughed a little. 'Oh, yes,' she said, 'but my lovely Lord of Cumberland saved my life, Sir Robert, after my poor husband was forced to leave Ormonde's Court in such a hurry. My lord gave us passage from Dublin in his ship...'

'The *Elizabeth Bonaventure*,' Cumberland put in. 'You remember her, Carey, we faced the armada in her and I've had a new mast fitted...'

'Thank heavens!' said Carey with complete insincerity. Oh God, this complicated everything horribly. Was she looking to get back at him? What had she told Cumberland? What had she told everyone else? The Court was a nest of gossip that made a ladies' flower-water party look like a collection of Trappist monks. Had any of what she must have been saying got as far as the Queen? Not directly, of course; the Queen was very unlikely to receive an Italian adventuress into her presence, despite the sweet wines....

Sweet wine. Essex had the farm of sweet wines and he would be looking for a suitable agent to run it for him. What would Essex make of Emilia, Carey wondered?

'How is your husband, Signora?' Carey asked, still sticking to English.

'Well,' she said with a little pout of her lips, 'the Irish...'ow you say?...zey drink like ducks but not appreciate good wine and when zey promise to pay, zey lie.'

'Tut,' said Carey.

'So, we are here now. At least ze English like to drink well... And perrrhaps...zey will pay?'

The opening was there, so he took it, simply on general principles, with no idea of where it might lead. And he did owe her something for the trick with the guns. 'I wonder if you've spoken to my lord of Essex yet, Signora?'

The faintest shadow crossed Emilia's face, followed by another diamond smile. 'Not yet...'e has been very...*occupé* with the Queen who is verry cross....To be a *mignon* is 'ard, no? 'Oo would do such a thing?'

And she tilted her head in a way which Carey suddenly found annoying. 'Mignon' had several loaded meanings on top of the simple translation of 'King's favourite.' In the context of the Scottish Court it meant the King's catamite. In the context of the English Court and the Queen...

'Indeed,' he agreed blandly.

'You could put in a good word for the Signora, Sir Robert, couldn't you?' said the ever-helpful Cumberland. 'My lord of Essex often speaks of how you saved his bacon with the Queen a year ago in France.'

'If I could get to see him, yes, perhaps,' Carey said. 'As he doesn't know I'm here...'

'You are friends wiz milord Essex?'

Emilia was looking intent, the way she had when they bargained in the summer. Carey couldn't help himself, he smiled cagily and spread his hands. 'He gave me my knighthood in France, Signora, and was my commander when we fought for the King of Navarre. He's also my second cousin.'

Her lips compressed. For some reason she was furious and Carey wondered why. It's all right, he wanted to tell her, if you're not trying to buy guns to sell to the Irish to be used against the Queen's soldiers, I won't cheat you. Of course, she might not be after just the farm of sweet wines from Essex; she was likely to be here for quite other reasons as well as the obvious one of espionage.

'M. *le député*,' she said to him with a nice curtsey. 'We must speak about this when my 'usband is 'ere, as I am only a poor little woman oo knows nossing of money or farms.'

Cumberland laughed, caught her shoulders and gave her a smacking kiss on the cheek.

'I love it when she talks English,' he said to Carey. 'It sounds so funny.'

Emilia's tinkling laugh told Carey a lot more than it seemingly did George Clifford. He didn't give the Earl of Cumberland much chance against the Earl of Essex if Emilia met the noble lord. From her sideways look at him under her remarkably long lashes, it seemed that she and her complaisant, well-horned husband might be willing to negotiate a fee for the all-important introduction to Essex. Possibly some of that fee could be in kind…

No, came the sternly righteous part of him. That's enough. You have to find a way to pay the men for the autumn if the Queen is too ill-humoured to give you your fee. And after what Elizabeth did for you in Scotland!

Could he take the risk of dealing with the Italian spies again? If he could find a way of spreading the responsibility a little as he had not been able to do before, perhaps? If he had some kind of authorisation? Perhaps he could talk to Thomasina again? There would be dancing that evening, another less cautious part of him thought, and perhaps I will dance with Signora Bonnetti again? Perhaps. No more than that, of course, but…

At least Elizabeth won't be watching, that part of him explained to the stern-faced puritan who came from Walsingham; she'd never find out….But that was another unexpectedly bleak thought. And she probably would, somehow.

Cumberland had started rubbing noses with Emilia. She laughed again and nipped his nose between her knuckles and he squawked.

'Be'ave, milord,' she said severely. 'What will Sir Robert think?'

'I know exactly what he's thinking, my little darling,' said Cumberland, piratical grin at full force. 'Aren't you, Carey?'

So she's told him, or he's guessed, Carey decided philosophically, so probably no chance of even a polite pavane with the Signora. Maybe for the best.

'Indeed, I am, my lord,' he said with diplomatic ruefulness. 'So I'd better go and see if my new servingman has made off with my Court suit. My lord…Signora…'

He bowed elaborately to both of them and plodded back through the mud to the horse-crammed kitchen yard of the little cottage that Cumberland had taken over.

There he found that Hughie Tyndale had done quite creditably. All three of the horses were munching away at nosebags, had been untacked and rubbed down and were tied up at the corner of the yard, next to Cumberland's carthorses and a string of pack ponies.

The packs with Carey's Court suit and jewels in it had been piled next to the wall and Hughie was squatting watchfully next to them, munching a pennyloaf with some cheese and drinking ale from a jack.

'We'll stay with my lord Cumberland tonight, Hughie,' Carey said as he pushed between the horses. 'Not sure where exactly, but we can hope to be in the dry.'

'Ay, sir.'

'Have you looked at my suit?'

'I had a quick look but Ah couldnae unpack it out here in case o' the wet, sir.'

'Quite right. Let's see if Clifford will loan me a dressing room or similar.'

The Earl of Cumberland was busy, said Mr. Simmonds stolidly, but had given orders that Sir Robert should have anything he wanted—except the delightful Signora, since, as his friend, the Earl wanted to make sure he did nothing rash to upset his headlong pursuit of romantical ruin.

Ha ha, George, very funny, thought Carey, oddly relieved. Simmonds showed him to a shed that was being used as a tiring room as it was dry and reasonably well-lit with a stone-flagged floor and bars on the window—no doubt a dry-goods store since it didn't even smell of salt fish or cheese.

He and Hughie carefully unwrapped the pearl-encrusted velvet doublet and hose from the hessian protecting it and hung it all up on a bracket on the wall. With Hughie's help he tried on the doublet and knew at once from the way Hughie went about it that the man had indeed worked for a tailor. No, the costly doublet was far too tight on the shoulders—he might even split a seam if he danced a volta and needed to lift the woman. Before they had finished deciding what to do about letting it out, a boy knocked and squeaked, 'Message for Sir Robert.'

'Eh? Who from?'

'I'm not to say, sir, I'm just to take you there.'

'Should I...er...shift my shirt to meet this person?' Carey asked hopefully, but the child shook his head vigorously.

'No, sir, just come straight along...she's in a hurry, she said.'

Perhaps it was the Signora wanting to cheapen over his commission for putting the Bonnettis in touch with the Earl of Essex? Perhaps she was bored with Cumberland? Perhaps she had fond memories of their dalliance in Dumfries? He certainly did.

'Just take the padding out of the armholes and wings,' Carey told Hughie cheerfully. 'It'll do the job and look fine. You know how to do it, don't you?'

'Ay, sir,' said Hughie, ducking his head, 'Ah'll come in fra the lining and reseam after though.'

Carey shifted the doublet up and down again, tight across the back too and flatteringly looser around the waist. Carlisle and the incessant riding and training was improving his figure even more than war in France had, but it was annoying that all the improvements were in places difficult to alter. No doubt about it, ten years of Court life had softened him badly despite jousting and tennis and swordplay. Now he was back in form again. That was pleasing and might please the Queen, too.

Carey smiled complacently at the half mirror nailed on the wall. He hadn't tried on his cannions and would have to hope they were all right; altering them would be even more complicated. He would have to use his riding boots as well or find and borrow some dancing slippers—it didn't really matter so much on progress, but still...Mind, his hose were in a poor state, having been darned several times by Barnabus. So boots were the better choice.

'You're sure I shouldn't change?' Carey asked, glaring at the boy severely. Whose child was he, anyway? Carey thought back fondly to his days as a page at the young Queen's Court, with his father, just before the Revolt of the Northern Earls.

'No, sir,' said the boy, luckily bright enough to understand what he was worrying about. 'Oh no, sir, it isn't Her Majesty, I'd make sure and tell you if it was and check for musk-scented boots too.'

'So I should hope,' said Carey, disappointed. He unbuttoned the heavy pearl-embroidered doublet and Hughie helped it from his shoulders, unlaced the sleeves, and turned it inside out before hanging it up.

Still buttoning up his old hunting doublet, Carey followed the page boy out of the cottage, along the rutted lane and down another lane to a small tithe barn. There he came upon another scene of chaos because clearly the place had been commandeered by all the mummers and musicians of the Court. On the ground floor, already eaten bare by the Court, bad-tempered choristers of the chapel in their livery coats were practising polyphony very poorly. In another corner, by some feed bins, were acrobats and tumblers, practising a complicated sequence of somersaults and jumps to build a pyramid. The master of the tumblers, a slightly built handsome Moor in a black brocade doublet and hose, was supervising with iron patience. The pyramid wobbled and collapsed.

'Try again,' he said, 'this time Master Skeggs as second rank base, and Will the Tun as first rank.'

The page boy was climbing a ladder in front of them that led to a half-loft still full of hay that made your nose twitch. When Carey followed him, he took a narrow path through the sweetly smelling piles of fodder to a nook at the back which had been laid over with rugs. There none other than Mistress Thomasina de Paris was sitting neatly with her knees folded under her in her white damask and gold tissue gown, with her costume trunks behind her.

Carey flourished a bow to her. 'Mistress,' he said, 'I have to say I was hoping to meet another Queen, but I would like to ask your advice on...'

She skewered him with a look. 'Tom,' she said to the page boy, 'go sit at the top of the ladder and...no, in fact, pull it up and sit next to it. Understand?'

'Yes, missus,' said the boy and forged a path back through the hay, looking determined.

Carey shut his mouth and looked quizzically at the Queen's Fool. She gestured for him to sit down and he decided against trying to sit on a rug as the points of his doublet were too tight to his hose to allow it. He perched on one of the boxes.

They sat in silence for a moment.

Just as Carey was about to open proceedings by asking conventionally after the Queen her mistress' good health, Thomasina took a sealed letter from the rug beside her and handed it to him without a word. She was looking immensely disapproving.

Carey held it in his fingers, looked at it. That was the Queen's personal seal, the small one. The one she never gave to anyone else.

Fingers a little unsteady, he opened it. The letter was in fact a warrant from the Queen, stating that Sir Robert Carey was her trusty and well-beloved cousin and acting in her behalf and requiring any who read it to assist him in any way he asked.

It wasn't the warrant for his deputyship; it was very much better than that. But it didn't say anything about what his office was nor why exactly he might need assistance.

Heart pounding, Carey refolded the letter carefully and put it in his inside doublet pocket.

'I have been asked to ask you...' began Thomasina judiciously.

'Mistress Thomasina, I know how Her Majesty's mind works insofar as any mere man can. Bear with me, please. If you are speaking on behalf of anyone other than our dread sovereign Queen Elizabeth, would you please say so now?'

Thomasina nodded her head once and then folded her lips. Carey counted twenty of his heartbeats because they were going faster than normal. 'Thank you, mistress. You were saying?'

'I have been asked to ask you to investigate a...a death that happened some thirty-two years ago.'

What? Carey didn't say that. He tried to think whose death, then asked, 'Before or after I was born?'

'Do you know the month?'

'The Queen was godmother at my baptism, I know that, but it was a little late for some reason. My mother always said I was a summer baby and bound to be lucky.'

'In which case the death happened after your birth. It was on the 8th September in the year of Our Lord 1560.'

There was something about the date, but he wasn't sure what. Something important to be sure, family stories from when he was very little, family gossip, something about his Aunt Katherine's gown being ruined on the hunting field. Something that had caused arguments between his father and mother. Carey closed his eyes for a moment. He had been such a little boy, still in skirts, riding experienced barrel-shaped ponies, youngest of a string of seven boys and two girls that lived. Only Philadelphia was younger than him, and he was hardly ever noticed except by his wet nurse, which suited both him and Philly very well indeed. What was it?

He opened his eyes and smiled. 'I deny it,' he said. 'The bill is clean, I was nowhere near. I have an excellent alibi from my wet nurse, as well as being hampered by my swaddling bands.'

Mistress Thomasina looked unamused.

'This...death changed many lives,' she said, obviously expecting him to have heard of it nonetheless. 'It happened only a few miles from Oxford, at Cumnor Place.'

'Cumnor?' Damn it, what was it about that name?

Thomasina rolled her eyes. 'I suppose most of our generation were never concerned by it and your parents wouldn't speak of it,' she said, pouring wine from a flask into a small coral cup for herself and twice as much for Carey into a silver goblet. From a sandalwood box, she offered sweet wafers which Carey refused. 'I had no idea myself who Her Ma...who was being spoken of. I didn't even recognise the name of the victim.'

Carey said nothing, watching carefully. Who the devil had died thirty-two years ago; why all the mystery?

'I say death,' Thomasina was being judicious again, 'but at the time the word being whispered was *murder.*'

Well of course it was; that wasn't surprising. After all, why bother to investigate a death if you didn't think it was murder?

'Was there an inquest?'

'Oh yes,' said Thomasina, 'though it took a year to decide on death by misadventure.'

That and her tone of voice did send Carey's eyebrows upwards. 'A year?' Most inquests had decided within a week.

'Yes. It didn't matter, though. The suspicion was enough.'

Would the bloody midget give him the name? Why was he supposed to guess? He felt doltish at all these riddles, actually sighed for the brutal simplicity of Carlisle where people tended to tell you to your face that they hated you and had put a price on your head. He was quite proud of the fact that his own head was rumoured to be worth at least £10 in gold to the Graham surname.

Thomasina wasn't even looking at him anymore but into a corner where there was nothing but a particularly fine Turkish rug, woven with strange squared-off houses and birds.

'I told her to let it be, that the trail was thirty-two years cold and that no one really cared anymore....And she snapped at me that she cares and that as her goddamned nephew is so clever at ferreting out the truth of things that don't concern him, he may as well make himself useful in her behalf for a change.'

He grinned. That had the authentic ring of the Queen's voice. Thomasina was an excellent mimic. Carey could almost see his cousin's high-bridged nose and snapping brown eyes under her red wig, the red lead giving bright colour to her white-leaded cheeks.

Nephew. That was an important message to him in itself. He was also her cousin through his grandmother, Mary Boleyn, sister to the beheaded Ann. But he was the Queen's nephew through his father, bastard son of Henry VIII, and her half-brother. That meant that this was Tudor family business.

'Mistress,' he began as tactfully as he could, 'I'm afraid I'm too young and ignorant to...'

'This death is that of Amy Dudley, née Robsart.'

All his breath puffed out of his chest. Carey knew that name.

'The Earl of Leicester's first wife...' he asked, just to be sure, 'who fell down the stairs at Cumnor Place and...?'

'And died,' said Thomasina. 'Sir Robert, something happened two days ago that upset Her Majesty and put her clean out of countenance. She has been in a rage ever since and was even let blood out of season for it. When she had news that you were coming, she told me to...I was told to tell you to look into it.'

'Look into the death of Robert Dudley's first wife?'

'Or her goddamned murder, as the Queen calls it,' added Thomasina quietly.

'She knows it was murder?'

Thomasina nodded. 'But...but...' Carey was horrified. The Queen was telling him to look into it, a direct order. Usually she allowed at least the polite semblance of choice. Of all things the Queen could have ordered him to do, this was surely the most perverse, the most ridiculous, the most—well, for God's sake, the most dangerous. To him. He was being ordered to go and stir up a thirty-two-year-old nest of vipers. There had indeed been family gossip about it when Carey was a boy and worse than that. Carey knew that his father had quietly bought up and burned a number of inflammatory pamphlets published secretly by the English Jesuits until the presses could be found and destroyed. Those pamphlets accused the Queen and her then-favourite, Robert Dudley, of murdering Dudley's innocent wife between them. Other suspects in the case were, of course, Sir William Cecil; later Lord Treasurer Burghley; Christopher Hatton, the attorney general who danced his way into the Queen's favour and never married; even Lettice Knollys, the Earl of Leicester's eventual second wife and the Earl of Essex's scandalous mother. There had been something going on that his father dealt with when he was fourteen, something about a man called Appleyard, Amy Robsart's brother.

Quite possibly every single member of the 1560 Privy Council could be a suspect for the killing.

'But why?' he burst out. 'The woman has been in the ground for thirty-two years and...'

'In Gloucester Hall chapel in Oxford, in fact,' Thomasina corrected him.

'In Oxford and...Why now?'

'The last time she came to Oxford was in 1566,' said Thomasina, seemingly at random.

'Yes?'

'She's very clear, Sir Robert. She wants the death investigated and she wants you to do it, but she will not tell you why. She shouted at me when I pressed her about it.'

'But, mistress,' said Carey carefully, 'the Queen must know she is by far the most...er...the one most likely to be suspected as the murderer now as well as then. What were the words she used to you exactly?'

'You do it as you see fit, and you report to her through me—directly to her if necessary.'

'She knows that this is a very ugly swamp and she may not like the smells that come up if I stir the mud?'

Thomasina smiled shortly. 'She wants it done and she will have you do it.'

'And if I find irrefutable proof that she was the murderer?'

The midget's eyes were cold. 'She didn't tell me, but no doubt she would expect you to keep it quiet.'

He could do that, of course, he wasn't a fool, but God, he hoped he wouldn't have to. 'And what if it is simply that the evidence I find points to her?'

Thomasina shrugged which made her look both worldly wise and girlish. 'She didn't say. But how could it have been her, Sir Robert? Surely she would simply have married Leicester anyway once the wife was dead and gone, no matter what the scandal? If she'd done it? Once she had damned her soul that way, where was the problem damning herself again? You can only hang once.'

Clearly Thomasina had been worrying about it, too. She sounded reasonable, but…the Queen was a woman and therefore by nature unreasonable.

'I'll need to see the report by the coroner and the inquest jury's verdict and any witness statements,' he said, hoping to play for time while the documents were searched for and copied.

Thomasina reached into a box beside her and brought out a sheaf of papers which she handed to him. They were all certified copies, written in the cramped secretary script of one of the older Exchequer clerks.

'I have to say what I'm investigating when I ask questions. I can't possibly keep it secret.' Thomasina shrugged again. This was an impossible task, Carey thought with a sigh. 'Does Her Majesty know I haven't yet been paid my wardenry fee?'

Thomasina looked blank. 'You had two chests of coin from her…'

'They were free loans. This is my fee of £400 which I was also promised. Separate and different.' Nothing. 'Mention it to my loving aunt, will you, Mrs. Thomasina? Try and get it into her head that soldiers need to be paid or they won't fight, that's all I ask. And by the way…I wanted to ask your…advice on the Bonnettis.'

'The Italian spies?'

'Especially Signora Bonnetti.' He looked carefully into space. 'I am hoping to introduce her to my lord of Essex to help him with his farm of sweet wines. I want to be sure that the Queen has no objection.' Yes, by God. He'd learned a lesson in Dumfries.

Thomasina tilted her head. 'I will send you a message if there is a problem, Sir Robert. In the meantime…you'll do it?'

'I shall think about it,' said Carey, 'and then I shall give her an answer.'

This was the Queen's invariable answer to anyone who wanted her to do anything at all, in particular marry. Thomasina knew that, too, and smiled briefly. He was joking. He had absolutely no choice in the matter.

He stood and bowed to the Queen's Fool.

When he and the page boy had put back the ladder and climbed carefully down, he was nearly knocked over by two swordsmen hacking at each other with theatrical gusto. He circled the fight, saw it was simply the first veney against the second veney, and slipped out of the tithe barn where he found Hughie waiting for him.

They walked back to Cumberland's camp. On the way, Carey spotted an elderly laundress with a big basket of shirts and bought a new shirt for Hughie from her on the spot, had him change into it, and gave her the old one to try and clean. It cost the same as fine linen would in London but was clearly some kind of hemp. Hughie seemed pleased. They walked on, Hughie admiring the whiteness of the shirtsleeves.

'Is it true,' he asked, 'that the Queen canna stand a man wi' a dirty shirt in her presence?'

'Very true,' said Carey. 'She's notorious for it.' Hughie was chuckling. 'What?'

'Ah wis just wondering if she'd ever met the King of Scotland?' Hughie sniggered and Carey had to laugh as well. In the unlikely event of Her Majesty the Queen ever being in the same room as the young King, who rarely even wiped his face, let alone washed his body or shifted his shirt, a hail of slippers and fans would be the least His Majesty of Scotland could expect. For certain his subsidy from the English Treasury would suddenly dry up.

Hughie carried on, shaking his head, to the tiring room while Carey went in search of somewhere relatively peaceful with good light so he could read the inquest papers.

SATURDAY 16TH SEPTEMBER 1592,

LATE AFTERNOON

Carey was impressed when he looked at the work young Hughie had done on his doublet shoulders. The young man had unpicked the lining, taken out just enough of the padding and rearranged the rest to make room for Carey's extra sword muscles and then sewn it all up again as neat as you like. It seemed to be true he had been prenticed to a tailor.

'Well done, Hughie.' He put the watch candle down and felt for his purse. There was still a bit of money in it so he gave Hughie sixpence for the job. The amount of money he had seemed to be going down with its usual alarming speed. He wasn't yet ready to encase himself in Court armour of velvet and pearls so he wandered out into the crowded afternoon.

The Earl of Cumberland's men had finished enclosing the whole orchard in a large marquee, laying boards between the trees. Some of the later-fruiting trees still had apples, pears, and golden quinces hanging on them which scented the whole tent. The ones that had already been picked were being decorated with hanging pomanders and little silk bags of comfits. The banquet tables were against the further wall of the tent and the more open part of the orchard had been completely boarded over, with the raspberry and blackcurrant canes taken out, to make a dance floor. Her Majesty would dance that evening in the light of the banks of candles being carefully set up in readiness, but only a couple of them were lit so far.

Meanwhile in the other corner the musicians were tuning up and arguing over the playlist while the men of the chapel were still practising. Carey stopped and listened—Thomasina was right, there were only two tenors and one of them clearly had a bad sore throat and a head cold.

He was just thinking he should go back to the cottage tiring room and shift his shirt and change to his Court suit, when Thomasina swept in, followed by her two women who towered over her.

She stood on a stool and bade the choirmaster have his men sing an air for her, a piece of music which was ruined by the tenors any time they had a line to sing above *doh*. Carey was shaking his head at his cousin's likely reaction to the singing and wondering why the chapel master didn't simply change the air for something in a lower key, when suddenly Thomasina skewered him with a look.

'Could you sing that line, Sir Robert?' she snapped.

Carey remembered too late that she'd said something about his voice, bowed and smiled. 'I'm no great musician, mistress, and I'm sure the chapel master could find a much better...'

'He could if we were in Oxford or London, but not here where nobody can read music even if they can sing and we daren't let in any of the musicians from London. You can read pricksong, can't you?'

'Well, yes, but I...'

The brown button eyes glared again and Carey realised that there was probably some purpose to all this. He bowed again.

'I'll do my poor best, mistress.'

He got some very haughty looks from the chapel men who were understandably nervous at the idea of a courtier singing with them. That nettled him. He knew he could sing and in fact music had been one of only a few childhood lessons that could compete with football.

He stepped up to the candle and took the handwritten sheet of paper, squinted at it. A little tricky, but not impossibly difficult.

Mr. Byrd had him sight-sing the entire piece solo to a lute, then grunted and took him through it with the chapel men several times. The result was much better, he knew. With the spine of the music held for them by his voice, they could manage the complex interweavings required of them.

'Hmm,' said Mr. Byrd, 'well done, Sir Robert, very accurate.'

'This is new, isn't it? I feel sure I've never heard it before.'

Mr. Byrd and Thomasina exchanged looks and Byrd bowed. 'Thank you, sir, I have only just finished it.'

Could it have anything to do with the death of Amy Robsart, then? Surely not. It was only a piece of music, an air in the Spanish style, magically worked by William Byrd, an excellent chapel master, perhaps even as good as his predecessor Mr. Tallis. True, he was a Catholic, but he had miraculously survived a brush with Walsingham's pursuivants in the early eighties and had amply repaid the Queen for her backing of him.

Carey hummed through the whole thing again while he went to try on his dancing clothes. It turned out that the trunkhose and cannions of the suit were also a little tight but would do for now. Hughie had done wonders with his hard-used boots—stuffed rosemary and rue into them, polished them with beeswax and tallow, made them verging on respectable.

He had a little time before he needed to be in the transformed orchard. The inquest report and coroner's report were, of course, written in Latin which had been a subject that had never once won a battle with football. He knew French very well, which gave him the Norman French you needed for legal documents, but he could only struggle and guess with Latin.

So he walked over to the small stone village church where the Queen's secretaries would set up their office. He spoke to the Queen's chief clerk, Mr. Hughes, asking for someone who knew Latin but wasn't too busy. Hughes gestured at the row of men standing at high folding desks, busy writing. Carey walked past them intending to ask one of the greybeards who were experienced and fast, but then he spotted the second-to-last man, a gawky spotty young creature whose worn grey wool doublet was older than he was from its fashion. The boy looked up and blinked at him short-sightedly. On impulse, he stopped.

'What's your name?'

'John Tovey, sir.' He had a strong Oxford town accent.

551

'Can you translate this for me?'

The boy took the paper and blinked at it. 'This is quite simple. Are you *sure* you need it translated, sir?'

Carey smiled. 'You don't normally work for the Queen's clerks, do you?'

The boy blushed. 'I'm…I'm the priest's son here,' he stuttered, 'I…I came to help to…to…'

The boy's fingers were inky and had a scholar's callus on the right index finger, so he probably was a genuine clerk.

Carey fished out another groat, a little less than a screever in London would have charged. 'Go on,' he said, 'English it as quick as you can. I'm due at the dancing.'

John Tovey nodded, gulped his large Adam's apple against his falling band, took the documents from Carey and spread them out on his desk in the pool of light made by his couple of candles. The light in the church was poor. What followed was remarkable enough that Carey blinked his eyes at it. The boy simply laid down a fresh piece of paper, picked up and dipped his pen and started scribbling, with his finger tracing along the lines of Latin. No muttering aloud, no scratching out, he just wrote down the English for the fiendish Latin.

Carey looked around at the whitewashed walls and carvings. It had been badly damaged at some time in the past, no doubt at the time of the stripping of the altars. There were headless statues and the windows were boarded up.

'Carey!' boomed a voice behind him and Carey spun to see a large boyish man with a curly red-blond beard and wearing an eye-watering combination of tawny slashed with white. His doublet was crusted with amber and topaz, the white damask sprinkled with diamond sparks.

Carey's left knee hit the tiles as he genuflected. 'My lord Earl of Essex,' he said formally, genuinely pleased to see his lord.

Robert Devereux, Earl of Essex, favourite of the Queen, bustled across the aisle to Carey, gesturing for him to stand and slung an arm across his shoulders. Essex was a couple of inches taller and at least a hand's breadth wider than Carey, who was neither short nor narrow. Essex was a man designed by God for the tourney and he loomed and laughed loudly.

'Sir Robert, how splendid! I thought you were still in Berwick chasing cattle raiders...'

'My noble father ordered me south, my lord,' Carey said and on that thought, he remembered why he had been so anxious to see Essex. His stomach tightened. He had important information for the Earl about some investments of his and what Carey thought had really been going on. Unfortunately the news was very bad and Carey had been the Queen's messenger of bad news often enough that he was nervous about it.

'I heard about you being in some scandalous brawl in the Fleet Prison,' said Essex. 'What the devil have you been up to? Is it true you gave Mr. Vice Chamberlain Heneage a bloody nose?'

'It is, my lord,' Carey said and told him an edited version of the last few weeks of activity. Some of it made Essex tip his head back and shake the church rafters with his bellow of laughter. John Tovey jumped like a startled cat at the noise.

'But it was the matter that happened later which brought me here, my lord,' he added. 'I wanted to talk to you about some lands you've bought in Cornwall...'

Essex's face suddenly shut down, switching from a handsome boy's face to something quite masklike.

'I don't own any lands in Cornwall.'

'You don't?' Carey was shocked. He had been so certain that the code word Icarus meant the Earl of Essex.

'No. There was a man called Jackson hawking them about a few months ago—recusant lands with gold in 'em, he said—but I don't own any.'

'That's wonderful news, my lord,' Carey said, smiling with relief. 'You were absolutely right not to buy. I was very concerned because the whole thing was a lay to coney-catch...people at Court.' He had been on the verge of explaining his theory as to who had set the lay and why, but something stopped him. Essex wasn't looking at him and his arm was not heavy across his shoulders anymore.

'Hmm, shocking,' said Essex vaguely. 'Well, I didn't.'

Alternatively, Essex had indeed bought the lands but had heard rumours already about their worthlessness and was lying about it in hopes of selling them on. Carey studied his face. Most courtiers, like Carey, shaved or trimmed their beards short to a goatee or a Spanish-style spade-shape. Essex, blessed with a luxuriant bush of red curls, grew it as nature wished and combed and oiled it every day. It left less of his face to read. For all his easy manner, Essex was a true courtier. Carey couldn't be certain if he was lying or not.

'I'm sure plenty of men at Court have been caught by Jackson's Papist lay, but not me,' Essex added.

He had to do it. He had to warn Essex of the real source of the trouble, if only because his own fortunes were still bound up with Essex's.

'Perhaps Sir Robert Cecil will be disappointed,' Carey said very quietly, in case any of the other clerks working away at the desks by candlelight as the light faded had been paid to listen.

Essex's blue gaze felt like a blow on the head, but then he looked at the boarded higher windows of the church.

'Yes, he always is, poor crookback.'

Carey said nothing. Essex had been Burghley's ward as a boy and had grown up with Burghley's second son, Robert, who had suffered from rickets as a child. It had never been very likely that they would be friends.

'So,' boomed Essex, 'what are you here for, Sir Robert?'

Carey paused before he answered because he wanted Essex to help with the Queen's impossible order. 'I'm hoping for my fee for the deputy wardenship,' he explained, 'but Her Majesty wants me to do something else first.'

Essex grunted sympathetically enough and allowed himself to be drawn outside the church walls and into the watery dregs of afternoon. Clouds were marching up from the west in great armies which didn't bode well for the dancing later.

He explained the whole circumstance and Essex shook his head.

'Jesu, rather you than me,' he said. 'That's a nasty matter.'

'Did your stepfather ever tell you anything about it?'

Essex shook his head vigorously. 'No, nothing. Wouldn't even let his first wife be named in his presence.'

'Your lady mother?' Carey asked cautiously. 'Did she...er...?'

'You'd think she'd have been jealous of Amy Robsart, as my stepfather's first love, but she wasn't. She was jealous, exceedingly. But not of Amy Robsart.'

Carey said nothing. They both knew the woman Lettice Knollys had real cause to hate.

'I'll be seeing my lady mother later,' Essex said. 'I'll mention it to her if you like.'

'That would be very kind, my lord. I need all the help you can give. But surely the Dowager Lady won't be coming to Court?'

'No, no, of course not, the Queen won't have her. But she's staying in Oxford at the moment so I'll see what I can do...'

That was hopeful—if the Earl remembered his promise and if he actually kept it. Carey thought of mentioning Emilia's suit, but then decided not to. After all, she hadn't yet even offered him a proper fee for the introduction to Essex. There was a nervous cough behind him. Carey turned back to see John Tovey standing there in his worn grey doublet, holding a close-written piece of paper and looking scared.

'Mr. Tovey,' said Carey affably, 'Have you finished?'

'Y...y...yes,' stuttered the boy.'D...did you want me to sign the copy?'

Carey shook his head, took the translation and read it carefully; a little to his surprise, some of the Latin had meant what he had guessed it did. As the Earl was still standing there, avid with curiosity, Carey passed it to him and he read it, too.

'It all seems in order, Sir Robert. The jury found it was an accidental death.'

Carey was so surprised to hear Essex say this that he looked carefully to see if the Earl was joking. No, there was no twinkle in the blue eyes, no smile, but no puzzled frown either. Essex saw nothing wrong with the accounts at all.

'Yes, my lord,' he said after a moment's thought and didn't say any of the things that had struck him forcibly even while he had been struggling with the Latin. He caught John Tovey's eye and saw from the terror there that the boy knew who Amy Robsart was and had spotted what he had in the dry legal phrases. So he had better deal with that.

'I must go and meet the Queen,' said Essex. 'I'll do what I can for you, Sir Robert. I'll arrange for you to talk to my lady mother—I'm sure she'll be very happy to do it. But best not to mention the...

er...the property business to her. She won't be interested and might take it into her fluffy head to buy some, eh?'

There was an unfilial wink and a laugh and then the Earl turned and strode out of the churchyard, letting the gate bang behind him. Carey bowed to him as he went, honestly impressed at how well the Earl could fake genuine amusement. So that was who had bought up the Cornish recusant lands, was it? Of course Lettice Knollys' son would have done the business for his lady mother. It made a lot of sense. Carey wondered if Sir Robert Cecil yet knew that detail—he would undoubtedly find out. Perhaps it would be a good idea for Carey to be the first to tell him? Or perhaps not. He would likely be annoyed, and Carey didn't want Cecil to know how much he knew about the Jackson affair. Though he probably did.

Carey sighed at the weary complexity of Court life and turned to John Tovey, who was still standing there like a post, mouth open, Adam's apple working every so often. His spots were more visible in the dull daylight, but he had done a creditable and, more importantly, fast job on the Latin. Carey sat down on the stone bench overlooking the churchyard, the only part of the village not being camped on or grazed by the Court or its animals.

'Mr. Tovey, how old are you?'

'T...twenty, I think, sir.'

'Are you looking for a place as a clerk?'

The boy flushed—he was almost certainly not twenty but a couple of years younger at least.

'Er...yes. Yes, I am, sir.'

That was why rootless, penniless, but educated young men would come and clerk for the Queen on progress—in hopes of a cushy office job with perks. Some of them weren't disappointed.

'What can you do?'

'I...I...can read and translate Greek, Latin, Italian, French, and write good secretary hand and italic as well. I can cast up accounts in Arabic figures and I...I know something of medicine and herbs.'

'Your father?'

'Is...the priest here. He taught me first and then, after I was prenticed to an Oxford 'pothecary, I went as a servitor at Magdalen, though at first they wouldn't have me.'

'Why not?' There was a pause while the boy blushed ruby red and stuttered.

'I'm a b...b...bastard, sir.'

'Is that all? So's my father. Did yours acknowledge you?'

'Yes, sir, but he never married my mother for fear of the Queen. She...er...she d...d...doesn't like priests to marry.'

'Your mother?'

'Is dead, sir. A few years ago.'

'And you want to leave Rycote, seek your fortune?' He must, look at the place!

The boy flushed dark, gulped, and nodded convulsively once.

'Excellent. Would you like to work for me, Mr. Tovey, as my clerk? It would involve coming with me to Carlisle, I'm afraid.'

'Where's that, sir?'

'A long way north. Next door to Scotland.'

'Oh.' A pause. Then another convulsive nod. Carey stepped closer, put his hand on the boy's shoulder and gripped. 'Well then, if your father gives permission, I will be your good lord if you agree to be my man.'

The boy nodded and said 'Yes, sir,' firmly enough. They shook hands on it. As it wasn't a hiring fair there was no need to go and pay fees or sign indentures, though for form's sake Carey intended to talk to the lad's father. He hadn't at all meant to recruit a clerk as well as a henchman, despite his hatred of paperwork. However, he had to do something about what Tovey had read and unexpectedly understood. Bribing him sufficiently would cost a lot more than simply paying him wages every so often. And, anyway, if the boy was telling the truth about his accomplishments, he'd be getting a very good University clerk out of it.

'We'll go and see your father, shall we? Get his permission? Do you know where he might be?'

'In the alehouse,' shrugged the boy. 'He won't care.'

They passed the place on the way back to the orchard and young Tovey was correct: his reverend father was drunk, playing quoits with the blacksmith, the miller, and the butcher. Once he understood what his base-born son was telling him, he was blurrily delighted that Carey was employing the boy without his even having to pay a shilling for the office. Tovey knelt for his father's blessing and got a wave of the hand and a few mumbles for it.

The boy asked if he could go back to the church to finish some work for Mr. Hughes and be paid for it. This was entirely reasonable and saved Carey from having to find somewhere for the boy to sleep since the clerks always dossed down where they worked. The dusk was coming down fast and the air crisping as he strode to the orchard.

Carey didn't really want to go and dance, even if there had been any chance of dancing with Emilia again. But he had to, if only to kneel to the Queen as part of the crowd and make sure she saw him. Mistress Thomasina had kindly given him an excellent way of being conspicuous without importunity. But his head was buzzing with the implications of the inquest findings into the thirty-two-year-old death of Amy Robsart. No wonder the jury had taken a full year to report, and had done so in such a way as to satisfy both conscience and, no doubt, covert influence from the Queen, Dudley, and who knew where else? The whole pile of papers must have been quietly buried in the Oxford town muniment room. It was lucky Thomasina had been able to find it and give him a copy. He was a little surprised they hadn't been burned in a mysterious fire. Did she know what was in them? Maybe not; she wouldn't understand Latin.

Back in the little tiring room, Carey waited until Mr. Simmonds had come out, clad in a smartly brushed buffcoat with his cloak over his arm, ready to attend Cumberland at the dance. His Court suit was hanging up ready, smelling of rose petal powder with the clean shirt he had managed to pack in his hunting satchel when he left Somerset House the day before. He had kept it carefully for exactly this chance. He sniffed his armpits and frowned. Could he wash anywhere? Riding forty miles in a day was a sweaty business and he'd ridden in from Oxford in the morning as well.

There would be stews in Oxford for the naughty students, but none here in the little village. There would be hip baths in Norris' manor house which the Queen and her ladies would use. No doubt Essex was stepping into something organised for him right now. Where was Cumberland? A small pack of boys ran past him downhill, shouting in excitement about something going on in the duck pond.

He shucked his hunting doublet and hose, left them hanging

on another peg. Scratching fleabites from the last night at the inn, Carey ambled barefoot in his shirt down toward the village duck pond, singing the tune he'd just learnt.

A grey-bearded man in a sober black doublet and gown suddenly turned and stared at him as if he had spoken, then hurried after him.

'Sir,' he said, 'that tune. Did Heron Nimmo teach it to you?'

'Eh?' said Carey, irritated at being interrupted in his thoughts, 'No, the Queen's chapel master. Why?'

The man flushed and bowed. 'My apologies, sir, I mistook you for a friend.'

'I don't know anybody called Heron Nimmo. You should enquire of Mr. Byrd, perhaps. The Lord Chamberlain, my father, might know him if he's a musician?'

The man bowed again, muttered to himself, hurried away. Carey sauntered on down to the duck pond. He found Cumberland and half the Court there, busily wading into the pond and the stream feeding it and washing as best they could.

Villagers were lining the banks and watching with gaping mouths. Some of them were women, peeking round hedges and clutching each other and giggling. Grinning at the sight of the richest and most powerful men in the country splashing about naked in cold water for fear of a fussy woman of fifty-nine, Carey stripped off his own shirt, hung it on a post, and waded in.

The water made him gasp but it was quite refreshing. You had to be careful because the stones on the bottom were covered in weed and very slippery. Cumberland saw him and whistled.

'Christ, Sir Robert, who tried to slit your ribs?'

Carey looked down at the purple scar he had collected in the summer and completely forgotten about.

'A Scotsman with a knife. Cost me £20 to get my black velvet doublet mended afterward.'

Cumberland laughed. 'Where is he now?'

'In Hell, my lord, where do you think?' Carey answered coolly, since he had in fact killed his man to the great approval of the assembled Carlislers. The inquest on that death had taken twenty minutes and found it lawful killing in self-defence.

Cumberland slapped him on the back and offered him soap,

which Carey took. Just in that moment, as he bent to wash his armpits in the water, he half-heard a familiar sound and his body instinctively clenched and ducked, well before his mind could tell him what it was.

His foot caught on a slippery stone and he went over sideways with a splash, swamping Cumberland and two other Court sprigs, one of whom had been silly enough to put his clean shirt back on before he was well away from the water. Pure reflex made him grab the nearest thing from underwater, which unfortunately happened to be the Earl of Cumberland's leg. That took the Earl over as well.

Cumberland came up again, blowing water with weeds on his head, the light of battle in his eyes. Carey had to dive sideways to avoid a very accomplished wrestling grab by the Earl, which meant his shoulder went into the legs of somebody else and took him down as well.

The whole scene degenerated into a wrestling free-for-all. Carey climbed out of the shouting, splashing, yelling clump of nobility as soon as he could, quickly soaped his armpits and then was well-rinsed by the Earl of Cumberland pulling him back into the pond and dunking him. It took a very nice break-free taught him by Dodd to get out of the Earl's expert grip so he could use a willow branch to haul himself up and cough water.

The entire village was now gathered to watch the fun, including the quoits players, vigorous betting going on and the boys cheering on their favourites while the village dogs barked their heads off. The noise was amazing which meant Carey could speak quietly to get under the sound and penetrate to the Earl of Cumberland before he could be thrown again.

'Look there,' he said, pointing.

Cumberland stopped laughing suddenly, frowned. They waded across, shoving wrestlers out of their way to a willow root on the far side where some highly offended ducks were hiding as far up the tree as they could get in their webbed feet.

A crossbow bolt was buried deep in the wood, the notch bright and new.

That was the sound he'd heard. The snick of a crossbow trigger being released. He and Cumberland looked at each other. The bolt was an ordinary one from a hunting bow. Not one for small game, but for deer. The bolt was a good six inches long, heavy and sharp. If it had hit him it would probably have killed him.

'I was wondering what you thought you were doing,' said Cumberland thoughtfully. 'Thank you, Sir Robert.'

True, it could have been aimed at the Earl and not at him; they had been close enough together. And Cumberland too had enemies, notably the Spanish and the French and probably some inherited Border feuds as well. But when Carey felt which way the bolt's tail was pointing and traced the line of its flight across the stream, he thought it was at chest height where he had been standing in the moment he heard the trigger. Behind him had been a low wall and some bushes. Carey waded back across the pond as the wrestlers calmed themselves and started climbing out and drying themselves. Bets were being settled. He peered over the wall. The ground was soft but well printed with many feet and no way of telling among them.

'Or do you think it was you he was after?' The Earl was already on the bank, rubbing himself down with a linen towel. Carey shrugged and followed him, hoping to use the towel as well since he hadn't brought one.

'I don't know, my lord,' he said, blinking at the tree where the crossbow bolt was buried.

'Well, it wasn't an accident, that's sure,' Cumberland said, handing him the dank towel. 'With a bolt that size, whoever shot it wasn't after duck.'

Carey shivered suddenly but only because he was wet and the sun was setting. He rubbed himself briskly, finished, and pulled his shirt back on. Typically the Earl was now chuckling and shaking his head so his earring flashed.

'By God, Carell's done ye some good. That was fast. Do you find a lot people trying to kill you at the moment, eh?'

'Well yes, my lord, I understand the Grahams have my head priced at £10 in Dumfries.'

Cumberland hooted. 'Not nearly enough, the skinflints. I'll tell 'em to put it up to £50 at least.'

'Your lordship is too kind,' Carey said smiling, although he still felt cold. That was far away on the Borders where he rarely went anywhere without a padded jack reinforced with steel plates on his back, and Dodd behind him. For God's sake, this was Oxfordshire in fat, soft southern England. It wasn't supposed to happen, whoever the assassin had been aiming at. And who the hell had tried it?

***

Emilia Bonnetti was dousing herself in expensive rosewater to clean herself as there were no such things as proper baths in this peasant bog. She knew how persnickety the old English Queen was and had an intricately smocked fresh shift to wear under her stays. Her beautiful crimson silk gown had been left in Ireland, alas, that goddamned hellhole of a country. No doubt some uncouth chieftain's wife was wearing it now. Dante Aligheri was completely wrong: Hell was a green boggy place where the air was constantly damp from the equally constant rain and the people were charming, intelligent, sometimes remarkably good-looking but lethally unpredictable. Only God knew how near a thing it had been for herself and her husband; only she knew how nearly they had died.

She had borrowed a dancing gown from the wife of one of the musicians who probably made a very good thing out of it, seeing what the woman charged. The gown was tawny, which did not suit her colouring at all but would have to do as there was no choice. Her slippers were also borrowed, a different shade of tawny, and didn't fit properly.

She was in a peasant's main room, getting dressed with the few other women at Court who were neither ladies-in-waiting nor maids of honour; they were wives of lesser courtiers mainly. Maids of honour, pfui. Dishonour, more like. Emilia had heard of Raleigh's proceedings with Bess Throckmorton and was shocked. She had been a virgin when she married and it had taken some work to stay intact when her cousins came calling. However, once you were legally married and had given your man an heir, it didn't matter in the least what you did, in her view. Bonnetti himself was well aware of what she did and they often planned one of her campaigns together over a jug of their wine. On her part, she ignored his activities with chambermaids. They were excellent business partners. The wine made good profits when everything went well and the customers actually paid up; much more profitable was the trade in information. The barrels of goods and gold that went back to the Hague to pay for the wine would often have secret compartments with coded news in them from Signor Bonnetti to keep the stupid English Customs and Excise men and the pursuivants happy. Her own methods were better.

Tonight she had two quarries: one she had taken before, the tall chestnut-headed, disgracefully handsome cousin of the Queen, with his piercing blue eyes and his (she had to admit) quite polished manners. The other…well, she would have to be very careful not to actually catch that one or the whole plan would be ruined. She had only to wing him slightly, as it were.

Once that had happened…She pulled the corner of her eyes and carefully brushed on kohl to make them seem even darker. She never used belladonna for that purpose as she liked to be able to see what she was doing.

A lady's tiring maid was sewing in place the unfashionable square neck and small lawn ruff that stood up awkwardly behind her head. Even the woman's small attendance had cost her tuppence, for God's sake.

Emilia's hair was in an artful chignon—that had taken her hours to achieve—partly covered by a lacy little cap and her jaunty hat with a pheasant feather in it.

She had no pattens to protect her slippers from the mud, but Oxford's men had laid old rush mats on the path to the large tent that covered the orchard. The English were good at that kind of artifice because of their miserable climate. That whole part of the village was already filling with brightly dressed people, though the candles weren't lit yet. The banquet wasn't set either but you could hear the musicians tuning up.

It certainly wasn't time to arrive, so she retreated again and watched from the open horn window as the activity gradually built to a crescendo. She was watching for one man in particular, that chestnut-headed son of a king's bastard, an espionage plum she meant to pluck.

Emilia bit her bottom lip and frowned. Every time she thought of him, her stomach fizzed like a firework with anger and...well, yes, with desire. She was far too old and experienced to imagine that she was feeling love, but Jesu, her brain stopped working properly every time she looked at him.

No. She must concentrate. She had two aims. One was to be introduced to the Earl of Essex and begin the delicate process of impressing, attracting, and befriending him. She didn't know how much M. le deputé would want for that valuable connection, of course he hadn't mentioned a price, was himself far too wily.

She had had to leave her best pearl necklace with the musician's wife as a deposit and most of her bracelets and rings had been hocked either in Dublin or Oxford. At least she had her new gold and garnet necklace from George around her neck. Could she find something else Carey wanted? Perhaps? She hoped so.

Her fingers fumbled a little as she drew on her small kid gloves and pick up her fan. She had put extra red lead on her cheeks, knowing she would appear sallow in this goddamned tawny velvet that the pink and insipid Englishwomen liked so well. She had artless black ringlets escaping down her neck and a stylish hat... and she had herself.

And she would have Carey that night.

SATURDAY 16TH SEPTEMBER 1592,

AFTERNOON

Henry Dodd rode Whitesock and the mare into the main inn-yard at Bicester on Saturday afternoon and hired the luxury of a whole room to himself. He saw to his animals, ate steak and kidney pudding in the common room, and had a mug of aqua vitae to settle him for bed.

Then the barman looked sideways at him and asked, 'Where's your warrant, then what gets you half-price for booze?'

'Ah...' said Dodd, this being the first he'd heard of a warrant.

'Your horse has the Queen's brand on him,' said the barman, frowning. 'Stands to reason you've got a warrant unless you've prinked the pony.'

That sounded like something that meant 'steal.' Dodd frowned back. 'No, I haven't.' And in his view, he hadn't. He'd received the horse quite rightfully in the course of settling a dispute with the horse's previous owner, but they might not look at things sensibly down here in the mysterious South where nobody spoke properly or seemed to care what surname a man bore.

'Ay,' said Dodd, drinking his brandy, 'Ah'm riding wi' a message from ma Lady Hunsdon to her husband the Lord Chamberlain.'

Later he would remember the man sitting by the fire with a gaunt hawklike face and a wide-brimmed hat who looked up at that. At the time he didn't properly notice.

'Hmm. Where are you from anyway?'

'Berwick,' lied Dodd on general principles. None of the soft Southrons had heard of Carlisle and there was nothing wrong with a little misdirection. Especially as he didn't of course have any kind of warrant with him at all. For good measure he added, 'I serve the Lord Chamberlain's son, Sir Robert Carey.'

The barman was wiping the bar now, still not looking at him. Dodd smiled and lifted his mug to him, paid for his board and went upstairs. He was still dressed as a gentleman in a smart grey wool suit of Sir Robert Carey's and he carried a sword, but nobody knew better than him that he was in fact, thank God, no kind of gentleman at all and never would be. He was a tenant farmer and Sergeant of Gilsland, in charge of one troop of the Carlisle guard, that was all.

By the South's ridiculous way of looking at things, he had in fact stolen one of the Queen's horses from the Queen's vice chamberlain and he had no intention of explaining the circumstances to anyone at all until he had caught up with that bloody man Carey. He got into a bed that didn't smell too bad and fell asleep instantly.

He woke in the darkest part of the night with the thought 'Time to go,' ringing through his head.

He dressed quietly, getting better at putting on his complicated suit. Moonlight shone through the luxurious Southern panes of glass. Holding his boots, he went to the door, unbarred it, and found it had been locked on the outside.

'Och,' he said disgustedly and sat on the bed. No doubt there was someone sleeping on the other side of that door, waiting for him. Perhaps it was something to do with the damned warrant the barman had asked about. He went to the small glass window that opened onto the courtyard, which he knew had a gate that would also be locked at this time. The stables were directly below on this side of it, the kitchens on the other side. He needed at least one horse.

No help for it. Perhaps it was a pity to mess up the comfortable little room but there was really no help for it. From the moon's position he thought he had a couple of hours until dawn so best to get started.

Softly he tapped the floorboards—too solid. Then he tapped the wall between him and the next room. Withies, lightly plastered. He hadn't an axe but he did have a broadsword which he would now have to sharpen.

It took some strength and sweat to do it quietly, but he broke through the plaster low down behind the bed, smelling of where the bedbugs had their hiding places and then through the withies on his side, pulling them outward to a panicked exodus of creepy crawlies. The filling was only rubbish and then there were the withies for the wall on the other side. Working as quietly as he could, a giant rat up to no good, he weakened them with his sword and broke them, brought kindling over from beside the luxurious fireplace and built it up against them. Then he lit the tallow dip from the watchlight and lit the small bonfire. He had some aqua vitae left so he sprinkled it about around the fire to catch when it got hot enough.

He sat back on his haunches and watched the flames catch, enjoying the sight as always, the feeling of power as fire flowered where it shouldn't, then caught himself and pulled on his boots, buckled his sadly blunted sword on his hip and picked up his hat.

The flames were climbing the wall and had gone partly through.

He took the jack of ale left on the table and kicked through the wall bellowing 'Fire! Fire!'

A fat man in his shirt and two boys sharing the trundle bed in the next room started up, all shouting with fright. Somebody further away took up the shout.

Dodd slung ale all around the fire, but not on it, kicked some more of the wall, put his hat on his head and ducked through the flaming hole he'd made into the next room where the fat man was desperately scrabbling on his breeches and trying to move his strong box. The two boys had already opened the door and run. Dodd went through onto the landing, found a big man lying across his door just waking up and kicked him twice in the cods.

Then he went back to the merchant. 'Shall I help ye carry that, sir?' he asked politely, speaking as Southern as possible.

'Yes, yes...'

So he and the fat man in his breeks and shirt carefully carried the interestingly heavy locked box onto the landing, down the stairs crowded with other frightened customers, some of them in very fine velvets half put on.

He took the lead, elbowed through the throng, and helped carry the box out into the courtyard where there was a fine mizzle. It must have been dry recently for the thatch over his room was well alight now, billows of smoke going up and the rats coming out of the roof squeaking. The innkeeper was straining to open the big gates to let his neighbours in to help.

'Thank you, sir,' puffed the merchant, 'If I may give you...'

'Nay sir, glad tae help, I must see after my horse now.'

Dodd slipped away from the man and went into the stables where a brave but stupid boy was trying to lead the horses out without blindfolding them first.

Dodd went to his own nag and put his hat across the beast's eyes and put the bridle on. 'See ye,' he said to the frightened boy struggling in the next stall with a rearing kicking mare, 'Dinna let them see and they'll let ye help them.'

The boy put his statute cap across the mare's eyes and she started to calm down. Dodd got another bridle from the wall and put it over her head. He couldn't bring himself to grab a different horse, seeing as how none of them was a patch on Whitesock. The boy had followed his advice and managed to bridle two more horses.

'Ah'll take them out,' he said to the boy who was coughing hard and disappearing as the smoke filled the stable. 'Just unhitch the others and drive 'em before ye, then stay out of the stables.'

The hayloft above was likely to catch soon and Dodd didn't want the lad on his conscience as well. Then, slowly and gently, Dodd took four snorting horses through the door and out into the courtyard where he let all but Whitesock get away from him. They helpfully caused much more confusion there along with two hysterical dogs and an escaped pig, and disrupted the bucket chain. Bless the mare for her common sense; she headed straight for the open gate and he swung himself up on Whitesock shouting, 'I'll fetch her back!' and galloped straight out of the gate and up the road, leaving the other horses for dust and catching the mare's reins as he passed her.

Two miles up the road in the darkness he could still see the glow of the fire and could hear no hooves behind him. He started to laugh then. Well, it was funny. Here in the South nobody seemed to have the least idea about anything. Imagine thinking that locking the door on him would stop him?

SATURDAY 16TH SEPTEMBER 1592, EVENING

Hughie's ears were burning as Carey praised him for the work he'd done on that Court doublet. It had been a pleasure really; it was a lovely piece of work by a fine London tailor. It would be a pity to put a knife through it, and quite difficult as well because of the quadruple thickness, the heavy embroidery and pearls, the padding. So he wouldn't do that.

Carey changed his shirt and left the other on the floor as he hopped about putting on his hose. Hughie helped him into the canions and trunkhose, held up by a waistcoat of damask. The doublet weighed many pounds, Carey went 'ooff' and made a wry face as his shoulders took the weight, though he must be used to wearing a jack that weighed much more at about fifty pounds. Hughie then had to tie and retie the points at Carey's back three or four times to get them at exactly the right length so that they held the doublet and trunkhose together but allowed him to dance. Carey took his long jewelled poinard, having left his workmanlike broadsword in the Cumberland armoury.

Hughie coughed. 'Will Ah be attendin' ye at the dancing, sir?' he asked. He had brushed his woollen doublet and cannions, just in case. Carey's answer was a swift critical glance, sweeping Hughie head to toe and somehow making him blush again. There was a curt nod. It seemed Hughie passed muster.

They walked with a herd of other gallantly overdressed young men to the orchard which was now a glowing palace, the fruit still left on the trees making a sweet fresh scent to battle with the rose-scented candles and the raucous smell of men and wine.

The musicians sat and stood in a corner on the new boards of the dance floor. They were playing loudly—it would be a noisy night as the boards creaked and thundered under the boots and slippers of the Court.

Of course all the local gentlefolk were there with their unmarried daughters and sisters—the women tricked out in as much costly splendour as the men or indeed more, wearing tokens of their dowries. They gathered in shy drifts near the banquet tables and the high stands of candles.

The Queen wasn't there yet, nor were the great lords of her Court—the Earls of Essex, Oxford, Cumberland. Carey hesitated as he looked at the groups of henchmen and courtiers and then made some kind of decision, took up a place near the Earl of Essex's men. He started talking to a man with a sharp Welsh face.

Hughie stood behind him near the canvas wall, watching carefully, wishing his Edinburgh doublet was better fashion since all the other servingmen were very fine in good wool or even velvets with brocade trim.

Many of Essex's henchmen were in tangerine and white which suited nobody except the ones who were rosily ginger, and not really even them, Hughie thought critically.

They all waited, talking quietly while the music tinkled in the background, conducted by a short round man. Every so often he would pick up and play a different instrument.

Hughie jumped. Trumpets had sounded, the short man stood up and waved his arms, there was a rustle of tension, the sound of boots on boards. Hughie craned to see the red and gold livery of the Gentlemen Pensioners of Her Majesty's Guard. They fanned out and stood by the entrances and by the carved wooden seat with an awning of brocade lions set at the end of the dance floor.

Hughie was expecting the Queen next, but it was a herd of women, to the sound of pipes and viols. They were arm in arm, some of them older, eight of them juicy and pert in their teens and all wearing the Queen's black and white colours, designed to their taste. It was a fine sight and interesting for the mixture of French and Spanish fashion, with the big wheel farthingales coming in now even in Scotland.

The music stopped. More trumpeting. Men were shouting 'The Queen! The Queen!'

Hughie blinked. A broad long man in dazzling white with red hair and an impressive beard paced in slowly, leaning down to someone much shorter in black velvet and white damask blazing with jewels and pearls, who had her heavily ringed white hand tucked in the crook of his arm.

In a smooth sweeping motion, the whole mob of people in the tent went to both their knees. Nearly falling over, Hughie did the same, squinting to see the cause of it clearly.

Through the lanes of cramoisie, green, black, tawny, rose, and even daring sky blue, all the men with their hats off, went...

A smallish elderly woman entered wearing a bright red wig sparkled with diamonds and a small gold and pearl crown, different-coloured ribbons all over her black velvet gown with a huge Spanish farthingale under it. Her face was white with red cheekbones and her eyes snapping and sparkling black as they looked about around her people. Hughie's blood went cold as he realised he still had his hat on and scrabbled it off before she could see, leaving his hair standing up on end. The penetrating gaze swept past and didn't seem to have spotted him.

There was a loud shout of 'God save the Queen!' and all the people shouted it three times.

The Queen walked to the chair under her cloth of estate, turned about as she let go of the big man's arm, smiled down at her kneeling courtiers.

'My lords, ladies, gentlemen, and goodmen,' she said in a penetrating contralto voice. 'We thank you for your loving greeting and attendance upon us and hereby order you all to your feet in our presence, so we may enjoy the dancing arranged for our entertainment by our well-loved Lord Norris and Earl of Cumberland.' A round-faced man with a worried look stood up and bowed low to her. The Queen clapped her hands.

'Up, up, on your feet, all of you, never mind your knees,' she said with a magical smile. 'What shall we have first, Mr. Byrd? A coranto?'

The short fat man bowed and pointed two fingers. The musicians started up the dance-measure as the lines of courtiers quickly sorted themselves.

Hughie had no idea how to dance Court dances, though he could give a good account of himself at the Edinburgh fair day, which put him in mind of something he had done for Lord Spynie once at a Court dance and that had worked very nicely. Everybody had thought that the fat burgher, whose daughter Spynie had taken a fancy to, had gone outside for air and then died suddenly of a fit sent by God in punishment for his avarice.

Hughie watched as Carey joined the lines of dancers, smiling and talking to the small dark Welshman on his left. Hughie sidled along the wall to be nearer the musicians. He wanted a metal harp or lute string, that was all. You never knew when you might get the opportunity to earn your gold.

SATURDAY 16TH SEPTEMBER 1592, EVENING

Emilia watched Sir Robert Carey and calculated where she stood among the other women so she would be his partner for the measures halfway through the country dance that was next. Oddly enough, her prey seemed not to have noticed her yet. Perhaps he was being coy.

She fluttered her fan across her face, the last crimson remnant of what had worked for him in Scotland and smiled to him under her lashes. He acknowledged her with a polite tilt of his head but that was all. Had he been gelded by the Scots then?

She took hands with the provincial English girls on either side of her in their ugly provincial English gowns, stepped forward, stepped back, her borrowed velvet rocking around her hips with the other women's careful farthingales, stepped sideways, stepped back, such a boring dance, thank God she had a mind that learned such things easily, stepped forward, take hands with a spotty boy that had used far too much white lead on the spots, spin, dance a measure with him, spin again and back to the women's line, and so along by two partners.

At the far end she knew the Queen was in the line of women and at the other end was the ginger man, Essex, her mignon and no doubt her paramour, the wicked old bitch.

And step forward and back and sideways again. That bad man Cumberland was giving one of the prettier provincial girls the kind of smile he had given her across a hall in Dublin, and that was unfair, the use of a culverin to sink a rowing boat, for the girl was stricken by it like a rabbit at a fox. Perhaps she would be well-guarded by her menfolk.

Emilia sighed, spun, danced, stepped forward and back and then, quite unexpectedly, there was M. le deputé who had so helpfully and expensively sold her guns for Ireland. Well, he had sold them to her stupid husband who had been too excited at the thought of blackmailing the Queen's nephew to check them properly and so nearly brought about not just their deaths, which Emilia could perhaps have forgiven from Purgatory, but much worse, their ruin.

She smiled at him and wished for a feathered mask. He looked down at her gravely, spun her, danced, spun her again and all with the most depressing propriety.

Damn, damn, damn him, he was playing hard to get because there was a clear admission of guilt in his humorously raised eyebrow and the sparkle in his so-blue eyes.

Jesu, what an annoying man. Her stomach was fizzing again; she was lusting after him like one of the stupid provincial girls. That was not at all the way to do it. He was supposed to be hot for her, not the other way around. However, there was no question that she wanted more of what he had so scandalously and lustily given her in Scotland. She definitely wanted him. When they danced, her whole body had risen to him, trout to a lure. Goddamn him.

She smiled again with particular lasciviousness at the next man to spin her round, a willowy youth in pearl-grey satin. And then she quite consciously stopped herself. She had to bank her fires so they could work where they were really needed. But she still needed that valuable introduction to the Earl of Essex. Her satisfaction for the guns would have to wait. It was lucky she had a secret contact here.

She paced forward and back and sideways again and found herself dancing with the Earl of Essex himself, now in white satin and white velvet, sparked with diamonds, trimmed in gold. He blanked her completely. Should she dare to ask? No, the music was too loud and the Queen would see. She had to take the normal route, through Carey or another follower of the Earl. Damn. Of course, that was why Carey was playing hard to get, he had been ten years a courtier. He knew his worth.

She let the moment pass. At the last measure, cleverly timed, the Queen and Essex danced together. The Queen was a good dancer, light and brisk on her feet. Then Essex expertly played the part of a man in love and leaned solicitously over a woman at least thirty years senior to him, who giggled and flirted and Holy Madonna, had her stays scandalously low and her hair uncovered by a cap, as if a maid of fourteen. Disgusting!

The two bowed and curtseyed to each other—the Queen not very much and the Earl a great deal from his great height and the other dancers all clapped.

Emilia's feet were already sore and pinched in their borrowed dancing slippers and much-darned silk stockings. What could she bribe the Deputy with if not herself? She had only received one good necklace so far from Cumberland and it looked as if she would have to say goodbye to it now.

Hmm. She moved toward the broad-shouldered lad whom Carey had had at his back when he came in, instead of the lanky dour-faced man he had in Scotland. This one had a square raw-boned face and seemed only quarter-witted, but was wearing an Edinburgh cut doublet. He had been hanging around near the musicians, who weren't bad at all, considering. Now the youth was at the back, near the bowls of wine and mead, watching for the signal from his master.

It came—Carey caught his eye and made a move with his hand. The youth bowed slightly, turned and poured wine into a plain silver goblet he was holding. He took a quick mouthful, surprisingly well-trained to Court ways, then brought it over to his master, a small towel on his arm and offered it with a bow. Carey drank it off.

Then he turned to bow to the Queen, who said something to him that made him tense. Emilia was getting used to English after becoming quite proficient at the barbaric tongue of Scotch—the two languages were brothers after all. She was sure the Queen had said something about singing. Carey bowed again and moved through the crowds to the musicians where the men of the chapel were lining up to sing. Carey stood at the end of the row, took a sheet of music and squinted at it. He looked very odd there, gaudy in his pearls next to the plain chapel men with their black robes and white collars.

The fat music master was explaining the music, Emilia thought, saying something about writing it that very afternoon and would Her Majesty care to hear his poor rough first attempt sung for the very first time? The Queen inclined her head, said something which caused sycophantic titters of laughter among the courtiers.

Carey smiled like a man accepting a challenge to duel, opened his mouth, waited for the beat, and sang the opening, perfectly on the note. The boy-sopranos speared their way into his line and the bassos, other tenors, and altos came in. It was a Spanish air, newly set in the modern Italian way, but she hadn't heard it before. It was somehow both sprightly and wistful.

The words were English and didn't quite fit...she didn't understand them. Emilia closed her eyes. It had such a sound of the South, of the Mediterranean, you could almost smell the olive trees and dust in it, the hot dry sun in it. Ah, the sun.

Something made her look at one of the musicians at the back of the group. He seemed transfixed, a handsome greybeard, he had stopped playing his viol. A tear was tracking its way down his creased cheek.

Emilia turned away at once as the music casually knotted her throat. She had to catch a tear out of the corner of her eye with the corner of her handkerchief before it caused her kohl to smear. What had she seen there in that old man's face? Shocked surprise, then something raw, something full of longing. Did the air remind him, too, of olive trees and sunlight like a golden knife? Or perhaps of something else, a lover? Her tear had come from her longing for her children, not any stupid man, of course. They were lost to her, locked in their convent, unless she could bring off the coup she needed. Bonnetti didn't care because he was a man, he could get more. She would not.

Someone was singing solo now. The tune was complex but he had support from the pipes. Someone with a very fine strong voice, a clear tenor that allowed the notes to flow like water.

It was M. le député again. There he stood, sight-singing the complex tenor line and the bassos coming in again now to wind about the stem of his voice like dark green snakes.

There was another damned tear in her eye. Again! Because his voice did bring the blue blue sky of the South with it, somehow, the vivid intense lapis lazuli that you never saw in the grey North and she missed it and she missed her children....

She could not even cough. She had to stop breathing. She caught that tear, too, no more please, M. le député, my heart will not stand it and in any case it's all your fault that I'm still here in the Northern wastes.

Thank God the boys were singing now, one of them sharp from nerves, the men, too, weaving and parting and finally coming in sequence to an end against Carey's sustained note.

Just a little silence afterward, that heartbeat of silence the people needed to bring themselves back from the land of music, the highest compliment any audience could give. Then ordinary applause, the Queen smiling and clapping her embroidered gloves as well.

The adult musicians were grudgingly approving, the boys staring up at the Courtier. The senior chapel man shook Carey's hand. The Queen said something that sounded complimentary about her cousin at which Carey promptly stepped forward and went down on two knees to her, his lips moving although Emilia couldn't hear what he said.

The Queen laughed and gave him her hand to kiss which he did and stayed on his knees. Again his lips moved and the Queen tapped his nose playfully—but possibly quite painfully—with her new Chinese fan. He rose, bowed, stepped back, bowed again as the Queen too turned aside to speak to another person on his knees, looked wry and rubbed his nose, sneezed.

The Queen was now talking to Essex again and the chapel men started singing once more to the chapel master's nod, a song that only needed one tenor and was easy. Emilia started manoeuvring toward Carey through the crowds now sweating in the heat from the candles. Such a very fine piece of manflesh, she thought coldly, what a pity to kill him. But still, it had to be done. First Essex, though.

She barged neatly past two dowdy women making for the banquet table with jellies and creams. She got in front of Carey as he reached to take his goblet from his servingman. She made sure she was turned away from him so he would suspect nothing and he trod on the back of her gown as he was supposed to.

'Oh!' she squeaked as she heard the pop of one of her points. She turned and was surprised to see him, of course. 'Monsieur le deputé,' she trilled, 'May I speak to you?'

She said it in Scotch, on the grounds that she spoke that language better and it might give them a little privacy while not excluding the young servingman whom she had suddenly, just that moment, recognised as her contact. More of the English Court would speak French than Scotch, that was sure. Also she wanted Carey to remember their affair and even feel guilty, if possible.

He bowed slightly, his eyes hooded. 'I'm so sorry, have I torn your gown, Signora?' he asked. 'You know how clumsy I am.'

Like most men who called themselves clumsy, he wasn't at all. And he had apologised for his clumsiness before, in Scotland. Ai, her stupid heart had started beating hard again.

'No, no,' she told him. 'It was me, I was pushing in front of you because I want one of the rose almond creams that I love so much.'

He smiled, reached a long arm over the scrum of women and brought out a pretty little sugar paste bowl full of rose cream. Emilia took it quickly. It had a little carved sugar paste spoon sticking out of it and she started eating it immediately, very quickly and carefully. Actually it was wonderful, smooth and sweet and creamy with the scent of roses. The English were very good at this sort of delicacy thanks to their miserable cold climate.

She scraped up the last smears of cream and laughed. 'Delicious! And quite unobtainable in Italy, where you would need to freeze it first with snow or it would go off in the heat.' This time she was speaking French which was so much easier.

Carey's eyebrows went up; politely he responded in French.

'What a good idea, Signora,' he said, 'frozen creams—perhaps the Queen would enjoy them?'

Emilia shook her head, making the feather bob and the ringlets fly. 'Impossible, Monsieur, you must have high mountains that have snow in summer within one day's running distance and very clever cooks.'

'The cooks we have, and the runners,' smiled Carey, his eyes intent and patient. 'Alas, the snowy mountains, no.'

'Also to eat it you need good teeth or the cold makes them twinge.'

'Ah,' said Carey. 'In that case, perhaps not a good idea for the Queen.'

Emilia giggled. Of course, the Queen, like most of the sugar-loving English, had terrible teeth. Now then. How could she find out his price? Well, she could ask him. That might even be the best way to go.

She twined her arm into his confidingly and put the sugar plate bowl and spoon down on the banquet table. Her own teeth would certainly no longer stand up to crunching sugar plate.

'Monsieur, let me be frank with you,' she said. 'My husband

and I have contacts and knowledge of sweet wines.' They were still speaking French because she wanted to be understood by any embassy listeners. 'You are the Earl of Essex's man, who has the farm for sweet wines?'

'More than that. He knighted me, Signora.'

Even Emilia knew how important that was, how difficult it was for a man to be knighted at this Queen's Court, where the Queen was so stingy with honours and didn't even sell them like a civilized person.

'I can help him with his farm of sweet wines,' said Emilia. 'All I need is for you to introduce me to the Earl so I can introduce my husband to him. '

'Now? Tonight?' Like all courtiers he wanted to spin the negotiation out to get more than one bribe.

'Yes, or someone else will get it.' Suddenly there was sweat trickling down under her smock, it was hard to pretend indifference in this life-or-death matter.

'Do you want to buy the farm of sweet wines from him?'

Jesu, if only! 'No,' Emilia admitted, 'we want to manage it for him so he makes the most profit possible. We also want to import many very fine sweet wines from my country and sell them.' She left unmentioned how immensely valuable to many people might be information straight from the Queen's favourite, just in case he hadn't thought of that angle. 'If milord Essex does sell the farm to someone else, we can still work with him because he will still need to import sweet wines to drink.'

'Hmm...'

'I know we can find good wines at such low prices everyone will still make so much money,' Emilia added, 'perhaps a small commission for you...'

She let the sentence hang in the air and Carey didn't so much as blink at it floating past. He wasn't going to be fobbed off that way, it seemed.

'Fifty pounds cash,' said Carey, 'or the equivalent in jewellery. Now.'

'Now? Jesu Maria...'

He shrugged, a very French gesture Englished. 'You may be

able to find someone else to make the introduction,' he said still in French. 'They might even cost less. But this is your last chance until the Queen is back at Whitehall because after this, the Court will go to Woodstock and then to Oxford where there will be no women at the University entertainments. The Earl will be closeted with the Queen or attending on her and no one who isn't already one of his own or the Queen's will be able to meet with him.'

Oh God, he was right and he knew it. She bit her lip. He was right. How could she pay him if he was insisting on payment in cash down, not in kind? Which he was; she could see it in the cool set of his face.

She fumbled at her neck where the gold and ruby necklace Cumberland had given her gleamed—rightful plunder, he'd called it, from a Portuguese trader snapped up in the Bay of Biscay. She had a little velvet purse in her petticoat pocket: she took it out, put the gold necklace into it and waited. Carey must know exactly what the necklace was worth because that was the amount he had asked for, the greedy bastard.

She held the purse tightly, cocked her head a little against the uncomfortable standing ruff behind her head. In Ireland she had learned not to hand over the bribe before the paid-for favour had been done. Carey smiled, half bowed to her and headed across the dance floor, through a violent volta that was spinning and thundering on the boards. The musicians were sweating in the heat from the candles and the bodies as they played, but Emilia noticed that one of them was missing—the viol player who had wept at the Spanish air.

Mr. Byrd was looking very annoyed, speaking with the Earl of Essex. '...you can't trust any of these yokels,' he was complaining. 'He was only one of the Oxford waits but good enough to play for the Queen and this is how he repays me for the chance I gave him? Damn it, I was hoping to take him to London with us....Ah yes, Sir Robert, thank you for singing with us earlier.'

'Yes, indeed,' added the Earl of Essex. 'Her Majesty was very pleased with it, she told me so. Also she asked if your nose is better now?'

'It will be, my lord,' murmured Carey. 'When she has given me my warrant as Deputy Warden and, of course, my fee.'

Essex laughed. 'Good luck!' he shouted. 'You'd do better to sing with the travelling gleemen and save up your fees....'

Shut up about his goddamn voice, you stupid lout, Emilia thought, and smiled brilliantly at Carey.

'You nearly caused terrible damage to me, Sir Rrrobert,' she purred at him in English.

'I did?' said Carey, 'How, Signora Bonnetti?'

'Why you made me cry, rremembering the South, and that would have made my face all swollen and ugly.'

'Impossible,' boomed Essex gallantly in French, accented but fluent, 'No amount of tears could do that.' And, yes, he had swung from a stare at her cleavage to looking at Carey questioningly. Right. She had done all she could. Now he had to earn the necklace.

'Of course, my lord,' said Carey smoothly, already ahead of her. 'May I present the brilliant and extraordinary Signora Emilia Bonnetti, wife to the merchant Giovanni Bonnetti, who was arranging the wholesale import of excellent sweet wines to the Scottish Court, last time I met them?'

Essex smiled and held out his hand. Emilia took it and curtsied low, her lashes modestly lowered and, she hoped, a fetching blush on her cheek.

'And where is your husband, Signora?'

Where was the little man now? Oh yes. 'He is in Oxford, talking to the butlers of the colleges, I think.' They were all speaking French now. Most of the English were good linguists because who could possibly want to learn their awful ugly uncouth bastard tongue, the spawn of Dutch and French?

'He has reliable suppliers?'

'Of course, directly from Italy with no interference from the London vintners at all.' That interested the Earl—fewer middlemen meant cheaper wholesale prices, of course. And the London vintners were notoriously greedy in a land full of greedy men. 'He is very experienced with all kinds of wine and importing and exporting all kinds of things...You must talk to him, milord, because I am only a poor foolish woman....'

'But you are interested in the farm of sweet wines?' Essex asked with typical English unsubtlety. 'Which I hold?'

Emilia managed not to sigh. When in England... 'Yes, milord,' she said, 'of course. We are not wealthy enough to farm it directly for you, but we can manage the farm and bring in the very best wines from Italy.'

The price the Earl named was breathtaking and impossible. 'Plus one barrel in every ten as a gift to me, directly,' he added.

Outrageous! God, how greedy the English were. But in fact, it could be done, because the English couldn't grow drinkable wine in their horrible damp country but did drink wine, and in astonishing quantities. And there were things they made that you could send south—dull boring things like finished wool and iron guns and coal, that you could exchange for a lot of wine which the English wouldn't know was cheap.

'Milorrd,' she giggled, curtsied again. 'I would be honoured if I can speak to my husband about this matter and my husband, too, will be honoured but...'

They bargained carefully until the number of barrels they had to give the Earl was one in twenty. No matter. She had made the connection. Now she needed to strengthen it.

She offered her hand to the Earl, who gripped it with surprising strength, then turned it over and kissed the palm like a lover. He stood between her and the Queen so she couldn't see, but the meaning was plain. She tingled all over, caught Carey's cynical smile, also found herself smiling with pure delight. Hooked, by God, she could still hook them. She gave a little tremble as she curtseyed once more—ay, her poor knees and her pinched toes—fluttered her eyelids as she looked up at the towering gold and white of the favourite.

'Milord, I must not trouble you anymore with my foolishness,' she whispered.

He leaned in, gingery and pink under the white lead paste on his face. 'Will you join us for the card game afterward, Signora?' he breathed.

'I am a terrible card-player,' she lied. 'My poor woman's brain cannot even remember the points.'

'Perhaps I can teach you,' smiled the Earl.

'That would be such an honour, milorrd,' she said in English. 'Then yes, if you will 'elp me not lose too much and make my 'usband angrry. Thank you, thank you, milorrd.'

She stepped neatly away, retrieving her hand from the Earl's grip, and dived into the group of women trying to get a drink of spiced wine from one of the silver mixing bowls. Emilia's teeth were creaking with thirst in the heat, and as soon as she tasted the stuff they were drinking she knew she could make the sweet wine farm work for her, Signor Bonnetti, and even the Earl.

Carey stood behind her, blocking her escape from the group of women, so she finished the deal by handing him the black velvet bag with the necklace in it. His fingers explored it expertly to be sure she hadn't coney-catched him, then he smiled down at her as she curtseyed to him with her best modest smile.

'Are you happy, Signora?' asked the chestnut-headed reiver. She had to curtsey again while she sorted her thoughts. Would he be jealous? That would be nice.

"Oh very happy, M. le deputé, it is easy to see why the Queen loves milord of Essex. And you? Are you happy?"

He shook his head and put the bag containing fifty pounds' worth of gold and garnets that might be rubies into his inside doublet pocket. 'What is it that makes me fear we may never meet again?' he said with a creditable attempt at an abandoned lover's face, so Emilia had to laugh at him. He was quite right. He had cheated her, sold her bad guns, caused a nightmare in horrible Ireland, made the Spanish keep her two surviving children in the Flemish convent and forget their Italian, become prim, prosy, boring little Flemings...But still there was that thread of lust between them. Clearly they would not meet again—now that she had hooked the Queen's favourite—no matter what her stupid body felt about it. And she would try and find a way for him to die because he clearly knew too much about her and her husband. She might even be able to get her necklace back.

SATURDAY 16TH SEPTEMBER 1592, NIGHT

Carey went outside the hot tent to blow his nose properly and rub it. The Queen had practically broken it with the end of her fan and meant to as well. He had naturally taken the opportunity when he knelt to her of reminding her of the warrant for his office at Carlisle and his fee. She had told him he already had a very good warrant and should use it.

'Without any money to pay my men...?' he had begun pathetically and that was when her fan clipped the end of his nose so painfully his eyes had watered.

'Do as I bid you,' she had said, steely-eyed.

At least I've made sure that it's really the Queen who wants me to investigate the Amy Robsart death, he thought, trumpeting into his handkerchief again. And then along had come Emilia Bonnetti insisting on her introduction and even paying his fee with her necklace. He knew where she must have got it—perhaps Cumberland would be willing to buy it back? Perhaps not.

And Emilia had done it all very nicely, from the 'accidental' bump at the banquet table to her conversation with the Earl who was, as always, clearly in desperate need of ready cash. Carey just hoped the Bonnettis could find a good financier to buy the farm and actually do what Emilia said they could. The fact that they were obviously spies mattered not at all, so long as Essex used them carefully, the way Walsingham would. It was Walsingham who had taught Carey that the way to deal with spies and informers was to know who they were and keep them close so you controlled what they found out and what they told their handlers. Spies were only dangerous if you didn't know their identities and whereabouts. It was notorious that Essex was trying to take over Walsingham's networks and the Bonnettis would probably lead him to some very juicy information. Perhaps Giovanni could be turned, the way his brother the sword master had been. He hoped in a detached way that they would survive somehow, for Emilia's sake. What a woman!

When he went back in, he saw Hughie hanging around looking

nervous and smiled at him. 'Thank you,' he said. Hughie blushed and looked surprised.

'Ehm...?'

'I like a henchman who sticks at my back despite opportunities to dance with pretty girls,' Carey explained, pointing to the girls whirling between the trees. Some of the servingmen were partnering them since this was a jig, a dance for the common people. The Queen was fanning herself and talking to Essex again as she watched, her face alight with laughter.

'Ay, sir?'

'Nobody's trying to kill me around here,' Carey said, watching his face carefully. Had Hughie shot that crossbow? 'In Carlisle, though, it might be a serious matter if you weren't near me.'

Hughie looked distasteful. 'Ay, sir, Carlisle's all fu' wi' English Borderers.'

'Yes, true.'

Carey was very thirsty and knew the wine was too strong to do any good. What he needed was at least a quart of mild ale to wet his throat, but where could he find some?

'Hughie, go fetch me a flagon of spiced wine.' Hughie nodded and plunged toward the scrum around the wine and brandy barrels at the corner of the tent.

Carey left the marquee again and picked his way around the hedges to the musicians' entrance, where he found Mr. Byrd drinking tobacco smoke from a clay pipe and looking very disgruntled.

'I don't suppose you play the viol, too, Sir Robert?' he asked.

'No, Mr. Byrd, not at all. I was taught the lute but can't say I learnt it, since my playing is painfully poor.'

'And yet your voice is excellent, sir.'

'Thank you, but I can't take any credit for it. Simply a gift from God, for reasons that He no doubt understands.'

Byrd proffered the pipe, lifting his eyebrows, and Carey took it and drank some smoke. The tobacco was good although it had no Moroccan incense in it and it didn't make him cough, just smoothed some of the edges. Byrd smiled in the darkness.

'Yes, indeed, there's music for you. Who knows where it comes from or where it goes or why.' He sniffed and scowled heavily.

'Or musicians either.'

'Oh?'

'I'm one viol down in any case because the players from London had plague and have been forbidden the Court. So I hired me a replacement and now he's gone off somewhere, I don't know where.'

'I'm sorry I can't help you, Mr. Byrd.'

'His face is annoying me now, I'm sure I've seen him before. So what did you want, sir?'

'Er...would you have any spare mild ale anywhere about you to wet my poor dry throat?'

Byrd smiled again. 'We've got a proper Court ration, half a gallon apiece. You can have that damned viol player's pottle, if you like.' The chapel master even ducked back into the tent to fetch it for him and Carey took the large heavy leather mug, toasted Byrd, and gulped a quarter of it in one. That was better. It was very good, the manor's brewer had obviously taken care with it as the Queen herself was notorious for mainly drinking only mild ale. It was weak, refreshing, and slightly nutty.

'Did you know that Spanish air before you sang it?' Byrd asked. Carey shook his head.

'It was a pleasure to sing.'

Byrd bowed a little, looking thoughtful. 'Funny thing that,' he said in an awkwardly casual voice. 'The Queen asked for it particularly, but I didn't make the tune. She played it for me herself.'

'Oh?' Carey didn't say anything more, waited. Had Byrd been told to give him information?

'Yes, she picked it out on one of the lutes this afternoon and told me to set it at once so we could sing it this evening and then later in Oxford.'

'You did that in a couple of hours? I'm impressed, Mr. Chapel Master.'

Byrd smiled. 'It wasn't any trouble at all, just unrolled as easy as you like. Perhaps it could do with a little trimming, or perhaps more embellishment.'

'I wouldn't touch it...I thought it was perfect as it was.'

Byrd wagged a finger at Carey. The pipe of tobacco was finished; he had knocked out the dottle and put it in his belt pouch, but was showing no sign of going into the tent again. 'Only God is perfect, sir, that's what the Moors say, isn't it?'

Byrd was doing his best to look guileless so Carey resigned himself to having to probe. 'So what made an old Spanish air so important to the Queen, I wonder?' he asked and then added on impulse, 'She has asked me to look into an important but difficult matter for her and perhaps you can help me.'

Byrd nodded. 'Sir Robert, I have a few moments before we must play again for the tumblers.' They drew aside, away from the tent and also clear of the hedge. 'The air you sang was written on a piece of parchment, wrapped around something that looked like a piece of leather or a stick. I think it was found in the Queen's privy baggage when we arrived here and it put Her Majesty out of countenance. It seems there was music written on it and that is what she had us sing.'

'What else was written on the parchment?'

Byrd shrugged. 'I didn't see that, Sir Robert, only the Queen saw it. I glimpsed the staves when she opened it out to pluck it on her lute for me to transcribe.' Byrd patted Carey's arm. 'I know Her Majesty ordered Mrs. de Paris to find you and set you on the scent. She said she had heard you were as fine a sleuth dog as Walsingham and thanked God you were here. But that's all. She said nothing else about it, except that she has kept the parchment and bit of leather in a purse close under her stays.'

Carey nodded, bowed shallowly. 'Thank you, Mr. Byrd. If you find out anything else, please will you tell me?'

Byrd bowed back. 'Of course, sir.' He turned to the tent opening.

Carey had circled round and re-entered when the musicians struck up a bouncy martial tune with drums for the tumblers. The grave Moor with his walking stick was standing at the back, watching narrow-eyed as the boys and men danced and somer-saulted and swallowed swords and threw themselves at each other across the dance floor, and the boys climbed the trees and jumped off onto pyramids of men. Then Thomasina bounced from her place by the Queen's skirts to shouts and cheers from the courtiers and threw herself into the air, bouncing, turning, and then at last leaping high onto the top of the pyramid of men and boys where she stood on the shoulders of the topmost boy and breathlessly sang a lewd song of triumph.

He looked around at the bright crowd. Hughie was by the banquet with the other men-at-arms and servingmen like Mr. Simmonds, staring at the tumblers' show, the flagon still dangling empty in his left hand. He had clearly forgotten all about fetching spiced wine. Emilia was across the other side of the room, amongst Essex's followers, talking to a Welshman, Essex's current favourite. Thomasina was mimicking a different great man of the Court in each verse of her song and was doing a particularly good imitation of the haughty Sir Walter Raleigh who wasn't there on account of still languishing in the Tower for sowing his seed in a maid of honour. Idiot. Serve him right. The soft Devon accent and haughty head were unmistakeable, even when a midget only three and a half foot high did them. Carey had thoroughly disliked the man, had got into a fistfight with him over a tennis court back in the eighties, which had been smoothed over by his father. The progress following that had been remarkable in that Carey was consistently billeted with Raleigh, who was not yet at all important, and had had to share a bed with him a couple of times. They had come to an understanding eventually over card games, but still...What an arrogant fool.

The rest of his mind was turning over the Amy Robsart problem, the one the inquest report pointed to with such shocking honesty. Surely the Queen hadn't actually read that report? She was sitting under her cloth of estate now, laughing at Thomasina who was currently guying the hunchbacked Sir Robert Cecil. Mind you, there was no way of telling what the Queen was thinking; she had been at Court all her life and knew a thing or two about keeping her counsel.

Why the devil did she want the thing brought up again? Why now? Did it have something to do with the scrap of parchment written with music? Why?

The Queen was standing and holding out her arms to her people. All the Court went to their knees again, Carey included, just missing a lurking patch of mud with one of his knees and nearly staining his last remaining good pair of hose. He really hoped Hughie knew how to darn. Maybe when he met his father at Oxford, he could snaffle a few new pairs?

Her Majesty said a loving goodnight to her people and then paced out to the sound of trumpets, leaning on the arm of the Earl of Essex, who was looking pleased with himself. The Gentlemen of the Queen's Guard went ahead and behind, making red and gold borders around the maids of honour and the ladies-in-waiting, who were following the Queen, the younger ones rolling their eyes sulkily at having to leave the dancing so early.

Carey could see Emilia amongst the Earl's followers at the end of the procession, the tilt of her feathered hat unmistakeable. Ah well. Perhaps another time. (A lucky escape, you idiot, said the puritanical part of him.)

Carey caught Hughie's eye and beckoned him to bring over the flagon and pour for him. The lad started and looked guilty, dove into the scrum of servingmen by the large silver spiced wine bowl and disappeared. Finally he emerged, wading upstream against the flood of other servingmen, dodged a couple of whirling dancers, and came over. Carey lifted his silver cup and Hughie served him quite well, pouring carefully and using a linen napkin on his arm to wipe any drips.

When Carey sipped the wine, he nearly gagged—it was a spiced wine water, very sweet, mixed with brandy and spices and a hint of bitterness from the cloves. The attempt to hide its dreadful quality hadn't worked. Still it was wine, so he drank it.

As soon as the Queen had gone, the musicians had struck up an alemain and the roar of voices went up another notch. He watched the peasant dance for a while, wondering if he wanted to dance anymore.

God, it was hot. Carey changed his mind about dancing, moved out again into the darkness, feeling for rain first because he did not want to damage his (still only half paid-for) Court doublet and hose. There were torches on some of the trees so you could see something in the flickering shadows.

Carey was still thirsty, so he followed the sound of water back to the stream, tipped out half of the syrupy wine in his goblet and refilled it with water caught carefully from a small rapid over a mossy stone. You never knew with water, but he'd found in France that wine generally cleaned it well.

Sipping cautiously, Carey decided it was much better and even the bitterness of cloves in it was refreshing, like well-hopped beer. Away from the torches and candle-lit tent, the evening was still and some stars were coming out, powdering the velvet cloak of the sky with diamond dust. The evening must be much warmer than you'd expect at this time of year, despite the clearing sky. Carey was burning up in his Court suit.

He spotted the dim outline of the church spire and went toward it. The clerks would no doubt be bundled up asleep inside, along with other courtiers' servants, since there, at least, they wouldn't be rained on despite the hardness of the floor.

Once in the churchyard he wondered what he was there for, since he wasn't about to go and roust out John Tovey from his sleep just for the sake of it, after all. Still the church pulled him as he gulped the watered wine. Perhaps it would be cooler in there. He opened the door carefully, shut it behind him carefully and paced with great caution down the aisle. On either side were dozens of bundled figures, quite tightly packed, wrapped in their cloaks. Some had managed to beg, borrow, or steal straw pallets to ease the stone flags under them.

It wasn't cooler in here, damn it. He went up toward the altar, still too hot and still dry-mouthed with thirst. All the Papistic nonsense had been cleared away years ago, the altar had been moved so that it was a proper communion table, the saints of the altar screen had lost their heads and been whitewashed, the Lady chapel had no figure of the Madonna on the plinth at all, though there was a puzzling carved frieze of deer around the walls. They looked oddly alive, even seemed to move.

The soft snoring from behind him was forming itself into a strange rhythmic music. He looked up at the boarded windows, one or two left intact with the old style full of scriptural pictures for the illiterate. Those were their only way of learning the gospels as they were denied hearing the Word of the Lord by the Vulgate Latin of the old Mass. That you couldn't see the sky though the silvery light told him that the moon had risen. What were the reiving surnames up to on the Border? It was a church. Perhaps he should pray?

He drank again, took his hat off belatedly and thought about Amy Dudley née Robsart, poor lady. She had died on the 8th September 1560, the year of his own birth, perhaps not very long after he was born, a summer baby. He smiled, thinking vaguely of his wet nurse and how he had loved her when he was tiny, when his mother sometimes frightened him on her visits back from Court with his quite terrifying father. They had become better friends once he was breeched and he had realised how kind they were, compared to the parents of most of his friends.

He knocked back most of the rest of his wine, wondering why nothing seemed to ease his dry mouth, and sat on one of the benches against the wall. Nobody was sleeping there, perhaps because the stones were broken. There was more old destruction in the Lady chapel than the rest of the church. The plinth the statue had stood on still had a crescent moon, stars, and a snake carved on it.

Why was he so hot and thirsty after drinking so much ale earlier and then a whole flagon of watered wine? And another peculiar thing was that he didn't need a piss at all. His insides seemed to have turned suddenly into a strange desert.

And now something really odd was happening. The whitewashed stone of the church was seeming to billow around him slowly, as if it were only painted curtains at a play. The whitewashed walls thinned and thinned and swayed in and out and back and forth like the dancers, to the rhythm of the snore-music around him.

He couldn't stand the heat anymore and his head was hurting, his mouth glued with drought. He had to cool down. He fumbled for the buttons of his doublet, undid them with hands full of thumbs, then had to feel around the back where his poinard hung for the points and then he thought of taking his belts off, which he did, and then he broke a couple of laces and the doublet came away at last. He took the thing off his shoulders, wondering why it had got so much lighter and hung it on a headless woman saint holding a wheel.

He was still too hot and his eyes weren't working right. Everything was blurring and billowing in front of him, and the moon must be shining through a window somewhere because he could see well in the darkness, make out the outlines of snoring clerks and Court servants on the floor. The vest that held up his paned trunk hose and canions was making him hot now so he set about undoing the buttons and laces for that. It was a nightmare of inextricable buttons and laces so he broke the damned things and wobbled as he pulled those off as well and hung them on a saint holding a castle next to the pearl-covered doublet and stood there in his shirt with his hose dropping down and his boots still on. He burped.

Blinking, rubbing his eyes which were getting worse and worse, licking lips like leather with a tongue of horsehide and panting with heat, a small part of him finally thought to wonder, 'Am I ill?'

The last time he had felt so bad was on the *Elizabeth Bonaventure*, Cumberland's ship, chasing the Armada north through the storms of the North Sea. He had been hot, dry, dizzy, blinding headache...

Well, said the sensible part of him, it couldn't be a jail fever because that was what nearly killed me in 1588 and you never get it twice.

Was it plague? Christ Jesus, had he caught plague in London and brought it to the Queen?

His distant hands trembled as Carey felt himself for buboes, as his head started to swell to twice its size and then four times. No lumps, nothing. He wasn't bleeding anywhere either, but the furnace of his heart was pounding louder and louder like the drum for the acrobats and the church itself was dissolving around him into gauzy billowing curtains.

He had to get out. But he couldn't. He was standing still, his legs too far away to command. He was panting like a hound. He needed help. Was there anyone? The clerk? What was his name?

'Mr. Tovey,' he croaked, 'Mr. Tovey...'

He tried again, he couldn't shout, the voice that had flowed so well earlier was now a cracked whisper. He had to lie down or fall down. So he carefully put his goblet on the bench again and sat cross-legged on the flagstones as if he was in camp in France. His whole body had turned into an oven and at least the stones were cool. In fact they looked very inviting and as the stone church had somehow turned to a tapestried tent and billowing fine linen, so the broken stones of the Lady chapel were becoming pillows and bolsters specially for him.

He lay down full length on them, liking the cool and softness on his burning face.

There was quiet movement behind him. Somebody was lighting a candle end at the watchlight by the altar.

He moaned in protest, the light was far too bright as it came too close, it hurt his eyes. He tried to push it away, punch whoever was trying to hurt him with a spear made of light. Through tears he saw Tovey's bony anxious face, shape-shifting to a skull amongst the soft billowing stones and the saints singing headless.

'Sir Robert!' Tovey's voice cracked through his headache. 'Are you sick, sir?'

'Ah'm not drunk,' Carey told him. 'Don't think s'plague...'

Tovey flinched back for a moment but to his credit, didn't run. Carey felt a bony hand on his forehead, saw the frown, the candle brought close to his face, Tovey feeling his armpits and groin, oh God, do I have the tokens on my face? Carey wondered, because he felt as if there was a bonfire on each cheek.

Tovey frowned suddenly, one of his fingers brushed Carey's leather lips, then the damned candle came near again.

'Sir, please look at the candle flame,' Tovey said. The boy suddenly had some authority in his voice. Carey frowned at the yellow-white blaze in his eyes but did his best to look straight at it. Splots of light danced in his vision, strangely coloured, and the stone saints sang the Spanish air from earlier, rather well in chorus in a different setting.

Maybe it was plague after all? 'Don't...come...near...' he whispered. 'Get everyone out...Might be plague...'

The boy felt his forehead again as if he was a mother. He shook his head.

'Sir Robert, what have you drunk?'

''M not drunk...' He knew that. It took more than a couple of quarts of mild ale and a goblet of not very good spiced wine to make him drunk.

'I know.' The boy looked about, spotted the goblet, took it from the bench, sniffed the remnants in it, stuck a finger in them and licked it. There was recognition on his face, 'Mother of God,' he said, papistically. Then something in his expression hardened. 'Sir Robert, you've been poisoned.'

Had he? Good Lord, why? Or was it an accident when the poisoner was after bigger game? Fear swooped through him and the saints started singing a nasty discord. He reached up and grabbed the boy's woollen doublet front. 'Tell the Earl...of...' Damnit, who? Wossname? 'Essex, tell Essex. Don't le' the Queen...'

'I have to make you purge, Sir Robert,' he said. 'Get the poison out of your stomach...'

Rage gave him more strength than he realised, and he swiped the boy away, got to his feet. 'Tell...Essex first!' he shouted. 'Queen! Lord Norris! Don' le' 'er drink spiced wine....'

Burning with rage at whoever had done this, he started for the door, heard shouts, found more people around him, holding him back. Lots of them. He knocked a couple of them down, found his arms held, damn it, somebody swept his legs from under him and he landed on the stones, half a dozen people were sitting on him. He was fighting and roaring incoherently at them to stop the Queen drinking spiced wine and then Tovey's face with a fat lip and a bruised chin was close to him again and the mouth moving and making words and he finally heard the boy.

'Coleman and Hughes have already run to the manor house, s...sir,' said Tovey. 'We've warned her. If she hasn't already drunk it, she won't.'

It penetrated. Tovey was shakily holding a wooden cup and the other clerks were cautiously letting him sit up enough to drink. He was even more thirsty than before, dry as dust, dry as death. Interesting, who could have done it? Emilia? Hughie? One of the musicians or chapel men? Somebody else? Please God, the Queen was all right. She had survived so many attempts, many not recorded, let God keep her safe still...

Somebody else had arrived, was panting breathlessly, saying something to Tovey. 'Sir, the Queen's people have been warned,' he said slowly and clearly, 'P...please drink this, sir, we must purge you.'

He drank whatever it was and found to his annoyance it was salted water, spat it out. The young clerks still sitting on him and holding his shoulders were turning themselves into the singing saints and the whole church was billowing. He gulped more seawater, damn it, the storm was terrible, he was sinking through the floor and...ach...Jesu...

Suddenly the wisps of church had blown away and he was lying on something soft, saints holding his arms and legs whenever he tried to shake them off. Was he in heaven? Well, he couldn't hear harps though the singing of that Spanish air was starting to annoy him, no visible angels. Maybe? He was looking down on something that looked like a wonderful map made of cloth with green velvet grass and fringed trees and blocks of stone poking through. Perhaps he'd turned into a bird.

Green, came the thought, so not autumn.

'Sir Robert, please drink this, sir, please...'

Christ, he was thirsty. The lip of a wooden cup (they had wooden cups in heaven?) knocked his teeth and he smelled water, downed it in one. Seawater again, ach, salty...

His belly twisted and heaved and his body jackknifed. Sour stuff gushed out of his mouth. He couldn't see properly, everything was flaring and blurred, part of him was on a cloud somewhere high up, the other part felt the rough staves of a bucket and he puked into it helplessly.

'Again, please, sir.'

He drank again, hoping for plain water or mild ale, but no, more brine. Ach. He hated being sick, but sick as a dog he was, violently, coughing and sputtering disgusting bitterness. In a distant part of his overheated skull, the wry thought came: at least I don't have the squits as well, that's a small mercy.

'Good, that's better. Sip this please sir, just sip.'

He was cautious after the saltwater, but this time it was just well-water with a little brandy. He sipped, then gulped, had to puke again.

'This is good, sir,' Tovey's voice said soothingly. 'It's washing you out...'

There were voices above him, Tovey answering steadily. Somebody else looked in his face with the candle held near again, he recognised one of the older Gentlemen Pensioners, behind him one of the Queen's ladies in a fur-trimmed dressing gown, red-haired, didn't know which one, might be a cousin, tried to blink at the goddamned candle still blazing like the sun in his sight.

'You're right, Mr. Tovey,' said the lady-in-waiting. 'His pupils are fixed wide open, it must be belladonna.'

'The Queen?' He had to know. What if his aunt had had her usual nightcap of spiced wine?

'She's well, Sir Robert, she hasn't had any of this at all. She knows what's happened and we are searching Rycote now for the poisoner. Please sir, lie down.'

'I've brought my pallet for you, sir, please lie on it until we can move you.' Tovey's voice.

Really he preferred the stones which were cooler, but his stomach cramped and twisted humiliatingly again and Tovey's blurred angular face was wobbling and stretching, drawn upon the finely woven veils around him.

Looking down from his straw-smelling cloud was fun. He laughed at the sight of men on horseback, riding hell-for-leather across country along the line of the old Giant's Wall. He recognised the man at their head—good God, was that what he looked like in a jack and morion? Not bad, quite frightening in fact, and from the look of his face, he was in a rage about something.

Carey peered with interest over the other edge of the cloud to see more riders, a remarkable number, in fact. It looked like a full-fledged Warden raid, though for some reason all the riders were heading eastward rather than north or south, riding bunched in their surnames. From the quilting on the jacks there were Dodds, Storeys, Bells, a lot of Armstrongs, Grahams...good God, *Grahams*? Following him? What the hell was going on?

And somehow he saw in a flash what it was that had enraged him, which was Elizabeth Widdrington in nothing but a bloodstained shift, locked in a storeroom, with a black eye and a swollen face and dried blood on it.

The bolt of fury that drove through him at that sight knocked him right off his cloud and into the uproar of his body which seemed to be fighting the people trying to strap him to a litter. He could ride, he needed his sword, where the hell was Dodd...? More light blurred into his useless eyes making his enormous head hurt. Had he been struck blind? Dear God, please not?

Heavy weights coloured red and gold twisted his legs from under him and landed on his shoulders and hips, pinning him down. There was murmuring in the background. Someone with a foreign voice was advising caution, the delirium from belladonna or henbane could make a man four times as strong as normal....

The war drums were beating around him but he could still hear Tovey dropping to his knees and stammering something. What was he saying?

'Y...your M...Majesty?'

The fear in the boy's voice was what suddenly cut through his rage. Despite his agonising headache, his heat, the suddenly more distant rage, the drought, and the unsettling discovery that the world was really made of the finest, most delicate silk, Carey smiled.

'Robin, Robin, can you hear me, my dear?'

Yes, it was the Queen. He knew his aunt's voice, though when he squinted to see her she was a blotchy pink and white moon, framed by sable fur and topped with a thatch of grey-red. Red and gold lumps were next to her, behind her was a dark column with a doctor's cap.

He managed a grunt through a throat too dry to make any other sound and he couldn't think of words. Some of the rage was draining out of him, despite the pounding of his heart. Garbled foreign noises surrounded him. She was talking to Tovey in Latin and the boy responded, he couldn't understand a word of it, now the doctor was talking it too. Bloody hell, he hated learned people talking about him in Latin.

He felt the Queen's hand on his shoulder which was going numb because of the large Gentleman Pensioner kneeling on it.

'Robin, I have brought my own Doctor Lopez who is an expert in poisons, one of my lord Essex's physicians as well,' said the Queen's voice. He frowned. The last thing he wanted was a doctor—he didn't want to die.

'He has purged, Your Majesty,' said Lopez's nasal Portuguese voice. 'He has drunk some water. I recommend the empiric treatment of this belladonna poisoning, as suspected by Senhor Tovey. I 'ave a decoction of beanpods which has been efficacious in the past...' A click of fingers, somebody trotted off into the night, he heard them, what the hell was a decoction of beanpods?

He tried to shift the weight of the two Gentlemen Pensioners with their knees bruising his shoulders and couldn't. The Gentlemen were not scrawny young clerks to be knocked sideways like ninepins. There was another argument going on above him, this time in English.

'No, he certainly can't stay here. So long as this is no illness, not plague...'

Nobody thought it was plague, especially not Dr. Lopez. That was good to hear. The argument went on while he drifted in and out, sometimes on his cloud, sometimes wishing they'd stop holding him down so he could go and kill the bastard who had hurt Elizabeth Widdrington.

Cool bony fingers touched his forehead.

'Robin, listen. I'm having you moved into the manor house,' said the Queen in a voice that brooked no argument. 'We'll kick out one of Essex's pack of hangers-on and make room.'

She patted his cheek and he heard the rustling of dressing gowns as she left with her two ladies. It wasn't the first time he'd seen his aunt in her dressing gown, after all. Not that he'd seen her this time, since his eyes weren't working at all.

The weights came off his shoulders and hips, but something was tangling his wrists so he couldn't lift his arms. He tried to sit up, was pushed down firmly and a strap came across his chest. Goddamn it to hell, he had to get up, he didn't have time for this nonsense, he needed his broadsword, he had to save Elizabeth. He tried to shout, but couldn't, he wanted to piss but couldn't. He wanted to see but couldn't. He was hot as hell again and the world was turning back to silk veils as he somehow jerked high in the air, blinking at the shadowed stone forest of the church, the branches in their orderly stone patterns and the gargoyles laughing at him. Christ, where was his sword, where was Dodd? He was somehow bobbing along on his back, a stone lintel went past above him and now he was flying through the sky where the stars were and now he was on the other side of the fake painted silk walls of the world.

But this time he was looking at himself climbing a ladder to a wooden platform.

Two men were waiting for him in the cold sunlight, and a priest in a plain surplice, speaking the words 'Oh Lord, wash me of my iniquity, cleanse me of my sin....'

His own face was white, lips set in a line, but his eyes were sad. He heard himself speaking in the dawn to the small crowd waiting to see him die, apologising for his wicked rebellion against his most loving cousin, the Queen, thanking her for her gentle mercy to him of the axe, who was unworthy of it. Quite a good speech, really.

He saw himself turn, shuck off a worn green velvet doublet and kneel down to the block in his shirt and hose. He heard himself saying the Our Father in a creditably firm voice, words torn away by the wind, then bending to put his neck on the block and the headsman's axe swinging up, glittering in the sunlight.

The blow knocked him out of his dream again and back into his body where someone was making him drink something filthy-tasting. Meekly he drank it and let his miraculously still-attached head down to the pillow again, heart drumming wildly inside him.

Rebellion? Against the Queen? Good God. And it must have been a foul bill that he confessed to because the vision of himself had had no injuries, no signs of torture at all. How could that have happened?

It's a fever dream, he told himself somewhere deep inside himself where the drought didn't matter so much—both of them were fever dreams. And why had he been so badly dressed for his execution? His doublet had looked ten years old and hard-worn. That could never happen. Rebellion was as ridiculous as the idea that he could become so...well, so shabby.

Which was the last thought he knew as the clouds wrapped him in silk again....

SUNDAY 17TH SEPTEMBER 1592, NOON

Dodd hauled the horse back on its haunches and cursed. He knew he was going the wrong way again...you wouldn't think that riding northwest to Oxford would be so difficult. It hadn't been while he stuck to the Oxford Road, but last night had worried him and so he'd left the Roman street and followed a signpost that took him along a nice road amongst the plump coppies and fields full of cattle and pigs eating up the stubble before they burnt it, ready for winter barley.

That had been early this morning. After a couple of hours of hard riding, he had spent some time in a copse rubbing chewed bark into the telltale brand on Whitesock's hindquarters to stain it brown. It wouldn't fool anyone who checked properly, but would do for the moment along with the mud he slapped on top. Now it was noon and he was tired. He hadn't got any sleep on Friday night, had ridden hard most of Saturday, not got a full ration of sleep Saturday night, and here it was Sunday and he had no idea where he was. He knew the rutted track was taking him the wrong way, despite the waymarker that had pointed toward Oxford.

He would have struck off across country, but this land was separated out into little fields with newfangled tight-woven hedges and forbye; he didn't want to leave so clear a trail as a broken hedge and a crossed field. The lanes between them headed in half a dozen different directions at once and it was all strange country to him—he didn't know the lay of the land. He knew the right way to go, of course, even though the sky had clouded over, but the lanes wouldn't let him and most of the fields had been deeply ploughed or were still stubbled.

He was starting to feel very thirsty and both horses were tired and sulky from being ridden without a saddle. Now the track was heading downhill into a boggy little wood. He went with it in the hope that he could find a stream in it, slipped from Whitesock's back, and led him as well.

The wood closed around them. There were signs that there had been people living there, once long ago and some more recently, too. In one place there was an old fire and the marks of horses tethered to trees. In another he could see clear signs of wagons from only a few days ago. Perhaps there was some kind of manor house or village nearby.

Later Dodd wondered why he hadn't been more careful and decided that as well as being tired, the rotten Southern air had made him as soft and soppy as the Southerners and he deserved what happened.

The track came at the stream from around a small mound and stones made a rough ford. The trees were thick overhead so he couldn't see the sky and the horses pulled forward to the water so Dodd let them put their heads down to drink.

He was just looking at the deeper part in the bend behind him and wondering if there were any fish in it that he could tickle for his supper when something large and heavy landed on his shoulders and thudded on the back of his head.

Bright lights exploded and he went over like a toppled tree. He glimpsed an ugly scarred face with a broken nose under a morion helmet and a flash of bright orange-and-white rags, felt a hand across his mouth so he bit down hard and head-butted backwards at whoever was on his shoulders.

Next thing, two more heavy weights landed on him and his arms were wrestled up behind while his face went into the mud. Kicking and fighting as viciously as he could, he struggled to breathe, once even managing to rear up with the red rage all around him. Eventually another blow to his head took the world away into a deeper darkness than he'd ever known, although a part of him remained amused to note that he was still fighting as boots thudded into his ribs.

SUNDAY 17TH SEPTEMBER 1592, MORNING

The light was hurting Robert Carey's eyes even through his eyelids and two people were shouting at each other right next to him, hurting his sore head with the noise.

'...you ordered *my son* to investigate the Robsart matter...?'

'Who else could I ask, Harry? Walsingham is dead and none of the others...'

'My son! You put my son in danger of poisoning...?'

'I had to do it!' roared the Queen, 'I have to find out...'

'You did not have to find out anything, Eliza, for God's sake, you've let it lie thirty years, you could let it lie another thirty. Why the hell didn't you?'

'I could NOT let it lie, you old fool, look what they sent me!'

Silence. What? What did they send you? Who sent it? Carey fluttered his lids, only to find his eyes worse than ever, blurred and blazing with light that hurt him. He shut them again, tried to stretch his ears.

There was a long moment of silence and his father's heavy breathing, then the sound of creaking joints and popping knees as Lord Hunsdon knelt to the Queen.

'I'm sorry, Eliza.'

'Why?'

'For shouting at you.'

'You understand now? Why I couldn't let it lie?'

A heavy sigh. 'Yes.'

There was movement, rustle of skirts. 'What else could I do?' His aunt's voice had lost its full-throated roar suddenly and the blurred shape was merging with the darker shape, his father kneeling to her. 'I was horrified when I found it. What if it all came out now? And then I heard your boy Robin had turned up at Court and it seemed...it seemed as if God had sent him specially to help me.'

More creaking as Carey's father stood again.

'I'm so sorry he was poisoned, Harry. I never thought they would try such a thing, it never...Oh, Harry!'

The two figures merged into one. His father had his arms around the Queen and she was...good Lord, she must be crying into his chest, from the snuffling sounds.

Carey was too weak and dry even to moan. Ask her for my fee and my warrant as Deputy Warden, he thought as forcibly as he could. Go on, Father! Fee! Warrant! Ask!

Baron Hunsdon was rumbling again. 'There now, Eliza, there now. It's all right. I have the Gentlemen of the Guard checking all the supplies and some of my other men are asking Norris' servants and kitchen staff what happened. Mr. Byrd and Mrs. de Paris are making reports right now.'

'Be gentle...'

'Don't worry, I'm certain both Byrd and Thomasina are loyal, but they must be asked, you know. Somehow enough belladonna got into the flagon of spiced wine that Robin drank from to half-kill him and his henchman.'

What? Young Hughie had been poisoned, too? That was interesting.

The Queen sniffed and blew her nose. 'You're sure it wasn't the servingman? He's a Scot, after all.'

'I very much doubt it. It was pure luck he didn't die after drinking about half the contents of that flagon. Everybody thought he was just very drunk. Luckily he puked some of it up and after he collapsed, the other servingmen thought from his fever that it might be plague so they left him where he lay under the hedge. Once Tovey raised the alarm, of course, he was the first one we went looking for and we found him with the flagon beside him. It was very lucky that we did.'

'And you're sure it was poison?'

'Certain, Your Majesty. We fed the flagon's contents to a piglet which ran wild, then collapsed and died less than an hour later. Dr. Lopez says an infallible sign of belladonna poisoning is that the pupils of the eyes become fixed wide open and that light dazzles and hurts the victim. Hughie Tyndale is suffering from that, as well as Robin.'

So that was what was wrong with his goddamned eyes.

'The fever and the delirium are also typical.'

'Harry, your son...' The Queen was sniffling again which was very unlike her.

'What?'

'Your son insisted that the Earl of Essex be told before he would take anything to bring up the poison. He knew what had happened, but he was more worried about me drinking the spiced wine.'

There was a pause.

'Quite right,' came his father's voice after a loud harrumph. 'No more than I'd expect.'

'Oh, Harry...' The Queen's voice had a smile in it. 'I have a Court full of men who claim they would die for me, but so few of them who really would.'

There was another loud harrumph from his father, who seemed to have something stuck in his throat—a confounded nuisance, as far as Carey was concerned, as he needed his father to talk for him. Come on, Father. Ask her! Fee! Warrant! More money! shouted Carey in his mind, to no effect at all.

Through the watery flicker of his eyelids, he made out two blurred shapes embracing again. Very touching, you prize idiot, thought Carey in despair, why the hell won't you get me some more money and a proper warrant, you old buffoon? Or a customs farm or a patent? How about a monopoly on the import of sugar? That would be nice.

'Eliza, may I beg a favour?' His father's voice sounded tired.

Thank God, Carey thought. Come on, Father, you know how to do it.

'Of course.'

'Please, Eliza, for God's sake, will you make sure the boy's mother doesn't get to hear of this?'

Arrgh, thought Carey. Then after a moment's thought—well, yes, all right. Sensible.

Now there was something better than a smile in the Queen's voice, more like a giggle.

'I'll do my best, Harry, but you know that Annie has her ways of finding things out, just as I do. Nobody else need know since neither Robin nor his man actually died, thank God, so no inquest is needed and the Board of Green Cloth doesn't need to sit, or not officially. The poison was only in that particular flagon, not in the rest of the spiced wine.'

There was the sound of a woman's skirts on the rush mats again.

'In fact, I think the attempt was upon your son, not me.'

Hunsdon said nothing. 'And even so, brother,' continued the Queen

awkwardly, 'as soon as he's well enough again, you understand that
I want Robin to carry on with investigating the Robsart matter.'

Another pause and his father sighed. Now! thought Carey. A
piece of land. A nice monopoly on the sale of…oh…I don't know…
brandy…Come on!

'Will you let me tell him what…?'

'No. He has to work under the same conditions.'

'For God's sake…'

'Under the same conditions.'

'He's working blind. Literally now, as well as metaphorically.'

'I have a reason for what I do, Harry.'

'Excellent. What is it?'

'I want your son to have an open mind, not to make assumptions
about anything.'

'That could be dangerous, you know. Not just to his life, but to
you. He might find out by himself or work it out but come to the
wrong conclusion. Very clever boy, you know, in spite of the way
he treated his tutors, probably the brightest of the litter.'

By now Carey had gone beyond thinking in words. His head
was too full of pain and frustration at his father's incredible
dunderheadedness in not setting his penniless younger son up
for life. That was mixed with some pleasure at his father at least
acknowledging him as the brightest of his brothers—which he
knew already, of course, but it was good to hear it from his father's
mouth. Even if he did keep calling him 'boy' when Carey was over
thirty-two years old and had fought and killed.

Suddenly the Queen laughed her amazingly magical laugh.

'Brightest of the litter?' she chided playfully. 'Are you saying
he's a sleuthdog for tracking criminals?'

'Why not?'

'What does that make Annie?'

Hunsdon laughed too. 'Nothing wrong with bitches. Some of
my best trackers have been bitches.'

'And you, Harry?'

'Your Majesty's old guard dog, always at your heel.'

Creaking of joints meant Hunsdon had genuflected again. Well
done, Father, very courtly, Carey thought in despair, where's my

goddamned exclusive patent for the sale of silk ribbons, eh?

'Send Thomasina to me as soon as you can,' said the Queen's voice.

'Ah yes, before I forget…one of the matters we're investigating is the very fine gold and ruby necklace Robin had in his doublet pocket. His friend the Earl of Cumberland said it was a necklace he had given the Italian woman Signora Bonnetti.'

Somehow the Queen could make even a silence dangerously loud. 'Interesting,' she said at last.

'Signora Bonnetti, however, had left the dancing tent with the Earl's party by then and my lord of Essex says that she was playing cards with him while they discussed her husband's management of the sweet wine farm for him. Two of my own men who were there say this is true.'

'So the necklace was a fee for the introduction?'

'I think so.'

'Nothing wrong with that and quite a reasonable amount considering the value of the sweet wine farm. I remember Thomasina mentioned it to me earlier. Do you think the Italians are spies, too?'

'Probably. They were at the Scottish Court this summer.'

'Ah.'

Carey's lids fluttered again and he croaked, trying to explain that he didn't think it was Emilia who had poisoned him, despite it being with belladonna, but that she definitely was a spy.

At last they paid attention to him. He caught the Queen's smell of rosewater and peppermint comfits to sweeten her breath. She was leaning over him with a smooth ivory cup of water with brandy in it. Behind her loomed the wide shape of his father in black Lucca velvet and gold brocade as usual.

He'd better drink whatever the Queen was giving him. With enormous difficulty he lifted his head and gulped to soothe his leathery throat. Something bumped his teeth and he just managed to avoid choking on a large dark bitter-tasting stone, rattling around in the bottom of the cup.

'There,' said the Queen, letting his head rest on the pillow again, 'how are you, my dear?'

'Better,' he managed to say. And he did indeed feel better,

though for some reason there was a sharp uncomfortable pain at the base of his belly. The window shutters were closed so the room was not so full of painful light as it had been.

The Queen stroked his cheek. 'Your fever's gone,' she said. 'We'll talk later, Robin.'

The blur of black and white topped with red swished out of the room. Carey's father came closer to the bed.

'Well done, son,' he said, gripping Carey's bruised shoulder. 'She won't forget this. It's a good thing you'd stripped off your clothes and dropped your knife belt in the fever. You were in such a rage, laying about you and roaring about saving Elizabeth, it took every single clerk in the church to hold you down. But at least nobody's dead. Now let's hope we can keep it away from my esteemed lady wife, your mother, eh?'

'Yes, Father,' said Carey with difficulty. It had just occurred to him what the pain in his groin was. He urgently, desperately, needed a piss. Christ, he needed it right now!

'Father,' he croaked, 'Ah...pot...please?'

'Eh?' Hunsdon was deep in thought.

'A chamber pot?'

'Oh...ah...I'll send for a servant....'

'Now!'

Carey was sweating, so perhaps Hunsdon could see the urgency because he bent, looked under the bed and, thank God and all His holy angels, brought out what Carey needed, which was miraculously empty. It took a moment to let go but the relief almost brought tears to his eyes.

As Lord Hunsdon put the pot very carefully down on the rush mat next to the bed, Carey smiled. Amazing the way your body ambushed you and the joy in even the basest things when it hadn't been working for a while. He realised his father had gone to the door and he was afraid of being left alone, the first time he had felt like that since...must be the Armada year, when he was ill before.

'Father?'

Baron Hunsdon loomed over him again. 'I've sent for your new clerk,' he said. 'We've checked Mr. Tovey. I think it was a good idea hiring the boy—he's got sense.'

'Hughie?'

'Not out of the woods yet—he's in Lord Norris' servant quarters here. He must have drunk more spiced wine than you did. Dr. Lopez says whether he lives or dies depends entirely upon his humoral complexion and there's little he can do save prescribe his sovereign decoction of beanpods. The man so nearly died last night, we don't suspect him of the poisoning, though we haven't been able to find out much about him as he's Scotch. We've not made any progress on who actually did it, but the two prime suspects seem to be out of it.'

'How...long...?'

'Have you been asleep? Well, it's Sunday, you missed Divine Service in the church where you were fighting the poor clerks last night, missed a damned prosy sermon, and you're missing Sunday dinner to be followed by a very fine allegorical masque. It's Sunday afternoon.'

Carey groped for the water cup and his father caught his hand just before he knocked it over, put it into his fingers and poured more water for him. Carey tried to fish out the stone he'd nearly swallowed.

'Leave that, it's a bezoar stone against poisoning,' said his father, 'Dr. Lopez recommended it. The Queen's lent you her unicorn's horn cup as well.'

'Nearly swallowed...'

'I don't think you should eat it, I think it's actually a goat's gallstone. I'll drop it in the flagon.'

Carey couldn't make out anything in the blur, not the cup, not the flagon, not his father apart from as a large shape. The world was a dazzle that made his eyes hurt again so he shut them tight and frowned unhappily.

'Mr. Tovey thinks your eyes will recover by tomorrow,' rumbled his father. 'Dr. Lopez thinks it might take a couple of days.'

The full cup was in his fingers again so he drank the brandy-and-water mix. Now that he'd dealt with his immediate physical problems, he felt better. Slowly his mouth was getting less dry but he still had to keep his eyes shut.

'Father, would you close the bed curtains? Light hurts my eyes.'

'Can't see a damned thing in here, but very well.' The curtains swept across making the bed stuffy but the pain in his eyes reduced.

'That necklace...fee for introducing Emilia Bonnetti to Essex.'

'Want me to warn him about her?'

Carey hesitated. Perhaps that hadn't been a favour to his lord, after all? Would Essex understand how useful a spy so close to him could be? Or would he blame Carey? He couldn't decide. 'I don't know,' he admitted.

'We'll keep an eye on her. Young Cecil knows about her, too,' said his father. 'What happened with the bad guns you sold her in Dumfries?'

'I'm not sure but I think my lord of Cumberland got the Bonnettis out of Ireland just in time, unfortunately.'

'Would she bear you a grudge?'

He thought about it. After all, she was Italian. 'Probably, but once I made the introduction, she was in Essex's party and nowhere near Hughie. And I don't see why she would jeopardise managing the sweet wine farm by poisoning me. If it wasn't Hughie either, I can't think who else it could have been. Most of my enemies are in and around Carlisle now.'

'And the rest of them are creditors who want you alive,' growled his father. Carey said nothing because this was manifestly unfair even if it was true. 'We haven't had any luck with witnesses. They were all too drunk or busy dancing. Ridiculous bunch of popinjays.'

For some reason that reminded him of the incident at the duck pond. He told the story to his father, annoyed that he couldn't see Hunsdon's face for the reaction.

It was a mistake because Hunsdon sat down on the bed and took him through the story twice more. Carey's throat was dry again and he was suddenly exhausted.

'A crossbow argues against Signora Bonnetti because of the difficulty for a woman of drawing and carrying it. You say it was a deer-bolt?' Carey nodded once. 'So it must have been a full size crossbow. Hmm. I'll set a guard on your door, Robin, and I don't want you going out without at least three men with you.'

Carey shrugged. 'God looks after me always.'

'God likes us to look after ourselves as well, so He doesn't have to do all the work. Be careful in the Queen's matter, Robin.'

'What is it that she doesn't want you to tell me? What was the message she got with the music?'

He thought his father was smiling at his boldness. Well, it was worth a try. He got no answer though. His head was pounding again and he felt too tired to do anything else. Hunsdon patted his hand, lying on the coverlet. Carey felt the roughness of sword callouses there which could only mean his sixty-year-old father was still employing a swordmaster to play veneys with him regularly.

'I'll work on her, but she's a Tudor and she knows the value of information. She wants you to come at the Robsart killing with a fresh mind, since nobody else has got anywhere with it.'

'But Father, what if...'

'Ah, Mr. Tovey, thank you for coming.'

'M...my lord, how is he?'

'Very much better,' Carey said, 'thanks to you knowing what was happening.' Could that mean Tovey was...No. Surely not. Without the clerk's prompt action, he would probably be dead by now. 'But I still can't see a bloody thing at the moment,' he added resentfully. 'And do you know what happened to my Court suit, I left it hanging on a couple of saints in the church...?'

'Yes, sir, I got Mr. Coleman to help me bring it up before Divine Service this morning. It's hanging on the wall here.'

Well thank God for that at least, as the Court suit was probably worth more than the church building itself.

'My lord, Dr. Lopez wants a sample of Sir Robert's water...'

There were careful movements around the pot, someone was filling a flask. The pot was then removed and emptied, no doubt by one of his father's men. He didn't really care. He was falling asleep where he lay propped on pillows in the darkness of the bed curtains. He yawned and struggled to remember something else that was very important. Oh, yes...

'Father, where's Sergeant Dodd? Should be here by now.'

His father was moving, preparing to leave. 'I've been looking out for him,' came the rumble. 'No sign of him yet. I'll send him straight up when he arrives. Sleep well, Robin. I'll have a man at your door.'

Blackness welcomed him with strange dreams that broke apart and fought each other. One was of Elizabeth Widdrington holding him tight and him kissing her the way he had longed to since the Armada year. One was of a prison cell.

SUNDAY 17TH SEPTEMBER 1592,

LATE AFTERNOON

He woke up to a darker chamber, restless, his stomach aching and his head hurting again, so he sat up on the bed among the pillows and tried to think.

The important things were the inquest report and witness statements. Had Thomasina herself realised just how damning they were? The men of the jury had clearly been stout honest gentlemen because despite extreme pressure from powerful people, they had reported some things that made a nonsense of their obedient verdict of accidental death. Everyone knew that Amy Robsart had died of a broken neck. What everyone knew was wrong.

A little while later someone knocked. It was John Tovey, coming in carrying candles which hurt Carey's eyes. He got the fire going again.

'Mr. Tovey, I want you to go to whichever kitchen is serving the Queen and ask them for food for me and when you come back, bring your penner and paper. Make sure the food is taken from a common pot, no small meat pies or penny loaves, for instance.'

'Will you want me to taste the meal, sir?'

The lad caught on quickly; that was good. 'Yes please, Mr. Tovey, if you would. When you come back.'

'Yes, sir.'

Was Tovey the poisoner or in league with him or her? Very unlikely since all he'd had to do when Carey called him the night before was set up a cry of 'Plague' and leave him until he was dead.

Certainly the poisoner or his or her accomplice wouldn't instantly identify what was wrong and get him to purge. Besides, Carey had picked him out personally, almost at random.

By the time Tovey got back with more food from the Queen's kitchen, set up in one of the manor's parlours, Carey was hungry and bored. He'd tried reading his papers but he couldn't make anything out, in fact he couldn't even look out of the windows for the dazzle. Goddamn it. Although come to think of it, that was a very promising metaphor to use on the Queen sometime—being dazzled blind by Cynthia, the Moon Goddess and so on and so forth.

Tovey ate most of the bread, cheese, butter, and sausage plus a good half of the large wedge of game pie he'd brought. Once he started eating, Carey found his stomach and gullet were still sore from being sick and so he mostly just drank the ale.

'Mr. Tovey, where did you learn to spot belladonna poisoning?'

'Ah...my mother was a wise woman, sir. She taught me some things. When she died, I went to my father. He sent me to a good Oxford apothecary to prentice to him and learn my letters better than he could teach me.'

'And then?'

'My master taught me Latin as well as many other things and when he found I was an apt pupil he sent me to the grammar school. I was able for all things to do with letters so I went to study at Balliol, sir, as a servitor. He died of plague a little after I took my degree, alas. God keep him. He was a good and kindly master—we often spoke about the mysteries of alchemy and the different qualities of matter. I found it hard to get work in Oxford where there are so many clerks, so I went back to my father and that's why I came to clerk for the Queen's secretaries, in hopes of finding a place.'

'Good thing for me you did. Now then, those papers I asked you to translate. You understood the significance of them?'

Silence. Carey couldn't even see the boy's face, much less read it. His voice came as a whisper. 'Yes, sir.'

'Explain it to me.'

'I have friends at Gloucester College where she was buried. Everyone knows Lady Dudley fell down the stairs at Cumnor Place and broke her neck and everyone says she was murdered, but I didn't...I couldn't understand why the inquest found for accidental death.'

'Somebody very important told them to,' Carey said.

'Well yes, sir, but why then did they say she had neither stain nor bruise on her?'

'Go on.'

'She fell down the stairs and hit her head with two dints, one half an inch, the other a couple of inches deep so her skull must have been broken. How come she didn't bleed?'

'And?'

'And what, sir?'

Carey was surprised he hadn't spotted the other ridiculous thing. 'According to witnesses, her headdress was untouched and on her head.'

A pause. 'Oh.'

'Yes, oh. No bruises—possibly that could be because when she actually fell down the stairs she was already dead, though I doubt it. You can bruise for a while after death. No stains—maybe, just perhaps, her skin wasn't broken even though her skull was and so she didn't bleed. But her headdress untouched? With a two-inch dent in her head? I don't think so.'

Silence. Carey continued, 'They reported it truly even though they had been told what their verdict should be, because they were under oath. I assume that whoever was pressuring them didn't bother to read the whole report because if they had, I expect they would have sent it back to be rewritten.'

'Yes, sir. That's what surprised me.'

Carey didn't add what had already occurred to him about that, which was that the Queen had clearly not read it. The boy was frightened enough already.

'I don't need to tell you that everything in this matter must be kept most secret and not spoken of to anyone.'

'No, sir. I wouldn't dream...'

'There is one circumstance when you must speak of it and that's if I die suddenly for any reason at all without having finished my inquiries. If that happens you must immediately leave the Court, and lie low for a while. Take any papers with you and make sure you give them to…to…' Damn it, to whom? Who couldn't be suspected in the Amy Robsart killing? '…to my father or the steward at Somerset House. Understand?'

'Yes sir. Who is your father exactly, sir?'

'The Queen's Lord Chamberlain, Baron Hunsdon.'

A very loud gulp and then Carey thought he saw a smile. Or heard it rather, in the ambitious boy's suddenly eager voice. 'Really?'

'Yes, really. So please make notes.' There was a rustle and the soft click of a pen being dipped. 'And of course be very careful of poison for both of us. Is there a man on the door now?'

'Um.' Tovey went and looked. 'It's Mr. Henshawe,' he said.

A good man, Carey remembered him. He shook his head with his eyes still closed and frowned. 'That was one of the mysteries of the thing,' he said to Tovey, his restless mind drifting back to the puzzle the Queen had set him. 'Why wasn't Amy Robsart poisoned instead of being pushed down stairs? Certainly she was careful about what and how she ate, but even so…it wouldn't have been so very hard to do by an expert. The Papists insist that it was her husband, the Earl of Leicester, who killed her. But if it was him, why the devil didn't he poison her with belladonna or white arsenic or something? Yes, of course, there would have been rumours but the thing would have been uncertain enough that he would still have had a chance of marrying the Queen.'

No answer from Tovey who was probably too shocked.

'After all, killing his wife was a tremendous risk—why would he do it in such a way that would immediately look like murder and draw down suspicion on his head? Dudley was never the cleverest of men but he wasn't crazy and he wasn't stupid.'

'Did you know him, sir?'

'Oh yes, of course, he used to shout at me when I was a young idiot of a page in the sixties and seventies. Nobody ever spoke about his first wife but only fools of Papist priests ever thought it had been him that killed her.'

'They say it was him at Gloucester College, sir.'

'No doubt, being a notorious bunch of Papists there. How much recent history do you know, Mr. Tovey? I mean after the end of Holinshed's Chronicles, about the Queen's father King

Henry and his various…er…marriages?'

'Very little, sir. Only that the Queen is his daughter by Queen Anne Boleyn and that her older sister, Bloody Mary, was by the Spanish Infanta, Katherine of Aragon.'

'Well, the Queen lost her own mother, Anne Boleyn, my great-aunt, to the axe on trumped up charges of infidelity. The next of Henry's Queens died of a childbed fever, the Queen after that he divorced for ugliness, the Queen after that was executed for infidelity on a bill that probably was foul, and the one after that survived him but then died of childbed fever after marrying later.' Tovey said nothing. 'It's common gossip at Court that the Queen never wed to get an heir because she's in horror of marriage, because she believes that it's tantamount to a sentence of death for the woman. That's why she tries to protect her maids of honour from the marriage bed. She certainly loved Robert Dudley when she came to the throne and she might have been able to bring herself to marry for his sake, but after he had killed his first wife? Just the suspicion of it was enough to set her against it. He knew that and he wasn't stupid or reckless. If he had decided to kill Amy Robsart, the thing would have been done a lot better and would never have been known as murder, so he could in fact marry the Queen afterward and become King.'

'Y…yes, sir. Um…s…sir, isn't talking about the Queen like this treasonous?'

'Yes, it is,' Carey said, 'if she finds out.'

Silence. 'Yes, sir.'

Carey hoped that Tovey wouldn't take the bait held out to him in case he was somebody's spy, but you never knew. And you might as well add a bit of egg to the pudding.

'Of course, it's plain Amy was in fact killed no matter what the inquest says. And there are plenty of other suspects.'

Tovey moved restlessly. 'Sir,' he said awkwardly, 'I…I'm only a c…clerk and you haven't known me long. Should you be…er… opening your mind to me like this?'

Carey beamed at the area of blur where he was. 'Probably not,' he agreed, 'if you're working for someone else apart from me.'

'No, sir, of course not.'

'Mr. Tovey,' Carey admonished, 'if you aren't yet, you will be when word gets round you're my clerk now. The people who are likely to offer you money to pass information to them are Sir Thomas Heneage, the Earl of Essex, my father, Sir Robert Cecil— any number of people here and more once we get back to Carlisle.'

'I'll tell them "no," sir.'

'No you won't.' He could actually hear the click of Tovey's jaw as he shut his mouth after a shocked pause. Bless him, he was as a newborn lamb to the greedy wolves of the Court. Better educate him quickly.

'What you do is you tell me about it. Whoever it is, whatever they offer, you take it and then you tell me. Especially if it's Sir Robert Cecil. Don't be too quick, play innocent and shocked— they'll expect it. Let them pressure you, especially that bastard Heneage, but then give in. Whoever it is, whatever they ask, no matter how much money you're offered, you swear you'll tell no one, especially not me, and you'll work for them only, and then we'll decide together what I want them to know. I won't charge you commission on your bribes, so long as you tell me about each one.'

Another pause and then Tovey chuckled softly. 'Was that why my father was so happy not to pay a fee for the place as your clerk?'

'Absolutely. Don't let him drink all your bribes. And learn to lie.'

Tovey dipped his pen in a businesslike way. 'Shall I put my lord of Leicester at the top of your list of suspects?'

'Why not? Make five columns, head them *Nomine, quomodo, quando ubique, quare, cui bono.*'

'Name, how, where and when, why, whose benefit?'

Carey was quite proud of himself for remembering all that Latin.

'Yes, Walsingham's system. He taught it to me when I was serving him in Scotland, along with many other things. He always said that practically any tangle could be solved by asking *Cui bono*, who benefits? So, Dudley first. His best method was poison, despite Lord Burghley having a man placed in Amy's kitchen. Where and when was any where and any time since she was his wife. The why is obvious but the benefit—he could not benefit from the way the murder was actually done.'

The pen was slipping smoothly across the paper. 'Unless it was a double bluff?'

'I doubt it. He hardly bluffed at primero. I don't think he would bluff with the chance of becoming King.'

'You said there were other suspects?'

'Sir William Cecil, my lord Treasurer Burghley now.'

The pen stopped moving. 'Sir?' The fear in the boy's voice now did credit to Burghley.

'Write it down, Mr. Tovey.' Carey had an idea of what he would do with the paper later, despite the risk. 'In fact put in any of the old guard, the Privy Council of the early years, the men who danced around the young Queen. By blocking out the favourite, the killing of Amy Robsart benefited anyone who hoped to marry the Queen—therefore the Spanish, all of her suitors foreign or English. Hatton, possibly even Heneage. He had the Queen's eye once, I believe, for a couple of months.' He laughed at the thought. 'Burghley is top of the list because he was desperate to stop her marrying Dudley as they hated each other then and he would have lost his place the instant King Robert was crowned.'

He paused to let Tovey catch up. 'And then there's the most obvious suspect of all,' he said softly, 'the Queen herself.'

That stopped him. 'I'm not writing that, sir,' said Tovey.

'Put her down as 1500,' Carey agreed, harking back to the code name for the Queen that Walsingham had used. Of course the Queen probably knew it, but it kept the thing decorous. The fact that Tovey wrote it down without arguing further showed he had a brain and could use it.

Because the fact was that the Queen was by far the most likely suspect. Not as she was now, a wise and politic prince, but as she had been in Carey's father's stories of the early days of her Court, when Carey himself had been a baby in swaddling bands in his wet nurse's arms. When the Queen had been a wild laughing young woman with red hair, a flaming temper, and the power to draw men like moths to a flame. That she was ruthless enough to kill her lover's wife could not be doubted. But was she foolish enough, impetuous enough? Had she done that?

He shook his head. If she had, why ask him to investigate? Why not, as his father had advised, leave it lie another thirty years until she was safely dead and nobody cared anymore?

Since the Queen was a woman, she might have any number of reasons, but from the information that Byrd had given him, Carey rather thought that someone else knew for sure who had done it and had sent her a message demanding money along with some kind of token proving he did. Which made things look very bad for the Queen, indeed. Had she really done as her far stupider cousin, Mary Queen of Scots, had done? As her father had done? Had she murdered to clear her path to marriage?

He shook his head, which was aching again. If it really had been the Queen who killed Amy Robsart, how had she done it and kept it secret so long? She was constantly surrounded by her women and had been even when she was running wild with Robert Dudley. The Papists were always claiming that some bastard or other was hers, even one of his father's own byblows had been taken up in France as the Queen's baseborn son, but nobody who knew anything about the Court ever believed a word of it. And if she had done it, surely she would have done a better job, just as Dudley would have? There would have been somebody available to swing for the murder, surely? Carey could think of half a dozen ways the Queen could have quietly abolished Dudley's first wife, not one of which involved pushing the woman down a few stairs. That was why, if he even thought about it, he had assumed what most people now at Court did, that Dudley's first wife had been unlucky or unwell and the thing truly was an accident. Until he read the inquest papers.

If she was being blackmailed about it, she might well ask him to investigate—but surely then she would have given him the message with the Spanish air on it and the token, whatever that was, and told him to quietly find and kill the blackmailer. Surely?

He was feeling tired again, surprisingly so. Sitting in shadows with only one candle lit for Tovey and his eyes shut was making him sleepy. He realised he had been silent a long while.

'Is that all, sir?' Tovey asked hopefully.

'Yes, thank you. I think I'll go back to sleep now though it's far too early. It's infernally boring not being able to see but that might help my bloody eyes recover.'

'It might, sir. M…may I advise you to cover them when daylight comes? Your eyes pain you because they have no defence against the sunlight and too much light might actually damage them and blind you permanently.'

'Jesu.' That put fear in the pit of his stomach. 'Is Mr. Henshawe on guard at the door?'

Tovey checked. 'Yes, sir. And I've brought my pallet and I'll sleep here tonight.'

'Good. Has Sergeant Dodd arrived?'

'No, sir, when I fetched the food, your father's under-steward said my lord was sending riders out along the London road to see if he'd fallen off his horse, as he must have left London early on Saturday. '

Carey frowned. That didn't sound at all plausible; Dodd had practically been born on a horse. But perhaps he was in some kind of trouble. You never knew: after all, who would have thought Carey might end up being poisoned in the Queen's Court? Dodd's absence was worrying—surely he wouldn't have decided to simply head north and bypass Oxford altogether? Even if he'd walked from London to Oxford, he should have been here by now.

***

Somebody knocked on the door. Carey was instantly awake, feeling for a dagger under his pillow where there wasn't one, blinking in the darkness of the brocade bed curtains with a pattern of fleur de lis. He heard Tovey's voice murmuring.

'Mrs. de Paris to see Sir Robert,' said one of Thomasina's women.

'Let her in, Mr. Tovey,' called Carey with resignation, groping at the end of the bed for his dressing gown and finding none. What was the time? He wasn't sure because when he peered through the curtains the room seemed brighter than it should have been with just one blurry watch-candle in it. He heard people talking. 'Damnit, Mistress Thomasina, wait a minute, I'm only in my shirt…'

Tovey handed him a fur dressing gown of his father's, marten and velvet, which Carey pulled around his shoulders, opened one of the bed curtains and sat with his legs crossed.

The door was opened a little by Mr. Henshawe, and Carey could make out the small colourful blur of Thomasina still in her tumbling clothes.

'Sir, would you like me to make notes?'

'No,' said Thomasina's high-pitched childlike voice. 'Please leave us.'

Tovey stood where he was. Carey heard him swallow. 'Er…?' he said. Carey was liking the scrawny clerk more and more. 'It's all right, Mr. Tovey,' he said. 'Mrs. de Paris is an old friend.'

Tovey bowed awkwardly and went out into the passage to stand with Thomasina's women.

Carey felt Thomasina jump up on the bed like a man mounting a horse and then she sat with her legs folded under her, looking like a small lump of forest of tawny and green brocade in the general blur. He smiled in her direction.

'Next time your spiced wine tastes bitter, Sir Robert, may I suggest you throw it away?'

Her voice was withering.

'At the time,' he admitted, 'it never occurred to me that anyone would try and poison me, but from now on I'll bear it in mind.'

'Good.'

'Why are you here, Mistress? It's late. And I think you weren't even born when Amy Robsart died…'

'No, I remember the accession bonfires and getting drunk on spiced ale with my older brother,' she said. 'Perhaps I was about two or three at the time as it's one of my first memories.'

Good Lord, she was older than he was. Astonishing.

'Of course, I wasn't then in Her Majesty's service nor even imagining such a thing. I'm here, Sir Robert, to find out if the Queen can help you in your quest.'

'She can come and break the matter fully with me, tell me about the message that upset her, so I know where I am.'

Silence. 'She won't. Not yet.'

Damn it, he hated it when people wouldn't tell you what you needed to know. But there it was, neither his father nor Thomasina would disobey the Queen just to make his life easier. So he shrugged.

'Is there anything else I can do?'

'While I'm stuck in this room and not able to see, I might as well keep busy. I want to interview all of Her Majesty's Privy Councillors that served her then and are alive now.'

'Oh?' Carey couldn't make out her face but he didn't need to. He could imagine the expression on the midget's face. 'Who do you want to start with?'

In for a penny, in for a pound, Carey thought. Let's see if my loving aunt, against all her normal habits, actually means what she says.

'My Lord Treasurer Burghley,' he said simply.

Well at least Thomasina didn't laugh at the idea of the Queen's penniless and frankly quite lowly cousin and nephew interviewing the person who in fact administered the realm for her and also ran the Queen's finances, who was the chief man in the realm whatever the Earl of Essex thought, and had been since the Queen's accession.

'When?'

'If he's here at Rycote, now. Tonight. If not, as soon as he can come.'

Instead of a grim laugh, a flat refusal, or a placatory platitude, Thomasina said simply, 'Very well, Sir Robert, I shall arrange it. He's here, so don't go back to sleep.'

Well, he hadn't expected that. She hopped off the bed like a sizeable cat and trotted to the door.

Jesu, thought Carey, what have I asked for? I didn't expect to be given it!

Burghley arrived only twenty minutes later. Carey had wrapped himself in his father's dressing gown, feeling every limb as heavy as if he had just chased a raiding party across the Bewcastle Waste for two days. He was still sitting on the bed because the bed curtains gave him some protection from the light. He had also fastened a silk scarf across his eyes. Partly it was to protect them from the extra candles Tovey had lit so he could take notes, partly for dramatic purposes. He was nervous. Carey knew the Lord Treasurer, of course, had oftentimes seen his aunt lose her temper with her faithful servant and throw things at him. Walsingham had told him a few interesting tidbits but had respected the man greatly, despite his pragmatism and their many disagreements over how best to deal with Papists.

Burghley limped in, wincing from his gout and the man with him had an odd, quick uneven gait. Ah yes, Burghley must have brought his second son whose body was clenched and hunched from the rickets he had suffered in his youth, despite the careful supervision of three or four doctors.

'My Lord Treasurer, S…Sir Robert Cecil,' announced Tovey in awed tones. Carey stood for them, bowed, then felt behind him for the bed and sat again quickly, drawing his legs up. He had actually nearly overbalanced, his brain felt battered and bruised, and his mouth was dry again.

'My Lord Treasurer, Sir Robert, I am very grateful to you and honoured at your coming here. I apologise, my lord, that my temporary disability has prevented me from coming to you as would be more appropriate,' he said formally.

'Yes, yes, Sir Robert. Her Majesty asked me to speak to you about these matters but alas, I doubt very much that I can help you,' said Burghley's voice. It was a deep voice and paradoxically able to make very dull subjects verge on interesting. Even Scottish politics became comprehensible when Burghley explained them, a remarkable and essential talent. Carey remembered the Lord Treasurer once explaining to him many years ago why it was that his debts kept mounting up. Probably his father had asked him to. Carey vaguely remembered that the lecture was about what four shillings in the pound interest could do given time. Burghley seemed to think that because he was interested in the clever Greek ways of planning cannon fire and siege towers and had read that manuscript Italian book about card play, he could understand accounting. He probably could, he just…wasn't interested. Burghley had given up eventually.

Tovey brought up the one chair with arms and a cushion for Lord Burghley. Sir Robert Cecil quietly took a chair without arms that had been foraged specially from one of the manor's storerooms. The room was too small for any more furniture with the big bed in it, the clothes chest, and Tovey's pallet folded on top of it. Tovey was using the window sill as a desk.

'I have asked my clerk, Mr. Tovey, to keep a note,' Carey said and heard the creak of the starched linen ruff when Burghley nodded.

'Good. Good practice. My son will do the same for me.'

Carey wondered if the two records would look anything like each other. The chair creaked on its own note as Burghley settled himself in it.

'May I offer you wine, my lord?' Carey asked, then smiled, 'though I may say I've been a little put off wine myself.'

It was annoying that he couldn't see Burghley's expression, that pouchy wary face with the knowing little smile.

'Alas, Sir Robert,' Burghley said, 'Dr. Lopez has warned me off wine of any sort and I am sentenced to drink mild ale and nothing else apart from a foul and superstitious potion made of crocus-bulbs as penalty for my gout.'

Carey made a sympathetic noise. 'How is your gout, my lord?'

'Bad,' was Burghley's short answer. 'Very painful. Get to the point, sir, Her Majesty will be waiting to cross-examine me after this meeting.'

Carey paused. He wanted straight answers and wasn't about to start a verbal fencing match with the finest exponent in the kingdom.

'The point, my lord, is *cui bono*,' he said, plunging straight in. 'Who benefits? There are those who would say that you were the one man who benefitted most from Amy Dudley's murder.'

Both Sir Robert Cecil and Tovey sucked in their breaths with audible gasps. Carey sat with his legs folded, his father's marten and tawny dressing gown round his shoulders and the scarf over his eyes and felt...good God, he was enjoying himself dicing with death again. His hearing seemed to be getting better as well–the cannonfire and shooting muskets and dags in France and on the Borders had blunted his hearing, taken away his ability to hear bat squeaks and noticeably dulled soft music for him. Perhaps with his eyes not working properly he was paying more attention to what he could hear. He had known the moment Tovey's pen and Sir Robert Cecil's pen had stopped their soft movements across paper.

'Explain yourself,' said Burghley with cold fury in his voice.

'My lord, with all due respect...' Carey began, knowing very well what the lawyer's phrase meant, as did Burghley. 'I am sure I am not the first person to point that out. From what I know of the first few years of Her Majesty's blessed reign, she was very far from being the wise sovereign lady that she now is. She was, God save her, a flibbertigibbet, a flirt, and very disinclined to any business of ruling at all. She ran riot with Robert Dudley and other men of her Court in the first few years. It was a matter of desperate import to you and all her wiser councillors that she marry as quickly as possible so that she would have a man to direct and guide her and calm her unstable woman's humours.'

A pause. Tovey cleared his throat. 'Sir, d...did you want m... me to...'

'Record all of it, Mr. Tovey,' Carey ordered firmly. 'I will repeat it to Her Majesty's face and take the consequences.'

There was more creaking of chin against linen ruff. Someone, probably Burghley, was shaking his head.

'There was no shortage of good mates for her,' Carey went on, quoting his father. 'Philip II of Spain offered for her and could not be rejected outright, several German and Swedish princes offered who were unexceptionable except that the Queen didn't like them. Even a carefully chosen English nobleman might have been a possibility. Unfortunately the Queen had fallen head-over-heels in love with her horsemaster, Robert Dudley, the son and grandson of traitors, much hated by the older noble families and a man of very little common sense. He was the worst possible lover she could have chosen but she would not listen to reason.' The silence in the little chamber was oppressive.

'He was also utterly opposed to you, my lord, and your careful diplomacy, had no understanding of the financial situation which was in a desperate state, and was moreover an intemperate man who loved war, although he himself was disastrously untalented as a general.

'You, my Lord Treasurer, were in terror that the Queen would persuade Dudley to leave his wife and scandalously marry her, making himself king. This you saw as likely to drop the realm straight into civil war as the nobility picked their own candidates for the Queen's husband and called out their tenants. In point of fact, the Northern Earls did revolt a few years later with the Howards at their head. And the Earl of Leicester hated you, my lord, and so with him once crowned, you would have lost your place and the realm gone to rack and ruin even if civil war was somehow avoided.' Somebody was breathing hard and Carey knew it wasn't him, though his heart was pounding. God, this was fun—should he be enjoying himself so much?

'So, my lord, logic clearly shows that you were the one man who gained most by Amy Dudley's death in the manner by which it occurred....'

'Don't be ridiculous, Sir Robert,' snapped Burghley. 'Amy Dudley's death cleared Leicester's way to the throne. However she died, the fact that she was dead made him a widower with no impediment to marriage. When I heard what had happened I was in the worst despair I have ever been in my life because I was sure they would marry immediately and that all would fall out exactly as you have suggested. In fact I started selling land and books so I could move to the Netherlands again if necessary. Amy Dudley was my best bulwark against Leicester's kingship. I had men placed in her household to guard her, one in the kitchen against poison, one as her under-steward, and I was paying a fortune to one of her women, I forget the name, to keep me informed. I had all the letters to and from Cumnor Place opened and read, I took every precaution to keep Leicester's wife safe and alive, and the bloody man somehow managed to kill her anyway!' Burghley was shouting by the end. Carey thought from the sound that he was leaning forward, quite possibly prodding the air with a finger as he often did.

'So, who did kill her?'

'Her husband, Sir Robert Dudley, the Earl of Leicester, the obvious suspect, the man who wanted to be king.' Burghley was still shouting and Carey wondered if his face was going purple.

'With respect, no, my lord,' said Carey calmly. 'It's my belief that the Queen would not, could not marry a man who had killed his wife, no matter how, no matter why.'

'Of course she would. She was on heat for him, it was a disgraceful sight.'

'So why didn't she, my lord?'

'What?'

'You say Leicester must have killed his wife so he could marry the Queen. Once he had done it, why didn't they marry?'

'God knows, perhaps God managed to drive a particle of common sense into the Queen's head, because God knows none of the rest of her council could.' Carey was momentarily entranced at the implied idea of Almighty God sitting on the Privy Council presided over by Burghley. 'Or perhaps she realised that the scandal would destroy her. It was then only seventy-six years since the Queen's grandfather ended the civil wars between York and Lancaster by taking the throne. There had been a decade of trouble, religious turns and twists, Queen Mary burning hundreds of good Protestant men and women, the Exchequer exhausted, the currency debased, the...'

'So, my lord, you say that you did not kill Amy Dudley in such a manner that the Earl would be blamed and thus the Queen would refuse to marry him?'

A fist came down on the arm of the chair. 'No! That would have been madness! To take such a risk, take away the one thing putting a brake on Leicester's cursed ambition? Never! Thank God, the Queen realised that a man who would kill one wife might also kill another wife, just as her father had, and that pulled her back from the disastrous marriage, much to Leicester's disappointment.'

'But you could have done it?' Carey pursued, knowing he was dancing on the lip of a volcano.

'I had and still have the power...the men...to do such things,' said Burghley's voice, heavy with menace. 'As a general rule, I do not use it. As a general rule.'

Carey smiled back at the threat. 'You're sure it was Leicester, not realising that the Queen would react the way she did.'

There was the faint rustle of lifted shoulders. 'I said so at the time and have said so since. It was that bloody man she fell in love with, clearing away the main impediment, despite all I could do to protect her.' The chair creaked. Carey wondered for the first time if Burghley might have been a little in love with the Queen all those years ago as well.

The Queen's first Councillor must have read his mind.

'Of course I loved her, Sir Robert,' he rumbled into his ruff. 'We all did. She was a marvel, a joy, a gift from God. She was enraging and magical, every room she entered was suddenly full of sunshine and lightning, a slender pale creature with a war-beacon of hair and the temper of a king and that laugh...God, yes, Sir Robert, I loved your aunt from the time I first saw her in her brother's reign. I always knew I could never have her as my own. Yes, I hated Dudley because he made her happy and made her laugh and I could not—although I could indeed make her safer. And that was all I wanted. All I still want. All I have ever asked of God is that she should outlive me.'

Carey found that he was wordless. He had never expected cautious dull old Burghley to have such passion hidden in him, much less speak of it.

'The Earl of Leicester killed Amy Robsart, his unfortunate wife, married before he realised he had a chance of a kingdom, while Princess Elizabeth still had two lives between her and the throne and a question over her legitimacy. He killed the woman because he was a stupid but ambitious man and he did it to clear his path to the throne.'

Burghley was creaking to his feet, making it clear that the interview was over. From the sound, Carey thought the still-silent Sir Robert Cecil was helping him. He tried again.

'My lord, that doesn't work. *Cui bono*, remember? How could Leicester have gained from killing Amy that way?'

Burghley paused. 'I told you, I had men looking after her. He had no other way....'

'Had there been any attempts at poisoning her? Any mysterious fevers?'

'She was ill, certainly, she had something wrong with one of her breasts that pained her, but not enough to kill her.'

'But had there been previous attempts to...'

'No.'

'None?'

'No.' Burghley did seem to pause. 'I would never have taken the risk of killing Amy Dudley,' he said again, but more thoughtfully this time. For a moment Carey wondered if something new had occurred to him after all this time. But then the door slammed.

However, his chamber wasn't empty. Somebody else was close

to the bed and it wasn't Tovey because the smell was different and the movement even more awkward than Tovey's.

'Mr. Secretary Cecil,' Carey said politely to Burghley's hunchback second son whom he had nearly forgotten because the man had said not a word. 'What do you think of this?'

Cecil's voice was higher and a little breathless because of his back. 'I think it's a very interesting problem, Sir Robert, but I believe what my father says. Killing Amy Dudley to lay the murder at Leicester's door in the hope that it would put the Queen off Leicester...no. Far too great a gamble for him, Sir Robert, and my father never ever bets on anything but a certainty.'

Carey had to admit he had no understanding of this way of thinking. Surely a gamble was the finest thing in the world, the breath of life and excitement even if it did go wrong? As he had to admit, it often did for him. But that made all the sweeter the times when it actually worked.

'While Leicester was married, he couldn't have the Queen. As soon as he was free, my father was sure the Queen and he would marry. That they didn't is a mercy he has always attributed to the direct intervention of the Almighty. And that's the beginning and end of it,' Cecil added. 'Meantime, I understand that your remarkable Sergeant Dodd has not yet arrived, which is causing you some concern.'

'Yes? Do you have any news of him?' Carey was a little surprised. In the cockpit of the Court, he was in the opposing faction to the Cecils, that of the Earl of Essex. Why was Sir Robert Cecil, secretary to the Privy Council, offering him useful information?

'I do.' Cecil sounded amused. 'Sergeant Dodd rode out of the wreckage of one of Heneage's secret London houses with one of Heneage's post-horses under him and another as remount. That was on Saturday morning.'

Carey couldn't help it. He shouted with laughter. 'Good God, what happened? He didn't raid Heneage's...He did?'

'Yes, Sir Robert, it seems he did, in alliance with the King of London and your extraordinary lady mother and her Cornish... ah...followers.'

Carey was too stunned to speak. Surely to God she hadn't

set Dodd on to conduct a private reprisal raid on Heneage in the middle of London? To teach him a lesson on not plotting against her husband and sons? Had she?

'The official story is a little different. It seems that the rabble Heneage was employing there had kidnapped several people, including your young lawyer, and there was a riot during which Dodd, your mother's...people, and a few upright men loaned by the King of London freed the prisoners and accidentally set the house on fire.'

That was definitely Dodd. He had a worrying weakness for accidentally setting things on fire.

'Fortunately not much damage was done, only a couple of deaths and peace was restored. Luckily. Oh, and another of Heneage's houses blew up the same night.'

Carey shook his head in wonder. She had! Did his father know?

'Very fortunately, your lady mother had let me know that the riot was likely and so I was able to be present and help broker peace and so the matter is now, as far as I am concerned, closed.'

'Mr. Recorder Fleetwood?'

'He concurs.'

This was fascinating. Was it possible that his mother had managed to form an alliance with Burghley's promising second son? His father was always neutral in Court factions and he, of course, was the Earl of Essex's man who was also Heneage's notional lord, unfortunately. His mother had deliberately reached out to involve Burghley's politic son in Dodd's revenge against Heneage, it seemed. And it looked as if she had got away with it.

However, it was very worrying now that Dodd hadn't made it to Oxford. With a post-horse and remount, Dodd should have arrived on the Saturday evening, around the time Carey was puking his guts up to get rid of the poison, or early on Sunday morning. So long as he hadn't been stupid or ignorant enough to stay the night at one of the regular post-inns along the Oxford road, of course...Ah.

'I don't suppose...' Carey began cautiously. 'You didn't notice any post-inns on fire as you came from London yourself?'

Cecil paused before he answered. 'Curiously enough, there was one we passed this morning that was still smoking and had half its roof burnt off, but fortunately no one died.' Carey said nothing. 'We didn't inquire about it. I'll send a man down to talk to the innkeeper.'

'Thank you Mr. Secretary. For...er...everything.'

'Please don't mention it. I was delighted to make a better acquaintance of my Lady Hunsdon and Sergeant Dodd.'

Again the door banged, more quietly this time, and Carey frowned, absentmindedly pulled the annoying scarf off his eyes, only to find his eyes still pained by the candles Tovey was using. 'Mr. Tovey,' he said, 'did you note down what Mr. Secretary Cecil said?'

Tovey's voice was struggling to sound unmoved. 'Yes, sir.'

'Please burn that page.' He waited until the crackle of paper and the smell of smoke reached him and Tovey pounded the ashes in the fireplace where a fire had been laid but not lit.

What was the time? Somewhere near midnight? Damn, damn, damn it. Where the hell was Dodd? What had happened to him? The man always seemed to be made of boiled leather and very sharp steel but he was only human.

Carey pushed the covers back and got out of bed, intending to get dressed and roust out some men to canter down along the Oxford road and find out what had happened at that post-inn.

Then he fell over the chair Burghley had sat in, blundered into the chest by the wall, and stubbed his toes painfully. While he was still cursing that, there was another knock at the door. Tovey moved to open it a little and there was a murmur of argument. Tovey turned his head, his voice even more nervous than usual.

'It's Mr. Vice Chamberlain Heneage to see you, sir.'

SUNDAY 17TH SEPTEMBER 1592, NIGHT

Carey was standing on one leg, holding his toes. Jesu! Heneage! Come to make a complaint, no doubt, damn damn.

He hopped to the bed with the dressing gown flapping, knocking over the little table by the bed as he went and climbed in gratefully.

'I'm resting, Mr. Tovey,' he hissed. 'Tell him to go away.'

More conversation. 'Sir, Mr. Vice Chamberlain says that Her Majesty has sent him and he must speak with you.'

Heart thumping with annoyance and tension, Carey sat up again, wrapped the dressing gown tighter round him. His knuckles had recovered from breaking Heneage's nose at the beginning of September, but still…Had the man come to demand satisfaction? Was that why Cecil had told him the bare bones of what Dodd and Lady Hunsdon had been up to while he had been riding for Oxford and snoring in the post-inn on the way? It sounded as if Dodd had introduced some of the Borderers' ways of settling disputes to London, and as an officer of the Queen's law, he could not possibly approve of it. Officially.

'Mr. Tovey,' he said loudly, 'I am at a disadvantage here. Please make notes and if Mr. Heneage does not behave himself as a gentleman should, would you be so good as to tell Mr. Henshawe to remove him and then fetch my father?

Heneage came through the door with the predictable clerk at his back. Carey couldn't make him out either.

'I think you are hardly in a position to lecture me on the behaviour of a gentleman, Sir Robert,' he sneered nasally.

'Quite true, Mr. Vice,' Carey said. 'I find the presence of the man who tried to use my older brother against my father and then beat up my henchman does annoy me enough to make me forget my manners. What do you want?'

Heneage plumped himself down in the chair that Carey had just tripped over.

'You wished to speak to me, Sir Robert,' he said sourly. 'Her Majesty told me to come and so here I am.'

'I don't believe I did. You weren't a Privy Councillor in 1560 were you?'

'I was far too young. I didn't even come to Court until 1563.'

'Why are you here then?'

'Mrs. de Paris insisted as well.'

'Why?'

A pause. Heneage's voice when he spoke again was full of compressed fury. 'I know very well that you set your man Dodd to burn my Southwark house in complete defiance of Her Majesty's peace and…'

Carey managed a laugh, carefully measured for maximum insult. 'I certainly did not, Mr. Vice. I'm afraid I wouldn't have the balls. If, which is not admitted, Sergeant Dodd had anything to do with quelling the riot at your house caused by your negligent employment of deserted ex-soldiers and other riffraff, I'm sure he did it in order to preserve the Queen's peace, not break it.'

'Make him drop his lawsuit.'

Carey laughed again. 'Mr. Vice, you wildly overestimate my control over Sergeant Dodd. If he chooses to drop the lawsuit, he will and if not, then not. My interference would certainly not convince him to stop and may well provoke him to continue. I think you discovered what a stubborn independent man he is for yourself, didn't you?'

'The thumbscrews would have worked eventually,' said Heneage.

Carey paused because he was too furious to speak for a moment, though he kept the smile on his face. It might have become a little fixed.

'I doubt it, sir. Mr. Tovey, see Mr. Vice out…'

'I'm not going until I've told you what I need to.'

'Then perhaps you could come to the point? Hmm?'

Carey's fists were bunched in the sheets and if he hadn't been blind he might well have punched the bastard again. It was taking him an immense amount of effort not to jump out of bed and try anyway. Speaking in a voice lower than a shout was actually making his throat hurt.

'I wasn't at Court in 1560 but I…know someone. Someone the Queen set on to investigate the Robsart death before you, when she was in Oxford last time.'

It had been in 1566. Who had that been? Carey wondered at the back of his anger.

'So, give me Dodd and I'll tell you about him.'

Christ almighty, Carey realised distantly, is he just trying to provoke me or is he serious?

'Dodd is riding a stolen horse with the Queen's brand on him and no warrant. He shouldn't be hard to find. Tell me where you've told him to hide out and I'll do the rest.'

Carey's jaw was hurting from the way his teeth were clenched. Dear God, it was hard to sit still.

'Goodbye, Mr. Heneage,' he managed to say at last. 'I know you're accustomed to cheapening over men's lives. I am not.'

'He found out a lot, this man,' Heneage pursued. 'He's very good at it. He found out something he's never told.'

'What?'

The sound of a shrug. 'Give me Dodd and I'll give you him.'

If he says that again, I surely will hit him, Carey thought through the roaring noise of his temper in his ears. Also I don't know where Dodd is. He took the scarf off his eyes and squinted at the shadowed blur before him.

'Go, Mr. Heneage. Go now. Mr. Tovey?'

Tovey had already gone to the door and was speaking to someone standing outside. A large shape appeared in the candle dazzle, a smear of black-and-yellow Hunsdon livery.

'My lord Hunsdon left orders that his son wis no' to be annoyed,' said the Berwick tones of Ross, Hunsdon's sword-master who must have replaced Mr. Henshawe for the nightwatch. 'On account of it being a danger to his health and the health of the annoyers forbye. I hope your worship will see the sense in it.'

Heneage stood, walking out with his clerk. At the door, typically, he turned again to sneer.

'Why do you make your life so difficult, Sir Robert? My informer has made a good thing of what he found all those years ago.'

'It would be pointless trying to explain my reasons to you, Mr. Vice,' said Carey, 'since I would first need to explain to you the meaning of the words honour, loyalty, and friendship. Good night to you, sir.'

Ross gestured the man out and at last he went.

Carey leaned back on the pillows, feeling frighteningly weak and shaky. Fury was exhausting when you had to sit still and not hit anybody. He actually felt dizzy.

'Sergeant Ross, please don't let anybody else in until tomorrow.'

'Can't do that, sir, Mrs. de Paris is here to speak to you and she's brought supper from the Queen's own table. I can't keep her out.'

'I'm not hungry.'

'That's why I'm here,' came Thomasina's squeaky but extremely firm voice. 'The Queen sent me to be sure you eat all of it. She knows what you're like.'

'What I really need is a large tot of brandy...' Carey hinted.

'Not at all,' said Thomasina. 'Dr. Lopez was very clear about it. Nothing but mild ale for you to ease the strain upon your sanguine and choleric humours...'

'Christ!' roared Carey, 'If I could just see...'

'...which are clearly still disordered. And it's just as well you can't see, ain't it?' said Thomasina as she climbed onto the chair. 'Otherwise I'd be calling the cleaners to sweep away Heneage's teeth and balls, eh? What a fool that man is.'

A tray was placed on the bed next to him by her woman and good smells came from it to distract him. He recognised a mess of rhubarb and prunes which were clearly on prescription from Lopez who must have the usual doctor's faith in purging. He groped up a napkin and tied it round his neck to save his father's dressing gown as he ate.

'Who the hell was the bastard talking about?' he asked with his mouth full of pottage and bread. 'Do you know, mistress?'

'No, but I'm sure the Queen does and I'll ask her the minute you finish your dinner.'

'Did you get a record of that meeting, Mr. Tovey?'

'Y...yes, sir.'

'Good. Make a copy of it for my father. Make a copy of the meeting with Lord Burghley as well.'

'Yes, sir.'

'I'm impressed at your ability to keep my Lord Treasurer from his bed, Mrs. de Paris,' Carey admitted. 'When can I speak with the Queen?'

'When she chooses.'

Instead of protesting, Carey attacked a couple of very good braised quail in wine with his fingers and teeth. 'Why the devil is she being so coy?'

No answer from Thomasina. And the quail had been stuffed with prunes as well. Jesu, he'd have the squits soon. He felt carefully amongst the dazzle and found a penny loaf to mop up the sauce. It was enraging, having to fumble around for food and he snarled at Thomasina when she offered to feed him. He found the salat of autumn herbs was too messy to eat and he didn't like herbs much anyway, couldn't understand why the Queen seemed to be so addicted to them, ignored the goddamned rhubarb. Tovey brought a bowl and ewer over to him and he washed grease off his fingers and face. Please God he never got blinded permanently or ever again.

'I don't know how much more I can do before I'm better. I want to go and visit Cumnor Place,' he said to Thomasina. 'But I don't see the point if I can't see. Most of the people I want to talk to are dead or otherwise unavailable.'

The chief of those he wanted to talk to was, of course, the late Earl of Leicester. Despite what he had said to Burghley, Leicester was the second most likely suspect still.

'When's the Court removing to Oxford at last?'

'We're going privately to Woodstock palace tomorrow so that the Queen can rest for a few days and deal with business before she makes her full public entrance on Friday.'

'The word was that the Queen was in Oxford a month ago— why has it taken so long?'

'Yes, we were due in August, but they had some cases of suspected plague and we took a detour while the town was checked. That's why we've doubled back on ourselves from Rycote to Woodstock again. There haven't been any more cases in Oxford.'

'Where is Cumnor Place, by the way?' Carey asked casually as he absentmindedly picked up the horn spoon and started eating Dr. Lopez' medical dish. At least they had put sugar and spice in it.

'It's about ten miles from here, due south,' said Thomasina.

'And from Oxford?'

'About three miles, southwest. But the Queen would prefer you to wait until you're fully recovered.'

'Of course.' He drank more ale and then yawned. Thomasina clapped her little hands together briskly and a woman came and took the tray. He yawned again, rubbed his face.

'Sleep well, Sir Robert,' said Thomasina. 'I'll bring you more Privy Councillors to question in the morning.'

'Thank you, mistress,' said Carey, suppressing another yawn.

Once the door had shut behind her, he beckoned Tovey over to the bed and whispered to him very quietly. 'Would you do me a favour, Mr. Tovey? Would you take this ring to the Earl of Cumberland? I lost it to him yesterday at a very peculiar game of chess and only just remembered.' It was his ruby ring with his initials carved in it that the Queen had given him for daring to take the news of Mary Queen of Scots' execution into Scotland. He almost never hocked it. Tovey wouldn't know its meaning but Cumberland did and would almost certainly be game for what he purposed. Be damned to his blindness, horses have eyes, after all.

Bless him, Cumberland was there quickly, swaggering in wearing a particularly loud combination of red and tawny, no doubt for the masque Carey had missed.

'What's this I hear about you having been struck blind for general venery, Sir Robert?'

'Somebody put belladonna in my spiced wine last night. Was it you, my lord?'

'Damn, I never thought of that. Good idea, though. What were you playing at? You introduced my luscious Emilia to m'lord of Essex and next minute she's gone off with him and you're puking and raving all over the church. Completely wrecked my plans.'

'And mine. I'm sorry to tell you, my lord, that my eyes should get better soon enough but at the moment I can't see properly which is a confounded nuisance as I have a lot to do.'

'And what do you want me to do?' Cumberland sat on the side of the bed and gave Carey back his ring. 'Break you out again?'

'Yes, my lord,' said Carey and explained his plan.

The Earl put his head back and laughed. 'By God, Carey, I'll say this, you're reliably entertaining. Two hours before dawn do you?'

'Yes, my lord. Thank you.'

'The Queen will know by sun-up.'

'She can hardly complain when I'm simply obeying her own orders.'

'She most certainly can, as you know as well as I do. Never mind.

I'll see you tomorrow.' Cumberland laughed again as he walked out past Sergeant Ross. Carey beckoned the swordmaster over.

'Where's my father?'

'He went to Oxford as soon as he was sure you would recover, sir. He left about midday.'

Carey told Ross what he planned and why. 'I don't intend to try evading you if you want to stop me,' he told the man. 'But I hope you won't.'

'Your father ordered me to see you wisnae annoyed, sir,' Ross pronounced. 'Seems I'd be annoying you if I tried to stop you.'

'Exactly, Sergeant.'

'So I'll come with ye, sir.'

In the worrying absence of Sergeant Dodd, that was quite a comforting thought. Carey turned over and lay down in the welcome darkness of the curtained bed, only to have to get up again as Dr. Lopez's prescriptions did their work. Finally he got to sleep, and was grateful not to remember any dreams.

MONDAY 18TH SEPTEMBER 1592, MORNING

Somebody had left the door open and he was freezing cold, shivering. The blankets had crumbled to useless papery things and some evil bastard had clamped a black helmet over the whole of his head so it was hard to breathe or see because whoever had done it was hitting the helmet over and over with a hammer.

Dodd tried to turn over and punch him and somebody poked a gun in his ribs. His fingers felt for his knife and found nothing but goosebumped skin and some painful bruises, plus his knuckles hurt.

'Och,' he muttered and tried to open his eyes. They were clamped shut which froze his arse even more with fright. Was he blind? Blindfolded?

The banging on his head was getting worse now. Shaking, he put his hand up to his eyes and found crusting all over them and crusting around his nose which he thought might be broken. The bit at the end of his nose was bent. Damn it, somebody had broken his nose. Again.

Before he could think too much about it, he gripped his fingers on the bent part and twisted it back to where it belonged.

Bright white pain flared through the middle of his face and then faded down through red and violet to a dull brown. His nose was bleeding again but not too badly and he could breathe a bit better.

From the feel of them, his lips were busted and a front tooth was loose but not lost. Whoever had kicked him had done it more than once but not aimed well.

The wind was blowing a gale and he was freezing cold. With straining hard work he could turn over and curl up a bit in the rustling leaves and sticks and stones and bright spikes of bramble and twigs.

His mouth was shockingly dry. And he was naked. Bare as a peeled twig. That was why he was so cold. The bastards hadn't even left him a shirt to keep him decent.

Dodd lay still in the little dip full of leaves that his body had apparently crawled into by itself at some time during the night. Something of what had happened was coming back to him. He had been watering Whitesock and the mare at the stream and somebody had managed to creep up behind him and hit him... or more likely, drop on him from a tree. Ay, that was likely since his horses hadn't noticed anything. Stupid bloody soft Southron horses, no Northern hobby would have let anyone ambush him like that.

He thought he'd done his best, fighting in the fog of being hit on the head to start with, mainly by instinct. The front of his head was sore as well as the back so perhaps he'd managed to headbutt someone. He hoped so.

Lying in the darkness of his sealed eyelids in the little stand of coppiced hazels from the smell, Dodd felt the black ball of rage in him that never really went away. It was in the pit of his stomach, swelling. It worried part of him even though the heat of it was giving him strength.

Somebody—several somebodies—had dared to rob him and beat

him like a dog. They had taken everything. Carey's loaned suit, his boots, his shirt, his sword that he was fond of, his knife that he'd had since he was a boy and lost several times in mad card games or bets on horse races, but always won back, his hat, his nice new horses reived from Heneage himself...Christ, they'd even taken his underbreeks. And they must have spent quite some time kicking him once he was on the ground too, the bastards, though they'd made the mistake of failing to slit his throat while they had the chance and for that they would pay. All of them would pay. Firstly in money and fire, and then in blood as they died screaming and, if he was feeling merciful, he might not wipe out their entire families unto their babes and seventh cousins. Possibly. If they died painfully enough.

Rage was making his breath come short and he still couldn't get his blood-caked eyes open and find out if he really was blind. Though from the racket the bastard birds were making over his head, he knew it was probably dawn.

Cursing to himself he worked his tongue and snorted to get some spit up, then rubbed and peeled away some of the blood on his eyelashes. His head was full of metal from the blood smell. His whole body hurt, but he didn't think he'd broken any bones— maybe there was a rib busted from the way it hurt to breathe.

Obscurely he blamed the Deputy Warden. It had to be his fault for bringing him south from Carlisle and into foreign parts where they were barbarians and committed long-winded complicated suicide by beating him up and robbing him. Goddamn the bastards. And the Deputy and...

He actually heard the sticky sound as his eyelids parted and he could see past them into the world.

A lovely golden sunrise was stirring up the birds who were shouting at each other with no need at all, it being September. He hated them.

Slowly and carefully, Dodd sat up in the leaf litter and moss. He scraped his head on one of the hazel branches above and was chittered at by a squirrel with a nut in its mouth. Dodd reached for it to strangle it and stop the noise but it 'Kikikikkked' at him and escaped with a flirt of its russet tail.

While he waited trembling for all the various parts of him to stop banging and throbbing, he looked at the twigs above. There were cobnuts aplenty and more had fallen. He picked them out of the moss and broke them with his backteeth, ate a few. As the birds calmed down, he heard the sound of the stream nearby, which stood to reason since he couldn't have crawled very far.

His other eye wouldn't open properly because it was swollen. So he squinted his good eye and looked at his hands where the knuckles were raw and a cut in the web of skin between thumb and forefinger of his left hand so he had probably wrestled someone for a sword or dagger.

His knees and elbows were grazed, probably from crawling into the clump he'd been lying in through the damp cold night. Christ, he was cold. He pulled his knees up and wrapped his arms round them and shivered. He hadn't been this low since...Well, ever. He'd had uglier awakenings but never one more humiliating and lonely. Him! Henry Dodd, Land-Sergeant of Gilsland, husband of Janet, Will the Tod's red-headed Armstrong firecracker of a daughter, properly stolen from her father's tower one wild night and her laughing behind him on the galloping horse and her arms tight around his waist and her hands distracting him, ay, that was a warm thing to think of...Of course, lately he had been playing the part of a respectable gentleman in fine wool loaned him by the Courtier, but he was also the rightful winner of the feud between himself and Vice Chamberlain Thomas Heneage which counted for something. Him! Beaten up, stripped and left naked in a ditch to die of cold. They'd got his money too. Forged and true, they'd got the lot.

Jesus God, he was angry. His hands were shaking with it as well as the cold.

And he was affeared as well. What if the bastards came back to finish the job they had so foolishly left undone? What if they were working for Heneage? He didn't know who they were, mind, but if they came back...

He didn't know he was showing his teeth in a snarl. He wasnae deid yet and until he was, they were as good as dead themselves. Once he knew who they were.

All he could remember from the fog and rage of the fight was a flash of dirty orange and white. That was all. Not much to go on.

The sun was fully up now and starting to warm him a little but he sat and listened a little longer. Nothing at all except what you'd expect in a hazel wood turning over to autumn. A little rustling sounded like a blackbird; there were other brown birds still arguing in the further branches and from the sharp smell now attacking his slightly cleared nose, he'd used a fox run to get into the bushes.

Grunting with effort and his left hand cupped to keep his bruised tackle from brambles, Dodd eeled and crawled along the small stinking corridor through the dense brush until he shoved out into the morning sunlight by the banks of the stream.

The mud around it was well stirred up. Further away he could hear deer, nearby the animals had fled the man in their midst. Well he wasn't in a fit state to catch one for breakfast, so they could save their effort.

The brambles that had prickled him were heavy with berries so Dodd ate all he could reach of them and the riper cobnuts. Then he slipped and slid down the bank to the stream snickering at him over the stones of the little ford.

He looked about for tracks and signs very carefully. Yes, as he'd thought, there was a yew tree over the stream with a wide branch that hung over where he'd been watering his horse. Nobody there now, though the bark was scraped. He'd been unforgivably careless. The mud of the bank was rucked up, broken branches all around, a gash in the trunk of a willow tree where the horse had kicked. You could see there had been a fight.

Him against how many? Two? Three? Hard to tell with the way all the signs were over each other. He picked his way about the place on his tiptoes, squinting. There was a drier spot where the nettles were flattened and a few threads of grey wool caught on them. So that was where they must have laid him down while he was unconscious and stripped off his clothes. He could see where the heels of his boots had made dents in the soft mud and been dragged off by the bootprints of the man that did it. There was a scrap of good linen from his shirt there on a bramble.

Another scrap of thread, this time of a faded but once-virulent orange. Tawny they called it at Court. So he hadn't dreamed the orange and white clownlike clothes. Dodd felt the thread with his fingers—it was silky, so he kept it by wrapping it round his little finger like a ring. It might make a fishing line anyway.

It was easy to see which way the robbers had gone—at right angles to the stream, following a faint path but heading uphill, single file. Three, maybe four of them, and one very big and heavy, with big feet so it wasn't just something he was carrying. And unless Dodd had forgotten all he knew about tracking, that was the one who had reived his boots.

He found the deepest part of the stream, took a deep breath and waded in, stood there shivering with his toes clenching around the weed-covered stones while minnows investigated his heels. Then he carefully washed himself all over in the icy water, swearing and shivering at it until all the dirt and gravel was out of his various grazes and the blood from the blow to his head was out of his hair and beard and his eyes could open properly again, even the swollen one. His nose was still singing to him and his black eye had that stupid puffy stiff feeling. He drank deep of the water despite the way it made his teeth ache.

Just as he finished turning the water rust-coloured he noticed that the water coming toward him was swirling with little white clouds.

'Och,' he said quietly to himself.

He climbed out of the stream, careful of thorns in the leaf litter. Still shivering he squeezed his hair and shook himself all over like a dog, jogged on the spot and waved his arms. Jesu, he was cold, it was a sharp morning and had been a sharper night. He was hungry, too, despite the ball of rage in his stomach. He needed a fire by nightfall and since the bastards had taken his tinderbox along with everything else, that meant he had to find whoever was living upstream.

For a few seconds he stood looking at the blades of sunlight stabbing through the turning leaves and thought wistfully of the faeries magicking his own tower into reach and him going there and Janet putting salve on his grazes and bandaging his head for him and giving him another shirt and wrapping him warm by the fire in blankets of her own weaving. And him then calling out his surname and her surname and anyone else who owed him a favour and taking a fiery bloody revenge on anyone he could find in orange-and-white velvet.

Monday 18th September 1592,

Before Dawn

Carey and Cumberland were old hands at slipping away illicitly from the Queen's Court. When he arrived at the door of the small bedchamber, Cumberland found Carey was already awake and irritably instructing Tovey on the art of helping him dress. They hadn't lit any candles although the sky was overcast so the night was very dark. Carey however seemed to be able to see without difficulty.

Cumberland led the way out of the manor house and they picked their way over servants and page boys sleeping in all the corridors while their Courtier masters shared beds and had to dice for pallets in the bedrooms. The courtyard was filled with tents and tethered horses, four of them being led out by Kielder, the most discreet of Cumberland's grooms. Carey picked the second best mount out of deference to the Earl and unthinkingly jumped to the saddle.

'I thought you said you were blind?' accused Cumberland as Carey adjusted his stirrups.

'Only in daytime, my lord,' Carey said, highly pleased. 'I can see like an owl now.'

They walked the horses out through the gate, past the Yeoman of the Guard whom Cumberland had bribed, found the southward road and put their heels in.

After getting lost among the maze of lanes only twice, they found Cumnor Place was tidily kept but quite empty-looking in the grey dawnlight. There were no grooms hurrying about to feed horses, nor kitchen staff nor bakers, nor smoke from the chimneys. Hunsdon's excellent swordmaster, Nathaniel Ross, knocked on the least ivy-choked door. An elderly man slowly opened another door to one side of the house and came shuffling out to blink at them.

Carey was already squinting and shading his eyes though the sun wasn't up yet. Cumberland spoke to the man.

'Well,' he answered dubiously, 'You don't look like them sturdy beggars. What do you want?'

'Goodman,' Carey put in, 'my name is Sir Robert Carey and the

Queen has charged me with investigating a matter that happened here many years ago...' He handed down his warrant upside down and the old man didn't turn it.

'Ah yes, the death of Lady Dudley. I wasn't here then, sirs.'

'May we look around the house where it happened?'

'I'll have to ask my mistress, Mrs. Odingsells.'

'Is that the Mrs. Odingsells who attended Lady Dudley back then?'

'Yes, sir, nearing a hundred years now.'

'Are her wits...Is she able to talk to me?'

'Dunno, sir, I can but ask her. Sir Anthony Forster pays me and my wife to take care of her, sir, she won't leave. Says she likes it here and...well, I'll ask her.'

'Thank you, Mr....?'

'Forster, sir, I'm a cousin of Sir Anthony's.'

The kitchen door banged open and a clucking mass of chickens and ducks came out and spread themselves to peck at the overgrown cobbles of the yard, followed by a plump woman in an apron and cap.

Cumberland and his groom had already dismounted and Kielder took the horses and tethered them to a ring in the corner. When Carey dismounted as well, Cumberland saw that he was letting his horse lead him and he tripped on a pothole. The old woman following the fowl stopped still and stared with her mouth open, then started curtseying anxiously.

'S'all right, Mrs. Forster,' said the old man, 'They're from the Court, not the monastery. I'll just go ask the mistress.' He set off to a different door, still holding the warrant. While they waited, Carey cursed under his breath and wrapped a silk scarf around his eyes again.

Forster came back without the warrant. 'Mistress says she in't ready to receive you yet, sirs, but you can look to your heart's content.' His voice was deeply disapproving. 'Here's the keys cos it's all locked up.'

Carey clearly couldn't see where the old man was holding out the keys, so Cumberland came forward and scooped them up, offered Carey his arm to be led. Carey swore again and shook his head, but took it.

'Remind me never to go blind again, my lord,' he muttered through his teeth, ramming his hat down on his head to shade his eyes. It was very clear to Cumberland that his friend should have stayed in bed and given himself time to recover.

'I know what you're doing, Carey,' he said quietly. 'But why the hell are you doing it?'

'The Queen told me to, my lord.'

'Ah.' Cumberland started to whistle a very rude ballad about the Mother Superior of Clerkenwell Convent, that famous London bawdy house.

They walked across the courtyard, Carey tripping on a couple of chickens who were fighting each other over a slug, and Cumberland found the door that the old man had pointed to.

'According to all official accounts, this is where Amy Dudley fell down the back stairs from the long gallery, broke her neck and died,' Carey explained.

The door was swollen with damp and needed a firm shove from Cumberland's shoulder. Inside the stairwell the only light came from a large boarded trefoil window. Once in semi-darkness again, Carey took the scarf off and blinked around, looked up the famous staircase.

The steps went up along the wall from the small square hall, turned sharp left at a small landing, up again and right to a doorway. The stairwell had been built onto the end of the long gallery, probably for convenience so that family members could come straight out into the courtyard. The door they had come through was large and the stairs were in a line with it so they went forward, stepping carefully on the slippery stones spattered with white. There was a clatter of wings. Cumberland looked up and felt a chill down his neck as he saw little leather gloves hanging from the roof beams and a few bony heaps on the floor. The air was chokingly musty.

'Ugh,' he couldn't help saying. 'Bloody bats.'

Carey shrugged and went forward.

Had anybody been in here since they took Amy's body out and locked the door? Cumberland wondered. 'I expect it's haunted too,' he added, trying to make light of it. 'Stands to reason she'd walk.'

Carey said nothing to that either. Probably nobody had been here since the 8th September 1560. They must have locked the door and left it. Carey put his foot on the stairs, stamped a couple of times in case the wood was rotten, and went up to the turn. He stopped, blinked, peered to his right and started fumbling with the keys.

Cumberland had shaken himself like a dog and went up the stairs to find Carey opening another small door from halfway up which seemed the start of a small corridor. It was dark, lit only by what light came through the door behind them.

Carey went through the little door, having to stoop, and followed the narrow passage which led to another door. That one wasn't locked, only latched, but it hadn't been opened for a long time and creaked. Mainly because he didn't want to be on his own with a possible angry female ghost, Cumberland followed.

Carey was looking out into the dimness. They were high up in the high-beamed great hall of Cumnor Place, clearly also unused for decades, standing on the narrow musicians gallery. The small door they had come from must have been for the musicians' use, so they could come in from the back stairs and not bother the family or the rest of the household. Treading extremely carefully and looking out for holes, he stepped onto the gallery, creaked to the rail, and looked over. Cumberland followed, teeth bared.

Below, benches and trestle tables for feeding a large household were stacked against the panelling and spattered with white, the high walls festooned with old swallows' nests and the carved beams of the roof well-inhabited with creatures that rustled and moved. The lantern window gave only a little light due to ivy but some slats of wood were broken and a couple of pigeons fluttered out in a panic. Cumberland had a sensation of eyes watching him and hoped devoutly it was only rats.

'A desolation and an habitation of owls,' Carey quoted conversationally to the Earl who nodded without commenting in case his voice shook. They went back to the door they had come through and along the short corridor that connected with the stairs leading up to the long gallery.

Once back on the landing at the turn of the stairs, Carey looked about him carefully. Cumberland took his tinderbox out, but Carey touched his arm.

'No need, my lord, I can see better without it.'

'Damn it's dark in here,' said the Earl. 'Are you sure?'

'Quite sure.'

'What if she...er...'

'If Amy Robsart's ghost turns up, I'll be delighted, my lord. I'll be able to ask her directly who killed her and save myself some trouble.'

Cumberland knew his short laugh wasn't very convincing. He was starting to sweat as Carey stood still and looked about. Why wasn't he getting on with it, whatever it was?

Suddenly Carey moved. He went up the steps and touched something on the wall at a little lower than his chest height.

'Look at this, George,' he said in a soft voice full of suppressed excitement.

Cumberland was doing his best not to think of the rustling bats above and the probable rats below. He didn't mind rats, didn't like bats....What if the rustling wasn't bats? What if it was...? What was that? Carey's sudden movement had made his heart thud, and he followed his friend, felt the small round hole Carey had somehow seen.

Well, that certainly was interesting. They both knew—from the way the edges of the hole were punched inward but the wood not broken—exactly what it was.

Carey was looking about for the bolt, but found nothing. He put his finger in the hole, followed its flight down the stairs to the turn where they had been standing, with the door to the minstrels' gallery behind them.

Carey's eyes narrowed and he stepped backwards through the small door again, looked up, blinked and smiled.

'Would you give me a boost, my lord?'

Sighing, Cumberland went through the door, couldn't see anything at all up above the wall which Carey seemed to find of interest. He went on one knee and let Carey use his thigh as a step, which was less painful than using his cupped hands for the boost.

Nobody had bothered to finish plastering the musicians' corridor. Above where the wall ended on the inside was the darkness of the roofspace and beams above. Carey had caught one of the supporting beams there and was pulling himself up into the space, knocking down choking dust and mummified owl pellets in a rain on Cumberland.

There was a triumphant 'Hah!' Either Carey had taken leave of his senses or he had found something. There was a clatter, a grunt from Carey, scraping, and then the madman dropped back to the floorboards with something large in his hand.

That something was a crossbow. It was probably brother, or more likely grandfather, to the crossbow that had been fired at the two of them at the duckpond the day before; a large hunting bow, no need for a windlass to wind it up if you had the strength to bend it, but very lethal.

'What the...'

'This was hidden behind one of the roofbeams, hooked on a nail.'

Carey was triumphant, holding the rusted thing, covered in nameless white and black stuff, insects and spiders bailing out as fast as they could. He waved it, set it to his shoulder, and took aim at the hole in the wall that Cumberland could no longer see. Cumberland's gorge suddenly rose because he had looked at the other end of the bow. It was dented, some small threads caught in the splintered wood there.

Carey saw it too and his eyes narrowed as he looked carefully at the place where the steel of the bow crossed the wood of the stock. To Cumberland's horror he pulled off a couple of the caught threads, put them carefully in a leather purse he kept in his doublet sleeve pocket.

'Hmm.' he said.

'Jesu,' was all Cumberland could say.

'According to the inquest report, before she broke her neck, Amy was already dead from two large dents in her head, one two inches deep, the other one inch deep.' They both looked at the crossbow. 'See here? He fired at her, missed, then when she tried to run past him and out the door, he hit her on the back of the head with the crossbow hard enough to kill her. The stock itself made the two-inch dent, the metal bow the one-inch dent.'

'Jesu.'

In the pause, Cumberland thought that now if ever would be the moment for Amy's ghost to show herself. But she didn't. All the movement came from Carey who leaned the crossbow, stock down, against the wall and went up the second set of steps, turned right at the top of the second set of steps where there was a much larger carved door.

Another search through the keys eventually found the one that opened it and they looked into a very fine long gallery running above the wing of the manor house that adjoined the hall. That, too, had shuttered windows but it seemed in better condition, though it was dusty and smelled pungently of mice and rats. Thank God there were no bats. Somehow it didn't...feel haunted.

Carey was frowning. 'So. Somebody shot at her with the crossbow, she tried to get out the door at the bottom of the stairs, which meant she had to run past him, and that's when he hit her with the crossbow.'

Cumberland nodded. It made sense of a gruesome kind.

Carey stepped out into the long gallery where Amy Dudley had walked on rainy days and probably practised dancing. He paced all the way to the end, where there was another locked door, blinking rapidly when he passed a window that let daylight squeeze through the shutters. The portraits and hangings that must have been there once had long since been taken away. Only the things built in were still there, like the window seats and the carved linenfold panels on the walls.

Carey moved purposefully back to the long gallery door onto the back stairs. They stood looking down into the entrance hall.

'Right, George. I'm Amy...'

'And very pretty you are, too...'

'Thanks, my lord,' said Carey drily. 'You are the assassin.'

'Grr.'

'So you stand inside the musicians' door until you hear the sound of my steps.'

Cumberland did as he was asked with great theatricality. Carey came down the stairs slowly, stopped on the landing. Cumberland stepped out from the musicians' door, aimed an imaginary crossbow because he didn't feel like picking up the one that probably killed Amy Dudley.

'Kerchunk!' he said, firing an invisible bolt at Carey.

'By some fortune, you miss at point-blank range and I see you. Then I run *down* the stairs past you...'

Carey came down the stairs past Cumberland who mimed hitting him on the head with the imaginary crossbow.

'And down she goes and breaks her neck in the bargain,' finished Carey looking annoyed. 'It's wrong. It can't be right.'

'Makes sense to me.'

'But why would she run past the doorway where a man was standing who had just tried to kill her? She could have turned and run up to the long gallery again, screaming blue murder and escaped through the door at the other end.'

'Tried to fight him?'

'Don't be ridiculous, my lord, she's a woman.'

'My wife would.'

'Your lady wife is made of stronger stuff.'

'Your lady mother would, too.'

Carey sighed. 'All right. I don't know where the dents on her head were, back or front. They might have been on the...No, the inquest report would have said so, said they were on her face, not her head. She must have run past him...no.' Carey shook his head irritably.

'What's the problem? You've found the murder weapon. Amy Robsart was killed by someone who tried to shoot her with a crossbow bolt and then used the crossbow to bludgeon her when he missed. You should be pleased. You've solved a thirty-year-old mystery.'

'No, I haven't, I've made it worse.'

'How?'

'For God's sake, my lord, why didn't she run back into the long gallery?'

'Panicked?'

'When you panic, you run away from the danger, not straight past it!'

'Not necessarily,' said Cumberland who believed he had never panicked in his life.

'You do!' Carey went back to the small door and looked at it again, seemingly found nothing that pleased him. He went back up to the long gallery door, opened the door, looked through it, locked it again, came down the stairs, counting them, checked the bolt hole in the panelling, went past Cumberland and clattered on down the stairs to the bottom. Through the open door to the courtyard, they could see Forster waiting for them.

MONDAY 18TH SEPTEMBER 1592, MORNING

Dodd decided to take a closer look at the clear trail left by the robbers before it rained or something. He knew he was conspicuous in his unpeeled state and also completely unarmed, but he needed to move to keep warm and he might as well do that by finding out more about his enemies.

He found the narrow path again with the footprints and some hoofprints from Whitesock, a tail hair on a branch. The path turned, went two ways. Upstream there was a dog turd, downstream the footpads' feet, and Whitesock's hooves continued in a different direction, heading south.

Dodd went carefully and quietly along the path by the stream. His feet told him that the path had once been a better-made road because it had smooth blocks of stone in places, some robbed out, some covered in weeds. It wasn't as deep down as the Giants' Road up on the borders, though. He bent to look at the stones more carefully. One was freshly chipped by a shod horse's hoof.

He carried on up the path, his feet already prickling and sore from the stones and twigs. Once the soles of his feet had been like leather, when he was a wild boy, but he still knew how to go quietly.

He smelled them first. There were men somewhere up ahead, smoking.

His nose tingled. He recognised that smell. The bastards had stolen his pipe and expensive henbane of Peru, mixed with that magical Moroccan incense that made the world soft-edged and his rage far away. He scowled. Jesu, what he would give for a pipe and some smoke to drink.

He slipped among the stands of bracken and gone-over shepherd's purse and mallow. There had been buildings here once, the path had a tumbled masonry wall beside it and a great multi-trunked yew tree growing from it.

It was a while since he'd needed to do it, being senior enough now that he could send Bessie's boy or Bangtail up a tree for him, but you never forgot how. He circled the tree to be sure there weren't any crows in it, found a place to start. He hoisted himself up onto a branch and then climbed slowly to the crown of the tree, and then out along a branch where he lay down and got his breath with the sun dappling on his bare back.

They were sloppy. Imagine leaving a tree that gave an overview of their tower? It wasn't a tower of course; they didn't have those in the soft South. Below he could see crooked flat stones and lumps of stone sticking out of the earth at angles. Ahead was another well-robbed wall. Beyond that was...

Once it must have been a small monastery, a hive of industry, no doubt, full of monks. The roof was gone and the walls showed the old blackening of fire and the green flourish of plants breaking it apart. Perhaps the monks had rebelled against King Henry's men and so been burned out. That had happened in other places.

By squinting and leaning over, Dodd could just make out the two men standing on a bend in the path. It wasn't so hard. Every so often puffs of smoke went up from them and he could hear quiet talk.

Past them, further on, where the monastery gatehouse must have been, there were signs of thatch having been added to some of the building which was roughly planked along one side.

Dodd nodded to himself. They had a bolthole, that was why they were so bold. Who was their headman? He'd give a lot to know that and his surname. For a moment he thought about carrying on round the place and working out where the weak spots were.

He was more tempted to stay in the tree and wait for nightfall and then go in quietly and slit some throats. It was a very attractive thought, but in the end that would be stupid. He might well slit a few throats but at some stage someone would wake up or catch him and it stood to reason there were a lot more of them and then they wouldn't make the same mistake again.

Sighing, he climbed very carefully down the tree, sliding a little on the flaky bark, then retraced the path upstream. He stopped at the ford to drink as much as he could. He wasn't hungry anymore, the ball of rage in his gut was food enough really, as it had been in the past.

Then while he was drinking, he heard the rattle of dog paws trotting down the path toward him, smelled the dog himself too who was panting and snortling on a trail, and he heard a high voice speaking to the dog.

He stood still and thought for a second. He already knew there were people upstream who had goats or maybe even a milch cow. Why would they come down the path with dogs?

There was one obvious answer. Would he run or would he meet them? That was obvious too. He looked about for a soft place and when he'd found somewhere behind a bush without too many thistles and brambles, he lay down there, curled up and shut his eyes.

MONDAY 18TH SEPTEMBER 1592, MORNING

Once out in the early morning sunlight, Carey shaded his eyes and cursed, then irritably wrapped his scarf round them again, rammed his hat back on his head.

'Mrs. Odingsells will see you now, sir,' said the man, 'Though she's not very happy, I'll tell you. It's a good thing you're not a black-haired man, is all I can say.'

'I am,' said Cumberland.

'You're too young, sir, both of you are, Mrs. Odingsells was very particular about it.'

They followed Forster in through the door to the opposite wing where the great doors to the hall were and then up a larger set of stairs that led on to a corridor in the inhabited part of the house.

They went into a chamber with a very large curtained bed,

with the curtains pulled back and the shutters half open. The smell of old lady in the room was not too bad, Cumberland thought, quite similar to the Queen's under all the rosewater, although the chamberpot was clearly unemptied.

Propped up on the linen pillows was a bony form in a knitted jacket and embroidered cap. Her hair was white, her eyes yellowed and milky with cataracts, and her beak the most powerful part of her face which had mostly fallen away back to the skull. Carey's warrant lay on the bed, now right way up.

'So Her Majesty is trying again, is she?' she demanded in a stronger voice than Cumberland expected.

'Er...yes, mistress,' said Carey, sweeping off his hat in a bow, removing the scarf.

'Sit down, sit down, both of you boys. What's your name?'

'Sir Robert Carey, mistress,' he explained, 'seventh son of my lord Baron Hunsdon, Chamberlain to...'

The old woman had sucked in a breath.

'Henry Carey?'

'Yes, mistress.'

'Why isn't he here then, eh?'

'I'm not sure, Mistress Odingsells, I think he's supervising the Queen's move to Oxford on progress.'

'I didn't like the man she sent last time she was there, whatsisname? Slimy villain for all his fancy gown.'

Carey had sat on the chair by the bed, Cumberland modestly took the clothes chest by the door, the better to escape if necessary.

'Kept shouting at me and hectoring and then offering money. Stupid man. Must have been a very good liar to get the job. So. What do you want, my lad? *I* didn't see who did it, you know. I was playing cards, God forgive me.'

'Do you know the man's name? The one who questioned you before?'

The wrinkled lips pinched together, then smacked apart.

'No, and I'll have forgotten yours by tomorrow. Ugly tall man, black hair and eyebrows, one of Lord Shrewsbury's crew, I think. The Queen was at Oxford.'

'Well, can you tell me the story of Lady Dudley's last few days?'

'I can,' said the old lady and shut her lips.

Carey smiled. 'Please will you, mistress?'

'Perhaps. Why should I?'

'I have a warrant from Her Majesty.'

The old lady lifted the warrant and squinted at it from the side of one eye. 'Queen's seal, give aid and so on. Yes. So what? Might be a forgery.' Carey said nothing. 'And why would she want it all dug up again after thirty years?'

'I don't know, mistress,' said Carey with surprising humility. 'She won't tell me. She won't tell me anything, which is extremely annoying.'

The old lips stretched in a smile.

'It's a puzzle isn't it? And the man most folk say was the murderer died four years ago.'

'Do you mean my lord of Leicester?'

'Of course,' said Mrs. Odingsells, 'Who else? Not Sir Richard Verney nor Bald Butler as the Papist book said, they weren't anywhere near. And yet it wasn't right.'

Cumberland was suppressing the urge to shout 'Stop talking riddles!' Mind you, it would be interesting to hear about the thing that changed the Queen's life forever from someone who was there. Not as interesting as a sea battle, but still interesting.

'Mistress, please, would you tell me the tale, starting with about a week before, around the 1st September 1560?'

The old lady shut her eyes. 'I suppose I'll get no peace until I do.'

'I'm afraid not, mistress.'

The eyes snapped open. 'Well the last thing I want is peace. So there!'

'Yes,' said Carey quietly, 'It's very dull being blind, isn't it? A... an accident happened to my eyes on Saturday and I own I have never been so utterly undone with tedium as since then.'

She laughed a little. 'What's wrong with 'em? French pox?'

'Someone put belladonna into my wine.'

'Tut. You see, that was why I always thought it couldn't have been my lord of Leicester. Yes, Sir William Cecil had a man placed in the kitchens, but it would have been easy enough to get round him and do the deed.'

'I think so too,' Carey said.

'Hmm. Good. Why didn't you die?'

'I was very lucky, mistress. Or perhaps I should say that God must have watched over me?'

That's right, thought Cumberland, give it a bit of Godly piety, that should unlock the old oyster.

'Hah! Such arrogance. So why didn't He watch over poor Amy?'

'I don't know, mistress. I'm not privy to His counsels. Perhaps God never meant Her Majesty to marry, as she says now.'

There was a cynical look on Mrs. Odingsell's face. 'So why didn't He find a way that didn't mean killing poor Amy?'

'In fact, you might say, in order to stop the Queen marrying Leicester, God only had to keep Amy alive.'

Mrs. Odingsells slowly shook her head, looking pleased with herself.

'Not necessarily.'

'What do you mean?' Carey's voice had gone down to a murmur.

'Something was afoot. Something…I didn't know. A messenger arrived from my lord Leicester and put Amy all in a tizzy. She ordered a new gown from her tailor and then when a new message came before it was ready, she sent me into Oxford to have her best velvet gown refashioned, to put gold brocade on the neck. She wouldn't let me read any of the letters. She burnt them. Then she wrote three herself, though her penmanship was poor. I thought Leicester was planning to visit her but…'

'Did he?'

Again the slow shaking of her head. 'He hadn't seen her for months. A year maybe. *He* didn't visit her.'

Cumberland missed the inflection but Carey didn't.

'Who did visit her?'

There was a very long silence while Cumberland said nothing and rather thought Carey was actually holding his breath.

'According to the inquest papers, she wanted the house empty for the day,' Carey prompted finally. 'She sent everyone else to the fair at Abingdon, but you refused to go and she was angry about it.'

'I knew poor Amy was terribly worried about something. It was very important. But she never killed herself, she wouldn't do that, no matter what wicked men say. Never never. Amy was a good Christian woman, she spent hours on her knees praying for the wisdom to judge rightly.'

Another long pause.

'She did love her husband, you see,' creaked the old voice sadly, 'In spite of everything. She loved him. She knew he didn't love her, never really had, and she knew he was completely enchanted by the Queen but...she still loved him.'

Carey was tense as he sat, poised. Cumberland had to admire his patience and wondered where he'd got it.

'As for going to the fair...' The old creaky voice was far back in the past. 'The youngsters were all for it, I wasn't. I liked peace and quiet then. Go to Our Lady Fair at Abingdon on that Sunday... No! I don't think so. Only the ungodly would go to a fair on a Sunday. There was to be a football match as well and why should I watch something so boring and unseemly?'

To Cumberland's surprise, Carey didn't explain to her what fun football was—but then no woman could possibly understand such things. Even his wife thought football was a waste of time.

'I refused to go and we had an argument about it. Mrs. Owens was going to stay with her but Mrs. Owens was deaf as a post and not too firm in her wits. Amy screamed at me that I would spoil everything, but I held fast and then finally she told me...She was meeting two courtiers. She would not say why but the meeting was vitally important. So I offered to help her dress for it and at last she said I could stay so long as I never moved from the parlour, on my honour.' There was a long creaking sigh. 'And I never did, till it was too late.'

'Do you know who were...'

'The two courtiers? One was your father, Henry Carey, the other one of the Queen's women. I didn't know them, of course.'

'Did you see them?'

Mrs. Odingsells nodded. 'Through the window of the parlour, through the glass so I couldn't make out the faces. I saw Amy curtsey low to them, call the man my lord Hunsdon. He helped the lady-in-waiting down from her horse and they went up to the Long Gallery to speak.

'I played cards with Mrs. Owens, trying not to listen. I didn't leave the parlour as I had promised.'

'What did you hear?'

A heavy frown and her lips puckered, a movement deeply carved into her mouth and chin.

'I heard nothing, they must have been talking quietly. Then doors opening and then a sound...a crack. A cry. Feet. Something like a cook splitting a cabbage. Then a woman's voice crying, screaming 'No! Oh no!' Scraping, thudding. A man's shout. Running feet. Then a long pause and I looked at Mrs. Owens who hadn't heard a thing and said, 'What was that?' and she shrugged and bet me a shilling that the next card would be low.

'Then I heard nothing more and as there were no more cries and I was annoyed at losing four shillings to Mrs. Owens who was not a good player, I didn't do anything until I heard the hooves galloping away.'

'What did you see of the lady-in-waiting?'

'She was wearing forest green with a brown velvet gard along the kirtle hem, I think. Quite a plain hunting dress. She had a headtire and a linen cap on her head and under it black hair as far as I could tell. She had...she was very pale.'

'And you didn't know her?'

'Neither of them, they were blurred by the glass. I only knew your father because of Amy greeting him by name.'

Carey rubbed his temples. 'Mrs. Odingsells,' he said very softly, 'did you ever find out who the lady-in-waiting was?'

Another long pause. 'I guessed eventually. After the inquest.'

'And?'

'I will die before I tell you or anybody. That's what I said to the evil black-haired bastard that came and tried to bully me in 1566 and I say it to you. So now.'

Carey took breath to speak, to argue with her.

'I'm an old woman,' shouted Mrs. Odingsells, partly sitting up in bed. 'I'm old but I know you, Mr. Topcliffe, I've lived too long but anything you try with me will kill me anyway so you can do as you like and be damned to you!'

There was spittle on her lips. Carey stayed where he was.

'Mistress, I'm not Richard Topcliffe.'

'Get out and be damned...! You're not?'

'No, mistress. Sir Robert Carey.'

'Oh.'

'What did Topcliffe do?'

'He was here before, the last time the Queen was at Oxford, when I was still young and could still see. He came and questioned me and he asked the same questions as you, but when I wouldn't answer, he shouted and roared and threatened. Nothing came of his threats however, and he didn't get what he came for. Oh no.'

Carey was leaning forward, his elbows on his knees, squinting at Mrs. Odingsells who had her hands clasped to her breast. As far as Cumberland could make out in the dimness, Carey was pale.

'What were the courtiers discussing with Lady Dudley?'

The bony old shoulders lifted and dropped. 'They didn't tell me.'

Carey's eyes narrowed. 'But you know?'

Mrs. Odingsells said nothing. Cumberland listened to her breathing as Carey let the silence stretch, but Mrs. Odingsells was too old to be worried by it and simply glared back at him.

At last Carey tilted his head in acknowledgement. 'Is there anything else, anything at all you can tell me of that day?'

'It was a nightmare after we found her, I couldn't believe she was... There were people all over the place, coming and going, messengers to the Court, to Sir Anthony, to my lord of Leicester. The undertaker came from Oxford with his best hearse to pick up Amy and most of the village was there gawking and getting in the way, trampling about in the gardens and orchard and stealing apples and quinces. Dreadful. They buried her in one of the colleges of Oxford and the inquest spent a year debating what had happened. Pah!'

'That's a very long time for an inquest?'

'Well the foreman of the jury was one of the Queen's own men so you couldn't expect them to come up with anything other than they did, but the rest of the jury was decent solid men from this county. And then...' She paused and looked as if she was about to add something else but whatever it was, she shook her head again and shut her eyes.

'I'm tired now, Mr. Top...Carey, please leave.'

'Yes ma'am,' said Carey with surprising meekness, stood up and went to the door. Cumberland followed him. 'Thank you for speaking to me. If there is anything more you want to say...'

'Yes. Tell your father that I would like something tidied up. I cannot control what will happen to my possessions when I die, which will be soon, please God. Be sure you tell him to come here himself as I will speak to none other, not even you. Good-bye.'

As Carey made a Court bow to the old lady, Cumberland could make out the milky eyes, wide open, staring hard at him, assessing.

Once back in the corridor and the bedchamber door shut, Carey went along the corridor to the carved door at the end, opened it. There was the long gallery, seen from the other end, their own footsteps in the dust. Carey shut it again, felt his way back with his eyes squeezed shut in the light from the small windows along the courtyard side.

Then he stood, staring down the great stairs for what seemed an hour. Cumberland had no idea what was going on in his friend's head except it seemed to be making him absentminded.

'Do you know who was the lady-in-waiting with your father?' he asked, more to break the silence than anything else. Carey started slightly and squinted at him.

'I'm not sure.'

'But you suspect...?'

'There's a family story. My father's sister, my Aunt Katherine, was one of the Queen's senior ladies-in-waiting, and there was a story about a green hunting kirtle of hers being somehow damaged a month or two after I was born.'

'You think it was your aunt?'

Carey paused. 'Yes, I do. But not my Aunt Katherine.'

For a moment Cumberland couldn't work out the inference and when he did he sucked in his breath as if he'd been punched in the stomach. Only not with surprise because, after all, there had to be something like that going on.

Carey's father, Henry's by-blow and the Queen's half-brother, had brought Elizabeth Tudor to Cumnor Place, disguised in her half-sister's plain hunting kirtle, probably wearing a black wig. The Queen had been at Cumnor Place on the morning of the

8th September 1560, the day her rival Amy Robsart had been killed.

Carey found he was gripping the banisters with his left hand, the fingers of his other pressed hard into his temples to try and ease the headache. Something inside him was fighting to be heard. After a moment he breathed deeply and relaxed because this still wasn't the answer.

How could the Queen possibly benefit if her lover's wife was killed by a crossbow bolt, especially if she was actually present? The Queen was the sharpest, most intelligent woman he had ever met, apart from Elizabeth Widdrington. Would she set an assassin with a crossbow to kill Amy Robsart and actually be there to watch? The idea was ridiculous.

He shook his head again and groped his way slowly down the stairs, followed by a silent Cumberland. As they went into the courtyard and he tied the scarf on again, pulled the brim of his hat down against the sunlight, he said quietly,

'I don't need to tell you to keep quiet about this, my lord.'

'Christ, no!' said Cumberland with feeling, offering Carey his arm again. 'I've forgotten already. You deal with it. I'd rather take on three Dutch sea-beggar fighting ships in a rowing boat.'

'Thank you, my lord.'

'Please don't mention it again,' Cumberland said firmly and beckoned for Kielder to bring up the horses. Carey called Ross over and the swordmaster went over to the stairwell where Amy had died, came back with a heavy sack.

'Where are we going now?' Carey asked as he felt for his horse's girth to tighten it.

'I've had men at Oxford setting up an encampment in a field north of the city wall, just past that alehouse with the good cider. It's handy for the Schools and Balliol, there's a stream and it's not too marshy. We'll stay there.'

'Why not in one of the colleges?'

'Don't be wood. Unless you fancy going three in a bed with strangers...'

'No, my lord,' said Carey, climbing into the saddle with much more effort than usual. He was suddenly infernally tired, was thinking longingly of going to bed, alone, and staying there. 'I've done that.'

Cumberland laughed.

It was only three miles to the outskirts of Oxford but by then Carey's head was having nails pounded into it by invisible carpenters. The bedlam of Oxford's streets didn't help. The High Street, Cornmarket, and Broad Street were filled with scaffolding, stages, fences, and the noise of hammering and shouting made Carey feel physically sick again. He set his teeth, drove his horse on and let the animal follow Cumberland's lead. At some stage the Earl must have quietly put a leading rein on the animal, which was humiliating, but otherwise Carey didn't know how he could have stayed with the party. At last they turned aside through a gate and Cumberland shouted for grooms. Carey slid from the saddle, forced his knees straight and stood holding onto the horse's reins, the world dissolving into a bedazzlement of light and noise that he could make no sense of. The horse dipped his head and nudged him, nickered with concern.

'Are you all right, Carey?' It was the Earl's voice.

'Yes. No.' He had to admit it. 'I need to rest.'

More bellowing by Cumberland, who seemed to think there was a gale blowing, and a man with a comforting Glasdale accent arrived to lead Carey to a tent behind the main ruckus, and to a pallet laid on a bed of sweet rushes. The man helped Carey with his doublet and boots, helped him to drink more mild ale and gave him a magnificent bear fur rug which he pulled over his head to keep out the light.

Despite the frightening exhaustion of his body and the pounding in his head, Carey's mind was whirling. Could the Queen have got to Cumnor Place that day? If she had been hunting at Windsor Castle, she most certainly could. In her late fifties she could still ride like the wind for hours and leave her courtiers behind in the hunt. Windsor to Cumnor was only thirty miles and with a remount she could have done the distance in a few hours. But why? For what conceivable reason could she have disguised herself in Aunt Katherine's hunting kirtle and ridden out with his father to see her lover's wife?

Not to kill the woman. That didn't make sense. Thirty years

ago, the Queen had been much younger, of course, so probably more impatient, more ruthless, less cautious...but...

Unlike Mary Queen of Scots, she had a brain. He couldn't believe she had plotted to kill Amy. Although Henry VIII had committed judicial murder of inconvenient women at least twice in his marrying career, Carey couldn't believe it of the Queen. Not for morality's sake, but for expediency. What a king could get away with, a queen couldn't, as the Queen of Scots had proven.

He needed more evidence, and to talk to more people. Could Thomasina fetch him Topcliffe? Would Topcliffe tell him the truth if she did?

And he simply must do something about finding Dodd, who must either have headed straight for the Border with his loot or got into serious trouble. If ever he needed to be up and about, now was the time and his bloody eyes and head and body weren't cooperating.

And who had poisoned him? Emilia? Surely not. Hughie? Unlikely. Someone unknown? Why? Emilia perhaps? He knew his father would have taken care of the lad and intended to find him as soon as he could, ask a few questions. He would be sure to warn the Earl of Essex, though there was no chance Emilia would try to poison the Earl. However, it would be embarrassing for everyone if other bidders for the management of the farm of sweet wines suddenly started dropping dead.

Carey awoke once into daylight, heart pounding. Sunlight was shining through the canvas of the tent, he could see the shadow of a man sitting by the flap and another on the other side to stop anyone coming in that side. Although the painful light made him shut his eyes immediately, he smiled, quite comforted. George Clifford had a simple view of most things and a mysterious assassin was one of them. You put men in the way.

Something had woken him. Something loud in his mind, but there was no sign from the two men on guard that there had been a real noise of a blade slicing through a neck....And his heart was beating like a drum, his shirt drenched, cold shivers down his legs.

Christ! It was the half-remembered fever dream from Saturday night. Or no, it was another installment of it. He had been shaving himself carefully in a small mirror in…Yes, definitely a stone cell, though quite well lit. His hand was steady, but looking into the mirror he had seen an older man, hair retreating a little up his temples, streaks of grey in the chestnut, a pouchiness to his face that he had seen in men who drank too much too often. His shirt collar was frayed and had been badly darned. He was facing the axe, he knew it, was sad about it but not angry. He had made many stupid mistakes and had unforgivably let himself be talked into rebelling against his royal cousin and aunt. He could not quarrel with the sentence, only hoped the headsman would be good at his job. If only Elizabeth Widdrington…The face in the mirror stopped pulling the razor over the sides of his face and just stood staring. If only he had married Elizabeth Widdrington.

Then it was as before, the shock his watching self felt at the worn green velvet doublet, the glitter and swing of the axe, the sound that had woken him…

He was sitting up now, all the hairs on his body prickling upright. Was that why he rebelled? Because he didn't marry Elizabeth Widdrington? Why hadn't he? It was the one thing he wanted most in the world, he was quite clear he would trade anything at all save his honour for her. Had she turned him down? Had she died?

Was this a prophecy from God? Had he been sent a warning? What was he supposed to do with it?

Slowly the strange feelings down his legs and in his heart calmed and faded, leaving him exhausted again. He didn't like sleeping during the day but he didn't want to get up. What was he supposed to do? What did God want?

He knelt on his pallet with his eyes tight shut against the light. As he couldn't think what to say to God, he just recited the Lord's Prayer and hoped the bit about leading him not into temptation would do the job, whatever it was.

Of course, it was clear that the Queen would consider accusing her of being the actual killer of Amy Dudley as treason plain and simple. Would she have him executed? Perhaps not, although the Tower was a distinct possibility. But he didn't think that of her because it didn't make sense, even if the Queen actually was at Cumnor Place when it happened.

He growled softly to himself with frustration, lay down again and instantly fell asleep.

Then somebody prodded him awake and he blinked into the dazzle at a small person in a small but stunning cherry red-and-gold wheel farthingale with a tiny black doublet bodice and a raised cambric ruff behind her head like a saint's halo.

'Well, Sir Robert,' came Thomasina's voice, 'What have you been up to?'

'Ah um...' moaned Carey, wishing his head would stop pounding. He shut his eyes against Thomasina's outfit. 'I'll tell you, Mrs. Thomasina, on condition you stop any other bastard waking me up and let me sleep.'

'Certainly,' she said.

And so he told her the whole story of what he had found at Cumnor Place and what Mrs. Odingsells had told him, including her wish to see his father. He didn't say anything about what he thought of the matter. Thomasina sat perfectly still while he spoke and then nodded once. She settled back on her cushion with her legs crossed and he heard the click of ivories as she started playing dice with herself. No doubt it was her full set of crooked dice, highman, lowman, bristleman, quite hypnotic. His eyes fell closed again and he slept.

MONDAY 18TH SEPTEMBER 1592, MORNING

Dodd waited, forcing himself to breathe slowly in the prickling leaves and stones. There was a crunch of wooden clogs, but quite light, perhaps not a man...The dog was snortling about and came right over to Dodd. He stayed still where he lay, let the animal sniff him all over, heart beating.

A wet nose thrust into his face and started licking his face, chin to forehead, slobbering his beard hairs the wrong way.

'Ach, awa' wi' ye!' he complained and shoved the dog off. The dog put his paws on Dodd's shoulders and panted in his face, so Dodd stayed where he was and reached out to pat the dog's hairy flank. 'Ay, what d'ye want?'

'Goodman,' said a girl's voice on the other side of the bushes, 'Are you all right?'

'Eh…nay, lass, Ah've got nae clothes nor gear and yer hound's droonin' me…'

Silence. Then: 'Are you a foreigner?'

Dodd sighed deeply and said it again more Southern, which hurt his lips and face.

'Oh. Are you very much hurt?'

Considering the battering he'd taken, he'd been very lucky with only a possible busted rib and nose. But…

'Ay, Ah think ma leg is broken.'

'Oh no, I'm so sorry. The robbers must have jumped you at the ford, didn't they?'

'Ay,' Dodd said, thinking fast, 'Ah'm no' a pretty sight for a lass. Ha' ye any breeks wi' ye?'

After more tiring translation, a bag was thrown over the bushes and in it Dodd found a rough hemp shirt and woollen breeches. He pulled them on at once, hoping the other man's lice wouldn't be too ferocious.

The dog had lain down beside him, watching with his nose between his paws and his eyebrows working as Dodd looked about for a belt. There was none, nor shoes nor clogs neither. He sighed, having a shrewd idea what was going on.

'I'm decent now,' he called and the girl peered around the bushes.

She was a grubby little creature, about seven or eight years old and her greasy brown hair hanging out under a smeared biggin cap. Impossible to say if she would ever be pretty.

'Oh, Goodman,' she said with a polite curtsey, 'I'm ever so sorry about the robbers, they're terrible wicked men. My granny says, would you like to come and stay at our house until you're recovered?'

'Ah have nae money,' Dodd explained. 'I could likely get some in Oxford town but the robbers took a' I had on me.'

It was a real nuisance having to repeat everything he said more Southern. His right leg was the one more bruised from the kicking so that was the one he decided would be broken.

'It's all right,' said the child with a smile that seemed hard work for her. It certainly never reached her eyes. 'My granny says it's our duty to help poor travellers attacked by the robbers.'

'Ay,' said Dodd, careful to keep his suspicion off his face and not ask why they didn't try a bit of warning then. And also how it came about that she had clothes for him. 'Would ye...ken...d'ye know the name of the reivers...the robbers' headman...their captain?'

'No, Goodman,' said the child in a pious way which told Dodd that she did. 'They're wicked men.'

Dodd made a great palaver of getting up, screwing up his face and groaning loudly in a way he never would if his leg actually had been broken. Then he leaned heavily on the child's shoulder as he hopped along the path with the dog padding quietly ahead of them.

After only a mile or so uphill they came to a tiny little bothy with low walls and a roof of turves and branches, not even respectable thatch like the remains of the monastery. An old lady in blue homespun was sitting on a stone by the door knitting and she looked up and smiled toothlessly as Dodd came hopping along with her granddaughter.

He made the motion of taking off his cap to her but of course he wasn't even wearing a statute cap which made him feel as if he was still naked.

'Missus,' he said respectfully, 'yer grandaughter says I can come and recover ma strength with ye, which I'm grateful for, but I'll tell ye now I havenae money with me for the...bastards took the lot includin' ma breeks.'

'They do that so you won't chase them,' said the old woman. 'Can you work, Goodman?'

Dodd made a helpless expression. 'A little, missus, but I think I've broke me leg.'

That got only an unsympathetic grunt from her and the child left Dodd to wobble on one leg and went to whisper fiercely in the carlin's ear. Another grunt and a chomping of jaws. Before he fell over or had to put his leg down and give the game away, Dodd grabbed the bush he was standing next to. He had felt unaccountably dizzy for a moment there which was odd. Still maybe not surprising, considering the battering. He had already sworn a mighty internal oath that he would never ever come to the soft safe South again, where people beat you up but didn't bother to kill you.

The old woman's eyes were narrowed in their crumpled beds and her jaws worked again. 'Who's yer master?'

Dodd had thought hard about this inevitable question. What would be the best thing to say?

'Missus, I dinna ken...know ye and I'm grateful for the duds ye've lent me, but until we're better friends I'd be happier in my mind not to gi' ye my master's name, seeing he's a courtier.'

The old eyes were narrowing and the child's as well. You could see they were related.

'Is he rich?'

'Not him, his family,' said Dodd truthfully, 'but Ah dinna ken if they'd ransome me...'

That was a dangerous thing to say because there were people on the Border who would just slit your throat if they thought you weren't worth anything. On the other hand, it was worth it to see the reactions—disappointment, guilt, then...

'We wouldn't ask for ransome, Goodman, we're not robbers and you're not our prisoner,' said the old woman, working hard to look pious. 'We only want to help you.'

'I'm sorry, missus,' Dodd said, with as charming a smile as he could get his bruised face to stretch to. 'I meant a reward, payment for yer trouble...'

The carlin smiled and nodded, the child continued her very hard stare.

Ay, thought Dodd with some satisfaction, I know ye, missus, and how you're placed and what you're up to.

In fact, there was no chance whatever that a little cottage with a garden and...yes...from the smell, goats...could have survived next to a troop of broken men like the bastards who had temporarily bested him, without they paid blackrent of some kind. They were the carrion crows to the wolf pack of the broken men. What did he want the wolves to know? That was the question.

Monday 18th September 1592, noon

Captain Leigh was playing dice with the old Spaniard in the still watertight monastery parlour, when little Kat Layman came trotting in ahead of John Arden who was drunk again. Her grim little face was less tight than usual which meant she had good news. She curtseyed nicely to him and waited to be spoken to, manners he had taught her with the back of his hand.

She took the cup of watered wine he always offered and sipped it, no expression.

It was stupid really, but Edward Leigh found the child unnerving sometimes. She was so unchildlike.

'Now then Kat,' Leigh asked, rubbing the large bruise on his chin where their most recent target had punched him, 'What have you found out?'

'His name is Colin Elliot, he's a Northerner which I knew anyway because you can't hardly make out what he do say.' Leigh nodded encouragingly. 'He was taking a message to his master which is a courtier and one of the Earl of Essex's men.'

Leigh stopped breathing and looked over at Jeronimo, sitting still with the dice cup still poised between his long fingers. His cadaverous hawk of a face was intent. Was it possible the Spaniard had been right?

'Where was he headed?'

'Oxford, of course, he says if the Queen ain't there yet, she will be and his master is at Court to get money and a warrant out of her because he hasn't any, no tower nor land, he's just a bloody courtier with a smooth tongue.'

Leigh nodded carefully. The Court was at Oxford and so was the Earl, only ten miles away. Holed up in this old monastery for the last few weeks, it had been hard to get news. But perhaps at last, at last they could move.

Kat was still speaking. '...and he hurt his leg or it got hurt when you was kicking him, he says it's broken, so he can't work much... He says "canna," you know, and he's good with his hands and with stock so he says he'll help as much as he can until he's well and his master's father will give a reward for him if my granny will send me off to Oxford to tell him.'

'He's a good fighter,' slurred John Arden whose black eye was flowering well, 'took five of us to take him down. Could we get him to join us?'

Leigh shook his head. He didn't want another fighter, he wanted someone who had connections with the Earl of Essex. And that, thank God, despite all his doubts, he seemingly had at last. Now how could he parlay the Northerner into what he really wanted, much more than a simple reward or ransome?

'*Katarina, cariña,*' said Jeronimo, 'who is the father of this courtier the man serves?'

'He told me not to tell the robbers but it's my Lord Hunsdon, the Queen's Chamberlain.'

Leigh blinked in awe at Jeronimo. 'You were right,' he said. 'His master is Captain Carey.'

Jeronimo nodded, took a deep breath, then winced and rubbed his stomach where it was swollen.

'We've got him this time,' he said in French so the child wouldn't understand. 'You can ask him for an audience with the Earl.'

The Earl of Essex owed him a large amount of back pay, owed all of them, and Leigh intended to get it. If necessary he would have marched his remaining men down Oxford High Street in their once-fancy tangerine-and-white livery and demanded his rightful pay from the man he had trusted while that man was in the act of licking the old Queen's arse for her. In fact that had been his original plan.

'All right, Kat,' he said to her, handing over a bag of bread and apples from the remains of the monastery orchard. 'I'll likely come and take a look at him myself, so don't be alarmed.'

Kat's face looked cunning. 'Will you be fierce?'

'Roaarrr!' Leigh shouted, showing his teeth as he used to at his little brothers and sisters. This unnatural child didn't even flinch. 'I'll be fierce, Kat, so make sure you tremble and run away.'

She nodded disdainfully, hefted the bag, looked in it and scowled.

'I want paying. I want money, not just food.'

'Kat,' said Leigh, pulling her nose to nose with him by her kirtle, though not roughly, 'I told you, we're only here because we fought and died for the Earl in France for eighteen months and got not a penny of the shilling a day he promised us, not one penny, though he spent plenty on pennants and livery and feasting.'

She glared straight back at him. 'I want a shilling like you promised. You got all the money from that Northerner, give me some.'

'What if you're lying? What if he's lying?' Leigh was still nose-to-nose with the child.

'Can't help it if he's lying but I'm not,' retorted the child, 'and he said he'd lost the suit his master gave him to look more respectable than his homespun and he wished he hadn't looked so rich and there'll be the devil to pay for that too and there was money in it too, plenty of money.'

Nick Gorman was wearing the man's suit now because it fit him best and it was certainly a gentleman's suit. Smithson had his hat, being in most need of one. The money was Leigh's now, naturally, as captain.

He let go of the fistful of rough kirtle he'd been gripping. Kat straightened herself and her apron with a brow of thunder.

'Give me my shilling,' she said shrilly. 'You'll just drink it and I need it for my dowry.'

'Don't make me angry, Kat.'

'*I'm* angry! I bring you things you didn't know that are important like he's a Northerner and who his master is and everything and you won't even give me a shilling like you said!'

'We could burn you and your old hag of a grandam out of your hovel!' Leigh shouted, outraged at being defied by a little girl. 'I could send Harry Hunks down to you, do you want that?'

The ferocity of the child's glare actually stopped him.

'Don't be like that, sweeting,' he said after a moment in the kindest voice he could muster. 'Of course, we won't burn you out, you just made me cross.' Nothing. Stony brown eyes stared steadily back at him. He gave her a comfit of sugarpaste taken from a rich packtrain a week before. She held it in her fingers and didn't even taste it, curtseyed silently and went out of the monastery parlour where Arden was waiting for her.

Jeronimo was shaking his head. 'You should have paid her,' he said in the French he found more comfortable. 'She's right, she needs a dowry. It was only a shilling.'

Leigh shrugged; he was the captain, not the Spaniard. 'I need it more than she does. How am I going to afford the ribbons we need otherwise?'

Jeronimo said nothing, only winced and drank more of the brandy after adding laudanum that he kept in a small bottle in his doublet pocket. He only had one arm, his right had been taken off above the elbow with the sleeve neatly folded and sewn up. Perhaps the arm that had been broken by a musket ball and cut off many years ago still pained him as sometimes happened. His doublet had once been a very rich silk brocade and had worn well, but his shirt and falling band were as frayed and grubby as everyone's was. Perhaps he was ill: his dark skin had a greyish tinge that Leigh didn't like, though he had no fever.

They finished the brandy and Leigh decided that he, John Arden, and Harry Hunks, the biggest man they had who was nursing bruised ballocks from the Northerner's final headbutt, would go and chat to this Colin Elliot they had caught. Jeronimo he left in charge of the rest of the men, despite the fact that he was Spanish, because after you had fought together for a while, things like that didn't matter anymore and the Spaniard was owed money by the Earl of Essex too. And the Spaniard had certainly been a captain in the past and knew how to do it, which was more than Leigh felt he did, even now.

So with the cold autumn sun already westering, they sauntered down the overgrown cobbled path to the cottage. Leigh knew that they could follow the path northwards for a couple of miles and find the village of Cumnor with its haunted, almost-empty manor house, then three miles north of that would take them to the city of Oxford. The Spaniard had found the place for them and it couldn't be bettered.

The dog set up a-baying at Harry Hunks, whose real name was Percival but had been given the name of a famous London fighting bear because of his size and ferocity. Harry Hunks growled back at the dog and showed his teeth, at which the animal whined and hid behind the cottage.

The old woman came out still toothlessly chewing some of the bread her granddaughter had brought. Kat however was nowhere to be seen.

'Where is he?' shouted Leigh at the old woman, for general effect. 'I know you've got him hidden, where is he?'

'Backyard sir,' she quavered. 'He's mending the chicken coop.'

Stupid old bat, why had she given him a job that involved a weapon? They tramped round the tiny cottage, Harry Hunks deliberately squashing some of the winter cabbages already planted, out into the little yard where the chickens pecked and the muckheap teetered.

The Northerner's face and swollen nose was colouring nicely and he held his right leg awkwardly out to one side, tied with long hazel poles to keep it straight. He was weaving withies in and out to darn a gap in the side of the chicken coop. He stopped to look at them, didn't stand but did duck his head. Leigh couldn't see a hammer in his hands but assumed he'd have a knife to cut the withies.

The Northerner watched them from under his brows, his plain long face sullen. He was sizing them up, Leigh felt, including Harry Hunks, no doubt noting their Essex livery of tangerine and white despite its raggedness.

'Colin Elliot?' Leigh said as firmly as he could.

'Ay,' he said. 'May I help ye, sirs?'

That was civil enough for a Northerner, perhaps someone had been teaching him manners. Leigh had fought with a few Northerners.

'Good day, Goodman,' said Leigh, doing his best to charm. 'I hear from little Kat Layman that some wicked robbers attacked you at the ford. I came to see if there was anything we could do?'

Just for a second the man's eyes flickered and then his face became even more mournful.

'Ay,' he said. 'And they took ma maister's suit that he lent me, these duds arenae mine, sir, ma wife's capable o' much better. And ma boots forbye.'

He looked disgustedly at his bare toes. His feet certainly were wide. Harry Hunks had been delighted with his share of the pickings and was wearing the boots now. A little too late, Leigh wondered if Elliot had noticed this.

'So who's your master?'

'Sir Robert Carey, sir.'

Leigh nodded. It was wonderful news if true, but was it true?

'Yes,' he said, 'I think I met your master in France when he was a captain. One of the Earl of Essex's men? A very able captain, I think.'

The Northerner finished the end of the withy, put down the coop and sat back. 'Ay,' he said, 'I heard he wis knighted when he was in France wi' the Earl.'

Lucky bastard, Leigh thought, who had once hoped to be knighted as well. 'King of Navarre took quite a shine to him too, offered him a place, I believe.'

The Northerner shrugged. Fair enough, it was unlikely Carey would share anything of that sort with his henchmen.

'Tell me, my memory's not too good I'm afraid, your master's a dark man, isn't he? Black hair?'

Contempt crossed the Northerner's face briefly. 'Nay, sir, he's got dark red hair which he calls chestnut and blue eyes. And he's allus dressed verra fine though he canna pay his tailor.'

Leigh had to smile. That was Carey all right. 'He had one entire packpony for just his shirts, I remember, until the Earl of Cumberland got them off him for a night attack.'

The Northerner's mouth turned down at the ends. 'Ay, sir. It's shocking.'

'So clearly I must help you get a message to Captain...er...Sir Robert Carey. Where do you think he'll be?'

'At Court wi' the Queen, wherever she is. Oxford, I heard.'

'And the message you were carrying?'

'Dinna ken, sir, it was a letter. The robbers got it nae doot along o' ma purse and ma silver and ma sword,' said the Northerner bitterly.

Thank God nobody was actually wearing the man's sword, Leigh thought, though it was a good solid weapon, clean, oiled, and would have been sharp if it hadn't been used for something like gathering firewood. He wondered what had happened to that letter.

'Do you know what was in the letter?' he asked and the Northerner shrugged, looking highly offended.

'Cannae read, sir. Ah can make me mark and puzzle oot ma name but nae more, sir. I can fight, though. Ay, I could fight.' He looked gloomy and rubbed his broken leg.

Leigh clapped the dejected man on the back.

'Mr. Elliot,' he said encouragingly, 'I'm sure your leg will get better soon enough. And I'm sure that as soon as we find Sir Robert and explain things to him he'll...er...he'll see you properly equipped again.'

'Ay, he might beat me though.'

'Oh I don't think so, goodman, not his style at all.' Leigh had never seen Carey flog a man for anything less than unauthorised looting or rape. Generally the sheer volume of noise he could produce when he was angry did the job just as well. 'I'll send someone to Oxford to find Sir Robert,' he went on, 'We'll soon sort you out.'

'Ah doot he'll mind ye,' he moaned. 'He's a courtier.'

'Well true,' said Leigh. 'but my experience of Carey as a captain is that he did his best to keep his men alive and paid, even if he occasionally came up with mad plans to achieve that.'

At which point the Northerner gave a brief bark of laughter before turning sullen again, which was what convinced Leigh that he had actually struck gold at last.

'Is there anything else?'

'Ay, sir, I had a good post horse under me and a remount when the...eh...the broken men took me, and the nags might be runnin' loose. I wouldnae want the broken men tae have the benefit of them. There's a gelding with a white sock and a chestnut mare.'

That was interesting: they'd found the mare not far from the ford, but the other horse must have bolted further, perhaps heading for home. He'd send a couple of the boys out to track and find the animal; they needed horses desperately.

As he walked back to the monastery, he thought hard. Why the devil hadn't his men found that letter? Admittedly, it had been a scramble at the ford and at one point the blasted man had almost got away—he fought better half-stunned than most men fully fit.

However, once they'd got him down they had stripped and searched him thoroughly, finding no papers, which was a surprise. Jeronimo had said he was connected with Essex which was why they had switched the waymarker stones so they could ambush him.

He called the men together. There were twenty-five of them left from the fifty men he had taken with him to France. It had been a long hard road back from France after the Earl betrayed them. The ruined monastery had been by far the best billet they'd had since Arles. They were in some of the Earl of Oxford's neglected hunting forest and in the autumn there was a good amount of forage, including hazelnuts, mushrooms and berries, plus the game of course. But they only had two horses left of the twenty fine beasts that had gone to France.

Leigh sighed as he looked at his troop, all of them bony and bearded, grubby and ragged, very different from the strong brave young men who had followed him from their villages. Four of them, including Jeronimo, were strangers he'd picked up in France. A couple of them had persistent coughs that wouldn't go away, several of the boniest also had squits that wouldn't stop. All of them had a harder look in their eye than he liked to see. He sighed again. He had changed too. An older man looked back at him when he trimmed his beard and he knew he was going bald on top. War hadn't been anything like that glorious adventure the Earl of Essex had so eloquently convinced him to expect.

'Gentlemen,' he said quietly, 'is any of you hiding a letter that the Northerner was carrying? A letter to Captain Carey? Some of you may remember him from France?'

Nobody said anything.

'You know I need to see anything of the kind.' Silence. Nobody was blushing, some of them were looking suspiciously at each other.

Leigh felt the stirring of the angry unhappiness that had settled around his gut sometime during the first months in France, felt it twist around his entrails. Just in time, Nick Gorman who had got the Northerner's suit to replace his remnants of Essex's livery, stepped forward.

'There was this in the doublet pocket, sir,' he said, holding out a stained bit of paper. 'I didn't know it was important.'

Leigh took the paper, glanced at it but it was all numbers. A cipher of some kind.

'Jeronimo, can you break codes?'

The Spaniard shrugged, stepped out of his place ahead of the line and took the paper. "I don't know, Señor," he said, squinting at it, "Perhaps in Espanish, but...I can try."

'Thank you.' For a moment Leigh stared worried at Jeronimo. 'It turns out you were right about the Northerner. Do you know anything about Captain Carey yourself?'

'The son of Henry Carey, milord Hunsdon?'

'Yes.' The Spaniard smiled radiantly at him, quite shocking in his normally tense face and said something that sounded like *Gracias a Dios.*

'Why? Do you know him too?'

"No Señor, I know of hees family. From when I play lute for the Queen."

A likely story. Leigh had instantly dismissed Jeronimo's colourful past as the usual nonsense old soldiers spouted. He thought about the problem. Whom should he send to Oxford with the all-important letter? He could go himself and also try and buy the ribbons they needed, but that meant leaving the men without a leader and that always meant trouble. He could send John Arden but with Arden there was a good chance that he might pop into an alehouse for half a quart and not come out again until all their money was spent. On the other hand, Arden was probably the best second-in-command he had, though he was standing there with his hip cocked, one hand on his sword and a bleary expression on his puffy once-handsome face. He was certainly better than Leigh at planning a fight, should probably have been the captain, but didn't want the office. He preferred to get drunk every afternoon rather than worry about supplies and getting the men paid. Although it beat Leigh completely where he was getting his drink from.

Leigh sighed again. He couldn't rely on any of the others and besides it would be better for Carey to be contacted by someone he knew, so it had to be him. He would leave Arden in charge along with Jeronimo and hope for the best.

'Nick,' he said, 'I'm afraid we'll have to swap clothes so I look more respectable and nobody realises what we are. You can have the suit again when I come back. And in the meantime I want you, Tarrant, and Clockface to go and find the Northerner's remount, a good gelding with a white sock. As it came from the South it's probably heading back in that direction, trying to find its home and we don't want that, do we?'

Gorman nodded philosophically and then remembered and tipped his hat. 'Yes, sir.'

Meantime Leigh had to make sure the Northerner didn't take it into his head to make for Oxford on his own, barefoot as he was. He would have to be locked in at night, possibly chained, only they didn't have any such things, of course. He'd just have to send Harry Hunks down to the carlin again and tell her to keep the man in the pit at night.

MONDAY 18TH SEPTEMBER, 1592

Kat was munching stolidly through one of the crusts from the bread she brought back from the soldiers while Dodd did the same more cautiously because some of his teeth still felt loose. She had just finished counting up on her fingers.

'There's twenty-one of 'em,' she said, scowling with the effort. 'Then there's Captain Leigh and John Arden and Jeronimo and Harry Hunks.'

Even Dodd had heard of Harry Hunks. 'A bear?' he asked.

'What?'

He explained about the famous London fighting bear of the Eighties that could still be found engraved on horn cups and plates and in stories told on ballad sheets, though he'd died nearly ten years ago. Barnabus had told him all about the star of the bearbaiting.

Kat scowled even more. 'I hate him,' she said. 'He's like a bear but he's bad. He's horrible. John Arden is nice and gives Granny nice things he finds in the monastery and she gives him her apple aquavitae. Captain Leigh is stupid and stingy and mean and I hate him too.'

'Jeronimo?'

'He's a furriner,' Kat said dismissively, 'a Spaniard who's dark and skinny and hisses through his teeth sometimes.'

'Ay,' said Dodd.

'So there's too many of 'em. What can *you* do?'

Dodd contemplated telling her, but decided not to in case she changed her mind again and went back to the soldiers.

Kat had come to him as he awkwardly dug a trench from a sitting position, using a small wooden trowel, for the old grandam to plant more winter cabbages in. Kat was still carrying her bag with the bread in it and her cheeks were flushed with fury and her eyes steely slits.

'If I tell you about the men at the old monastery, will you promise to kill them?' she had demanded. 'Especially Captain Leigh?'

Well that was easy enough. 'Ah cannae promise I'll do it,' Dodd told her, 'but I promise I'll try.'

She paused, thinking about it.

'Yes well,' she said after a moment, 'you don't have to do all of them, just Captain Leigh.'

'Ay.'

'He promised me a shilling for what I could find out and didn't pay me last time and he didn't pay me this time so he owes me two shillings for my dowry and I hate him.'

You've a cousin in Carlisle, Dodd thought, highly amused and wishing the Courtier was there to manage the conversation with an angry little maid. She cocked her head on one side.

'So I'll tell you everything the captain told me not to tell anyone and then you can decide how to kill him.'

Dodd had listened carefully while the child spilled out her fierce heart to him. It seemed the tale of the broken men was a disgraceful one of noble promises unkept, but common enough. You hardly ever got paid for soldiering, bar what you could steal or kill for, everyone knew that. It seemed that the unfortunate Captain Leigh still hadn't worked it out.

'What happened to the last messenger they caught?'

'Oh, he was all right. They just knocked him out and took his stuff and then when he was a bit better, Captain Leigh came along and said they'd got his duds and message back from the robbers and off he went again, on foot of course, as they had his horse. They got some wagons a while ago too and they were pleased with that and the men guarding it didn't fancy a fight and ran off back to London.'

'So Leigh will use me to get hisself an audience with the Earl of Essex?'

'I suppose so. He thinks he can talk his lord into paying him.'

Dodd laughed once at this and then clamped down again. It was a serious matter. The men of Leigh's troop had put a brave on him but they hadn't killed him when it would have been easy to do it. At first he had taken this as an insult like Heneage's, that they thought him some nithing that need not be feared for vengeance. But perhaps it hadn't occurred to them that he might be a man of parts, even if he was in a foreign county. On the other hand, he intended to get his gear back, particularly his sword, his knife, and his boots. His hip felt very strange without the weight of a weapon on it and his feet were already cold and sore.

Who would go to put the bite on Carey? He hadn't seen the Spaniard, but had seen the drunken walk of John Arden and the large shaggy man with a slight limp that had looked coldly at him. Probably Leigh would go himself as he already knew Carey from France. Hmm. That would be good.

'Whit happened to the monks in the monastery when the King's men came?' Dodd asked.

Kat shrugged. 'My grandam said they were just a few stupid old men and boys by then and they tried to fight so they all got killed and they burnt some of the monastery. So it's haunted, of course.'

'Ay, do the soldiers ken that?'

'Grandam told Captain Leigh when he came but he laughed at her and said he didn't think so. But it *is* haunted.'

'Ay.' Dodd rubbed his bottom lip with his thumb. The glimmerings of an idea was coming to him. For complexity and madness it was one nearly worthy of Carey himself; perhaps being near the

Courtier was causing him to catch courtierlike ways of thinking. Still.

'Grandam told the boy Nick Gorman when he came to get cheese from us, she warned him about the ghosts of the burnt monks and he didn't laugh. Captain Leigh came and told her off, he said no good Protestant believed in superstition like that and Papists couldn't hurt Godly men like them anyway.'

Dodd tutted. He'd never heard of a ghost that cared about such things.

'Kat,' he said, 'I want ye to go back to Captain Leigh and act verra nice tae him. Can ye do that?' She frowned, opened her mouth to say something. 'Not to be friends again but to find things out from him. I want ye to find oot who he's sending tae my master and what he's doing next. And get me some paper.'

'Can you write then?'

'Ay, but dinna let on.'

It was a useful test. If she came back with paper as he hoped, then he'd know he might trust her which was important for the most complicated part of his plan. If she came back alongside Leigh demanding to know why he'd lied about his ability to read, then he might be in for another leathering but he'd know what he needed to about Kat. Her face had suddenly fallen.

'But what about your leg? How can you kill Captain Leigh with that?'

'Whit about it?'

She looked at the splint and then stopped. He put his finger on his lips and winked and got from her the first real smile he'd ever seen on her face.

Then she dusted crumbs from her greasy kirtle and jumped to her feet and trotted determinedly away with her wooden clogs clacking on the cobblestones of the path.

The old woman came out later and watched him at his digging with her hands on her hips.

'Will ye have that ready by this evening, Goodman?' she demanded.

'Ay,' he said, 'the dog's helping.'

The dog had done some digging and found a greenish bone

which he was gnawing on quite happily. Suddenly he lifted his head and sniffed the air, then whined nervously, pawed the bone back into the earth and skulked round to hide behind Dodd.

The carlin went out to the front of the cottage and Dodd could hear the big bearlike man called Harry Hunks tramping to the front door in Dodd's own boots. The sound of talking came to him. Quick as he could, he hopped over to listen by the path and caught Harry Hunks' last sentence.

'…and make sure he sleeps, we don't want him getting out.'

'The pit will hold him, Harry, he's broken his leg.'

'Make sure he don't get out or I'll burn your cottage.'

'Captain Leigh wouldn't like that.'

'Then I'll kill your dog.'

Nothing more, so Dodd hopped back and sat down by his trench just in time. Harry Hunks loured round the side of the cottage and pointed at him.

'You!' he shouted. 'You stay put or I'll break your other leg.'

Dodd did his best to look cowed, touched his capless head and quavered 'Yes, sir!' at the big lout. Harry Hunks turned about and stamped away, damaging Dodd's good boots by kicking a hole in the hurdles of the goat pen as he went.

Dodd's belly gave a great growl and grumble then which wasn't surprising since he hadn't eaten all day. He went over and shoved back the inquiring goat's head that instantly came through the gap.

'Missus,' he called, 'ye'll need tae move yer goats.'

The grandam came out the back of the cottage, saw the damage and shook her head. Then she hobbled over and put a halter round the billy kid's neck. There was a nanny kid as well that she haltered and the two others were nannies with still-heavy udders.

The grandam dragged the two half-grown kids back toward the cottage, both protesting at being separated from their mothers. The nannies pushed through the gate to follow.

'You can herd the nannies, if you're minded to, Goodman,' shouted the carlin.

'Ay missus,' said Dodd, who caught the nannies by a horn each and looked them in the long-pupilled eyes. One said 'Neh!' in a testy way, so she was the one he led ahead of the others and they came quietly enough. It was as well to respect rank among goats as well as men.

Kat had joined them by the time the goats were in their tumbledown shed beside the cottage and Dodd had already mended the hurdle. She was looking smug and she whispered at him,

'Can you milk goats?'

The question irritated him. Of course he could milk goats, he could milk anything with teats and had once milked a sow for a bet and nearly got his nose bitten off. 'Ay,' he said.

'Can Mr. Elliot help me with the milking, Grandam?' asked Kat artlessly and the old woman nodded. The day was cooling and Dodd wondered where the pit was where he'd sleep that night. He hadn't expected that there would be room for all three of them in the bothy with its yard-high walls, quite apart from the propriety of it. The child brought a stool and two good big earthenware bowls to the shed, sat down and started on the younger nanny's udder, pulling at the teats roughly and impatiently. Dodd squatted by the older one, rubbed her flanks, butted his head a couple of times where a kid would nuzzle and made a quiet goat noise. Then he licked his fingers and wibbled the teats, rubbed the spit on. As soon as the first few drops had oozed out, he started the rhythmic work with his hands which he hadn't done since he went to Carlisle. It took him right back to his boyhood when he'd had four goats to milk every morning and evening. The goat let down her milk almost at once and he soon filled the bowl with warm milk to the brim. Then because his stomach was griping him something terrible and he wasn't convinced the carlin would waste any supper on him, he ducked his head and milked a stream of warm creamy milk straight into his mouth.

He stopped when he saw that Kat was staring at him.

'Whit?' he asked, wiping milk off his beard.

'How did you fill it up so quickly?' the child asked, still wrenching away at the other goat's udder in a way that made Dodd feel sore in the teats he didn't have. Had nobody ever taught her?

'Tell ye what,' he said, 'let me finish her off and ye can tell me what Captain Leigh is planning.'

She gave him the stool and he squatted down again, butted

the nanny's pungent flank and let her poor udder rest a little. The bowl was hardly half full and only with the thin first milk, none of the cream. He patted and rubbed her neck and waited.

'So why aren't you getting on with it?' demanded the angry child.

His mother had taught him to milk goats this way, God rest her, and so he told the angry child what she had told him.

'Because ye'll get more milk by kindness than ye will any ither way. They won't give ye the milk if ye hurt 'em or mek 'em sore.'

Kat's eyes narrowed suspiciously. 'What do you mean?' she demanded, 'They've got food. Nobody's beating them.'

He teased the teats a little with his wetted fingers.

'Ay, Kat, listen, the milk's for their kid. Ye've got to fool 'em you're their kid, then they let out all their milk not just the thin stuff.' He did it again. 'So what's Captain Leigh planning?'

She was still scowling. 'I tore some clean paper out of a book in the parlour when Captain Leigh went to look at your other horse that they found, the one with the white sock and I got it from John Arden that him and Jeronimo are in charge along of Harry Hunks when Leigh goes off to Oxford in the morning to find your master and the Earl of Essex too. The Queen's not there yet.'

Dodd raised his eyebrows. Carey had been talking about the Queen being at Oxford for a month but then she was a woman. He held out his hand for the paper and took it—nice thick creamy stuff it was, with a pretty border of flowers. Some monkish thing, no doubt. He'd forgotten to ask her to find ink, but some charcoal was a better proposition, less complicated than a pen.

'You heard about Grandam keeping you in the old monk's cellar until Captain Leigh comes back.'

'Ay.'

'He's going to buy *ribbons*!' she spat, her face twisted in fury, 'with *my* money!'

That was when the younger nanny decided to let down her milk and the drops came, so he took the teats and started milking two steady streams into the bowl.

'How far is it tae Oxford from here?'

'I don't know.'

'How long does it take ye to walk to market there then?'

'Maybe two hours?'

'How d'ye ken…know?'

'Well when we go to market with the cheeses we start before sun up and when we get there the gates are open and the market's started.'

Maybe six or seven miles then. He could run that in an hour and a bit, given a reasonable path and not too many hills. However, he didn't like to think of what that would do to his poor soft feet. He wasn't about to do it if he had a better plan, which he did. And besides, he wasn't crawling back to Carey in rags and bare feet and no sword. Not him.

'How will yer grandam be sure I'll let her put me in the cellar?'

Kat smiled patronisingly. 'She'll put wild lettuce juice and valerian and poppy pod juice in your pottage tonight.'

'Ay?' He sighed. 'Where's the cellar then?'

The bowl was full and milk still coming so he took that straight into his mouth as well. It was deliciously creamy. Kat stared at him 'Could you do that for me?'

She was a skinny little mite with a hungry face—why hadn't he thought of that before? She looked like his littlest brother, the one he'd often taken down into the pastures to steal milk for after the Elliots killed his father and took all their herds. So he beckoned her nearer and pointed the goat's teat at her open mouth and the jet choked her a little but she got quite a lot down. She smiled at him.

'Grandam says it's all got to go to cheese to sell in Oxford for the rent money to the Earl of Oxford, and the bastard soldiers are likely to do even more damage before they go so she'll likely need more money for that and to pay them off too.'

'Ay,' said Dodd, 'broken men are hard on everyone. Ye've got a good couple of bowls there now if we dinna spill it.'

On his insistence they wiped down the goats with wisps of hay and fed and watered them, they had salt licks from their palms as well. All goats were mad for salt. Then he got Kat to show him where the monks' cellar was.

It was in the pile of stones that said this had been a part of the monastery and the cellar was actually a stone-lined pit that they might have used for grain or even tanning. It was deep enough that he wouldn't be able to climb out of it without a ladder or something similar, though there were gaps between some of the stones to put your toes in. You had to hope there was some kind of roof to put over it and that it wouldn't rain in the night or you'd be floating by morning. There was dried bracken at the bottom on the least muddy bit. Dodd had seen worse prisons.

'Does she put a hurdle across?'

Kat waved at a hurdle of withies, next to the ladder. The important point was whether the grandam would chain him to anything but he couldn't see any chain or ring down in the pit itself so he devoutly hoped she wouldn't.

'You can't get out, my dog will stop you,' Kat told him. She turned her back on him to give the dog a hug and play with his ears so Dodd took the chance of dropping a few things into the pit that might come in useful later.

Then they went and collected the bowls, took them into the cottage where the carlin nodded approval at the amount and set them on a stone shelf at the back that was probably looted from a church as it was marble.

'You're a good stockman, then,' Kat's grandam said.

'Ay, missus,' he said to her politely, touching his nonexistent cap, 'Ah am.'

'Come in and have supper,' she said which caused his stomach to make an almighty comment that got all of them laughing.

It wasn't so bad a place to live; dry and snug and it had a tiled pavement with rushes over it. The roof wasn't high enough for him to stand upright but it was high enough for the little old woman. A modern chimney of stolen bricks was in the corner for the fire and a pot hanging over it, so the place wasn't nearly as smoky as the turf bothies he had spent his teens in. There was hardly even enough smoke to make you cough.

Dodd squatted next to the fire where the carlin had a stone bench and Kat had her milking stool, took the wooden bowl of pottage and the wooden spoon. He took a few spoonfuls which was hard on him since it was good stuff with some bacon in it, even, beans, lentils, even carrots. He had a bit of old bread as well, so he made the most of it.

The dog was prowling about the yard to keep the foxes off

the chickens. When the carlin went to tap some of her own wine from a barrel at the back of the cottage, he put his head quickly out the top half of the door and dumped most of his pottage on the ground, whistled softly through his teeth.

He had to squat down again quickly and happy snortlings told him the dog was slurping up the drugged pottage.

She came bustling back with a horn cup of her elderflower wine so he took that and it was excellent, such a pity she'd put laudanum in it too.

'Ah've a need for the jakes,' he said yawning deliberately.

'Dungheap's behind the cottage.'

He knew where that was, so he caught Kat's eye as he went to the door, cocked his head.

She was a cunning little piece. She waited until he finished, then came out with his wine cup.

'She's put more sleeping potion in it,' she hissed at him. 'She didn't see you finish the pottage.'

Dodd tipped out the wine and refilled it with water from the water butt. He'd been busy while he'd squatted at the furthest end of the dungheap.

He showed Kat the charcoal writing on the nice paper.

'Ye know the way to the market in Oxford, ay?' he said to Kat who nodded intently. 'D'ye know the man that rules the market, one of the Mayor's men, mebbe?'

'You have to pay him even if you don't sell nothing,' she sniffed.

'Early tomorrow morning, I want ye to walk tae Oxford, fast as ye can. Go to the market clerk or whoever it is, curtsey, call him sir, say ye've bin sent by a…a man-at-arms in service to Sir Robert Carey, son of Lord Hunsdon, and give him that paper. Tell him where ye live and a' that and warn him of the broken men. But be sure and gi' that bit o' paper tae somebody of worship, official, mind? Naebody that disnae wear a gown.'

She nodded slowly. 'Why?'

'Ye asked me tae kill Captain Leigh for ye?' he reminded her. She nodded, eyes narrowing with suspicion. 'How'd ye like to watch him hang for coining and maybe horsetheft, eh?'

Her eyes went round and her mouth opened in delight.

'Really? Truly?'

'Ay. This letter is laying information agin him. I happen tae know that a lot of the money that he's gonnae be spending on ribbons is false coin. That's a hanging offence, is uttering false coin. And he'll be riding a reived horse forbye.'

She blinked in puzzlement and then nodded firmly. 'I'll do it. I know the way really well and once when Grandam was ill I ran to the 'pothecary in the Cornmarket and got laudanum for her.' Dodd didn't tell her the final refinement to a plan that he was quite modestly proud of. Suddenly she laughed. 'Did you really steal the white-socked gelding?'

'Ay,' he said heavily. 'It wis a mistake.'

MONDAY 18TH SEPTEMBER 1592,

AFTERNOON

For the first time since Saturday, Carey woke feeling more like himself. The day had greyed over and so the light wasn't so bad for his eyes; besides, he fancied that they were improving a little. He was also hungry.

John Tovey appeared when he stuck his head out of the tent to see who was about and came to help him on with his doublet.

'Any idea where my henchman is, Mr. Tovey?' he asked the boy who seemed to be as bad at tying points as he was good at penmanship.

'Um...sorry, sir,' said Tovey, fumbling about at the back of Carey's doublet, 'Who?'

'Hughie Tyndale? He was poisoned at the same time.'

'Ah. My lord Earl said your f...father had taken him into the rest of his household when they moved into Trinity College.'

'Excellent. Go find me some food and then we'll take a walk round the corner and talk to him.'

Tovey came back with a couple of pies and bread and ale which Carey demolished at speed. He then strapped on his sword and poinard, crammed his hat as low on his head as he could and stepped outside the tent, past Henshawe sitting whittling something and the Earl at his peculiar chess play and various rehearsals for a masque going on.

The traffic would be far too bad to bother with a horse, so Carey simply walked out of the makeshift gate between the bright flags onto the muddy rutted path that joined Broad Street which went alongside the old Oxford city wall and was at least cobbled for the horse market there. The alehouse on the corner with the lane that went down to New College was crammed with menservants shouting at each other. The schools and the Bodleian library loomed opposite.

Even in the annoying dazzle Carey could see the men in his father's livery at the door of Trinity College, tucked between a field and a small bookshop. He went straight over, made a few enquiries and ten minutes later was unbolting the chamber door where Hughie was still recovering.

The window was shuttered and although Hughie didn't rate a proper fourposter bed, somebody had rigged up a curtain of old-fashioned tapestry with pointy hatted women and moth-holes.

Hughie looked pale and frightened, which was an odd sight in a young man as large and well-shouldered as he was, with his black hair and square shuttered face and his beard starting to come in strongly.

When he blinked at Carey he tried to get up, but Carey stopped him with a raised hand.

'Hughie, don't trouble yourself, I came to see how you were doing.'

'It wisnae me, sir,' growled Hughie in Scotch. 'Ah tellt 'em, Ah didnae spike yer drink...'

No doubt his father had made sure the lad was well-questioned, but Carey had better methods. He pulled up the stool and sat himself down, blinking and rubbing his eyes.

'I've only just been well enough to get up,' he said affably. 'How are your eyes doing?'

'Mebbe I've bin struck blind,' muttered Hughie dolefully, 'I cannae mek out...'

'No, that's what belladonna does to you, it seems, fixes your pupils open so you can't see in daylight. Dreadful stuff. It's lucky I didn't drink as much of that flagon as you did. You should start being able to see properly again tomorrow.'

'Ay?'

'Oh yes. Now I'm completely certain it wasn't you who put the belladonna in my booze, but you must have seen who did it because...'

'But I canna remember, sir, I'm so sorry.'

That might be true. Carey couldn't think how he'd got to the church and couldn't remember much of what happened there either, apart from the puking which he would have preferred to forget.

'Well we'll start with your last clear memory and see what more you can remember? Do try, there's a good fellow, you're my only chance at tracking down whoever did it.'

'Ay,' Hughie looked very gloomy, his jaw was set. 'I wantae ken that masen.'

'All right. Do you recall me sending you off for spiced wine?'

It was like pulling teeth. Hughie remembered the girls dancing the country dance. He remembered seeing Carey speak to the pretty Italian woman and he remembered heading for the spiced wine bowl and pushing through the other servingmen. He couldn't remember any more.

'Did you see who was serving?'

He shook his head, there were too many people around the table, he couldn't get through.

'So how did you get your flagon filled?'

He'd passed it forward to the table and got it back filled with spiced wine...

'Ach,' he said, scowling, 'that's when it happened.'

Carey nodded. 'They wouldn't take the risk of poisoning the whole bowl, it had to be very specific. So when whoever it was saw you with the flagon, he knew you were my man, he blocks your path to the spiced wine and he helpfully gets it filled then adds the belladonna. The idea, I think, was that you would be blamed for it.'

'Ay?'

'Well of course. It's only because you illicitly drank enough to half-kill yourself that my father doesn't have you banged up in the Oxford jailhouse right now.'

There was a long thoughtful pause while Hughie digested this.

'Ah hadnae thocht o'that, sir.'

'No? Well, think about it now. You bring me wine which is poisoned, ideally I die and it's only thanks to God that I didn't, and then as my henchman who brought the wine, you would be the first and probably last suspect.'

'But I didna...'

Carey leaned forward, blinking at the young man's sullen face and wishing he could see more clearly. 'Hughie, I'm sure you didn't but if I was dead and you unpoisoned, you would be in very big trouble no matter how innocent you were. I can't guarantee that my father wouldn't have you put to the question to find out what had happened; he's a decent man and doesn't like that kind of foreign rubbish, but he would be very upset if he had my corpse to bury. To put it mildly.'

More silence. 'Ay, sir,' said Hughie heavily. There was some kind of rage smouldering in him somewhere. Carey hoped Hughie would put the rage to good use—by finding the poisoner, for instance.

Carey stood and clapped a hand on the young man's shoulder. 'I'll talk to my father, make sure he releases you to me once you're better. Think about it. Oh and Hughie...'

'Ay, sir?'

'I'm a very tolerant man, you know. I served at Court for ten years before I decided it would be more fun to do some fighting on the Borders. I know how Courts work and I know how the King of Scotland's Court works as well because I was there with Walsingham years ago and I've been back a few times since. The only thing I don't forgive in a man of mine is lying to me. Understand?'

More silence.

'If you're taking money from someone to keep an eye on me and report back, I don't mind at all—so long as you tell me about it.'

Nothing. Carey nodded and crammed his hat further down

over his eyes. 'See if you remember anything more, drink plenty of mild ale and if you feel up it you can be back at work for me tomorrow. God knows, Mr. Tovey my new clerk doesn't know one end of a doublet from another.'

Not a glimmer of a smile, the saturnine young face was clearly masking a brain that was thinking furiously.

Quite pleased with himself, Carey went out and found Tovey sitting on a window ledge peering out the window into the quad. His face was wistful.

'Happy memories, Mr. Tovey?'

'Yes, sir. Though I was at Balliol not Trinity, and working my keep, I loved it here.' The shy smile among the spots was like that of a man remembering an old love. 'All the books, it was just...It was heaven here. So many books to read.'

Carey nodded politely. While he liked reading and enjoyed romances like the *Roman de la Rose* or adventure stories like Mallory's *Morte d'Arthur,* he usually got restless after an hour or so. He wasn't a clerk.

'Let's go find one of my brothers,' he said. Tovey hopped down and trotted after him obediently.

Luckily the one he found was George who was unenviably in charge of organising the Hunsdon household. The household was enormous even on progress and spilled out of the main college quad and into the gardens behind. George was Hunsdon's heir, in his forties and very harassed by the lack of provisions.

'What?' he snapped irritably when Carey asked him the question for the fourth time. 'You want to know whether your man Dodd's turned up and also about Aunt Katherine's riding habit thirty years ago? For God's sake, Robin, why?'

'For a good and sufficient reason,' Carey said. His hat was helping the dazzle but he was getting another headache and his guts were in a sad state, no doubt thanks to Dr. Lopez' prescriptions. And he was now seriously worried about Dodd— none of his father's men had any idea whether he had been found yet. It was as if he had been stolen away by the faery folk. And Carey did not personally want to think about a faery that could do that to Dodd.

Carey passed a hand down the leg of the horse that seemed skittish, while his elder brother gloomily checked the hay stores which had clearly been got at by rats and possibly humans.

'I don't know what the devil happened to her skirt,' said George pettishly. 'And as for Dodd, my bloody wagons left London ten days ago with food supplies and they haven't arrived yet either. Maybe the sergeant ran off with them.'

Not impossible with Dodd, but unlikely, Carey thought. The skittish gelding next to him blew out its lips and hopped a bit. Running his hand down again, Carey found the hot sore place on the knee which he suspected would need a bran poultice. He pointed this out to George who wasn't pleased to hear about it as he was also short of horses. In Carey's experience nobody, in any situation, ever had enough horses.

'Come on, George,' he insisted, 'I'll leave you alone if you tell me. You must remember more than I do and I remember quite a fuss years later. Aunt Katherine's riding habit?'

'God, I don't know,' snorted George, sounding very like a lame horse himself, 'I'm not so bloody interested in fine clothes as you, I don't...'

'I don't wear kirtles, George,' Carey said coldly, wishing his brother wasn't so pompous. 'I'm asking for a reason. Do I have to show you my warrant?'

'Oh. That. Well...' George sighed and stared at the ground. 'Far as I can remember she was at Court early in the Queen's reign. Lettice hadn't come to Court yet. I was a page still, and yes, her riding habit went mysteriously missing. And then one of her tiring women was complaining that it was ruined but then the Queen was very kind and gave Aunt Katherine a dress length—a whole twelve yards—of fine green Lincoln wool, and arranged for her own tailor to make a new habit for her.'

'Anything else? How was the kirtle ruined?'

'Got splashed with blood or something. And the headtire had been lost as well. Aunt Katherine probably fell off her horse and didn't want to admit it, she was never a very good rider.'

Yes! Carey stood stock still, staring into space. 'I don't remember

Aunt Katherine ever liking the hunt,' he said carefully. 'What style was the headtire?'

George shrugged. 'She was very old-fashioned, usually wore French hoods that went out with Bloody Mary, I don't know.'

Carey's heart was pounding and the hair was standing up on the back of his neck; it was like what you felt when you saw a chorus of Kings in your hand and a fat pot on the table.

George was still droning on. 'Sorry, brother?'

'I said, Robin, if you'd care to listen for a change, that Aunt Kat was very upset about it and so was Father and he told us not to mention it at all.'

'Right.' That fitted too. Carey decided he had to find his father and talk to him. 'Where is Father?'

'He's out with some men, trying to find out what happened to the pack train—and your Sergeant Dodd as well. He was saying if you hadn't been so infernally careless and got yourself poisoned, you could have been very useful. He wants to know when you think you'll be fit to ride?'

Leaving out the detail of where he had gone that morning, Carey shrugged. 'Maybe tomorrow if my eyes are better. I'm quite busy too, you know. In addition to the warrant matter, I'm also trying to find out who poisoned me. Thank you, George.'

He walked carefully out of the Hunsdon camp, still trailed by Tovey, with the sunlight peering under a sheet of dirty linen cloud to dazzle him again and make his head hurt. He would have to find out from Cumberland who was serving the spiced wine on Saturday and then talk to the man to see if he could remember any of the people crowding round the table. Meantime his head was buzzing because he had thought of a possible reason for the Queen to be at Cumnor Place on the 8th September 1560. It was far-fetched but it made better sense than the notion that she would personally murder Amy, that was sure. He might have to go back to Cumnor Place and press Mrs. Odingsells for whatever it was she had kept. And his Aunt's missing headtire made sense of something else.

Unfortunately the new explanation once again made a prime suspect of Lord Burghley.

MONDAY 18TH SEPTEMBER 1592, NIGHT

Back with the Earl of Cumberland's encampment, he found the man who served the spiced wine who was understandably extremely nervous. It took some time to calm him enough to get any sense out of him at all. He said he was certain there had been no woman at all amongst the servingmen wanting spiced wine for their masters, which took out Emilia's direct intervention. As for which of them had passed forward Hughie's flagon—the man had no idea at all, blinked helplessly at the flagon Carey showed him and said he'd filled hundreds that looked just like it, he was sorry, sir, but...Carey sighed, gave him thruppence for his time and promised him another ninepence if he could remember anything else.

Carey would bet a lot of money that whichever man it had been, he'd left Rycote on Saturday night, but so had plenty of other people. Or had he? There were so many servingmen, henchmen, and general hangers on at Court, even on progress, the poisoner could easily have stayed with the Court if he kept his nerve.

He was restless and out of sorts. He couldn't even enjoy playing cards with Cumberland when he could hardly make out the pips. Darkness fell which eased him somewhat. And so Carey sat and drank mild ale in the little alehouse on the corner of the Hollywell Street, staring into space, trying to filter out the noise of a lute being played by an idiot and some extremely bad singing.

The hammering and sawing died down and the workmen started filling up the alehouse, spending their wages. Flocks of students moved restlessly along the street in their black gowns, arguing and drinking and, occasionally, fighting.

Somebody else got hold of the lute, somebody who could actually play the damned thing because he started by tuning it. No alehouse lute was ever in tune. When the man began playing, Carey sat up and put his mug on the table.

It was the Spanish air he had sung at Rycote. The tune didn't have the same arrangement that Byrd had given it, but it was still the same wistful melody. And the man playing the lute was the man who had disappeared from Byrd's music consort on the Saturday night after hearing Carey sing.

Carey's neck felt cold. Had he put the poison in Carey's booze? Why would he do that? He'd annoyed Mr. Byrd by leaving the musicians' consort—that didn't say he'd left the whole party.

The man finished playing that air and then played two other tunes more. Despite applause and calls for more from the workmen, he put the lute down and walked out of the alehouse without even passing a hat round.

Goddamn it, he needed a man at his back, he wished he hadn't sent the yawning Tovey off to his bed. At least Tovey could have run to Trinity College and rousted out Sergeant Ross and a few Northerners to arrest the man.

No help for it, he couldn't afford to lose the man so Carey put his half-finished ale down and followed. At least now that the streets were fully dark apart from occasional public-spirited lanterns on college gates, his eyes worked very well. He could see as clearly as if it were a moonlit night and not as overcast as it was.

The man walked purposefully along the road to New College, went into the tiny boozing ken next to it, picked up the violin there and played that. Once again the Spanish air rang out, followed by two more tunes and the man left once more.

Carey pulled his hat down, wished he'd bothered with a cloak and pretended to be staggering drunk as he followed the man on down the lane that eventually wound up passing by Magdalen deerpark where he turned right and came back along the High Street.

There were a lot of inns and alehouses on the High Street and the man went into each one, played the Spanish air and a couple more tunes, then left without passing a hat round or accepting any of the beer offered to keep him in the place.

He stayed and ate the ordinary at the London Inn on the southward road from Carfax, then off he went again, having maybe one quart of mild per five boozing kens and playing the Spanish air at each of them. And there certainly were an amazing number of inns and alehouses in Oxford. Studying must be thirsty work.

Just as Carey was loitering in a doorway on the corner of St.

Giles after a foray to the Eagle & Child where the alewife had scowled at both of them, he saw a looming pair of shoulders and a statute cap pulled down low on Hughie's saturnine young face.

'Ay, sir,' said Hughie, when Carey caught up with him, 'I came to find ye because I minded me of something. The hand of the man that gave me the flagon back…it was…Ah…ye ken, his fingernails wis long and he had rough ends tae his fingers.'

Carey paused, his heart lifting. Hughie was screwing up his eyes and frowning and Carey knew that the very little light from the torches on the college gates was still bothering him.

'Hughie, well done!' he said, clapping the man's shoulder, 'That's wonderful because I think I may be following the villain. Come with me.'

They went into the White Horse where the musician was just setting down the house lap harp and being applauded. There was a flicker over his face which could have been fear. As far as Carey could tell he had a square handsome old face, grey beard and hair; a solid-looking, dependable man, not at all what you might expect a musician to look like. He didn't even have a drunkard's red nose. Perhaps he and Hughie could lay hands on the man?

Then he heard a quiet cough behind him, turned and found Sir Robert Cecil sitting in a corner booth. Cecil lifted his quart to Carey.

'Sir Robert,' said Burghley's second son, 'I'm glad to see you up and about again.'

'Thank you, Mr. Secretary,' said Carey warily.

'May I get you anything?'

In the corner of his eye, he could see the greybeard musician moving toward the back of the alehouse. Under his breath he said to Hughie, 'Is that him?' Hughie made the indeterminate Scotch sound 'Iphm' which probably meant he wasn't sure. 'Go after him, keep him in sight,' Carey hissed. 'Do it quietly.'

'Ay sir,' said Hughie with a shy smile, and went over to the bar.

Cecil had already beckoned the potboy. Carey certainly couldn't ignore a Privy Counsellor in favour of an old musician, so why not? He had run out of money again, having come out with only a shilling in his purse. 'Thank you, sir, I'll have brandywine.'

At Cecil's gesture, he sat down in the booth facing the youngest member of the Privy Council. Meanwhile Hughie had carried his jack of ale straight over to the musician, tapped him on the shoulder and asked him in a harsh slurred voice how you set about playing a harp, it was something he'd always wanted to do. The greybeard paused and then warily let Hughie sit next to him and started showing him how to tune the instrument.

'Ye have to do that, eh?' said Hughie, after a big gulp of ale. 'Why?'

'No sign of Sergeant Dodd yet?' Cecil asked while the musician stared at the lad and clearly struggled to find words to explain something so obvious. Carey shook his head.

'My father's gone south again to try and find him.'

Cecil smiled. 'I wanted to tell you that I found a distraught innkeeper at the post inn that had its roof burnt off on Saturday night. He had been suspicious of Dodd because he was, of course, riding one of the Queen's horses but didn't present his warrant to get half-price booze.'

'Ah.'

'By his account, he locked Dodd into his room, and put one of his men on guard, planning to alert the authorities in Oxford.' Carey winced slightly. 'Yes, indeed. The mysterious fire started in the wall between Dodd's and the next chamber. However when I had my pursuivant find and question the merchant in that room, a Mr. Thomas Jenks, he insisted that Dodd was clearly a man of worship and no horsethief, had very kindly helped him carry out his strongbox when his two pages had run away, helped his young groom in the stable to get the beasts out, refused any reward and behaved very gentlemanlike all round. Mr. Jenks last saw Dodd make an impressive flying leap onto the back of his horse and chase a bolted nag out of the inn gates.'

Carey laughed outright. Sir Robert Cecil smiled. 'And then, I'm afraid, the trail goes cold again. Nobody between the London inn and Oxford has seen hide nor hair of him—they would have noticed him because he would have been riding without a saddle, of course.'

Hughie and the musician were getting along famously. Hughie had the harp on his lap and was clumsily twanging the strings. He started a song, some Scotch caterwaul about corbies which was Scotch for crows and no crow could have made a less musical noise than Hughie when he sang. Even Cecil winced at it and glanced at the barman, while the musician closed his eyes in pain. Something niggled Carey about Hughie then. What was it?

Hughie was looking soulful. 'Oahh,' he said, 'I've allus wanted to be a musician. I love tae sing. What would lessons cost?'

The potboy sniggered while the musician stoutly explained that a shilling an hour was the minimum possible amount.

Sir Robert Cecil was speaking again. 'I even had my people check further south and on the Great North Road in case he decided to go home without visiting you in Oxford but again, no traces.'

Carey lifted his silver cup to Cecil. 'I'm indebted to you, Mr. Secretary,' he said formally, wondering why Cecil was being so pleasant to him and what he wanted in exchange. 'Thank you for taking such trouble over it.'

'Not at all,' Cecil was genial, 'I feel a sense of responsibility for Sergeant Dodd's troubles. I realise now I should have warned him not to...er...reive any of Heneage's horses that had the Queen's brand on them, but I'm afraid it never crossed my mind.'

Carey nodded. 'Why should it, Sir Robert? Only someone who had to deal with Borderers regularly would know what they're like with good horseflesh.' Should he mention to Cecil the musician he had been following, who so liked the Spanish air? No. Perhaps not. After all, Cecil's father had suddenly become a major suspect in Amy Dudley's murder again. And goddamn it, both Hughie and the musician had gone. They must have left the place by the back door to the jakes while Carey's attention was on Cecil.

'Her Majesty is in a terrible temper. If she were not the Queen, I would go so far as to call it a foul mood.' Cecil paused. The pause was a polite opening for Carey to tell Cecil what he had been up to.

Carey continued to say nothing. It wasn't easy to do in the face of Cecil's tilted face, his grotesquely curved back disguised by the clever cut of his doublet and gown. Cecil shifted on the bench and winced slightly.

'I understand you brought something back from Cumnor Place today,' said Cecil. Of course Cecil had spies everywhere, just as his father did. It was part of the game of Court politics.

'Quite so, Mr. Secretary,' Carey said evenly, 'I did. I believe it was the murder weapon. A crossbow.'

Cecil raised his eyebrows as if this was new to him. 'Did you find Lady Dudley's damaged headtire?' Of course he would have read all the paperwork by now and seen what Carey had seen.

'No, Mr. Secretary, I didn't.'

Cecil nodded. He hadn't expected Carey to find it, he was making a point. There was a long silence again. 'I may be able to help you in your quest,' Cecil said slowly, 'I am not without... resources of my own.'

Carey thought very carefully about this. There was more to it than simple information exchanged for assistance. Carey was the Earl of Essex's man and of all the great men at Court, it was well known that Essex and Sir Robert Cecil hated each other. At least, Essex despised Cecil whom he occasionally teased about his hunchback. Cecil, it was obvious to everyone except Essex, virulently hated the Earl.

On the other hand, Cecil was as loyal to the Queen as his father and did, indeed, have resources of his own. Although it was Essex who had hurried to take over Walsingham's intelligence networks when Sir Francis died in 1590, Cecil was where the pursuivants and intelligencers went when they got tired of dealing with Heneage. He was even more close-mouthed than his father so it was impossible to know how much information he had access to, but Carey's guess was that he would be a lot better at the work than Essex was, who tended to boast. And Cecil had been behind the subtle coney-catching lay of the Cornish lands, Carey was certain of it.

Yet when Lady Hunsdon had taken that colossal risk to pay back Heneage for covertly attacking her husband through her son, she had deliberately involved Cecil in the business. And Mr. Secretary Cecil had cooperated.

Cecil would want to protect his father, might even be acting on his father's orders. And what if Essex found out? Nonetheless, some gut instinct was telling him to talk to Cecil.

'She wasn't shot?' Cecil wasn't really asking a question.

'Of course not. She was struck hard on the head with the end of the crossbow and broke her neck as she fell down the stairs.'

Cecil nodded. 'The Earl of Leicester?'

Carey shook his head. 'I really doubt it, sir. Why would he set on a man to shoot his wife with a crossbow—so clumsy, so risky—when a little belladonna could have sufficed as it nearly did for me?'

'No, I've never thought it was him either. So. Interesting. I will leave it in your capable hands, Sir Robert. Do not hesitate to call on me if you need any…er…advice or assistance.'

'Thank you, Mr. Secretary,' Carey said with a polite tilt of his head. 'I will.'

Cecil smiled, a sweet and charming smile that lit up his saturnine face. 'Have you ever considered a place on the Privy Council?'

Carey shuddered. 'Good God, no, sir! I had rather go back to France and fight for the King of Navarre.'

'Why not?'

'Too many meetings, too much paperwork. And I hate paperwork.'

Cecil laughed. 'It is an acquired taste, I admit. I only acquired it perforce but now I find it quite entrancing.'

'It would be good to have such an influential position,' Carey admitted. 'And I'm honoured you think I might be suitable, Mr. Secretary, but I'm afraid that the Queen knows me far too well and would never appoint me.'

Cecil tilted his head and raised his cup in toast. 'To your continued freedom from paperwork then, Sir Robert.'

Carey touched cups with him. 'And to your expert navigation of it, Mr. Secretary.'

MONDAY 18TH SEPTEMBER 1592, NIGHT

Hughie and the old musician walked down the lane at the rear of the White Horse, the musician going ahead to lead the way to his lodgings where he had brandy and a variety of instruments for Hughie to try.

Hughie was in a quandary. His first impulse was simply to get out his stolen harpstring and throttle the man in vengeance for daring to try and poison Hughie's prey without Hughie's permission—and nearly poisoning Hughie into the bargain. Why, why had he done it? The itch to know was as urgent as the itch to kill. The jeering voice inside was with him on this one—shouting at him to hurt the old man, make him suffer, find out if anyone else had been set on to kill Carey.

Despite Carey's gift for making enemies on the Border and at the Scottish Court, Hughie didn't think there was any real competition for the £30 in gold he expected to reap once Carey was dead and buried.

Perhaps he'd even have a lesson with the old fool. His interest in learning to sing and play an instrument was genuine. When you saw the mewling idiots who could impress the girls with their warbling and strumming, music couldn't be so very hard to learn. It was just noise that went up and down to a beat, wasn't it?

Now the musician had turned down a very narrow wynd; Hughie paused at the corner, loosened his knife. It occurred to him the musician must have marked him to give him the poisoned flagon in the first place and so...

He swayed back as the cosh came at him from a shadowed doorway on the other side of the wynd where the musician had been waiting.

Hughie laughed for sheer delight—knocked the cosh away with a sweep of his arm, then dived straight forward with his large left hand splayed, caught the man's throat and shoved him back against the wall. A knee in the man's groin finished the matter.

'Ay,' Hughie said, 'we do have business, but ye canna beat me in a fight.'

The musician was hunched over creaking for breath. A light punch in the kidneys put him on his face and Hughie knelt on his back, forced his left arm out on the ground and pinned the wrist, then started sawing at the man's thumb with his knife blade, which was shocking blunt; he'd have to sharpen it.

'No! No!' screamed the man, 'Please!'

Hughie stopped sawing. There was only a cut. 'Why did ye try tae poison me?'

'Not you,' gasped the man, 'your master, Hunsdon's boy.'

'Ay?'

'He knew Heron Nimmo's song, I thought...But he's a spy, he'll ruin it all.'

'Ay?' said Hughie, 'All what?'

There was a pause. Hughie shrugged and started sawing at the man's thumb again.

The jabbering took a while to get through because Hughie was intent on the pretty way the dark blood came out, but at last he stopped and listened. And then he let the weeping old man sit up and even wrap a handkerchief round his thumb and spoil the nice look of it.

'Och, shut yer greeting,' Hughie said, tossing his knife up and catching it. He found a likely looking cobble stone and started sharpening the blade—how had he let it get so bad? 'Start at the beginning. Say it slow.'

The musician took a long shuddering breath and did as he was told. Hughie listened carefully. It was an astonishing tale, stretching back into the past well before Hughie's own birth during the troubles that ended the mermaid Queen of Scots' wicked Papistical reign.

At the end of it, Hughie laughed. 'Och, so all ye want is tae kill the English Queen? Is that all?'

The musician goggled at him. Hughie shrugged. 'I'm a Scot,' he said, 'what do I care fer yer witch Queen, eh?'

The musician stammered something about treason. ''Tis nae such thing for me,' Hughie explained, 'if she goes, in comes the King o' Scots and that'll be a fine thing for me.' Especially if he could take the credit for it. Though King James, who was notoriously against bloodshed, might take a poor view of the man who did the deed, however much it might profit him.

'A'right, a'right,' he said to calm the old man's begging. Seemingly it all had to do with a great friend he hadn't seen for years, who made the song, or some such. Hughie couldn't be bothered to work it all out. 'Ah'm no worried about yer killing the Queen, but ye willna take another shot at Sir Robert Carey, d'ye follow me? Eh?'

The musician nodded, eyes like a hanged man's, beard full of turnip peelings, doublet smeared with shit, his hand cradled.

'I swear it,' he said. 'Nothing more against Carey.'

For a moment Hughie was tempted to tell the old fool what he himself was about, but why? Knowledge was gold. There was no need to give it away free.

They shook on it. 'Off ye go then,' Hughie said, dismissing him with a gesture. 'Dinna cross me again.'

Once the musician had stumbled off down the alley, Hughie brushed himself down and set off in the opposite direction, back to Broad Street.

He found the White Horse inn again, but no sign of Carey who must have gone back to his bed. It was a very tempting thought, he was unusually tired.

The candles and the fire in the grate bothered Hughie's sore eyes and he wasn't feeling very well, so he was turning to leave when a shadowy twisted figure in one of the booths beckoned him over.

The gentleman Carey had spoken to respectfully wasn't ill-looking under his tall hat, and his doublet was a smart black brocade: well cut and padded to hide his hunchback, clearly London tailoring and very skillful. The cloak was tidily folded beside him.

'Are you Hughie Tyndale?' asked the man.

'Ay, sir,' he said, a little nervous.

'Your master Sir Robert Carey has gone back to the Earl of Cumberland's camp. How did it go with your music lesson?'

'Och,' said Hughie with a genial smile. 'It wisnae very good and then I want tae another ale house and tripped on the way out, muddied maself something terrible.'

The man's face was sharp as an Edinburgh merchant. 'Set ye doon,' he said in passable Scots, 'Ah've a mind tae speak wi' ye. What's yer right name?'

Hughie said nothing and shrugged though his heart was beating hard. The man smiled shyly.

'I've an idea yer right name is Hughie Elliot, youngest brother to Wee Colin. Is that right?'

It was the password he'd been given by the man who said he

was working for the Earl of Bothwell.

'Ay sir,' he said. So this was the man who was supposed to be his contact in England. A rich hunchback. Well, so be it.

'What were you to do for me?' asked the man.

'Nobbut send ye tidings of Carey's doings in the West March,' Hughie told him and the rich hunchback nodded gravely. 'And then after a year and a day, when I've killt him, let ye know so ye can warn the goldsmith to give me ma gold.'

The shadow of something that might have been amusement crossed the hunchback's face.

'Indeed? Can you cipher, Hughie?'

'I can read and write, if that's yer meaning, sir?'

The rich hunchback brought out paper and some pieces of graphite and showed him what ciphering meant. It was a way of putting signs or numbers instead of letters in a system which meant you could still read it. Hughie was impressed at the cleverness of it.

'How do I send ye messages, sir? In the dispatch bag to Berwick?'

'Certainly not,' said the hunchback. 'Do you know Carlisle at all? No? Well there's a man there called Thomas the Merchant Hetherington that will do anything at all for money. Go to him when you get to Carlisle and show him this token.'

It was a blood jasper, carved with the image of a snake. A nice piece.

'That's the Serpent Wisdom. He'll know then that he's to take your letters and send them south with his own letters to London. They'll reach me.'

'Ay, sir.'

'Oh and Hughie, please hold off on killing Carey, would you? Remember your pension stops when he dies.'

'Ma pension?'

'Certainly. I'll instruct Thomas the Merchant to pay a shilling to you for every letter I receive.'

"Och." It would take a great many letters to equal the £30 in gold he was owed for Carey's head. Six hundred in fact. But still... It was money in the hand not the bush, as it were.

'Ay, sir,' said Hughie, carefully tipping his cap to the hunchback. 'Thank ye, sir.'

'I'll look forward to your reports with interest,' said the hunchback.

'Ehm…Who should they be addressed to?'

'Mr. Philpotts at the Belle Sauvage inn, Ludgate Hill.'

'Ay? What shall I do till I get yer money, sir?'

'See if Carey will pay you,' said Mr. Philpotts lightly. 'You'd better go now, he wants you to help him with his doublet.'

As Hughie turned the corner and saw the chequered Cumberland flags he thought to himself, 'I'll kill him when I choose, not when ye say so, Mr. Hunchback Philpotts.' It was exciting to be earning money for letters though. He'd come a long way since the bastard Dodds burnt out his whole family when he was but a wean, a long, long way.

TUESDAY 19TH SEPTEMBER 1592, 2 A.M.

Captain Leigh struggled awake in the black night before dawn, heart thumping, his sword already grabbed from its usual place by the side of his bed. He stood there, listening for a moment.

A horrific shriek rang out that was neither an owl nor any creature being eaten by a fox. Then there was a thunder of running feet and shouting, then horses…

He already had his hose on and he pulled his buff jerkin over the top of his shirt, drew the sword and ran outside into the burned monastery's cloister. A large shape galloped past him and nearly knocked him over. Another shape cannoned into him in the dark and tried to punch him. The smell of booze told him who it was.

'Goddamn it, I'm the captain!' he shouted at John Arden who sheepishly let him up. A man in a shirt ran past screaming blue murder, another couple of men were scrambling up onto a lookout place like milkmaids chased by a mouse.

The horse in the cloister reared and kicked, another galloped past neighing with panic. Leigh grabbed for its mane and it tried to bite him. Both nags galloped out the gate into the forest.

In the murk, more men appeared groggily, some with their buff jerkins on, most without their boots. One was hopping on one leg with a nasty gash in his toe.

Finally someone got the lantern alight again which only helped a little as the night was so dark.

'It...it's ghosts, sir. Burnt monks.'

'*Al infierno con esos capullos,*' hissed somebody behind him. Leigh spun to see Jeronimo stamping across the flagstones with a loaded crossbow clamped under his shortened arm, a torch in the other, his buffcoat and boots on and his morion on his head. At that moment Leigh knew the man was not lying about having been a *terceiro* of the third Imperial Spanish legion as he boasted.

They checked the carrels below the monks' dorter which was in use as their stable. Three of the horses had bolted, leaving only the Northerner's Whitesock still there, pulling at his tether. Leigh went to him and managed to calm the animal down, gave him some hay to eat. The doors had been broken outwards.

Eventually under Leigh's bellowing and Jeronimo's withering scorn, the men gathered together, sheepish and cold. Harry Hunks was there, blinking, looking witless and still in his shirt.

'God's teeth!' shouted Leigh in disgust, 'Christ save us if we ever do find ourselves attacked in the night. None of you will. The only man among you that wouldn't be dead right now is Don Jeronimo.'

Jeronimo flourished a bow. The men didn't like being compared unfavourably to a foreigner and one of them muttered rebelliously.

'Speak up, Smithson,' Leigh snapped.

'It was ghosts, sir, I heard 'em singing.'

'I saw one, it was white, sir, and it moaned.'

A gabble of frightened stories broke out. Allegedly the burned monks had been singing the Papist hymn for the dead.

'For God's sake, it was probably just another one of you idiots, blundering about screaming in the dark.'

'All the watchlights went out, sir, all at the same time. And then there was Papist singing. It's the burned monks, sir.'

Leigh rolled his eyes. Nothing annoyed him more than superstitious nonsense about ghosts. He should have seen ghosts by now if they existed and he hadn't. So they didn't. It was clean contrary to good religion in any case—the dead slept until judgement when most of them would be damned. It didn't matter whether you buried them or not, they slept. How many piles of bodies from battles or camp fevers had he supervised being burned or buried? If ghosts walked, there should be troops of them following him and following the men he led, ghosts of innocent people they had killed or burned. He shivered for a second. Of course, he would be among the damned.

'Look,' he said, trying to get them to think, 'The old monks are dead and gone fifty years ago at least.'

Somebody muttered. 'Don't matter to ghosts.'

'I saw it, sir, it was white and moaning, sir.'

'I expect that was Mr. Arden, hungover, trying to stop you killing each other in your fright.' Arden smiled a little.

Leigh was thinking hard. He sent some men out to catch the bolted horses again, beckoned Smithson over and they walked quickly down to the old witch's cottage in the ruins of the monastery gatehouse. If that bloody northerner wasn't in the monk's pit, he'd flog the bastard.

The dog was snoozing in the yard, lifted an ear and one eyelid at the sound of their feet, gave a short lazy 'Woof!' and went back to sleep.

They found the turfed wickerwork roof over the mouth of the pit and peered in.

The man was asleep there, curled up in a rough old blanket and snoring. The light from their lantern woke him and he lifted his head and put up his hand against the dazzle.

'Ay, whit d'ye want?' he snarled. 'Can Ah no' get ma sleep?'

'Was it you causing trouble?' Leigh demanded.

The Northerner propped himself on his elbow and scratched his brown hair vigorously.

'Ay,' he sneered, 'Ah've wings to fly and Ah flew over ye and shat upon ye for entertainment.'

Leigh let the hurdle drop again. They went back to the old monastery and tried to clear up and sort out the mess. Leigh decided he had to run some proper exercises for his men. They'd got soft sitting around here. In France they would never have let a couple of bolted horses and a few shrieks from an owl spook them so badly.

But nobody was dead. That was what finally convinced Leigh he was only dealing with superstition and stupidity. If the Northerner had done it, surely he'd have slit a few throats, it stood to reason?

It was past sunrise before he was in the Northerner's respectable suit which was tight at the waist, the Northerner's fat purse full of gold angels in the crotch and some counted out into the front pocket. Whitesock was in perfectly good health despite the night, though the saddle from one of the other horses didn't fit him properly. The other three were no doubt out in the forest eating yew and whatever else they could find that would poison them. The men would have to find them, he didn't want to delay any longer.

The Oxford road was only a mile away, near Cumnor Place. As he prepared to leave he beckoned John Arden to his stirrup. Jeronimo was sitting slumped on a stone bench, his crossbow discharged now, his face grey and unreadable.

'Listen, John,' he hissed at his old friend, 'stay sober, stay in charge, make sure nothing else happens. If that Northerner gives trouble, knock him out but don't kill him. This is our one chance for our pay, you understand?'

Arden was clearly already drunk. He blinked owlishly up at Leigh.

'I know that, Captain,' he slurred, 'I won't get drunk.'

Leigh shook his head and put his heels in.

TUESDAY 19TH SEPTEMBER 1592, MORNING

Dodd had gone to sleep again after the excitement of the early morning and he only woke when the old woman heaved the hurdle off the top of the pit and threw pebbles on him.

'Whit?' he asked, annoyed.

'Where's my granddaughter?' she demanded shrilly, 'What have you done with her?'

'Eh?' he blinked as stupidly as he could, 'What could I do wi' her, missus, I've bin in this pit all night? D'ye see her here?'

The carlin set her toothless jaw. 'Then what was all that shouting? Did that frighten her?'

'Mebbe, missus.' Even if she hadn't known all about it, Dodd would have bet that it wouldn't frighten young Kat. 'I dinna ken.'

'Well you can stay there today, I don't trust you.'

Dodd shrugged, spotted his feet and pulled them cautiously under the rough blanket he'd been very grateful for last night. 'Suits me, missus,' he said and she stamped away. He could hear the goats protesting as she milked them and led them out to feed, muttering all the while.

Then he lay back with his head on his arms, blinked at the sheep's wool clouds caught on the cold blue sky and smiled quietly to himself. It had been fun last night. Getting out of the pit had not been easy, but he had once raided gulls' nests on the cliffs by the sea when they were starving and had learnt how to climb with his toes and wedge billets of wood between gaps in the stone. The poles of his splint had come in useful, tied together at the ends, to push the hurdle-roof off the top of the pit. Little Kat had been waiting for him in the blackness and cold before dawn, snuggled next to the snoring dog and he had taken her on his shoulders and had her tell him the way to the main Oxford road so he'd know it later. Once she was off, trotting up the road determinedly in her clogs in a way that reassured him, he'd turned back to the old monastery and set about seeing to it that Leigh didn't beat her to Oxford city.

In the days when his feet had leathery soles and he was smaller and lighter, he could move like a shadow. He was no longer a boy but he could still put his feet down softly and he did that, slipping through the clearer parts of the undergrowth in his loose woollen breeks, the shirt and the blanket under his arm, mud smeared in stripes and splotches over his face and chest.

There were only two guards set, chatting in the darkness by their watchlight at the bend in the road, smoking his tobacco. Getting past them had been almost insultingly easy. And then he had free rein over the sleeping men in the monastery. After he had taken a knife out of the boy's scabbard, hanging by his bed in the dorter, he carefully trimmed the wicks on the watch candles so they'd go out a few minutes later. He broke the tethers of the horses that weren't Whitesock by scorching the rope first with a watchlight and then he broke the bolts open by levering with one of the halberds. And then he'd cracked the nags over the backside with the pole of the halberd and let out a good Tyneside yell. His throat still hurt from it. He had the shirt over his head and the blanket round his shoulders and he'd spent a happy few minutes running through the shadowy dorter shrieking about the burned monk, singing the one piece of plainchant he knew which was some nonsense his mother used to sing to get them to sleep. 'Dee is eery, dee is iller, solve it sigh clum in far viller!' he'd intoned, finishing by howling and then shouting 'Alarm!' and 'Ghosts!' for good measure. Once the darkness was full of frightened men in their shirts running about and punching each other, he'd pulled the shirt down properly and tied the blanket round his waist under it and done a bit of running and punching himself.

As a final flourish he'd run directly across the cloister screaming and out the gate while the dimwitted Captain stood there blinking with his sword in one hand and the lantern in the other. The old Spaniard came out then with his crossbow on his shoulder and Dodd picked up speed into the darkness.

Then came the hard part. As he ran he stripped his shirt off again and picked up a branch to drag behind him and pounded through the woods as fast as he could back to the old carlin's pit, doing his best not to shout when he bruised his foot on a stone or trampled through brambles.

At the edge of the pit he'd used the blanket to wipe the mud off his sweating body and face, dropped it and the shirt into the pit, let himself down on the wedged billets of wood and the stone he'd propped against the wall, pulled them out and used the two poles from his splint to manoeuvre the hurdle back over the top of the pit, leaving it dark. And then he'd groped about, found the shirt and blanket, pulled the shirt over him, dropped onto the bracken and wrapped the blanket round him, panting hard as he heard Leigh's boots approaching.

He hadn't had time to put the splints back on his leg for effect but he hoped they wouldn't notice. It seemed they hadn't and they'd been fooled by his imitation of the noises Carey normally made at night. He'd stay meekly in the pit now and hope like hell young Kat would get to Oxford in time. He'd done all he could, mind, he couldn't think of anything else he could do for the moment.

After some more thought he sat up again and looked at his feet. They were a sad sight, bruised, muddy, still bleeding in a couple of places. He pulled the thorns out with his fingernails and as he didn't have any water to wash them with, he carefully pissed on them which stung but at least left them cleaner. Then he strapped the splints on again. After that there was no sound from the old woman so he might as well go back to sleep as there was no chance she would feed him.

Yet she did. She woke him with more thrown pebbles and then let down a pail with bread, cheese, and a quart of ale which Dodd assumed would be full of valerian and wild lettuce. He was thirsty from all the running around and needed his rest, so he drank half of it. And had to admit that the old woman's green goat cheese was excellent, maybe better than Janet's.

Ay, Janet. He'd have some tales to tell her of the south. She'd laugh her spots off, his freckled leopard of a wife and then he'd see to her, ay, he'd see to her well and perhaps he'd plant a child in her this time.

He was dozing in the middle of a particularly pleasant daydream of something unusual he could do with fine goat's cheese if his wife would only cooperate, when the branch he'd dragged behind him to hide his tracks came over the edge of the pit and landed in front of him.

He'd hidden the stolen knife by driving it into the earth between two stones and so he stood and moved closer to it.

A man in a morion was standing near the dressed stones at the edge of the pit, idly pointing a loaded and cocked crossbow down at him one handed. His other sleeve was folded up short.

'Señor Elliot,' said the Spanish accented voice.

'Ay,' Dodd said after a moment. The man had him cold, nothing he could do about it, so he sat down on the pile of bracken and crossed his legs.

'Last night,' said the Spaniard, hissing in through his teeth like a man hiding that he was wounded, 'it was very *divertido*, eh? An excellent *camisado* attack.'

Dodd shrugged. 'It wasnae me, whatever it was,' he said, more for form's sake than anything else, as he didn't expect this one to believe him. 'What's a camisado attack?'

The bony hawk face smiled briefly. 'A night attack. We call it camisado because the attackers have shirts over his armours so they look equal as the sleepers.'

'Ay?' said Dodd, interested. You wouldn't call a night attack that in the Borders, of course, because everyone would be wearing jacks, whether they'd been asleep or no. These Southerners were pitiful, really.

'The thing is strange,' said the Spaniard, 'No deaths. None killed. Why not, Señor Elliot?'

Dodd shrugged again

'I watched with admiration,' said the Spaniard, 'one man against twenty-five idiots, what a chaos!'

Dodd said nothing, didn't see the point.

'My name, Señor Elliot, is Don Jeronimo de la Quadra de Jimena.'

He said it as if it should mean something to Dodd, as if he was stating his surname, but of course Dodd didn't know anything about Spanish surnames.

'You are Don Roberto Carey his man, yes?'

Did don mean sir in foreign? 'Ay,' said Dodd.

'He send you find me?'

Dodd almost said no, but then he thought it might be more interesting if he lied. So he did that. 'Ay sir,' he said, 'but he didna tell me why. I was tae bring ye to him.'

The man frowned so Dodd sighed and said it again more Southern. He knew Carey would back him, whatever this was about. The grizzled soldier nodded slowly. Then he took out the bolt and released the crossbow string, squatted down at the edge of the pit. Dodd watched with interest as he filled his clay pipe one-handed with Dodd's expensive medicinal tobacco and started smoking.

'I like this herb,' said the Spaniard, 'very good. Did Don Roberto tell you anything?'

'Why would he?'

'No. What do you intend tonight?'

Dodd had never heard such a cheeky question in his life. What did the foreigner think he'd say?

'Sleep,' he said coldly, 'as I did last night.' He was watching the Spaniard from below so the shape of the face was different, but then as Jeronimo turned his face away and winced for some reason, he suddenly knew him. It was the man who had stared at him at the Oxford road inn. He almost said something about it but then he decided it could wait. If Jeronimo was the one responsible for all the pain and aggravation he'd suffered since Saturday night, Dodd didn't want him alerted to his doom. And when Dodd caught a whiff of the smoke from his pipe, he could have killed him just for the tobacco.

'Señor, let us tell a little tale. Shall we say that some...yes, some *diablito* creeps into the burned monastery and cause chaos, what is his purpose?' Dodd shrugged. 'You could have slit some throats, taken back your sword. But no. So what was your purpose?'

'I didna do it,' Dodd told him. 'I was asleep.'

Jeronimo sighed. 'Señor,' he said, 'I know you are a man of virtue, I know you are more than you say. Perhaps I talk to Captain Leigh of what I see and you not play your game again. Perhaps I hamstring you.'

Dodd had to hide a flinch. Cut the cords at the backs of his legs so he couldn't walk? Christ, please, no. But Jeronimo could do it, if he had enough men on his side. Dodd had no doubt that he would be willing to do it.

'Or you cure my childish curiosity,' said the Spaniard with another hiss of pain, adding more of Dodd's tobacco to his pipe and puffing. No more of the smoke was coming into the pit, it was all going upwards, damn it.

The maddest part of his plan came back to him. Maybe? Dodd stood up. 'Whit d'ye think to the Captain, Don Jeronimo?' he asked.

The Spaniard shrugged. 'He is adequate though not very bright. He is *flojo*. Lazy. I come to England with him for protection, company. There must be a captain and I do not want it. I was many things, Señor, a musician, an assassin, a soldier, a Courtier, a captain, a hero, a cripple, many many things. I have no desire for being a captain again. I have other business here. And I will die soon.'

'How d'ye know?'

Jeronimo sighed, put down his pipe on a stone and pulled up one of his canion breeches to show his thigh. His leg was covered with ugly black spots and sores. Dodd felt sick. Was it plague? No. Couldn't be. He'd be lying down, not walking around waving a crossbow.

'It is a canker. I asked a physician in France, a good one, though a Jew. He had seen such things. It was first one mole, it bled, it itched. Then it grew, it had children. Some become sores. Now I have pain and stones in my *estomago*, now I have a thing like a rock in my liver and I bleed sometime like a woman.'

'Och,' said Dodd, because he couldn't help it. His legs felt wobbly. He hated sickness, hated it. Men with swords you could fight. What could you do against black spots or a rock in your belly? Bleed like a woman? From his arse? Och God.

Jeronimo smiled slightly. 'So, all men die and I will die soon. I hoped once it would be bravely, in battle. It makes no matter. But I have a business in England now. When I was young and clever and very stupid, I try to please my natural father with a great deed—but it went badly. Later I lose my arm and my music, I think this pays for it, but when I make confession to a priest last Easter, he say no. I must make it right.'

Jeronimo shrugged and grimaced. 'I should go to a more easy priest. But he was right so I set off to do it, and here I am.'

'Ay,' said Dodd, cautiously, wondering what was coming next.

'Don Roberto is son of el conde Hunsdon, no?'

'Ay.'

'Hunsdon is a bastard and so I am too. He is bastard of the King, me...Less important. I must see his sister, the Queen,' said the Spaniard, 'That is all.'

Dodd's jaw dropped. 'See the Queen?' he repeated.

'Si, Señor, Her Majesty the Queen Isabella of England.'

'Why?'

'My business, Señor. Can your master manage such a thing?'

'Ay, he could,' Dodd said instantly, seeing no call to disappoint the old madman. 'But why should he? Men pay hundreds of pounds for a chance just tae talk to the Queen.' Jeronimo nodded.

'It is sure,' he said. 'She will wish to see me. All I need is the man to...ah...to connect.'

'But...' Madman, assassin? Why else would a foreigner want to speak directly to the Queen? Dodd set his jaw. 'Why?'

Jeronimo tutted. 'Only give me your word of honour you will speak to your lord, Señor Elliot.'

Dodd folded his arms and looked up narrow-eyed at the man. 'And?'

'I will let you go, free you.'

'No,' he said.

'Why no?'

'Ah dinna ken who ye are nor why ye might wantae see the Queen, but I can guess since you're Spanish. So ye can go to hell.'

'I will not harm her, not a hair of her head.'

'No.'

'I swear it on my soul.'

'No.'

'Why so much trouble, so much chaos and no killings, Señor Elliot? How can we agree?'

Don't threaten my hamstrings, Dodd thought, don't put me at risk of hanging, drawing and quartering. Instead he showed his teeth. 'Let's call vada and I'll see your prime,' he said, a phrase he had picked up from Carey. 'Help me and I'll think about it.'

'I will bring the ladder.'

'Och,' Dodd shook his head at the man's ignorance. Still he was nobbut a foreigner, he couldn't help it. 'Nay, I'll want more than that.'

'Indeed? What, Señor?'

Dodd told him, leaving out some important details in case this was all some elaborate ploy of Leigh's to interrogate him. Jeronimo started to laugh which got a sour look from the old woman as she came past with her small flock of goats. Then the Spaniard took his hat off to Dodd and walked away, leaving Dodd with nothing to do but worry that he'd been coney-catched himself and that Leigh would come back from Oxford and slice his hamstrings so his legs would be like a broken puppet's, unable to stand. And Christ, bleeding like a woman from a rock in your belly. It made his skin shiver just thinking about things like that.

TUESDAY 19TH SEPTEMBER 1592, MORNING

Somebody was shaking Carey awake. It was Ross. Carey sat up, feeling groggy which was a very strange experience because normally he was awake before dawn and out of bed immediately. Was this how Dodd felt every morning? Poor man. The night had been full of complicated incomprehensible dreams about Elizabeth Widdrington.

'You've a lady visitor, Sir Robert,' said Ross, looking amused. 'Best get up and look tidy.'

Carey rubbed his face, wondered who it was. Couldn't be the Queen, she was at Woodstock palace by now, resting, and she'd roust him out to visit her, not the other way round. Couldn't be his mother, please God, she should be on the high seas on her way back to Cornwall. Couldn't be Emilia as she had been such a hit with the Earl of Essex. God, he was stupid this morning. If only there was some potion you could drink which would wake you up.

'Who is it?'

'M'Lady Blount, sir.'

'Who?'

'The ex-Dowager Lady Leicester.'

Jesus Christ, Lettice Knollys as was, his cousin. The woman who had snaffled the Earl of Leicester from the Queen. It came back to him slowly that Thomas Blount, one of her son's hangers-on, had scandalously become her third husband.

'What? What's she doing here? She's not supposed to come to Court, the Queen can't stand her.'

Ross managed not to smile. 'Well sir, the Court's not arrived yet officially and nor has the Queen so she's here to see her son, I expect.'

'Oorgh. What time is it?'

'Half past eight o'the clock, sir. My lord Earl of Cumberland said not to wake you.'

'That late?'

Carey swung his legs to the floor as the camp bed creaked its straps under him. How on earth had he slept so long? Normally he was awake the minute dawn came, no matter what time he went to bed. Was he hungover?

Hmm. Perhaps still a bit poisoned. But at least his eyes weren't as bad as they had been. The light coming through the tent walls wasn't actually hurting him. He rubbed his face again, felt bristles around his goatee.

'Do you know how to shave a man, Mr. Ross?'

'Not really, sir. I'll send for some hot water and a razor.'

'Please apologise to Lady Blount and explain that I'm not in a fit state to see her yet but I'll be as quick as I can. Get her sweet wine and some wafers and sweetmeats if you can find any.'

Twenty minutes later, wearing a fresh shirt belonging to the Earl of Cumberland (who owed him at least five from the abortive *camisado* attack in France a year before), beard trimmed, cheeks shaved, hair combed, hat pulled down low against the grey daylight, clean falling band and his forest green hunting doublet unbuttoned at the top in the fashionable melancholy style, Carey breezed into the marquee where Lady Blount was sitting, magnificent on a cushioned stool which was entirely drowned by her large wheel farthingale.

'My lady cousin,' he said making a full Court bow with a flourish of his hat, 'how delightful to see you here!'

She was the daughter of his aunt, Katherine Knollys, she of the lost riding habit, and the mother of the Earl of Essex by her first husband Walter Devereux. She had earned the Queen's undying hatred because, after her husband, the first Earl of Essex died conveniently in an Irish bog of a flux, she had firmly set her cap at and succeeded in stealing the Queen's only real love, to wit, one Robert Dudley, Earl of Leicester. She had been a beautiful woman in her youth, flame-haired, white skin, blue eyes, but had got quite stout recently. She made no concessions to this and creaked in a low cut pointed bodice plunging into her vast farthingale in eye-watering yellow brocade and emerald-green velvet. Her feathered hat was tilted on her white cap and her famous red curls peeked out under it, quite possibly helped by alchemical magic. Her face was well made-up so she looked like a child's poppet with her white skin and red cheeks, and her hands were heavy with rings. She no longer looked so similar to the Queen as she had in her youth because the Queen was still slender and she was not.

'Well Robin, what have you been doing to yourself?' she cooed maliciously. 'Are you hungover again? You really shouldn't drink so much…..'

Carey smiled with equal sweetness, 'No, Coz, somebody put belladonna in my drink on Saturday night,' he said. 'Was it you?'

She ignored this. 'What is it my lord son tells me about my gold-bearing Cornish lands?'

Carey sighed. Somebody had to have bought them—clearly he was right and the Earl had been buying them on behalf of his mother.

'If my lord Earl of Essex was repeating what I told him,' he said slowly and clearly so as not to overtax her very womanly brain, 'the lands were a lay set by a coney-catching Papist called Father Jackson and are about as worthless as land can be.'

'Of course they're not, Robin, I have seen the assays. You really mustn't try and lower the price on them, I expect dear Henry wants to snap some up cheap the way…'

I don't really have the time or the inclination for this, Carey thought, how can I get rid of the old bag?

'Perhaps you would like to discuss this with my mother,' Carey said, 'She's the one who spotted what was going on. She's at sea now, I think, but I'm sure my father would…'

Carey knew perfectly well that his mother and Lettice hated each other. Lady Blount tightened her mouth which was wrinkled exactly like an old purse.

'I'm asking you, Robin.'

Don't call me Robin, Carey thought and smiled again because he'd been on the verge of commiserating with her about the failure of her speculation. His father had suffered a few: you can't speculate in property without occasionally making a costly mistake.

'Lady Blount, if my mother says the lands are worthless, they're worthless. And they're in Cornwall where I doubt you're willing to go to find out.'

'Why not? Where is Cornwall anyway?'

'About four hundred miles west and south of here.'

'Really? Are you sure?'

'Er...yes, cousin.' He decided not to try and explain the details because it would probably melt whatever passed for a brain under her fake red curls. 'And I'm very sorry, but I'm not completely recovered from the poisoning and...'

He wasn't being entirely truthful. He felt tired but now he was more awake and in the dimness of the pavilion, his eyes were behaving themselves at least.

'Well that wasn't why I came.' Lettice was staring sideways at him now. 'I heard from my son that you were looking into the... er...the death of my late second husband's first wife.'

Carey paused. Surprisingly, the Earl must have kept his promise. 'Yes, my lady cousin, I am. Very reluctantly but the Queen ordered it.'

'Reluctantly?'

'The thing happened thirty-two years ago, the year I was born in fact.' To his unkind satisfaction he saw Lettice flinch slightly. 'That's how long poor Amy Dudley has been dead and buried. I know Her Majesty set someone on to look into it in 1566, but he got nowhere...

'Topcliffe certainly did get somewhere,' Lady Blount contradicted him. 'He just never said what he found, only I think he's been blackmailing the Queen about it very cleverly.'

'Oh?' Now that was very interesting. Was that why Topcliffe was mysteriously untouchable, no matter what he did? 'Do you know what he found out?'

Lettice shrugged her powdered white shoulders and then looked cunning. 'Maybe you should ask what he found, not what he found out. Just knowing something wouldn't be enough, would it?'

Carey perched himself on a table and wished for wine, his throat was infernally dry again. 'Sergeant Ross,' he called, 'could you find me a boy to fetch us some wine…some more wine? Not spiced, please. And some breakfast for me.'

After last Saturday night, Carey doubted he would ever again be able to stomach spiced wine; just the thought of it made his gorge rise.

Lady Blount had clearly finished the first plate of sweetmeats and looked disappointed when the boy trotted in with a plate of bread and cheese alongside a jack of good rough red wine, then brightened when he produced another silver plate of wafers and comfits. Carey didn't like sweetmeats and they pained one of his back teeth every time the Queen made him eat one. He soon felt full so he let Lettice munch on the other half of the penny loaf and only took a bit of cheese himself. However, the wine was Italian and better than usual so he drank that.

'Do you know what thing Topcliffe found, Lady Blount?'

'No, of course not.' The kohl crusted eyelashes batted at him. 'And I would tell you if I did, Robin, because nobody likes Richard Topcliffe despite the way he gets lands off the Papists.'

Carey suppressed a sigh. 'So was it Topcliffe you wanted to talk to me about, my lady?'

She made a face. 'Ugh no, he's a horrible man. My son wanted me to tell you something my lord Leicester said to me once when he was drunk.'

She paused significantly. What would she want for the information? 'Yes?'

'Of course, you know this is secret. This is very, very secret. I've never told anybody this, not even my darling Robin until now.'

'Yes?'

'So you won't tell Her Majesty who told you?'

'I can't promise that, my lady. If she asks me the question direct, I will tell her of course.'

The pouchy rosebud lips tightened. Then she shook herself. 'Well, I don't see why I shouldn't tell you, the scandalous old cat. Especially if she's digging it all up again.'

'Hm?'

'My lord husband...' said Lettice drawing the words out slowly and Carey worked to keep the impatience off his face because it would only encourage her, '...my lord of Leicester said once after dinner that it was damned unfair, the whole thing had nearly been arranged, Amy would divorce him, and if he ever found out who murdered her before she could set him free, he would kill the man with his own hands, for taking his Eliza from him. There.'

She sat back and looked pleased with herself.

'A divorce?' Carey breathed. It was obvious, but he had only just started to wonder about it.

'Yes,' said Lettice. 'Good King Henry did it twice of course, so much less upsetting than finding someone guilty of adultery and beheading them. It was before Bess of Hardwick divorced her husband and it would take an Act of Parliament but still...What couldn't happen was my lord of Leicester doing the divorcing or the scandal would be too much and Convocation would block it. The Queen didn't want any trouble like that, she was so hot for him. So the plan was for Amy to ask for an annulment on grounds of non-consummation.' Lettice nibbled a third wafer like a greedy squirrel and winked. It was a frightening sight.

Carey's lips were parted at this brand new angle on the story. 'But...' he began.

'Convocation would have granted it—they'd been plumped specially. Parliament would have granted it if Amy petitioned because they were desperate for Her Majesty to marry and get an heir even though they hated the Earl. She was getting old, after all, she was 27 in 1560. Amy would be given a nice pension and some property and be free to marry again while she could still have children and my lord of Leicester would become King.'

Now that made a lot of sense. A lot more sense than the notion of the Queen being so insane as to murder her lover's wife.

'So perhaps Burghley did the...'

'Fooey,' said Lettice unexpectedly, 'I don't think Burghley did anything because he didn't know. Nobody knew. Just the Queen, Amy, and Robert Dudley. Nobody else at all. They made sure the musicians played loudly when they were planning it and they didn't speak in English and sometimes they wrote to each other

but then they burnt the letters. It was a secret. Amy was still at
Cumnor Place but she sent letters saying that she was willing to
talk about bringing a petition for divorce. She was just dickering
for more money and a nicer manor house and more land. She
wouldn't come to Court; she didn't like it, said she didn't want to
be bullied out of her money.'

Lettice pursed her lips again and leaned forward confidingly.
'She was a dreadful girl, dull, twitter-headed, greedy, obstinate.
I never liked her and I certainly didn't know anything about all
this at the time. And she was so pious. Robert laughed about how
worried she was about having to swear in court that they hadn't
consummated their marriage because they had, she just never
quickened, no matter what she did, she was barren. But she was
terrified about hell and damnation for swearing it falsely. That
drove the Queen mad.'

Carey kept to himself his immediate thought that the Queen,
whose indecisiveness drove every one of her servants crazy with
impatience, had well-deserved to face the thing herself.

'And then...the stupid girl fell down the stairs or somebody
pushed her and the whole thing fell apart. Poor Dudley was the
one everybody thought did it so he couldn't even marry the Queen
though he was free.' Carey nodded and Lettice smiled smugly. 'Of
course, it was lucky for me because then I could marry him, not
the Queen.' A shadow passed over her face. 'I wish she would let
me come back to Court now he's dead. It's not fair of her, is it?'

Carey shook his head sympathetically.

'I so love to see all the new fashions and hear the new music.
My son tells me the news of course and I advise him and his wife.
Poor Frances. She's so brainy for a pretty girl. It's terrible for her
really. She's pregnant again, you know?'

Lettice finished the last wafer and sat back as far as she could
in the gaudy cage of her dress.

'Hmm. What did my Lady Essex think about the Cornish lands?'

'Oh, she has no idea. She wouldn't let poor Robin so much as
ride down to look at them, said her father taught her that anything
that looked too good to be true probably wasn't true, the boring
old creep. So he missed out on them.'

Carey nodded again, thinking better of Lady Essex. He, too, had learned that maxim from Walsingham.

'She'll be sorry when the gold starts to flow,' said Lettice brightly, nodding her head so her feather bobbed. 'I'll tell my lord son I've told you about the Queen's divorce and he can tell you anything else he learned from his stepfather. You know, my lord of Leicester was a wonderful father, he taught Robin to hunt and ride—even after his own poor little boy died, he was kind to his stepson. I remember once when...'

Carey smiled and nodded at a very fond tale about the young Earl of Essex's first pony. He had forgotten how boring Lettice Knollys could be but he now had to get rid of her urgently because Dr. Lopez's potions were summoning him.

'My lady cousin,' he said with as much unctuous sincerity as he could ladle into his voice, 'I am so grateful to you for coming all this way and telling me this extremely important secret. I am truly amazed at it.'

Not really, more amazed he hadn't thought of it before. Lady Blount looked pink-cheeked and happy and creaked obediently to her feet as Carey offered his hand to help her up.

'Please don't tell anyone at all what you've told me,' he warned.

'Oh don't worry, Robin, not even my lord Treasurer Burghley, though he's such an old friend and he was asking me the other day. You know he was the one who introduced me to my lord of Leicester after my lord realised the Queen would never really marry him?'

Which put Burghley squarely back in the dock for the murder of Amy Robsart, despite all his protestations. If Amy had agreed to petition for divorce that would ultimately make Dudley king and Burghley would have been out of a job the same week. Desperate men do desperate things. In 1560, the then-Sir William Cecil had not yet made his fortune from the Treasury and the Court of Wards. It was all very clear. The Queen wouldn't like it coming out at all though and what about Mr. Secretary Cecil? Speaking of which, why on earth had she set all this in motion anyway? Why hadn't his father warned him?

Carey bowed Lettice, Lady Blount out of Cumberland's pavilion, blinked longingly at the men playing veneys in the central area of the camp while Sergeant Ross ran the sword class with his usual combination of wit and bullying. Unfortunately he had an urgent and probably unpleasant appointment with the jakes.

Tuesday 19th September, 1592

Some time later, Carey ambled into town again to see if he could spot the musician he had been following the previous night. His eyes did seem to be getting better—he had to squint and things were a bit blurry but at least he didn't have to tie a scarf across them. He was in search of a good tailor in case he could find a better doublet for ordinary wear than his green one and perhaps one of the short embroidered capes that were all the rage and possibly one of the new high-crowned hats…Passing Carfax he heard a great deal of shouting as a short puffy man was arrested for coining and horse-theft. The man's face was purple; he kept shouting that he was Captain Leigh on urgent business. His henchman, a big louring thug, suddenly broke free of the two lads holding him, knocked down a third and took to his heels down the London road. A few people gave chase but didn't try too hard on account of his size and ugliness. Carey didn't fancy it himself. Meanwhile, the horsethief had been cold-cocked on general principles and hauled off to the Oxford lockup.

The first tailor he found on the High Street was showing some very good samples of fine wool and Flemish silk brocades in his window, so he wandered in and asked questions. Alas, the prices were even more inflated than in London and the man explained smugly that he couldn't be expected to produce anything in time for the Queen's Entry on Friday as all his journeymen were working flat out already. And there were only two other tailors in Oxford town.

Carey picked up one of the little wax dolls showing the latest French fashions in women's kirtles, looked deeper into the shop which was full of men sitting cross-legged stitching at speed. 'Who is the oldest man here?' he asked idly.

The harassed man in thick spectacles frowned. 'I am.'

'When did you do your prentice piece?'

'In 1562. I cry you pardon, sir,' he added with the sharp voice of someone who spends his days sitting down, worrying. 'I have fully worked my time as an apprentice and journeyman and I am simply not able to fill any more orders at all at any price...

Carey smiled. 'I was just wondering if I could ask you a question or two, Mr. Frole.'

It was a pity, he would have liked to order a couple of alterations to his Court suit to make it a little more in fashion, but never mind. Hughie could do it when he was better.

'I'm looking for the tailor who made gowns and kirtles for Lady Leicester,' he said. 'Not Lettice Knollys, but Amy Robsart, his first wife. Did you work for her?'

The man went pale and his eyes flickered. Suddenly he was sweating.

'No sir,' said Frole shortly, 'I didn't. I have only been in business as Master Tailor these last ten years and...

'Do you know who was her tailor?'

'It was Master William Edney in London.' The man shut his mouth like a trap. Carey watched him, wondering how to get him to open up.

'Mr. Frole, I know this is a sensitive matter despite being as old in years as I am myself. Were you prenticed in Oxford?' The master tailor nodded. 'I know gossip travels around the 'prentices. Is there anything at all you can tell me about the end of August 1560, anything about Lady Dudley...? I have been asked by the Queen herself to make enquiries.'

The man was looking narrow-eyed and suspicious. Carey sighed. 'I believe she set another man, by name Richard Topcliffe, to find something out about it only six years after Lady Dudley's death, while Her Majesty was on progress in Oxford the last time. But the man has an ill reputation and I'm certain he...

'He had a warrant,' said Frole. 'Do you?'

Carey took it out of his doublet pocket, his heartbeat quickening.

'Did Topcliffe offer money which he didn't pay or did he grab people and beat them up until they told him what he wanted to hear?'

'Both,' said Frole, thin-lipped, and held out his hand. Carey handed over the warrant which Frole read quickly and gave back.

'We told him all we knew which was that Lady Dudley was in a hurry to have a new gown although she already had plenty of the best quality. She had ordered a new one from London but it hadn't come. This was the first week of Spetember and she sent her best bodice, kirtle, and gown into Oxford by her woman Mrs. Odingsells to have the collar changed to stand up and have gold lace put on it, very costly. We did the work while she waited, for Lady Dudley intended to wear it in a few days.'

'Who did the work?' Carey asked, 'you?'

Frole shook his head. 'One of the journeymen, she was too important a customer to risk an apprentice's work. He died of plague in '66. Mrs. Odingsells paid for it in gold at once. Just as well, really.'

'How about her headdress? Did that need altering?'

Frole shook his head. 'Her headtires all came from London as she didn't like the shop here. I believe they were very old-fashioned, from the boy-King's reign. I never met Lady Dudley, you know, she was always at Cumnor Place, waiting for her husband.'

'Did Topcliffe let slip anything interesting?'

Frole gave a cautious look. 'He was an evil man, broke my best friend's fingers so he couldn't continue in the trade. He went off to Cumnor Place after he spoke to us and I heard him boasting in an alehouse that night that he had found something that would make him a great man at Court—he was the Earl of Shrewsbury's man then—and comfortable for the rest of his life. He said other things that I can't repeat about the Queen, terrible obscene things. But at least he had lost interest in us prentices and took himself off back to London the next day, following the Court.'

Carey nodded. Terrible obscene things—Topcliffe was notorious for the way he spoke of the Queen and yet nothing was ever done about him. Generally the Queen rightly had a short way with anyone who was offensive about her in a way that often made them shorter by a head or another important limb. So what gave Topcliffe his extraordinary immunity? Blackmail, surely. But with what?

'Mr. Frole,' he said to the unhappy-looking tailor, 'I am very grateful to you. If you have any further memories or ideas, please tell me—you can find me with the Earl of Cumberland while the Queen is here or by means of the Lord Chamberlain if I am gone north again. He will make it worth your while.'

Frole bowed Carey out of the shop and he stood in the street and havered between heading off down the London road to look for Dodd and continuing his sweep of Oxford. He even had five pounds from the Earl of Cumberland won on a bet as he left. George Clifford had been loudly offering to take Carey on as a permanent general purpose gleeman and fool if he got tired of soldiering in the starveling and dangerous Debateable land. George had explained how Carey would only have to wear a cap and bells on Saturdays and would have his very own kennel with the dogs...Carey had thrown a pennyloaf at the Earl on this point and challenged him to a veney which he had narrowly won.

Did he want to spend it on overpriced ale and beer? Well, yes, he did and he could kill two birds with one stone if he went round the multitude of Oxford taverns. So that was settled. He would do that and then he'd take a horse and ride down the road, see if he could spot where Dodd had gone. Or find his body, which was starting to look more and more likely.

TUESDAY 19TH SEPTEMBER, 1592

It took a lot of work to wait in that pit without doing anything. Dodd drank the rest of the drugged ale and dozed, filling his head with lurid pictures of the welcome his wife would give him when he got back to Gilsland and what he would do and...Well, it passed the time, didn't it? He had heard little Kat coming in, her clogs slow and tired and her stout lie that she had climbed a tree to avoid a pig in the forest when she was looking for more cobnuts and then got stuck in the tree. Her Grandam shouted at her and sent her to card wool in the cottage with no dinner, which made Dodd feel

727

sorry for the little maid. His guts were churning with nerves about what he would do that night. After all, a mere night raid, a bit of fun running about shrieking and spooking horses, that was easy. His plan for this night was a lot more ticklish.

Still. He couldn't go back to Carey without at least his sword and his boots. So there was no help for it and if everything went well he'd be bringing a lot more than just his sword and his boots. He might be able to make something of a show. He dozed off again, smiling to himself.

There was a clatter at the lip of the pit and Dodd jumped to his feet. Jeronimo was there, letting down the ladder, smiling enigmatically in the dusk. 'Captain Leigh and his bullyboy have not come back from Oxford as they said they would, John Arden is drunk, and the men are afraid they have been tricked again. I spoke with your *pequenita* when I carry her the last mile, she was much tired, she said she had been questioned but then went away. She says it is sure Captain Leigh was taken because she heard him shouting.'

Dodd allowed himself a grim smile as he stepped onto the cobbles of the yard. For all the odds against it, that part had worked, at least.

'Where's the old woman?'

'I said her stay in her cottage with the child. She has the dog beside her and barred the door.'

'Ay.' She'd come to no harm from him, but who knew what might happen? 'She fears Harry Hunks might try again to seduce her granddaughter.'

'Good God,' said Dodd, disgusted, 'She's nobbut a child.'

Jeronimo shrugged. 'They have no man for protect them.'

Dodd had the stolen knife in a belt he had woven himself from the bracken fibres. He bent and scraped up mud, swiped it over himself. 'Who's got ma sword?'

'Garron has it, he won it at dice.'

'Tch,' said Dodd. 'Big, small?'

'Young,' said Jeronimo with a wolfish smile, 'and frightened.'

* * *

With Jeronimo and his loaded crossbow at his back, Dodd quietly climbed the tumbledown monastery wall and padded forward to where the lad who had his sword was supposed to be on guard. He was leaning against a tree, dozing.

Jeronimo said something that sounded rude in foreign. Dodd paced quietly to the tree, put his arm softly round the lad's neck from behind and squeezed. There was only a brief struggle before he went heavy against Dodd's arm.

Dodd let him down gently, turned him, put his knee into the back and used the lad's scarf to tie his hands and feet together like a deer carcass. Then he unstrapped his sword belt from the lad, put it back on at a notch tighter than normal and drew his weapon. That was when he found that the stupid child hadn't cleaned it or oiled it or even sharpened it since he got it. So he used the boy's lank greasy hair to oil the blade again which woke him up with a squawk and a smooth cobble to sharpen it as best he could. Dodd had already taken the boy's boots off and chucked them into the undergrowth since they were far too small for him, and so he stuffed the boy's mouth with one of his own tattered socks.

'Ah've let ye live since ye're nobbut a lad,' Dodd told him conversationally. 'Ithers may no' be sae lucky, dinna push it.'

From the wild eyes the boy hadn't understood a word of this but Dodd didn't have time to strain his larynx talking Southron. The lad should be able to work his way free by which time it would all be over, please God.

Dodd straightened, with his sword warm and comfortable in its rightful place on his hip, and headed for the monastery parlour where there was a fire in the hearth and a powerful smell of booze.

There was the second in command, John Arden, slumped in a chair with an empty horn beaker in his hand and a barrel of brandy before him.

It went against Dodd's grain to slit a man's throat sleeping, which forebye would be messy. Instead he removed the man's sword and poinard, put the long narrow poinard blade to the thick neck and grabbed a sticky doublet-front to shake him awake. He was reminded of Robert Greene a few weeks ago, for it took some doing.

'Arah, wuffle,' said the man at last, focussing blearily on the long shine of his own dagger at his throat.

'Ay,' said Dodd sympathetically, 'Ye've a choice. Ye could allus surrender and gi'me yer word. Or not.'

There was a pause while the man's drink-sozzled brain fought to understand. Then his body gave slightly.

'Quarter,' said the man. 'I surrender. My name's John Arden.'

'Good man,' said Dodd with the friendliest face he could manage. 'Pit yer hands behind ye.'

They tied Arden to his seat and Dodd took the sword and knife. He liked the poinard which was clearly of good Italian make, so he slid it on the back of his own belt, where Carey wore his. He would have nothing to do with a nasty long pig-sticker of a rapier so Jeronimo took the sword.

They walked into the monastery's cloister with its central yard and Dodd went up the stairs to the dorter. These lads weren't used to setting any kind of proper guard. They were drinking and dicing. Those that were still asleep, he tied up. Those that were awake he asked politely if they would prefer to surrender or die on his sword. Most of them were sensible. One arrogant young man thought he ought to fight for honour's sake and died honourably with Dodd's sword down through the centre of his skull while he was still struggling to pull his unoiled blade out of its scabbard.

The others stared wide-eyed as Dodd wrenched his sword out of the bone and grease with his foot and cleaned it again. Jeronimo crossed himself awkwardly and muttered something Latin over the young man as his heels drummed. Of course, all Spaniards were Papists, they couldn't help it, but he didn't see the point in praying for someone you'd just sent to Hell. It felt as it always did when he killed someone: hard labour and a sense of satisfaction that it was the other man and not Dodd that was dead.

'Ay,' he said, 'anybody else?'

They all shook their heads. 'Come down to the yard and I'll talk to ye,' he said, turned on his heel and walked back down the worn stairs with the painted pictures on the walls. His back prickled. He was showing he had no fear of them, though of course he did. That was the moment when they might have rushed him if they'd been Borderers. Which they clearly weren't, but still, you never knew. That was the thing about fighting. You never knew.

He methodically went from the lookout place to the rickety watch tower, taking more surrenders. Finally he stood in the yard with his sword still in his hand. He faced eighteen frightened young men with only Jeronimo to back him, smoking his goddamned tobacco again, face shadowed and intent and the crossbow dead steady in his good hand. Only two of them had their buff coats on and had lit torches.

'Yer previous captain is in jail in Oxford,' Dodd told them. 'His lieutenant is tied up and has surrendered. Now then, I have a proposition...'

'What about that God-rotted Spanish traitor?' demanded a hollow-eyed man with a cough and flushed cheeks.

'He's my ally,' said Dodd coldly, 'and the ainly decent soldier among the pack of ye dozy idle catamites. Ye can be polite tae him or fight me.'

'Or fight me,' said Jeronimo, with a lazy smile. '*Pendejos*. Assholes.'

'I have a business proposition for ye,' Dodd continued. 'Here I am, I've taken the lot of ye and it would ha' bin easier to cut all yer throats and save myself a lot of bother. It's only thanks to my kindness ye've still got gullets to gobble wi'. So. Now. I'm making myself yer captain. Is there anybody here wants tae tell me no? And make it stick?'

Behind him, Jeronimo made a noise between a snort and a laugh.

'I mean it. I'll fight any man of ye that wants the captainship instead o' me. Come on.' There was a moment of balance while Dodd waited, consciously breathing out and relaxing. He didn't think a man of them had the ballocks to try it, but you never knew.

At the corner of his eye, he saw movement, saw something before he knew what it was, something raised to strike from the other side and so he slipped out of the way, ducked, brought his sword round almost gently and cut the man's head part off. There was no thought in the movement at all.

The others sighed as John Arden collapsed to his knees, dropping the veney stick in his fist, blood pumping in a fountain from his neck and a look of surprise on his face. Dodd watched him as he crumpled over into the black pool of his life. That was a nice stroke, probably one of his best. You rarely got the neck so neatly that you cut through because it was a small target and there was so much meat and bone in the way, you usually got the shoulder or the jaw by mistake.

'Ay,' he said, 'anybody else?'

They huddled together like the scared boys most of them were.

'What about our pay from the Earl of Essex?' shouted one of the youngest. 'That's why Captain Leigh went to Oxford.'

'Och God, is that what it was?' Dodd said, scratching his ear which was sticky. 'Was that why Leigh was sae hot for the Deputy Warden?'

'He was going to get us into the Queen's procession and then petition the Earl in front of all the people and Her Majesty herself!'

For a moment Dodd was honestly flummoxed. 'Did ye truly think it would work? That ye could just walk into a procession like that?'

'He was going to buy us white-and-orange ribbons so we could fit in,' said another lad.

'And then we got you and he was going to talk to Captain Carey about us.'

Dodd shook his head sadly. 'Ye never had any chance of getting any of your pay nae matter what,' he said explained, 'for the reason Essex has nae ready cash to pay ye and even if he did, he's got no reason to do it.'

'But he promised us,' wailed the youngest boy.

'Listen,' said Dodd, patiently, 'the Earl of Essex is a lord and he disnae give a rat's shit for any of ye. Ask him if ye like. Jesus, as yer new Captain, *I'll* ask him, but trust me, ye willna get what's owing. You went to fight and if ye didna keep any plunder, then ye'll take home nae more than stories.'

He looked about at the young dismayed faces and felt pity for them. 'But,' he shouted, 'if ye follow me as yer Captain, I can get ye home if ye're so minded or it might be if ye dinna care to go home wi' nothing, I could find ye places as fighters at Carlisle, where I'm from. I willna promise it, but if ye can back a horse and heft a pike, there might be a place for ye in Carlisle. I willna promise it, but if ye come, ye'll get a share of the Deputy Warden's fees and ye'll have a place in the mostly dry and food ye can mostly eat. What d'ye say?'

Another babel of voices broke out while Dodd waited for them to settle it amongst themselves, ready to fight if they decided to rush him together. If they did that, he could only give himself a medium chance so he stayed ready with his sword still out. He cleaned it again before John Arden's blood dried.

What was Carey's main problem? Not money as he thought, because money could always be stolen. No. It was that he did not have enough men that would fight only for him. And here Dodd had a solution if Carey was clever enough to take it. And if not, well, he might take the men over to Gilsland anyway and put his wife in charge of them. They had been easy meat for a night raid but they must be good for something or at least might shape up with some shouting and kicking.

And the raiding season was fast coming, already here. God only knew what outrages had happened in the Debateable Land or what the Grahams or the Scottish Armstrongs had been up to, or, God sakes, the Maxwells and the Johnstones, no doubt at each others' throats again and lesser surnames taking the scraps.

This was something Dodd had been thinking hard about. He had seen what it was like in the South, where there were no pele towers but there were orchards and fat cows and sheep and sure, there were broken men and troubles, but still mainly people who could live their lives without being raided. It made them soft, true. But a sudden decision had come upon him that afternoon while he thought of Janet and the child he fully intended to plant in her the minute he got her on her own in their tower. He wanted his sons and daughters to grow up where the cows were fat and there were orchards, not raiding and killing the way he'd had to all his life.

And how could you do that? Well, among other things, clearly you needed soldiers, men who were not related to anybody they were fighting. Men who would do what they were told and not hold back in a fight because they were swapping blows with their brother-in-law. Men who had no feuds. That was hard to achieve on the Borders from the way all the surnames went at the marrying and breeding and killing there. But here, right here, he had the start of a solution. So.

Dodd had already taken the swords he could find. The lad Nick Smithson was leaving the huddle of young men, coming toward him with an eating knife laid across his two palms. Dodd waited, said nothing but shook his head when Smithson made to bend the knee to him. The lad genuflected anyway and Dodd let him.

'Sir,' said Smithson, 'Mr. Elliot, we would like to ask you to be our Captain.'

He offered Dodd the knife and Dodd put his sword in his left hand and took the knife with his right as dignified as he could.

'Ay,' he said. 'Now. My right name's not Colin Elliott, that's the name of my blood enemy in Tynedale. My true name is Sergeant Henry Dodd, headman of Gilsland and I'll be your Captain under my own lord, Sir Robert Carey. Understand?'

He had all of them line up and swear allegiance to him, the old way, kneeling, their hands in his while he looked at their faces. Some looked a little shifty but most seemed relieved. It was hard to decide things for yourself, but harder still to know in your heart that the man who was leading you couldn't or wouldn't do the job properly. He knew what that felt like. So they had been easy meat for him and had now got themselves a captain who could do the job.

'Get yerselves ready to move out,' Dodd said. 'We'll leave tomorrow morning at dawn. We'll take everything with us. I want all of ye to take turns on watch.'

The only thing that still annoyed him was that he hadn't found his boots yet. Ah yes, Harry Hunks had been wearing them, of course, and he must have gone to Oxford with Leigh so his boots were probably being damaged kicking against the door of the Oxford lock-up.

***

Leaving Jeronimo in charge to set watches and start the business of packing up, Dodd sheathed his sword and limped down the path back to the old woman's bothy in the hope he could lay hands on some scraps of cloth or leather to wrap round his feet which were feeling even more sore and cold now the excitement was over.

He felt much better. Certainly when he first woke up in the forest he'd been determined to kill all of them, but it was better that he'd only had to kill three of them and now had eighteen men sworn to follow him. He had his sword on his hip again, the comforting weight of it across his shoulder and he had a nice new poinard as long as the courtier's blade, which he'd envied. Carey would teach him how to use it properly, that useful-looking two-handed sword and dagger work. He'd wake up the old woman and tell her and Kat to be ready to move as well.

He paused. There was a commotion coming from the goats' shed and something was wrong with the entrance to the cottage, there was...

He smelled the fresh blood before he saw it and felt rather than saw the battle axe coming down on him.

His body flung itself sideways and rolled, followed hard by a huge bear-like shape and another chop from the axe. Christ, that was Harry Hunks, taller even than Carey or his dad, broad and big as Richie Graham of Brackenhill and twenty years younger. Dodd rolled again and struggled up in a nest of nettles, panting.

Harry Hunks was named after a bear and was as big as a bear, but he fought like a serious man. No roaring, he was quiet as he came after Dodd again, battle axe in one hand, short sword in the other, teeth gleaming in a fighting grin, eyes catching little flashes of light in the dark of his eye sockets.

Dodd's sword was in his right hand, the poinard in his left, he backed up, not at all liking what he saw. The big man wasn't moving heavily, he was light on his feet, almost bouncing like a child's pig bladder. And that axe...most Borderers only used an axe if they couldn't afford a proper sword or billhook, it was a much harder weapon to get the mastery of and you needed to be big and strong.

Harry Hunks came after him again, Dodd dodged as the axe came whistling down past his chest, just missing his shoulder, you couldn't block that with a sword. He turned, sliced sideways but Harry Hunks wasn't there any more.

The goats were creating a bedlam of noise, there was a bit of starlight, occasional moonlight. Dodd's mouth drew down angrily. It was his own fault. The night had been too easy, he should have realised that and no doubt Leigh had somehow got out and was even now re-establishing who was in charge of his troop of men, knocking heads together. So Dodd didn't have long to kill this bear of a man and get away. And it had to be done because it looked like the bastard had killed someone, whether the carlin or the child he wasn't sure but he could smell the fresh blood on the man's axehead...

Again, it was his body saved him, not quite ready for Hell yet. He dropped to his knees as the axe came whistling from nowhere exactly for his neck. He rolled again as one of his own boots tried to kick him in the face.

Goddamn it, Harry Hunks had his boots.

Dodd's eyes narrowed and he finally stopped thinking. He came in and out a couple of times, feinting to see where Harry Hunks' weaknesses were but he didn't have any. Each time Dodd's sword bit nothing but air as Harry Hunks moved just enough out of the way and while Dodd was off balance with the missed blow, he nearly lost an arm and then his nose. You didn't get wounded by a battle axe, you got dead, there were no first bloods, no second chances.

Harry Hunks came after him again and he tripped, stubbed his foot on a stone and nearly had his crotch split while he went over his shoulder and up again behind a tree.

The tree took the full force of the battle axe again, the axe stuck for a second, but when he tried to slice the man's arm as he tried to free the axe Dodd nearly ended up spitted on a short sword.

Jesu, said the little cold voice at the back of his head, this one's bigger and faster and stronger than you and he's better. He's going to kill you.

He dodged again behind another tree and ran, turned tail and ran like hell for the clearing by the old stone shed and the ruins of the monastery gatehouse.

TUESDAY 19TH SEPTEMBER 1592, NOON

Carey was just deciding that it had been a mistake to try quartering the alehouses of Oxford for any clues to Topcliffe or Dodd, mainly because there were so many of them and he couldn't find the musician again. His head was pounding from the grey daylight in his eyes and his stomach turned at even the smell of wine. Nonetheless it was past time to get a horse and remount and go down the London road in search of his man.

As he turned his back on the High Street with its forests of scaffolding and hurrying men with ladders and hammering and sawing, a page in Cumberland's livery came running after him. 'Message, sir!' shouted the boy. 'Message for Sir Robert Carey!'

The lad gave him a folded letter with the Vice Chamberlain's seal. Carey opened it, skimmed the Italic.

'Sir Robert, I have just arrested your man Dodd on a charge of horsetheft and forgery. Please reply by this messenger, with your terms.' It was signed by Heneage.

For a second, fury scorched through him as he stood with his hand on his swordhilt. The boy read his face and stepped back nervously.

'Is there a reply, sir?' asked the lad. Carey stared at him for a moment. Heneage must have just caught Dodd and come straight over to Cumberland's camp to gloat because otherwise, why would he send one of Cumberland's pages?

'Yes, please tell him I will meet him at Carfax to discuss terms with him when I have consulted my father. An hour from now.'

The boy bowed and ran off, heading up the Cornmarket. Carey took a circuitous route but headed out of town for the Oxford lock-up, jingling what was left of Cumberland's five pounds in his purse.

A little to his surprise, it wasn't a trap. The guard was as bribable as usual and unlocked the little cell with great ceremony. Carey's eyes still weren't working properly and sunlight was coming in at the barred window so at first he only thought that the suit he'd lent Dodd had taken some damage and there must have been a fight, which made sense.

'Come on,' shouted the guard, 'Get up to your master, Dodd, don't sit about.'

The man didn't turn his bare head, which was balding. 'My name,' he said with dignity, 'is Captain Leigh, I am a gentleman and I've never heard of anybody called Dodd. I demand that you set me free immediately.'

Carey nearly exploded with laughter. By God it was hard to keep a straight face. Then he thought to lean in and ask,

'Then how did you come by that suit?'

Leigh lifted a shoulder. 'I won it from a man called Colin Elliot.'

Carey grinned and nodded to the man to lock up again. Then he went to visit the Jailer and made him richer by five shillings.

'No, sir,' he said, 'By information laid. A small girl brought this letter from a Mr. Colin Elliot, informing the Sheriff's man that this is Dodd, a notable horsethief and forger, wanted by Vice Chamberlain Heneage. We checked his horse and found it had the Queen's brand though a bit coloured over to hide it and there was no proper warrant. His purse had several forged angels in it so the information was correct. Unfortunately his henchman got away, but we have informed Mr. Vice.'

Carey took the smeared bit of parchment decorated with blue flowers. The charcoal scrawl was Dodd's horrible penmanship and Colin Elliot was his usual *nom de guerre*. Reading the script, Carey almost cheered at the elegance of its contents.

'Where's the little girl?'

'She got away, ran south. Said she lived to the south of Cumnor Place.'

So at least until yesterday, Dodd had been alive and scheming to get someone else arrested for horsetheft in place of him. They must have been within a couple of miles of each other when he and Cumberland were poking about at Cumnor. Meanwhile he could rejoice at the splendid way Dodd had dealt with the problem of the horse he had stolen from Heneage's stable.

'I'd like to talk to my man,' Carey said to the Jailer.

'You can't bail him,' he said at once, 'Mr. Heneage's man was very particular about it.'

'No, that's all right, I'll have a word with his honour later. I just want to talk to him.'

Another shilling got him back inside the cell with a quart of beer to share. Leigh seemed grateful for it and very willing to talk especially once he focussed and recognised Carey from France.

Half an hour later, he had the full sorry tale and Leigh's desperate petition that he ask the Earl of Essex for their pay. He insisted that the man he knew as Elliot was being held in a pit—not chained, of course, not at all and the pit was not at all uncomfortable, quite dry in fact—but had a bad leg. Some mysterious trouble with the horses had broken out in the night and Leigh had been delayed in setting out with only the stolen horse to mount...His lieutenant would be fully capable of keeping the prisoner safe and all Sir Robert needed to do to free him was promise to get their pay. They were owed a lot of it, a full year's service in France and not a penny from the King of Navarre either.

Carey had been financially crippled himself by soldiering for the Earl of Essex but had at least gotten a knighthood out of it and was in any case used to debt. He nodded sympathetically, promised to try and sort out the mistaken identity with the Vice Chamberlain but had not given his word on the matter of pay. He couldn't. He knew perfectly well that the Earl of Essex wasn't going to pay anyone.

Meantime it sounded as if Dodd was healthy enough and would stay put for a while. It was a relief that he wasn't a corpse with a broken neck in a ditch somewhere. Carey thought about enlightening Heneage and then decided not to—why make trouble? Presumably once Heneage bothered to go and visit the man he would know Dodd had given him the slip again and Leigh would have to be released as the bill was spoiled. Carey smiled as he set off for Trinity College and then frowned because he had decided it was time to talk frankly with his father.

He was distracted by the sound of singing from the church halfway up Cornmarket and went in to hear it. These weren't the chapelmen, but a choir of boys, anxiously practising a very complicated piece in Latin with five parts. They were good but they hadn't quite got it yet. He stood at the back of the church, holding his hat, far away from the candles so as not to be troubled by them, thinking.

The signs all pointed in one direction. Well perhaps two. Carey realised that was why he had a headache. He would rather think that Burghley had done the deed, fearing Amy Robsart's divorce from Dudley and Dudley as king—quite rightly. But there was a much better suspect if Amy had balked. Possibly two of them.

He had lost track of the music with his anxious thinking, found that his fingers were holding his hat tightly enough to bend the brim. He wanted to broach the matter privately with the Queen but knew that was both unwise and impossible. He would have to talk to his father; there was no help for it, but he didn't want to because he was actually afraid of what might happen when he did. Was this where his dreams of being in the Tower on a charge of treason had come from? Were they just devilish phantasms or true warnings? How could you tell? Was that why his doublet in the dream had been so worn and faded? Would the Queen execute him for high treason just for asking?

Surely not. But he wasn't sure. He wasn't even sure if he could ask his father. He didn't mind if his father lost his temper and hit him, though he really didn't want to get in a brawl with the old man. And he certainly didn't want to be locked up by him. There was a polite cough beside him and he realised that someone had come in and was standing next to him, a round man in the Queen's livery gown.

'The tenor's good,' said Mr. Byrd, 'Perhaps I'll poach him for the chapel men. Not as good as you, sir, he don't have your round tone.'

Carey tilted his head at the compliment though as always when being told he had a good voice, he didn't feel he could take the credit.

'It's a pity you weren't born of lesser stock, sir,' Byrd went on, 'we could have made something of you.'

'Hmm. I'd have enjoyed that trade, Mr. Byrd, though my instrument playing is atrocious.'

'Lack of practice, no doubt.'

'I truly did try with the lute…I don't know. Singing seems so natural and playing the lute so complicated. I can tune it and make a perfectly reasonable sound but it's wooden, lumpish. I can hear the fault but I can't mend it.' That was true, he had been very disappointed not to be able to master the lute as he wished.

'Hmm. Fighting practice won't improve your playing, veneys coarsen your hands.'

'Perhaps.'

Byrd smiled. 'I remembered something that might help you, sir, so I'm pleased to have found you. You know the musician who ran away on Saturday night?'

'The viol player you hired from the waits?'

'Yes. I finally remembered when I'd seen him before. It was when I was a singer for Mr. Tallis at the Chapel Royal, he used to play for the Queen then. It was in the early part of her reign, but he and his Spanish friend that played the harp and the lute, they ran away from Court, didn't even collect their arrears of pay and we never saw them again.'

Carey frowned. 'When did they do that?'

Byrd shook his head. 'I'm not sure, sir, I think it was very early, perhaps the summer of 1560.'

Carey blinked. 'His friend was Spanish?' It was common enough then to have Spaniards still at Court, since there had been so many of them during the Queen's sister Mary's reign. 'Do you know the names?'

Byrd shook his head. 'I can't remember, I'm afraid. I remember his Spanish friend better, a very handsome proud man, like a hawk. He could play any stringed instrument like an angel but his voice was worse than a crow's. He was base-born, his father was a Spanish grandee.'

'What was the viol player's name when you hired him?'

'Sam Pauncefoot. That's what he told me last week—he may have changed it.'

'To Pauncefoot? Thank you very much, Mr. Byrd. I'm not sure what I can do with this, but it might fit in somewhere.'

There was no point waiting any longer, Carey had to go and see his father. He wanted to know what had happened to Emilia's necklace which he needed to sell for ready funds and he urgently wanted to borrow some men to go looking for Dodd, and most importantly, he needed his father to tell him the truth for the first time in thirty-two years.

Outside an immense arch was being covered with canvas and

painted. He stood squinting at it sightlessly, his hat pulled down against the watery daylight. Where did a Spanish musician fit in?

He had to talk to his father. He set off, walking fast, trying to make out the pattern forming in his head somewhere just out of reach. And what was the worst that could happen? Well his father might well lose his temper at what Carey was going to put to him. Probably would, in fact. If what he suspected was true, then he wasn't at all sure what he himself would do.

Once on Broad Street he went in at the gate of Trinity College where the usual porter and one of his father's under-stewards were sitting glowering at each other.

For a moment, he hesitated. He had a bit of money. He could hire a horse from Hobson's stables in St Giles, ride to Bristol in probably no more than a day, take ship for the Netherlands and sell his sword there or to the King of Navarre…

He'd wondered about it before; he always did. It was a dream of freedom he had acted on the summer before last, going to France with the Earl of Essex in the tidal wave of enthusiasm that the Earl had somehow generated. He had done well there, learnt that the Court was stifling an important part of him.

So he didn't have to confront his father, he could just go. Dodd was no longer worrying him; he didn't believe a word of the damaged leg, he thought the problem with the horses last night was definitely thanks to Dodd who would clearly cope perfectly well without him. So he could join a crew of Dutch sea-beggars and raid the coast of Northumberland and carry off Elizabeth Widdrington from under the nose of her foul husband and make her a widow in the most satisfying way possible. He could. He knew he could. He was able for it, wanted it, what was standing in his way?

He had his hand on his swordhilt again which was making the porter eye him fishily.

'Your father is here, sir,' said Mungey the steward.

What if his father hit him and he lost his own temper like that misunderstanding when he first arrived in London?

Carey smiled sunnily at the college porter and unbuckled his swordbelt, lifted it off and laid the ironmongery on the wooden counter in front of him.

'Look after these, will you?' he said. 'Mr. Mungey, where's my father?'

'In the walled garden, sir, he was asking for you.' Both of them were blinking nervously at the bundle of Carey's sword, poinard and eating knife before them. Carey felt odd with no weight on his hip, but much happier. He paced out into the quadrangle as if marking out a battlefield.

TUESDAY 19TH SEPTEMBER 1592, EVENING

Harry Hunks was coming after him, breathing hard but not shouting, Dodd's own stolen boots crushing the brambles and stones that were ruining Dodd's bare soles and toes, too close, too fast for such a big man, Christ, come on move, ye bastard.

He sprinted the last bit in the open, legs and elbows pumping, mouth open and gasping, and at the last second jumped over the pit he'd been in. Its ladder was still sticking out, but he cleared it, landed in a soft muddy bit and rolled again to his feet, turned and...

Yes! Harry Hunks was teetering on the stone edge of the pit, heavy for such a leap and he fell in, scrabbling as he went.

Dodd swapped sword and dagger so the poinard was in his right, went in a crouch to the side of the pit where the ladder was, stuck his sword in the earth where he could grab it again if he had to. Harry Hunks came up the ladder, he heard the creaking and puffing. Just before his head would clear the top of the pitwall, Dodd reached out, grabbed his hair and stabbed the man in the eye with the poinard, hard as he could, felt the soft jelly, the slight resistance of the bony back of the eye socket and then the give as the blade went into the man's brain and stuck in the bone of his skull on the other side.

The hilt was wrenched from his fist as Harry Hunks roared and struck blindly for him, then toppled backwards into the pit, screaming and clawing at his eye. He landed with a thud and a clatter and then his back arched and his feet drummed and the smell of shit told Dodd he was dead.

Dodd sat down next to the pit, gasping for breath and shaking. Christ, that had been close. Christ. All he could do was sit there and pant until the shaking had gone down a bit.

Then he wiped his wet hands on the ground, looked down into the pit and wondered if he wanted that poinard back at all. He'd leave it in Hunks' head until he decided. But he had to get up and find who Harry Hunks had killed before he arrived. He avoided looking at his feet and forced himself up onto still-trembling legs.

The goats were wildly indignant but unharmed. The old woman lay across the door of her cottage, nearly cut in two by the axe, her cooking knife in her hand unbloodied. Dodd pulled the old body away from the door and called softly through into the darkness, only a few embers of fire still lighting it. Was she still alive?

'Kat?' he said, 'Kat, I killed the big yin, are ye there, hinny?'

Nothing at first. For no reason he understood, his belly swooped and clenched itself against his backbone. Was the brave little maid split in two as well?

Then there was a stealthy sniffle. 'Kat, I'm coming in, will ye no' stick me? I'm tired and ma feet are sore.'

They were burning with pain, bleeding badly from their stickiness, cut to ribbons when he sprinted desperately away from Harry Hunks. He ducked and limped in, leaving prints on the tiles under the rucked up rushes. The sniffle had come from under the marble shelf where the bowls of goatmilk were still sitting to let the cream rise for cheese.

Dodd sat down next to the place, cross-legged, partly to have a feel of how bad his feet were and partly so as not to get stuck by the little maid in her panic.

'Kat,' he said conversationally, 'how many were they? Ainly Harry Hunks or another man as well?'

No answer.

'I killt Harry Hunks. He's in the pit I was in, but deid, ye follow? D'ye want tae come and look and be sure?'

Her head poked out with its grubby little cap sideways and her face covered in mud. 'Is he completely dead?'

'Ay. I put a knife in his eye. Was he alone?'

She nodded grimly, not a tear shed, still shaking. 'I think so, he tried to come in for me and Grandam kicked him and he pretended to go away and she made me hide and then...and then...'

'He come back wi' his axe?'

'He chopped her and then he was feeling about for me and I shut my eyes because I heard you whistling as you came back and I prayed to the Lady very hard...'

Good God, had he been *whistling*? The South was having a terrible effect on him and he would never ever come here again.

'So nobody else?'

She shook her head.

'Did ye see Captain Leigh taken?'

A lovely smile broke out across her grim little face. 'I did and he went purple and shouted and that was when I just moved away so they wouldn't make me stay with them and talk to Captain Carey and I ran back as quick as I could but I was very tired.'

'I've taken over the broken men as Captain, we're packin' up and leavin' for Oxford in the morning. I came to ask you if ye'd care to come wi' us.'

She was staring at his poor feet now, making a face. 'Tsk,' she said, 'How will you walk?'

He gave a grim snort of laughter. 'I willna, I'll ride. And we'll take the goats and sell 'em.'

She nodded. 'We can take the cheeses too. What about the curds? Can I give them to Wolfie, he loves the curds and there's no point straining them for...Oh!'

Dodd was slightly ahead of her. He tried to beat her out of the cottage door but his feet were too painful and she slipped past him and out into the darkness and then he heard a scream. He was swearing and wincing and hobbling after her now that he wasn't fighting for his life and the fighting rage wasn't carrying him, and he found her weeping over the lump of dead fur and meat that was all that was left of the poor dog. She certainly wept more for the dog than for the grandam which showed you something, he supposed.

Since he was up and out he limped over to the pit and found

Harry Hunks still lying there on his back with the poinard sticking out of the eye.

The ladder was unbroken so he put it straight and went down carefully, unreasonably scared that the big man would suddenly rear up and attack him again like the Cursed Knight in the ballad. But Harry Hunks was cooling now. Dodd hauled the poinard out and cleaned it by driving it deep into the earth a couple of times; its point was a little bent. That would have to do, he'd sort it properly with an oil rag and a whetstone when he had the time.

Then he set to pulling his boots off the man's feet and managed it finally. He felt about in the man's old doublet and found the little luckcharm Janet gave him and that made him smile. He didn't know what was inside the little leather pouch and he didn't want to know, but he felt quite pleased with it and his wife for playing his enemy false for him. There were a couple of shillings that he took and the buff coat which was too big but would at least make him a bit more decent than the hemp shirt and ragged breeks he had on. Climbing up the ladder again took most of what was left of his strength and then when he tried to put the boots on again he found that his feet were so swollen, it hurt too much.

'If you didn't give me that message then Harry Hunks wouldn't of killed Wolfie and my Grandam,' said Kat, standing by the dead dog, hands on hips, narrow-eyed. 'Would he?'

Dodd was too tired to deal with this. 'Ay, and Harry Hunks is deid, I killed three ither men this night and now I'm master of them all and Leigh will hang for horsetheft and forgery. Whit more d'ye want?'

'I didn't know Wolfie would get killed!' Her voice was going up in pitch and it went right through Dodd's head. He could almost hear his temper snap.

'No, ye didn't. That's because ye don't know what will happen when ye set out for vengeance,' he shouted, 'ye canna ken until the fight's over which side will win.' He was nose to nose with the little maid; full credit to her, she didn't flinch. 'People die and ye canna help it, no matter if ye love 'em or no'...*Especially* if ye love 'em! D'ye hear me?'

He stopped, realised he had hold of the front of her kirtle

and let go, turned away. Somebody tapped him on the shoulder. 'What?' he snarled.

'Thank you for killing Harry Hunks,' said Kat with great dignity. 'It wasn't your fault about Wolfie and Grandam. It was mine.'

'Och no, hinny,' he said, and knew she wouldn't believe him, would never ever believe him. 'It was Harry Hunks that did it.' And me, he thought.

She shook her head, went to the back of the cottage and came back with a bucket of water the old woman must have drawn, ready for the morning. She dipped a pitcher out for their drinking water. Then gratefully he put his feet in and the water went dark.

'Do you think I could marry you?' she asked after a moment, 'I'm good at cheese and butter and I've got some bits of monkish gold I found and a shilling to my dowry?'

Dodd managed not to sputter. 'Ah...no, Kat, I'm a married man mesen and ye're by far too young for me but I'll see ye wed tae a good man of yer ain if ye like. When yer old enough.' She frowned, puzzled so he said it more southron and she went and dug a hole in the floor under the place with the curds and pulled out a leather bag and slung it round her skinny body.

'I'm ready,' she said. 'You can't bury my grandam the way you are, so we'll set fire to the cottage and that'll do it.'

She had good sense. Dodd got his poor feet dry again, hobbled out and pulled the dog's corpse into the cottage to lie next to the old woman. Harry Hunks could be buried by the foxes and the buzzards and ravens. Then they got the coals under the earthenware curfew going again, both lit handfuls of dry reeds they pulled from the thatch and the roof was dry enough, so the fire flowered where they lit it all about and it made him feel better. There was something clean about fire. He knew a couple of prayers from the Reverend Gilpin but he'd never seen the point in them. He told the ghosts of the Grandam and the dog not to let Harry Hunks walk and he warned God not to play the little maid false again.

TUESDAY 19TH SEPTEMBER 1592, AFTERNOON

Henry Carey Baron Hunsdon, Lord Chamberlain to Her Majesty Queen Elizabeth, first of that name, was sitting in the college garden, looking at the fallen leaves clotting the grass and worrying. He had his walking stick with him which he generally didn't use in public because he hated to admit that he had arthritis in his knees, as if he were old.

He saw his seventh son before Robin saw him, as his bench was in a shadow between yew trees. The boy...no, even a fond father had to admit that the youngest of his sons was long past full grown, in fact, in his prime: tall, well-built with a breezy swagger that he supposed his sons had picked up from him since they all had it. In fact, of all of them, Robin reminded him of nothing so much as himself when he was a young man, although with the useful addition of his wife's ingenuity. He knew he didn't have that wild streak. He was profoundly grateful that Mary Boleyn had been so much less determined than her sister, that she had been married off to the complaisant William Carey while pregnant with him, the King's bastard. If she had hung onto her virtue the way her younger sister Ann had done, well, he might have been King Henry the IX and had a much worse life, his sons would have been Princes of the Blood Royal and even more trouble than they were anyway. Or more probably they wouldn't even exist because he would have been married off as a child to some thin-blooded crazy barren Hapsburg or Valois Princess, or God forbid, Mary Queen of Scots herself and then...He shuddered. No Annie Morgan to marry in a whirlwind. Being a King.

Thank God for bastardy, that was all he could say. His half-sister and cousin, Anne Boleyn's volcanic daughter, wove and politicked her way to the throne and was the finest Queen any nation had ever had since...Well, no nation had ever had such a Queen. Some fools might have been resentful at being barred the throne; he was not, he loved his firecracker of a half-sister and would do anything for her. Which was why he was Lord Chamberlain, of course, in charge of her palaces and her security, in charge of protecting her sacred person. It was the uttermost trust she could place in anyone. People called him nothing but a knight of the carpet, but when it mattered he had taken Lord Dacre's hide in the revolt of the Northern Earls. What did he care if men thought him a fool? It made them less careful of him when they plotted.

And here he was, looking at his youngest son who was now a danger to the Queen. He was digging up the early days of her Court when she had been, frankly, a menace, a cocotte, and a flirt who scandalised the Court and the nation and the foreigners in Europe as well. And Robin was doing his considerable best to stir that dirty puddle on the Queen's own orders.

Insanity. He had urged her to leave it, not to repeat the deadly mistake of 1566, her previous visit to Oxford. So she had used his youngest son as her tool because he had a fine mind and Walsingham had taught him a few things during those months he had spent at the Scottish Court with Walsingham's embassy and then nineteen months in France for polish, also with Walsingham's household. Three months he had taken to learn fluent French, a very diligent student for the first time in his life, and then sixteen months to cut a scandalous swath through the French ladies of the Court that even the French had found noteworthy. Perhaps he too had left a scatter of unknown bastard Hunsdon grandchildren among the French aristocracy, adding English yeast and Tudor blood to Parisian style.

Hunsdon smiled. He hoped so. And the boy had spent an astonishing amount of money as the French grandes dames taught vanity, luxury, and extravagance to an apt pupil. His time in a Parisian debtor's prison had taught him very little about economy, something about power.

And here he came, a little off balance because he wasn't wearing his sword.

Hunsdon frowned. Why? Why had his son disarmed? Had he worked it all out or made a terrible mistake?

He was on his feet, thumbs in his swordbelt, unaware how much his broad frame made him look like his royal sire—although he had never suffered the gluttony born of misery that had swelled King Henry and given him leg-ulcers and turned him into a monster.

Robin came right up to him and genuflected very properly and respectfully on one knee to his father. Hunsdon had to resist the impulse to raise and hug his son who had been so near death from poison only a couple of days before. He was wary. Generally, his son was only that respectful when there was trouble brewing. Or he wanted money.

Robin stood in front of him and hesitated. Their eyes were on a level. It was always a surprise when the baby of the family did that to you.

'Well?' said Hunsdon, guessing one reason why his son might have left his sword behind.

'Was it you, my lord?' Robin's voice was strained and soft in the quiet garden, his face unreadable. 'Was it you killed Amy Dudley for the Queen?'

For a moment it was hard for Hunsdon to speak.

'If it was you, father,' Robin went on gently, 'If it *was* you...I'll take my leave and say no more about it.'

This was tricky. The Queen had used a good young hound to find an old trail and he had done very well, far better than she could have expected. But he had to be careful. The Queen had given her orders. On the other hand...

'Do you really think I could have done a such a dishonourable thing?'

'For your sister the Queen? Yes. I would do it for Philadelphia if she needed me to.'

Hunsdon couldn't help smiling although it might be misinterpreted. Robin and Philly as the two youngest had always been close and had constantly got into terrible scrapes together. Only the absolute cold truth would do here, that was obvious, although it had to be edited.

'Well, Robin, it's true I would have done it if she asked me, despite the wickedness and dishonour, but the fact of the matter is that she didn't ask me to and I didn't kill Amy Dudley. On my word of honour.'

Robin looked no happier, standing tense with his fist where his swordhilt would have been.

'I had hoped you would say you had done the killing, father,' came Robin's voice, softened to a breath of sound that the wind in the red and yellow leaves could cover, so he had to strain to hear it.

'Oh? Why?'

'Because otherwise all I can think is that the Queen did it herself.'

Hunsdon nearly gasped. It was clear Robin had worked out a great deal of what had happened at Cumnor place in the year of his birth. But he didn't have all of it.

'No,' Hunsdon said positively, 'I'm not saying she wasn't capable, but no. She didn't.'

'Nor ordered another man to do it?'

'No. My word on it, Robin, she didn't.'

'But you and she were both at Cumnor Place when Amy Dudley née Robsart died.'

It was a statement not a question. Hunsdon's eyes widened as he saw how he had been trapped and he couldn't help a shout of laughter. Damn it, the boy was bright. Carey didn't join in with the laugh.

'You were there to discuss the divorce, the Queen's Great Matter,' Robin went on remorselessly, using the term Cromwell had used for Henry VIII's long-ago divorce from Katherine of Aragon. 'Amy Dudley would petition Parliament and convocation for an annullment of her marriage to the Earl of Leicester, on grounds of non-consummation. Amy was being difficult about it so the Queen decided to convince her in person. And so she dressed up in Aunt Katherine's riding habit, put on a black wig and a married woman's headtire, and rode out from Windsor to Cumnor Place thirty miles away, under cover of hunting. You went with her because really you were the only person who could. A man to protect her, but her half-brother so there could be no suggestion of impropriety. You would agree on the deal for freeing Dudley and perhaps make a downpayment in gold. It was a deadly secret, for if Burghley had realised what was afoot, he would have put a stop to it immediately by blocking the annullment in Parliament and Convocation, much as the Pope did thirty-odd years before. It was ironic, really. Nobody would have given Dudley the divorce, but they might have done it for Amy given enough oil and pressure, because there was no breath of scandal whatever against Amy and she had borne no children in ten years of marriage.'

He was good, damn, he was good. Hunsdon watched Carey's face and his heart swelled with pride. Carey had started to pace, squinting a little when the sun poked through the clouds.

'Amy lived so quiet a life, so carefully, she couldn't be treated the way Anne Boleyn was and have charges trumped up against her. She had to sue for her divorce. And the Queen decided to visit her personally to get the agreement.'

'Not quite,' Hunsdon said softly.

'Amy was in a panic that week, trying to get clothes fine enough to feel confident in. She had one gown ordered from London that didn't come in time, altered another to put gold lace on the collar. That's what told me it was the Queen for sure, that she had to dress fine. You might say it was for her husband, true, but gold lace wouldn't have impressed Leicester. A beautiful French lady once told me that women dress for other women, not men.'

Hunsdon said nothing. He was back in the past, when he was young and the finest tournament jouster at the Queen's Court, when the Queen was young. How often had he actually noticed what any woman was wearing?

'So you and the Queen rode to meet her at Cumnor Place, since Amy couldn't or wouldn't ride herself. You took remounts, rode thirty miles across country at top speed. Meanwhile Lady Dudley had bidden all her servants out of the house for the meeting, sent them off to the Abingdon fair though some of them didn't want to go. She was alone apart from a couple of her women playing cards in the parlour.'

It had been a wild ride, the Queen egging him on, challenging him, risking her neck for joy, taking hedges and ditches on her fine hunter, named Jupiter, a fire sprite, light in her sidesaddle, laughing as their horses ate the miles with their legs.

'And then...'

Hunsdon put up his palm to stop him. 'Robin, you're very nearly right. But...I must ask Her Majesty before I break the matter fully with you? Do you understand? I simply can't...'

Robin had taken out his warrant. 'So why did she tell me to dig? Come on, father, this authorises you to break silence.'

'This is dangerous ground,' Hunsdon rumbled, 'Trust me, Robin. It was neither me nor Her Majesty...'

'Then who was it?'

'We don't know.'

'You must know. You were there!'

'We tried. I tried when it happened, but I lost him, had to get back to the Queen. Unfortunately, the Queen hired Richard Topcliffe from the Earl of Shrewsbury in '66 when she came to Oxford. He must have found something and I know he turned against her and...'

'He's been a licensed monster ever since.'

'He has. He was very clever. Whatever it was he found, he took it to one of the Hamburg merchants at the Steelyard and sent it overseas. If he ever dies unexpectedly or is arrested or word gets out, the box will be sent unopened to the Jesuits at Rheims who will know how to embarrass the Queen with it.'

'Burghley? Surely if he'd known a divorce was in the wind, he might have organised the murder to stop...'

Hunsdon shook his head. 'I don't think so. It would have been safer to block it in Convocation and Parliament. Cecil was never a gambler, he has only ever bet on a sure thing. If he was going to murder anyone, it would have been Dudley, I think. And not a bad idea at that, if he didn't mind being hanged, drawn, and quartered for it.'

'But it only had to be made obvious that Dudley had killed her. Burghley could have seen to a verdict of unlawful killing from the inquest and put Dudley in the Tower no matter what the Queen thought. She wasn't so secure on her throne then; she would have taken notice of her entire Privy Council and her magnates calling out their tenants.'

'Would she? I doubt it, Robin. You didn't know her then. She learnt a lot from the troubles of her cousin Mary Queen of Scots.'

'The only thing I don't understand is why the Queen took the risk of meeting with her at all.'

'Amy Dudley was an appallingly obstinate woman, no doubt how she trapped a Dudley in the first place. She was a God-fearing dull woman who loved her husband deeply and could never understand how Eliza could fascinate men, the magic she had—still has, for God's sake. Amy struggled terribly with her conscience, I think because she would have to testify on oath that the marriage had not been consummated when of course it had been. She was just barren.' Hunsdon sighed. He could no longer see the matter as he had as a young man. 'She kept changing her mind and asking for more money, more guarantees and she insisted she had to meet the Queen and see her sign the agreement. Nobody would do as a go-between, it had to be the Queen herself. Eliza was furious about it.'

'I'm sure.'

'They looked extraordinarily alike, you know, red hair, white skin. Amy was like the Queen diluted with milk. I'll ride over and see Her Majesty tomorrow, to talk about the arrangements for Friday and I can ask her...'

'Can I ride with you?'

Hunsdon was surprised. 'Robin, won't you be bailing Sergeant Dodd and negotiating with Heneage...' Robin's grin of triumph did his heart good to see, as he hadn't been looking forward to dealing with Heneage for the man's release. He bellowed with laughter when he heard what had happened.

'Colin Elliot? He's called himself...?' Hunsdon knew more than he really wanted to about the Border surnames and he knew that there was a vicious bloodfeud between the Dodds and the Elliots which had burst out with spectacular nastiness in the 1570s after the Revolt of the Northern Earls. Wee Colin Elliot was a very dangerous raider and headman about the same age as Robin.

'Yes,' said Robin, 'Dodd always uses that name as an alias: it means anyone who knows him gives himself away with shock and any crimes he might commit are blamed on Wee Colin by the ignorant.'

'Excellent. You can certainly ride with me to Her Majesty tomorrow, Robin, if your eyes are recovered completely.'

'They're much better, thank you father, though to be honest I was never blind, only dazzled. I could actually see better in the dark. That's how I found the murder weapon at Cumnor.'

'You found the crossbow? Where was it?'

'High up in the space between the passage ceiling and the roof of the hall. The man came through the little door to the minstrel's gallery.'

'I know that, damnit, I chased him. How the devil did he have time to hide the crossbow there, I thought he threw it away? We spent a day looking for it with blood hounds a couple of days later.'

They stared at each other and came to the answer at the same moment.

Hunsdon felt the blood leave his face. 'Oh my God, there were two of them.' He actually staggered at the enormity of what he had done all those years ago. Robin was at his shoulder at once, supporting him to the bench again, holding his arm. Hunsdon's legs had suddenly gone to water.

'I left her alone,' he croaked, 'I chased after the man I saw and I left her alone with a killer...'

'Father,' came Robin's distant voice in the roaring, sounding worried, 'He didn't kill her, didn't do anything...'

Hunsdon shook his head slowly. Suddenly there was a band around his chest and his left arm was aching. I need to be bled, he thought distantly, I'll see Dr. Lopez when I can.

Robin was anxiously patting his hand and looking around for a servant.

'I have...some physic in my sleeve pocket,' Hunsdon wheezed.

Carey felt for it, pulled out the little flask, poured some of it into the cap.

'That's enough,' Hunsdon said, took it, pinched his nose and drank it down. While Robin fumbled his flask back, Hunsdon waited for the pounding to subside and the roaring to quiet.

'Father,' said Robin tactfully, 'You mustn't blame yourself. In the event, she wasn't killed!'

'You're right,' Hunsdon said with an effort, 'But I was an impulsive fool and I chased the man that had shot at Amy and then clubbed her down with his crossbow while Eliza tried to help Amy. I didn't catch the bastard, even then I wasn't fast enough and all the time the man had a confederate. Well, if I didn't know it before I know it now: Almighty God wanted her for Queen.'

'What did the Queen do while she was alone?'

'I'm not sure. She must have been crazy with the shock for she took off your Aunt's headdress that she was wearing and put it on Amy's head—I suppose to make her respectable because Amy's was dented beyond wearing. She supported Amy on her skirt I think, from the way it was dirtied and used it to wipe off the blood that came out of Amy's ears and eyes. I forced her to leave the woman though she was crying with frustration and we rode away. Stupidly, I made her throw away the bundle she had made, into a bush by the old monastery, and that was one of the few times she obeyed me. I wish she hadn't.'

'I expect that bundle was what Topcliffe found in 1566.'

Hunsdon shook his head. 'Perhaps. I went back with bloodhounds, I told you, Robin. We didn't find the crossbow and nor did we find that bundle. They must have tidied them up and taken them away.'

The pain was subsiding from his arm and the invisible iron band was loosening. Hunsdon suddenly felt exhausted.

'So why on earth did she suddenly bring it all up again?'

Hunsdon shook his head again, trying to clear it, his brain was no longer working. 'I'm sorry, Robin, I have to get to my bed. Would you...er...accompany me?'

'With good heart, Father,' Robin said, considerably more filial than normal—must still need money. He gathered up Hunsdon's stick and supported him on his arm back across the garden and with some trouble up the stairs to the Master's lodgings. Hunsdon's manservant came to help him undress and bring him watered brandy. Hunsdon could hear them muttering to each other, that he had had a couple of these attacks before, that Dr. Lopez thought it was a syncope of the heart and had prescribed an empiric dose of foxglove extract to reduce Hunsdon's choleric humours. Of course my choleric humour is unbalanced, he thought, there's my devil of a sister to deal with.

'Don't go to the Queen tomorrow, sir,' Robin urged. 'You need to rest first. Please?'

'Nothing wrong with me,' growled Hunsdon, leaning against his high-piled pillows. 'Just need bleeding. I'll see a barber surgeon tomorrow and go in the afternoon.'

'But...'

'Damn it, I can still play a veney, I shall be perfectly well tomorrow. I'm just overwrought at the moment, what with the progress, Her Majesty's tantrums, your bloody inconsiderate and careless drinking of poisoned wine and now this...'

Robin grinned exactly like the boy Hunsdon had so often had to shout at for running away to play football with the stable hands and dogboys and occasionally beat for more serious crimes. 'There may well have been two of them but God looked after Her Majesty as He always seems to look after me.'

'Can't think why, it must be a time-consuming business keeping a bloody fool like you safe...'

Quite surprisingly Robin put his arms around his father's shoulders and hugged him tight. Hunsdon gripped back which eased his heart a little more.

WEDNESDAY 20TH SEPTEMBER 1592,

EARLY MORNING

They had left well before dawn from the old monastery, with two of the three remaining horses drawing two of the three carts still left from the Lord Chamberlain's provision train. A couple of the men had run in the night after refusing to dig graves for the three men of the troop Dodd had killed there. He had sixteen men following him and they walked reasonably well for the ragged starveling creatures that they were. No doubt they had done a lot of walking.

Nobody except Kat had got any sleep—she was curled up in a blanket on one of the carts. The rest of them had spent some time making themselves as tidy as they could and their weapons as clean and sharp as they could under Dodd's tongue-lashing. What had come over him, he wondered? It was only a few months since he had furiously resented Carey's ridiculous whims in the matter of cleanliness and tidiness, but here he was forcing his new followers to clean and sharpen their swords, knives or pikes and their faces as well. He himself spent an hour cleaning and straightening his new poinard and his familiar friendly sword, sharpening them and oiling them.

All three of the carts had a mark he recognised instantly: the mad duck of the Careys, or, as Carey called it, the Swan Rampant. The two remaining carthorses were in bad condition, mainly from neglect and bad feed, so Dodd set two stronger men to each cart to help it along on the rutted track north from the monastery, and four of the ones he thought might make trouble to pull the third cart and really give them something to moan about.

They had reached Oxford city gate after it opened and joined the queue of farmer's wives laden with produce to sell, some nasty covert looks from them as well. Dodd was comfortable on the bare back of the mare he had part-ridden from London, bandages round his feet, Harry Hunks' large buffcoat making him a bit more respectable and his recovered hat on his head. And he had his sword at his side and his own boots in the cart next to Kat.

He didn't dismount to talk to the sheriff's man at the gate, noticing a couple of the Queen's Gentlemen Pensioners of the Guard behind him. He did strain his Adam's apple to talk Southern.

'Ay've the baggage train sent up from London by may lord Baron Hunsdon that wis waylaid by sturdy beggars. These men helped me get it back.'

'And you are?'

The goats at the back being led by the youngest man, rightly suspecting something was up, started making a racket and trying to escape. The gateman was eyeing him with distaste.

'And you are?' he repeated.

Dodd drew himself up to his full height and glared down at the man. He knew the black eye and bruising that flowered green and yellow on his face and nose were hardly helping him but why should he care?

'Ma name is...' he started, then caught himself. 'Ach...Mr. Colin Elliot, Sir Robert Carey's man.'

Now that got a reaction. The gateman turned and shouted at

one of the lads quietly collecting weapons from the men wanting to come into the town. The boy touched his forehead and pelted off and Dodd and his party were waved aside into the space by the gatehouse, where another merchant was protesting about paying so much tax.

Dodd sat back and tried not to doze. It was hard work being a captain, that was sure, especially when you had no wife to threaten people with. And his belly was rumbling too—when was the last time he had a decent meal, he wondered? Saturday?

There was a stir and a shout: Carey was riding through the crowds at a trot, followed by four mounted liverymen of his father's, his face full of delight. Dodd was appalled to find that he was glad to see the courtier too, so he scowled and his mouth turned down with the effort of not smiling back.

'By God!' shouted Carey, 'Mr. Elliot, I'm very happy to see you at last. That wicked man Dodd is safely locked up in the town jail. Now is that the baggage train my brother so carelessly lost?'

'Ay, sir, I think it is, there's a bit left o'the supplies.'

'Do you know who took it?'

Dodd was trying to communicate urgently without words. Carey's eyes passed over the men behind him who were looking self-conscious.

'Nay sir, but these lads helped me...ehm...get the supplies back.'

Eyebrows up, a look of perfect comprehension on Carey's face.

'Spendid, splendid! My lord father's in Trinity College and my brother will be very happy to hear that at least some of the train is here. Do you know what happened to the carters bringing it?'

'Ah think they went back tae London, I dinna think they was killed.'

'That's a relief. Perhaps they'll turn up again at Somerset House. Now then, gentlemen, I think I recognise some of you from France.'

Dodd made a few introductions, ending with the Spaniard who swept off his hat in an accomplished Court bow. 'Don Jeronimo de la Quadra de Jimena,' he said.

Dodd hadn't often seen Carey do a double take. 'Indeed?' he said, responding with a fractionally shallower bow. 'The musician?'

Something in Jeronimo's lean weary face settled and hardened. '*Si, Señor*,' he said, '*El músico*.'

759

'Ehm...' Dodd put in with a clearing of his throat. With great reluctance he slid down from his horse and hobbled into a corner of the yard, beckoning Carey to follow him.

'What happened to your feet, Sergeant?' Carey asked, looking at the rags Dodd had wrapped around them.

'Ah'll tell ye the whole of it over a meal, sir, but first I want ye tae arrest Don Jeronimo and keep him safe.'

'Why?'

'He's asked for a meeting wi' the Queen...'

'He has?'

'And he says she'll grant it.'

Carey's eyes narrowed and he took breath to shout an order. 'Take him quietly,' Dodd put in, 'so the lads arenae upset by it.'

Both of them moved toward where Jeronimo was waiting, his back set against the guardhouse wall, eyes hooded.

'He helped me for nae reason but that he wanted tae talk to ye. I think he was the one convinced Captain Leigh to come this way in the first place and I seen him at the inn the night before the bastards took me and robbed me in the forest.'

'Of course they're the sturdy beggars who have been making the Oxford road so dangerous.'

'Ay, sir, I wis careless and they had me easy an' ma suit and horse and ma boots and sword. They're wanting their pay fra the Earl of Essex and had nae ither way of making a living. I cannae say I wouldna do the like in their place, though I'd do it better, I hope.' He vaulted back onto the mare to save his feet again and scowled at them.

Back with the little knot of worried looking men, Carey went over to Jeronimo, leaning on his wall, and made himself extremely affable, speaking French to the man. That was amazing, in Dodd's opinion: how Carey could suddenly switch into speaking foreign, easy as you like. Mind, when you looked at Jeronimo carefully, you could see he was hollow-eyed and often drank his medicine now. Perhaps it was true he had a canker.

They walked their horses together up a street with a roof over it that was high enough so they didn't need to dismount. They were tactfully escorted by Hunsdon's liverymen to Trinity College, whatever that was, tucked away on the other side of a wide street that must be taking the place of a moat for opposite was the patched and pierced old northern wall of the city. Oxford was an interesting place, full of huge archways and pictures made of canvas and behind them were good sturdy houses and a number of places that looked like monasteries with high walls and gatehouses like mansions. Quite defensible, for a wonder. However, now that he'd seen London, Dodd wasn't easily impressed.

As they went past the gate into the courtyard, Carey spoke quietly to the porter and Dodd heard the sound of the gate they had come through being locked and barred. Jeronimo looked up at him. 'Do not arrest me when the men can see,' he said quietly. 'Wait, settle them. I give you and Don Roberto my parole that I will not try escape until I have seen the Queen.'

The business was done quickly. The other men were shown into the college hall to eat a late breakfast from the remains left by Hunsdon's servants. Jeronimo waited as four large liverymen appeared and surrounded him.

He deftly unbuckled his swordbelt one-handed and handed it to Dodd who took it grimly.

'I surrender to you, *Señor* Dodd,' he said. 'I ask only that I may speak to the Queen.'

'With all due respect, Don Jeronimo,' Carey said, 'I don't think she will agree.'

'She will, Señor,' said Jeronimo, reaching with his only hand into his doublet pocket and taking out something quite small, wrapped in old linen. Carey took it and opened it. Dodd could just glimpse it was a richly embroidered woman's kid glove, badly stained with brown and with one of the fingers cut off. He could also see the breath stop in Carey's throat as he took it.

Carey's eyes were a bright cold blue as he stared straight at Jeronimo for a long silent minute.

Jeronimo inclined his head. 'If you give her that, Señor, she will see me. If you do not...' He shrugged elaborately. 'I will die soon in any case and then she will never...know something she has wanted to know for many years.' He smiled gently, his dark hawk of a face as arrogant as Carey's. 'In the end, it will not matter; all will be as God decides.'

Carey tucked the little package into his own doublet pocket, holding the Spaniard's gaze for another minute, something unseen in the air between them. Then Carey turned and issued a blizzard of orders.

Kat had woken up while all of this was going on and watched with frank fascination, her pointed chin on her arms on the side of the cart.

'So that's why he helped you, was it?' she asked without surprise. 'I did wonder.'

Jeronimo went quietly and Dodd made introductions to Carey who smiled and said nothing about yet another waif added to his father's household. The goats were inspected and approved of by the Steward, although the young billy kid was likely to meet his inevitable fate soon.

And the inevitable time came when Dodd had to get down from his horse again. He sternly refused a litter but took a dismounting block and tried not to wince. He still couldn't put his boots on and so he followed a servant to one of the downstairs rooms usually lived in by scholars. When Carey offered him a shoulder, he took it and soon found himself seated on the side of a comfortable half-tester bed, next to a small fire in the hearth, his feet soaking in cool salted water with dried comfrey and allheal in it, which stung like the devil, and drinking a large jack of excellent ale. The chamber gave onto a small parlour that had another chamber leading off it where there was a pile of packs and Carey's Court suit hanging up on the wall. Dodd started to explain to him what had been going on but when he started yawning every other word and losing track, Carey called in the barber surgeon who had been sent to bandage Dodd's feet.

'The story can wait. I'll be riding out with my father immediately,' he said, 'Get some sleep, Henry and...by God, I'm pleased to see your miserable face again!'

Carey clapped Dodd on the back and went through the parlour to clatter down the stairs. The barber surgeon peeled off the clouts, cleared out a lot of thorns and a sharp stone splinter while Dodd drank more ale and wished the man in hell, then put clean linen socks on him and bowed himself out.

Dodd found a decent linen shirt waiting for him on the bed

and was pleased to put it on rather than the filthy hemp shirt and woollen breeches although no doubt the lice would be sorry. He was too tired to be hungry, ignored the platter of pork pie, bread and cheese and finished the contents of the jug of ale. He fell into bed, asleep almost before his head hit the pillow.

His last thought was a question as to what the hell it was Carey had been up to while Dodd had been busy, which had made him look distinctly pale and unhealthy, coupled with a forlorn hope that he might let Dodd sleep for a couple of days at least.

WEDNESDAY 20TH SEPTEMBER 1592,

LATE AFTERNOON

Sunset was coming through the small glass window as Dodd woke because someone had just come into his room.

Yes, it was Carey. Dodd knew he hadn't slept nearly long enough, but he didn't see the point of complaining about it. Carey's face was unreadable, closed down into the affable, slightly stupid-looking mask he wore when he played primero for high stakes.

'Ay,' sighed Dodd, 'what now?'

'Sergeant, I hate to have to tell you this but we absolutely must visit the stews.'

'Eh?'

It turned out to be one of the strangest experiences of Dodd's life and it was only a pity he was too tired and hungry to enjoy it properly. He had to get dressed again in a respectable suit of wool that Carey said was borrowed from the Under-steward and apologised for it being well out of fashion as it had been handed on from Carey's father. Dodd didn't care; at least it wasn't as tight and uncomfortable as Carey's previous loan, now being worn by Captain Leigh in jail.

Dodd had leather slippers to put on and low pattens to save them from the disgraceful cobbles and he wobbled painfully across Broad Street and down a tiny alley with the sign of a magpie hanging on an alehouse at the corner. Did none of the scholars here know that horse muck was good for gardens and making gunpowder?

They went into a little house that smelled of woodsmoke and was full of sly-eyed women with very low-cut bodices, but Carey swept straight past them, for a wonder.

The next thing was shocking. They were in a room full of shelves with a tiled floor and Carey proceeded to strip off all his clothes as if he were about to go for a swim, even his shirt. An ancient attendant folded his doublet and hose and handed him a linen cloth which he wrapped around his hips like someone in an old religious picture. Then he put on a new pair of wooden pattens from a row by the wall. Firmly ramming down his multiple suspicions and wondering if he was in fact delirious and hallucinating, Dodd did the same and clopped after Carey along floors that got hotter and hotter until they were in a small room with a brazier in it. Several other men were sitting about on wooden benches—old men, mainly, with grey beards, wrinkled stomachs and twiglike arms, a few spotty youths like peeled willow wands and with a tendency to peer.

The heat from the brazier was fierce and Dodd could feel the sweat popping out all over him.

'We never got round to doing this in London, which is a pity as they're much better there,' Carey said conversationally, as if it was the most natural thing in the world to take off his linen cloth, fold it and sit on the edge of the bench on it. He stretched his legs negligently in front of him, peering at one of the white scars. 'This will do.'

'Ehm...whit the...why...?'

Carey didn't meet his eyes. 'Sovereign for bruises and damage generally, helps sweat out poisons and so on and so forth.'

Dodd had never heard of a medical treatment that required you to get this hot though he had heard of some alchemists curing the French pox with mercury and sweating.

'Och,' he said, doing as Carey had done so he didn't burn his arse on the planks and tried not to fight the heat as the sweat started dripping off him in rivers. You had to admit it was sort of relaxing.

'We're lucky it's the men's day today,' Carey said. 'Otherwise we'd have had to pollute the Isis.'

The older men and youths left a little later and Carey opened his eyes and smiled lazily at Dodd who was dozing where he sat.

'Now then,' he said, 'what have you been up to, Sergeant, apart from recruiting a sorry pack of my lord Essex's deserters for the Carlisle castle guard?'

'Ay,' Dodd said, sticking his jaw out, 'but they are nae related to onybody, are they? And they can shape up or die.'

Carey laughed. Dodd told him the story. Carey was a good audience, exclaiming with anger at Dodd being ambushed, laughing at his description of Kat.

'That's the child in the cart?'

'Ay. How is she?'

'Still asleep as far as I know, with the wife of the Trinity College cook looking after her. Last I heard she was insisting she had to stay with you.'

Dodd carried on with his tale until he brought it to the death of Harry Hunks and his own decision to leave the ill-starred monastery.

'If ye ask him, d'ye think the Earl of Essex will pay his men at last?'

Carey's expression became unhappy and he looked away.

'Ay, well, their stupid captain's plan was tae get into the procession in their stupid tangerine and white rags and ask him in public why he betrayed them?'

'I gathered something of the sort from the unfortunate Captain Leigh. It would not have been allowed, believe me.'

Dodd said nothing although he suspected that with the number of alleyways and passages in Oxford town and some men who weren't too fussy about what they did, it might be easier than Carey thought.

'I dinna think they expected more than tae humiliate him and perhaps get the Queen to pay them instead.'

Carey made a non-committal grunt.

Dodd sat up, despite the puddle of sweat on the floor under him and the way he was starting to get dizzy with the heat.

'Sir,' he said sternly, 'they should be paid. They ainly went wi' the Earl because they believed him. The maist of them are not fighting men, or they werenae, they was younger sons of farmers that wanted adventure and found that fighting wisnae as he painted it. And the maist o' them died and not one o' them was paid aught but promises.'

'There are plenty of others like them,' Carey pointed out with typical aristocratic callousness.

'Ay, sir,' said Dodd, clenching his jaw with outrage. 'And the more shame to the lairds for it. None o' the Grahams or the Armstrongs or the Kerrs would do the like. Take a man that wis happy at the plough and make a soldier of him and then leave him to die or rot or starve.'

'How's it different on the Borders?'

This showed a Courtier's bloody ignorance, in Dodd's opinion.

'I've niver bin aught but a fighter,' he told Carey. 'Raised tae it. Ay, ma mother sent me to learn ma letters wi' the Reverend Gilpin but I could back a horse and shoot a bow long before. I killed ma first man when I wis nine, in the Rising of the Northern Earls...'

'So did I,' said Carey, softly enough that Dodd nearly didn't hear it.

'Ay?' he said, surprised and a little impressed. 'Well, if I was to take some foolish notion in ma heid and gang oot tae the Low Countries or France or the like and sell my sword, it wouldnae be sae great a change for me, I wouldnae be made different, ye ken.' He couldn't quite catch the words to pack his anger in, the way it grated on him how the young men who had turned sturdy beggars and robbers had been betrayed, even though they'd beaten him up in the quiet Oxfordshire forest. How he knew they would mostly find it hard—bordering impossible—to return to their villages, even if they got their back pay. 'There's a difference, and it's... Och. Ye'd ken if ye kenned.'

Carey stood up and mopped himself with the cloth, then tied it round his hips again. 'Yes,' he said quietly, 'It's like hunting dogs. Once you've hunted with a dog, he never can really go back to being nothing but a lapdog. There's always something of the wolf in him afterwards.'

It was a good way of putting it. 'Ay,' said Dodd, standing up himself and wincing; some of his deeper cuts were bleeding into the wooden sandals. 'Like a sheepdog if it goes wrong. Once it's tasted sheep, ye must hunt wi' it or kill it, ye canna herd sheep wi' it again. So that's what's been done to the lads, they dinna ken themselves but I doubt if more than one or two of them can go back tae being day labourers or herdsmen or farmers.'

'No,' said Carey.

'Will ye pay 'em?'

'I can't give them their backpay. If they want to come north, they might be useful and then I'll find a way to pay them.'

Dodd knew that was the best he was going to get and he knew he trusted the Courtier more than the high and mighty Earl of Essex.

They went through to the next room which was even hotter and full of clouds of steam from idiots like Carey sprinkling water on the white hot coals in the brazier. Dodd couldn't stand it for more than a few minutes, scraping himself with a blunt bronze blade. He did Carey's back and Carey did his which felt odd but also pleasant, like somebody scratching your back for you after you'd been wearing a jack for a couple of days. Which thought took him on to thinking of his wife and then he had to put his towel back around his hips and think of other things before he embarrassed himself.

'We might have time for a girl,' Carey said, deadpan.

'I wis thinking o' me wife,' Dodd said with dignity. It was the truth too so Carey's cynical laugh was very annoying. Then they were out in the dusky garden and going into a kind of tent lit by candles. Odd. There was a glint of green water—it covered a big square pond like a fish tank.

And then the next thing was that the bloody Courtier had pushed Dodd into the fish pond with an almighty shove. The cold water made him gasp and he dog-paddled to the surface again filled with vengeance just in time to get a faceful of spray as Carey jumped in next to him. He coughed and spluttered and trod water as Carey splashed past on his back. The wooden pattens were somewhere at the bottom.

'Whit the hell did ye...'

'Didn't want another argument,' Carey said, blowing water out of his mouth like a dolphin on a map. Dodd found a place where the water only came to his chest and there were indeed fish in the tank but not too much weed or slime. The fish immediately started nibbling at his feet and legs and he tried to kick them away. 'It's the final part of the treatment. You'll feel a lot better for it.' The man was looking insufferably smug again.

A suspicion struck Dodd. He suddenly remembered the other purpose of stews, the one that didn't involve women.

'Is this yer way of getting me tae take a *bath*?' he demanded furiously, '*Again*? Not a month after the last one?'

Carey sniggered and so Dodd went after him, ducked him, held him under then decided not to drown the bastard because he was too tired to deal with the consequences. So he let go and climbed out by the mosaicked steps. Carey stood coughing, shaking his head and still bloody laughing, the git.

A little later he was dry, skin glowing, feet in another clean pair of linen socks which had been very helpfully put on by one of the girls who had patted them dry and tutted sympathetically and even put a green salve of allheal on. They were drinking brandy in the stews' parlour while Dodd waded into an excellent dinner of steak and kidney pudding with potherbs, followed by a figgy pudding with custard that filled most of the corners in his belly. However, he had maintained a dour offended silence throughout and continued it as they walked back to Trinity, trying not to limp. Carey was not in the least concerned.

'See you in the morning, Sergeant,' he said in the upstairs parlour that overlooked the large courtyard that Carey called a quadrangle for some reason. There were a couple of straw pallets and some blankets by the fireplace, so it seemed some servants would be sleeping there. It was nice that Dodd had an actual bedchamber. 'We're riding out before dawn.'

'Och,' said Dodd, wishing he could have a day off too.

At least there was ale and bread and cheese waiting for him

in his chamber, and a manservant came in to help him undress, a luxury he still found suspicious but was grateful for as his eyes had started shutting by themselves again. He went to sleep with his skin still feeling very peculiar and his hair damp.

THURSDAY 21ST SEPTEMBER 1592, DAWN

Mrs. Odingsells always woke at dawn, even though the fog that filled most of her world meant she only knew when it was full light. Her window faced east and she left the shutters open so that when the weather was bad enough she could see the threatening colour of dawn a little.

She was always amazed at how tiring it was to lie down all the time. She had a girl come from the village most mornings to help her dress and sit in a chair by the window but lately the trembling had got too bad and she couldn't make her legs work. Why the Devil couldn't she die? She prayed most nights to die and welcomed each cough and sniffle in the hope that it might be bearing the gift of a lungfever. She was not afraid of death, had hopes that her faithfulness might count for something with Almighty God, with whom she intended to have words in any case. She was not even very worried by pain.

So why was she still alive, she wondered? She had borne two children to Mr. Odingsells in the 1550s during the boy-king's reign, only to have all three carried off by the English sweat. It was an old horror now, well-scabbed over. With no heart for another husband, she had become a gentlewoman to her distant cousin Amy Robsart when she made her very good match. And then Amy, too, was mysteriously struck down. She had stayed at Cumnor Place afterwards, thanks to the kindness of Sir Anthony Forster, and lived a quiet and prayerful life on her small jointure, running the manor for him, with occasional visits to Oxford and Abingdon, reading mainly scripture and the Church Fathers. She had a long memory and a good one: she remembered the bonfires for the Princess Elizabeth's birth, had in fact got drunk at the feasting and danced with the young man she had liked then, who only got himself killed in France. Yes, she would have words with the Almighty.

She had outlived everyone she loved so what was she doing here? Was it about the Queen's matter, from decades before? In which case...perhaps there was hope that the pleasant young man would have passed on her message to Her Majesty.

She knew he had as soon as she heard the hooves of several horses in the courtyard, heard old Forster with his voice full of fear greeting the man with the rumbling voice. She remembered that voice, remembered it very well and managed to sit up in bed. More than two horses, three or four, she thought, including a pony from the shorter stride.

She pulled on a bedjacket she had knitted herself a decade before, of silk and wool mixed—against scripture, of course, but very practical. With infinite effort she rearranged her pillows so she could stay sitting up, then felt for the sewn silk packet she had kept on a ribbon round her neck all this time, safe. That ill-affected man Topcliffe had tried to find it to take it off her years ago but she had convinced him the papers were burned.

Forster soon knocked on her chamber door and she bade him show her visitors in.

It was the man and the woman again. The same two. She squinted sideways, lining up the tiny patch of her eye that still worked. There was Henry Carey, even more like the King in his age, older and greyer, of course. There was the woman she had never actually seen before but had heard, screaming. She was wearing a black wig again. Forster withdrew.

'Mrs. Odingsells, with your permission, we wish to make use of your hall...' began Hunsdon courteously.

'Well?' That was the woman, the strong contralto voice, accustomed to command.

'Your Majesty,' Mrs. Odingsells said steadily, for hadn't she practised in her imagination for this meeting many times? 'Please forgive me for not rising, my legs no longer obey me.'

The woman stepped forward. 'Do you have them?'

Mrs. Odingsells nodded. 'Yes. Please use whatever you want

of this house—Mr. Forster will help you.'

'All this time?' said the Queen in wonder. 'Why did you keep it? Why not burn it?'

Her bedroom was not cold; there was a curfew over the fire, to keep the coals hot. Mrs. Odingsells looked sideways at it, not able to see it any more.

'I couldn't. I tried to many times, especially when that evil man Topcliffe tried to take it. But...It was in your handwriting, signed by you, Your Majesty, and by poor Amy. And...I thought you might want it one day.' She couldn't see, of course, but she thought the Queen coloured.

'Why? To remind myself of how near I came to losing my kingdom?'

She did understand. Mrs. Odingsells smiled joyfully into the fog where the Queen loomed. 'Yes, Your Majesty. Nothing good could have come from poor Amy forswearing herself, breaking her Bible oath. No amount of gold or land or manors could have made that right.' She didn't add that the Queen's love for Robert Dudley was the mystery of the age, considering how he had treated Amy who loved him too.

'No.' The Queen was agreeing with her. 'I think that poor Amy saved my life and my kingdom that day.'

It was time. Slowly, with fingers that trembled and fumbled no matter how hard she tried to control them, Mrs. Odingsells lifted the little packet on its ribbon over her head and held it out. The Queen took it, her long slender fingers cold and smooth. The paper crackled as she opened it out. She took a long breath.

'Hmm. Good penmanship,' said the Queen after a moment in a self-satisfied tone. Mrs. Odingsells nearly laughed. Amy's handwriting had been poor so the Queen must have been her own clerk that day and done it well. 'I thank you heartily, Mrs. Odingsells, both for your discretion and your faithful keeping of this to give to me. Is there anything we can give you or assist you with in token of our thanks?'

'No,' said Mrs. Odingsells. 'It was my duty to keep it safe and now you have it once again, perhaps the good Lord will call me to Him at last.'

There was another long pause, and a sharp movement from Henry Carey. 'God speed,' said the Queen. 'Thank you, Mrs. Odingsells.'

The two of them walked out leaving a sense of empty space behind them. Mrs. Odingsells called in Mr. Forster and told him to let them do whatever they wanted within reason.

Once out in the passage the Queen looked down at the single sheet of paper. Written on it, in her own excellent Italic, was her agreement with Amy Dudley née Robsart that Amy would petition Convocation for the annulment of her marriage on grounds of non-consummation and in return receive large estates, a pot of gold, a manor house and a house in London and a pension from the Queen. Both parties had signed it, of course, but...Harry was staring at it, appalled. In all the hurry, thirty-two years ago, they had both clean forgotten the agreement they had come for and now...

'Where's the other one?' he whispered. 'There were two copies.'

There had to be two copies. One for Amy, one for her. Two copies, both signed by both parties. Mrs. Odingsells had only handed over one.

The Queen shook her head, refolded the paper and put it under her stays, then walked down the stairs swiftly and out into the weedy courtyard. Her lady-in-waiting Mary Radcliffe and Thomasina her Fool had already gone into the old hall to supervise its tidying and sweeping. The horses were tethered in the corner. To be so free of attendants—as always it made her feel light and giddy. She had her brother get out his tinderbox and light the stump of candle in it so she could burn the paper she did have and stamp the ashes into the mud. The other copy...Well, that would have to wait. Perhaps she would set young Robin on to find it one day.

Then she had the final argument with her brother about the meeting she had planned. It didn't matter what he said. She had to receive the old musician who had plotted so carefully to meet her. She must finish what she could of the business at last. Obviously she couldn't do it at Woodstock, so full of courtiers and spies, nor at Oxford. There was a fitness in things and for all Henry's spluttering about the risks, this matter must be finished where it started.

Thursday 21st September 1592, Morning

It was full light when Dodd woke up to someone knocking on the door. That was some comfort.

'Whit the hell...?' he growled, confused into thinking he was still in London.

'We leave in about half an hour, Sergeant,' came Carey's voice filled with his usual loathsome morning cheerfulness.

Dodd rolled out of bed, used the jordan under it and slowly got himself dressed. There were good thick knitted hose with it to go over the linen socks, so he took a chance and pulled on his boots that someone had already done a good job of mending and polishing. It wasn't what you could call comfortable but it was bearable; he would just have to hope they were riding, not walking. He went into the parlour where there was food ready on the table, neither Tovey nor the Scotsman visible. He gulped down more mild ale and fresh bread and cheese.

In the quadrangle were horses and men and Carey efficiently sorting them out. Nobody was wearing buff jerkins or helmets or jacks but they all had their swords and were looking smart. Dodd's own sword was at his hip and he felt much the better for it. To his surprise, Don Jeronimo was also there, on a horse with his only hand loosely attached to the saddle so he could still use the rein; one of his feet was tied to the stirrup. His face was unreadable under his hat but he looked worryingly humorous.

Dodd mounted without touching the stirrups, despite it being so early, then leaned over and unbuckled the stirrup leathers, handed them to a surprised groom. 'They'll ainly mek ma feet sore,' he told the lad who didn't look like he'd understood.

'So,' he asked Carey, 'where are we gangen tae, sir?'

'Not far, about four miles from here.'

They went through the College gate, walked along the wide road where they must have markets, down a narrow road past another of the odd-looking monkish fortresses, curved along the line of a high wall, over a bridge and then they went to a canter in a body, Don Jeronimo constantly surrounded by Hunsdon's liverymen. Dodd recognised several typical Border faces among them, though their speech was from the East March.

They had to slow down soon. The road into Oxford was choked with people and packtrains coming the other way, so they used the verge, where it wasn't too muddy, and pounded along. It was mostly a broad road, well-built perhaps by the same giants that had built the Faery's Wall that once was the Border line. Dodd recognised the look of the stones and some of the waymarkers carved with square letters in foreign.

They turned aside only a little south of Oxford so it was hardly any time at all before they were clattering into the courtyard of a mansion that had clearly been closed up and not much inhabited for a long time, from the grass growing between the stones and in the gutters. As usual there was no proper tower and it was not defensible but there were four horses tethered in the corner: two beautiful hunters, a palfrey and a little pony.

'Where's this, Sir Robert?' he asked.

'Cumnor Place,' Carey told him, 'about a mile and a half north of where you were being held. This is where Amy Dudley née Robsart was killed.'

Dodd had never heard of the woman so he concluded that it was some dirty business Carey had got himself tangled in. And the south must be getting to him: he hadn't even thought how to steal those very pretty and unattended four horses in the corner.

Jeronimo had slumped in the saddle but when Hunsdon's liveryman untied his foot and reached over to tie his wrist to his belt instead of the saddle, he looked around himself as if recognising the place. Then he swung his leg over the horse's neck and jumped down forwards, only staggering a little as he landed. Dodd dismounted the same way and managed not to yell when his boots hit the ground.

And then they were going into the hall which seemed to have been hastily swept, though the tables were still piled on one another and the benches stacked by the wall.

On the dais sat Carey's father with two, no, three women beside him. One looked like a child but had a face that was somehow not childish. She was sitting cross-legged in tawny velvet at the feet of a black-haired elderly woman in a green woollen kirtle and a gown of velvet, who was sitting a little behind Hunsdon. In front of her and on a better chair was another older woman in richer clothes, with red hair.

Carey made an odd little half-bob, then bowed to his father. Dodd copied him, less elegantly. Jeronimo paced in, surrounded by Hunsdon's men, his face haughtier than ever. His dark eyes travelled along the people in front of him and he let out a half-smile. Then he stepped forward and went gracefully to both his knees and stayed there, ramrod straight.

'I have been asked by the Queen to question you, Señor Jeronimo de la Quadra de Jimena,' gravelled Lord Hunsdon, chin on his ruff. 'Her ladies-in-waiting here will carry the account back to her.'

Jeronimo tilted his head slightly but said nothing.

'Please tell me why you have asked for audience with the Queen and where you got the…item you gave to my son, Sir Robert Carey.'

'Milord,' said Jeronimo, 'the last time we meet here you chased my friend a mile down the road. It is thirty-two years since. Now I am old and dying. I have a canker growing in me and I bleed. I have come to make right what I did that day.'

'Go on.'

'I am the bastard son of Don Alvaro de la Quadra who was the Spanish ambassador at Her Majesty's Court then. I was a young fool of eighteen, good with the lute, good with the harp, very very good with the crossbow. All stringed instruments were friends then.' He smiled as if remembering a long-lost lover. 'My father bought for me a place among the Queen's musicians from Mr. Tallis so I could spy on the Queen. I was proud for the work.'

Jeronimo smiled. 'At that time I truly believe that the Holy Catholic Church was the only refuge of mankind, the only dwelling of God, and that all heretics must die.' He shook his head in wonder. 'Since then I learn better. But I was a young idiot.'

'Indeed.'

'*Entonces*, milord, while playing my lute I hear Her Majesty who was then so beautiful and scandalous and in love with her horsemaster, speak with her lover about how to deal with his wife. Perhaps she thought I would not understand Italian. She wanted the woman to divorce him but it must be done with much care in case Sir William Cecil hear of it and make a stop. But the wife was being difficult, stupid.

'Milord Leicester sent me with a letter to his wife ordering her to divorce him and stop delaying. She read it while I waited for an answer and then she began to cry. What could I do? I was a young idiot and not ugly—she was pretty and distressed. I put my arms around her and held her. And so I was lost.

'No; alas, milords, I never took her to my bed but I certainly sinned with her in my mind. She was a virtuous woman. We talked much and she told me she wanted to kill her rival. And...'

There was a concerted gasp from everyone.

'She wanted to kill the Queen? And you told her how it could be done?' Hunsdon barked, leaning forward.

Jeronimo bowed a little and coughed. 'Of course.' Everyone in the hall shifted position in some way. The black-haired woman with the tiny woman beside her crossed her arms. 'I told her to bring the Queen with as few attendants as possible to the manor where she lived very sad and lonely for her husband and that if she can do this, my friend and I will do the rest. And for the first time she smiled at me and said, yes, she could do it. And we kissed.' He smiled, his eyes crinkling.

'Did your father know?'

'Of course. I spoke with him immediately. He was still trying to bring about the marriage between the young Queen and his master, King Philip II. He knew that the horsemaster was a fierce heretic and a fighter, desiring war. He believed it is a disaster for Spain if they marry.

'And when I put it to him, he could see how it solved all. I kill the scandalous Queen, the last Tudor. There will be two contenders with a good claim: the Queen of Scotland, a Guise, or His Most Catholic Majesty himself through his marriage to the Queen's ugly older sister. If there is war, it is in England, not in the Hapsburg lands, but there was no reason to think the Queen of Scots will fight for her English throne as she then was still the Queen of France, married to the young King who was unwarlike.' Jeronimo shrugged. 'I knew it might mean my death but I was young, I no believed I could die. I was in love with the poor Lady Dudley and I thought that when the Queen was dead, I would challenge Leicester to a duel and kill him and so take her for my own. It was very romantic.

'So my friend warned me when the Queen took a good galloper and a remount for a hunt in Windsor Great Park and when you, milord Hunsdon, did the same to go with her. We slipped away from the Court and rode to Cumnor Place. My Amy had arranged it all. We were there first, I wait in the darkness of the musicians' passage with my friend keeping watch. I never see the Queen arrive with you, milord, I was in the dark behind the door. They went into the Long Gallery to meet Amy and discussed the divorce. She agreed, they signed paper, there was gold. It took a long long time. And then, as we had agreed, the second door opened to the back stairs where I was waiting. I had my crossbow wound and ready.

'I hear them come through the door, my eyes accustomed to darkness; I step out and I am dazzled by the light through the window. I see the woman in front with her red hair and the gold on her collar and I shoot at her. Somehow, I miss. She tries to run down the stairs to me, screaming in English but I do not understand so well. I step back, I take my crossbow by the stock and I strike her down the side of her head and she falls like a sack down the stairs and that is when I know who she is.' He paused, breathed carefully, his voice husky. 'I still can see my beautiful Amy crumpled at the turn of the stair, her neck bent on the wall. You, milord, had put behind you the other woman, the one I had only seen as having black hair, you had drawn your sword and so I turn and stumble back through the gallery where my friend is waiting. But I cannot move for shock, he is a faster runner than I and I climb up into the rafters as milord Hunsdon thunders past me, chasing him.'

'Si, Señores, I could have wound my crossbow again and killed the black haired woman too, but why? What was the point? I couldn't think, I believed she was only a lady-in-waiting. I looked at her as she knelt by my Amy's body, crying over her body, trying to stop the blood coming from my Amy's ears and eyes. I climbed up to hide the crossbow among the roofbeams, climbed down again and I saw she was taking off the broken headdress, using it to mop the blood, try to make all clean. I saw her take off her own headdress and place it on Amy's head where there were two terrible dents from my crossbow. Perhaps to hide it.

'And then milord came back and he pulled her to her feet. She had rolled all together in a bundle, the headdress, her gloves dirtied with blood. They argued, he ordered her to ride and called her "Your Majesty" and that, Señores, was when I understood that she was the Queen but wearing a black wig and someone else's kirtle. I stood there, turned to stone as I heard their horses gallop away.

'Later I found the bundle in a bush. I kept one of the gloves, the bloody one, and my friend took the other and the headdress. ER was embroidered on the gloves and they were the finest gloves I had seen. Then when my friend had stopped my weeping and I could think again, we rode back to my father.'

Jeronimo's face darkened. 'My God, my father was furious. He would not let us in the house, told us to go and lie low and he will do what he can. We hid in the Spanish embassy for a while. Then we went to Oxford where my friend had his family. We lived there a while and then when the Queen came back to Oxford six years later and the place was full of pursuivants and that evil man she hired to hunt us down, I rode to Bristol and took ship for the Low Countries where I learned other things than lute-playing.'

'You could simply have told me this, Don Jeronimo,' said Hunsdon, 'Why do you insist on seeing the Queen?'

Jeronimo was not paying attention to him, looking hard at the women beside him. He narrowed his eyes and then smiled.

'If I could be received into Her Majesty's Presence, if I can have such favour though not deserved,' he said quietly staring into space, 'I will say this to Her Majesty: I am not now the hot-headed young idiot that I was. Now I am a cold-headed old idiot. I have a canker that came from a mole that broke open and bled. My liver is full of stones, there is a rock in my stomach. Soon I will take to my bed and die in pain and then I will go to Purgatory to answer for all the men and women I have killed in my life. For my *querida* Amy, I have already paid much. It is just.

'I will say this to the Queen: Your Majesty, I ask pardon that I tried to kill you. I am happy that I failed but I am also sorry that because I so stupidly killed your horsemaster's wife, the scandal meant you could not have him. A very strict Jesuit confessor sent me back to England to make amends. And so here I am. I beg your forgiveness with all my heart. You may take me and execute me if you like, you will do me a favour.' He paused in the silence. 'He was a clever Jesuit, I think.

'This I will say to the Queen for the end: now I thank God you were incognito so I made such a mistake. And then I will wait for Her Majesty's judgement and mercy.'

He bowed his head and there was silence. Hunsdon leaned over to talk to the women beside him and then lifted a hand. 'We will consult on it.' A nod to his men and Jeronimo was helped to his feet and led out of the hall, walking slowly as if he was in pain. At another nod from Hunsdon, Carey went with them.

'Sergeant Dodd,' said Hunsdon after a moment, 'I understand from my youngest son that you have dealt in your inimitable way with the troublesome band of sturdy beggars who took my supply train and beat up my men and that you propose that my son take them into his service.'

'Ay, sir,' said Dodd after a moment to collect his thoughts. 'They wis only raiding because they had nae ither choice, being betrayed in France by the Earl of Essex and getting none of their pay.'

Hunsdon's eyes were hooded. 'We will offer them the chance to go back to their villages near Hereford. If they choose not to, Sir Robert will take half and I'll send the other half to Berwick to my other son who is Marshal there.'

Dodd shrugged. It was eight men not sixteen for Carlisle, but he supposed the Captain of Berwick Castle would need unattached men as badly as they did. He was glad Hunsdon saw the advantage there.

The black-haired woman with the tall hat cleared her throat. 'Sergeant Dodd, my mistress the Queen asked me to...talk to you about what has been happening.'

'Ay, missus,' said Dodd warily. 'Milady.'

The woman beckoned him so he went over, trying not to hobble, and did the best bow he could over her hand. She looked far too old to be any of the women constantly pestering Carey's father and son to bed them so perhaps she did work for the Queen. You could tell she was a powerful character with that beaky nose and the snapping dark eyes and you'd think there would be clashes. The other woman was sitting back, talking to Hunsdon.

She took him through the entire past four months in detail, since Carey had arrived at Carlisle to be Deputy Warden to his brother-in-law, clearly knowing far more about the various happenings on the Border and in London than any lady-in-waiting really ought to. She laughed at some of Dodd's comments which emboldened him so he gave her more stories than he normally would. Her laugh was delightful for all her age and the fact that her teeth were stained.

'Sergeant Dodd,' she said eventually, 'I take it that you approve of Sir Robert Carey and his various...actions?'

Approve? That was a little strong. 'Eh, he's canny but he takes mad plans in his heid,' Dodd said cautiously. 'He's a bonny fighter but he's allus a Courtier, no' a Borderer and that holds him back.' In the corner of his eye, Dodd caught a brief flash of a smile from Lord Hunsdon and wondered why. Conscientiously he added, 'Mind, he's no' himself at the moment, he seems...eh...a little unwell.'

'Perhaps you could tell him that I already spoke to Mrs. Oding-sells before you arrived. I personally received from her the... document she kept for me all these years, so faithfully.'

'Ay missus,' said Dodd, with no clue as to what she was talking about. The lady nodded once, seemingly approving, then smiled again.

'He will understand. I have made provision for her as well although she insists she needs nothing. Now then. This matter of Don Jeronimo,' continued the lady, narrowing her eyes. 'Do you think I should advise Her Majesty to see him?'

'Good God, no!' snapped Dodd. 'He says he's sorry for it all but there's a long plan here. He's the one brought the broken men here tae Oxford, he saw me at the inn on the Oxford road, heard me say I wis Carey's man, and then he took me prisoner in the forest, easy as ye like. And then he comes and helps me escape and take over the troop...I dinna think it wis kindness nor to make amends. And why was he at the Oxford inn at all? Eh? What had he been at before? He says he tried to kill the Queen thirty years gone and he got the wrong woman, his ainly love.' Dodd's lip twisted in a sneer. 'Och, the puir wee manikin, whit a sad tale to be sure.' Dodd stabbed the air with his forefinger. 'He's a Papist—he admits he tried it on once, you tell the Queen *hang him today*!' Dodd realised he was shouting and toned it down so as not to frighten her. 'He said she'd be doing him a favour.'

Hunsdon banged with his stick on the floor. 'Well spoken, Sergeant!' he boomed.

The lady-in-waiting smiled. 'Thank you for your advice, Sergeant Dodd. My lord Hunsdon, I think we are done here.'

Hunsdon harrumphed. 'Indeed, I shall indict him on a charge of high treason...'

'Och for God's sake,' groaned Dodd, goaded beyond endurance by this stupid Southron way of doing things, 'He's said hisself the bill's foul, ye have him, string him up now and be done wi' it. Ah'll dae it for ye if ye're too...'

'Sergeant, the laws of the Border and the laws of England are different. We can't simply string a man up here without trying him first...'

'A'right, give me a crossbow and five minutes and...'

The lady-in-waiting was almost laughing again. 'Sergeant, then we would have to arrest you for murder.'

'What? Och, no, see, I took a shot at a deer in the forest and what a pity, I missed and hit...'

'No, Sergeant.'

'But he's *foreign.*'

Both Hunsdon and the lady-in-waiting were laughing outright now. Dodd took a deep breath and set his jaw so no more words would escape for them to make fun of. It was obvious they were stupid fools with no idea of how to deal with a dangerous bastard like Don Jeronimo, because of living in the soft south no doubt. So it would be up to him. He knew Jeronimo would understand and so would Carey and if the worst came to the worst he could always join his Armstrong brothers-in-law in the Debateable Land.

Suddenly there was a confused noise outside. Dodd heard Carey's shout and instantly drew his sword, ran as fast as he could hobble out of the hall.

There was a scene of chaos in the courtyard. The horses were plunging about, one of the Borderers had already caught one and mounted, Carey was lying on his back holding his face. Dodd struggled over to him.

'He's awa'?' he asked.

'Oof,' said Carey, obviously part-stunned as he climbed back on his feet, shaking his head and feeling his jaw where there was blood coming from his lip, 'Bastard!'

'Ay,' said Dodd.

'He started to puke, I went to help him and he decked me and ran. Caught one of the horses, got on board and off he went. He's not as sick as he makes out.'

'Ay,' said Dodd.

The two Borderers were galloping down the path into the forest and Dodd was completely certain that they wouldn't catch Jeronimo.

There was a sound behind him. Hunsdon was in the courtyard, looking furious; behind him were the women.

'We'll ride back to Oxford,' he ordered. 'Now.'

'Och no, we can quarter the forest with enough men...'

'We must first escort the ladies back to Woodstock palace. Then we'll find Don Jeronimo.'

Well that was more Southron stupidity; give the women a couple of men to help them and send them off out of the way while everybody else found Jeronimo and accidentally killed him where no bloody lawyers could see. For a wonder, the ladies-in-waiting were not arguing at all; the two women were already at the mounting block, being helped into the side-saddles, one on the handsome hunter, the other on the pretty palfrey, while the tiny person with the unchildlike face was already on her white pony, her face thunderous and what looked like a small throwing knife in her hand.

'Ay but no' by the Oxford road,' Dodd said, resigned to losing Jeronimo for the moment.

'Why not, Sergeant?' asked Hunsdon.

'Because Jeronimo can use a crossbow and we dinna ken if he's got one or no' and he knows this forest well for he's been living here for weeks. All he needs is a tall tree and a clear shot and ye're deid, my lord Hunsdon.'

'Harrumph.'

'Do you know the paths in the forest?' Carey asked. Dodd had to admit he didn't, he hadn't had a chance to learn them. 'In that case, ma'am, I think the Oxford road is still the best way. It's reasonably good, the trees are not close to it, we can use the messengers' path to avoid the crowds and we can bunch up close.'

The black-haired lady was looking very annoyed as she controlled her big horse, but not particularly frightened. 'Very well. But honestly, Robin, I'd thought better of you.'

Carey's face was comically downcast. 'You're...you're right, ma'am, he made a complete fool of me.'

Dodd had found his own horse without the stirrups, sheathed his sword again and jumped to the saddle, then wished for a lance and a good bow. There was something quite wrong with Carey, seeing he was so meek. It was worrying.

Hunsdon's two Berwick men came back looking frustrated and, of course, without Jeronimo. Hunsdon ordered them out in front as scouts, the men bunched up around the women with Hunsdon on one side of them and Carey and Dodd on the other and they took the path that led from Cumnor Place to the Oxford road with Dodd's back itching furiously and his heart thudding. He didn't even have a jack or a helmet and if Jeronimo could find himself a crossbow and some bolts he could do terrible damage from the close woodland around them.

A little to his surprise, they reached the road without anyone shooting at them and from there they went to a canter and then a full gallop with one of Hunsdon's men out front shouting at the people on the road to make way, make way! The red-haired woman was looking uncomfortable and frightened, the child-sized one was narrow-eyed all the way, but the black-haired woman seemed to be enjoying herself and even Dodd had to admit, she rode very well in her fancy side-saddle.

They got back to the bridge in record time, but instead of going into any of the colleges, they rode straight on through the crowded streets, bowed through at once by the gate guards, and trotted right up wide St. Giles to the northward road. From there it was perhaps ten miles to a village Carey called Woodstock. There, overlooking the valley, was a small fancy castle, probably once defensible but quite decayed now. It was surrounded by tents and horses. The ladies-in-waiting immediately disappeared into the castle. Then Hunsdon turned his horses and they took it easier as they rode back down the road to Oxford at last.

Dodd and Carey took their horses to the stabling at the back of Trinity College themselves and walked them round the courtyard a few times to cool them down. It was only mid-morning and no grooms to be seen, of course.

'Whit were ye talking about wi' Jeronimo when he got ye?' Dodd asked casually as he rubbed his horse down with a wisp of hay. Carey was still looking pale as he did the same and kept rubbing his chin where a very well-aimed bruise was darkening the point of it. His lip was puffing too. You had to admit, a Court goatee gave a good target to aim at if you wanted to knock a man down.

'I was talking about music,' he said in a puzzled voice. 'I said I'd sung the Spanish air he'd sent to the Queen as the signal that she was willing to meet him. I hummed it for him. He said he was hanging around Oxford to hear it, but then he came on you at the inn and decided it would be easier and safer to take you prisoner and use you directly as a lever. He asked me if anyone else had known it and I said no, but then I remembered...goddamn it!' Carey had gone even paler. He was standing like a post staring into space while his horse stamped uneasily. 'Goddamn it to Hell and perdition.'

'What?'

Carey took a deep breath and shook his head. 'I'd forgotten about it. I'd just learnt the tune and was humming it when someone...an old man asked me if I was sent by Heron Nimmo. That's how I heard it. Of course, that was Jeronimo if you pronounce it the Spanish way. But I had no idea what the old man was talking about so I told him, no, the Queen wanted me to sing it specially.'

'Ay?'

'About an hour later, someone tried to shoot me with a crossbow. It was pure luck they missed. And that night someone put belladonna in my spiced wine and nearly killed me.'

'Ay?' Well, that explained the pallor and slowness. Poison? Jesu, that was a new one even for Carey. 'Did ye tell Jeronimo those things?'

'Yes, I asked him if it had been him with the crossbow and the belladonna on Saturday, and why he had been trying to kill me not the Queen, not that I minded, of course. Moments later, he started puking and then when I came to help, he hit me.'

'How? His wrist was roped to his belt.'

'With his stump—it must have a leather and iron cap over the end from the way it felt.'

'Och!' Dodd was reluctantly admiring.

'Then while I was stunned, he part-drew my sword with his teeth and sawed through the rope, then he was gone. Damn it.'

'Would ye know that old man again?'

'That whole Saturday evening is very blurred. I don't know. Jeronimo said there were two of them that tried to kill the Queen, his friend and him. The friend who had family in Oxford and gave him shelter. And now I think about it, I wonder if he was the musician from the Oxford waits that played cello for Mr. Byrd when I sang the song again and then disappeared halfway through the Earl of Oxford's ball. Mr. Byrd was very annoyed. I even drank his ration of ale.'

They were silent a moment. 'I'll tell my father,' Carey said. 'We'll let the men comb through the forest with dogs, I doubt they'll find Jeronimo. He'll be in Oxford meeting his bloody friend...What was his name? Sam? Punch...no Pauncefoot. Right. We'll get them cried at the Carfax and St Giles.' Carey smiled wanly at Dodd. 'Even out in the courtyard, I could hear you shouting at the...the lady to hang Jeronimo immediately. That was good advice, but it probably helped make his mind up to escape.'

'Ay,' said Dodd bitterly, wondering when someone would listen to his good sense soon enough to do something about it.

Thursday 21st September 1592, Evening

It was a hopeless business, trying to search Oxford for just two men, even if one of them had only one arm. The place was full of strangers, not just courtiers and their attendants and hangers-on, but also scholars and lecturers and readers, all there ahead of the start of Michaelmas term to cheer the Queen, along with any peasants from the surrounding countryside who could bring anything into the market to sell. Oxford roared with people and horses, pigs, goats, sheep, cattle, innumerable chickens and geese, barrels, carts...Dumfries had been more chaotic but there were far more people in Oxford which was a bigger town to start with.

Dodd was fascinated by the idea of the colleges, fortresses where you went to learn things from books. He had never heard of the like, although he vaguely thought that the Reverend Gilpin had studied Divinity somewhere like Oxford. He had a look at Christ Church which was where the Queen was going to stay and thought it well-defensible so long as no one had cannon. However, the proposed processional route was a nightmare, lined with painted allegorical scenery, any one of which gave beautiful cover for a man with a crossbow and no shortage of high windows in the houses either.

Halfway through the afternoon it started spitting with rain but then stopped. Dodd was sitting at a table in the White Horse on Broad Street in a private room at the back with Lord Hunsdon, Carey, Lord Hunsdon's steward Mungey, the Captain of the Queen's Gentlemen Pensioners of the Guard and some other men, including Carey's two new servants, the skinny clerk Tovey and the large dark Scot who was as pale and unhealthy-looking as his master. Dodd gave the man an ugly look: he didn't like Scots. The Scot gave him an ugly look right back: no doubt he had his nation's usual irrational hatred of the English. His voice was pure Edinburgh but there was something about him that tickled Dodd's memory.

The Captain of the Queen's Guard was speaking, Dodd forgot his name. He was deputising for Sir Walter Raleigh who was still in the Tower of London for getting a Maid of Honour with child and then marrying her without the Queen's permission.

'Her Majesty will not cancel her entry into Oxford.' Nobody looked surprised though Dodd was. He had heard that the Queen was nervous about her safety and very careful of poison. 'That's final.'

Hunsdon and Carey looked at each other. 'Did you bring the Royal coach?' Carey asked.

'Yes we did, although she hasn't used it yet. She hates it, claims it makes her feel seasick,' said Hunsdon thoughtfully. Dodd agreed with the Queen, he hated coaches too.

'Well then, I'd persuade her to at least ride in the coach. That makes it much harder to shoot at her and the coach should stop a crossbow bolt.'

Hunsdon nodded and his clerk made a note. 'She won't like it, but she will do it,' he said.

'Would she wear a jack or a breastplate?' Dodd asked. 'For when she's out of the coach listening to speeches? The King o' Scotland has a specially padded doublet for entries and the like.'

Everyone exchanged looks. 'It was hard enough to get her to do it in '88,' said Hunsdon, 'for Tilbury. There's no reason we can give now and I think she won't do it. It would look mistrustful of the people.'

Dodd wondered why a sovereign Queen cared about that. He sighed. 'We just have tae find them, then,' he said.

As the futile search wore on into the night, Tovey and Tyndale were not much use; Carey was looking more and more glum and said very little. It seemed Tyndale had had a chance to catch Jeronimo's friend the night before but had messed it up. At last it was Dodd who called a halt and they went back to Trinity College. They drank a late night cup of brandy by the fire in Dodd's chamber while Tovey and Tyndale got themselves settled for the night in the parlour.

'Dinna fret yersen,' Dodd said awkwardly to the Courtier who was staring at the flames with a remote expression on his face. 'Onybody might ha' made that mistake wi' Jeronimo.'

'It never occurred to me that he might hit me with his stump.'

'Nor to me,' Dodd said, though he hoped he would have thought of it. Still, as Jock o' the Peartree had established, the Courtier was soft.

'Come on, Henry, what would you do to find Jeronimo and his friend before they kill the Queen?'

'I wouldna bother searching the town the day,' he said after a moment's thought. 'I would search her route but yer dad will do it anyway. What I would do is think like Jeronimo. He hasnae kin in Oxford but his friend is one of the waits, so we need to keep a good eye out for them. But yer dad will do that too. So. Where would I put myself to kill the Queen?'

'Somewhere high. No shortage what with all the displays and allegorical arches around, not to mention the buildings.'

'What would I use?'

Carey's laugh was humourless. 'A crossbow, a dag, Christ, a dagger will do if he can get close. She's only flesh and blood.'

Dodd narrowed his eyes and thought. He'd never actually assassinated anyone, in the strict sense, but you couldn't deny, it was an interesting problem. You had to be close, within about ten feet to have any hope at all of hitting the target. Or you needed to know exactly where she would be and lay a trap of some kind. His money was on a trap. Everyone knew her route through Oxford— down the Woodstock Road, St. Giles, Cornmarket, Carfax, and on down to Christ Church.

They talked it over for a while and then went to bed because it was late and they had to be up before dawn. They had come up with a large number of outlandish ideas, including gunpowder, which even worried Dodd. He was shocked to hear Carey praying quietly before he fell asleep.

FRIDAY 22ND SEPTEMBER 1592, MIDDAY

Unlike her cousin who was up before dawn, though at least not too happy, it seemed the Queen did not like mornings. She got up at about seven o'clock and spent the next hour and a half dressing, heard Divine service, and then, on the Lord Chamberlain's insistence, delayed all morning by dealing with papers and business with Lord Burghley and his son while Oxford and its environs was searched again.

No sign of Don Jeronimo nor his friend Sam Pauncefoot. After a quick dinner around noon, Carey and Dodd left Tovey and Tyndale with Hunsdon's liverymen and rode north to Woodstock. There they found the Queen, magnificent in a black velvet bodice and black velvet kirtle trimmed with pearls, ribbons, diamonds, rubies, and peacock feathers, a high cambric ruff standing behind her head and her small gold crown pinned to her bright red wig in a cobweb of diamonds, in a very bad mood. There was something familiar about the beaky nose and the shrewd eyes but Dodd couldn't place it, put it down to Carey being related to her.

They were given royal tabards to wear and ordered to ride alongside her coach. Dodd wished for a jack or breastplate: he was only wearing a wool doublet and not even the buffcoat he had taken from Harry Hunks on the specious grounds that it smelled too bad. The bloody tabard was nothing but embroidered silk, of all useless things. At least Carey had managed to find a couple of secrets to put under their hats, iron caps that fitted over your skull and were devilishly uncomfortable but at least gave you a chance if somebody hit you on the head.

The Queen was helped into her coach by Lord Hunsdon who was looking tired himself. She sat there, glowering. The large green and white coach, flying the Royal standard like a castle, jerked off along the rutted road, creaking and groaning like any cart though there were leather straps that supposedly made it more comfortable. There were eight stolid carthorses in silk trappings drawing it, with plumes on their heads. Nice beasts too, much the biggest Dodd had seen since Carey's tournament charger was sold to the King of Scots: heavy-boned, powerful and big-footed. They had hairy feet, perhaps there was Flemish blood in them? There were two black geldings, a half-gelding and three mares, originally piebald but dyed black, sixteen to seventeen hands high, their tails docked and plaited up and their coats shining with...

'You're supposed to be looking out for Jeronimo. Pay attention to the crowd and the Queen, not the bloody horses,' growled Carey out of the side of his mouth and Dodd coughed and dragged his eyes away from the alluring horseflesh.

His heart was beating hard and slow and his back itched and so did his head under the iron cap. He didn't like any of this though the first mile or so was easy enough: along a road that had been tidied up, the undergrowth cut back from the road properly and some holes filled, lined with peasants from the villages, all cheering for all they were worth and waving tree branches and the occasional banner. About halfway down, the louring grey clouds clenched and dumped their rain so the courtiers in the train all covered themselves with cloaks. Neither Carey nor Dodd had brought one so they got wet.

Then they came to a bridge where a large group of men were waiting on foot, some wearing bright red gowns trimmed with marten and behind them more men in black and grey gowns and some in buff coats which Dodd looked at enviously. Their ruffs were sadly bedraggled.

'Vice chancellor of the university, the doctors of the colleges.' Carey muttered to him.

The Queen ordered her coach stopped and said she would hear speeches so long as they were short. She stood on the step of it with two of her grooms holding her cloth of estate over her head to keep off the rain. The vice chancellor knelt to her on the stones of the bridge and made a speech in foreign that seemed long to Dodd. He then gave her a bundle of white sticks with more speechifying and the Queen speechified right back in more foreign and gave the sticks back too. Then one of the others knelt to her and spoke even more in foreign and then, thank God, the lot of them arranged themselves ahead of the coach, the rain dripping from their nice gowns going pink from the red dye running, and walked ahead into Oxford.

There was rain dripping off Dodd's nose too and he carefully tipped his hat so the rain collecting in the brim wouldn't spill down his back. At least the weather made a gun unlikely: who could keep a match alight in this? Though if Jeronimo or his friend had a wheel-lock dag...No. Carey's only fired properly one time in four, you wouldn't risk it. Even a crossbow would be chancy if you let the wet get at the string.

Another half mile down the road, you could see a very wide street where another road joined from the north, with another of those odd monkish fortresses of learning, flying a lamb and flag on its banners. More men, this time the mayor with his chain and the aldermen—even Dodd could spot that. They made speeches too, but this time in English and a bit shorter, thank God. They too went into the procession with the mayor and the vice chancellor exactly level at the front and a little bit of shoving behind them between the aldermen and the red-gowned doctors of the colleges.

Now the procession went down past a church and into the lead-roofed street called Cornmarket. The streets were lined with young men in their gowns and odd-looking square caps from the days of the Queen's father. They shouted 'Hurrah!' for the Queen and threw the caps up as the Queen went past, which frightened the life out of Dodd for a second who thought they might be throwing stones.

The street's cobbles clattered and groaned under the iron-shod wheels of the royal coach, and Dodd caught a glimpse of the Queen looking very tense under all her red and white paint. She beckoned Carey over. He actually dared to argue and was clearly told to shut his mouth. Carey moved his horse around the coach so he could speak to Dodd, his mouth in a grim line.

'She says she's feeling sick, so she's going to stop the coach at Carfax. And she knows the risk....'

'Ay,' he said, 'there's a tower there.'

'She won't get out of the coach but she'll stop there as long as she can. She thinks it will be quite a while because one of Essex's pets, Henry Cuffe, is the Greek Reader and will be making a speech in Greek to her.'

What was it with lords? Why did they like speaking foreign so much?

'Can she no' ride on and have Cuffe come tae her later?'

'She could but she won't. She ordered me to flush the Spaniard out at Carfax for she won't have this nuisance all through her visit to Oxford.'

'Och.' Dodd saw the young Scot's face behind and below Carey looking as if he was actually enjoying himself. Carey must have told the lad to stick around on foot as backup which Dodd doubted was a good idea.

At that point the rain stopped, blast it, and the sun came out. Typical southron weather, you couldn't even rely on it to rain when you wanted.

Carey was thinking the same. 'Now she'll insist on getting out,' he said gloomily. 'She says she's near to puking with the motion of the coach already.'

'Och,' You had to say this for the King of Scots, coward as he was. He wouldn't do any such thing. And the result? Nobody had succeeded in killing him yet, despite plenty of good tries and a couple of kidnap attempts.

The crowds were closer now, held back by the Gentlemen of the Guard, the Beadles of the university in their buffcoats who had joined them from the university procession and Hunsdon's liverymen as well. There were townsfolk as well as black-robed scholars, shouting and cheering the Queen and waving their hats.

At least the Cornmarket's lead roof had kept some of the rain off and would stop any attempt from above. It was nicely decorated with allegorical people standing on it to greet the Queen by singing, half naked, painted gold and silver, still streaming with rainwater and shivering. The coach had to stop so the standard could be taken down as the roof of the coach just went under the roof. The corn merchants were lined up on either side in their best, the only dry spectators of the day, cheering the Queen.

The coach came out again onto the square crossroads with the tower and there was more messing about while they put the standard up again. Yet more men were waiting in their doctor's robes and hats, all of them tense. The coach stopped near the tower, which would make a shot from its roof more difficult. Good. Dodd brought his horse round behind the coach, too many people pressing forward to see the Queen. Carey was staring around anxiously, squinting to see if one of the chilly half-naked painted people on the roof of the Cornmarket was armed. The light was suddenly bright and sharp between the banks of grey.

Somebody pulled on Dodd's stirrup and Dodd scowled down

at that bloody Scot Carey had hired, Hughie Tyndale.

'Ah've seen him, the greybeard that filled the flask wi' poison, there. He's there!'

'What?' Dodd couldn't work out what the man was talking about. He was pointing at the crowd. There was a bunch of schoolboys in their best with their schoolmasters holding them back with whips, but no greybeard visible. Carey's head craned round, he was squinting. Nothing.

Dodd stared hard at the top of the tower, couldn't see anything there either. A movement caught at the corner of his eye, he couldn't see who had suddenly bent in a bow. Then he heard a kind of scraping rolling sound under the roar of the crowd that bothered him. Tyndale's dark face was there, looking ready to run.

'Under the coach, Sergeant,' shouted the lad, sprinting backwards. There was a disturbance going toward the tower.

What was under the coach? From his horse's back, Dodd couldn't see, so he slid sideways to the ground and bent and peered.

Something round and metallic was there, smoke coming out of it...

Dodd's gut clenched hard and his mind slowed down and went cold. Quite calmly he looked at the grenado under the Queen's coach. His horse behind him was stamping. No, it was worse, it was made of metal. It was a petard.

'Git her oot!' he shouted and threw himself down in the mud on all fours, scrambled under the belly of the coach. As he did that he heard creaking, more cheers and then the straps went up a bit. Someone must have helped the Queen down from the coach. From underneath, beyond the deadly iron ball with its burning fuse, Dodd could make out people kneeling and the large velvet folds of the Queen's kirtle.

Damn it, he didn't even have gloves. He grabbed for the petard, it rolled away, he stretched and grabbed again, caught it, brought it toward him, fanned away the choking smoke, saw that the fuse was nearly down to the priming chamber and tried to pull the whole fuse out with his fingers, scorched them, couldn't do it. He grabbed his hat off, pulled the secret from his head and then carefully brought its iron edge down on the smouldering bit of fuse, cut the hot coal away and stubbed it out on the stones. As soon as it was cool, he pulled the fuse out with his teeth. Then he tipped the petard over and let the fine black priming powder scatter on the stones, then the charge smelling of bad eggs, rubbed wet mud on everything.

At that point the world speeded up again, he felt sweat dripping down his face and he heard more foreign windbaggery resounding from one of the kneelers to the Queen. All he could tell about it was that it was a different sort of foreign from the usual with a lot of oy-sounds in it so he supposed that was Greek.

Somebody was pulling on his boots, he eeled out backwards and bounced up ready to punch whoever it was and found Carey facing him. He held up the petard ball and saw Carey go as white as paper. Beside him was Jeronimo, for God's sake...Smiling?

'Bien, mi bravo! Benga, está en el torre!' said Jeronimo, 'Hombres, vamonos!'

'But...'

Carey was already shoving through the crowd to the tower, Hunsdon's men let him through, Jeronimo after him and Dodd scrambling behind, still holding the empty petard. Empty of powder but full of metal balls and scraps of iron.

There was a man lying unconscious at the door which was open. Dodd heard Carey's boots, saw Jeronimo's boots and sprinted blind up the narrow spiral staircase because he didn't know if this was another elaborate trick or what was going on. First you put a petard under the Queen's coach which was an excellent target whether the Queen was in it or not and then you...

Well, then of course you sat somewhere high up and shot into the confusion caused by the explosion.

He got to the platform at the top of the Carfax tower. Jeronimo was advancing on an old man standing by the parapet holding a crossbow. The old man had shaved recently from the pale skin round his mouth and one of his thumbs was bandaged.

'Amigo mio,' said Jeronimo, panting for breath, 'Sam, no la mates, por Dios!'

The old man's face crumpled for a moment. 'Stop,' he whispered, 'Let me finish it for you. I've waited so long.'

Jeronimo shook his head. His remaining hand was open as he

advanced, unarmed. The old man set the crossbow stock to his shoulder, aimed squarely for Jeronimo's chest.

Dodd threw the iron ball under arm. It skittered on the flagstones curving leftwards. Carey swung down with his sword from the other side and in that moment Jeronimo charged, the crossbow twanged, and as the men crashed together, Jeronimo's stump lifted, punched under the old man's jaw and into his throat.

Both of them thudded to the ground, the greybeard choking blood from his broken windpipe and Carey's sword stuck in the bone of his shoulder. Other men were coming up the stairs too late, the Scot at the back, typically. Dodd left Carey to pull out his blade, peered over the parapet, caught Hunsdon's eye and gave him the thumbs-up.

Below them, interminable Greek oratory continued and the Queen stood on the rug-covered cobbles beside her coach, glittering in the sudden sunshine, smiling and nodding attentively at the speech.

The old man was taking a while to die, Carey's blow had only broken his shoulder blade. But he was drowning in the blood from where Jeronimo had punched his throat with his iron-capped stump, turning blue like a hanged man, threshing and straining to breathe. Dodd glanced at him briefly to make sure he wouldn't get up again. Carey had turned Jeronimo on his back and found the bolt sticking out of his chest with water and blood leaking out.

The Spaniard was smiling. 'Eh...Lucky,' he said, 'She is well, the Queen?'

'Yes,' said Carey. 'We thought you were trying to kill her as well.'

'No. Pardon that I struck you yesterday, Señor. When you said... poison...I knew poor Sam was still trying to finish the business after thirty years.'

'It was meant for the Queen after he heard your song?'

The blood was bubbling from around the bolt and more was coming out of the Spaniard's mouth, staining his clenched teeth.

'I think so. Last night I tried...to change his mind. But I was too sick to reach him. It took me all my strength to reach Oxford, I had none to find where Sam had gone.'

Jeronimo shook his head. 'I put the music and a finger of the

Queen's glove in her baggage as it passed me on the road to Rycote and asked to speak to her, to confess to her. If she would, she must cause it to be sung. I am so sorry I never heard it sung by you, Señor, because I was busy with Captain Leigh and his men to take your man prisoner after I found him at the inn.'

Carey shook his head a little.

'*Pobre Sam*,' said Jeronimo, his voice creaking and fading now as the blood filled his lungs. 'He loved me and I did not love him. I was cruel to tell him to wait for my music to be played. So long a wait. I think he was taken by the Queen's inquisitor and so lost the headdress and other glove he kept.' Carey nodded. 'And so this...a petard, a crossbow. He had meant to try at Rycote as well, in my memory, but when he thought you were her spy, he used his poison on you, Señor, instead.'

'Perhaps I should be more grateful than I am, Señor.'

Jeronimo smiled again. 'It has fallen out better than I ever hope,' he whispered. 'I will not die screaming in bed of my canker, and Sam will be with me in Purgatory. Instead a death of honour. Ask the Queen, if she forgives me, of her mercy, have a Mass said for our souls.'

A frown passed over Carey's face. 'Well...'

'Yes, superstition, you say. I will know the truth sooner than you, Señor. Only put it to your Queen. Please.'

Carey ducked his head. Dodd folded his arms and waited, scowling at Hunsdon's men and the Gentlemen of the Guard now uselessly crowding the top of the tower to keep them back. Soon both Don Jeronimo and his old friend were dead.

***

The Queen passed on down to Christ Church, cheered by the scholars and went immediately to the privy chamber to rest and hear reports. A couple of hours later, with their soaked tabards handed over to be dried and brushed down, Carey and Dodd were brought in to see her sitting under her cloth of estate in the professor's parlour she was using as her presence chamber with the Earls of Cumberland, Essex and Oxford attending, along with her ladies-in-waiting, including the red-haired one from Cumnor.

Dodd was in a terrible state of nerves which seemed to amuse Carey. 'Now you see why I made you go to the stews the other night?' said the cursed Courtier whose fault it was. 'If you were doing this the way you smelled that night, the best you could hope would be that any lapdog she threw at you wouldn't bite you. Though my main worry was that you might then throw it back.'

'Och,' gasped Dodd, trying to stop his knees knocking. For God's sake, he wasn't this afeared of the King of Scots, was he? Well he might be, if he was going to meet him. But this was a powerful Queen who had been ruling since before he was born and had a short way with people who offended her.

The Gentleman of the Guard led them in and Carey bowed three times with tremendous elegance and then knelt on both knees. Dodd managed one bow, nearly fell over his own boots and landed with a thud on his knees on the rush matting which hurt.

'Well, Sir Robert, I see you have redeemed yourself,' came the Queen's voice, very sardonic, somehow familiar...

'Your Majesty is most kind and understanding. If I may mention...'

'You did well with the quest I gave you, but then you fell for an extremely simple trick which could have been very dangerous to me. I will give you both your warrant and your fee, you can be certain of it, and in good time. But not today.'

Carey's shoulders sagged a little, though he didn't look surprised.

'Then, ma'am, may I present Sergeant Henry Dodd of Gilsland who dived under Your Majesty's coach this afternoon to grab the petard there and put the fuse out and then helped stop the assassin on Carfax Tower.'

'Yes, indeed,' said the Queen's voice, sounding very amused. 'Sergeant, your advice yesterday was excellent although I could not have followed it, even if my cousin had not let Don Jeronimo escape. And it seems in the event that it was better so.'

The face was familiar too. Dodd blinked at the beaky old woman under the red wig and suddenly recognised her. Put a black wig on her and she was the black-haired lady-in-waiting. Now he thought of it, that woman had had ginger eyebrows. Jesu, he had shouted at her only yesterday, wagged his finger at her. Jesu. Oh God. Why the hell hadn't Carey warned him?

His horror was obviously leaking onto his face, because she laughed. Jeronimo must have known who she was despite her black wig. That's why he said what he said, broke his parole. He only gave it until he saw the Queen, after all. God, oh God. What would she do to him for shouting at her like that?

'Come here, Sergeant.'

He didn't want to shuffle about on his knees, so he stood up, stepped forward hiding a wince, and knelt again nearer to her, smelling both old lady and rosewater and the incense caught in the velvet of her gown.

'We have persuaded my lord the Earl of Cumberland of your merit and so, Sergeant, we are very happy to present you with this, as a small token of our thanks for your service to us this day.'

It was a parchment scroll. Dodd took it and nearly dropped it. The Queen was smiling at him. Something was snuffling at his other hand and he looked down to see a little fat lapdog licking it.

'Felipe likes you,' she said. 'High praise. I, too, like you Sergeant Henry Dodd and am still in your debt for your actions today. I had considered a pension but Sir Robert thought you would prefer what is in the deed there.'

She gave him her hand, covered in white lead paste and powder and heavy with rings, so he kissed the air above it. Then she nodded to him and he realised he was supposed to stand up and back away. He managed it, just about. What had come over him? While he knelt again just in case, and also to take the weight off his feet, the Queen smiled at Carey, too.

'Robin, I know you won't approve, but I have also written to ask the French ambassador to dedicate a special Mass for the repose of the souls of Don Jeronimo de la Quadra de Jimena and Sam Pauncefoot. Mr. Byrd will arrange the music for it.'

'Your Majesty...'

'Please be quiet, Robin. You know my opinion on the matter which is that there is one God and Jesus is His Son and the rest is argument over trifles. Now you may go.'

Outside on the staircase, Dodd blinked down at the parchment in his hand. Was it a thank you letter? A warrant?

'Aren't you going to open it, Sergeant?' Carey asked, grinning stupidly.

He did. Bloody foreign again. But then he saw the word 'Dedo' and then the word Gilsland. What? He looked up at Carey.

'They're the deeds to Gilsland,' Carey explained. 'You now own it outright, freehold, with the messuage appertaining. She got it off the Earl of Cumberland in exchange for cancelling one of her loans to him.'

'The deeds...' There was his name in foreign. Henricus Doddus, Praetor whatever that was. 'To me?'

'Yes. Gilsland is now legally yours. You were Cumberland's tenant-at-will, now you are the freeholder of the land and the tower, to you and your heirs in perpetuity unless you sell it.'

Dodd's heart was pounding. 'Ye mean I dinna owe rent?'

'No. You have the expenses of maintenance of course, but Gilsland is now yours. Blackrent is your own decision.'

'Och.' He couldn't take it in. What would Janet say? By God, she'd be ecstatic, none of her brothers nor even her father was anything more than a tenant-at-will. Now he could not be evicted legally. Illegally, of course, he could be turned off it if he couldn't defend it, but he was now safe from a landlord's whims and lawyers.

'Of course it won't change much now,' Carey was still blathering, 'and I hope you'll continue in the castle garrison as sergeant of the guard as well as of Gilsland. But in due course...when...er...the King of Scots eventually comes in and not for a long time, of course, but eventually...you will have a secure title to your lands. Much better than the Grahams, for instance, who are in fact simply squatting on the Storey lands. It could be very important.'

Dodd managed to get his mouth to shut and looked back down at the deeds and then at Carey again. He blinked around himself at the stairs and a world suddenly changed forever by a bit of parchment in his hand.

He couldn't yet say thank you to Carey, in case he greeted like a bairn so he coughed several times and said gruffly, 'Ay sir. Ay. I'll need tae think about it. Ehm...where now?'

Carey grinned with perfect understanding, which was annoying. 'Back to Trinity College to pick up my clerk and my manservant and some supplies and horses, gather up the new men.'

'Ay, and then?'

'North,' Carey was laughing, 'north for Carlisle. God knows what the surnames are up to, it's the full raiding season. We might make York by nightfall.'

HISTORICAL NOTE

Spoiler warning!

All historical novelists rely on proper historians to inspire and guide them. Often one particularly well-written and well-researched book becomes the main reference—if I'm lucky enough to find one. As I've said before, the whole of the Carey series of books was inspired by George Macdonald Fraser's marvellously funny and accurate history of the Borders, *The Steel Bonnets*. For the account of Queen Elizabeth's ceremonial entry into Oxford in September 1592, I used the contemporaneous account in Nicholl's Progresses [The Grand Reception and Entertainmen of Queen Elizabeth at Oxford, 1592]—and yes, it was indeed raining.

Amy Robsart, Lady Dudley died on Sunday 8th September 1560. Her suspicious death changed Elizabeth's life story and the history of her reign. For *An Air of Treason*, I used a recent account of the mystery by Chris Skidmore titled *Death and the Virgin: Elizabeth, Dudley and the Mysterious Fate of Amy Robsart*. Chris Skidmore has remarkably tracked down the original coroner's report into her death and prints it in an Appendix—in full, both Latin and an English translation. It makes eye-opening reading because it was clearly not a broken neck that killed Amy Robsart. There is also a throwaway comment in the wildly inaccurate Catholic propaganda libel 'Leicester's Commonwealth' where it says 'she [Amy] had the chance to fall from a pair of stairs and so to break her neck, but yet without hurting of her hood that stood upon her head.' [Skidmore] This intrigued me despite the fact that pretty much everything in 'Leicester's Commonwealth' is a fancifully scurrilous attack on the Queen's favourite that would put modern tabloid journalists to shame for venom and lack of interest in veracity. But what if that bit was based on truth?

There are other intriguing tidbits for which there is unimpeachable documentary evidence: why did Lady Dudley send all her servants out of the house on that day—a very unusual and quite daring thing for a wealthy and respectable woman to do? She had only two women with her who were ordered to stay in the parlour. Why was Amy in such a panic over her clothes, ordering a new outfit from her tailor and then, when it didn't arrive in time, sending another one into Oxford to have gold lace put on the collar? Who was she trying to impress?

I'm not a proper historian, I'm a novelist. I like to look at what the record says—and then speculate wildly about what might really have happened while trying to stay true to the era and the characters of the people I'm writing about. So that's what I did.

I hope you enjoy the result—as painstakingly uncovered by that 'concentrated essence of Elizabethan' Sir Robert Carey and his much put-upon Sergeant Dodd.

GLOSSARY

A fortiori – stronger, moreover

Alchemy – the unacknowledged illegitimate grandfather of modern chemistry; an intellectually satisfying and logical theory of matter which featured four Elements and held that gold was the pinnacle of matter and could be made to order by using the Philosopher's Stone. Unfortunately, like many such theories, it was completely wrong. They found it was a little more complicated than that.

Apothecary – drugstore/druggist

Aqua vitae – brandy

Barnard – proposed victim of a coney-catching lay (scam)

Bartalmew's fair – London pronunciation of St Bartholomew's Fair. Please note that no 'fair' is ever spelt 'fayre'.

Board of Green Cloth – committee in charge of administration and discipline at Court and within three miles of the Queen's person (within the Verge)

Boot, the – instrument of torture popular in Scotland which used wedges and hammers to break the victim's legs

Boozing ken – a small alehouse, often full of thieves etc (Thieves' Cant)

Border reiver – armed robbers on the Anglo-Scottish Border, organised in family groups called surnames who used the Border as a means of escape

Buff jerkin – long sleeveless jacket made of tough leather, originally from buffalo

Carlin – old woman (Scotch)

Carrels – study rooms in a monastery or library

Chess – there have been various manifestations of chess over the years; one form of Medieval chess had a queen that could only move one square at a time in any direction. The modern mobile or puissant (powerful) queen was introduced some time around the sixteenth century and may have been a compliment to Elizabeth. When two pieces of equal power were in position to take you could throw dice to decide which piece won

Chorus of Kings – a winning hand at Primero (Aces were low)

Cloth of estate – a square tent of rich cloth traditionally set up over any seat occupied by a monarch

Cods – testicles, as in codpiece

Coining – forging money

Colloped – cut into chops

Coney-catch – con-trick (thieves' cant)

Counsels – old-fashioned way of saying, trusted advice, hence Legal Counsel and Counsellor.

Cramoisie – dark purple red, a very popular colour in Elizabethan England.

Culverin – medium sized cannon with a long barrel

Dag – large muzzle-loading pistol, decorated with a heavy ball on the base of the handgrip to balance the weight of the barrel and hit enemies with when you missed

Daybook – diary

Debateable Land – area to the north of Carlisle that was invaded and counterinvaded so often by England and Scotland that in the end it became semi-independent and a den of thieves, as often happens.

Dominie – Scotch for a teacher

Dorter – dormitory

Faggots – bundles of firewood, hence also the name of a kind of traditional English meatball made with offal

Falling band – plain white turned down collar, Puritan style

Farthingale – like a crinoline, a petticoat shaped with steel or wooden hoops to make the kirtle stand out in a particular shape; bell-shaped early in the reign, then more or less barrel shaped by the 1590s.

Footpad – mugger

French hood – a style of headtire popular in the 1550s

French pox – syphilis

'Greeted like a bairn' – cried like a baby

Groat – coin worth four pennies

Harbinger – scouts sent out ahead of the Court on progress, specifically to requisition lodgings and food for it

Headtire – woman's stiffened headdress which went over her linen cap, mandatory for married women

Henbane of Peru – an early name for tobacco

Henchman – a male servingman or hanger-on, often providing muscle and armed back-up to a lord, although a young page might be called a henchman as well

Humoral complexion – the personal mix of the humours which dictated your character and which caused disease when unbalanced – Sanguine (Blood), Choleric (Yellow Bile), Melancholic (Black Bile) and Phlegmatic (Phlegm).

Incognito – in disguise

Insight – portable and saleable household goods

Jack – padded jacket interlined with metal plates

Jakes – outside toilet

Kinchin – child (Thieves' Cant)

Kine – old plural of cows

Kirtle – skirt over the petticoats

Lay – scam (thieves' cant)

Limner – painter in colours, also meant a miniaturist

Lye – the all-purpose cleaning agent, made by passing water through woodash repeatedly, a powerful alkaline. Used to make soap as well.

Morion – high curved steel helmet, standard in sixteenth century

Mort – woman (Thieves' Cant)

Muliercula – little woman or midget

Nae blood tae his liver – it was believed that the blood in your liver gave you courage—hence lily-livered, said of those whose livers were pale. No doubt cirrhosis did make you cowardly.

Nipped that bung – stole that purse (Thieves' Cant)

Ordinary, the – fixed price meal at an inn

Papist – Catholic

Parole – after surrendering, a gentleman would give his word (parole) that he wouldn't try to escape

Patent – a monopoly on the sale of some luxury granted by the Queen in the later years of her reign as a way of rewarding courtiers without costing herself anything, very unpopular with the ordinary people who had to pay inflated prices as a result

Penny loaf – bread roll. A one pound loaf of bread had its price fixed at 1 d but with the inflation of the late sixteenth century and high wheat prices, the loaf shrank though it still cost a penny

Phlegm – mucus or snot, the cold and moist Humour, one of the four Humours of the body and a constant problem for the English who were renownedly Phlegmatic

Pinniwinks – Scottish term for thumbscrews, a conveniently portable instrument of torture which broke the victim's fingers

Playing a veney – exact equivalent of a kata in Karate or pattern/tul in Taekwondo, this was a set series of sword moves practised with a partner so as to build up strength and agility. To keep the deathrate down, pickaxe handles with hilts or veney sticks were used.

Poinard – long thin duelling dagger with an elaborate hilt, big brother to a stiletto

Polearm – any weapon involving a long stick with something sharp on the end

Praemunire – the short name of the statute of Henry VIII which forbade as treason any appeal to an authority higher than the king's i.e. the Pope

Punk – whore

Pursuivant – literally chaser, someone who acted for the state in tracking down spies, criminals, and traitors. Often freelance and unscrupulous

Quod Erat Demonstrandum – as was demonstrated, QED

Red lattices – the shutters of any place selling alcohol would be painted red

Rickets – soft bones caused by Vitamin D deficiency in childhood, common among the Elizabethan upper classes if they allowed their childrens' diet to be supervised by physicians who advised against fresh vegetables (too Cold of Humour) and fish (too lower class).

Run wood – wild, mad

Screever – professional scribe, later a pavement artist

Serjeant-at-law – a senior lawyer with special privileges, appointed by the Crown, roughly equivalent to a QC today

Sleuth dog – hunting dog specially bred for tracking

St. Paul's Walk – the aisle of old St. Paul's Cathedral where fashionable young men would parade up and down in their finery.

Starlings – the piers of London Bridge

Statute cap – blue woollen cap that all common men had to wear so as to support the wool industry – a statute more honoured in the breach than the observance

Stews – Turkish bathhouses (descending ultimately from Roman baths) that tended also to be brothels.

Strilpit wee nyaff – untranslateable Northern insult meaning 'weakling'

Surety – a Border system whereby the headman of a surname would hand over a lesser member of his family as a hostage for the good behaviour of another member of the surname

Swan Rampant – this was indeed apparently Hunsdon's badge and looked as described.

Terceiro – elite Spanish soldier

Teuchter – incomprehensible Northern insult

Tiring room – dressing room (from attire)

To wap – to fornicate, as allegedly in 'Wapping', a notorious haunt of whores

Upright man – gang leader

Utter barrister – outer barrister. At this time a lawyer who had been called to the Bar (of the court) and could stand outside it, thus having the right to be nearer to the judge than mere attorneys or solicitors (which then meant the equivalent of ambulance-chaser). Later they became the only people who could speak before a judge in court.

Venery – persistent naughty, sexual behaviour. Now called sexual addiction, very common.

Veney – exact equivalent of a kata in karate or pattern/tul in tae-kwondo, this was a set series of sword moves practised with a partner so as to build up strength and agility. To keep the death-rate down, pickaxe handles with hilts (veney-sticks) were used.

Wittol – idiot

Wood – wild, mad